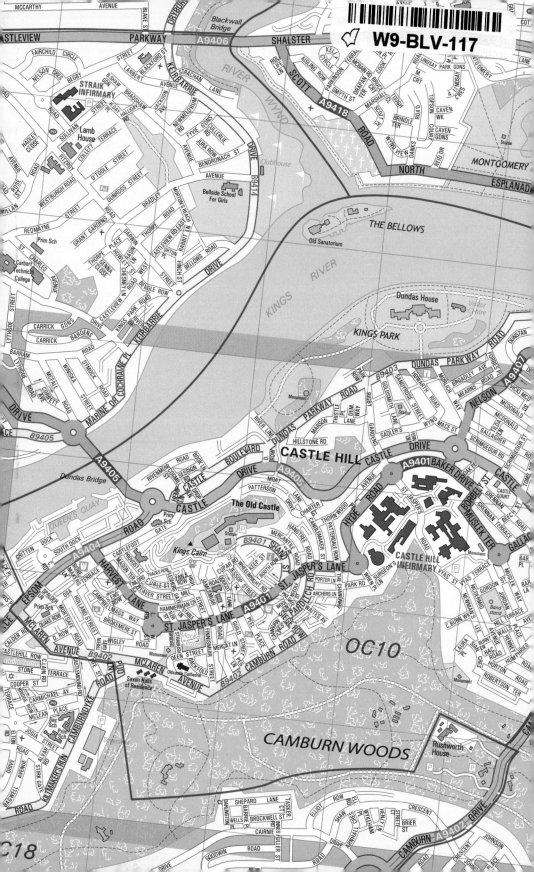

A DARK SO DEADLY

BY STUART MACBRIDE

The Logan McRae Novels
Cold Granite
Dying Light
Broken Skin
Flesh House
Blind Eye
Dark Blood
Shatter the Bones
Close to the Bone
22 Dead Little Bodies
The Missing and the Dead
In the Cold Dark Ground

The Ash Henderson Novels
Birthdays for the Dead
A Song for the Dying

A Dark so Deadly

Other Works
Sawbones (a novella)
12 Days of Winter (short stories)
Partners in Crime (Two Logan and Steel short stories)
The 45% Hangover (a Logan and Steel novella)
The Completely Wholesome Adventures of Skeleton Bob
(a picture book)

Writing as Stuart B. MacBride
Halfhead

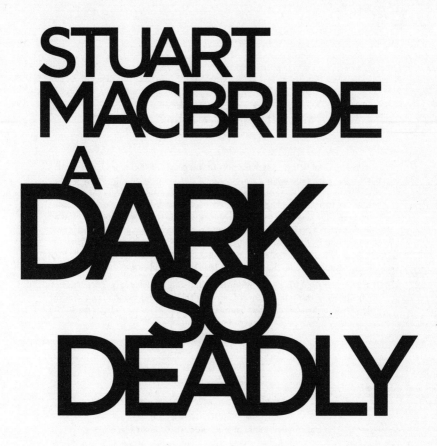

STUART MACBRIDE

A DARK SO DEADLY

HarperCollins*Publishers*

HarperCollins
PUBLISHERS
Since 1817

The quotation from the public information film *Stay at Home* appears courtesy of the British Film Institute © Crown Copyright (1975). The quotation from William Blake's *Songs of Innocence* – The Chimney Sweeper (1789) is taken from the British Library's first edition copy.

HarperCollins*Publishers*
1 London Bridge Street,
London SE1 9GF

www.harpercollins.co.uk

Published by HarperCollins*Publishers* 2017

Copyright © Stuart MacBride 2017
Endpaper detail shows map of Oldcastle © Stuart MacBride

Stuart MacBride asserts the moral right to be identified as the author of this work

A catalogue record for this book is available from the British Library

ISBN: 978-0-00-749468-2

Set in Minion

Printed and bound in the United States of America by LSC Communications.

Find out more about HarperCollins and the environment at
www.harpercollins.co.uk/green

17 18 19 20 LSC/C 10 9 8 7 6 5 4 3 2 1

For Sue.

Without Whom

As always I've received a lot of help from a lot of people while I was writing this book, so I'd like to take this opportunity to thank: Prof. Sue Black, Dr Roos Eisma, Vivienne McGuire, and Dr Lucina Hackman, all of whom do excellent work at the University of Dundee's Centre for Anatomy and Human Identification; Sergeant Bruce Crawford who answers far more daft questions than anyone should ever have to, as does Professor Dave Barclay; Sarah Hodgson, Jane Johnson, Julia Wisdom, Jaime Frost, Anna Derkacz, Sarah Collett, Charlie Redmayne, Roger Cazalet, Kate Elton, Hannah Gamon, Cait Davies, Damon Greeney, Finn Cotton, the eagle-eyed Anne O'Brien, Marie Goldie, the DC Bishopbriggs Super Squad, and everyone at HarperCollins, for doing such a stonking job; Phil Patterson and the team at Marjacq Scripts, for keeping my cat in shoes all these years; Catherine Pellegrino, and Sandra Sawicka for translational help; and let's not forget Cecelia Lynch, or James, Duncan, Katy, and Liz Shannon who helped raise money for two very worthy causes, and Matt Patterson whose wallet makes several guest appearances. And thank you to Tony Dykes of the British Film Institute for permission to quote *Stay at Home* within these pages.

Of course, there wouldn't be any books without bookshops, booksellers, and book readers – so thank you all, you're stars.

And saving the best for last – as always – Fiona and Grendel.

— exhibit A —

1

The wall whispers to him with splintered wooden lips. *'They'll worship you. They'll worship you. They'll worship you...'*

Its words fill the gloom, rolling around and around and through him, pulsing and pulling. *'They'll worship you.'*

Why?

Why can't he just die?

'They'll worship you: you'll be a god.'

Is this what gods feel like? Thirsty. Aching.

Every muscle in his stomach throbs from the repeated heaving. Every breath tastes of bile.

Bile and dark, gritty wood smoke. Filling the low room with its stained wooden walls.

'They'll worship you: you'll be a god.'

He slumps back, making the rusty links of chain rattle and clank against each other. Heavy around his throat. Heavier where it's bolted into the wall. The wall that talks.

'You'll be a god.'

He can't even answer it, his mouth is desert dry, tongue like a breeze-block, blood booming in his ears. Boom. Boom. Boom.

So thirsty... But if he drinks the foul brown water in the jug, he'll be sick again.

'A god.'

He turns his face to the wall. Finds a silent crack in the wood. And stares through into the other room.

'They'll worship you. They'll worship you.'

Through there, it's bright: a mix of light and shadow as someone stands on their tiptoes to slot another pole of fish into the rack. Herrings, splayed open, tied in pairs at the tail, their flattened sides like hands. Praying.

Help me…

He opens his mouth, but it's too dry to make words. Too burned by the bile.

'They'll worship you.'

Why can't he just die?

Up above, high above the poles of praying fish, eight fingertips brush a blade of sunlight. They run their tips along its sharp edge as the body they belong to sways in the darkness. Caught in the breeze from the open door. Head down – like the fish – arms dangling. Skin darkened to an ancient oak brown.

'You'll be a god.'

Then the person on the other side disappears. Comes back with a wheelbarrow piled up with sawdust and small chunks of wood. Dumps the lot in the middle of the room. Stoops to light it. Stands back as pale tendrils of smoke coil up into the air. Backs away and closes the door.

Now the only light is the faint orange glow of the smouldering wood.

'You'll be a god.'

He slides down against the wall. Too tired and thirsty to cry. Too tired to do anything but wait for the end to come.

'They'll worship you…'

Why can't he just *die*?

— bodies of the lesser god —

Then the little girl with the lizard's tail jumped into the air with a *whoosh!* "I've got it!" she shrieked. "We can make an enormous pie out of all the bits of hair and beard!"

Ichabod scowled at her. "That's a horrid idea," he said, because it was. "No one wants to eat a cake made of hair."

"Ah, but the hair of the Gianticus Moleraticus is *magical* and tastes of everything you like in the whole world! Gumdrops and sausages, baked beans and chocolate biscuits, custard and ham." She scooped up a big handful of hair and shoved it in Ichabod's mouth. "See?"

But to Ichabod it just tasted of hair. The little girl was clearly insane…

R.M. Travis
The Amazing Adventures of Ichabod Smith (1985)

And if some motherf*cker gonna call the police?
I'm-a grab my nine-mill and I'm-a make him deceased.

Donny '$ick Dawg' McRoberts
'Don't Mess with the $ick Dawg'
© Bob's Speed Trap Records (2016)

2

'POLICE! COME BACK HERE, YOU WEE SOD!'

Only that wasn't really right, was it? Ainsley Dugdale *wasn't* a wee sod – he was a dirty great big lumping hulk of a sod, hammering his way along Manson Avenue. Ape-long arms and short legs pumping, scarf flittering out behind him, baldy head glinting in the morning sunshine.

Callum gritted his teeth and hammered after him.

Why did no one ever come back when they were told to? Anyone would think people didn't *want* to get arrested.

Squat grey council houses scrolled past on either side of the street, lichen-flecked pantiles and harled walls. Front gardens awash with weeds. More abandoned sofas and washing machines than gnomes and bird tables.

A couple of kids were out on their bikes, making lazy figure eights on the tarmac. The wee boy had sticky-out ears and a flat monkey nose, a roll-up sticking out the corner of his mouth – leaving coiled trails of smoke behind him. The wee girl was all blonde ringlets and pierced ears, swigging from a tin of extra-strong cider as she freewheeled. Both of them dressed in baggy jeans, trainers, and tracksuit tops. Baseball caps on the right way around, for a change.

Rap music blared out of a mobile phone. *'Cops can't take me, cos I'm strong like an oak tree, / Fast like the grand prix, / I'm-a still fly free...'*

The wee girl shifted her tinny to the other hand and raised a middle finger in salute as Callum ran past. 'HOY, PIGGY, I SHAGGED YER MUM, YEAH?'

Her wee friend made baboon hoots. 'HOOH! HOOH! HOOH! PIGGY, PIGGY, PIGGY!'

7

Neither of them looked a day over seven years old.

The delights of darkest Kingsmeath.

Dugdale skittered around the corner at the end of the road. Almost didn't make it – banged against the side of a rusty Renault, righted himself and kept on going, up the hill.

'RUN, PIGGY, RUN!' Little Miss Cider appeared, standing on the pedals to keep up, grinning as she flanked him. 'COME ON, PIGGY, PUT SOME WELLY IN IT!'

Her baboon friend pedalled up on the other side. 'FAT PIGGY, LAZY PIGGY!'

'Bugger off, you little sods...' Callum wheeched through the turn, into another row of grubby houses. Low garden walls guarded small squares of thistle and dandelions, ancient rusty hatchbacks up on bricks, the twisted metal brackets where satellite dishes used to be.

'COME ON, PIGGY!'

The gap was narrowing. Dugdale might have got off to an impressive sprint start, but his long game wasn't anywhere near as good – puffing and panting as he lumbered up Munro Place. Getting slower with every step.

'HOOH! HOOH! HOOH!'

He crested the hill with Callum barely ten feet behind him.

The street fell away towards a grubby line of trees and a grubbier line of houses, but Dugdale didn't stop to admire the view: he kept his head down, picking up a bit of velocity on the descent.

The wee kids freewheeled alongside him, Little Miss Cider swigging from her can. 'RUN, BALDY – PIGGY'S GONNA GET YOU!'

One last burst. Callum accelerated. 'I'M NOT TELLING YOU AGAIN!'

Dugdale snatched a glance over his shoulder – little eyes surrounded by dark circles, a nose that looked as if it'd been broken at least a dozen times, scar bisecting his bottom lip. He swore. Then put on another burst of speed.

'NO YOU DON'T!'

'HOOH! HOOH! HOOH!'

Closer. Eight foot. Seven. Six.

Here we go...

Callum leapt. Arms out – rugby-tackle style.

His shoulder caught Dugdale just above the waist, arms wrapping around the top of the big sod's legs. Holding on tight as they both crashed onto the pavement, rolling over and over. Grunts. More swearing.

A tangle of arms and legs. Then something the size of a minibus battered into Callum's face.

Now the world tasted of hot batteries.

Another punch. 'GET OFF ME!'

Callum jabbed out an elbow and connected with something solid.

'HOOH! HOOH! HOOH!'

'FIGHT, PIGGY, FIGHT!'

Then the pavement battered off the back of his head and a fist slammed into his stomach. Fire roared through his torso, accompanied by the sound of a thousand alarm clocks all ringing at once.

He swung a punch and Dugdale's nose went from broken to smashed.

'Gahhhh!' Dugdale reared back, blood spilling down over his top lip. He lashed out blind, eyes closed, and that massive fist came close enough to ruffle the hair above Callum's ear.

Distance. Get some distance.

A big black Mercedes slid past, the sweaty-sweet scent of marijuana coiling out from the back windows, a deep *BMMTSHHH*, *BMMTSHHH*, *BMMTSHHH* of hip-hop bass rattling the air. It stopped in the middle of the road, where they could get a good view of the fight. But did anyone get out to help? Of course they sodding didn't.

'KILL HIM, PIGGY, FINISH HIM!'

'HOOH! HOOH! HOOH!'

Callum scrabbled back against a rusty Volkswagen. Yanked out his handcuffs. 'Ainsley Dugdale, I'm detaining you under Section Fourteen of the Criminal Procedure – Scotland – Act 1995—'

'FIGHT! FIGHT! FIGHT!' The kids pulled up their bikes, blocking the pavement, making an impromptu brawl-pit in the space between the Volkswagen and a garden wall. 'COME ON: KILL HIM!'

'Shut up!' Back to Dugdale. 'Because I suspect you of having committed an offence punishable by imprisonment, namely the—'

'HOOH! HOOH! HOOH!'

'GAAAAH!' Dugdale lunged, but not at Callum. He grabbed the wee girl by the throat and yanked her off her bike.

Her tin of cider hit the deck and bounced, sending out a spurt of frothy urine-coloured liquid. 'Ulk...' Eyes wide, both hands clutching onto Dugdale's forearm, legs pinwheeling and kicking at the air.

Oh sodding hell. And things had been going so well right up till that point.

'No, no, no!' Callum scrambled to his feet. 'That's *enough*. Let the girl go.'

Her wee mate hurled his roll-up. It burst against Dugdale's chest in a little hiss of sparks. 'LET HER GO, YOU DIRTY PAEDO!'

'Come on, Dugdale ... Ainsley. You don't want to hurt a kid, right?' Hands out, open, nice and safe. 'You're not that kind of guy, are you?'

'PAEDO! PAEDO! PAEDO!'

Callum hissed the words out the side of his mouth. 'You are *not* helping.'

Dugdale stuck out his other hand. 'Money!'

'Come on, Ainsley, let the girl go and—'

'GIVE US YOUR MONEY!' He gave the girl a shake, sending her legs swinging wildly as her face turned a darker shade of puce. 'NOW!'

'OK, OK. Just let her breathe.' Callum dug out his battered old wallet. The one with the threadbare lining sticking out. He took the last tenner and crumpled fiver from inside. 'Here.' He placed the cash on the floor.

'Is that *it*?' Dugdale glowered at the two sorry notes. 'ALL OF IT, OR I SNAP HER NECK IN HALF!'

Baboon Boy's chant died. 'Paedo...?'

The kicks were getting weaker: those Nike trainers barely moving.

Her wee friend snivelled. Wiped his top lip on the back of his sleeve. 'Please, mister. Don't hurt my sister...'

'That's all the money I've got, OK? Now let the girl go.'

Dugdale growled, then chucked the little girl at Callum.

He ducked for the fifteen quid as Callum dropped the tatty wallet and caught her wee body before it hit the pavement. And that's when everything slowed down.

The tatty wallet bounced off the paving slabs, spinning away, its torn lining waving like a flag.

'Aaaggggh...' She hauled in a huge whoop of air, both hands wrapped around her throat – as if Dugdale hadn't done a good enough job throttling her and she was having a go herself.

But Dugdale didn't snatch up the money, he kept on going, smashing into Callum and the wee girl, sending them slamming back into the Volkswagen. Rocking it on its springs.

A fist connected with Callum's ribs. Arms and legs tangled. Flashes of sky, then concrete, then rusty metal, then sky again.

Then bang – everything was at full speed again.

Callum yanked the pepper spray from his jacket pocket. The little girl wriggled her way out from between them, trainers digging into his thigh as she went. Callum flipped the cap off the spray and thumbed the button, sending a squirt of burning pepper stink out at Dugdale's face.

Missed.

Dugdale didn't. He rammed his hand into Callum's crotch, grabbed hold, and *squeezed*.

Oh *God*...

But when Callum opened his mouth to scream, all that came out was a strangled wheeze – eyes wide as every single ache and pain in his body disappeared, replaced by the thermonuclear explosion going off in his scrotum. It raced out through his stomach, down his legs, up into his chest – a shockwave ripping out from ground zero as Dugdale twisted his handful like a rusty doorknob.

Oh sodding Jesus...

Dugdale let go, but the nuclear war still raged.

No...

Water filled Callum's eyes, making the word go all soft focus, but the pain remained pin-sharp. He lashed out with the pepper spray, swinging it in an arc with the button held down.

Someone bellowed in pain.

Then scuffing feet.

Argh...

The clatter of a very large man tripping over a fallen bicycle.

A dull *thunk*, like a watermelon bouncing off a coffee table.

Oh that *hurt*...

'BLOODY PAEDO!' Some more *thunks*.

'Come on, leave him!'

Thunk, thunk, thunk. 'BLOODY BALDY PAEDO WANKER!'

Ow...

'Willow, come on! Before he gets up!'

The sound of someone spitting.

'Grab the cash, Benny. No, you spaz, get the wallet too!'

Then trainers on concrete, the rattle of bicycles being dragged upright, and the growl of tyres fading away into the distance.

One last cry of, 'PIGGY, PIGGY, PIGGY!'

The sound of that big black Mercedes pulling away now the floor-show was over.

And silence.

Callum cursed and panted and wobbled his way up to his knees, one hand clutching his tattered groin.

Sodding ... for ... *ooogh*...

Deep breaths.

Nope. Not helping.

He scrubbed a hand across his watery eyes.

Dugdale lay on his front, one hand behind his back the other limp in the gutter. His face looked as if someone had driven over it with a ride-on lawnmower.

Callum dragged himself over and slapped on the cuffs. 'You're nicked.'

Ow...

'Little monsters...' Never mind saying *thank you* – no, that was too much to hope for these days, he'd only saved her life, not as if it was *that* big a deal – but did they have to take his sodding wallet?

Dugdale twitched and groaned, eyes still closed, the blood crusting on his battered nose. A swathe of red crossed his face, following the pepper spray's less than delicate path, swollen and angry looking. Like the lump on his head. It was going to be impressive when it finished growing – about the size and colour of a small aubergine. Probably have himself a gargantuan headache when he finally woke up. Maybe concussion too.

Good. Served him right.

Callum pulled out his mobile, staying where he was – standing, hunched over almost double, one hand on his knee, holding him upright as he dialled.

Three rings and then a woman's voice came on the line, sounding small and concerned. *'Hello?'*

'Elaine, it's me.'

'Callum? Are you OK? You don't sound OK. Is everything OK?'

He gritted his teeth as an aftershock rippled its way through his groin. 'No. Can you phone the bank? I need you to cancel my debit and credit card. Someone's snatched them.'

A sigh. *'Oh, Callum, not your dad's wallet...'*

'Don't start, please. It'll be bad enough when McAdams gets here, don't need you kicking the party off early.'

Silence.

Yeah, way to go, Callum. Smooth. Nice and understanding.

He took a deep breath. 'Sorry, it's... I'm not having the greatest of days.'

'I'm not your enemy, Callum. I know it's been difficult for you.'

Understatement of the year. 'All I get is snide comments, nasty little digs, and crap. It's been three solid weeks of—'

'It's for the best though, remember? For Peanut's sake?'

Peanut.

He closed his eyes. Tried to make it sound as if he meant it: 'Yeah.'

'*We need the money, Callum. We need the maternity pay to—*'

'Yeah. Right. I know. It's just…' He wiped a hand over his face. 'Never mind. It'll be fine.'

'*And we* really *appreciate it, me and Peanut.*' A pause. '*Speaking of Peanut, you know what he'd totally love? Nutella. And some pickled dill cucumbers. Not gherkins: the cucumbers, from the Polish deli on Castle Hill? Oh, and some onion rolls too.*'

'They stole my *wallet*, Elaine. I—'

'*I didn't ask to get pregnant, Callum.*' A strangled noise came down the phone, like a cross between a grunt and a sigh. '*Sorry. I don't… There are times when I need a bit of support coping with all this.*'

Support? *Seriously?*

'How am I not supporting you? I put my hand up, didn't I? I took the blame, even though it was nothing to do with—'

'*I know, I know. I'm sorry. It's…*' Another sigh. '*Don't worry about the Nutella and stuff, it's only cravings. I'll make do with whatever's knocking about here.*'

He limped over to the garden wall and lowered himself onto it with a wince. Took yet another deep breath. Scrunched a hand over his eyes. 'I'm sorry, Elaine. It's not you, it's… Like I said, I'm having a *terrible* day.'

'*It'll get better, I promise. I love you, OK?*'

'Yeah, I know it will.' It had to, because it couldn't possibly get any worse.

'*Do you love me and Peanut too?*'

'Course I do.'

A shiny red Mitsubishi Shogun pulled into the kerb, the huge four-by-four's window buzzing down as Callum levered himself up to his feet. His crumpled suit and crumpled body reflected back at him in the glittering showroom paintwork.

'Got to go.' He hung up and slipped the phone back in his pocket.

'Constable Useless.' A thin, lined face frowned through the open car window, its greying Vandyke framed by disappointed jowls. The chin-warmer was little more than stubble, matching the patchy salt-and-pepper hair on that jellybean of a head. 'Do these old eyes deceive me? Did you *catch* Dugdale?'

Callum wobbled up to his feet, one hand on his ruptured testicles, the other holding onto the Shogun for support. 'Oh: ha, ha.' Another wave of burning glass washed through him, leaving him grimacing.

'He's been unconscious for a couple of minutes. You want to take him straight to the hospital, or risk the Duty Doctor?'

Please say hospital, please say hospital. At least there a nice nurse might have an icepack and a few kind words for his mangled groin.

DS McAdams raised an eyebrow. 'I am shocked, Callum. Didn't he have enough cash? No nice bribe for you?'

'Sod off, Sarge.' He let go of his crotch for a moment, pointing off down the hill. Winced. Then cupped his aching balls again. 'Pair of kids got my wallet. We need to get after them.'

'If I had to guess. The reason you're hunched in pain. You have met *The Claw*!' He held up one hand, the fingers curled into a cruel hook, then squashed an invisible scrotum. 'Dugdale's claw attacks. Crush and squish, the pain is great. Bringing hard men low.'

Callum stared at him. 'They – got – my – wallet!'

The frown became a grin. 'A well-turned haiku. It is a beautiful thing. You ignorant spud.' He actually counted the syllables out on his fingers as he spoke.

'For your information, *Sarge*, I've never taken a bribe in my life. OK? Not a single sodding penny. No perks, no wee gifts, nothing. So you can all go screw yourselves.' He limped over to the back door and swung it open. 'Now are you going to help me get Dugdale in the car or not?'

'That's the trouble with your generation: no poetry in your souls. No education, no class, and no moral fibre.'

'Thanks for nothing.' He bent down. Winced. Clenched his jaw. Then hauled Dugdale's huge and heavy backside across the pavement and up onto the back seat.

'He better not bleed. On my new upholstery. I just had it cleaned.'

'Tough.' Some wrestling, a bit of forcing, a shove, and Dugdale was more or less in the recovery position. Well, except for his hands being cuffed behind his back. But at least now he *probably* wouldn't choke on his own tongue. Or vomit.

Mind you, if he spewed his breakfast all over Detective Sergeant McAdams' shiny new four-by-four, at least that would be something. Assuming McAdams didn't make Callum clean it up. Which he would.

Git.

Callum clunked the door shut, hobbled around to the passenger side and lowered himself into the seat. Crumpled forward until his forehead rested against the dashboard. 'Ow...'

'Seatbelt.' The car slid away from the kerb.

Callum closed his eyes. 'Think they turned right onto Grant Street.

14

If you hurry we can still catch them: wee boy in jeans and a blue track-suit top, wee girl in jeans and a red one. About six or seven years old. Both on bikes.'

'You got mugged by toddlers?' A gravelly laugh rattled out in the car. 'That's pathetic even for you.'

'They're getting away!'

'We're not going chasing after little kiddies, Constable. I have *much* more important things to do than clean up your disasters.'

'That's it. Stop the car.' Callum straightened up and bared his teeth. 'Come on: let's go. You and me. I battered the crap out of Dugdale, I can do the same for you.'

'Oh don't be such a baby.'

'I'm not kidding: stop – the – car.'

'Really, DC MacGregor? You don't think you're in enough trouble as it is? How's it going to look if you assault a senior officer who's dying of cancer? Think it through.' The car jolted and bumped, then swung around to the left, heading down towards Montrose Road. 'And any time our workplace badinage gets too much for you, feel free to pop into Mother's office with your resignation. Do us all a favour.' He slowed for the junction. 'Until then, try to behave like an *actual* police officer.'

Callum's hands curled into fists, so tight the knuckles ached. 'I swear to *God*—'

'Now put your seatbelt on and try not to say anything stupid for the next fifteen minutes. I'll not have you spoiling my remarkably good mood.' He poked the radio and insipid pop music dribbled out of the speakers. 'You see, Constable Useless, sometimes life gives you lemons, and sometimes it gives you vodka. *Today* is a vodka day.'

The jingly blandness piffled to a halt and a smoke-gravelled woman's voice came through. *'Hmmm, not sure about that one myself. You're listening to* Midmorning Madness *on Castlewave FM with me, Annette Peterson, and today my extra-special guest is author and broadcaster, Emma Travis-Wilkes.'*

McAdams put a hand over his heart, as if he was about to pledge allegiance. 'Today is a *caviar* day.'

'Glad to be here, Annette.'

'A champagne and strawberries day.'

'Now, a little bird tells me you're writing a book about your dad, Emma. Of course he created Russell the Magic Rabbit, Ichabod Smith, *and* Imelda's Miraculous Dustbin, *but he's probably best known for the children's classic,* Open the Coffins.'

'A chocolate and nipple clamps—'

'All right! I get it: everything's just sodding *great.*' Callum shifted in his seat, setting his testicles aching again. 'One of us got thwacked in the balls, here.'

'That's right. He's given joy to so many people, and now that he's … well, Alzheimer's is a cruel mistress. But it's been a real privilege to swim in the pool of his life again.'

'Pfff…' McAdams curled his top lip. 'Listen to this pretentious twaddle. Just because she's got a famous dad, she gets to plug her book on the radio. What about *my* book? Where's *my* interview?'

'And it's lovely to see these memories light up his face, it's like he's right back there again.'

'Cliché. And, by the way, unless his face is *actually* glowing like a lightbulb, that's physical hyperbole, you hack.'

Callum glowered across the car. 'We should never have chipped in for that creative writing class.'

McAdams grinned back at him. 'My heart: creative. My soul, it soars with the words. Divinity: mine.'

'Wonderful stuff. Now, let's have a bit of decent music, shall we? Here's one of the acts appearing at Tartantula this weekend: Catnip Jane, and "Once Upon a Time in Dundee".'

A banjo and cello launched into a sinister waltz, over a weird thumping rhythm as McAdams pulled out of the junction, heading left instead of right.

Silly old sod.

Callum sighed. 'You're going the wrong way.' He pointed across the swollen grey river, past the docks and the industrial units, towards the thick granite blade of Castle Hill. 'Division Headquarters is *that* direction. We need to get Dugdale booked in and seen to.'

'Meh, he'll keep.' That skeletal grin had widened. 'It's a vodka day, remember? We, my useless little friend, have finally got our hands on a murder!'

3

The first drop of rain sparkled against the windscreen, caught in a golden shaft of sunlight as McAdams' huge four-by-four slid past the last few houses on the edge of Kingsmeath. A second drop joined it. Then a third. Then a whole heap of them.

McAdams stuck the wipers on, setting them moaning and groaning their way across the glass, smearing the rain into grubby arcs. He pinned his mobile phone between his shoulder and ear, freeing his hand to change gears. Accelerating up the hill. 'Yeah. ... Yeah, Dugdale was there. ... No. ... Not a word of a lie, Mother: the new boy *actually* caught him. That's right: his anonymous tip-off paid off.' He cast a glance across the car at Callum. 'I know, I know. ... Ha! That's what I said.'

Callum folded his arms and pushed back into his seat. Stared out of the window at the dull green fields and their dull-grey sheep. The ache in his groin wasn't a full-on testicular migraine any more, it'd settled to more of a dull throbbing – each pulse marking time with the groaning windscreen wipers. 'Oh you're both *so* hilarious.'

'What did we say about you keeping your mouth shut?' Back to the phone. 'No, not you, Mother: Constable Useless here. ... Yeah, yeah. Exactly: an actual murder. How long has it been?'

Probably never see his wallet again.

McAdams put his foot down, overtaking a sputtering Mini. 'You on your way? ... Uh-huh. ... Yeah, I couldn't believe it either. Since when does the great Detective Chief Inspector Poncy Powel hand over a murder investigation to the likes of us? ... Exactly.'

More fields. More sheep.

OK, so it was just a scruffy, tatty lump of leather and the lining was falling apart, but it had sentimental value.

Bloody kids.

'Did he? … No! … No!' Laughter. 'And did you? … Sodding hell. … Yeah, he'll *love* that.'

Bloody Dugdale too.

He was just visible in the rear-view mirror, lying there with his mouth hanging open, face crusted with blood and bogies. Well, if Dugdale died in custody there was no way Callum was taking the rap for it. If anything happened it was McAdams' fault.

Accepting blame for Elaine's cock-up was one thing, but McAdams? He could sod right off.

'Uh-huh. We're about … five minutes away? Maybe less? … Still can't believe it: a real murder! How long's it been? … Right. Yup. OK. See you there.' He poked a button on his phone's screen then slid the thing back in his pocket, big smile plastered across his skeletal face.

'Am I allowed to ask where we're going?'

'No.'

Git.

McAdams took one hand off the wheel and pointed through the windscreen. 'We go where life rots. Where man's discarded dreams die. We go … to *The Tip*.' Fingers twitching with each syllable.

A large white sign loomed at the side of the road: 'OLDCASTLE MUNICIPAL RECYCLING AND WASTE PROCESSING FACILITY'. Someone had scrawled 'TWINNED WITH CUMBERNAULD!' across the bottom in green graffiti.

The Shogun slowed for the turning, leaving the well-ordered tarmac for a wide gravel road acned with potholes and lined with whin bushes. Their jagged dark-green spears rattled in the rain.

It was getting heavier, bouncing off the rutted track as McAdams navigated his shiny new car between the water-filled craters and up to a cordon of blue-and-white 'POLICE' tape.

He buzzed down the window and smiled at the lanky drip guarding the line. 'Two cheeseburgers, a Coke, and a chocolate milkshake please.'

A sigh and a sniff. Then Officer Drip wiped her nose on the sleeve of her high-viz jacket, sending water dribbling from the brim of her peaked cap. 'Do you *honestly* think it's the first time I've heard that today?'

'Cheer up, Constable. A little rain won't kill you.' He nodded at the cordon. 'You got our body?'

'Depends. You on the list?' She dug a clipboard from the depths of her jacket and passed it through the window.

McAdams flipped through the top three sheets, making a low whistling noise. 'There's a *lot* of people here. All for one dead little body?'

'Oh you'd be surprised.'

He printed two more names on the last sheet in blue biro, then handed the clipboard back. 'There we are, right at the end. Now be a good girl and get out of the way. It's the opening chapters: I need to draw the readers in, establish myself as the protagonist, and get on with solving the murder.'

Constable Drip frowned at their names, then into the car. Her mouth tightened as she stared at the bloodied and unconscious Dugdale lying across the back seat. 'Looks like you've already *got* a body.'

'Oh, this one's not dead, it's just resting. DC MacGregor decided to try his hand at a little police brutality.'

'MacGregor...?' She peered at the list again, then across the car, top lip curling. 'So it *is* you.'

Callum stared right back. 'Don't: I'm not in the mood.'

She shook her head, stowed her clipboard away, then unhooked a length of the tape barricade and waved them through.

McAdams grinned across the car at Callum. 'My, my, Constable. You just can't stop making friends, can you?'

No.

'That offer of an arse-kicking is still valid, Sarge.'

'Yes, because people don't hate you enough already.'

The Shogun pitched and yawed through the potholes like a boat. God knew how big the rubbish tip was, but from the wide, lumpy road, it stretched all the way to the horizon. A vast sea of black plastic, gulls wheeling and screaming in the air above – flecks of evil white, caught against the heavy grey sky.

And the *smell*...

Even with the car windows wound up it was something special. The rancid stench of rotting meat and vegetables mingled with the sticky-brown reek of used nappies, all underpinned by the dark peppery odour of black plastic left to broil in the sun.

McAdams slipped the four-by-four in behind a line of police vehicles and grubby Transit vans. Had to be, what, eight cars? Twelve if you counted the unmarked ones. About three-quarters of the dayshift, all out here playing on the tip.

The sarcastic half-arsed-poetry-spouting git was right: this was an awful lot of people for one dead body.

McAdams hauled on the handbrake. 'Right, Constable, make yourself useful for a change and go fetch us a couple of Smurf suits, extra-large. Ainsley and I need to have a little chat.'

A chat?

'He's *unconscious*, Sarge. He needs a doctor. I told you he—'

'Don't be stupid.' McAdams turned in his seat, staring through into the back. 'Give it up, Ainsley, you're not fooling anyone.'

Dugdale didn't move.

'Don't make me come back there, because if I have to...'

One of Dugdale's eyes cracked open. 'I'm dying. Got a brain haemorrhage, or something.'

'You have to have a *brain* to have a brain haemorrhage, Ainsley. What you've got is a lump of solid yuck wrapped in ugly. Now, Constable Naïve here is going to sod off like a good little boy and you're going to tell me *all* about what Big Johnny Simpson's up to now he's walked free.' McAdams made a dismissive little waving gesture in Callum's direction. 'Go on, Constable. Two Smurf suits, at the double. I won't ask again.'

One punch in the face. Just one. Right in the middle of his smug, wrinkly face...

What was the point?

It wouldn't change anything.

So Callum gritted his teeth and stepped out into the stinking mud. Closed the car door. Counted out his own muttered haiku. 'Away boil your head. You patronising arse-bag. I hope you get piles.'

Out here the smell was eye-watering. Like jamming your head in a dead badger.

He turned up his collar and hurried through the slimy mud to the nearest Transit van, sheltering in the lee of its open back doors. From here, Oldcastle lay spread out beneath the heavy grey lid of cloud like a cancer beneath the skin. The vast prow of Castle Rock loomed out from the other side of the valley, wound round with the ancient cobbled streets of Castle Hill; the dark sprawl of Camburn Woods peered out from its shadow; the warehouses, shopping centres, and big glass Victorian train station punctuated Logansferry to the left of that. Spires and minarets stabbed up between the slate roofs on the other side of the river, like some vast beast was trapped under the surface, trying to claw its way out. And on *this* side: the grubby maze of council houses, high-rise blocks of flats, and derelict terraces of Kingsmeath; the rest of the city, hidden by a line of trees at the edge of the tip.

Quite a view for a rancid mass of black plastic bags and mouldering filth.

He reached into the Transit and helped himself to two large blue Tyvek oversuits, two sets of plastic bootees, a pair of facemasks and matching safety goggles. What every well-dressed Scene of Crime officer was wearing this, and every other, season.

One of them appeared from the other side of the van, the hood of her SOC suit thrown back to reveal a sweaty tangle of dark brown hair. Her thin, pale oval face shone with sweat. She took a swig from a leopard-print Thermos, the words coming out on a waft of coffee breath with a faint side-order of Aberdonian. 'Oh, it's *you*.'

'Don't start, Cecelia, OK? I get enough of that from McAdams, don't need the Scene Examination Branch chipping in.' He tucked the suits under his arm. 'We're here for the body.'

She curled her top lip. 'Which one? Started digging at nine this morning and we've already turned up four of the things. Seven if you count those.' She nodded in the vague direction of a red plastic cool box and helped herself to a wad of paper towels. 'Three left feet, severed just above the ankle.'

'Well ... maybe their owners aren't dead? Maybe they're limping about somewhere, wondering where their other shoe's gone?'

'Urgh. I'm melting in here.' Cecelia scrubbed the paper towels across her damp face, turning it matt again. 'Bet they don't have this problem in G Division. Bet if you go digging in a Glasgow tip all you turn up is rubbish. Can't open a bin-bag in Oldcastle without finding a sodding corpse.' A sigh. 'Have you got any idea how much work it is to process crime scenes for *seven* different murder enquiries, all at the same time?' She ticked them off on her fingers. 'One stabbing, one shotgun blast to the face, one God-knows-what, and I'm pretty sure the body we found over by the recycling centre is Karen Turner. You know: ran that brothel on Shepard Lane? Beaten to death.'

At least that explained why most of Oldcastle Division was in attendance, picking their way through the landfill landscape.

'Wow.' Callum frowned out at the acres and acres of black-plastic bags. Suppose it wasn't *that* surprising the tip was hoaching with corpses – if you had to dispose of a body, where better than here? Clearly the city's criminal element didn't approve of littering. 'Maybe we should set up a recycling box at the front gate, so people can dump their dead bodies responsibly?'

She puffed out her cheeks. 'We should never have started digging here. Just asking for trouble.'

'So, come on then: which one's ours?'

'Body number three: the God-knows-what. That way.' She pointed her Thermos at the middle distance, off to the right, where a handful of blue-suited figures was wrestling with a white plastic tent. 'And Callum?'

He turned back to her. 'What?'

'I know it wasn't you.'

What wasn't…?

She rolled her eyes. 'There's no point standing there looking glaikit. You didn't cock-up that crime scene, Elaine did.'

Oh.

Heat bloomed in his cheeks. 'No she didn't.'

'Yes she did. Elaine worked for me, so I *know* it wasn't you. One more strike and they'd have fired her.'

He tucked one of the Tyvek suits under his arm. 'I've got no idea what you're talking about.'

Cecelia shook her head, sending a little trickle of sweat running into the elasticated neck of her suit. 'You're a daft sod, Callum MacGregor.'

True.

'Bye, Cecelia.' He turned and marched back to the Shogun.

McAdams was still in the car, mobile clamped to his ear, so Callum struggled into one of the SOC Smurf suits – zipping it up to the chin, hood up. Stood there in the manky mud, rain pattering off his Smurfy shoulders and head.

Come on, you lanky git. Get off the phone.

A rattley green Fiat Panda lumbered its way up the track towards them, bringing a cloud of blue-grey smoke with it. Dents in the bonnet, dents in the passenger side, a long scrape along the driver's door and front wing. Duct tape holding the wing mirror on.

Great, because having to deal with DS Sodding McAdams wasn't bad enough.

The Panda spluttered to a halt behind McAdams' immaculate Castleview Tractor, and its driver peered out through a fogged-up windscreen as the wipers made angry-donkey noises across the glass.

Mother.

She looked right at him and the smile died on her face.

Oh joy.

He gave her a nod. As if that was going to make any difference.

Mother struggled her way out into the rain.

The sleeves of her black fleece were rolled up to the elbows, exposing two large pale forearms – tattoos standing out like faded newsprint against the doughy flesh. A dolphin. Two swallows holding up a little banner with 'LOVE NEVER DIES' on it. A thistle and a rose wrapped around a dagger. What looked like a tribute to the Bay City Rollers – all mullets and tartan scarfs. She glanced about, sending her mass of tight ginger curls bobbing. Sniffed. 'Where's Andy?' Apparently completely unfazed by the rain.

'DS McAdams is in the car, making some calls.'

Her eyes narrowed. 'Have you been upsetting him?'

'Upsetting *him*? He wasn't the one Dugdale tried to neuter! Come on, Mother, how come every—'

'Ah yes, Andy said you'd had a run-in with The Claw.' A tiny smile. 'And how many times do I have to tell you: you haven't earned the right to call me "Mother". As far as you're concerned it's Boss, Guv, or Detective Inspector. Are we crystal?'

'It wasn't a "run-in", Dugdale resisted arrest. Violently. And *for the record*,' Callum pointed at the back seat of the Shogun, where Dugdale was now sitting up, 'I said we should take him to the hospital, but DS McAdams refused.'

The tiny smile grew. 'Nobody likes a clype, Constable.'

A clunk and McAdams emerged from the car. 'Mother...' A frown. 'MacGregor, why are you wearing that SOC suit?'

Callum looked down at his blue Tyvek body. 'You told me to get two Smurf—'

'One for me and one for *Mother*, you idiot. Why the hell would we want you messing up our crime scene?'

He clenched his fists. Stepped forwards. 'You think I won't—'

'All right, that's enough.' Mother held a hand up. 'Andy, we're going to cut the wee boy some slack on account of The Claw. He can come with us.' The hand came down again, till it pointed at Callum. 'Don't make me regret this.'

'Yes, Boss.'

'Now go find someone to keep an eye on Ainsley here,' she nodded at Dugdale in the back seat, 'and fetch me a Smurf suit. We've got a dead body to gawp at.'

4

Wet bin-bags shifted beneath his feet, popping and crackling, crunching and slithering in the rain. Hard not to imagine the surface opening up and swallowing them whole. Pulling them further and further down to drown in its reeking depths.

God that was cheery.

Mother and McAdams struggled on beside him, clinging on to each other to stay upright on the bin-bag sea. They must have made quite a sight: all three of them, dressed in matching blue outfits that were about as flattering as a dose of dysentery, shuffling their way through the rubbish towards the SOC tent.

It stood, a grimy shade of white, poking out of the bin-bag ocean like an iceberg. Or some vast grubby tooth.

Mother sniffed behind her mask. 'What do we know about our victim?'

'Nothing.' McAdams picked his way past a slimy mass of something. 'DCI Powel was even more inscrutable than usual. Probably got his nose out of joint because he had to hand it over to us.'

'Poor darling. Still, as long as it's a murder and we're investigating it, I'm happy.'

McAdams let go with one hand and placed it against his chest, launching into a wobbly but not unpleasant baritone:

'People dismembered with axes and chainsaws,
Someone's been strangled with wire or some string,
A stabbing, a beating, a fresh torture victim,
These are a few of my favourite things...'

'Oh, *very* good. I like that.' She struggled on a couple of steps. 'Thought you were on haikus today.'

'Decided to branch out a bit.'

A cordon of yellow-and-black tape encircled the SOC tent, the words 'CRIME SCENE – DO NOT ENTER' rippling and spinning in the wind. Every gust making the plastic tape growl. Water ran down the tent's walls, dripping off the sagging roof.

Mother motioned to Callum and he held up the cordon so she could duck under and slip inside. McAdams stopped right next to him, voice low, just audible through the facemask. 'In the three weeks you've been here, you've done nothing but moan, whinge, and disappoint. But if you compromise my crime scene, I'll make you wish Dugdale still had your balls in his fist. Understand?'

Callum just stared back.

'Good.' He turned and pushed through into the tent.

Count to ten.

Don't let him get to you.

Deep breath.

Callum pulled his shoulders back and followed McAdams inside.

Rain thudded against the tent's roof. The wind moaned through the gaps in the plastic, making the walls shudder. Technically, you could have parked a couple of patrol cars in here and still had room for a police motorbike, but instead it was home to a small diesel generator and four workplace lights on six-foot stands.

The stench was something special – so thick it was almost chewy, trapped by the tent's walls and roof, amplified by the warmth of decomposition, and soured with diesel exhaust fumes.

Four figures in the full Smurf kit were kneeling around a hole dug into the rubbish, right in the middle of the tent.

Mother joined them and clapped her hands, raising her voice over the rain and the generator. 'Come on then, what have you got for me?'

One of the figures straightened up with a groan, both hands pressed into the small of his back. 'Mummy.'

She pursed her lips. 'I don't mind a little informality, young man, but that's going a bit too far.'

'Not you.' He pulled down his facemask, showing off a round sweaty face with tiny pursed lips. Like someone had pumped a cherub up on steroids and pies. 'In the hole: it's a mummy. Your actual, curse-of-the-Pharaohs, from-the-leathery-mists-of-time, mummy.'

'Really?' Mother inched her way to the very edge and peered down.

'Or it might be a daddy. Difficult to tell without unfolding the limbs, and I get the feeling they'll snap off if we do that. Teabag tends to frown on our dismembering corpses before he's had a chance to post mortem them.' He dug out a scrap of cloth and dabbed at his shiny face. 'Gah. Like a sauna in here.'

McAdams stepped up beside Mother. 'Ah...'

Callum crept around to the opposite side of the hole, bin-bags shifting beneath his blue-booteed feet, and leaned out over the edge.

The SOC team had shored up the sides of their excavation with sheets of corrugated iron, which held back the mass of garbage, but did nothing to stop the grey-brown liquid seeping out underneath it.

Their body lay on its side at the bottom of the hole, about eight feet down, where the liquid was deepest. Elbows tight in against its ribs, hands drawn up to its chest, knees hard up against them, feet tucked in to the body. Its neck was bent hard forward, so the face was completely hidden by the hands and knees. So far, so murdery, but it was the skin that gave it away. Instead of being all blotched with mould and falling apart it was creased and leathery. Darkened to a dirty mahogany. The only ear visible had shrivelled up till it resembled a dried apricot, clinging to the side of its bald head.

Callum raised his eyebrows. 'Now there's a sight you don't see every day.'

Mother's fists clenched at her sides. 'That rotten, two-faced, lying *bastard*!'

The oversized sweaty cherub in the SOC suit wiped his glistening forehead. 'At a guess, it's got to be about, what ... a thousand years old?'

'I should have known! Thought they'd finally given me a proper murder, but *no*. That was asking too much, wasn't it?' She turned and stomped out of the tent.

McAdams didn't follow her, just shouted over his shoulder instead. 'Where are you going?'

Her voice faded away into the distance. 'To tell DCI Powel exactly where he can stick his thousand-year-old mummy!'

The only sound in the tent was the hammering rain and the growling generator.

'Hmmm...' McAdams squatted down, one hand on the bin-bag next to him. 'The body's naked. Wonder what happened to all the bandages.' He glanced up at the Cherub. 'It's a mummy, it should be all wrapped up.'

'Don't look at me.'

Callum eased himself down to his haunches, holding onto the top of a corrugated sheet. No way he was risking an eight-foot plummet into a paddling pool of rancid bin water. 'They've got a mummy just like it in Elgin Museum. On display, naked in a big bell jar. Some Victorian bloke brought it back from Peru: suppose he unwrapped it so the viewing public could get a good look at a real-life dead body.' A small smile shifted against his facemask. 'We used to go there when I was a wee boy. Me and Alastair would…' Yes. Well. The less said about that the better.

McAdams grunted, then stood. Turned to face the sweaty cherub. 'Don't suppose we've got any clue who dumped it here, do we?'

One of the other Smurfs looked up from the contents of a ruptured refuse sack. 'Nah. Back in the good old days, there'd be envelopes and letters and newspapers all through this stuff – dates and addresses in every bag. Now?' He shook his head. 'Recycling: bane of our lives.'

McAdams wiped his hands together. 'Soon as Dr Twining's seen the remains, get them bagged, tagged, and down the mortuary. And if he gives you any grief about it being a waste of his valuable time, tell him tough. Don't see why we should be the only ones.' A click of the fingers, held high overhead, as if McAdams was summoning a waiter in a sitcom. 'Constable MacGregor: we're leaving. Turns out this is more of a short story than a fully-fledged novel.'

Callum stayed where he was, sniffing the air. 'Can you smell that?'

'I said, "We're *leaving*."'

'No, underneath all the rotting rubbishy smell, there's something else. Wood smoke? Like there's been a fire?'

'Don't look at me.' The Cherub shook his head. 'Fifteen minutes in here and you go nose-blind. Can't smell a thing.'

McAdams' voice boomed from outside the tent: '*CONSTABLE MACGREGOR! HEEL!*'

The Cherub shrugged. 'His master's voice.'

Don't suppose it mattered anyway. What was one extra smell on top of all the others?

Callum stood, wiped his gloves on his legs, and slipped back out into the rain.

Halfway back across the slippery bin-bags, his phone launched into its default ringtone. Sodding hell. He peeled off his right glove and fought the bare hand into his SOC suit. Pulled out his phone. Kept on walking. 'Hello?'

'*Ah, hello. Am I speaking to Detective Constable Callum MacGregor?*'

He checked the number. Nope, no idea who it was. 'Can I help you?'

'*Good, good. This is Alex from Professional Standards, we'd like you to pop in for a wee chat.*'

Oh God.

'How does tomorrow morning sound? I know it's taken us a while to get round to it, but better late than never, yes?'

No.

'Tomorrow morning?'

'Excellent. Let's say... Oh, that's lucky: I can fit you in at seven. First thing in the morning, then you can get on with your day without having to worry about it.'

Might as well get it over with – like ripping off a sticking plaster, wrenching all the hair out with it. 'Right. Yes. Seven tomorrow morning.'

After all, what was the worst that could happen?

They could fire him. Prosecute him. And send him to prison.

'Good, good. See you then.' Alex from Professional Standards hung up.

It would be fine. It would.

Callum put his phone away. 'Yeah, you just keep telling yourself that.'

He crunched his way through the bin-bags to McAdams' shiny new Mitsubishi Shogun. The lanky git was leaning on the roof of Mother's scabby Fiat Panda, one hand making lazy circles in the air as she peeled herself out of her Smurf outfit. Probably working on new ways to make Callum's life even worse. As if it wasn't bad enough already.

Professional Standards.

Gah...

He yanked open the passenger door and pinged his blue nitrile gloves into the footwell. Tore off his SOC suit and bundled it up.

They didn't have anything on him.

They *couldn't* – he hadn't done anything.

Yeah, but when did that ever stop anyone?

He scowled at his crumpled suit. What was the point taking it back to the station and sticking it in the bin, it was just going to end up right back here anyway. Callum hurled it away. It spun, unfurling in mid-air like a shed skin, before tumbling to the filthy ground.

And when he turned back to the car, there was Dugdale grinning at him from the back seat.

'Oh ... sod off.'

The municipal tip shrank in the rear-view mirror. McAdams shifted behind the wheel, dug a packet of gum from his pocket and crunched down a little white rectangle. 'Right, you know what's coming next, don't you?'

Sitting behind him, Dugdale scowled out of the window. 'I want a lawyer.'

'Not talking to you, Ainsley, I'm talking to our special little friend, Constable Crime Scene here.'

Callum folded his arms. 'If it's more haikus, I'm putting in for a transfer.'

'Don't let me stop you. First call all the museums. See whose mummy's gone.'

He stared across the car. 'Oh you have *got* to be kidding—'

'One of them's lost a mummy. I'll bet if you beaver away *super* hard for the next two or three months, you'll find out which one.' He smiled. 'Unless you're too busy resigning, of course? Wouldn't want to get in the way of that.'

'Oh for... Why can't Watt do it?'

'Because, dear Constable Useless,' McAdams turned a smile loose, 'I don't like *you* even more than I don't like *him*.' The smile widened. 'It'll be good for you: character building.'

Callum turned to face the passenger window. 'I'd like to build your character with a sodding claw-hammer.'

'Did you say something, Constable?'

'I said, "Yes, Sarge."'

'Good boy.'

And a nail gun.

Dugdale was still wearing the same scowl, but he'd swapped his clothes for a white SOC suit, bare toes sticking out of a pair of manky grey flip-flops. And he'd washed the dried blood off his face. That would be a bonus when his duty solicitor finally appeared.

Callum stood on the concrete apron and waved him goodbye as a Police Custody and Security Officer led him away, steering Dugdale down the corridor and into the cell with 'M6' stencilled on the thick blue door.

The cell block rang with the sound of someone screaming what sounded like passages from the Bible. All 'thee' and 'thou' and that.

Raw breezeblock walls painted a tired magnolia, with a blue line all the way around it, straddling the bright-red panic strip. A dozen cells in this block, most of them occupied, going by the A4-sized whiteboards mounted next to each closed door. Three assaults, two indecent exposures, a theft from a locked-fast place, a shoplifter, one breach of bail conditions, an attempted murder, and Dugdale.

'*VERILY, SAYETH THE LORD, FOR YE SHALL FEAR MINE WRATH!*'

The PCSO stepped back out into the corridor and clunked the cell shut. Printed, 'RESISTING ARREST, ASSAULT, ARMED ROBBERY', on the custody board, each word smaller than the last as she ran out of space, finishing with a scrawled '& CONSPIRACY 2 PTCoJ'.

'*AND YE SHALL BE SORE AFRAID IN THE TIME OF DARKNESS! FOR LO, IT IS THE WORD OF THE LORD THAT COMES FOR THEE!*'

'Oh shut up, you fruitcake.' The PCSO stuck her marker-pen back in her top pocket and looked Callum up and down. 'Something we can do for you, Constable?'

'*YEA, FOR HE IS THE DARKNESS AND HE IS THE LIGHT!*'

'Can you give me a shout when his solicitor gets here?'

'*AND ALL SHALL KNOW HIS WRATH! THESE ARE THE END OF DAYS, AND—*'

She clicked down the viewing hatch on M3. Tutted. Then, 'Come on, Phil, I thought we had an agreement.'

A muffled, '*Sorry.*' came from the other side of the door.

'Should think so too, disturbing all our other guests. Poor Ken's trying to sleep.' She clicked the hatch up again. Turned to Callum. 'They picked him up on Chamber Street, "The End Is Nigh" placard in one hand, his "original sin" in the other.'

Lovely. 'So, Dugdale's solicitor…?'

She shook her head. 'Now Kenneth, on the other hand, tried to smash his mother's head in with a china dog from the mantelpiece. Spaniel, I think it was. She wouldn't let him go to the pictures. He's forty-six.'

'Yeah, but Dugdale…?' Eyebrows: up, winning smile: on.

'I can't.' A sigh. 'Oh, don't look at me like that, it's orders. "DC MacGregor is not to be given access to custodies or their representatives without a superior officer being present."'

'You are *kidding* me!'

'All contact is to be managed through DS McAdams or DI Malcolmson.'

'I can't talk to anyone without McAdams or Mother holding my hand?'

'Nothing to do with me, it's…' She turned away. 'If you were them, would you want to risk it?'

5

'Yes, I understand that, but I'm asking anyway: do you now, or have you at any time, had a human mummy in your museum?'

The smell of chicken curry Pot Noodle coiled its way across the office, warring against a taint of cheesy feet and yesterday's garlic.

From up here, on the third floor of Division Headquarters, the view should have been a lot better than it was: the back of a billboard streaked with pigeon droppings. Rusting supports featured a dozen small grey feathered bodies, strutting about and adding to the stains.

'*A mummy? What, like an Egyptian one?*' The young man on the other end of the phone sounded about as bright as a broken lightbulb. '*Nah. No. Don't think so.*' Think, think, think. '*Maybe?*'

Callum turned his back on the window, one hand massaging his temples, the other gripping the phone tight enough to make the plastic creak. Fighting hard to keep his voice reasonable and level. 'Can you check for me? It's important.'

The room was divided up into six bits, each one sectioned off with a chest-high cubicle wall – their grubby blue fabric stained with dribbled coffee and peppered with memos from the senior brass and cartoons cut from the *Castle News and Post*. Six cubicles for six desks, two of which were laden with dusty cardboard boxes and teetering piles of manila folders.

Almost every horizontal surface was covered in a thin grey fuzz of dust.

The top of Dot's head was just visible above the edge of her cubicle, pale-brown hair swept up in a weird semi-beehive do. Schlurping noises marked the death of yet another freeze-dried soy and noodle product.

31

A tiny kitchen area sat in the corner behind her, complete with kettle, microwave, and a half-sized fridge that gurgled and buzzed. Throw in a sagging assortment of ceiling tiles, scuffed magnolia walls littered with scribbled-on whiteboards, the kind of carpet that looked as if it'd been fished out of a skip, and you had the perfect place to dump police officers while they waited for their careers to die.

Or were too stubborn to realise that their careers already had.

'Pffff... Suppose. I'll see what I can do. Hang on, gotta put you on hold.' Click, and an elevator muzak version of 'American Idiot' dribbled out of the earpiece.

Callum printed the word 'dick' in little biro letters next to the museum's name. It joined a long, long list.

Dot wheeled her chair back till she could peer around her cubicle. 'Callum, you on the phone?' Her scarlet lipstick was smudged and a shiny dot of gravy glittered on one rounded cheek. For some reason she'd decided it was a good idea to dress up in what looked like a black chef's jacket, only with shiny silver buttons and silvery edging.

He held up the receiver. 'On hold.'

'Don't fancy making a chocolate run, do you? Only the machine on the fifth floor's got Curly Wurlies.'

'Can't: I'm on *hold*.' He waggled the phone again to emphasise the point.

'I'd go myself, but I'm avoiding Detective Superintendent Ness. She found out I scratched her new Nissan Micra with Keith. Please?'

His shoulder slumped. 'Dot—'

'Pretty please? Got the doctor at three, need to keep my morale up.'

A voice growled out from the opposite corner: 'For Christ's sake!' Watt stood, glowering over his cubicle wall at them. He'd swept his dark floppy hair back from his high forehead, securing it there with enough product to stick a hippo to the wall. Sunken eyes. Squint teeth. A sad excuse for a beard that looked as if he'd made it himself out of ginger pubic hair. 'Will the two of you shut up? Some of us are trying to *work*.'

Dot narrowed her eyes at him. 'Oh, I'm sorry Detective *Constable* Watt, are we disturbing your sulk?'

He stuck out his chin and its wispy covering. 'I am *not* sulking, *Sergeant*. I'm preparing for a deposition, OK? Now will the pair of you shut up and let me get on with it?'

'All I wanted was a Curly Wurly.'

'Fine! Fine. You know what? Here...' He dug into his pocket and hurled a fiver in Callum's direction. It fluttered and tumbled in mid-air, falling to the manky carpet six feet short. 'Go. Get her some sodding chocolate. Just do it quietly.'

Callum held up the phone again. 'Is this thing invisible? I'm – on – *hold!*'

'*Aye, hello?*' The Scottish idiot on the other end cut 'American Idiot' dead. '*Hello? ... You still there?*'

Finally. 'Hello. Yes.'

'*Right, I've had a word with Davey: he can't remember a mummy, but he's only been here a year longer than me. Marge's been here for donkeys', but she's on holiday till the twelfth. Gone to Norwich for a BDSM festival. You want me to give her your contact details so she can drop you an email when she gets back?*'

Callum folded forward until his forehead rested against his keyboard. Don't swear. Don't swear. 'That would be great. Thanks.'

'*Yeah, OK.*' And the line went dead.

He hung up.

Dot's chair squeaked across the room. Squeak. Squeak. Squeak. Until it was right next to him. When he looked up, she smiled. 'So ... chocolate?' She fiddled with the wheelchair's push rims, twisting the whole thing left and right. All coy and fluttering eyelashes. The left leg of her jeans was stitched closed and trimmed off, just below where her knee should have been.

Suppose a little help getting some chocolate wasn't too much to ask for.

He closed his eyes for a moment. Then nodded. 'Yeah. Could do with a break anyway.' He pushed back from his desk. 'Curly Wurly, coming right up.'

She nodded at the list sitting next to his phone. 'No luck?'

'You got any idea how many museums there are in Scotland?' He stood, bent over and scooped Watt's hurled fiver from the floor. 'Then there's all the universities and private schools with natural history stuff in display cases. Never mind private collections.'

'You want a hand?'

He blinked. Turned back to her.

At least *one* person on the team didn't treat him like something they'd stepped in. 'Thanks, Dot.'

'Don't get all emotional about it. I'm only helping so you'll be my chocolate monkey.' She wiggled her fingers above her head, cackling it out: 'Fly free, my pretty!'

Over in the corner, Watt gave a frustrated wee scream.

*   *   *

Callum slumped his way up the stairs. Two years since they stopped doing proper meals in the canteen. Two years and the stairwell *still* smelled of boiled cabbage.

His phone went off as he reached the fourth-floor landing. Sodding hell.

He dragged it out. 'What?'

There was a pause. Then a high-pitched man's voice squeaked in his ear. *'Mr MacGregor? I'm calling from the Royal Caledonian Building Society's Fraud Prevention Department. I need to ask you a few security questions. OK?'*

Callum glowered at the wall. 'No, it's not OK.'

'I'm sorry, have I called at a bad time?'

'Someone's just nicked my wallet, and I've got no idea who you are. I'm not giving you my security details. You want to help? You prove who *you* are by answering *my* security questions.'

'I ... I don't think we're allowed to do that.'

'Tough. What's the third, fifth, and first letters of my mother's maiden name?'

'Errr... Look: why don't you call us, then? That way you'll know it's not a scam. You'll find the number on the back of your cards.'

'On the back of my *stolen* cards? The cards I don't have?'

'Ah... Right.' What sounded like an argument echoed up from the floors below, followed by a door clunking shut. *'Well, maybe you could pop into a branch and they can help you?'* Was that a note of hope and desperation there at the end? *Please* go away and become someone else's problem.

'Yeah. Why not.' He hung up and clunked his head against the wall. Breathed in the cabbagey smell. Then opened his eyes and swore. No wallet meant no cards. And the little sods had wheeched off with his last fifteen quid, leaving him with... He rummaged in his pocket and came out with two pounds fifty-six in change, a button, and a Mint Imperial that had gone all hairy with pocket fluff. So Elaine could have a jar of Polish pickles *or* a jar of Nutella, but not both. And forget the onion rolls.

Because it wasn't as if he could steal the change from Watt's fiver.

Could he?

He puffed out a breath. Of course he sodding couldn't.

Callum lumbered up the stairs to the fifth floor. Pushed open the door. And froze.

DCI Powel was standing right in front of him, mug in one hand, manila folder tucked under his arm, phone in his other hand. A big man with ears to match, silver-grey hair swept forward from his temples to cover the bald bits. Smart suit with matching tie. He narrowed his eyes. 'Hang on a minute, Margaret, there's someone I need to talk to.' He lowered the phone.

Callum backed away, into the stairwell again, but Powel followed him.

'Well, well, well, if it isn't our very own answer to Mr Bean: Detective Constable Callum MacGregor.'

'Guv.'

'I hear you managed to catch Ainsley Dugdale this morning, Constable. He's one of Big Johnny Simpson's goons, isn't he? That's a first for you, isn't it? Big Johnny won't like that.'

Don't rise to it.

'And we all know how much you *love* Big Johnny Simpson, don't we?' A massive finger rose and poked Callum in the chest. 'Don't think I won't screw you to the wall for that, Constable. I don't put up with dirty cops in my division.'

Callum curled his hands into fists. 'Permission to speak freely, Guv?'

'Not a chance.' He leaned in closer, bringing with him the stench of aftershave and dead cigarettes. 'I don't like you, Constable.'

'You hide it well, Guv.'

Was that a twitch of a smile?

Then Powel backed off, turned and marched away down the stairs. 'Enjoy your meeting with Professional Standards, tomorrow. I'll bring in a cardboard box so you can empty your desk afterwards.'

Clunk. The door closed, and Callum was alone again.

'And screw you too, Guv.'

Powel's voice echoed up from the landing below: 'I'm still here, Constable.'

Of course he was.

6

Callum logged off his steam-powered computer, stretched, yawned, slumped in his seat for a moment, then hauled himself to his feet.

The office's fluorescent lighting buzzed overhead, giving everything the warm and welcoming ambience of a horror film. Shame he was the only one there to enjoy it.

One more yawn, a sigh, and a rummage in the bottom drawer of his desk for the paperback-sized Tupperware box he'd stuck in there first thing this morning. He went back in for the dog-eared hardback copy of *The Monsters Who Came for Dinner*. Checked his watch. Just gone two. With any luck the lunchtime rush at the building society would have petered out by now, but if it hadn't at least he'd have something decent to read.

Callum pulled on his jacket and stuffed his sandwiches in one pocket, crisps in the other. Right, time to—

The office door swung open and McAdams loomed into the room.

Sod.

McAdams frowned. 'And where, exactly, do you think *you're* going, Constable MacGregor?'

So near, and yet so far. 'Lunch, Sarge.'

'Lunch? Off to hide in the park reading… What is that, a kid's book?'

'It's a *classic*.'

'Maybe if you're six years old.' He checked his watch. 'And you don't have time. That mummy needs its home found. Get your arse to work.'

Again with the sodding haikus.

'I've *been* working.' Callum picked up the list, all eight pages of it, and shoogled it. 'Now, I'm going to waste my contractually mandated lunchtime in the building society, trying to get them to give me some of my own money, so I can buy food for my pregnant girlfriend. That all right with you?'

McAdams snatched the list from his hand and flicked through the sheets. Frowned. 'Constable, why do these museums have the word "dick" written next to them?'

Ah...

'I'm waiting, Constable.'

Right. Yes. Er...

Ah, OK: 'It's not "Dick", Sarge, it's "D.I.C.K." Database Incomplete – Currently Checking. Most of them don't have an electronic register of all the exhibits in storage, so they're getting back to me.'

McAdams raised an eyebrow, making a line of wrinkles climb its way up his forehead. '"Checking" doesn't start with a K, Constable.'

Innocent face. 'Doesn't it, Sarge?'

'But I appreciate the creative effort.' He pointed at the empty desks. 'Where's Captain Sulky and The Wheels?'

'DC Watt's off to a deposition – that schoolteacher they caught rubbing himself against old ladies in the big Waterstones. DS Hodgkin has a doctor's appointment.'

'Hmmm...' McAdams' mouth pulled down at the edges. 'Ah well, I suppose it can't be helped.' He clicked his fingers. 'You, with me. Mother's office. Now.'

What?

They weren't going to fire him, were they? They couldn't. Professional Standards hadn't even questioned him yet. They couldn't fire him till *after* that, surely?

Or maybe they could.

Callum took one last look around the miserable little office – with all its stains and dusty surfaces – then followed McAdams out into the corridor, across the hall, and in through the door opposite. The one with a small brass plaque on it, marked: 'DETECTIVE INSPECTOR MALCOLMSON ~ DIVISIONAL INVESTIGATIVE SUPPORT TEAM'.

Mother's office was a bit nicer than her team's, but not by much. It was just big enough for a scarred Formica desk, a line of filing cabinets down one wall, a whiteboard on the other surrounded by pictures of cats cut out of an old calendar, and a single chair for visitors.

Mother was behind her desk, sooking on the end of a biro, but a uniformed PC stood in the middle of the room, at attention: black trousers; big black boots; black fleece with her ID number on the epaulettes; black, police-issue bowler under one arm. Her curly black hair was pulled back in a bun, exposing the dark skin at the nape of her neck.

OK… Maybe they weren't going to fire him. Maybe they were going to arrest him instead.

Mother wrinkled her mouth around the pen and stared at Callum. 'Is this it?'

McAdams propped himself up against a filing cabinet. 'Everyone else is out.'

'Suppose he'll have to do.' She turned. 'Constable Franklin, this is Detective Constable Callum MacGregor. Not the brightest spade in the undertaker's, but he's all ours. For our sins.' Another grimace. 'Callum, this is Constable Franklin. She's joining us from E Division. That means you're no longer the new boy. You will show her the ropes. You will be nice to her. And most of all,' Mother poked the desk with the sooked end of her pen, 'you will *not* lead her astray. Are we crystal?'

Babysitting. Even more joy.

'Yes, Boss.'

'Good.' Mother plucked a sheet of paper from her in-tray and held it out. 'Now, if neither of you have anything better to do—'

Callum stuck up his hand. 'Actually, Boss, I—'

'—and I know for a fact that you *don't*, you can chase this up.'

Constable Franklin took the piece of paper. 'Ma'am.' The word was forced out, resentment dripping from that one syllable like burning pus.

'Tell me, Constable, do you have a fighting suit?'

'A fighting…?' It must have dawned, because she nodded. 'Yes, ma'am.'

'Good. You're a DC now: change out of that uniform. You look like you're about to arrest someone.'

A twitch, a tightening of the hands into fists. A breath. Then: 'Ma'am.'

Oh yeah, babysitting this one was going to be *bags* of fun.

'Off you go then.'

Franklin turned on her heel, face all pinched and flushed. Narrowed her dark-brown eyes and bared her teeth at Callum. 'Do we have a problem, *Detective* Constable?' Voice like a silk-covered razorblade.

Wow. She was just … wow. Completely … like a *model* or something. Not just pretty, but totally—

'I asked you a question.' She curled her top lip, exposing more perfect teeth. 'What's the matter, never seen a black woman before?'

'I… It… No.' He blinked. Stood up straighter. 'I mean: no. No problem. Welcome on board.' He stuck out his hand for shaking, but she just pushed past and marched from the room, slamming the door behind her.

'Bloody hell...' Callum leaned against the wall.

'I know. Magnificent, isn't she?' McAdams grinned at the closed door, then laid a hand against his chest. 'Skin like warm midnight. Her eyes are moonlit rubies. Her heart: frozen steel.' A sniff. 'See if I hadn't already ticked "threesome" off my bucket list?'

Mother smiled. 'Congratulations. Anyone I know?'

'Nah: Beth got someone from her work. Miranda. Nice lady. Presbyterian, but *very* open minded.' He frowned at Callum. 'Still here, Constable? Haven't you got an angry detective constable to babysit?'

'Yes, Sarge.'

Sodding hell.

Bright yellow diggers and tipper trucks lumbered about on the massive Camburn Roundabout, rearranging it's grass and earth into swathes of rutted mud. The Vauxhall's windscreen wipers made dying-squid noises as Callum took the first exit. He snuck a glance out the corner of his eye at the simmering lump of resentment sitting in the passenger seat.

She'd ditched the uniform in favour of a black suit with weird puffy shoulders, a white shirt, and thin black tie. As if she was on the way to someone's funeral. 'What the hell are you staring at?'

He snapped his eyes front again. 'Nothing.' Yellow-brick cookie-cutter houses stretched out on either side of the road. Bland, safe, and predictable. 'Actually...' He bit his lip. 'If you don't mind my asking...' Deep breath. 'What did you do?'

She turned and gave him the kind of look that could strip flesh from the bone.

'I mean, you know, to end up working for DI Malcolmson?'

DC Franklin faced front again.

'Only, it's not usually—'

'Do you always talk this much?'

'Just thought, if we're going to be working together, we—'

'Let's get something perfectly clear, Detective Constable MacGregor: I am not your friend. I am not your colleague. I am someone who will be out of here very, *very* soon.' She shot her cuffs, making them exactly the same length where they stuck out of the sleeves of her shoulder-padded jacket. 'I don't intend to spend the remainder of my career lumbered with a bunch of dropouts, has-beens, and never-weres.'

The houses gave way to greying fields and austere drystane dykes. All hard edges softened by the incessant drizzle.

Franklin pulled out her phone and poked away at the screen. Glowering down at it in silence. Ignoring him.

OK, well no one could say he hadn't tried.

About three miles south of Shortstaine, a pair of dark lines swooped out from the tarmac, dug through the roadside verge and punched a hole through a barbed-wire fence. A patrol car sat twenty yards further down, parked up on the side with its flashers going.

Callum indicated and pulled in behind it. 'There's a couple of high-viz jackets in the boot, if you want to... OK.'

She was already out of the car, stalking her way across the verge and down into the field beyond.

'Fine. Catch your death of cold, see if I care.' He helped himself to one of the fluorescent-yellow monstrosities and followed her. Arms out to keep his balance on the slippery grass slope.

A hatchback sat about a hundred yards into the field, on the other side of the fence, at the end of those curling dark lines. Its front end had made friends with a chunk of rock, leaving the bonnet twisted like a sneer.

Franklin was halfway there already, back straight and rigid. Presumably because the stick rammed up her backside was of the extra-large variety.

Callum picked his way down the hill until he stood beside her.

The hatchback was an old Kia Picanto – the kind that looked like a roller-skate on steroids. Originally blue, it was now a muddy grey, with deep scratches along both sides where the barbed wire had raked it. A 'Police Aware' sticker covered most of the driver's window.

Franklin stared at the car, then pulled out a sheet of paper and stared at that instead. Then back to the car. 'Is this *it*?'

Callum walked over to the back window and peered in through the rain-flecked glass.

Inside, the car was a mess. Not just the usual burger wrappers and sweetie papers, but splashes of paint and crusts of what looked like plaster dust. A tool bag lay in the rear footwell, next to two drums of flooring adhesive and a packet of slate tiles.

A voice behind them: 'HOY!'

Callum turned.

A young bloke in uniform was stomping his way across the field towards them, one hand holding the peaked cap on top of his head.

'YOU! WHAT THE HELL DO YOU THINK YOU'RE DOING? GET AWAY FROM THERE!'

Franklin waited till he was six feet away, before hauling out a standard-issue warrant-card holder. 'Constable. Care to explain why I'm wasting my time with a road traffic collision?'

PC Shouty peered at her warrant card, then pulled a face. 'No offence, but could you not have introduced yourself back at the roadside and saved me a trip down...' The expression on Franklin's face must have finally worked its magic, because he shut his mouth with an audible click. Blushed. 'Sorry?'

Her voice got even colder. 'I'm listening.'

'Yes. Right.' He pointed at the car. 'Someone called it in this morning, no sign of the driver or any passengers.'

She stepped closer, looming. 'And I give a toss, because?'

'The boot! There's a body in the boot and we thought ... well, *I* thought – thinking isn't exactly Tony's forte – but—'

'There's a body in the boot?' Her eyes widened. 'YOU BLOODY IDIOT! Why haven't you cordoned off the scene? Where's the common approach path? Why aren't you logging visitors? And where the buggering *hell* is the SEB?'

He backed off a couple of paces, hands up. 'Whoa. It's not like that. I mean, it's not fresh or anything, it's just, you know, dead, and we—'

'THERE ARE HUMAN REMAINS IN THAT CAR, YOU MORON! Call the pathologist, *now!*'

'No, it's like... Look.' He sidled around to the boot of the car and popped the hatchback lid. Swung it up with a gloved hand. 'See?'

Callum leaned forward and frowned.

There, nestled in amongst the dustsheets and a bucket full of plasterboard fragments was a human body. It lay on its side, arms folded so the hands were pressed against its chest, knees hard up against the hands, feet hard up against the bottom. Head bent forward sharply, so the face was almost completely hidden by the knees. Skin shrunken and wrinkled, the colour of ancient leather.

He groaned. 'Not another one.'

Franklin bared her teeth. 'Is this supposed to be a *joke*, Constable?' She poked Callum in the shoulder with a rock-hard finger. 'A bit of a laugh at the new girl's expense?' Gearing up for a good bellow. 'WELL, IS IT?'

And there it was again, that smell. Much stronger here than it had been back at the tip, where it had to fight with the stench of a hundred million rotting bin-bags. The rich, warm, but slightly bitter tang of wood smoke, so strong you could taste it at the back of your throat.

'Constable! Constable MacGregor, I'm talking to—'

'Will you shut up a minute?' He snapped on a pair of blue nitrile gloves. Reached in and prodded the body. Solid, as if it'd been carved from a chunk of oak, then dipped in the peatiest whisky in the world.

When he straightened up, Franklin's eyes were wide, her whole person trembling as if she was about to pop.

Before she could get started, he dragged out his Airwave handset and called Control. 'Aye, Brucie? I need a check on a Kia Picanto.' He rattled off the registration number and colour, then clunked the boot shut in the intervening silence.

Franklin squared her puffed-up shoulders. 'Now you listen to me, *Sunshine*, I will *not* be spoken to like that! How dare—'

'*Okeydokey.*' A thick Dundonian accent crackled out of the Airwave's speaker. '*Yer car's registered to a Glen Carmichael, eighteen Walsh Crescent, Blackwall Hill. Twenty-four years old. Ooh, looks like he lives with his mum. You wanting the postcode?*'

'Has he got prior?'

'*Couple counts of housebreaking-and-robbery when he was twelve. Suspended sentence. And an ex-girlfriend got herself a restraining order when he was fourteen. Sounds like a lovely wee lad.*'

'OK, thanks, Brucie.' Callum put his Airwave away. Grinned at Franklin. 'We turned up a mummy at the tip this morning, just like this one. Probably nicked from a museum. The Kia's owner has form for breaking into places he shouldn't and helping himself to things that aren't his. Are *you* thinking what I'm thinking?'

'I see.' She shot her cuffs again. 'Well, don't just stand there – let's go pick him up.'

7

'Shhh, you're doing great.'

Is he? Then why does he feel so terrible? Why does he just want to lie down and die?

The water around him is cold, but that's not why he's shivering.

A sponge dips into the dark brown liquid, then runs gently across his chest, clearing away the thin white rime of salt. Dissolving the crystals back into the brine.

The wall whispers over the sound of trickling water. *'They'll worship you: you'll be a god.'*

Then the sponge dips into the water again, presses against his forehead sending rivulets running down his lined face.

'They'll worship you: you'll be a god.'

'Are you thirsty?' The voice is kind, worried. 'Do you want something to drink?'

He tries to shake his head, but can only tremble. No. No more of the foul water.

'I know it's bitter, but it's good for you. Full of herbs and minerals. Here...'

'You'll be a god. You'll be a god. You'll be a god.'

A metal cup presses against his cracked lips, and he hasn't got the strength to keep his jaw clenched shut. Sour liquid fills his mouth, catches the back of his throat. And he coughs, splutters the water out, feels it dripping from his chin onto his chest.

'They'll worship you.'

His body rocks back and forward, sending out little waves across the bath.

Why can't he cry?

43

Only it's not really a bath, is it? It's a large metal trough, big enough for three people, let alone one living skeleton. All the joints are rusty, dark brown as if the thing is bleeding, rivets standing out like nipples on its cold metal skin.

Why can't he just die?

'You'll be a god, and they'll worship you.'

'Shhh...' A warm hand on his forehead. A gentle touch and a soft word. 'It'll all be over soon.'

8

Walsh Crescent curled in on itself like a snail shell. Mostly bungalows, but every now and then a second storey sprouted from a converted attic. Box hedges, gravel driveways, nameplates on the garden walls. Pretensions of grandeur. One even had a pair of three-foot-high lions perched either side of the drive, their whitewashed surfaces cracked and showing the concrete below.

No view to speak of, but a nice enough street.

Sitting in the passenger seat, Franklin scowled out at the suburban enclave.

Callum pulled up outside number 18. Killed the engine. Sat there with his wrists draped over the steering wheel. 'Look, I know arresting idiots for stealing mummies from museums probably isn't what you signed up for, but this is all they let us do.'

She didn't move.

'And trust me, this is a lot more interesting than what we're usually lumbered with. At least there's genuine dead bodies involved. Even if they are a thousand years old.'

Franklin let out a low sigh, then unclipped her seatbelt. 'I'm here because I punched a superintendent in the car park.'

'In the car park?' Callum smiled. 'There's a euphemism I've never heard before. Sounds painful.'

'He deserved it. Next thing you know: no more Edinburgh for you, pack your bags, you've been posted to Oldcastle.' Sounding about as pleased as someone who's just discovered their routine check-up has turned into emergency root-canal surgery.

'Welcome to Mother's Misfit Mob.' He pointed through the windscreen. 'Shall we?'

They climbed out into the drizzle and hurried up the path to number 18. Stood beneath the little portico waiting for someone to come answer the bell.

'So?' Franklin stuck her hands in her pockets.

'So what?'

'What did *you* do?'

'Oh...' Well, she was going to find out sooner or later. 'I cocked up. Contaminated a crime scene, because I wasn't paying attention. Too busy trying to get a conviction.' A shrug. 'You know Big Johnny Simpson?'

'Never heard of him.'

'Well, he walked on a murder charge. Because of me. And no, I'm not happy about it.' At least *that* part was true.

'So the team's a dumping ground for the unwanted and the incompetent. That's just great.'

'I wouldn't say—'

The door opened. 'Hello?' A middle-aged woman squinted out at them, hair piled on top of her head, a red pinny smeared with grey stains covering polo-shirt and cords. She wiped her hands on a dishtowel. 'Sorry, I was in the studio. Can I...' Her shoulders dipped as she looked them up and down. 'I'm flattered, but I honestly don't want any copies of *The Watchtower*, leaflets about the Bible being a guide to modern life, or a discussion on accepting Jesus into my heart. So if you don't mind.' She tried to close the door, but Callum stuck his foot in the way.

'Mrs Carmichael? Police. Is Glen in?'

'It's Ms, and no.' Her nose came up. 'Now, if you'll excuse me, I've got clay on the wheel.'

Franklin held out her warrant card. 'There's been an accident: we just found your son's car in a field south of the city. He's not in it. We're worried for his safety.'

A hand fluttered to her mouth. 'Glen...'

'Now can we come in?'

The kitchen was warm enough, every surface covered with pots and bowls and mugs. Some less wonky than others.

Callum stuck the kettle on to boil, then picked up a blue mug with a white rim. 'These are very good. Did you make them yourself?'

Ms Carmichael sat at the small kitchen table, worrying at her clay-greyed dishtowel. 'Is Glen all right?'

Franklin pulled out a chair and sat down opposite her. 'We don't know. We've been in contact with the hospitals and doctors' surgeries, but nothing so far. He's—'

'Oh God...' Her eyes reddened. 'Glen.'

'Let's not jump to any conclusions.' Callum pointed out through the kitchen wall in the vague direction of Shortstaine. 'We didn't see anything in the car to suggest he's badly hurt. He's probably just lying low and feeling a bit bruised and stupid.' That, or Glen had massive internal injuries and was drowning in his own blood somewhere, but his mum *definitely* didn't want to hear that. Nothing wrong with leaving people with a little hope.

Franklin sniffed. 'Ms Carmichael, your son had something in the boot of his car that we're concerned about. Something that didn't belong to him.'

She stiffened. 'My poor wee boy could be lying dead in a ditch and you're here accusing him of *stealing*?'

Callum put teabags in mugs. 'I know it sounds a bit insensitive,' he gave Franklin a pointed look, 'but we've got to investigate this kind of stuff. It's important.'

'It's because of those burglaries, isn't it?' She poked the table with a clay-greyed finger. 'He was *twelve*, OK? Just a kid. His dad, God rest his useless little soul, ran out on us the year before. Glen had a hard time adjusting.' A shrug. 'His therapist said he was just trying to get attention. Pushing me to see if I loved him enough to put up with all his crap.'

The kettle grumbled to a boil, spouting steam into the air.

'It wasn't even money he took. It was stupid things: a standard lamp from next door, a bust of Daley Thompson from the sports centre, all the cutlery from Terry's Bistro on Minerva Road. It wouldn't even have been a thing if the bloody sports centre hadn't insisted on pressing charges.'

Callum fished the steaming teabags out and dumped them in the bin. 'What happened with the girlfriend?'

'Gah...' Ms Carmichael stared at the ceiling for a moment. 'Angela. He wouldn't leave her alone. Always buying her little presents and writing her little notes. Following her home from school.' She looked down when Callum put a mug of tea in front of her. 'I tried to talk some sense into him, but you know what teenage boys are like – all hormones, spots, and erections. Her parents called the police, and he was in trouble again.'

The fridge was mostly full of yoghurt and chardonnay, but there was half a pint of semi-skimmed that looked reasonably fresh, so Callum stuck it in the middle of the table. 'Nothing since?'

She wrapped her hands around her mug. 'It took a while, but he grew up a bit. Got over his dad abandoning us for some leggy tart in the roads department. Started doing well in school again. Went to university and got an MA in business management.'

'Sounds like a bright kid.' Callum passed Franklin a slightly wonky green mug, but kept his eyes on Ms Carmichael. 'Is it OK if we take a look at Glen's room?'

'What?' She blinked at him. 'Oh, yes. Right.' She scraped her chair back and stood. Led them out of the kitchen and down a small corridor to a room at the end with 'SECRET EVIL VILLAIN LAIR' printed on a sign hung on the door beneath a radiation symbol. She opened it and stepped to one side, mug of tea clutched to her chest. 'Of course, by the time he graduated no one was hiring. That's the recession, isn't it?'

The floor was barely visible through the patina of discarded socks, T-shirts, jeans, and pants. Walls covered in bookshelves – science fiction and fantasy paperbacks, mostly. A TV hooked up to a PlayStation. A poster of a young woman in a bikini, riding a motorbike. Never mind leathers, she wasn't even wearing a crash helmet. Some people just didn't take basic safety precautions. A collection of photographs pinned to the wallpaper, above a small computer desk that was heaped with envelopes and bits of paper. And a double bed covered in more clothes.

Every breath in here tasted of stale digestive biscuits and mouldering cheese.

Ms Carmichael shrugged. 'Don't look at me, I told him when he turned sixteen: you're a grown-up now. You tidy your own room, or you live in a pigsty. Your choice.'

Franklin picked her way into the middle of the room. 'Was Glen interested in museums?'

'When he was little we'd go to the art gallery, and we'd laugh at all the statues and their naked willies, but other than that...' A shrug.

'Hmm...' She leaned over the desk and pulled a photo from the wall. Held it out. 'Is this him?' Her finger hovered over the central figure in a group of three. It looked like a selfie: three young men, all with grins and tins of lager. Checked shirts and tan braces.

The one on the left had a full-sized Grizzly Adams beard, two squint teeth dominating his smile, all crowned by brown hair cropped close at the sides and floppy on top. He'd got one of those piercings, where they stuck a big round plug in the lobe to stretch it wide – making a dirty big hole. As if he was a Masai tribesman, instead of a peely-wally wee bloke from Oldcastle with a lumberjack fixation.

The one on the right's arm snaked out of the picture – so he'd be the photographer – a shoulder-to-wrist tattoo of Clangers, Soup Dragon, and the Iron Chicken blurring into a colourful mush where the lens couldn't focus. Long hair pulled back in a ponytail. A variety of studs spread about his nose, eyebrow, lip and ears.

And the one in the middle looked as if he'd inherited his great grandad's haircut and glasses. Though where he'd got the massive soup-strainer moustache from was anyone's guess. He was straightening his bow tie, showing off an oversized steel wristwatch on an oversized leather strap. More piercings.

Ms Carmichael squinted at the photo. 'No, that's his friend Ben. Glen's the one on the left with the ridiculous beard.' She grimaced. 'Why these hipsters all want to look like old men from the thirties is beyond me. But there you go.'

'I see.' Franklin produced her notebook. 'Can you tell me what your son was wearing when he left the house this morning?'

A snort. 'This morning? He's not been back here for six weeks. Him and his friends have been staying at the flat they're doing up.' She sighed, looking around the room with its explosion-in-a-laundry-basket décor. 'Brett's got a degree in environmental science, Ben's got a BA in aqua-culture, and none of them can find jobs. Recession.'

Franklin scribbled something in her notebook. 'And where is this flat?'

'They bought it at auction. The man who lived there killed himself in the living room – bank was foreclosing on his mortgage.'

'Yes, but where is it?'

'Hold on, it'll be in here somewhere...' Ms Carmichael rummaged through the piles of paper on the computer desk, before emerging triumphant with what looked like a council tax bill. 'Flat twelve, one thirty-five Customs Street, Castleview, OC twenty-one, six QT.' Then she turned and put a hand on Callum's arm. 'You're sure Glen's ... not *hurt*?'

He gave her his best reassuring smile. 'We'll let you know as soon as we hear anything.'

'Why did you have to lie to her?'

Callum shrugged, slowing the car at the junction. 'What did you want me to tell her: we've no idea if your wee boy's dead or not? Think that would've helped?' The bridge over the River Wynd made a graceful cobbled arc above the water, marking the border between Blackwall Hill's twisted knot of housing estates, the Wynd's well-ordered Georgian streets, and Castleview's functional industrialisation. All of it grey and miserable in the drizzle.

He took a left at the next roundabout, down a long drab street – blocks of terraced flats, punctuated by shopping centres with more boarded-up windows than new shops.

'What if Glen Carmichael turns up dead from a punctured lung, or a ruptured spleen?'

'Then he'll still be dead whether she's panicking about him or not. Let her have... Oh, hold on.' He slammed on the brakes and pulled their manky Vauxhall into a space between a delivery truck and a skip.

'What the hell do you think you're—'

'I'll only be a minute.' He scrambled out of the car. 'Honestly, five tops.' Callum clunked the door shut, waited for a bus to grumble past, then hurried across the street and into one of the few shops still open.

The Royal Caledonian Building Society's carpet was going threadbare in the middle, drawing a straight line from the door to the counter. A large middle-aged lady sat behind the bulletproof glass, reading a copy of the *Castle News and Post*. She looked up as he reached the counter and pulled on a smile about as natural as a porn-star's breasts.

'How can I help you?'

Callum thumped his warrant card on the countertop. 'Someone stole my wallet and I need you to give me some money from my account.'

She made a face, as if he'd just slapped a used nappy down in front of her. 'I'll have to speak to the manager...'

The sharp-faced woman pulled on her glasses and peered at her computer screen. 'Well, Mr MacGregor, you'll be glad to hear that we appear to have recovered your cards. Someone tried to use them to redeem a number of items at ... let me get this right ... at a "Little Mike's Pawnshop"? In Kingsmeath?'

Little sods were probably trying to get hold of samurai swords, crossbows, and ninja throwing stars.

Callum crossed his fingers. 'Did they find my wallet?'

Please, please, please, please.

She poked at the keyboard. Frowned. 'I'm sorry, I don't actually have that information. But the proprietor *has* destroyed the cards, and as there's been no successful purchase made on the account, there won't be any excess to pay.' The frown turned into an expectant smile, as if she was waiting for congratulations and a round of applause. 'We'll get new cards issued to you in the next couple of days.'

'A couple of days? But I need to buy—'

'I'm sorry, but the cards have to be reissued from head office. I'll flag it as urgent, but it'll still take a couple of days. Now is there anything else I can assist you with, Mr MacGregor?'

'Yes: I need to take some money out of my savings account.'

'Ah. I see…' She made the same face as the woman behind the counter.

Franklin glowered at him as he lowered himself into the driver's seat. 'What happened to "five minutes, tops"?'

'Don't start.' He hauled on his seatbelt and started the car. Pulled away from the kerb. 'Just been bent over a bank manager's desk for the last quarter of an hour, being shafted without lubricant. And do you know what for? Fifty-three pounds and seventy-two *sodding* pence.' He held up the tiny handful of notes and coins. 'Because *that's* all the money we've got.'

Down to the end of the road, and right onto the main road.

'It's my sodding money! Why do I have to beg for my own fifty-three quid? How is that fair?'

Franklin shook her head. 'Do you do anything other than moan?'

'I'm not moaning, I'm ranting. It's different.' He took a right, into another street full of tenements, heading towards MacKinnon Quay. 'How much did we pay to bail those thieving gits out? Billions. Whole sodding country up to its earholes in debt, people losing their jobs and their houses, all so they can enjoy their bloody yachts and champagne!'

A smile. 'Do you *honestly* think the manager of a wee building society sub-branch, in a nasty little shopping centre, in a crappy corner of the mediocre cesspit that is Oldcastle, has a yacht?'

'That's not the point.'

Straight through at the roundabout and onto Customs Street. It skirted the edge of the docks, with their large blue cranes and towering tanks of offshore mud, all secured behind a twelve-foot-high fence topped with razor wire.

Just past the harbour, a row of small cottages – jammed in tight as teeth – lined the left side of the road, but the houses opposite were a lot less quaint. They were built into the side of the hill, about six feet above road level: the kind of buildings councils put up to punish people for being too poor to afford somewhere better to live. Long, brutalist rows of grey flats, four storeys tall.

Oh, they'd made an *attempt* to tart them up, put brightly coloured cladding on the top floor, arranged big concrete planters out front on the four-foot-wide strip of grass that separated the flats from the vertical drop to the road below. But the cladding was chipped and faded, the planters cracked and full of weeds, the grass a patchwork of yellow and brown – landmined by generations of terriers and Alsatians.

Callum slowed the car. 'Which one is it?'

She checked her notebook. 'Number one thirty-five.' Then tapped a finger against the glass, as if she was counting time for a very small orchestra. 'One fifteen. One sixteen. One seventeen…'

'Glen and his mates had three university degrees between them, and they bought a flat down here? So much for modern education.'

'One twenty-two. One twenty-three…'

'Suppose they spend six months doing it up, who'd be daft enough to buy it when they've finished?'

'One twenty-eight. One twenty-nine…'

'Bunch of idiots.'

'One thirty-two. Thirty-three…' She pointed. 'That'll be it there. Top floor.'

Callum parked outside, next to a dilapidated Transit van with, 'Danny & Mike ~ Children's Entertainers' on the side. Someone had daubed the words, 'THEYZ PEEDOFILES!!!' underneath, in what looked like blue Hammerite.

He climbed out into the rain. Locked the car soon as Franklin joined him on the pavement. 'You ready?'

She rolled her eyes. 'It's a wee boy with a degree in business management, Constable MacGregor, not Osiel Cárdenas Guillén.' Franklin climbed the steps up to ground level, disappearing from view.

A sigh, then Callum followed her.

Down at road-level, the cottages opposite acted as a windbreak, but up here the drizzle came down sideways, driven in on frigid gusts. MacKinnon Quay sat off to the left, then the grey water of Kings River, then the green line of Dalrymple Park with its big granite monument on the other side. Castle Hill lost in the low grey mist.

On a good day it was probably quite some view, but this wasn't one of them.

Franklin jabbed a finger at the intercom. Then grimaced and pulled it clear. She sniffed the end of her finger and grimaced again. Wiped it on the rough grey wall.

Callum took out a biro and used it to press the button marked 'SERVICES'. Holding it down until someone inside finally got tired of the noise and let them in. He smiled at her. 'Trick of the trade.'

Inside, the corridor was lit by a single flickering bulb in a flyblown fitting. Concrete floor, walls painted magnolia above waist-height and a grubby green below it. The smell of frying onions mingled with the hospital stink of disinfectant. An open stairwell led up into the gloom.

Yeah, Glen and his mates were definitely kidding themselves if they thought *anyone* was going to buy their flat.

Franklin led the way upstairs.

And Callum tried not to stare at her backside, he really did, but...

Heat rose up his face, making his ears tingle. Yeah, probably better not to ogle his new teammate's rear end. But it *was* magnificent.

Across the first-floor landing and up another flight of stairs. And there it was, right in front of him again.

Stop it!

Pregnant girlfriend, remember? Even if she had been off sex for the last five months.

Yeah, but...

No. No staring.

He cleared his throat. Stared at the wall instead.

The second floor was almost identical to the first – two pairs of red doors, some with welcome mats, some with browning spider-plants and dying ferns in pots. Numbers on the doors. Plastic or brass nameplates.

A little old man cracked his door and glowered out at them. 'You from the Council? About time. Tell those bloody hooligans to turn their music down! Can't hear myself think in here.' He slammed the door shut again.

OK.

Callum hurried past, trying *very* hard not to ogle Franklin's bum as she climbed the last two flights and stepped out onto the third floor.

She reached into her jacket, came out with a pair of purple nitrile gloves. Snapped them on. Frowned. 'Are you all right, Constable? Your face is all red.'

'It... I... Just, you know, the stairs and that.' He cleared his throat and snapped on his own gloves: blue. 'You want to kick the door in, or shall we do it the old-fashioned way?'

'Hmm.' She knocked.

A skylight sat in the middle of the ceiling, right above the void in the stairwell. A scuffling scratchy noise followed two blurred outlines across the cloudy glass. Seagulls?

He shifted his feet, locked his eyes on a spot six inches above her head. 'So who's O'Neil Gillen, when he's at home?'

'Osiel *Guillén*, not O'Neil Gillen. AKA: El Mata Amigos, the Friend Killer. Mexican drug lord.' Franklin knocked again. 'Hello?'

She squatted down and lifted the letterbox.

Music pulsed out onto the landing, Led Zeppelin hammering on and on about giving someone a whole lotta love.

'Hello?' Another knock.

Callum wrinkled his nose. 'Can you smell that?'

Sort of a cross between rancid sausages and pine air freshener.

'Mr Carmichael? Police. I need you to open this door. Mr Carmichael?' She glanced up at Callum. 'Is it just me, or does this scream "dead body" to you?'

He took a step back. 'Two choices: we dunt it in, or we go get a warrant.'

'Hmmm.' Franklin let go of the flap, cutting off the music. 'Dunt it.'

'My thoughts exactly.' He raised a foot and slammed it into the wood, just below the handle. The whole thing rattled in its frame. One more. Then a third and the door sprang open, battering into the wall. It didn't bounce back.

The smell got a hundred times worse.

The music got a lot louder too – thumping away from somewhere deeper inside the flat.

Oh yeah, there was certainly something rotten in there.

Percussion solo.

Franklin gritted her teeth and stepped into the hallway. 'THIS IS THE POLICE! I WANT EVERYONE IN THE FLAT TO STAY WHERE THEY ARE!'

Gloom filled the hallway.

A sheet of plasterboard slouched against the wall, the bottom edge bowing under its own weight, anchored there by two big ten-litre tubs of magnolia paint.

She crept through the door at the end of the hall.

Callum followed her into a reasonably sized living room. Two windows should have given a view out across the harbour and the river, instead they were completely covered with... Yup, that was hardcore pornography. What little light filtered through it picked out the shape of a platform ladder, a collection of hand tools, and a stack of paint pots. A wallpaper table in the corner bent slightly under the weight of a tool belt, three electric drills, and a small, portable CD player – not quite turned up full volume, but close to it.

Franklin switched the thing off.

Now the only noise was the droning buzz of fat lazy bluebottles making drunken circles in the rancid air. The little dead bodies of their fallen comrades crunched beneath Callum's feet.

'GLEN CARMICHAEL?' She reached into her jacket and came out with an extendable baton. Christ knew where she'd been hiding that. A flick of her wrist clacked it out to full length. 'HELLO?'

Callum pulled out his pepper spray. 'COME ON, GUYS, LET'S NOT PLAY SILLY BUGGERS!'

Two bedrooms led off from the living room, their windows similarly coated in bits of porn mag. One of them looked almost finished – the walls smoothly plastered and painted a neutral beige. The other was stripped back to the bare breezeblocks.

The kitchen was awash with pizza boxes and takeaway containers. A bong, half-full of dirty water, sat on the unit by a sink mounded with dirty dishes. A stack of empty lager tins that was taller than Callum.

Three university graduates and they *still* lived like teenaged boys.

The smell had been much stronger in the corridor than it was in the rest of the flat.

He stopped in the middle of the living room. 'Where's the bathroom?'

She frowned at him.

'These flats didn't go up in Queen Victoria's time, did they? So where's the bathroom?'

Back into the hall, where that big sheet of plasterboard leaned up against the wall.

He hefted the paint pots out of the way, then grabbed the plasterboard and pulled, dragging it over to the other side.

A flat panel door. That would be the bathroom.

Callum turned the handle and it swung open inwards. He—

Oh dear God, the *smell*...

It crashed out into the hall like an avalanche, the dark-sweet taint of rotting meat riding on a wave of cloying pine.

Behind him, Franklin made little retching noises.

He reached for the light switch and clicked it on.

About a million bluebottles leapt into the air, buzzing and swarming, battering at the bare lightbulb. Setting it swinging.

The room was just big enough for a white bathroom suite, which looked brand new, with a shower above the bath. Dark water filled the tub, the surface flecked with floating mats of white and orange mould. A crust of brown made a tidemark around the rim, tiny crystals that glittered in the swaying light.

There was someone in the bath, lying facedown, skin all blackened and swollen. Crawling with little white things where the body's shoulders protruded from the water.

Franklin stepped up beside him. 'Christ...'

Yeah.

And then some.

9

Callum stuck his notebook back in his pocket, stepping out of the stairwell and into the drizzle. The view hadn't improved, if anything it was worse. Low cloud and mist hid everything on the other side of the river, reduced the MacKinnon Quay to little more than a collection of random shapes.

The whole world rendered in shades of grey.

Getting dark too.

Oh no... He checked his watch: just gone half six. The Polish deli would be closed. No pickled cucumbers, onion rolls, or anything else.

So much for Elaine's cravings.

Yeah, he was going to be popular when he finally got home.

He scuffed along the path then down the stairs to road level, made his way past patrol cars and manky Transit vans. Someone had finger-painted a big willy in the dirt across the back doors of one, complete with hairs.

McAdams' shiny red Shogun took pride of place in front of the Willymobile, engine running, inside lights on. Callum limped over to the thing and slid onto the back seat. Closed the door on the cold dreich evening. 'God, it's perishing out there.'

Sitting in the passenger seat, Mother took a sip of something in a large wax-paper cup. 'Well, well, well, if it isn't Detective Constable MacGregor.'

He sighed. 'What am I supposed to have done *now*?'

Her sidekick turned the blowers down and turned in his seat. 'You kicked in the door. Didn't call for permission. You should know better.'

'You're very welcome, *Sarge*.' Callum cupped his hands over the heater mounted between the seats, trying to get some feeling back in his

fingertips. 'If it wasn't for me you'd still be investigating odds and sods
– I brought in a murder, OK?'

Mother still hadn't turned around. 'What makes you think it's a murder,
Callum? Man falls over in the bath, drowns, happens all the time.'

'And did he accidentally drown in the bath, before or after dragging
a big sheet of plasterboard and two tubs of paint in front of the bathroom door?' Callum poked at the heater. 'Can you turn this thing up?'

McAdams fiddled with the dashboard and warmth flowed. 'What
about the door-to-doors?'

He produced his notebook. 'Sixty-three flats in the immediate
vicinity. Twenty-four of them did nothing but complain about their
neighbours, thirty-one wouldn't answer the door or weren't in, and nine
want their hats re-tinfoiled. Not one of them had a single thing to say
about Glen Carmichael or his mates.' Shrug. 'Well, other than the
downstairs neighbour complaining about Led Zeppelin playing on a
loop, full blast, for the last two days.'

'Interesting...' Mother tapped her fingers along the wax-paper cup.
'Officially, I should reprimand you for breaking into a crime scene
without authorisation, Callum, but our new girl put her hand up to it.
Said you were dragged along against your better judgement.'

McAdams snorted. 'I didn't even know you had one.'

'So you, my little man, may have a sweetie.' Mother dug into her
pocket and produced a bag of jelly babies. Held them out.

Callum helped himself to a green one. 'Thanks.'

She put the bag away. 'I always love this bit. Forensics are going
through the scene, we don't know who the victim is, there's a killer
on the loose. Excitement. Adventure. And...' She frowned. 'Can't
remember the end of the quote, but you know what I mean.'

McAdams nodded. 'The main plot is unfolding. What we need now
is a flashback from the killer's perspective then some sort of investigative
montage to show how much research the writer's done.' He clicked his
fingers again. 'Constable MacGregor, get yourself and your new best
friend DC Franklin back to the lair. I want a murder board ready to
go by ... I'm in the mood for pizza, so call it an hour and a half. And
get a lookout request on the go for Glen Carmichael and his two mates
while you're at it. Most people stick to rubber duckies in their bathtub,
a dead body requires a bit more explaining.'

Ah. 'Sarge, I was kinda hoping to go home and—'

'Oooh.' Mother made a sooking noise. 'And you were doing so well,
Callum. I even gave you a jelly baby.'

'Time to be a team player, Detective Constable.'

His shoulders slumped. 'Yes, Boss.'

Yeah, Elaine was going to kill him.

The wet road hissed beneath the pool car's tyres.

Franklin frowned out of the window. 'I thought Division Headquarters was that way?'

'*Technically*, yes.' Callum took a right at the roundabout, heading back along the boundary between Castleview and The Wynd. 'Just got a quick errand to run first.'

'Oh for God's sake.' She closed her eyes. 'Is this what it's going to be like, Constable? All moaning and "wee errands"?'

'Five, ten minutes tops. I swear.' After all, the traffic wasn't too bad for a Tuesday. 'Someone stole my wallet this morning. A guy might have it at a shop in Kingsmeath.'

A sigh. A shake of the head. 'Thought you were supposed to be a police officer.'

'I was trying to save a little girl's life: that OK with you?' Up and over the Newton Bridge, and back into Blackwall Hill again, with its modern sprawl of cul-de-sacs and middle-class housing estates.

'By losing your wallet?'

Past the lights, the road opened up into dual carriageway, everyone sticking to the outside lane to avoid Oldcastle City Council's award-winning collection of potholes. 'I didn't lose it, it was stolen.'

'This isn't helping us put a murder board together.'

'We'll be fine.'

'They're only going for pizza, we—'

'I've done *loads* of murder boards: it'll be fine. Trust me.'

She pursed her lips. 'And why on earth would I do that?'

Fair point.

Montgomery Park drifted by on the right-hand side, a bunch of big white marquees with tartan stripes already sprouting on the grass around the boating lake.

'OK. Full one hundred percent honesty time: the reason everyone hates me, is they think Big Johnny Simpson bribed me to sod-up a crime scene so he'd get off. But I *didn't*. Not a penny. Ever.'

She frowned at him. 'Is that supposed to make me feel better? That you're incompetent instead of corrupt?'

'I'm not incompetent!'

'Could have fooled me.'

'Fine. I was trying to share, but why don't you just sit there in sulky silence. See if I care.' He clicked on the radio. Let it drown out her pouting.

'*...headline the main stage on Saturday, of course, it's Oldcastle's very own Donny "Sick Dawg" McRoberts! Donny, my man, good to have you in.*'

A fake London patois burst out of the speaker, not quite good enough to conceal the Kingsmeath burr underneath. '*Yah, it's* Sick Dawg, *right? Donny's what me foster mum called us, and you ain't my mum, bro.*'

'*Ha, ha. Right. Yeah, I got you, man. Respect. "Sick Dawg" it is...*'

The massive Blackburgh Roundabout loomed before them. Burgh Library sat on a hill in the middle, all lit up like a 1960s idea of a spaceship – glass and concrete, curving walls and wonky rooflines. The Kingsmeath side of the roundabout was ringed by seven massive tower blocks, eighteen-storey headstones soaring above a scrubby patch of woodland. More *1984* than *Star Trek*.

'*So, "Sick Dawg", welcome to* Deathbed Discs *on Castlewave FM, where we find out what tracks you'd take with you to the grave. And you're kicking us off with "Stan" from Eminem's fourth album,* The Marshall—'

'*Yah, I been thinking about it, right? And I'm-a not about that no more.*'

Callum swung the pool car around the outside lane, then took the first turning into Kingsmeath.

It was as if someone had turned down the lights, leaving the buildings in gloom. Rows and rows of council houses. Tenements. Grey faces and grey buildings.

'*You're not?*'

'*Nah, man. I go to my grave I'm not gonna be surrounded by stuff from the oldtimers, you know what I'm sayin'? Nah: I'm-a play my own stuff, bro. You know, from the heart.*'

'*OK...*'

An old couple stood on the pavement, screaming at each other, a wee dog cowering on its lead as they yelled.

'*Well, why don't we just play the song anyway. It'll give us time to completely abandon all the music your publicist told us you wanted to talk about and reprogramme the whole show...*'

Fake rain clattered out of the speakers, followed by Dido singing over a heavy bassline.

Franklin made a little growling noise then jabbed her hand out and turned the radio off. 'Bloody rap music.'

After that she kept her mouth firmly shut all the way through the bleak housing estates, past a dilapidated playing park – the swings and roundabouts reduced to slumped blobs of fire-blackened plastic – past Douglas on the Mound with its scaffolding-shrouded spire and vandalised graveyard...

It wasn't until Callum pulled into a potholed car park that she opened it again. 'Is this it?'

The car park was bordered on three sides by what were probably billed as 'single-storey retail units with excellent potential!' but looked more like something off the news when a riot's just passed through. Three of the eight were boarded up; all were covered in a tattoo of graffiti; all had the kind of metal grilles over the window that were meant to roll up out of the way, but probably spent all their time firmly locked in the down position. A newsagents, a chip shop, a convenience store that looked about as welcoming as a shallow grave, a charity shop, and right at the far end: Little Mike's Pawnshop. The sign above the frontage boasted, 'WE BUY AND SELL ALL MANNER OF THINGS!' 'CASH FOR GOLD!' 'PAYDAY LOANS AT EXCELLENT RATES!!!' 'EST. 1995!'

Callum parked in front of it. 'Won't be long.'

'Oh for... You're here to redeem some manky family *heirloom*?'

'Five minutes. Promise.' He climbed out into the rain. Ducked his head and hurried inside.

The door made an electronic *bleep-blonk* noise as it swung closed behind him. Shelves lined the walls, packed with other people's things. Free-standing display units turned the shop into a labyrinth. Old video game consoles, a collection of musical instruments, microwaves, hairdryers, boxed cutlery, vases, what looked like a brass urn with 'IN MEMORY OF AGNES MAY ~ BELOVED MOTHER' engraved on it. All of it marinating in the gritty stench of dust and mildew.

Callum picked his way through the maze to the counter, where a wee fat man was bent over a copy of the *Castle News and Post*. His white shirt was just a bit too big for him, the collar and cuffs stained and frayed. A maroon waistcoat with buttons missing and brown stains down the front. Bald head glinting in the shop's dim lighting.

'You Little Mike?'

The man behind the counter looked up, squinted, then pulled on a pair of small round glasses. 'I am indeed, young sir, welcome to my emporium of delight.' He swept a chubby hand from left to right, indicating his second-hand wares. 'How may we assist you this drizzly September evening?'

The door made its *bleep-blonk* noise again and Franklin appeared, as if by magic. 'Are you not finished yet?'

'Ah, I see.' Little Mike smiled like an indulgent parent. Then he folded his paper and moved it off to one side, revealing the glass countertop. A collection of rings and watches sparkled against dusty purple velvet. 'An engagement ring for the lady, perhaps?'

Franklin stiffened. '*What?*'

'Definitely not!' Warmth bloomed in Callum's ears. 'Someone tried to use my credit and debit cards in here today. You destroyed them.'

He sighed. 'A shame. You make such a lovely couple.' A finger poked the glass. 'Are you sure I can't tempt you?'

'Did they leave my wallet behind?'

'Or, how about this?' He grabbed something from beneath the counter and stuck it on his head then went back and fiddled a clip-on bow tie into place. 'See? It's a fez and bow tie. You can dress up like Doctor Who, for parties. Isn't that fun?'

'Have – you – got – my – wallet?'

'No? Ah well.' He covered the glass top with his newspaper again. 'The young lady and gentleman concerned *did* have a wallet with them. A rather tatty affair, with the lining hanging out.'

Oh thank God. 'That's it! That's the one.'

'I see... Well, perhaps I can help.' He disappeared through a door in the back.

Franklin picked the urn from its shelf. 'Who pawns their mother's ashes?'

'Here we are.' Little Mike was back, holding a shoebox. He set it down on the countertop and pulled out a couple of wallets. 'Real leather, look at that stitching, have you ever seen anything so magnificent?'

'What? No. I don't want another wallet, I want the one those little sods stole from me!'

A pained smile. 'I'm sorry, the young lady and gentleman only handed over the cards, not the wallet. But I can do you a *very* good deal on a new one if—' His eyes went wide behind the little round glasses and he bustled out into the shop. 'If I may?' He held his hands out in front of Franklin.

She gave him the urn.

'Thank you. Mr May would be most distressed if I allowed his mother to leave the shop without him.' Little Mike polished a speck of dust from the urn with a hanky, then returned it to its shelf. 'Now, is there anything else I can interest you in, while you're here? An electric guitar, perhaps? Or how about the sensual delight that comes with an electric foot spa?'

Callum held out his hand. 'Where are the bits of credit card?'

'Ah, of course. You wish to make sure I haven't indulged in anything illicit. Quite proper.' He pulled out a carrier bag and tipped the contents of his wastepaper basket into it. 'Don't worry: as it's loose items, I don't have to charge you for the bag. Now, if I can't tempt you with my esoteric pre-loved wares, I think I might close up for the night. So, if you don't mind...?' He swept a hand towards the door.

They shuffled through the maze to the exit.

Callum stopped with one hand on the handle. Frowned back into the shop. 'The building society said they were trying to redeem something when you cut up the cards.'

'That is correct, yes.'

'What?'

One of Little Mike's eyebrows made a break for freedom. 'Ah... I'm afraid I can't—'

'If you're about to invoke pawnbroker-client confidentiality, don't bother. What did they try to redeem?'

'Very well.' He shook his head, then turned and led them back through the stacks and display cases to a collection of brightly coloured plastic. 'Items F-twenty-three to F-forty-six.'

There was a sandpit, a collection of squeaky toys that looked as if they belonged in a bath, a Wendy house, a kid's tricycle far too small for either of the little monsters to ride. An off-grey teddy bear with only one ear, scuffed button eyes, and stuffing poking out of his side. There were other bits and pieces, but nothing suitable for anyone over the age of three.

Franklin gave Little Mike one of her finest scowls. 'You *pawn* wee kids' toys?'

He sighed. 'Some people, this is all they have. If they can't pay their bills, their rent, if they can't buy food for their children, what do they do? You want them to go to loan sharks?'

'They're kids' *toys.*'

'I know. But what can *I* do, turn them away hungry? Let them get thrown out on the street? So I pawn their children's toys, and I know they'll never come back and redeem them, and I know they're worthless, but I do what I can.' He took off his glasses and polished them on the frayed edge of his shirt. 'This is what real life looks like from down here at the bottom, officers. Foodbanks and pawnshops. Who else is going to help these people?'

Callum frowned down at the collection of plastic tat.

A hand on his arm. 'Come on, we need to get that murder board done.'

He puffed out his cheeks. 'How much to redeem the toys? And I'll need their address.'

10

Callum stuffed the multicoloured rocking-horse-shaped-like-a-fish thing in the boot with all the other toys. Closed the lid. Turned and leaned back against the car.

Little Mike rattled down the grille over his pawnshop's front door. Wrestled a thick padlock into position. Then turned and lumbered away into the evening.

A shaft of sunlight broke through the heavy cloud, the low beam of golden light pulling a rainbow from the drizzle. Making the graffiti-wreathed shopping centre shine.

The car's horn blared.

Right.

Callum peered in through the rear window and there was Franklin peering back at him, reaching over from the passenger seat to lean on the horn again.

Mouthing the words, 'Hurry up!'

Funny how some people could start off looking extremely pretty, only to get less and less attractive the more time you had to spend with them. At this rate, by the end of the week, Detective Constable Franklin was going to resemble the underside of Quasimodo's armpit.

He sighed and climbed in behind the wheel. Cranked the engine. 'We've got plenty of time.'

She checked her watch. 'DS McAdams said an hour and a half, thirty minutes ago. We're, what, twenty minutes from DHQ. That leaves—'

'*Plenty* of time.' He navigated his way through the potholes and back onto the road. 'Just got a little stop to make on the way.'

'God's sake!'

'It's on the way. Won't take five, ten minutes tops.'

'Gah!' She swivelled in her seat to give him the full-on glower. 'I've just started with this team and I am *not* going to let you screw it up for me.'

'Seriously?' Left at the junction, onto McGilvray Place with its boarded-up terrace and abandoned building site – just foundations and pipes sticking out of the ground to mark the death throes of the local construction industry. 'What happened to, "I'm not wasting my career with you losers"? Thought you wanted nothing to do with us.'

'Let's get something straight, Constable, I'm out of here first chance I get. But until then, I'm going to do the job. *Properly*. Not whatever half-arsed version of it you think you can get away with.'

'It'll take *five* minutes.' A right, onto Munro Place, taking the car up the hill. 'Then we'll hit Division HQ and *I'll* do the murder board, OK? And you can feel free to clype on me anytime you like.' After all, it wasn't as if Mother or McAdams could hate him more than they already did.

He slowed for a moment next to the rusty Volkswagen, where Dugdale had deployed The Claw, then over the crest of the hill and down the other side.

Left at the bottom.

Callum checked the slip of paper with 'Little Mike's Pawnshop ~ Pre-Loved Goods & Personal Finance Solutions' in flowery script along the top and, 'Brown : 45B Manson Ave.' scrawled beneath it in biro.

Number 45 was on the outside edge of a set of five identical squashed grey council-issue boxes. Each one semidetached, split down the middle – A on the left, B on the right – ten homes per block. Someone probably thought arranging them into wee groups like that would foster a sense of community pride and spirit. It hadn't. A ruptured sofa sat outside the house next door. The one beyond that had a washing machine as a garden ornament, the porthole door open to show a collection of crumpled lager tins. Knee-high weeds from the front door to the garden wall.

Callum parked out front. Hauled on the handbrake. 'Five minutes. You can use the time to compose your formal complaint about me.'

She just scowled at him.

He slipped out of the car, turned and stuck his head in again. 'One of these days, the wind's going to change.' Then clunked the door shut and marched off before she could say anything back.

The garden gate was rusted solid, so he hopped over it onto a path of cracked paving slabs with grass growing in off-green Mohicans between them.

No doorbell.

He gave the chipped wood three loud hard knocks.

The light was on in the living room, shining through a pair of lace curtains. Shadows moved about inside.

Another three knocks.

And a voice came from the other side of the door. Young, female. *'Go away.'*

'Mrs Brown?'

'If you're from the bailiffs, you can sod off. I don't have to open the door!'

'It's not the bailiffs, it's the police.' He held his warrant card up to the spyhole. 'See?'

A groan. Then something thunked against the door at head height. *'He doesn't live here, OK? I kicked him out* six weeks *ago.'*

Callum put his warrant card away. 'Who doesn't live here?'

Franklin was checking her watch, making a big pantomime of pointing at the thing and then pointing at him.

'Go away.'

'I've got some stuff for you, OK?'

'I'm not in.'

Why bother?

Callum marched back to the car, popped open the boot and hauled out an armful of kid's plastic toys. Dumped them just over the garden wall and went back for another load. Adding to the pile until the boot was empty.

The last thing was the raggedy teddy bear, with its missing ear and herniated stuffing. Plastic tat was one thing, a well-loved teddy bear was another. No way it was getting dumped in the weed-ridden grass.

He returned to the front door. Knocked. Held Teddy up to the spyhole.

Some muttered conversation inside, then the door opened a crack, the chain glinting in the hall light. A thin face peered out at him, blonde hair pulled back tight. She didn't look old enough to leave school, let alone have two small kids. There was a huge bruise on her cheek, dark and angry against the pale skin. She blinked at the bear. 'Mr Lumpylump?'

She shifted, and there was child number three – a baby cradled in her arms, wrapped in a tatty Power Rangers blanket. Face a rounded pink blob, making snuffling noises.

A small child wailed somewhere behind her, sounding as if someone was removing its fingers with a blowtorch. Child number four.

The woman didn't even flinch. 'Shut up, Pinky.'

'I redeemed the rest of the kid's toys. They're in the garden.'

Her hand reached through the gap between the door and the frame, fingers trembling. 'Can I have him. Please?' She licked her lips.

'Look, all I want is my wallet back, OK? There's no money in it anyway, it's just a tatty old wallet that's falling apart. Like the bear.' He gave Mr Lumpylump a wee shoogle, making him dance. 'It's important to me.'

She blinked up at him. 'I don't have it. I don't have any wallet.'

'You could check, though? Ask your children?'

Behind her, the toddler wailed some more, as whoever it was turned the blowtorch on their toes.

'They're not here.' She reached out until the frame and door dug into her arm. Straining for the manky teddy bear. 'Please...?'

What was he going to do, hold a kid's teddy to ransom?

Callum passed her the bear and she snatched it from him, yanking it back inside the house and slamming the door.

He knocked again. 'Hello?' Rested his forehead against the door. 'Hello?'

Silence. Not even the wailing.

Great.

What was the point of trying to help people? Why did everyone have to be so ... so *selfish*. And nasty. And horrible?

One last try.

He pulled an official Police Scotland business card from his pocket wrote, 'IF YOU FIND MY WALLET, PLEASE LET ME KNOW' on the back, and slipped it through the letterbox.

Probably be sod-all use, but what other option did he have?

Callum trudged back along the path. Clambered over the rusted gate.

'Hoy, mister?' A young girl's voice, hard with defiance and a broad Oldcastle accent.

He turned.

The little monster from this morning. The one who'd swigged cider from a can. The one Dugdale had used as a human shield. The rotten wee sod who'd stolen his wallet.

She'd ditched the baseball cap and tracksuit top for a T-shirt with a vampire Womble on it, but not the attitude. 'What you doing here, Piggy?'

He nodded at the pile of plastic things.

Her eyes widened. 'Whoa! You got Pinky's toys back?' Then her internal coolometer must have kicked in, her grin turned into a bored expression and a shrug. 'Yeah, so?'

'Swap you for my wallet.'

'Ain't got no wallet, do I? Chucked it.'

His whole face crumpled. 'Oh for...' What was the point? Of course she chucked it, with the credit cards cut up, why would she hold onto it? Wasn't as if there was any cash in there. His shoulders drooped. 'Sodding hell.'

'Don't know what you're greetin' about. Just a crappy old wallet, innit?'

'It was my father's. Only thing I've got of his.'

'Yeah?' She spat into the weeds. 'Well, *my* dad broke my arm then ran off with one of mum's friends.'

'*Mine* disappeared when I was five.'

'I was *four*.' Always had to have the last word, didn't she? A competition for who had the crappiest childhood.

'Well *I* grew up in a care home. Beat that.'

Aha, she couldn't, could she. At least *she* had a mother. Though going by the bruised face, her mum's taste in men hadn't improved any.

He narrowed his eyes. 'It's Willow, isn't it?' At least, that was what her wee brother had called her when she was kicking three shades out of Dugdale's head. 'Any idea who's been hitting your mum?'

Willow's back stiffened. 'I ain't no snitch, Piggy.'

'Course not.' He produced another business card, stuck his mobile number on the back, and laid it on top of the wall. 'But if you're worried about her or anything...' A shrug. 'You know.'

The lace curtains twitched open, and there was Willow's mum, standing with a toddler on one hip. She had the tatty old teddy bear clutched to her chest like a bible.

Not the kid's bear, hers. Pawned to pay for food, or rent.

How depressing was that?

Callum climbed in behind the wheel. Frowned. Shook his head. Then started the car.

Franklin stared at him. 'Well?'

'No idea.' He pulled away from the kerb, keeping one eye on the rear-view mirror.

The little girl stood and watched them all the way to the corner, then disappeared from view.

'This was all for your stupid wallet, wasn't it?'

He pulled out his Airwave, poking at the buttons with one hand as they navigated their way back towards the real world. 'Control? Can you do a PNC on a Ms Brown, forty-five B Manson Avenue, Kingsmeath? See if anyone's been bothering her.'

'Aye, will do. Hang on.'

'Thanks.' He stuck the handset on the dashboard, took them out past a dilapidated community centre – doors and windows boarded up with damp-swollen chipboard – and onto Montrose Road. Pottering along behind a Fiat Punto barely doing twenty miles an hour.

'For God's sake, at least put the blues-and-twos on.' Franklin reached for the button mounted on the dashboard, marked, '999'.

Callum slapped her hand away. 'Are you off your head?'

'We're going to be late!'

'You press that button and the dashboard camera comes on.' He pointed at the little rectangle of plastic mounted against the windscreen, hidden by the rear-view mirror. 'And the GPS starts recording. And it all gets stored for the courts, or in case there's an accident while you're wheeching through traffic. Lights and sirens are for emergencies *only*, not because you're in a hurry.'

She curled her hand against her chest, as if he'd stabbed it with a fork and scowled at him. 'Where is it then? This magical wallet?'

A stone settled in his stomach, cold and heavy. 'They threw it away.'

'Waste of sodding time.' She checked her watch again. 'Thirty-six minutes to get back to Division Headquarters and make up a murder board.'

'Will you stop moaning on about—'

'DC MacGregor from Control, safe to talk?'

He picked up the handset and pressed the button. 'Go ahead.'

'Aye, right: your woman's a Miss Irene Brown, twenty-three years old. Done for possession four years ago, got off with a caution. … Hmm… Looks like that's the last known address for one Jeremy Barron, Jezza to his mates, AKA: Jerome Barton, James Broughton, and Jimmy Bishop. Bit of a scummer from the look of it. Assault, robbery, assault, aggravated assault, possession with intent, serious assault, two counts of sodding about in public with a knife.' A clicking keyboard rattled out of the speaker. *'Looks like she's got a bit of a history with violent scumbags. Poor woman couldn't pick a nice bloke out of an empty room if you Sellotaped a balloon to his forehead.'*

Twenty-three years old, with four kids.

And a dirty big bruise on her face.

No wonder she clung onto her teddy bear like that.

Her daughter, the horrible Willow, had to be at least seven years old, so that meant Miss Irene Brown must have been about sixteen when she'd had her.

What a life: trapped beneath a landslide of pregnancy and violence.

Callum tapped his fingers on the handset's plastic case. 'Do me a favour: put a grade one flag on the house, OK? Just in case this Jerome Barton comes back again.'

'Pfff, can't promise anything, but I'll see what I can do.'

'Thanks.' Callum slipped his Airwave back in his jacket. Took a left at the roundabout and onto the Calderwell Bridge.

Halfway across the river, Franklin sighed. 'OK, *now* can we go do this sodding murder board?'

'And *that*, is that.' Callum pinned the last photo to the corkboard and stepped back, hands on his hips.

Not a bad job, even if he said so himself.

The murder board took up a whole wall of the Divisional Investigative Support Team office. One whiteboard cut up into sections with that thin magnetic tape stuff, all headings spelled correctly, details on the corkboards to either side of Glen Carmichael and his fellow graduate property developers. Ben Harrington with his massive moustache, Brett Millar and his Clangers tattoo. Photos, potted bios, previous brushes with the law, list of known friends and associates. Schedule for the flat from the auctioneer's website along with PNC details for the previous owner.

He checked his watch. 'Done with five minutes to spare.'

Franklin stayed where she was, perched on the edge of her brand-new desk. 'Is that *it*?' A sniff. 'I always thought a murder board would be more... I don't know. Like on the TV.'

'TV people wouldn't know a murder board from a Christmas list.'

The door banged open and in stormed Watt, floppy fringe plastered to his forehead, mouth scrunched up into a twisted pouting sneer, wee pubey beard bristling as he hurled his soggy jacket into the corner. He graced Callum with a glare, then shifted it over to Franklin. 'Who's this?'

She stiffened her back. Drew herself up to full height.

But the door thumped open again before she could lay into him and Dotty wheeled herself into the office. 'Oh don't be such a *princess*, John. I said I was sorry.'

Might as well do the introductions.

Callum hooked a thumb at Franklin. 'Watt, Dotty, this is our new recruit: Detective Constable Franklin, from E Division. Punched a superintendent, right in the car park.'

Watt wiped his hands down his face and flicked the drips at Dotty. 'I'm bloody *drenched*!'

'It was an *accident*.'

'No it sodding wasn't! You aimed for that puddle on purpose.'

'Franklin: the soggy tit with the beard is Detective Constable Watt. He clyped on his last team at G Division, so the high heedjins had him transferred to Oldcastle. And *we* are graced with his presence, because none of the other teams will work with the grumpy little git.'

'I didn't know you were standing there.'

'This is because I wouldn't get you chocolate, isn't it?' Watt grabbed his mug from his desk. 'Get your own damn chocolate!'

'The young lady in the wheelchair is Detective Sergeant Dorothy Hodgkin. *She's* here because some wee radge fancied a high-speed pursuit in a stolen Beamer. Dotty lost her leg above the knee in the crash. Her wheelchair's called "Keith": don't ask.'

'I *will*.' Dotty bared her teeth at Watt. 'And you know what? I *was* sorry, but I'm not now. You're a sour-faced, childish, chippy, miserable scumbag, John. No wonder nobody likes you.'

Callum shrugged. 'As you can see, we're all one big happy family.'

'Oh, ha-ha.' Watt turned his scowl back on Callum. 'I bet he's not told you why *he's* here, Franklin, has he? He—'

'Everyone thinks he took a bribe to cock-up a crime scene. I know.' Franklin folded her arms. 'So is everyone on this team a reject? What about McAdams and Malcolmson?'

Dotty wriggled her way out of her jacket. 'DS McAdams has terminal bowel cancer. They *so* want to send him off on the sick, but he won't go. And DI Malcolmson is just recovering from a massive heart attack.' Dotty held her arms up, flashing victory signs like Richard Nixon. 'Welcome to the Misfit Mob! Abandon hope, all ye who enter here.' She wheeled herself across the manky carpet tiles to Franklin and stuck out a hand with a fingerless leather glove on it. 'Dorothy. Dot or Dotty to my friends.'

After a wee pause, Franklin shook it. 'Rosalind.'

'Rose for short?'

'No.'

'Oh...' Dotty wheeled herself back to her desk. 'Ah well.'

Callum swept his hand around the room. 'And that's us. All the other departments think we're useless, the bosses give us boring or horrible cases, and this is the first exciting enquiry we've had since, well, *ever*. But if you—'

'Knockity, knock.' The door swung open and in waltzed McAdams, a stack of four pizza boxes balanced in one hand. 'Behold, little ones, Mother and I have returned. Lo, I bring *succour*.' A grin. 'Well, one ham-and-pineapple, one meat feast, a four seasons, and a pepperoni, but it's the thought that counts.' He dumped the boxes on the nearest desk. 'I trust you've all been beavering away, advancing the plot and revealing character through action rather than exposition…' A frown. 'Constable MacGregor, why are you still here? Go home.'

Callum pointed at the whiteboard with all its lines and data. 'But you said—'

'Detective Constable Franklin!' McAdams patted her on the back. 'Excellent job on the murder board. Very thorough.'

Her cheeks darkened slightly. 'But I didn't—'

'Nonsense. Credit where it's due.' He picked a sheet of paper from the nearest desk, crumpled it up and hurled it at Watt.

It bounced off his floppy fringe. 'Hoy!'

'What did I tell you about signing off at the end of a shift? I just checked the logs and *apparently* you're still on duty from yesterday.'

Watt cleared his throat. 'I was busy.'

'I don't care if you're King Busy, ruler of all the Busy Bee people in Busy Buzzy Bee Land: *sign out*! I'm not authorising any overtime till you get that through your pointy wee head.'

'But. Sarge—'

'No.' McAdams glanced at Callum. 'Thought I told you to go home, Constable. You've got a full day tomorrow: all those museums to phone.'

'Oh you are *kidding* me! I was the one who—'

'To each man his task, according to his merits. Some more than others.' A wink. '*You*, for example, can leave the murder investigation to the professionals.'

Callum bit his bottom lip. Arms trembling. Hands curled into fists.

'*Good night*, Constable.'

He took a step forward.

McAdams grinned.

And there it was: he *wanted* a punch on the nose. With Franklin, Watt, and Dotty as witnesses, McAdams could go to Professional Standards and get him suspended at the very least. It wouldn't look very good at his review tomorrow either.

Deep breath. Callum forced his hands to open. 'Fine.' Grabbed his coat. 'But I'm taking one of these with me.' He helped himself to a pizza box, warm against his fingertips, and marched out of the door.

'Elaine? Hello?' Callum balanced the pizza in one hand, propped his bike against the wall, and clunked the front door shut. Slipped out of his soggy jacket and kicked off his wet shoes. Left soggy-sock footprints on the laminate flooring through into the kitchen. 'God what a day. Utterly soaked.'

The sounds of some sort of cookery programme oozed out through the closed living room door.

At least the backpack was waterproof. Callum unloaded it onto the kitchen table, raised his voice so she'd hear him in the lounge. 'DID YOU HEAR? THEY SAY IT'S GOING TO BE THE WETTEST SEPTEMBER ON RECORD.'

No reply.

'ELAINE?'

Nothing.

He stuck the Tupperware box for his sandwiches in the sink. Took today's note and put it up on the fridge with all the others she'd sneaked in with his lunches over the last month – little inspirational quotes, terrible puns, and the occasional dirty joke. Most came with a drawing. Today's was a rotund badger with teeny legs, taking a bite out of a pig, above the legend, 'I Love You More Than Desmond The Badger Loves Bacon'. Which was nice to know.

Callum flicked through *The Monsters Who Came for Dinner*, smiling at the old familiar illustrations.

Come on: there'd be plenty of time to read it after dinner.

He emptied his pockets, stripped to his pants, and threw his fighting suit in the washing machine. Set it to tumble dry.

Stuck his head back into the hall. 'YOU WANT TEA?'

Nope. Whatever she was watching, it had her.

Callum stuck the kettle on and the oven too. Wandered through to the lounge.

Some posh English bloke with curly hair and big nostrils filled the TV screen – wandering through a forest somewhere, banging on about how tasty squirrels were if you cooked them in a nice ragout.

Elaine was curled up on the sofa with her back to the door, wearing her comfies, a tartan fleecy blanket pulled over her enormous pregnant bulge. A bowl rested in her lap, containing a mixture of marshmallows and crisps.

It wasn't a big living room: barely enough space to take a three-seater sofa and an armchair; a fake coal fire that groaned and flickered; a coffee table with a collection of wooden ornaments on it; a TV, complete with squirrel-mongering celebrity chef; and four floor-to-ceiling book-shelves stuffed to overflowing with novels.

Their blinds were open, the darkness on the other side turning the window into a mirror – reflecting back one thin pasty body in blue underpants. The lights in the houses opposite twinkled through Callum, making him sparkle like the world's least scary vampire. Then the eight o'clock train to Edinburgh rumbled past, its glowing windows making rectangular spotlights sweep across the back garden. Searching.

He crossed the room and closed the blinds, before anyone on board became overwhelmed with desire at the sight of his ancient Marks and Spencer's lingerie going a bit baggy in the elastic. 'I got pizza for tea. Well, technically I *stole* pizza, and I know it's not Nutella and pickles, but—'

A grunt rattled its way free and Elaine sat up. 'What? M'wake!' She blinked at the room. Then the TV. Then Callum. Brushed the long brown hair from her eyes. 'What time is it?' Cracked a huge yawn, showing off a proper Scottish set of fillings. 'Why are you in your pants?' The corners of her eyes wrinkled. 'What happened to your *face*?'

'It's just gone eight.'

'You look like someone ran over it with a washing machine.'

'I've got pizza.'

'Gah...' Another yawn. Then she held out her arms. 'I had a horrible dream. You abandoned me and Peanut because we got ugly and you didn't love us any more.'

'You're not ugly.' He hugged her and planted a soft kiss on her fore-head. 'You're beautiful. You smell of cheese-and-onion, but other than that, you're safe.'

Callum picked one of Elaine's discarded mushrooms and put it on his own slice, adding to the pepperoni. Sat back on the couch and stuffed in another mouthful, trying not to get any on his tartan T-shirt and joggy bottoms.

'Urgh...' She grimaced at him. 'You eat like a wheelie bin.'

'Yronlygelous.' The words all mushed up as he chewed.

Sitting on the bookshelf, the flat's phone launched into a tinny rendi-tion of the *South Bank Show* theme tune.

Elaine curled her top lip. 'Sod off.' She pointed at the plate resting on top of her bulge like a makeshift tabletop. 'We're eating!'

'If it's your mum, I'm telling her we're not in.'

'Let it go to voicemail. They—'

'Can't. What if it's important?' He stuck his plate back on the coffee table and hauled himself out of the couch, walked round the back to the bookcases. Sooked his fingers clean and picked up the phone. 'Hello?'

Silence.

'Hello?'

Still nothing.

He checked the caller display: 'NUMBER WITHHELD'.

'OK, I'm—'

Click.

Elaine turned and looked over the back of the couch. 'Who is it?'

'No idea, they hung up.' He put the phone back in the cradle. 'Probably some auto-dialling PPI tossers.'

Probably.

'Callum, while you're up?'

'Mmm?' He turned away from the phone.

'Any chance you can grab the raspberry jam from the kitchen? I think it'll go great with these anchovies.'

He tried not to shudder, he really did...

— every day we live —
is a day closer to the day we die

Sometimes, the worst thing you can imagine – and I mean the worst thing you can *possibly* think of – that's just the start. Because things can always get worse, dear reader. And in my experience they usually do…

R.M. Travis
The Monsters Who Came for Dinner (1999)

Damn right you better fear me, cos I'm about to break free,
You better f*ckin' hear me, there won't be no all-clear: see?
I'm-a sharp like a shark, ma bite's worse than my bark,
I attack from the dark, cos violence is ma trademark,
Think that you're tough? You ain't even in the ballpark…

Donny '$ick Dawg' McRoberts
'Unrequited Love Song Number 3'
© Bob's Speed Trap Records (2015)

11

'...another six arrests in the Holyrood sex-ring investigation. Weather now, and there's more rain on the way, sorry, but it should clear up by the weekend for our very own Tartantula Music Festival in Montgomery Park! Fingers crossed. And if you haven't got your tickets yet, stick around – I've got just the competition for you.'

Callum marched back into the bedroom, scrubbing his hair dry on a pink towel.

'*This is* The Very Early in the Morning Show *and you're listening to me, Jane Forbes, on Castlewave FM, because you're sexy, intelligent, and looking* fabulous *today!*'

He grimaced at the naked creature in the mirror, then hauled on a pair of pants and yesterday's suit trousers. Maybe not so fabulous. Especially now the bruises Dugdale gifted him had darkened to a deep lustrous purple, ringed with blues and greens. Lucky he hadn't cracked a rib.

'*Right, we've got Sensational Steve's Breakfast Drive-Time Bonanza coming up in thirty minutes, but that gives us loads of time for yet more stonking tunes!*'

Elaine peered out from under the duvet. 'Tmmsit?'

'Half six. Go back to sleep.' A clean white shirt and red clip-on tie.

'No, m'up. M'up.' She let loose a massive yawn. Sat up and had a scratch, long brown hair all flattened on one side.

'*Let's kick off with a Tartantula festival favourite: Nearly Blind Vera, and their new single "Swarm".*' What sounded like a full orchestra belted out of the speakers, swelling to a—

Elaine thumped her palm down on the clock radio and swivelled her legs out of bed. Shuffled out of the room in pink bunny slippers, rubbing at the small of her back. 'Pfff...'

He pulled on clean socks and dry shoes, dragged a comb through his hair. Scowled at the purple stains on his forehead and chin. Wasn't exactly the best impression to make at a Professional Standards review, but what choice did he have?

Callum knelt by the side of the bed and dragged out a big file box. Rummaged inside for the maroon half-size ring-binders buried under the flat's insurance schedule, the mortgage documents, and the HP agreement for the telly.

Elaine's voice belted out from the kitchen. 'Did you stay up half the night reading again?'

'Maybe.' He tucked the binders into a small backpack, plucked the copy of *The Monsters Who Came for Dinner* from the bedside cabinet, and wandered through. 'You don't have to do that.'

'Yes I do.' She lumped a couple of slices of white from the bread bin onto the chopping board and slathered them with spread. 'You want cheese-and-pickle, or egg?'

'Go back to bed, it's fine.'

'Just because I'm stuck here with Peanut, doesn't mean I'm useless.'

Callum stepped behind her and kissed the back of her neck. 'No one thinks you're useless.'

'You'll have to have cheese-and-pickle, we're out of eggs.'

The flat's phone launched into its semi-classical theme tune again.

She froze.

'It's OK, I'll get it.' He marched through to the lounge. Grabbed up the phone. 'Hello?'

Nothing.

Checked the caller display. Same as last night. 'NUMBER WITHHELD'.

'Who is this?'

Silence.

Click.

Yeah, that was getting old very quickly.

He turned, and there was Elaine, holding out a little Tupperware box in one hand and a banana in the other. 'Who was it?'

'Automated-dialling PPI nonsense again.'

'There's a mini Mars Bar in there too. You know.' She lowered her eyes. 'To keep your strength up.'

He tucked the box and banana into his backpack. 'It's just a boring wee meeting with Professional Standards, it'll be fine. Promise.' That sounded confident, didn't it? Completely unlike the lie it was. He replaced *The Monsters Who Came for Dinner* in its bookshelf slot, grabbed a tatty paperback at random: *The Beginner's Guide to Shoplifting*, and added it to the pack.

'Callum...' She put a hand against his chest.

'What can they do? They've got no evidence – they can't, because I didn't *do* anything, did I?'

She gave him a little pained smile. 'We love you.'

'I know.' A kiss on the cheek. 'Got to go, don't want to be late for the rubber heelers.'

Callum shifted in his seat.

The waiting room was ... disturbingly neutral. Blue carpet, magnolia walls, a row of four soft-ish chairs along one wall, a sideboard-sized filing unit thing on the other – complete with the obligatory pile of well-thumbed, ancient magazines. A water dispenser in the corner. A framed painting of Oldcastle's skyline rendered in all manner of bright and unnatural colours.

He checked his phone – 07:13.

Oldest interview technique in the business – leave your victim to stew for a while. Let them work themselves into a state of nervous exhaustion worrying about what you knew.

Well, tough: they knew sod-all. Because there was sod-all to know.

The only thing up-to-date on the sideboard was a copy of that morning's *Castle News and Post*, the banner headline: 'BODY FOUND IN CASTLEVIEW FLAT' above a photo of the craphole Glen Carmichael and his mates were doing up. There was an inset pic of three figures standing outside the main entrance while SOC Smurfs shuffled past in the background. McAdams, Franklin, and right in the middle – staring straight at the camera – his own face. Looking tired and fed up. So they were right: the camera didn't lie. All three of them got a namecheck, though they'd managed to spell McAdams' name wrong. Which was nice.

Right underneath the main story, was 'DRUG DEN UPSTAIRS MADE LIFE A LIVING HELL', a 'shocking exclusive with Murder Flat's down-stairs neighbour!' continued on page six. There was always someone.

Callum dumped the paper and dipped into his rucksack instead, pulling out *The Beginner's Guide to Shoplifting*. Settled back to read the first short story. A bit heavy on the adverbs, but other than that, it was OK.

He was just starting the second one when the door through to the office opened and a middle-aged man in uniform poked his head out. His hair had abandoned its post, retreating to a defensive position around both ears, a set of jowls lightly blued with stubble. A pair of evil-scientist glasses, all narrow with silver frames. He smiled. 'Ah, Callum. Good, good: in you come. Sorry about the wait.' He held the door open and gestured inside.

'No, it's fine.' Callum stood. Stuffed the book in his backpack. 'Gave me a chance to catch up with my reading.'

'Good, good.' He moved aside, then closed the door behind Callum. 'I know we should have done this weeks ago, but you know what it's like. Busy, busy.'

It was a small-ish office, with a desk on one side and a round table in the middle. Some filing cabinets. A coffee machine. A small digital video camera on a tripod.

'Please, please, take a seat. Coffee? I'm having one anyway...?'

'Thanks. Just milk.'

'Perfect.' He wandered over and started pushing buttons and inserting cartridges. 'So, Callum, I understand you're going to be a father in two weeks' time. How exciting. Most fulfilling thing you can do as a man.'

'Well—'

'There you go. One white coffee.' He sank into the chair next to Callum's. 'I can't abide all this "flat white" nonsense, can you? Oh,' he stuck his hand out, 'Chief Inspector Gilmore, we spoke on the phone yesterday, but you can call me Alex.'

OK...

'Chief Inspector.'

'Ah, almost forgot.' He raised himself half out of his seat and pointed a remote control at the camera. A little red light blinked on. 'There we go. Can't do these things without a proper record, can we? The Boss would have my guts for garters. And I understand your good lady is in the job too?'

Callum closed his mouth, then opened it again. 'Well, yes. I mean, she's on maternity leave, but—'

'Let me see now...' He checked a notepad. 'Ah, here we are: Constable Pirie. Elaine. You know, I had an Aunty Elaine when I was wee. Lovely lady, used to give us Advocaat every Christmas because she thought it wasn't alcoholic. And I see she's been seconded to the Scenes Examination Branch?'

What?

Chief Inspector Gilmore held up a hand. 'Sorry, *your* Elaine, not my aunt. How's she getting on? Weird cravings, I'll bet. My Pauline used to chew the rubber hose from the spin dryer. That dates me, doesn't it? Amazing our sons didn't come out with two heads. How's the coffee?'

Was the man some sort of idiot? How...

Callum sat back in his seat.

No, of course he wasn't. Didn't matter what crime novels and TV dramas said, you didn't get to be a chief inspector without having a considerable amount of grey matter packed between your earholes. The rambling avuncular act was all about putting people at ease and off their game at the same time.

Well that only worked if you didn't know he was doing it.

Callum took a sip. 'It's great. Thanks.'

'Better than the stuff from the canteen anyway. So, Callum: tell me all about Big Johnny Simpson.'

'Well...' He cleared his throat. 'I want to start by saying I've never taken a bribe in my life. Ever.'

'That's the spirit.' Gilmore raised an eyebrow. 'But...?'

'No, no buts.' He picked his rucksack off the floor and upended the contents onto the table. Three burgundy ring-binders, a Tupperware box, and a banana. He retrieved his lunch and pushed the binders towards Gilmore. 'Bank statements. Well, building society statements, but it's the same thing. Feel free – go through them with a nit comb. And if you want to contact the Royal Caledonian, I'll tell them you've got free rein to look at any account I've got.'

'I see. That *is* awfully kind of you.' Gilmore stacked them into a neat pile on one side. 'But in the meantime,' a smile pulled his jowls up at the edges, 'why don't you tell me all about Big Johnny Simpson?'

'Urgh.' Callum dumped the rucksack on his desk. Collapsed into his seat. Powered up his computer. Grabbed his desk phone and called the control room.

'*Aye, Aye?*'

'Brucie? Any word on my lookout requests?'

'*Hud oan, I'll check...*'

The office was empty, no sign of Dotty or Watt-the-Moaning-Dick. They'd been at the murder board, though: no mistaking Watt's drunken-spider scrawl.

Didn't look as if they'd made a whole load of progress. The column headed 'OPEN TASKS' had gained a bunch of actions allocated to the pair of them, more on the bottom waiting for someone to take them on. Mostly interviewing friends and family of the three amateur property tycoons. Franklin's name appeared on the list only once: 'ATTEND POST MORTAM ~ 10:30'.

God's sake.

'You still there? Aye: Benjamin Harrington, Brett Millar, and Glen Carmichael – no sightings. You could get yourself a warrant and see if they've used their bank cards?'

'Thanks, Brucie.' Callum hung up, then hauled himself out of his chair and over to the board. Wiped the word 'MORTAM' out and wrote 'MORTEM' in the gap. Chief Inspector Gilmore might have been putting on an act, but Watt wasn't. He truly *was* an idiot.

'And what exactly, my dear Constable Callum, are you up to now?'

Wonderful: Haiku Boy.

Callum corrected the spelling of 'INTERVIEW COLLEEGES'. 'I'm fixing the murder board.'

'You keep away from that, young Callum. That's for grown-ups.' McAdams settled on the edge of Dotty's desk. 'While we're at it: what time do you call this? It's ten o'clock. Shift starts at seven a.m., not whenever you feel like it.'

'You know fine well where I was.'

A grin. 'Ah yes, Professional Standards.' He put one hand on his chest. 'They interview cops, who are dirty and bent, / To punish their sins, till they wail and lament, / Then cast them down low, in the dirt at their feet, / And I do hope they fired you, cos that would be sweet.'

'Yeah, go screw yourself, Sarge.' Callum chucked the whiteboard marker back onto Watt's desk, then sank behind his own. 'What happened with Dugdale, he cop to it?'

'That's no longer your concern, Constable.' McAdams checked his watch again. 'When the lovely DC Franklin gets in, you can give her a lift to the overflow mortuary. You're going there anyway.'

Oh *great*.

He sagged back in his seat. 'I am?'

'Of course you are. As a minor character you've been farmed out onto a subplot: discovering which museums have lost their mummies. Mother's even made you *SIO*. Isn't that fun?'

'Gah...' Callum covered his face with both hands. 'I hate you all.'

'And they're post-morteming your first mummy at half ten this morning. Don't be late.'

*   *   *

'No, don't put me on hold, I just need to know if... Hello? Hello?' A pan-pipes version of 'Green Sleeves' rattled out of the phone's earpiece. Wonderful.

Callum printed the letters 'D.I.C.K.' next to the museum's name. Third one in fifteen minutes.

There had to be, what, a dozen active murder investigations in the division right now? And what was he doing? Sodding stolen mummies.

The office door clunked shut.

Probably bloody Andrew McAdams, back for another gloat. Maybe he'd come up with another *hilarious* poem. Oh ha, ha, ha.

Dick.

Franklin's face appeared over the top of Callum's cubicle wall. 'Where's everyone else?'

He held the handset away from his head and frowned at it. 'Is it just me? Am I hallucinating and this isn't *really* an actual phone? Is that why I'm the only one who can see it?'

'Somebody's touchy.'

'Yes, hello?' A little voice replaced the pan pipes. '*We've checked and we've never had a human mummy here. We've got a mummified dog and a stuffed polar bear in storage, if that helps?*'

'No. Thanks. You've been a lot of help.' He hung up and stuck two lines through the museum's name. Sat back and massaged his temples.

Franklin sniffed. 'So?'

'So *what*?'

'So where is everyone?'

He pointed at the murder board. 'Off interviewing Glen Carmichael's mates.'

'Ooh, there's stuff on the board.' She disappeared from view. 'Wait a minute, how come *I'm* down to do the post mortem?'

Callum stood.

She was in front of the murder board, hands on her hips, frown on her face. 'What, I'm stuck in the mortuary with a decomposing corpse while you're all off interviewing people? Thank you very sodding much!'

He pointed at the list of tasks. 'If you didn't want to do it, why put your name down?'

'I *didn't*. None of this was on the board last night.'

Hmm... 'You didn't mark up the actions with Watt and Dotty?'

'No. We ate the pizzas, then Mother told me to head off and not come back in till quarter past ten, as I'd been here till late.'

Lovely. So even though he'd been here three weeks longer than she had, Franklin got to call DI Malcolmson 'Mother' while he had to call her 'Boss'. *And* she got a lie-in.

Franklin sniffed again. 'What's wrong with *your* face?'

'Nothing.' He picked his coat off the back of his chair. 'Get your stuff, we're off to the mortuary.'

The pool car slid along Camburn Road, following the edge of the woods. They made a thick blanket of green: leaves and bushes trembling in the rain. There were people in there, on the paths and tracks that wound their way between the trees – walking dogs, wheeling push-chairs, jogging. A wee girl on a bicycle...

Callum slammed on the brakes.

'Aaargh!' Franklin lurched forward against her seatbelt, both hands slapping onto the dashboard – bracing herself. 'What the bloody hell do you think you're—'

'Just be a minute.' He stuck on the hazard lights and scrambled out into the downpour. Flicked his collar up as he jogged between the puddles and in under the canopy of branches. Wiped the rain from his face. 'Willow.'

Her dirty-blue anorak was frayed at the cuffs and shoulders, hood thrown back, gold ringlets stuck to her shiny face. Pink cheeks and Rudolf nose. 'Sup?'

Raindrops pattered on the leaves above them, like a million tiny drummers. The occasional drip made it through the canopy, splashing into a puddle big enough to drown a toddler.

He cleared his throat. 'Is your mum all right?'

'Been waiting on you for ages, Piggy.'

'Did Jerome come back and hit her again?'

Willow tilted her head on one side. 'You perving on my mum?'

'No.'

'Why? What's wrong with my mum?'

'It's OK, I'll keep your name out of it. No one will know you told me who hit your mother.'

'Get bent, Piggy. I ain't no snitch.' She balanced on the pedals, shoogling the bike from side to side to stay upright. 'You got them toys for Pinky from the wee creepy guy with the pawnshop. Why?'

'Because.' Callum shrugged. 'No one should have to pawn their kids' toys just to stay afloat. No matter how much of a pain in the arse those kids are.'

She almost smiled.

'Willow, your dad – the guy who broke your arm when you were four – what was his name?'

'How come you always asking questions, Piggy?' She pedalled around him in a slow circle. 'Nosey, nosey, nosey: oink, oink, oink.'

'Just interested.'

'Always sticking your nose into other people's stuff and that.'

'Hey, it's OK if you don't know.'

'Course I *know*.' She did another lap. 'You saying I don't know?'

'Lots of people have no idea who their dad is. No shame in that.'

'Yeah, well I know: and I ain't no snitch. But see if he ever comes back? I'll break *his* arm.'

'Sure you will.' Callum turned in place, facing her as she circled.

'Break his little bitch legs too.'

A seven-year-old girl, with blonde ringlets. And the worst thing was: she probably meant it.

'You don't have to *be* like him, Willow. You can be so much better than that. Hell: put your mind to it and you can be anything you want.'

'You're a nutjob, Piggy.' She pedalled away a couple of feet, then dug into her pocket and came out with a small blue bag – the kind dog-walkers used to collect moist, soft, stinking presents – and chucked it to him.

Please don't let it be warm, please don't let it be warm…

It wasn't. And what was inside wasn't cold and squidgy either, it was a thin, flat rectangle.

Callum opened the bag, and there it was: one tatty leather wallet, the lining dangling loose from one side like a Labrador's tongue. A smile pulled at his face, but when he looked up Willow was already fading into the distance, pedalling for all she was worth.

He took a deep breath and bellowed it out anyway: 'THANK YOU!'

Then the car horn blared from the roadside behind him. Franklin, being her usual patient charming self.

Right.

He puffed out a breath and slipped the poo-bag in his pocket.

Time to visit the dead.

12

'Thanks. Thanks a lot. And now I'm late.' Franklin sat in the passenger seat, arms crossed, scowling.

'It's only just gone half ten.' Callum swung the pool car around the roundabout and into a shabby industrial estate. Past boarded-up business units with empty car parks and rusty chain-link fencing speckled with ancient carrier bags – their colours bleached and brittle. Through puddles the size of lochans, sending arcs of spray up onto the pavements. Windscreen wipers thumping back-and-forth across the glass. 'It's like going to the pictures: first fifteen minutes is all adverts and trailers.'

'I happen to *like* the trailers.'

Yeah, she would.

Left, past a garage selling shiny four-by-four flatbed trucks, and down to the end of the road.

A thick line of green bushes – at least twelve foot tall – stretched out from either side of a big automatic gate topped with razor wire. An intercom unit sat in front of the gate, mounted on top of a big concrete bollard. Callum pulled up beside it and wound down his window. Pressed the button.

Its speaker crackled and popped, then hissed something unintelligible at him. So he stuck his thumb on the button again and held it there till the gates squealed and rumbled their way open.

The pool car rocked its way over a speed bump and into the compound.

If the architect was going for warm and welcoming when he designed Oldcastle's overflow mortuary he'd done a sodding rotten job of it. The building looked like something out of a Cold War thriller – a concrete bunker with tiny windows along its length. A Transit van sat outside the loading bay, down the far end, two men in grey overalls manhandling a plain gunmetal coffin onto a gurney.

It wasn't the only vehicle there – a handful of manky pool cars had been abandoned as close to the mortuary's front doors as possible. Because clearly police officers weren't waterproof.

Callum parked on the periphery of the clump. 'There you go: five minutes. They'll still be going on about switching off your mobile phone and getting a drink and a snack from the lobby.'

'You're an idiot.' She climbed out into the rain and slammed the door behind her.

'So people keep telling me.' He locked the car and followed her inside.

They'd decorated since last time, the smell of fresh paint fighting against several plug-in air fresheners and the dirty-bowel-like stench of decay. All the posters were new too – motivational landscapes and quotes about peace and forgiveness. As if that was going to do any good to the poor sods who had to come all the way out here to identify their dead child's body. The wee stainless-steel reception desk hadn't changed, and nor had the big dusty rubber plant in the corner. Its thick waxy leaves like slabs of green liver, aerial roots searching the walls for sustenance.

A little old man lounged behind the desk, tongue poking out of the side of his mouth as he wrestled with the *Castle News and Post* crossword. The effort must have been quite something, because his wrinkles were even more tortured than normal, his hair a mixture of silver and cigarette-tar yellow.

Callum went over and had a look. Poked the newspaper. 'Three across, "Decapitated".'

The old man glanced up, showing off a pair of dark, glittering eyes. 'It doesn't fit.'

'It does if you spell "Robespierre" properly, Dougal. Three Es, two Rs and an I.'

'Oh.' He made the correction, then put the paper to one side. Grinned at Franklin with a big grey wall of perfectly straight false teeth. 'Well, well, well, when DS McAdams called to say you were coming over he didn't tell me you were such a beauty.'

She bared her teeth back at him, but it wasn't a smile. 'Where's the post mortem?'

'Ah, straight to business.' Dougal winked. 'I like that in a woman.'

'Do you also like a punch in the throat?'

'I wouldn't say no to a little light spanking. But maybe I should just show you through to the cutting room?'

'Maybe you should.'

Dougal stepped out from behind the reception desk and led the way through a pair of double doors and into a long corridor with doors opening off either side. 'We've got a full house this morning. Yesterday must've been buy-one-get-one-free on dead bodies.' The door at the end opened on an aisle between two sets of refrigeration units – big rectangles of stainless steel, each one covered in a grid of metal hatches. Four high, eight wide. Each hatch was about the same size as an oven door, only they didn't contain Christmas dinner.

Well, hopefully not anyway.

One of the hatches lay wide open so the two guys from the loading bay could wrestle a body bag out of the gunmetal-grey coffin and onto a sliding drawer. The contents all bendy and awkward.

Dougal waved as they passed. 'Let's not drop the guests, guys.'

A nod. 'Dougie.'

'Bodies, bodies, and more bodies.' He glanced back over his shoulder at Callum. 'It's the same every time you lot go digging about in the tip. Think you'd have more sense.'

At the end of the block, Franklin stopped. Stood there on the damp grey floor with her mouth hanging open. Staring. 'Holy mother of hell...'

From here, the full size of the room became apparent. A mini warehouse, with row after row after row of refrigerated units in it.

She gave a low whistle. 'How many bodies have you *got* here?'

'One hundred and twelve.' Dougal stuck out his chest, sounding every inch the proud father. 'But we've got space for three hundred and sixty, including the freezers. A seven-three-seven falls out of the sky at Oldcastle airport? We can take every single passenger, a full bendy bus, *plus* two football teams as well.'

And what a fun weekend *that* would be.

Callum followed the pair of them into the visitor's changing room, with its rows of lockers, racks of blue wellington boots, boxes of gloves and other assorted paraphernalia. Slipped off his shoes and stuck them in a locker. Helped himself to a pair of size-nine wellies. 'Who's doing the mummies?'

'The mummy?' Dougal scrunched up his wrinkles, then peered at a clipboard hanging on a hook by the door marked 'DISSECTING ROOM ~ SAFETY EQUIPMENT MUST BE WORN BEYOND THIS POINT'.

'Mummies. Two of them.' Callum pulled a plastic apron from the roll by the door and unfurled it. Slipped it over his head and tied the ties. 'Came in yesterday?'

'Right. Right. Well … OK, you've got Lucy Compton.'

'Never heard of her.' He helped himself to a pair of safety goggles.

'New APT. This is her first week. Young lass, you'll like her.'

Callum stared at him. 'Can we at least *pretend* we're taking this seriously, Dougal? I want a pathologist, not some wee Anatomical Pathology Technician just out of nappies.'

Franklin yanked an apron from the roll. 'What, she's not good enough just because she's a woman?'

'I don't care if she's a man, a woman, or a transgendered squirrel – she's not a pathologist!' He watched Franklin make a cat's breakfast out of tying on her apron. 'You've ripped the plastic.'

Dougal shrugged. 'Don't look at me. All I know is we've got two pathologists on duty and four bodies to PM today. Four to do tomorrow, and four more the day after that. Assuming no one else dies in the meantime. You want to moan at someone? Talk to Teabag and Hairy Harry.'

'Oh don't you worry, I will.'

Franklin tore off another apron and tried again. Finally got herself sorted out with goggles, wellies, a surgical mask, and gloves. Crossed her arms and shuffled on the tiled floor. 'Well?' Looking about as comfortable as a Seventies TV star in a police interview room.

Callum snapped on a pair of blue nitrile gloves. 'Have you been to a post mortem before?'

Her nostrils flared. 'Why, because I'm a weak and feeble—'

'Fine, *sod* you then.' He nodded at the door. 'Come on, Dougal, let's not keep Detective Constable Franklin waiting. She's keen to see her dead body being hacked apart.'

Dougal opened the dissecting room door and stood back to let them past.

A dozen cutting tables sat in a row down the middle, the air redolent with eau de mortuary. CCTV cameras hung from the ceiling above each one, their black bulbous eyes ready to capture the most intimate and thorough violation anyone would ever experience.

One table was surrounded by half a dozen people doing their best not to look like plainclothes police officers and failing miserably. They'd donned the same safety gear as Callum and Franklin, a couple of them laughing, two looking serious and boot-faced, two taking notes as a tall thin man in purple scrubs arranged a collection of trainers and shoes on the stainless-steel surface. Someone in green scrubs followed him, taking photos – the flash turning everything monochrome for a moment, before the colour seeped back in.

Down at the far end of the room, a dark body lay beneath a set of industrial extractor fans going full pelt. Not that it made much of an impact on the stench. But then it was difficult to imagine what would. Tip three gallons of Febreze in here and it would still stink of perforated bowels and rotten meat.

Someone in green scrubs was washing the body with a sponge, wringing out dirty grey water into a drain set into the floor.

Franklin took a deep breath and stiffened her shoulders. 'That our victim?'

'Shall we?' Douglas offered her his arm, as if they were off to the ball.

She ignored it and marched off, back straight, wellington boots making week-wonk noises on the stained floor.

The far wall was home to a long line of sinks and taps, with a glass wall above them looking in on a viewing gallery. A wee bloke with a red Henry hoover shuffled about inside looking as if he was in need of a post mortem himself.

Only two other tables were occupied – as far away from Franklin's corpse as possible – and both of them sported a mahogany-coloured body, curled up on its side. One of which was being circled by a small figure wearing pink scrubs. Dark curly hair pinned up in a lopsided bun, purple nitrile gloves, surgical mask.

That would be his brand new APT then.

Ah well.

He wandered over. 'Hi. You Ms Compton?'

She stopped and turned to him. 'No, I'm not, sorry, I'm not Ms Compton, who's Ms Compton?' She'd put her pink scrubs on over a black-and-grey stripy top. Its sleeves were rolled up just far enough to expose an inch of yoghurt-pale skin between them and the purple nitrile gloves. Not Ms Compton pointed at the curled body. 'Sorry, I know it's not my case, but I saw the mummies over here and I thought "that looks interesting", I mean I always loved those films when I was little, you know with Boris Karloff all wrapped up in bandages exacting revenge on the archaeologists who dared to disturb his tomb?' The words were delivered like machine-gun fire, in a cheery unplaceable Scottish accent. 'To be honest, I'm supposed to be consulting on

92

another case about some severed feet, but the heart wants what the heart wants.' She stuck out her hand. 'Ooh, and it's Alice, by the way, Alice McDonald, technically it's *Doctor* Alice McDonald, but that sounds a bit uppity doesn't it, so just Alice is fine, all gets a bit confusing doesn't it, maybe if everyone in the world wore name badges it'd be easier, what do you think?'

Yeah … this one was a freak.

He shook her hand, warm and slightly sticky through his gloves. 'Detective Constable Callum MacGregor.'

'Right, yes, great, good name, couldn't get much more Scottish, could you, not with a name like that, well, I mean it *could* be, if your middle name was Angus or Hamish. Is it?'

'You said you're consulting on a case. You're not a pathologist are—'

'Oh no, not a pathologist at all, I'm here doing Behavioural Evidence Analysis, which is what we call profiling now, because if we call it profiling people think it'll be just like the movies where the forensic psychologist says, "Whoever killed all these women and ate their uteruses was a white middle-aged man with one leg shorter than the other and an unnatural affinity with the music of Johnny Cash", because it doesn't work like that and lots of people like Johnny Cash but never kill anyone, though I'm not a fan myself. Do you see?'

No.

'Err...' Wait a minute. Forensic psychologist. Alice. Rambling. He lowered his own surgical mask and the dirty-brown smell of the mortuary swelled in his nostrils. 'Dr McDonald? It's me, Callum. I was on the Birthday Boy investigation, five years ago? You were consulting.' No reaction. 'I was on DCI Weber's team?'

She lowered her own mask and shared a slightly painful smile, as if she'd got something bitter caught between her back teeth. 'Ah, sorry, it's nothing personal, but I tend to just see a big sea of faces when I'm up giving presentations and then there's all the different investigations all over the country and there must have been at *least* three thousand police officers over the years, probably more, and I would love to be able to remember them all, but I haven't got that kind of brain, and I get a bit nervous when I'm up there, so I'm picturing you all in your underwear if that's—'

'Dr McDonald?' A figure appeared at Callum's shoulder, green plastic apron pulled on over a smart dark-grey suit. Half of his face was hidden behind a surgical mask, but there was no mistaking the voice or sticky-out ears. Detective Chief Inspector Powel. 'They're ready for you.'

Alice the weirdo waved at him. 'Hello, Reece, I was just admiring Callum's mummies, aren't they great, did you ever watch Boris Karloff when you were little?'

He barely inclined his head. 'DC MacGregor. I thought they were supposed to fire you this morning?'

'Nope.' Callum leaned against the cutting table. 'You'll just have to try a little harder next time you fit me up.'

Powel cricked his head to one side, then back again – like a boxer getting ready to fight. Then turned back to the professional nutjob in pink. 'Professor Twining's ready to begin, so if you want to come have a look before we take the feet out of their shoes…?'

'Yes, of course, the feet, duh, sorry got distracted. Do you think we should all have name badges, because I think we should all have name badges…' Her voice faded into the distance, swallowed by the background growl of the extractor fans as Powel led her away.

Callum stuck two fingers up at the DCI's back.

I thought they were supposed to fire you.

Dick.

And how could she not remember him? *He* remembered *her*. Mind you, she did stand out a bit, what with her whole 'Day-Pass-From-The-Asylum' shtick.

Still, it was nice she'd been interested in his mummies, because no one else seemed to give a sod.

Callum folded his arms. Searched the room for Franklin and her amazing exploding temper. She was standing in the corner, scribbling away in her notebook as the APT finished washing down the swollen corpse.

So, could be worse. At least he wasn't marinating in the Marmite stench of a decomposing body, like Franklin. No, *his* remains just smelled of… What?

Callum leaned in and took a sniff, but it was just the usual ever-present stink that permeated the mortuary: bleach, bowels, and decay. Which was odd – when they'd opened the car boot yesterday there'd been a distinct smell of wood smoke. And a hint of it back at the tip, with Mummy Number One too. Unless *this* was Mummy Number One. Kind of difficult to tell them apart.

He inched closer and tried again.

The scent was still there, lying under everything else. Like the old armchair his grandad used to smoke his pipe in. Puffing away, getting the scent of sandalwood and cherry deep into the leather.

Someone cleared their throat behind him. 'Can I *help* you?'

He flinched up. Smoothed down his thin plastic apron. 'Just...' Warmth tingled in the tips of his ears, as if he'd been caught snogging the remains instead of just sniffing them. 'Callum MacGregor, I'm Senior Investigating Officer.'

'Oh aye?' She was a large woman, compact and powerful looking. The kind of person that could pick up a fridge and beat you to death with it. Her green scrubs looked fresh out of the packet, but her arms looked fresh out of Barlinnie – covered in DIY tattoos. She leaned on the chunk of machinery she'd been wheeling across the mortuary floor. 'You sure?'

'*Yes.* Are you Ms Compton?'

She flexed her muscles. 'Lucy.'

'OK, Lucy.' He pointed at the body. 'Does this smell of wood smoke to you?'

She pulled down her mask, revealing a mole at the corner of her mouth. Sniffed. 'Oak. And...' Another sniff. 'I'm going to go with beechwood.'

'What about the other one?'

Lucy shifted the machinery over to the other cutting table, bent over the curled body and filled her nostrils. 'Definitely beechwood and oak. This one's a lot stronger.'

That would be the one from the car boot. Maybe lying about in the tip for God knew how long masked Mummy Number One's natural smell?

The APT went back to her trolley and pushed it next to the cutting table. Clunked on some sort of footbrake, then fiddled about with pins and levers until a big C-shaped arm swung out from the main unit. It had a box on either end, each about the size of small microwave.

'Right.' She handed him a heavy blue apron. 'Stick that on and we'll get some X-rays done.'

'X-rays?'

She looked at him as if he was a very thick little boy. 'Well we're not going to actually post mortem them, are we? They're *mummies*. Priceless relics of a long-dead civilisation. Cause of death isn't going to do you a hell of a lot of good, is it? Or are you planning on climbing into your DeLorean and travelling back to ancient Egypt with an arrest warrant?'

Yeah, she had a point.

'Now,' the APT pointed at Mummy Number Two, 'help me get it sitting up and we'll see what we can see...'

13

'I know it's not nice, but you need to eat it. It's good for you.'

The spoon is cold against his cracked lips, its contents hard and gritty.

He'd raise his hands and bat the spoon away, but his arms don't work any more. They don't even float in the water, just sink into its filthy depths to lie against the steel tank. *Nothing* works.

Can't even hold his own head up.

So the Priest holds it up for him, a warm hand on the back of his neck.

'Don't worry, I'll help.'

The other hand forces his mouth open, then pours the grit inside.

It sits there, in his mouth, like tiny stones. Sticking to his tongue and cheeks. Making him gag and cough. But there's not enough breath left to shift anything.

The walls are louder now, singing at the top of their splintered lungs: *'They'll worship you: you'll be a god. They'll worship you: you'll be a god. They'll worship you: you'll be a god.'*

Their voices send a tremor rattling through him, shaking his teeth, making his ribs ache.

'Shhh...' A hand strokes his forehead. 'Shhh...'

Then a kiss.

'I think it's time, don't you?'

Oh God please let it be time to die. Time for the pain to go away. *Please.*

'They'll worship you, They'll worship you...'

'Come on.'

The water falls away and he's being carried, arms and legs swinging in the cool air, rivulets of brackish water falling to the floor. There's almost nothing left of him now. Nothing but skin and bone.

'They'll worship you: you'll be a god.'

The singing walls swim and pulse around him, worshipping. And finally he makes the transition into the other room. The one where the fish hang in silent prayer.

Even the walls are quiet in here. Reverential. Waiting for the blessed relief.

Soon he'll be dead and all this will be over.

'Here we go.' Gentle hands lay him on the stone floor.

High up above, a sliver of grey sunlight dances with dust motes. Spiralling and swirling.

There's a pressure on his ankles, but not much more than that.

Then the squeal of wood on wood and his legs raise themselves off the ground, then his hips, his back, and finally his head leaves the earth. He sways gently, ascending to heaven with his arms dangling either side of his ears.

Swaying and rising.

Up and up into the darkness.

Up and up into death's comforting embrace.

He opens his mouth to say thank you, but all that comes out is a cascade of little gritty pellets.

The Priest smiles up at him, a thick rope held in one hand. 'You'll be a god...'

A god of skin and bone.

14

'And one more...' Lucy stepped back and the machinery buzzed again. Then clunked. 'OK, all done.' The muscles in her arm rippled as she pushed the portable X-ray machine's arm out of the way, making the tattoos dance. 'Now all we have to do is download the data, format it, and you'll get your glimpse into the ancient past. Might take a while, though.'

He puffed out his cheeks. 'Thanks.'

A grin. 'Who did you piss off?'

'Hmm?'

'To get lumbered with this. No one asks for a PM on a thousand-year-old mummy unless they're being punished for something.' She flipped off the footbrake. 'So who did you piss off?'

Callum forced a smile. 'Pretty much everyone.'

'Thought so.' Lucy took hold of the handles and shoved, setting the X-ray kit rolling. 'You can wait here, in the smell, or you can come through to the IT lab. It'll be warmer. With seats.'

'Yeah.'

'Wise choice. Oh, and on the way? There's a drinks machine in the APTs' lounge, I'll have a hot chocolate.'

Cheeky sod.

A dull buzzing thrum ran through the lab, mingling with the soft whirr of desktop computers, and the *ping-click-ping-click* of a small electric heater.

Callum took the last slurp from what the machine claimed was a white tea.

It had lied.

He stuck the empty plastic cup on the desk and shifted in his seat. Closed his book and put it down.

'Any good?'

He looked up. 'Hmm?'

'*The Beginner's Guide to Shoplifting.*' Lucy pointed. 'Any good?'

'It was OK.'

'I had a mate who was great at shoplifting. You name it, she could swipe it: food, booze, electric toasters. Made off with a bass guitar once.'

'Yeah, it's more a collection of short stories than a how-to guide.' He stood and stretched, little knots cracking across his spine. 'Pff...' Sagged. Checked his watch. 'Which way to the toilet?'

'Use the disabled: down the hall, on the left. I'm guessing another fifteen minutes? Servers are running like treacle today.'

'What happened to your mate, the shoplifter, she get caught?'

'Married a Glaswegian and emigrated to Newcastle.'

Callum wandered over to the door. 'Might make some calls too.'

Lucy went back to her computers. 'Wouldn't mind another hot chocolate if you're passing...?'

'See what I can do.'

Sodding hand dryers never worked.

He wiped his hands on his trousers as he made his way down the corridor to the far end. A window looked out over the mortuary car park – the reception area just visible in the middle distance.

Callum pulled out his Airwave and called Control. 'Any news on Ainsley Dugdale?'

'*Give us a minute.*'

The rain hadn't let up any, it still hammered down from a slate-coloured sky trying to batter the earth flat. It sparked back from water-logged potholes, bounced off the parked cars and...

A big man staggered out of the reception doors, both hands clutched over his face.

Was that blood?

It was.

It poured through his fingers, staining the white shirt above the disposable green apron.

'*Aye, Ainsley Dugdale: released on bail pending trial in six weeks' time.*'

'What? How the hell could they let him out on bail?'

The big man lurched against one of the pool cars and stood there, shoulders hunched in the rain, blood turning his shirt dark pink.

'How should I know? You want details? Speak to the officer in charge: DS McAdams. Anything else?'

'Yes. I got a PNC on one Irene Brown yesterday, I need a list of all known associates going back about … seven, eight years?'

'You're kidding, right?'

'No.'

A sigh battered out of the speaker. Then silence.

Out front, another man joined the first – picking his way between the puddles with a newspaper, or maybe a file folder held over his head as a makeshift umbrella. He stopped beside Captain Bleedy and patted him on the back.

There, there, poor thing.

Ah well, wasn't Callum's problem. 'You still there?'

'No, I've jetted off to Barbados for piña coladas and a barbequed lobster.'

He headed back down the corridor. 'Well?'

'I've got eight different names on here and according to the flags there's about another three that aren't on the system. One armed robber, two drug dealers, one got done for raping a nurse, one unlawful remover, one attempted murderer, and two aggravated assaulters. Well, they've all got charges for that, but two of your woman's mates didn't branch out into anything else. Or they never got caught.'

Eleven violent scumbags, and Irene Brown was barely in her twenties.

Little Mike was right: this is what real life looks like from down here at the bottom.

'Can you email me the details? Names, dates, convictions, everything you've got.'

'Urgh…' Another big put-upon sigh. 'Fine. Anything else, Your Majesty, or can I go back to working my fingers to the bone?'

Yes. Away boil your head.

'No. Thank you.' Callum stuck the handset back in his pocket.

Why did everyone have to be such a prima donna?

He paused at the entrance to the technicians' lounge. There was no point getting another tea from the machine – once poisoned, twice shy – but the hot chocolate couldn't be all that bad if Lucy was having another, so—

The door leading through to the dissecting room burst open and DCI Powel stormed into the corridor with his monkey ears bright red.

He turned and jabbed a finger at his own feet. 'IN HERE NOW!'

Franklin stepped in after him, shoulders back, chin up, jaw clenched.

Powel's voice dropped to a growling whisper soon as the door shut behind her. 'I do not care what you got away with in Edinburgh, but you do *not* assault members of *my* team without *serious* repercussions. Do you understand?'

She glared back at him. 'With all due respect, sir—'

'I SAID, DO YOU UNDERSTAND?' Bellowing it out, spittle flashing in the overhead lighting.

'Yes, *sir.*' There it was again: that burning-pus tone.

'Now you will wait here and you will not move a muscle while I go check on the man you assaulted. And while I'm gone I want you to have a good hard think about how screwed you are.' Powel barged past her and back into the dissecting room again, slamming the door on his way.

Franklin bared her teeth. 'I will rip your bloody balls off, you...' She must have realised she wasn't alone, because she clicked her mouth shut and turned her glare on Callum instead. 'What the hell are *you* looking at?'

He wandered over, hands in his pockets. 'Let me guess: the guy with the busted face...?'

'I don't answer to you.'

'Never said you did.'

She paced the width of the corridor in two steps then turned and did it again. 'What is *wrong* with you people?'

'Me people?'

'He grabbed my arse! Of *course* I hit him!'

Ooh...

Callum stuck his head on one side. 'Let me guess – big guy with sideburns and a wonky eye? DS Jimmy Blake. AKA: Blakey the Octopus.'

'And do you know what he called me when I hit him? An "effing darkie bitch"!' She thumped her hand against the wall.

'No.' Callum frowned. 'Blakey said, "effing"?'

'Oh shut up.' She went back to short-form pacing again.

The door thumped open, and there was Powel, suit darkened across the shoulders and legs. He hooked a finger an inch from Franklin's face. 'You. With me. Now.' Then turned and marched off.

She caught the door. Took a deep breath and went after him.

She was a pain in the backside, but still...

Callum followed the pair of them into the dissecting room's foetid air, across the stained floor to the cutting table covered in naked disembodied feet. It was surrounded by plainclothes officers, shuffling about and avoiding eye contact. Fidgeting. Looking shifty and embarrassed about the whole thing.

Blakey was a pillar of indignation off to one side, a wad of green paper towels clutched to his nose, shirt stained a lovely Ribena red all down the front.

Powel stopped right in front of him, and did the pointing-at-his-own-feet thing again. 'Detective *Constable* Franklin. You will apologise to DS Blake and you will do it now.'

She stood where she was told, muscles writhing along her jawline.

'*Now*, Constable!'

Franklin took a deep breath, opened her mouth—

But Callum got there first. 'Sorry to interrupt, Guv, but I'm sure this is all just a big misunderstanding.'

Powel didn't even look at him. 'This is none of your business, MacGregor.'

'Let's *imagine* for a moment that DC Franklin was the victim of a serious sexual assault in the workplace. She'd be well within her rights to defend herself, wouldn't she?'

At that, Powel turned. 'She attacked DS Blake.'

'There's a reason they call him "Blakey the Octopus", Guv.'

Blake took the towels from his face. His left eye pointed about ten degrees off from the right one, but both of them had already gone a dark shade of pink. 'I nebber tudged her!'

Ooh... Yeah. Mental note: *never* try to cop a feel of Franklin's bum. She'd completely flattened Blake's nose, leaving a squint lump of bloody gristle behind.

Franklin bared her teeth. 'You lying, sexist, *racist* scumbag!' She took a step forward, hands snapping into fists again.

Callum grabbed her arm. 'We can easily check, Blakey.' He pointed up at the dark CCTV globe mounted above the cutting table. 'Big brother sees all.'

'Ah...' Blake stared up at the camera.

'So maybe what *actually* happened is you slipped on the wet floor and tried to break the fall with your face?'

Blake pressed the towels against his nose again. Looked down at his feet. 'I slibbed ad fell.'

Callum held his arms out, like he was about to accept applause for a magic trick. 'There you go: told you it was nothing but a silly misunderstanding.'

'What was *that* supposed to be?' Franklin paced the length of the APTs' lounge, between an off-grey sofa and a coffee table covered in tabloid magazines, one arm jabbing in the general direction of the dissecting room.

Callum poked buttons on the vending machine, setting it whirring and clunking. 'You're welcome.'

'I'm *welcome*? Well thank you *so* much. He grabbed my arse!'

Oh joy.

A plastic cup clunked down in the dispenser, then the hissing and gurgling started.

'He grabs your backside – that's sexual harassment. If you'd *reported* him, that would've been it: Blake gets hauled up in front of Professional Standards for being a dirty sex offender. End of.' The machine stopped its noises, so Callum extracted the scalding hot cup and pressed the buttons again. 'But no, you had to lash out. You break his nose – that's assault. Now it's *you* in front of the rubber heelers and everyone thinks *he's* the victim.'

Gurgling and hissing.

'That what you want?'

She stopped pacing. 'So you just swan in and save the poor powerless black woman, do you? Because *you* know best.'

He stared at the ceiling. 'I give up. I really do.'

'The Great White Saviour rides again!'

'For God's sake... Do you *never* stop? All I've done since you got here is try to be nice. I was just looking out for a member of my team, OK? Even though she's hell-bent on leaping feet-first into the sodding wood chipper!'

She threw herself down into the sofa. Sat there seething. Looked away. Closed her eyes. Then let out a barely audible, 'Thank you.'

He picked up one of the scalding cups and held it out. 'Here.'

Franklin took it. Held it in her lap as her head fell back against the back of the couch. 'Why do so many white guys see a black woman and think she's going to be an easy shag? You think it's hard being a police officer? Try doing it when you're a woman, you're black, you're attractive, and everyone thinks you're "gagging for it".' She ran her spare hand across her forehead. 'If I'm sleeping my way to the top, how come I'm still a sodding constable?'

Callum smiled. 'If it's any consolation, I don't think you're in the least bit attractive.' He took a sip of burning-hot chocolate. 'Oh, I did for two or three seconds when I first met you, but soon as I got to know you? Not a chance.'

She gave a little laugh. 'When I was fourteen my geography teacher tried to feel me up in the stationery cupboard, said he'd always wanted to try a black girl. Wasn't the first to chance his arm and he wasn't the last.'

'Did you break his nose too? Or...' Callum sniffed. Wait a minute. He sat on the other end of the couch. 'That's why you got lumped into Mother's Misfit Mob, isn't it? You said you punched a superintendent – all hands was he?'

Franklin held up her cup in salute. 'Welcome to the world of hyper-sexualisation.'

'Yeah: they can't fire us. They *want* to, but they can't. So they chuck us all together and drip-feed us crappy nothing cases till we get fed up and quit.'

'*And* he was married.'

Callum had another sip. Lucy was right – the hot chocolate wasn't anywhere near as bad as the tea. 'How you getting on with our body in the bath?'

'You know what I should've done? I should've agreed to go to that hotel with him and recorded him being a sleazy git. Then sent the tape to his wife. Let's see Superintendent Neil Lambert slither his way out of that one.'

'Nice to know your first thought was revenge instead of blackmail.'

She gave her forehead a little slap. 'Blackmail. Damn – why didn't *I* think of that?' Franklin sagged in her seat. 'Our body's a Caucasian male, five eleven, difficult to tell how old. Turns out the water in the bath was a *very* heavy brine solution with leaves and flowers and herbs and spices thrown in. Little bits of bark. His lungs are full of it too, so he was alive when he went in. You think you're a bit wrinkly after half an hour in the bath? Our victim looks like he's about ninety.'

'At least all that salt will have preserved the tissue.'

'Only the outside layers. Didn't stop his stomach bursting in the water. Gah...' She had a little shudder. 'God, I *hate* post mortems.'

'Shouldn't have transferred to Oldcastle then, we're up to our ears in them.' He punched the buttons for a third hot chocolate. 'What do you reckon to Glen Carmichael and his mates being responsible? Three of them, killing the guy in the bath together – holding his head under till he stops struggling. Or it could be one of them. They fall out, fight, same result.' The machine hissed and gurgled. '*Or* maybe they get their hands on a load of dodgy drugs? One of them has a catastrophically bad trip so they try to sober him up in the bath. But he drowns. They panic and do a runner.'

She pursed her lips. 'Makes sense. Three blokes, stuck in that flat for months together, the windows all covered with hardcore pornography, getting drunk and wasted. Can't expect sensible decisions from—'

The door battered open and Lucy staggered to a halt on the carpet tiles. 'Callum?' A bit out of breath, but grinning too. 'You are *not* going to believe it.' She hooked a thumb over her shoulder, tattoos rippling. 'Digital X-rays have finished processing. You've got to see this!'

OK.

He peeled himself out of the couch and followed her down the corridor to the lab.

Lucy pointed at a large computer monitor sitting on a desk covered in empty Quality Street wrappers. 'Look.'

He hunched over and squinted at the screen. It was filled with human bones, the skin reduced to pale wisps of grey around them. The X-ray had been taken from the side, showing the body curled up with its elbows in, hands against its chest and knees against them, neck bent so far forward that the front of the skull was obscured by the kneecaps. Definitely one of the mummies. 'And?'

'This is *so* cool.' She clattered her fingers across the keyboard and the image zoomed in on the jumbled monochrome mess where the face met the kneecaps. 'See?'

'No.'

'I thought it was an artefact on the machinery – some of the APTs X-ray all sorts of crap for a laugh and if they damage the equipment it shows up on the digital prints – so I checked the anterior plates.' The tip of her tongue poked out between her teeth as she typed, and the picture changed to a close-up that was little more than a mess of white lines and grey masses. '*Now* do you see?'

Callum squinted, forcing the image out of focus, letting it... There. OK, those were the eye sockets, there were the cheekbones, difficult to pick them out from the leg bones, but not impossible. That made those the nasal cavities, and *they* would be the teeth.

Oh.

He sank into the office chair. Of course: it was obvious now. 'The hard white blobs in the mouth.'

'Yup.' Lucy grinned at him, eyebrows way up her forehead. 'I'm no expert on ancient Egyptian burial rituals, but I'm pretty sure Tutankhamun didn't go to his grave with a mouth full of NHS fillings.'

15

'Are you actually *hiding* in here?' Franklin stood in the doorway, holding the door to the disabled toilets open with her foot.

Callum gave her a grunt, then went back to the sink. Stuck a folded paper towel against the open neck of the disinfectant bottle and upended the thing till it soaked into the off-grey paper. 'I'm not hiding, I'm busy.' He dabbed the damp tissue against the wallet, blotting away a stain.

'Mother's here.'

'Course she is.' More blotting. The stuff was working even better than Lucy had promised. OK, so his dad's wallet would never look new again, but at least it didn't stink like the inside of whatever bin Willow Brown had fished it out of.

'Callum?'

'It was covered in cigarette ash and something I'm hoping was mayonnaise.'

'She's told Dr Jenkins she wants both mummies post-mortemed ASAP. Our bath body's gone back into the fridge till they're done. He's starting the first one in fifteen minutes.'

'Good for you.' Callum dumped the paper towel in the bin and moistened another with disinfectant.

'Well? Aren't you coming? Thought you were SIO?'

'What's the point?' He opened the wallet and started on the inside surfaces. Wiping the square of clear plastic covering the faded photo that took up the whole left-hand side: a happy family, all four of them grinning away at the camera, those bright summer colours faded to autumn tones of brown, orange, and yellow. Not quite in focus. Posed around a picnic table, blue sky, sea, and white sand just visible behind them.

'So you're *sulking*?'

'Like you can talk.' He dabbed away at the other side. 'They're never going to let me be Senior Investigating Officer for a triple murder. A detective constable running down a serial killer? No chance.'

Franklin shook her head. 'You've been inhaling too much of that disinfectant, there's only two murders, not—'

'The mummies have been smoked. That's probably to dehydrate and preserve them. And what do you do before you smoke something? You salt it to draw out excess moisture. You *brine* it.' He wiped off a crusty smear of red that looked more like tomato ketchup than blood. 'And what did we find floating in a bathtub full of brine?'

When he looked up, Franklin was standing there with her mouth hanging open.

One last go with the soggy paper towel. 'Exactly.' He wiped the wallet dry with a fresh sheet, then dug into his pocket for the cash he'd begged out of the building society yesterday. Slipped it into the slit where the lining was hanging out. 'Our victim was a work in progress.'

'Sodding hell.'

'And God knows how many more bodies he's got out there.' The plastic window was cool beneath his fingertips, its surface scratched in a few places, enough to blot out small sections of the photo beneath. All four of them, just out of focus, smiling their last recorded smile together. 'Mother's going to have her work cut out holding onto the case, never mind me. They'll fly in an MIT from Strathclyde and we'll be back where we started – low-level drug dealers, loan sharks, and pimps.'

Franklin peered over his shoulder. 'Whose are the ugly kids?'

Cheeky sod.

He pointed. 'That's my brother Alastair and me.' Two little boys with matching haircuts and freckles. 'We were five. Mum and Dad at the back.' Mum with her long pale-blonde hair and heart-shaped face, kind blue eyes. Dad with his dark curly mop-top, dimpled chin, and big broad smile. The whole family was dressed for the beach in shorts and flip-flops. T-shirts with cartoon animals on them. A fox for Alastair, an owl for Callum, a cat for Mum, a dog for Dad. Sunburn for everyone. 'Two weeks on a caravan site just outside Lossiemouth.'

Franklin gave a low whistle. 'You've got an identical twin?'

All those years ago...

— Callum —

'Da-ad, he's touching me again!'

Dad just sighed and turned the radio up, singing along with Mum. Both of them belting it out at the top of their voices as countryside slipped by the car windows. Green fields beneath a dark-grey hat of clouds.

Sitting in the back seat, Alastair grinned his gap-toothed grin. Then reached across and poked Callum again.

Rotten little bumhead.

'Da-ad!'

Dad didn't look around. 'If you two don't cut it out, I'm going to pull this car over. That what you want? You want me to pull over? Because you know what'll happen if you make me do that.'

Alastair stuck his tongue out. His shaggy bowl-shaped haircut was paler than usual, more freckles on his nose and cheeks. A cartoon fox on his brown T-shirt. Tartan shorts and grass-stained knees. Bare feet all sparkly with sand, just like Callum's.

The song on the radio finished, Mum joining in right to the very end. She put her hand on Dad's leg. 'I love that one.'

The man on the radio sounded like he'd eaten a whole nest of bees. *'An oldie, but a goodie – Jimmy Perez and the Mareel Boys, with their breakthrough hit, "Mothcatcher Blues". For an extra five bonus points, name the year that topped the charts.'*

Mum snorted. 'Easy: 1986. Give us a *hard* one, Scotty.'

'Da-ad?' Callum leaned forward and tapped him on the shoulder.

'And don't forget we've got – and I'm mega excited about this – the one, the only, the Krankies! They'll be here in fifteen minutes to tell us all about Monday's heee-larious episode of K.T.V. It'll be fan-dabi-dozi!'

109

'What did I tell you, Cal?'

'I'm Scott Kennedy and you're listening to the Golden Oldies Quiztime Special *on Castlewave FM...'*

'No, but I need to go wee-wee. I really do.'

'Now then, my little Quiztronaughts, who was the lead singer on this hit from two years ago? It's the Bangles, and "Eternal Flame".' Some sort of horrible old-people music jingled out of the radio – weird pings and things, with a woman being all soft and soppy over the top.

'We're half an hour from home, so you'll have to tie a knot in it.'

'But, Da-ad, I'm *bursting.*'

Mum shook her head, setting her pale-yellow hair swinging. 'Told you it was a mistake to buy him that tin of Fanta. It goes right through—'

'Don't start.'

'I'm just saying.' She pointed through the windscreen at a lumpy blocky building at the side of the road. 'Look, there's a public toilet. Stop.'

'I'm *not* stopping.'

'Fine. Well, you keep on driving, David MacGregor, and when Callum wees himself, *you* can clean it up.'

The lady on the radio sang about easing the pain. Which would've been nice, because right now there was a big balloon of pee swelling up in Callum's insides, sending stabby twinges all through his tummy right down to the end of his willy. *'Please,* Dad?'

'All right!' Dad thumped his hand on the steering wheel. 'All right, I'll stop. You happy now?'

'David, please, for *once* can we not—'

'No. That's perfect. I'm stopping.' The car pulled into the lay-by, bumping and rolling along the holey road, caravan lurching away behind it. 'There.'

Mum didn't sing along with the lady on the radio: she just sat there, in the passenger seat, with her arms folded, staring out of the window.

Dad's voice was stretched and twangy, the way it went before someone got spanked for being naughty: 'Alastair, do *you* need a wee too?'

'No, Dad.'

'Callum?'

'I'm sorry, Daddy.'

'Get out, Callum.'

He scrabbled with his seatbelt, pulled on his flip-flops, and pushed the door open. Hopped down onto the car park's holey surface.

The toilets were a low grey rectangle, sitting in front of a line of trees. Filth streaked the walls and the guttering sagged in the middle.

Someone had sprayed 'TORY SCUM OUT!' across the Ladies. There weren't any outside doors, instead a bit of wall was missing at both ends of the building, open and gaping. A cave, full of shadows and horrible smells.

Up above, the sky was dark as an angry cat.

Mum nudged Dad. 'Don't just sit there – go with him.'

'He's not a baby, Nicola. If he wants to go to the toilet he's damn well big enough to go on his own.'

Callum wiped his damp palms on the legs of his shorts.

Maybe he didn't *need* to go after all?

Maybe he could hold it in all the way home?

But that great big balloon just above his willy didn't want to hold it in. It wanted to pee it out, all down his leg if he didn't—

The car horn blared, and he jumped. Turned.

Dad scowled at him through the driver's window. Alastair grinned from the backseat.

Swallow. Turn.

You can do this, Callum.

You're a big boy now. Big boys can go to the toilet on their own.

He took a deep breath and crept into the Gents. Into the gloom. Into the manky-vinegar stink of old wee.

White tiles covered the walls, the lines in between them all dirty and yellow. Thick scratch marks ran across the brown floor, like something heavy had been dragged from one of the cubicles. Four of them huddled along the left wall, one with its door all splintered and hanging off. Urinals on the wall opposite. Sinks at the back.

A dripping tap went *plink, plink, plink.*

Callum hurried across to the urinals, unzipped his shorts and stood on his tiptoes.

Nothing happened.

Come on. Come on. Come on.

'Hello, little boy.' The voice was big and heavy, thick and slimy. Like a huge slug. 'You're a *pretty* little boy, aren't you?'

A thin stream of yellow piddle splashed into the urinal, wobbling up and down because Callum couldn't stop shaking.

'Such a pretty blond little boy.'

The Slug slithered closer, breath all heavy and panting.

'Please, my dad—'

'Shut up. Don't spoil it.' Closer. 'Are you a *good* little boy?'

Callum stood there, with his shrivelled willy in his hand. 'Please.'

111

'Mmm, I'll bet you are.' The Slug was so close now his butter-minty breath washed over Callum's face. 'This is going to be our little secret. If you tell anyone, I'll know. And I know where you live and I'll come get you. I'll kill your mummy and daddy and I'll *punish* you. Understand?'

He nodded. Bit his bottom lip to keep the tears in.

'Good.' A warm slimy tongue licked its way up Callum's cheek, slow and minty and wet. 'Now you're going to be very quiet and come with—

'Nah, *course* Labour's gonna win next year.' A man stumbled into the toilets, voice echoing back from the tiles. 'Stands to reason, don't it?'

Callum flinched.

The warm sticky breath disappeared and the slimy slug trail on his cheek went cold. Now the only thing left was the *plink, plink, plink* of the dripping tap and the jaggy sour smell of wee.

He fumbled his willy back into his pants. Zipped up with shaky fingers.

'They better win.' Another man – dressed in the same checked shirt and scruffy jeans as his friend – long hair dangling down round his face, cigarette poking from the corner of his mouth. 'Can you imagine another four years of these bawbags?'

No sign of the Slug.

Callum's breath shuddered out. He sagged for a moment. Then scuffed across to the sinks and washed his hands. Scrubbed a wet hand across the cold patch on his cheek. Dried himself on a greying curl of fabric hanging from the towel machine.

Stepped over to the exit.

And froze.

What if the Slug hadn't gone away? What if he was out there, just waiting for him? Waiting to grab him and take him away and punish him and he'd never see his mummy and daddy ever again and it would be horrible and...

The stabby pain was back. He hurried to the urinals, up on his tiptoes again, making little grunty noises as the wee went down the drain.

Then washed his hands again, cos Mum didn't like widdly hands in the car.

Both the guys in the grungy clothes were laughing at some joke about two nuns and a donkey that made no sense at all. Peeing and peeing and peeing like they'd drunk a whole bathtub full of Fanta. They didn't wash their hands either, just lit up cigarettes and sauntered out the exit with their hands in their pockets.

Callum wiped his sweaty hands on his shorts again.

Plink. Plink. Plink.

The sound of a car faded into the distance.

It would be OK. It would.

Dad would get angry about how long he was taking and come get him.

Then he'd shout at Callum, and maybe spank the back of his legs, but he'd scare the Slug away and everything would be OK again.

It would.

Callum swallowed.

Shifted from foot to foot in his gritty flip-flops.

Come on, Daddy. Come on...

It'd been *ages* now.

What if they'd got fed up, driven off and left him?

What if they'd forgotten he was here, in the toilets?

What if they never came back?

What if the Slug *did*?

Oh no...

Callum hurried outside.

Dad's car and the caravan were still there.

Thank you, thank you, thank you.

He'd never be naughty, ever again. He'd do everything Mum asked him. He'd tidy his room. He'd even be nice to Alastair the bumhead.

A rumble of thunder, off in the distance, mingled with the traffic noises from the road.

He ran fast as a rabbit to Dad's car and grabbed the door handle. But it just clunked up and down. The door didn't open.

Alastair must've locked it. Well, he was going to get a dead arm soon as Mum and Dad weren't looking. It wasn't *funny*: locking people out of the car when there was a horrible Slug slithering about trying to steal little boys like something horrid from a fairy tale.

Callum knocked on the window.

Tried the handle again.

Still locked.

Stood on his tiptoes, and peered in through the glass.

The bumhead wasn't on the back seat. Or in the footwell.

'Mum?'

She wasn't in the passenger seat. And Dad wasn't behind the wheel.

The car was empty.

'Hello?'

Another boom of thunder, loud enough to make him jump. They'd left him. They'd run away and left him.

How could they *leave* him?

Callum's bottom lip trembled.

He backed against Dad's car. 'Dad?'

They couldn't have left him. They *couldn't*.

It wasn't his fault he needed a wee…

'Mum?'

And what if the Slug came back? A drop of rain burst against the lumpy tarmac.

What if the Slug was *waiting* for him?

'Please…'

Another drop. Then another. And another. Thumping down on the car roof like the feet of a tiny monster. Soaking through his hair and his T-shirt.

Maybe…

Maybe they'd all gone for a wee too? But then he'd have seen Dad and Alistair, wouldn't he? In the Gents?

Or maybe they were in the caravan?

The breath rushed out of Callum, replaced by a smile. Yeah, that was it: they were in the caravan making cups of tea.

What an idiot. Of course they were.

Boiling the kettle on the little gas cooker.

He ran to the caravan's door. Twisted the handle and climbed inside. Clunked the door shut behind him.

Only there was no one there.

The smile died.

Callum checked under the table, checked the loo, he even checked the cupboards.

No one.

'Mum?'

A flash of white turned the caravan's insides black-and-white, then the thunder roared, rain clattering against the roof. Callum blinked. Rubbed a hand across his eyes. Stared out through the window at the front of the caravan – where the folding table and the benches that turned into Mum and Dad's bed were.

Someone was out there. A figure in the rain: big and hunched, moving with slow lumbering steps.

The Slug.

Callum ran for the caravan door and hauled the handle up, locking it. Backed away.

Another flash, followed by a deafening crash, like someone had jammed a metal dustbin over his head and battered it with a hammer.

He dropped to his knees and scrambled under the table. Curled up against the wall.

Don't move. Don't make any noise. Quiet and still as a mouse.

Outside, something scratched along the caravan's walls. It started over by the chemical loo, grinding and squealing across the metal, working its way slowly around, behind him, and past to the caravan's door.

Stopped.

Callum stared.

The handle twisted. Not far. Just a teeny weeny bit, till the lock stopped it. Twisted again. Then silence.

Maybe the Slug had given up? Maybe he'd gone away? Maybe he'd—

The whole door shook – banging and clattering in its frame.

'No!' Callum wrapped his arms around his head and bit his bottom lip till he could taste pennies. 'Go away, go away, go away...'

Then the noise faded, leaving nothing behind but the battering drone of rain on the caravan roof.

The Slug had given up.

He had to.

The caravan was *locked*, he couldn't get in.

A trembly sob rattled its way out of Callum. Safe.

And then that dark slimy voice crept through the caravan wall, as if the Slug's lips were right up against it. '*Your mummy and daddy don't love you any more. They say you're ugly and stupid and useless and they don't want you. So they've given you to me.*'

No. They wouldn't do that. They wouldn't leave him.

They couldn't...

'*You're* mine *now, little boy. You belong to me.*' Scratching noises against the wall. '*Now open the door and let me in.*'

A hand on his arm. 'Gah!' Callum flinched.

Franklin frowned at him. 'Are you OK?'

He let out a shuddery breath, looking down at the photo of the four of them in their holiday clothes. 'What?'

She pointed at the photo. 'I said, "You've got an identical twin?"'

He clicked the wallet closed and slipped it into his back pocket. 'A long time ago.'

16

Hairy Harry loomed over the wrinkled body on the cutting table, humming away to himself. A huge breezeblock of a man, with rounded shoulders and a bit of a gut on him. He'd tucked the last six inches of his Victorian-style beard into the top of his apron. A blue-camouflage bandanna covered the top of his head, his long furry ponytail poking out the back of it. Hairy Harry's voice was surprisingly soft and warm for someone who looked as if they ate live badgers. 'Now *that's* interesting...'

He reached into the open body cavity, coming out with a chunk of shrivelled black, holding it aloft like that baboon did at the start of Disney's *The Lion King*. 'Have you ever seen a liver look like that before, all dried out and wrinkly?'

Lucy shook her head and made another note on her clipboard.

'Fascinating.'

They'd laid the body out on its back, not so much uncurling the limbs as snapping them off at the dry brittle joints. Legs and arms, positioned either side of the smoke-coloured ribs.

Franklin had her own arms folded, voice so low it was barely a whisper. 'At least this one doesn't smell as bad.'

Hairy Harry went back in, coming out with what looked like a dehydrated snake. 'Well, well, well...'

Mother and McAdams stood off to one side, heads together, McAdams poking away at his mobile phone as she talked in hushed tones. Every now and then, she'd look up and stare at Callum. Then go back to conspiring with her poetry-spouting sidekick. Probably trying to figure out what crappy job to punish him with next.

'Amazing, when you think about it.' Hairy Harry stuck his gloved

116

hands on the hips of his purple scrubs. 'The only internal organs still attached are the heart and the lungs, everything else has been taken out, preserved, then put back in again. It's almost impossible to tell cause of death from the soft tissue, because there isn't any – it's all like beef jerky.'

The mummy's ribcage lay on a trolley against the wall, its covering of leathery skin too dried-on to remove like in a normal post mortem.

'No external sign of trauma, other than the discolouration around the throat – which *could* just be pigmentation from the preservation, but looks more like ante-mortem bruising to me. And then there's this.' He held up a little jar full of tiny discoloured spheres and gave it a shake, making them rattle against the glass. 'You'll need to get it tested, but unless I'm very much mistaken, it's silica gel. The kind of thing that comes in those little sachets they stick in bags, shoes, and handbags to sook up moisture and stop them going mouldy. His mouth was stuffed with it. More in the oesophagus, trachea, and sinus cavities. We'll have to rehydrate the stomach to find out, but I'm willing to bet we'll find some there too.'

Mother wandered back to the table. 'Excuse me, Dr Jenkins, I have to borrow Detective Constable MacGregor here.'

Oh. That didn't sound good. Whatever horror she and McAdams had come up with, it was about to spatter down on Callum's head.

'Please, it's Harrison. And by all means. The young man's a bit of a fidget anyway.'

Everyone's a critic.

She pulled on a smile. 'Thank you.' Then headed for the exit. 'Come on, Constable.'

Here we go.

Callum leaned closer to Franklin. 'Try not to punch anyone else, OK?' And followed Mother out, through the changing room, past the rows and rows of refrigeration units, across the reception area, and out into the rain.

She shrugged her shoulders up around her ears and hurried across the puddled tarmac to her battered Fiat Panda. Hurled herself in behind the wheel and beckoned at him from the safety of the car.

What would it be: door-to-doors in the freezing downpour? Digging into the archives for some obscure file that hadn't been seen for three generations? Talking to small children about road safety? Or maybe she was just going to fire him?

He high-stepped between the water-filled potholes, collar pulled up against the rain, and clambered in the passenger side.

A furry penguin hung from the rear-view mirror, along with a yellow air-freshener that smelled of chemical lemons. Inside, the car was a mess. Mud, grit, gravel, and old magazines in the footwells; plastic bags, a collection of cardboard wine-carriers full of empties, and for some bizarre reason a quarter-size inflatable sheep with sunglasses, littering the back seat. Dust coating the dashboard like a furry blanket. The bottles clinked and rattled as he thumped the door shut.

Ooh, sodding hell: it was like climbing into a very filthy fridge. Cold air nipped at his ears.

Mother stuck her hands in her pockets, her breath fogging in front of her face. 'Callum, Callum, Callum... What am I going to do with you?'

Oh great. She'd dragged him all the way out here for a bollocking. Could they not have done it inside in the warm?

'Thought I told you not to lead our new girl astray? And what do I find? She's running around assaulting detective sergeants on DCI Powel's Major Investigation Team. Care to explain yourself?'

What? 'How is this my—'

'I had Powel on the phone this afternoon, and he wasn't a happy hedgehog. Says after the assault you waded in and interfered with the victim – to wit one DS Jimmy Blake. Got him to change his story and say he slipped and battered his *own* nose to a wee bloody lump.'

'All I did was point out that the whole thing would be caught on the mortuary's CCTV system.' A shrug. 'For some reason, Blakey wasn't keen on anyone seeing it.'

'Right.' Mother nodded. Then sighed. 'Callum, I'm all in favour of sticking up for the team, I really am...'

'But?'

'But probably better get a copy of the footage. Just in case Powel or Blakey decide to make it disappear. Blackmail only works as long as you've got the negatives.' She grinned, then dug a paper bag out of her fleece pocket. 'Have a jelly baby. Hell, take two.'

He did. An orange and a yellow.

Mother shoogled down a bit in her seat and helped herself to a red one. 'And when you get the footage, pop past my office with it. About time someone tried to introduce Blakey the Octopus's nose to his rectum by first-class fist-express; I'm going to get some popcorn in.'

'Yes, Boss.' He popped the yellow baby into his mouth, chewed on its lemony sweetness.

'I don't know what to make of you, Callum, I honestly don't. One minute you're this vast pain in my backside, and the next you're saving Franklin from herself.'

He ripped the head off the orange baby. 'I didn't take a bribe from Big Johnny Simpson. Talk to Professional Standards – they're looking through every penny I've got. Yes: I cocked-up the crime scene, but I didn't do it on purpose.'

'Hmmm…' She chewed in silence for bit.

A squall of wind rocked the car, rain buckshotting the roof, setting it ringing.

Mother devoured another baby. 'They're going to grab this case off us if they can.'

Of course they were.

'Two victims mummified and a third brining, ready for smoking? That spells "serial killer" in eight-foot-tall flashing neon letters. There'll be a media outcry, public panic, press briefings, idiots hanging about outside Divisional Headquarters doing serious pieces to camera…' A yellow jelly baby lost its life. 'They'll want a superintendent running it.'

Callum wrote his name in the dashboard dust. 'Yes, but a superintendent won't want to get their hands dirty, will they? No, they'll want someone *else* to do the actual police work, in case it all goes horribly wrong. Plausible deniability.'

'Oh goody, a poisoned chalice. My favourite.' She held the paper bag out again. 'We're fighting for this one, Callum. It'll probably be the last chance Andy gets to put a killer away. I won't let them take that away from him.'

'We should run a dental records match on Glen Carmichael and his two mates. Just in case.' He popped a green jelly baby in, feet first. 'And Powel's got a forensic psychologist down to consult on his severed feet, Dr McDonald. She was the one they brought in to work the Birthday Boy case? We could tap her for some Behavioural Evidence Analysis.'

'What's that when it's at home?'

'They're not allowed to call it "profiling" because of the TV. Might help?'

'Not if it's Glen and his mates who're the killers…' A shrug. 'But what the hell. We'll get DNA and a facial reconstruction on the go too. I'll fight with our esteemed masters about the budget later.' She put the sweeties away. 'Anything else?'

Callum wiped the dust from his fingertip onto his trousers. 'When you dragged me out here, I thought you were going to fire me.'

'Did you?' A shrug. 'I just fancied a jelly baby – they always taste funny in the mortuary. Like death.'

Sharp salty cheese, soft claggy bread, smooth silky butter, and the tangy vinegar crunch of Branston Pickle. Callum sat in the APT lounge and chewed.

Elaine had stuck another little note in with his sandwich. Today it was a lumpy drawing of a flat fish, with a speech balloon above its head: 'YOU'RE MY SOLE MATE!', with the subtitle, 'BARRY THE FISH IS TERRIBLE AT PUNS', and a lipstick kiss.

He smiled at Barry, then tucked him into his jacket pocket – ready to join the others when he got home.

A copy of *Hey You!* magazine lay on the coffee table, all shiny and shallow. Apparently some plastic-faced, talentless, Z-list nonentities were celebrating the first anniversary of the renewal of their wedding vows! Picture exclusive! Oh my God! How exciting!

No wonder people turned into serial killers.

Still, it was his own fault for finishing *The Beginner's Guide to Shoplifting* that morning, instead of saving it for lunchtime. Could've had something decent to read instead of this.

He flipped the magazine open to a big photo spread of Mrs Plastic Face and her equally gormless-looking husband of eighteen months. Eighteen months married and they'd already reached the heady milestone of a vow-renewal anniversary.

Someone grunted their way down into the couch on the other side of the coffee table.

Callum took another bite. 'According to this, she's just signed a publishing deal: two million quid for four books.'

'How is that fair?' McAdams sighed. 'A book deal for an idiot who can't write her own name, / The public should know better, but they'll buy it just the same, / The publishers will lap it up, to boost their bottom line, / And if they'll publish crap like that, why won't they publish *mine?*'

Callum flipped the page again. 'Move over Pam Ayres, we have a new Poet Laureate.'

'Shouldn't you be doing something?'

'I am. I'm eating the sandwich my pregnant girlfriend made me for lunch.' He held up a finger. 'And before you start: I've already got the DNA sent off from all three bodies, got Lucy to X-ray their heads for dental chart comparisons, contacted Dundee University's facial reconstruction bods, asked the media department to send out "have you seen these men" posters for Glen Carmichael and his mates, and Dr Alice McDonald has agreed to pay us a visit as soon as she's finished drafting her preliminary report on Powel's severed feet.' Another bite of cheesy pickly goodness. 'So yes, right now I'm eating my lunch and reading about vacuous nonentities who spent more cash on a vow-renewal anniversary celebration than you or I will make in a year.'

'Just because Mother's softening on you, doesn't mean I am, Constable. And for the record: summary narrative is the hallmark of a lazy writer.'

He turned the page. 'Ooh, look here: it says she's bringing out a line of perfumes, that'll be nice, won't it? Silicone Implants à la Botox, a fragrance for women.'

'Fine.' McAdams stood. 'When you've finished your meagre repast, I want those dental records checked. And find out who they bought the flat from. Maybe he's the one in the bath. God knows I'd happily kill the idiot who sold us our house.'

'Sarge?' Franklin poked her head around the door. 'Sorry, but there's a Dr McDonald in the observation room asking to see the team. Says she's consulting?'

'That's me.' Callum popped the last chunk of sandwich in his mouth and sooked his fingers clean. Flipped the magazine shut and stood. 'Feel free to tag along, if you like.'

He sauntered out, past a frowning Franklin, and down the corridor into the observation suite. It was subdivided into booths by a series of half-height partitions, each area looking out over one of the dissecting room's twelve cutting tables. The booths all had their own whiteboard, DVD recorder, collection of uncomfortable plastic chairs, and TV screen.

Dr McDonald was sitting cross-legged on the floor right in front of the TV, still wearing her pink scrubs and stripy top, elbows on her knees, hands on her cheeks – holding her head up. Like a little kid watching cartoons. In front of her, the screen had a top-down plan view of the cutting table, a wrinkled leathery body lying dead centre curled up on its side. Figures flickered and swam around it, moving impossibly quickly, lurching in and out of frame.

She'd swapped her mortuary-issue wellies for a pair of red high-tops, and added a pair of glasses to her ensemble. The fast-forward post mortem reflected in their lenses.

She looked up as Callum walked in. 'I've watched it five times now.'

He waited, but nothing else was forthcoming. No babbling. No non sequiturs.

OK...

She unfolded her legs and stood. 'I'll need to see the crime scene.'

'I can probably swing that.'

McAdams marched into the room, followed by Franklin. Still no sign of Mother.

A big smile and McAdams stuck his hand out for shaking. 'Detective Sergeant McAdams, you must be Dr McDonald.'

She looked at the offered hand as if he'd grown a vast pale hairless spider at the end of his arm.

The awkward silence stretched.

He lowered his hand. Stuck it in his pocket instead. 'This is DC Franklin.'

'Before we start, here's how this works,' McDonald walked to the whiteboard and wrote 'VICTIMOLOGY' on it in red marker, 'I give you a series of educated guesses, based on the information you give me. If I don't know something I'll mark it as an assumption and you have to take anything based on that with a whole carton of salt. Agreed?'

'You're going to profile our serial killer?'

'OFFENDER BEHAVIOURAL INDICATORS' went on the board next.

'No, I'm going to give you educated guesses, remember?'

'CRIME SCENE INDICATORS'

McAdams leaned back against the partition wall. 'Go on then, guess away.'

'PSYCHOLOGICAL GEOGRAPHY / BOUNDARIES'

'From what we know right now, our suspect is *probably* a goal-orientated killer. It's possible preserving the victims turns them into some kind of fertility totem, but I don't think he kills them for sexual release. He kills them so he can mummify their bodies. That's his goal – it means something to him. *What* is the bigger question.'

'I'll settle for *who*.'

'Statistically it's going to be a white male, mid-twenties. He'll have access to a facility for smoking meat, and or fish, and experience in using it. You don't jump right into this kind of thing without practice.'

McAdams snapped his fingers at Callum. 'I want a list of every smokehouse in a twenty ... make it fifty-mile radius.'

Dick.

Callum made a note anyway. 'What about Glen Carmichael, Brett

Millar, and Ben Harrington? Any chance the three of them are killing as a team?'

Dr McDonald looked back at the TV, with its flickering ghosts. 'There's a chance, but it's not very likely. Two of them, maybe – one dominant, one submissive – but three would be *very* unusual. It's hard enough getting three men to agree on what pizza toppings to order, never mind how to select, kill, and preserve their victims.'

Fair enough.

She leaned in closer to the screen. 'Our offender's an artisan and an artist. This kind of work takes time, care, and skill. He's probably unattached, lives alone where no one can interfere with his work. He'll drive a big car, or a van – he needs to be able to transport the bodies.'

Franklin shook her head. 'We found one of them in the boot of a wee Kia Picanto – small four-door hatchback. You don't need that much space.'

'Not when they're mummified, but while they're still alive? You need more room.'

And Franklin explodes: in three, two, one… But she didn't. She just nodded.

'His post-murder activities are highly ritualised too. Removing the organs and preserving them separately, then stitching them back into the body cavity.' She wrapped the fingers of one hand into her hair, fiddling with the curls as her eyes narrowed and her voice dropped off to a murmur. 'You don't just mummify people for fun, do you, no you don't, you do it because you want them to live on in the afterlife, you deify them…' She let go of her hair and straightened. 'I wouldn't be surprised if there was some sort of religious upbringing.' She pointed at the whiteboard, where 'PSYCHOLOGICAL GEOGRAPHY / BOUNDARIES' was written. 'I need to know where the victims came from before we can work out where he's likely to live.'

Callum nodded. 'We're working on it.'

'Also,' McAdams took a marker from the shelf beneath the board and uncapped it, 'we need to decide what we're calling our boy. Can't have a serial killer novel with an unnamed antagonist.' He printed 'IMHOTEP' right in the middle. 'Before the tabloid newspapers come up with something more *lurid*.'

'Ah…' Dr McDonald bit her top lip. 'It's a nice thought, I mean I know we've got to call him something, but "Imhotep" doesn't actually work, does it, because Imhotep was Egyptian and Egyptian mummies are always preserved lying flat, and the curled body posture our suspect uses to pose his victims is more reminiscent of ancient Peruvian burial techniques, which results from a completely different cultural and religious background.' She shrugged. '"Paddington" would probably be more accurate, you know, strictly speaking, because of the Peru connection, I think we should definitely call him Paddington, it just makes a lot more sense.'

'And one final thing.' McAdams smiled. 'Aren't you going to say it?'

Dr McDonald wrote 'PADDINGTON' on the board. 'Aren't I going to say what?'

'It's a cliché of the genre, but the profiler always says it at the end of the briefing.'

A frown. 'Nope, you've lost me.'

'He *will* kill again!'

'Of course he will.' McDonald stuck the lid back on the marker pen. 'He's a serial killer, it's what he does.'

— Imhotep —

"Well, well, well," the God Wolf growled, "if I've not just caught the tastiest little morsel in the whole dark world."

"You can't eat me!" gasped Imelda. "I'm made of bones and stones and glass and groans, and if you eat me you'll get a *terrible* tummy ache and die!"

The God Wolf smiled at her. "I'll take my chances," he said. And swallowed Imelda whole.

R.M. Travis
Imelda's Miraculous Dustbin (1999)

Stay away from ma b*tches, they ain't down with no snitches,
I got me my riches, givin' punks like you stitches!

Donny '$ick Dawg' McRoberts
'Livin' Free Or Dyin' Tryin''
© Bob's Speed Trap Records (2014)

17

The God-In-Waiting sways gently in the smoke, head down, hands making delicate figure-eight patterns as it swings. No movement of its own, just that final rattling breath, then peace and stillness. Grace and purity.

It's time.

The racks beneath the God-In-Waiting are full of fish, hanging from their poles like the divinity above. He removes the poles, stacking them on the rack next door to cool. It'll be a good batch of smokies. They always are when a new god comes into being. Must be the air.

Or maybe it's the cleansed body, hanging above them as they smoke? Maybe it's the juices that drip like tears from the body as it takes on its final form? Whatever it is, the result is *excellent* fish.

Next is the scraper – just a plank of wood fixed on the end of a broomstick – he uses it to push the smouldering embers away, heaping them up against the far wall. Then stands beneath the God-In-Waiting.

It's beautiful...

Once Upon A Time

The man hanging on the wall has got nothing on but a kind of nappy, wrapped around his waist. His skin is a dark, rich wood, polished so much it glows against the cross. Someone's made him a hat of barbed wire, which must hurt something horrible.

A wobbly voice fills the air, echoing back off the church's stone walls. 'Sanctus, Sanctus, Sanctus, Dominus Deus Sabaoth...'

It's a pretty sound – even if the words are just made-up – floating above the pews, wrapping around the big wooden man. Maybe it makes him happier if people sing to him? He looks very sad.

Father's over by the altar, talking to the priest man. Both of them dressed in black, like crows – though the priest man's got on a kind of dress. Both are wearing those little white things around their necks. Dog collars. Both pretending to be something they're not.

'*Pleni sunt caeli et terra gloria tua. Hosanna in excelsis...*'

The man's been stuck to the cross with big metal nails, and there's holes in his side. Maybe that was mice? There's mice in Father's house and they eat holes in everything. Scurrying about in the dark. Leaving their little black presents behind.

'*Benedictus qui venit in nomine Domini. Hosanna in excelsis—*'

'*NO! NO! DAMN IT, OLIVER!*' A man's voice, not pretty and floaty, but hard and grating. '*How many times? It's pronounced, "ex-chel-cease". We're going to stay here and do it again and again until – you – get – it – right!*'

Father looks up at the gallery that runs above the back six rows of pews, where the organ is. Then down at him. 'Justin, thumb out of the mouth, eh champ?' He smiles. 'You're a big boy now.'

Justin's not his *real* name: it's from Father's favourite album, about a little boy who turns into a rabbit and has to save the world from the king of dead things. And Justin's as good a name as any.

He takes his thumb out of his mouth and wipes it dry on his T-shirt. 'Sorry, Father.'

'That's my boy.' Then Father shakes hands with the priest man and wanders down the apse. Ruffles Justin's hair. 'Come on, slugger, time to go home.' He turns and waves at the priest man as they leave the church.

'*Sanctus, Sanctus, Sanctus, Dominus Deus Sabaoth...*'

Down the steps in the warm sunshine, one hand on Justin's shoulder. Steering him to the car with its little Scottish flag fluttering on the end of the aerial. 'In you get.'

Justin does what he's told.

Gravel scrunches and crunches under the wheels as they leave the church grounds.

'Did you hear the singing, Father? Wasn't that—'

The slap is as hard as it is quick, snapping his head to the side, the sound like a gunshot going off.

'Don't you dare embarrass me like that again. Sucking on your thumb like a *baby*. That what you are? A baby?'

He blinks the tears back. Bites his lip. Lets the burning needles sink into his cheek. Don't cry. Feed off the heat. Don't cry. It'll only make it worse.

'You want to wear nappies and sit in your own filth again? IS THAT WHAT YOU WANT?' Little flecks of spit settle against the dashboard. 'ANSWER ME, DAMN YOU!'

Justin takes a deep breath.

Don't cry.

Feel it burn. Own it.

He stares down at his hands, curled in his lap. 'No, Father. Sorry, Father.'

'Good boy.' And just like that the storm passes, the clouds' shadows slip away and Father smiles at him again. 'Come on, why don't we go get some ice cream? We can bring some back for Mummy, she'll like that, won't she?'

Justin nods, even though it's not true. New Mummy doesn't like anything. She just cries all the time.

'And, slugger?' Father ruffles his hair again, the fingers warm and hard where they dig into his scalp. 'You stay away from church music, it's nothing but lies. See these?' He lets go of Justin and unhooks the white band from around his throat. Shakes it like a dead mouse. 'They call them a "dog collar" for a reason. They choke you. There's a chain that clips onto them, so you can go walkies. Because it's all lies: the churches, the hymns, the bible, the whole God-bothering holier-than-thou, deviant filth-mongering lot of them. Lies and liars.'

Justin doesn't move.

This can go one of two ways, and one of them ends with screaming and bruises and getting locked in the Naughty Cupboard – peeing blood for a week.

Father clicks on the car stereo, and the album picks up where it left off. A hissing of drums, then the man's voice comes over the top, quiet as treacle. '*You have to hide right here, right now, you have to stay so still, / Cos Justin, little rabbit boy, the night-time means you ill, / There's monsters here, there's monsters there, and they're prowling through the gloom, / Stay still and oh so quiet, or these woods will be your tomb...*'

Father squeezes his shoulder. 'Come on, champ, let's go get that ice cream.'

But not this time.

He stares up at the God-In-Waiting. It's not as beautiful as the wooden man on the cross, not yet, but it will be. It'll be better. So much better than a dead thing carved from a dead tree, hanging in a dead building.

It'll be a god...

He unhooks the rope from its cleat on the wall and takes the strain. Lowers the body, hand over hand, until it rests on the freshly cleared floor. Picks it up off the hot stone slabs – it isn't hard, the cleansed remains weigh almost nothing. The weight of sin is gone, purged, purified.

The God-In-Waiting is pale and soft, but that will change.

Everything will.

18

Callum shuffled the printouts together, then slipped them in a plastic folder. 'Thanks.'

Lucy shrugged. 'No probs.' A grin widened her face. 'Tell you the truth, I thought this was going to be a waste of time, but no way. My very first serial killer!'

He tucked the folder under his arm. 'Don't worry, there'll be plenty more where that came from.'

Franklin was in the hallway, outside the lab, standing with her back to the world – forehead resting against the wall, phone clamped to her ear. 'No. ... Because I don't. ... How am I supposed to know, Mark? I'm not a mind reader. ... No. ... I didn't... Urgh. Just forget it. Doesn't matter.' A sigh. 'OK, OK. I'll call you when I find out.' She hung up and stayed where she was.

Callum cleared his throat. 'You ready?'

She stiffened. Put her phone away. Turned. 'Do you eavesdrop on all your colleagues?'

He shook his head and marched off down the corridor. 'Don't know why I bother.'

Franklin didn't catch up to him till the car park, weaving her way between the puddles in the rain. She came to a halt in front of Mother's manky Fiat Panda. 'Is her face normally that colour?'

Mother was on the phone, eyes scrunched up, cheeks all flushed. Her mouth kept starting in on sentences, but never seemed to get more than a word or two into them before shutting again. Her other hand dug its fingers into her forehead, as if she was trying to force them through the skin into the bone beneath.

'Yeah...' Callum sidled towards the pool car they'd arrived in.

'Whatever that is, there's going to be repercussions and fallout. Don't know about you, but I want to be long gone before then.'

Franklin pushed past him to the pool car's driver's door. 'Keys.'

'Sorry?'

'Keys. Give me the keys, I'm driving.'

He raised an eyebrow. '*You* want to drive?'

'Just give me the damned keys.'

'So I'm going to sit in the passenger seat, and you're going to drive *me* around? Like I outrank you?'

'I'm not spending the rest of the day being dragged all over Oldcastle so you can run "little errands" like yesterday. Now: keys.'

Fair enough. He dug them out of his pocket and tossed them across to her. Walked around to the other side and climbed in out of the rain as she slipped behind the wheel.

Callum settled back in his seat. Stretched out a little. 'I could get used to this.'

Franklin took them through the rolling sea of ruptured tarmac and out into the industrial estate again. Past the boarded-up units, and onto the main road, heading back along the dual carriageway. The City Stadium loomed above the houses on the left, a lopsided bird's nest of steel, concrete, and glass, lording it over the 1950s-style rows of semi-detached two-up-two-downs.

It was nice not having to do all the driving for a change. Just sit back and watch the scenery slip by. Even if it *was* all grey and rain-streaked.

He dug his leprechaun-sized Mars Bar out of his pocket and took a tiny bite. Sweet, sticky, and chocolatey. 'This your first serial killer?'

'Of course it is.'

'Number four for me.'

Franklin looked at him across the car, one eyebrow raised. 'Four serial killers? Yeah, right.' She took them around the roundabout, the granite blade of Castle Hill just visible between the tall concrete buildings ahead. 'I'm not an idiot, constable. There's absolutely *no way* you've already worked three serial killer investigations.'

A big flat-fronted building went by on the left, little windows in a big granite façade.

'That's Woodrow Hospital. Four years ago, we got complaints of missing dogs in the area. Didn't really pay all that much attention.' He scooted down in his seat, following the hospital in the wing mirror as it faded into the distance. 'Then someone's granny disappeared.

Thought it was dementia to begin with, happens a lot with older people: they get confused and they wander off. Then another one went missing. And another. Took us six little old ladies to realise something was wrong.'

The looming green mass of Camburn Woods poked out above the rooftops, getting bigger.

Callum finished off his micro Mars Bar. 'Who's Mark?'

Franklin's jaw tightened. 'Mark is none of your business.'

'Turns out Pawel Sabachevich's parents moved over here from a little village outside Krakow when he was six years old. They brought his maternal grandmother with them. She wasn't very nice to Pawel. And twenty-three years later he abducted, raped, and strangled eight old ladies, dismembered their remains and fed them into the incinerator at Woodrow Hospital. He worked there as an assistant radiologist.' Callum crumpled up his chocolate wrapper and stuck it in his pocket. 'Nice guy. Well, if you overlook the whole murderous raping scumbag bit.'

The diggers were still at it on the huge flanks of Camburn Round-about – making mountains of mud, while a crane erected a lopsided metal trellis and high-viz figures sank into the mire. 'Then there was Ian Zouroudi.' Another shudder followed in the footsteps of the first. 'Gah... The whole team needed therapy after *that* one.'

'Just because I'm new and a woman, it doesn't make me an idiot.'

'Never said it did.' Camburn Woods reared up and swallowed the car, the thick branches reaching out over the dual carriageway on either side, leaves dark and dripping. 'From what I heard, it's all the mercury in the ground around here. Too big a dose and it screws with brain development.'

'Mercury.'

'We made most of Britain's mustard gas, right here in Oldcastle, for the First World War. Apparently it took a lot of mercury. And now we're the serial-killer capital of Europe. Pretty high on the list for birth defects too.' He sniffed. 'That was a fun day at antenatal class.'

Ruined buildings lurked in the woods to either side of the road, slowly dissolving into the bushes and ivy.

She frowned across the car at him. '*Three* serial killers?'

The world opened up in a blast of grey as the road emerged from the depths of Camburn Woods.

'Straight through the next roundabout and it's the third road on the right.' Two parallel lines of shops and flats followed them along the road, at least a quarter of them boarded up. Bookies and charity shops rubbing shoulders with places to sell your gold or pawn your kids' toys.

Callum pointed through the windscreen. 'That's us at the traffic lights.'

Franklin pulled into the turning lane and they sat there with the indicators clicking, waiting for the filter. 'So who was number three?'

'The Birthday Boy. You must've heard about that one: it was in all the papers. Sicko snatches girls just before they turn thirteen, takes photos as he tortures them to death, then turns the pics into homemade cards and sends them to the girls' parents every year on their birthday.'

She glanced across the car. 'And it's all because of the mercury?'

'Meh, what do I know?'

The lights changed and they pulled across the dual carriageway and into a curving street with a collection of cafés, hardware shops, a Sue Ryder and a British Heart Foundation, a newsagent, and finally the reason they'd come.

Franklin nodded. 'There we go.'

The McKibben Dental Practice had a frosted shop window, presumably so you couldn't see their victims writhing in agony, with posters either side of the main door depicting unfeasibly attractive people grinning away with unfeasibly white teeth. Franklin grabbed the nearest parking space, three doors down. 'I can't believe you've worked three serial killers.'

He clambered out into the rain. 'Go have a rummage in the archives at DHQ, there's stuff in there that'll make your hair curl...' He bit his lip. 'I didn't mean that to be—'

'I know what you meant.' She locked the car. Followed him down the pavement to the dentist's. 'And yes, it *is* naturally this curly.'

He shrugged. 'I quite like it.'

'Are you remembering what happened to Blakey the Octopus?' Franklin pushed through the door and into a warm reception room with seats around the walls of a little waiting annex off to one side. The faint aniseedy tang of oral disinfectant tainted the air. A rack of magazines was mounted on the wall – all the issues considerably newer and classier than the ones Professional Standards had – surrounded by more posters of halogen-white teeth.

'For your information, Detective Constable Franklin, I have a partner I love and she's pregnant with my child. So don't flatter yourself. I've got no intention of groping your backside or anything else.'

134

An unfeasibly blonde receptionist showed them her unfeasibly perfect teeth in a broad smile. Her voice was unfeasibly cheery too, but nearly as shrill as a dentist's drill. 'Welcome to the McKibben Dental Practice, how can I help you today?'

Callum flashed his warrant card. 'I phoned earlier. We need to speak to someone about Glen Carmichael's dental records.'

'Boss? We've got a match.' Callum switched his phone to the other hand and tucked the folder under his arm again. Rain dripped off the concrete portico that covered the shopping centre's rear doors, darkening the steps down to the car park. 'Took us three lots of dentists to get there, but according to the Leighton Road Dental Association in Blackwall Hill, our body in the bath is Ben Harrington. He's the one in the photo with the auld mannie haircut, glasses, and walrus moustache.'

Silence from the other end of the phone.

'Boss?'

The shopping centre car park was nearly empty, just a handful of old cars and a Shopper-Hopper bus picking up a load of OAPs with their wheelie trollies and battered umbrellas. Franklin was down there too, marching about in the rain, one hand making violent stabby motions in the air as she dumped a shedload of angry into her mobile.

Mother's voice sounded far away, muffled, as if she was talking to someone else. '*You can shift Harrington from the suspect column to the victim one. No, he's definitely dead.*' Then she was back. '*He was a Blackwall Hill boy, and seeing as you're in the neighbourhood…?*'

Oh joy. 'Death message?'

'*Good lad.*'

'Dr McDonald wants access to the crime scene.'

'*Meh. The Smurf Patrol have finished with it, so why not? Make sure she comes up with something useful though.*'

'Do my best.' He hung up.

The Shopper-Hopper gave its diesel roar and pulled into the traffic.

Franklin did another lap, jabbing away like she was trying to stab and bludgeon someone all at the same time.

With any luck she'd get it out of her system and there'd be none left to batter him with.

But just in case…

Callum nipped back into the centre and grabbed a couple of fancy pieces and two takeaway teas from the Costa by the lifts. Hunched his shoulders and hurried through the doors, into the rain.

By the time he reached the pool car, she was behind the wheel again, dripping and glowering.

So much for getting it out of her system.

He slipped into the passenger seat and held out his peace offering. 'Here. Tea, milk no sugar, and... Tada!' One paper bag. 'Got a billionaire's shortbread and a rocky-road brownie. You choose.'

The frown didn't shift. 'What's billionaire's shortbread?'

'Like a millionaire's, but there's bits of broken-up Crunchie in there too.'

She went for the shortbread, chewing with her shoulders dipped as the rain thumped down on the car roof. 'Not that it's any of your business, but Mark is my partner.'

Poor sod. Living with Franklin must be like trying to cross a minefield on a pogo stick every day. Blindfold. While sadists threw burning squirrels at you.

Mark was probably up for a medal. Or beatification.

Callum had a bite of brownie, sickeningly sweet, and washed it down with hot tea.

Franklin cracked a chunk off her shortbread. 'His work's hosting a dinner dance for charity Friday night, and apparently *I'm* being unreasonable because I can't tell him if I'll be there or not. Doesn't matter that I'm working a mass murder, no, the *important* thing is making him look good in front of his bosses.'

'Actually, a mass murder is when you kill four or more people in the same location without much of a gap between...' He cleared his throat. 'Sorry.'

'You're all the bloody same, aren't you?'

'Sadly.' A slurp of tea. 'What's he do, this Mark of yours?'

'Investment banking.'

And all sympathy for the guy died right there.

She finished her shortbread. 'It's not my fault I got transferred to Oldcastle, is it? I mean, it's not like I can commute here from Edinburgh. I'd have to get the five-thirty train every morning and I *still* wouldn't be here in time for a seven o'clock start.'

Callum balanced his tea on the dashboard and pulled out his notebook. Flicked through it. 'Mother wants us to drop in on Ben Harrington's parents and give them the bad news. Here we go: sixteen Brookmyre Crescent, Blackwall Hill. About five minutes away.'

'And I am *not* giving up my career, just to play house in a flat in

Portobello.' She bared her teeth, nearly as white as the dental receptionist's only with bits of chocolate stuck between them.

'I can drive, if you like?'

'Why do men have to be such selfish scumbags?'

A young mother slouched past the car, face slumped in permanent disappointment, pushing a buggy with a screaming toddler in it. Rain trickled from the straggly ends of her lank hair.

Callum had another bite of brownie. Kept his mouth shut.

Franklin sighed. Threw back the last of her tea. Then started the car. 'All I ever wanted to be was a police officer. I'm *not* resigning. Wouldn't give Superintendent Neil Sodding Sexual-Harassment Lambert the satisfaction.'

OK, at least this was safer ground than interfering in her relationship. 'So go to Professional Standards, make a formal complaint.'

'I did. Why do you think they transferred me?' She took them out of the car park. 'Which way?'

'Left, then right onto McAskill Road.'

'And yes, I shouldn't have hit him. I know.' The scowl deepened. 'Dirty, slimy, sleazy little prick got his complaint in first. Who are they going to believe, a black woman PC, or a white middle-aged male superintendent? Because you can bet it's not the woman.'

A lot of the shops around the centre had 'To Let' signs in the window, one advertising a closing down sale. One had its frontage all boarded up and a notice thanking customers for sodding off to Amazon instead of buying their books in a real bookshop.

'That's McAskill Road: take a right.'

She did. 'It's *never* the woman.'

The road dipped below a railway bridge, the inside scrawled with graffiti tags. A couple of older men huddled in a recess between the supports, sharing a cigarette and a litre bottle of supermarket blended whisky.

North of the line, Blackwall Hill broke out in coiled housing developments, little cul-de-sacs, and sweeping curved streets.

'Take Caldwell.' Callum pointed at the junction up ahead, past the pedestrian crossing. 'You want to deliver the death message?'

'Why, because I'm a *woman*?'

'On second thoughts, maybe a bit of compassion is in order. I'll do it. You can make the tea.' He held up a hand. 'And before you start, it's got nothing to do with "being a woman". You either deliver the death message and sit with them while they grieve, or you make the tea. One or the other. Turn right here.'

That took them onto a wide road with bungalows on either side, that bowed away to the left following the contours of the hill.

Franklin pursed her lips. 'Fine. You make the tea.'

'You sure?'

'Positive.'

It was a weird world when someone thought making four cups of tea was worse than telling a parent that their only child had been murdered. 'Brookmyre Crescent. That's us right there.'

She slowed for the junction, taking them into a dead-end road that cupped twenty or thirty houses in its coiled embrace. Some semidetached, some standing on their own. Most had been extended up into their attics, a few with converted garages, lots of lock-block driveways, wheelie bins arrayed on the pavements like guardsmen ready for inspection.

'Number sixteen: the one with the dark-blue door and hideous garden ornaments.'

Franklin parked outside it as the rain faded to a misty drizzle.

'Right, the mother's name is Christine, father is Tony. No brothers or sisters.'

She nodded. 'Christine. Tony.' Then undid her seatbelt. 'Let's do this.'

Callum followed her out into the damp afternoon gloom.

Number 16 was on the downhill side: a detached bungalow conversion with a room above the garage and dormer windows on the upper floor. Ivy growing up the wall around the door. A wooden wishing well sat in the middle of a gravel lawn, surrounded by gnomes in various rustic poses, and angry tufts of pampas grass.

Classy.

The gap between the house and next door's leylandii hedge was like a little picture postcard, looking down Blackwall Hill, across the river, and up to Castle Hill on the other side. A shaft of sunlight had made it through the heavy lid of slate-coloured cloud, turning the castle and its granite perch a warm shade of honeyed gold, all rendered in soft-focus by the drizzle.

Probably worth a fortune with a view like that.

Franklin leaned on the bell. 'Bet they're not even in.'

'Look, if you'd rather do the teas than deliver the death message, that's OK.'

'No, you idiot. There's no car in the driveway. Family living some-where like this? They've got more than one car.'

'Maybe it's in the garage?'

She tried the bell again. 'You've never had a garage, have you? It's not for keeping your car in, it's for storing all the crap you moved out of the last house and haven't taken out of the boxes six years later.'

No answer from inside.

'You might be right.' He checked his watch – 15:40. 'Better give it another ten minutes, though. Just to be safe.'

Franklin hunched her shoulders and turned her back on the drizzle. 'I'm not standing here, in the rain, for ten minutes.'

'So we wait in the car. At least it'll be—' His phone burst into life, belting out its anonymous ringtone. 'Hello?'

'Is that DC MacGregor, I hope so, this is the number he wrote on his business card and I mean he should know what his own mobile number is shouldn't he, mind you I suppose most people don't do they, after all, they don't phone themselves, so why would they remember it?' All done in a single breath.

'Dr McDonald. What can I do for you?' He followed Franklin back down the driveway.

'Psilocybe semilanceata.'

OK…

'What's that when it's at home?'

'Liberty Cap mushrooms, AKA: magic mushrooms, AKA: shrooooooms. We're halfway through Benjamin Harrington's post mortem and his stomach's full of them, well, not full-full, but there's quite a lot of them and they've not dissolved all that much because he must've died not long after taking them, which isn't surprising because it's still a lot of mushrooms to take in one go, but there's heaps of herbs and things in there as well, only they're going to take a lot longer to identify than the mushrooms, because magic mushrooms always look like magic mushrooms, don't they?'

Callum settled into the passenger seat. Clunked the door shut. 'Did he eat enough to kill him?'

'I don't think you can overdose on magic mushrooms, they've got an emetic effect, so you're more likely to vomit them up if you take too many, well, I suppose you could choke on your own sick, but that's not actually overdosing, is it? Anyway, they're running toxicology on the tissue samples from the two mummies to see if they've got any psilocybin in them, did you know they've got their own mass spectrometer here, it's amazing, I've never seen a mortuary with these kinds of facilities before, but Dr Jenkins says they were spending so much money sending samples away for testing that it made a lot more sense getting—'

'Doctor!' A bit rude, but at least it stopped her. 'There's a bong in the flat where the body was found – the shrooms might be Ben's. He takes too many, dies, Glen and Brett are too stoned to help so they panic and board him up in the bathroom then do a runner.'

Franklin frowned across the car at him, mouthing the word, 'What?'

'That's why they're rushing through the tox screen on the mummies, if there's psilocybin in the tissue samples, then we've got a link, and that's exciting, but I'd still like to see the flat if I can, can I?'

'Yeah. It's fine, SOCOs have finished with it anyway.'

'OK, I'll see you there, when's good, is now good?'

'Erm... No. We've got to tell Ben Harrington's parents that he's dead. And you're in the middle of a post mortem, remember?'

Franklin's phone launched into what sounded like Gilbert and Sullivan's ode about policemen being a poor put-upon bunch of sods. 'Yes? ... What, *now?*'

'Oh... Right, well, if you can give me a call when you've done that, that'll be great and we can get on with the geographical side of things and I suppose it won't hurt to spend a little time dealing with the severed feet case, and did I tell you we post mortemed the other mummy?'

'Is that the one from the tip, or the car?'

'The tip, and I think I know why it was thrown away.'

Franklin started the car again. 'Yeah, we'll be there soon as we can.'

Silence from the phone.

'Dr McDonald?'

'Sorry, dropped my chocolate biscuit. The mummy from the car was eviscerated and the internal organs preserved separately then stitched back inside. The body in the tip wasn't so lucky. He tried to preserve it whole, and mummification only works if you can dry out the remains faster than the microbes inside can decompose it.'

The gears made complaining grinding noises as Franklin performed a hurried three-point turn. She stuffed her mobile into a pocket. 'Put your seatbelt on.'

He covered the mouthpiece. 'Where are we going?'

'Someone's just broken into Brett Millar's house.'

'When was this?'

'Now. Right now. Neighbour just called it in.'

'—abdominal cavity is full of slippery moist organs and they go off incredibly quickly if you don't preserve them, that's why undertakers inject everything with preserving fluid when you die, because otherwise you'd

140

probably burst during the eulogies, and that wouldn't be very nice for the mourners, would it?'

'Any idea who broke in? Did the neighbour recognise them?'

'How should I know?'

'So my educated guess is that Paddington is one hundred percent committed to the end result. He's venerating these bodies by mummifying them, but they have to be perfect. This one wasn't, so he disposed of it and started again. That also means he's learning.'

Franklin put her foot down, sending pantile boxes whizzing past the car windows. 'Where am I going, and how do we put on the blues-and-twos in this thing?'

Callum pulled out his notebook and flipped it open, bracing his knees against the door and the dashboard. 'Walderswell Court. Right at the end, then left.' He reached out and poked a switch, setting the sirens wailing and the lights flashing.

'DC MacGregor?'

'Still here, Doc.'

'Please don't call me "Doc" it always makes me feel like I'm meant to be one of the seven dwarfs and I know I'm not the tallest person in the world, but I like to think I'm a bit bigger than that, and if you think about it—'

'OK, OK, sorry. Not Doc. You're definitely not one of the seven dwarfs.' After all, Snow White's roll call didn't go: Sleepy, Grumpy, Dopey, Doc, Sneezy, Happy, Bashful, and Bug-Eyed Crazy Weirdo Person.

'You can call me Alice, if you like, or do you prefer to keep things on a formal footing, sometimes that's better in a work evironment, isn't it, or does it just make me seem all distant and aloof, which would be bad, because I think we should operate as a team and—'

'No, that would be great. Alice it is.' He grabbed the handle above the door as Franklin threw them around the corner past another long sweeping row of houses. 'Go right at the end and it's second on the left.' Back to the phone. 'Was there anything else, Alice? Only we're wheeching across town trying to get to a break-in before the thieving scumbag legs it.'

'Oh, right. Sorry. That explains the sirens and things in the background, doesn't it? I'll let you go.' She hung up.

'Yup. Three hundred and sixty degrees of weird.' He put his phone away as the pool car screeched around the corner and into an older, less gentrified bit of Blackwall Hill. No more lock-block driveways and formation gnomes. No more attic conversions. Just street after street of identical semidetached bungalows, bristling with satellite dishes.

Franklin waved a hand across the car. 'Kill the siren!'

He clicked the button and she hit the brakes, just before the corner, swinging around onto Walderswell Court at a sensible thirty miles per hour. The police vehicular equivalent of whistling a casual tune to kid on you're not up to something.

The houses here were just a bit smaller than the ones on the road outside, jammed in just a bit tighter too. Number 32 was down the far end, next to a building plot. From the signage fixed to the site fencing, someone was chucking up two blocks of 'LUXURY STARTER FLATS!!!' where a pair of wee bungalows used to be.

Yeah, good luck selling those, stuck on the border between Blackwall Hill and Kingsmeath. You could see the dual carriageway from here... Wonder if that was where Brett and his mates got the idea to do up their flat on Customs Street?

Franklin coasted the last twenty feet, engine idling. 'How can we be first on the scene?'

'You drive like a maniac, what do you expect?' Callum popped open the glove compartment and took out the box of nitrile gloves, pulling two from the slot in the top like rubbery blue tissues. Tossed the box across to Franklin. 'Well, come on then.'

He climbed out into the drizzle and snapped his gloves on. Pulled out his pepper spray.

Across the road, a little old man peered out from between a pair of net curtains. Walking stick in one hand, phone in the other. That would be their informant.

Callum half crouched, half ran across the pavement and up the driveway to Brett Millar's house. No sign of forced entry on the front door. The handle was cold in his fingers ... and it wouldn't budge. Locked.

Franklin flattened herself on the other side of the door, extendable baton extended. 'Well?'

'Doesn't look like he got in the front way.'

She nodded at the other side of the road. 'Then how did Nosey Norman see it to call it in?'

Good point.

Callum pointed. 'Round the side.'

A six-foot wooden fence marked the boundary between number 32 and the building site, leaving just enough space for a narrow gravel path and a full-height gate. It was hanging off its hinges.

On the other side, a bush was flattened, as if someone had fallen into it. A smear of blood on the harling, probably left by sticking their hand out to break their fall. Oh yeah, this one was a master criminal. With any luck they'd be in the kitchen making themselves a bacon buttie.

Round the back.

The kitchen door was wide open, the glass in the bottom section smashed into regular safety-sized cubes.

Franklin held up a fist, then stuck one finger up and swept it in the direction of the back door. Clenched her fist again.

Callum stared at her. 'Are you off your head? This isn't the A-Team.'

A sigh, then she slipped in through the broken door, bent almost double.

God help us.

He followed her inside.

The kitchen was ground zero for a whirlwind of tins and smashed mugs, jagged shards of plate covering the lino floor, blood-spatters of tomato ketchup on the tiles above the cooker. A shattered jar of mayonnaise lying spent against the dented fridge.

Callum crunched through a drift of Special K. 'Wow. Someone's behind on their housework.'

Franklin did the ridiculous SWAT team signs again, then crouched her way out into the hall.

He wandered after her.

The hallway was a mess of thrown coats and hurled boots, the plasterboard dented where they'd hit the walls. Franklin did a slow three-sixty, then froze and pointed down the hall. Four doors: three shut, one wide open – bangs and crashes thumping out of it. Then a computer monitor bounced off the hall carpet, the display a spider's web of fractured glass.

She crept down the hall, baton raised and ready.

It would be a druggie, off his proverbials on coke, or crack, or jellies, or smack. Sees the house is empty and bingo – tries his hand at a bit of DIY *Bargain Hunt*...

Or maybe it was someone who knew Brett, Ben, and Glen? Someone who knew they might have a stash lying about. Or, going by the destruction, someone they owed money to.

Callum flicked the safety cap off his pepper spray. 'Shall we dance?'

Franklin raised an eyebrow. Looked at him for a moment, then smiled a nasty smile. 'Foxtrot or tango?'

Good. He smiled back. 'Let's see where the music takes us.'

She barged in through the open door. 'POLICE! ON YOUR KNEES, NOW!'

He thumped through less than a breath behind her, into the heart of a disaster. The wardrobe doors were ripped off their hinges, clothes everywhere; a computer desk smashed almost beyond recognition; single bed overturned, the slats cracked and splintered like broken ribs; a disembowelled games console, spilling its electronic innards across the floor; posters torn from the wall.

And there, in the middle of the hurricane, was a man – long greasy hair dangling down his back, sunken eyes, cheekbones you could carve granite with, wrists like two bones wrapped in pink cling film. Skin so pale every vein popped out like a blue-green worm. A solid ring of love bites around his neck. Filthy hoodie, filthy tracksuit bottoms, bare, filthy feet speckled with blood.

Full-on junky chic.

He had both hands above his head – probably not helping with the rotting-cabbage stink of sweat and that stale spicy base-note of old marijuana – holding a desktop computer covered in stickers, cables and a keyboard dangling from the ports in the back.

Captain Filthy just stood there, staring at them.

Franklin whipped the baton back into first-strike position. 'PUT THE COMPUTER DOWN AND GET ON YOUR KNEES!'

He bared his brown-grey teeth.

'I'M NOT TELLING YOU AGAIN: KNEES, NOW!'

'AAAAAAAAAAAAAAAAAAAAAAAAAAAAAAA!' The computer went flying, hurled full force at Franklin's head.

She ducked left, but it still caught her on the shoulder, spinning her one way while it went the other, cables flapping.

Captain Filthy lunged for Callum, arms out, hands like claws.

So he got a face full of pepper spray.

Oh crap…

Might as well have sprayed him with lavender floor polish, because Captain Filthy just kept on coming.

'AAAAAAAAAAAAAAAAAAAAAAAAAAA!'

Sodding hell.

A claw whipped past Callum's face, close enough for every dirt-caked fingernail to stand out in perfect focus. And then Captain Filthy was on top of him, snarling, little flecks of stinking saliva spraying against his face.

'Get off me!' He grabbed the guy's ear and twisted: nothing.

A dirty hand raked down Callum's cheek.

The stench of pepper spray was like a mask, choking off the air, blurring his vision as the tears started.

Captain Filthy wrapped his manky fingers around Callum's tie and pulled, trying to throttle him. Must have got a bit of a surprise when the whole thing just pinged free of its clips and came off in his hand, because he reared back, staring at it. Maybe he was distracted by all the pretty colours?

So Callum took a leaf out of Dugdale's book and grabbed Captain Filthy's crotch, digging his fingers into the tracksuit bottoms and crushing the contents. Twisting them.

Still nothing.

Then Captain Filthy threw the tie away and lunged.

Oh dear Jesus, this was it, he was going to die.

Those brown-grey teeth flashed in front of his face, dirty fingers digging into his cheeks.

Callum heaved upward, and the guy's head lurched past his, bashing into the bedroom floor, enveloping his face with that stinking greasy hair. Then knives and bees exploded through Callum's left ear, jerking him to the side, and warmth trickled down and around the back of his head.

'AAAAAAAAARGH! GET OFF ME!'

And just like that, the weight was gone.

'Sodding … *fuck*!' He sat up, one hand clasping his left ear – the fingers slippery and sticky all at the same time.

Captain Filthy was on his tiptoes, hauled back off balance by Franklin's baton as she worked it in around his arm – pulling him into a hammer lock. Blood made a thin red line down one side of her face. 'CALM DOWN!'

Worth a try, but it didn't work.

His mouth opened in a roar and he jackknifed forward, sending Franklin tumbling over his back and crashing into the overturned bed. Then he was off, one foot catching Callum on the way past and thumping him back against the carpet again.

Sodding hell…

He coughed, rolled over. Struggled to his knees. His left hand: bright red and dripping. 'Franklin!'

A little chunk of bloody gristle – about the size of a Wotsit – lay on the bedroom floor in front of him. Complete with the little dimple where an earring used to go.

'Franklin!'

A rattling clatter and she tumbled off the ruined bedframe. 'Bastard…'

His poor ear.

Callum snatched the bit up, clenching it in his fist. Lurched to his feet as Franklin did the same. Bared his teeth. 'He is *not* getting away!'

19

Out the back door.

The dirty little scumbag was halfway over the fence, leaving bloody footprints as he scrambled up and over the wooden panelling.

Callum tucked the chunk of his ear in his pocket and charged after Captain Filthy. Leapt up. Swung his legs over and dropped down the other side.

It wasn't another garden, it was a path, running straight downhill. Just the thing for little kids to break their necks skateboarding/cycling/rollerblading/sledging down. And Captain Filthy was well on his way, the dirty soles of his feet flapping as he ran.

Franklin cleared the fence and landed on the path, just ahead of Callum. 'Why didn't you pepper-spray him?'

'I did!'

Downhill.

It didn't take much to get going, arms and legs pumping faster and faster as gravity took hold. How the hell did they get planning permission to put a near vertical path down a steep hill? How was this possibly safe?

He leaned back, still getting faster.

Oh sodding hell, this was going to hurt when the inevitable happened and his feet went out from under him and he went tumbling over and over down the tarmac path battering into the garden fences on either side and why did the inside of his head sound like Dr Alice McDonald now?

'Aaargh!' Franklin passed him on the path, leaning back like he was, arms stretched out on either side as if she was about to take flight.

The path levelled out just for long enough to cross another residential street, houses flashing past on either side, and they were on the path again, running.

Captain Filthy was lengthening the gap.

Cannibalistic little sod was probably used to the thing, especially if he grew up here.

Bdumph.

Another residential street. More bungalows. More path. Then a set of bollards.

Oh. No…

No wonder there were bollards: that was Branton Street at the bottom of the path. Not a quiet cul-de-sac full of family homes, but a main road lined with shops.

Which meant all three of them were now hurtling full pelt towards the traffic.

A Transit van whizzed past the gap between buildings at the end of the path.

Callum hauled in a breath. 'DON'T BE AN IDIOT!'

But Captain Filthy wasn't listening. He shot between the bollards, still going strong.

There was a squeal of brakes, then a terrible metallic crunch. A horn wailed, accompanied by a car alarm. More screeching tyres.

Callum shifted his weight forward, leaning into it, gathering up a little extra speed, then snatched at the back of Franklin's jacket and skittered and slid on his feet about a dozen yards.

'Get the hell off me!'

They lurched out between the bollards and onto the pavement, still going fast enough to carry them out onto the road. A tricked-out hatchback slammed on its brakes, slithering sideways, just missing Franklin as they stumbled to a halt six feet out from the pavement.

'Wow…'

A ScotiaBrand Chickens van was parked halfway inside an Audi estate, its grille cracked and steaming in the Audi's crumpled interior. Curls of black were scrawled across the tarmac, ending in a Peugeot facing the wrong way with its rear wheels up on the pavement.

And right in the middle of the road was Captain Filthy. Just standing there. Arms dangling at his sides. Head tilted. Staring at the front end of a number 18 bus, stopped about six inches from his nose.

The bus driver still had both hands wrapped around the wheel, his eyes wide, mouth hanging open, shaking.

Franklin shook off Callum's hand.

The hatchback's driver's door opened and a young man clambered out – all spots and sideburns. His car's spoiler was bigger than he was. 'Hoy, you stupid *bitch*! What the fffff...' He pursed his lips into a perfect little bow as Franklin shoved her warrant card in his face.

Callum pulled out his cuffs, marched over to Captain Filthy, slammed him face-first into the bus and snapped the cuffs on. 'Go on: resist arrest. I *dare* you.'

Callum washed two paracetamol down with a swig of tepid water from a plastic cup. Shuddered. Slumped.

The treatment area wasn't huge – just big enough for an examination table covered in a white paper strip, a plastic chair, and a short section of work surface with cupboards above and below it. A little sink with advice on how to wash your hands, complete with diagrams!

Oh the sodding joy.

A pair of nasty green plastic curtains separated the treatment area from the waiting area. Well, they *called* it a waiting area, it was really just a line of seven plastic chairs, up against the corridor wall, underneath a sign saying, 'Non-Emergency Treatment Zone' and one of a mobile handset with a line drawn through it.

The curtains hadn't been closed properly, so it was all on show. Including Franklin, sitting right in the middle as if laying claim to the whole thing. Exerting her dominance by ignoring the 'Please Turn Off Your Mobile Phone!' sign.

Callum sniffed. Curled his top lip.

Why did disinfectant have to smell so bad? And why did it have to *sting* so much.

The whole left side of his face throbbed, bleeding into the sharp stabbing grating pulses from what was left of his ear.

Bloody Captain Filthy.

Franklin stuck the phone against her chest and stood. Wandered over to his intimate cubicle of doom and stepped inside. The blood on her face had gone, instead a wad of white gauze, about the size of a Post-it Note, was taped to her forehead above her right eye. 'What happened to the doctor?'

'You tell me. Little git slathered me in Dettol and iodine, said something about consulting someone, sodded off with the chunk of my ear, and I've not seen him since.' Callum shifted on the examination table, making it creak. 'How's the head?'

She pointed at the phone. 'I've got DS McAdams on, Custody Sergeant took one look at our boy and refused to take him into the cells till the hospital say he's not going to die from the drugs or choking on his own vomit.'

'We should be so lucky.'

'So they took him up to A&E, where they stripped him to do a full medical, and guess what?'

'He's off his nipples on cocaine.'

'Nope: they found a tattoo, from here,' she tapped her shoulder with her other hand, 'to here.' Then did the same to her wrist. 'Some sort of kids' cartoon characters. Clangers? Whatever they are.'

'You don't know who the Clangers are?' Some people had no appreciation of the classics. 'When Peanut gets born, he's being raised on a diet of Bagpuss, the Clangers, and Danger Mouse...' Callum scrunched his face up. Sod. Of course it was. 'The tattoo – it's Brett Millar, isn't it? He was breaking into his own house.'

'Got it in one. And when they pumped his stomach, out came magic mushrooms. *Lots* of them.'

No wonder the pepper spray didn't work. Could have dumped him in a bath of the stuff and he still wouldn't have felt it.

'There were other things in there too, leaves and flowers, so they've sent it all off for testing.'

'Just like Ben Harrington.' Callum massaged his temple, wincing as it pulled at the scratch marks. 'So much for Glen and Brett ganging up on him.'

'Might still be down to Glen Carmichael. He gets the other two stoned, eggs them on to eat more mushrooms than they can handle, then...' Her forehead creased. 'Still doesn't explain the herbs. Unless they thought they could get high from them too?' Then a couple of blinks and she snatched the phone back to her ear. 'Sorry, Sarge, I was checking on DC MacGregor. ... Yes, Sarge. ... I appreciate that, Sarge, but— ... Sorry.'

A young man in creased blue scrubs hauled the curtain back and joined them in the treatment area. Making it crowded. He cleared his throat and glared at Franklin. 'No mobile phones.'

She stuck two fingers up to him and wandered out into the corridor again. 'Yes, Sarge. ... Thank you, Sarge.'

'Honestly, some people think the rules apply to everybody but them, don't they?' He checked a clipboard. 'Now: Callum MacGregor?'

A nod.

'Right, I'm afraid we've got a bit of a problem with your ear.'

Of course they did.

'You see, our cosmetic surgery department were going to try and reattach the bit that was ... well, bit off. Unfortunate turn of phrase there, sorry. Only a wee girl's come in with third-degree burns. She tipped a boiling kettle all over herself. She's four.'

Callum slumped back against the wall. 'She going to be OK?'

'We hope so, they're taking her into surgery now. But she's going to need a *lot* of skin grafts. So...?'

He covered his face with his hands. 'You can't fix my ear.'

'I'm sorry, Mr MacGregor, but the little girl...'

'Yeah. I know. She needs it more than I do.'

'But I *can* stitch up the wound and give you some antibiotics and painkillers. Have you had a tetanus shot in the last ten years? Oh, and we'll need to take some bloods to test for Hepatitis and HIV.'

And to think, this morning a visit to Professional Standards was the worst thing that could happen.

20

Franklin kept sneaking glances at him across the car.

He frowned back at her. *'What?'*

'Nothing.'

The road in front was a long line of vehicles, slowly crawling along in a stop-start-stop-again line. Traffic going the other way was doing the same. Giving everyone time to enjoy the rain.

'How's the ear?'

'Sore. How's the head?'

She shrugged. 'I dodged the tower unit, it was the keyboard that got me.'

Then they listened to the windscreen wipers for a bit, until Callum reached out and clicked on the radio. 'Should be about time for the news. Unless you mind?'

'No.'

Something bland and unthreatening filled the car, the beat just far enough out of time with the wipers' *week-wonk* to be annoying.

'I can switch it off if you like?'

'Nah, it's OK.'

She was looking at him again.

'Look, there's obviously something, so—'

'Why didn't they send you home?'

His fingers drifted up to the wodge of bandage covering his poor tattered ear. At least it didn't hurt. Not right now anyway. Amazing what a wee injection of local anaesthetic could do. 'Going to be nearly six before we get there at this rate.'

The song on the radio dribbled to an end. *'Wasn't that spectonkular? You, my friend, are listening to* Crrrrrrrrrrrrrrrazy Colin's Rush-Hour

Drive-Time Club, *right here on Castlewave FM, and we're counting down the days to Tartantula! Oh yes indeedy-doody.'*

Franklin curled her top lip. 'Why do they always have to be wankers?'

'Going to be windup o'clock in fifteen minutes, but first here's Gorgeous Gabby with the Naughty News!'

'I think they grow them in special septic tanks.'

'Thanks, Colin. Police Scotland refused to comment on claims that a new serial killer is operating in Oldcastle, following the discovery of three mummified bodies yesterday—'

'Three?'

Callum let his head fall back against the rest. 'Didn't anyone tell you? Oldcastle Division leaks like a chocolate condom. At least it wasn't anyone on the team – we all *know* how many mummies we've got.'

'—appeal for calm. A house fire in Logansferry this morning was probably arson, according to Fire Brigade sources. A mother of four was rushed to hospital suffering from smoke inhalation—'

'Unless whoever leaked said there were three mummies instead of two, so no one would think the informant was on the team?'

'You're very cynical, Detective Constable Franklin.'

'—announcing road closures for this week's Tartantula Music Festival. Diversions will be in place from Friday lunchtime, add in all the planned roadworks south of the river on Saturday and we can expect significant *delays.'*

In Dante's *Divine Comedy*, Hell was divided into nine circles, each devoted to punishing a particular group of sinners. But up here, in the land of the living, it was roadworks and rush hour.

'And speaking of the festival, we managed to track down Oldcastle's very own Leo McVey earlier and asked him about Sunday's grand finale performance of his 1980s concept album, Open the Coffins.'

Franklin turned up the radio and a dark warm voice gravelled out of the speakers. *'Yeah, it's going to be great. I mean we've got some great acts joining us on stage: Lucy's Drowning, Mister Bones, Halfhead, Closed for Refurbishment, Catnip Jane, Donny Sick Dawg McRoberts, and loads of others, you know? Great.'*

The car crawled forward.

Callum puffed out his cheeks. 'It'll pick up a bit when we get onto the dual carriageway.'

'And we're not just doing highlights, right? We're doing the whole album, start to finish.'

Let's face it, the traffic couldn't get any slower.

A line of tail-lights, glowing like the fires of hell, flaring in the falling rain.

'The public's reaction's been great. It's kinda humbling that they still love it after all these years. And I'm loving strutting about like King of the Jungle again. Makes me wish I'd come out of retirement years ago.' A laugh, black as treacle.

Franklin smiled. 'I loved Open the Coffins. We listened to it non-stop when I was at university. Drove the woman downstairs mad...'

'And all the money's going to charity, right? Which is great. Everyone's giving up their time and their talent to raise money for Alzheimer's research, cos of Ray, you know?'

'Haven't heard it for ages.'

'—a terrible shame. I mean the book's genius, yeah? My kids loved it, my grandkids love it, I still love it. Open the Coffins: best children's book ever written, that's what I think.'

'Leo McVey there. And you can catch him this Sunday at Tartantula, but tickets are going fast, with all proceeds—'

She turned and frowned across the car at him. 'You didn't answer the question: why didn't they send you home?'

'—diagnosed with Alzheimer's last year. Weather now, and it looks like we're stuck with this rain till—'

He clicked the radio off again. 'What's the point of going home early? Won't bring my ear back.'

Besides, if he went home he'd have to explain what happened to Elaine. My earlobe and that gristly bit above it? Oh, nothing much: they were bitten off by a junkie. But at least my HIV test came back negative. Elaine? Hello, Elaine?

He shrugged. 'At least this way I get the overtime. Need all we can get with Peanut on the way. Do you have any idea how much it costs to raise a kid these days?'

Finally the roundabout onto the main road crawled into view. Buses and eighteen-wheelers sending up huge drifts of spray, drenching the smaller cars.

'Urgh.' Franklin crawled the car forward, bumper inches away from the people carrier they'd been stuck behind since leaving the hospital. 'All it ever does in this sodding town is rain.'

'Sometimes.' He drew a frowny face in the mist that crept up the passenger window. 'Did they get any sense out of Brett Millar?'

'Still off his face on mushrooms.' Franklin tapped her fingers against the steering wheel, syncopating with the windscreen wipers. 'They even tried giving him a shot of Narcan; didn't make any difference though.'

'Yeah, well magic mushrooms aren't opioids, are they? Not surprised it didn't work.'

'At least they tried.'

He drew angry eyebrows on the frowny face. 'So we've got Ben Harrington dead in the bath, Brett Millar's so high he can orbit the International Space Station, and Glen Carmichael is missing... You know what I think? I think the three of them aren't serial killers, they're victims. You saw how emaciated Brett Millar was. He's been starved.'

'When did you ever meet a fat junkie? Maybe he's...' Franklin closed her eyes and swore. 'Benjamin Harrington. We've still got to deliver the death message.'

'Oh for God's sake.' Callum peered through the rain-smeared windscreen.

Traffic was solid northbound, so getting over Calderwell Bridge was going to be a nightmare. He checked his watch. 'No point even trying till rush hour's gone. Stick to the plan: at least it's moving southbound.'

Assuming he hadn't just jinxed it.

'What if they find out from the radio, or some scumbag journalist doorsteps them?'

'They *won't*.' Fingers crossed, anyway. 'We pick up Dr McDonald and we head to the flat in Castleview. By the time she's finished poking around, rush hour will have died down and we can sling past Ben Harrington's parents on the way back to the station.'

Franklin edged them closer to the car in front, brow furrowed, eyes narrowed. 'Of course, the real question is: if Brett Millar's running about all over Blackwall Hill, out of his head on magic mushrooms, where's Glen Carmichael?'

'He's already dead.'

21

'AAAAAAAARGH!' The bucket sails through the musty air and bursts against the wall. Water makes a comet's trail, soaking into the bricks.

Where the hell is he?

He *should* be right there – chained to the wall, but he's not.

Instead, the chain sits on the ground, coiled like a snake. Venomous and treacherous. Useless. Four screws lie in the dirt, still in their Rawlplug shells, torn from the mouldering brickwork, letting the tie-up ring come free from the wall. It's still fixed to the end of the chain by its padlock. The traitorous useless chain.

'You had ONE JOB!'

He grabs it up and hurls it away into the gloom. It clangs and clatters against the long-dead boiler, hissing its way into a deceitful pile.

'AAAAAAAAAAAAAAAAAAAAAARGH!'

All that time. All that energy. All those sacred herbs *wasted*.

Weeks and weeks of work. Gone, just like that.

He grinds his teeth, whole body trembling, blood surging in his ears. *Whoom. Whoom. Whoom…*

How could he be so stupid?

Once Upon A Time

There's a jackdaw hanging on the fence behind the house. Like a little black kite, caught on its own strings. Wings outstretched. Beak hanging open. Eyes like marbles that've been rolled too many times on rough concrete and gravel, till they're all white and scratched.

The jackdaw is dead.

Everything dies.

He reaches out and touches its feathers. They're cold and soft.

Sometimes things die because they're old, or ill, and sometimes they die because Father makes them dead. Sometimes they get hung from the fence with wasp-eaten wooden clothes pegs. And sometimes they get buried in the cold dark ground.

Justin stands in the kitchen, sniffling. Outside the sun is going down, making the fields look like they're bleeding.

The fields are bleeding and the house is full of smoke.

And Father howls his anger at the walls. Using it like a stick to beat the smoke with. Only the smoke doesn't break as easily as Justin.

The kitchen door bursts open, bouncing off the wall, making the mugs and plates rattle in their cupboards. Father stabs a finger at him. 'It's those bloody jackdaws again!'

Justin doesn't move.

'Building their sodding nests in the bloody chimney...' His face is dark as the smoke, teeth shining like sharp white stones. 'Get the ladder.'

'I...' Justin licks his lips.

Father's hand is like a claw, fingers digging into Justin's arm, squeezing so hard it sends needles and pins and knives stabbing all the way up into his shoulder.

'Aaaaaagh!'

'You're making your mother *cry*. Can you hear her? Can you?' He shakes Justin, making his teeth clack together. 'CAN YOU HEAR HER?'

Faint, muffled sobs come from downstairs, working their way up through the floorboards like sad little seedlings looking for light. But there's no light up here, only blood and smoke.

'I'm sorry, Father, I'm sorry.'

Another shake. 'Then don't make me tell you again.'

A nod. Teeth biting his bottom lip. Blinking back the tears.

Father lets go and Justin *runs*. He runs out the back door and round the side of the house to the garage. Fights with the slippery doorknob. Stumbles into the darkness, wiping tears from his cheeks.

The ladder is bigger than he is, but he gets it down and hauls it out into the back garden. Sticks it up against the wall, so it reaches way up to the guttering. Shuffles his feet on the damp grass, his breath pink and cloudy in the fading light.

Father steps out onto the path. Looks at the ladder. Then looks at him. 'Well?'

Justin stares at his trainers.

'Up you go.'

'But the jackdaws hate me.'

'Of course they hate you. You're destroying their home and killing their babies.' Father smiles his nastiest smile. 'Why would they *like* you?'

'They'll peck my eyes out and I'll fall off the roof and I don't want to—' The fist is nearly too fast to see, but it smashes into his cheek like a hammer, snapping his head away, making him stumble and fall across the damp grass. The world sounds like symbols and drums. Then all the air whoomps out of him as Father's boot smacks into his tummy, lifting him off the ground and spinning him over onto his back. Rats gnaw through him, their little pink tails burning his insides.

He rolls over and curls up into a ball. Cries.

And finally, Father squats down beside him. 'Hey, come on, slugger. Dry your eyes, champ.' Gentle hands wipe the tears away. 'There we go. All better.' He helps Justin to his feet. Brushes the grass and dew from his jumper. 'You good?'

Justin nods. Don't tremble. Don't cry.

'Course you are: big boy like you.' He guides him over to the bottom of the ladder. 'Now up you go, and don't forget to kill the babies, OK? OK.'

He stands at the top of the stairs. Father must've left the basement door open again, and a bare lightbulb casts sharp shadows on the rough brick walls.

Justin's not allowed to step on the stairs. If he puts one foot on the stairs something horrible will happen. Father will make sure of it.

So he doesn't. He just stands there, with his face all swollen on one side and bits of stinky bird droppings and sticky blood on his hands. Looking.

New Mummy is there. She's sitting on the dirt floor with her back to an old radiator – all rusty and lumpy edges. She's got her knees drawn up to her chest, arms wrapped around them, face buried in her yellow hair. Shoulders quivering as she cries.

New Mummy must've been bad, because she's got no clothes on. She has to be naked and cold, because she's been bad.

It's like a lump of coal in the middle of his chest. You have to do what Father says. That's the Number One Rule.

Justin moves his foot and the floorboard groans beneath him.

Mummy flinches, like she's been slapped. Then stares up the stairs, eyes wide and soggy, ringed with red. The gag in her mouth has darkened to a deep blood red where the tears and bogies have soaked into it. And the chain around her neck sparkles like no diamond necklace ever did.

She makes … noises. All muffled by the gag. Strangly, angry, pleading noises.

As if he's the one who can help her. As if he isn't every bit as trapped as she is.

Justin reaches out and swings the door closed.

He's never making *that* mistake again.

There's only one thing for it.

The God-In-Waiting is gone and he's not coming back. Oh, he'll regret running away soon enough. Come crawling back, pleading to be released from his impurities, but as Mummy always found out, pleading never worked. Once you broke the rules you had to take your punishment, because that's how it works.

He had his chance at being a god and he threw it away.

Of course, there's very little chance of him being able to find his way back. The purification ritual is mind-expanding, but often makes the Gods-In-Waiting confused. As if their brains have been rewired to run on a foreign voltage. The signals from the real world get scrambled until they finally achieve divinity and all becomes clear again.

He won't be able to lead anyone back here.

Probably.

But probably isn't definitely, and that was one of Father's many lessons. You never trust a probably, because 'Probably' can't be trusted like 'Definitely' can. A thing is either dead or it's not, 'probably dead' isn't good enough.

So yes, there's only one thing for it.

He unscrews the cap of the petrol canister and pours it down the basement stairs.

It cascades like a little waterfall, making the air swim and wobble in front of him. The sharp heady scent of pear drops and sweet vinegar.

The living room smells of cloves and smoke, with its open fireplace full of twigs and bones. The jackdaws always win in the end. But they won't be back this time. He covers the mouldering furniture in unleaded, sploshes more on the dusty carpet. Pours what's left across the bathroom floor and into the kitchen. Upends it and gives it a little shake, getting the last dribbles out.

Steps out of the back door and into the rain.

Father would *not* be happy if he could see the garden. His precious vegetable plot disappeared under a war zone of brambles and nettles, battling it out for the last scraps of nutrients from the dark thick earth. The trees heavy with unclaimed fruit, rotting and wasp-riddled on the branches. The garden shed, where so many nights were spent learning not to be a bad little boy.

He dips a strip of fabric into the empty plastic container, strikes a match and puts it to the hanging end. Still enough petrol in there to soak through the scrap of T-shirt and turn it into a torch. Then the whole thing goes in the kitchen door, tumbling over and over, making the same fluttering roar as baby jackdaw wings when they're caught in their nest.

It bounces off the wall, and lands halfway between the kitchen and the living room. Blue flames rush across the floor in both directions, eating their way into the house. Popping and crackling like a baby jackdaw's bones when you hold one of their fluttering little bodies in your hand and *squeeze*.

Two minutes later the basement goes up, growling out its decades of pain.

He waits until the fire has taken hold, then goes back to the van.

It doesn't matter if the ex-God-In-Waiting leads them back here – there will be nothing left to find. And he will have moved on to somewhere new.

The only thing left to do is find someone else to take their place.

22

'Hold on, I'll put you on speaker.' Dr McDonald stood in the middle of the filthy room, dressed in the full-on Smurf outfit: booties on her feet, gloves on her hands, mask, and safety goggles covering most of her face. She had an oversized smartphone in one hand, held out at head height.

Scenes Examination Branch had left the windows alone – still covered with their layers of hardcore pornography, blocking out the evening light, leaving them to the mercy of the single lightbulb dangling from a wire in the ceiling. They'd left everything else as it was as well – the ladder, the wallpaper table, the power tools, the radio. The stack of empty cans in the kitchen and the half-full bong.

Most of the flies were gone from the floor though, so at least every step didn't scrunch.

And Callum's ear throbbed. So much for local anaesthetic. No one said the sodding stuff would wear off in less than an hour.

McDonald poked at her phone's screen and a semi-posh Scottish accent crackled out of the speaker. *'Can you hear me?'*

Franklin stood in the corner, notebook at the ready. But Callum leaned back against the wall, by the porn-covered window, with Cecelia. All of them done up in blue Tyvek oversuits with matching accessories.

Cecelia made a raspberry noise behind her facemask. 'To be perfectly honest, I find this more than a bit insulting.'

Callum shrugged.

'My team's been over this flat with the proverbial nit-comb. We *did* our job.' She folded her arms, her suit making crinkling noises with each movement. 'And for your information: Tina's confronting Yashnoor about having an affair on *Enders* tonight. In *ninety* minutes.'

He groaned. 'You'll be back in time for *EastEnders*.'

'I better be.'

Dr McDonald did a slow pirouette, showing the phone the flat. 'Say "stop" if you spot anything.'

'Ooh, is that pornography on all the windows? I wouldn't mind a gander at that.'

Cecelia shook her head. 'Pervert.'

'Who said that?'

'Hold on...' Dr McDonald turned the phone around, so they could see the screen.

A creased face blinked out at them – steel-coloured short back and sides, two prominent grey eyebrows, a matching moustache lurking beneath a puckered golf-ball nose. Little rectangular glasses. *'Greetings, minions of Police Scotland! Fear not, for your salvation is at hand.'*

'Bernard, this is Cecelia Lynch, head of the local Scenes Examination Branch. And standing next to her is DC Callum MacGregor and DC Rosalind Franklin. Everyone, this is Professor Bernard Huntly – he's a physical evidence specialist. A bit of an acquired taste, but he's annoyingly good at what he does so we put up with it.'

'Quite right too.' He gave them all a grin. *'Can you turn me up a bit, Alice?'*

She poked at the controls and Huntly's voice got louder.

'Well, why don't we cut straight through the meat to the bones beneath, Cecelia my love? Bloods?'

Cecelia pointed at the doorway by the kitchen. 'Biggest quantity was over there, and even then it was less than a teaspoon. Going by the little dots on the floorboards, it wasn't a gusher, more like a hammered thumb.'

'Semen?'

'I'd prefer an ice cream, if it's all the same to you?'

'Oh, we're feisty, are we?'

'Nothing in the living room, bathroom, kitchen, or hall. There's three sleeping bags in the bedroom, and they're like large down-filled condoms. Scrape them clean and you could artificially inseminate half of Fife.'

'So our three property tycoons were enthusiastic onanists. Everyone needs to have a hobby.' The little face pulled on a smile. *'That's why I wanted to see the pornography, Cecelia. Is it the sort of thing to*

encourage Ben, Glen, and Brett's nocturnal manipulations, or was it put there by whoever left a drugged body floating in a bathtub full of brine? Alice?'

Dr McDonald walked over to the window and held the phone up to the bits of magazines taped there.

'Hmm… Interesting.'

'You see something?'

'No, I just didn't think anyone actually bought dirty magazines any more. You can download all this for free from the internet, what sort of idiot pays for it?'

'It's all heterosexual, well, I mean it's mostly heterosexual except for the lesbian photoshoots and they're basically only there to appeal to heterosexual men, so what I meant is that there's nothing that would suggest the three of them were involved in a romantic way.'

Callum sniffed – the air still had that mouldering sausage smell. 'Unless they're overcompensating? Big display of testosterone: look how manly and laddish we are, and next thing you know they're all running around sharing sleeping bags and playing with power tools.'

'Does it really *matter*? No one cares if they were gay or not.' Cecelia pulled back the edge of her glove and checked her watch. '*Enders* starts in eighty minutes.'

'*Nobody cares* unless *that was why they were targeted, my dear Mrs Lynch. I'm going to need you to scrape out those sleeping bags after all – see if you can find evidence of sexual activity involving more than one person.*'

Her back bowed. 'Oh … lovely.'

Over in the corner, Franklin stiffened as her phone launched into a strangled rendition of 'Dancing in the Moonlight'. She snapped off one of her gloves and dug into her SOC suit, pulled her mobile out and turned to face the wall. 'Mark, this is *not* a good time.'

'*Now, to the bathroom! Our friend Imhotep had to fill the bath somehow and I fancy we'll find some DNA on the underside of the taps. Easy to contaminate with biological residue, not so easy to clean.*'

Dr McDonald carried Professor Huntly out through the door and into the hall. 'We're not calling him Imhotep, we're calling him Paddington, because of—'

'*The Peruvian-style mummies, yes, I know. But it's hardly a name with dramatic connotations, is it? "Paddington" isn't someone who abducts people, drugs them, drowns them in a bath of brine, then smokes them to a fine wrinkly jerky. Not unless those marmalade sandwiches of his*' were laced with psilocybe semilanceata. *And he wears a duffle coat! What self-respecting monster does that?'*

'But the team agreed—'

'*Paddington's* a stupid name for a serial killer, Alice. At least "*Imhotep*" has a bit of gravitas about it.'

'Bernard, you can't just waltz in and rename our killer!'

Cecelia hooked a thumb at the doctor and her phone. 'Are they always like this?'

'I have *no* idea.'

She slouched into the hall, after them. 'Your boy on the phone's a dick, but he's right. Paddington *is* a stupid name. Jack the Ripper wouldn't have got where he is today with a name like Paddington.'

There was no room for them in the bathroom, so they stayed in the hall.

'So why are you really here?' Callum leaned back against the wall, where the sheet of plasterboard used to live. 'Mother said SEB had finished with the crime scene ages ago. Nothing left for us to contaminate.'

'Ah...' Cecelia rubbed the tips of her gloved fingers together, making them squeak. 'Don't take this the wrong way, but—'

'Oh you have *got* to be kidding. You're here because of me?'

'The Powers That Be said you couldn't access the scene unless someone from my team made sure you didn't get up to anything. And I can see you making faces at me behind your mask, so don't.' She shifted her feet. Fiddled with her gloves some more. 'I know you didn't cock that last scene up, but everyone else thinks you're a liability.'

Of course they did.

He let his head fall back until it thunked against the wall. Winced as a thousand bees sank their stingers into his ear. 'Ow...'

'So tell them the truth, Callum.'

'I *can't.'* He lowered his voice, even though Franklin was still muttering angrily into her phone in the living room and there was no one else to hear. 'You said it yourself: one more strike and they'd fire Elaine. We need the money. If we didn't have her maternity pay coming in, with the mortgage, and the credit card debt, and all the stuff we've got to buy for the birth and babyproofing the flat, and everything else... It's two weeks away and we're nowhere *near* ready.'

Cecelia put a hand on his arm. 'Don't panic. Breathe.'

'We're not taking any chances. And *you're* not telling anyone.'

She gave his arm a squeeze. 'Still think you're an idiot.'

'Join the queue.'

Dr McDonald emerged from the bathroom, phone still in her hand. 'Mrs Lynch, can you do a complete swab of all the taps in the house? Especially the underside of the handles and knobs.'

'And the flush on the toilet too.'

'Sorry.'

Cecelia shook her head. 'Fine.' Then stomped off back to the living room.

Dr McDonald frowned behind her safety goggles. 'The three men here were targeted for a reason, we don't know what it was, but the flat's self-contained, a safe zone for Paddington to work, I mean no one's going to see in when you're on the top floor, are they, of course not, so he can do whatever he wants in here and no one's going to notice as long as he's reasonably quiet about it.'

Professor Huntly's voice boomed out in the narrow corridor. *'I've been thinking about your two other victims: the mummies. If you don't get anything from the DNA, you can try the fingerprints. It'll be cheaper than going for facial reconstruction.'*

'The question is: did someone gain access to the flat and decide Glen, Brett, and Ben would make good victims, or did he target them somewhere else and follow them back here?' She pulled back her hood and wrapped a coil of hair around two fingers on her free hand. Holding the phone out in her other like a Dalek's eye stalk.

Callum peered at the face on the screen. 'And we get their prints how? The mummies' fingers are like prunes.'

'Ah, my dear Constable...?'

'MacGregor.'

'I knew it was something like that. Their fingerprints are like prunes because they've been dehydrated. So how would one get them nice and plump again?'

Of course: 'Soak them in water.'

'Dear Lord, no, that would be a disaster. We soak them in glycerol. *Should make them lovely and soft too.'*

Dr McDonald twiddled with her hair. 'Of course, the fact that there's three of them makes it all a bit more difficult, I mean one person's easy enough to subdue, but three at the same time, when they're all young and fit, that would take a lot more doing, wouldn't it, you could restrain them individually, but then how do you do that without the other two stepping in?'

'Glycerol.'

'I'm surprised no one thought of it sooner. It's the obvious solution and a lot less expensive than extracting DNA from the tooth pulp cavity and sending it off for analysis.'

Well, it was worth a try.

'No...' Twiddle, twiddle, twiddle. 'I think they *knew* their attacker, they invited him into their flat and he brought the magic mushrooms with him, they sit around drinking lager and self-medicating till they pass out and after that Paddington can restrain them easily.'

''Scuse me.' Cecelia squeezed past and into the bathroom, carrying a large square metal case.

'OK, so we get the hands steeping in glycerol, what then?'

'*Then you run the prints. And you get a toxicologist to look at the tissue samples. A* decent *one, not some wet-behind-the-ears undergrad on work placement. I can probably give you some names if you like.*' On the little screen, Professor Huntly fluttered his eyelashes. '*Failing that, I'm available at very reasonable rates. ID the drugs and the herbs and you've got somewhere to start looking – he had to get them from somewhere.*'

'So the question becomes where did Paddington meet them, did they have a favourite pub or club, we need to get someone visiting the local bars and ask if Glen, Ben, and Brett were seen there with someone else, because he's going to have his own favourite haunts, areas where he likes to hunt, and if we can get an ID from the other two victims we might find a common denominator, don't you think?' She pulled down her facemask. 'Do you think we could leave here, because the smell is beginning to make me feel a bit sick.'

'*Wimp.*'

'Goodbye, Bernard.' She hung up and put her phone away. 'My arm was getting sore anyway.'

Callum lowered his facemask. 'You know we can just wait for Brett Millar to come down from his trip and *ask* him what happened.'

'We can, but what if he doesn't know what happened because he can't remember, or maybe the drugs he's been on have caused permanent brain damage, can you imagine what being force-fed magic mushrooms for days would be like, what it would do to your sense of perception?' Dr McDonald struggled her way out of her gloves. 'We have to work on the assumption that he's not going to be any help, that way if he *does* remember anything about the man who attacked them it's a bonus.'

Yeah, she had a point.

166

'OK. Well, what if they didn't meet the guy in a pub? He could work for the bank, if they're financing the refurbishment. Or a local estate agent, if they're looking for a valuation?'

'That's certainly worth exploring.'

And the list of people needing interviewed just ballooned to about three times its previous size. Mother would love that.

He took out his notepad. 'So, come on then, you've seen around the flat: who are we looking for? How do we spot him when we see him, assuming Brett Millar doesn't just wake up all bright-eyed and bushy-tailed tomorrow and give us a name and address?'

More hair twiddling. 'He was able to blend in to Glen Carmichael's social circle, that means he *could* be a bit hipstery. Think beard, lumber-jack shirts, skinny jeans, no socks, ironic tattoos, 1930s haircut, but not necessarily in that order. He's big enough to manipulate the unconscious bodies of three large young men and we're on the top floor, that's a lot of stairs to carry someone down to get them in your van. So he's strong. Capable. Not easily flustered.'

Through in the living room, Franklin was getting louder – the words impossible to make out, but the tone of voice was clear as a scream: *not* sodding happy.

'Assume he waits till the middle of the night to transport Glen and Brett, he still risks being seen by one of the other residents, or someone on the street. So he's confident too. He's got a story for every eventuality.' Alice tilted her head up and to the side, frowning at the plasterboard ceiling. 'He's had a lot of practice. And I'm not just talking about the mummy in the tip and the one in the car – these aren't his first victims. He's been doing this for a long, long time.'

23

The tattoo ripples like a flag across Father's back as he digs. Faded blue-grey lines and shapes. A little bird. A skull. A big pointy knife.

His spade bites into the black earth, spits out lumps onto a growing pile.

It's getting deep, the hole.

Deep enough that only Father's top half sticks out of it. Sweat all sparkly on his dirty skin. Not a big man, but powerful, like a bulldog. Not the one on the TV ads selling insurance, though, more like the ones Father's friends make fight in wooden pits in barns in the middle of nowhere.

All bulging muscles and dark blood.

Warm sunlight makes the garden shine, green and yellow and red.

And on the fence hang a dozen jackdaws, their bodies all stiff and dead.

But no one's digging them a hole.

'Come on, champ, out you go.' Father holds the car door open. He's wearing his dog collar again, all white and crisp against his freshly shaved neck.

Justin jumps down onto the sticky black tarmac.

The whole street smells like coal and treacle as the sun batters down like a fist. It sparks off the parked cars, so bright it's painful.

He makes sure not to get any tar on his new shoes. Father has been very clear on what'll happen if he does.

'Now, slugger, you know what to do.'

168

A nod. Then he bites his bottom lip and looks both ways – up and down the street – before skipping across the road. Like he's a little baby, instead of a grown-up six-year-old.

Normally it would earn him a beating, but not this time. This time it's what Father *wants* and if today goes well, Father will be happy and if Father's happy Justin's happy. So he skips.

The shops are boring, full of stuff no one could ever want: like pots and pans and carpets and things for cleaning dishwashers. But right at the end, by the bus stop, there's a sweetie shop.

It does other stuff, like boring newspapers and magazines, but the wall behind the counter is the best thing ever – rows and rows of old-fashioned plastic jars full of brightly coloured sweets with funny names like 'DIRTY TATTIES', 'POKEY FINGERS', and 'SOOR PLOOMS'.

The air tastes of excitement.

And perfume. Which is sort of like soap, only stronger and a bit chokey, and Father doesn't like it.

The smell's coming from a lady with yellow hair, standing with her elbows resting on the counter. She smiles down at him with shiny white teeth. 'Hello, little man, how can we help you today then?'

She's pretty. Yellow hair, heart-shaped face, little nose, sticky-out boobies. The kind Father always picks.

Justin blinks up at her. 'Ooh, are you a *angel*?' As if he doesn't know that angels aren't real. They're all madey up by liars, like Father says.

'Well, aren't you the wee charmer?'

'My mummy was pretty like you, but she had to go live with Jesus in the Heaven.' He sticks his bottom lip out and makes it wobble, like he's about to burst into tears.

'Oh, sweetheart!' The lady's face goes all wrinkly between the eyebrows and she hurries around the counter to hug him.

It's lovely and warm and she doesn't *really* smell soapy and chokey. She smells like sunshine.

'Where's your daddy?'

'I...' Sniff. 'I don't know. He went into a shop, but there was a doggy and I went to look at the doggy, and I can't remember which shop...' Justin works the sniffles into a tiny sob. Nothing too wet and snottery. Father didn't raise him to be a whiny little bitch.

She gives him another hug, soft and warm, then holds him at arm's-length and nods. 'How about we get you a nice sweetie, then we go looking for your daddy? I can shut up the shop for ten minutes. Would you like that?'

He pulls on his 'Brave Wee Boy' face. 'You *are* a angel.'

'How about … sherbet lemons?' She stands and clatters a handful of yellow pebbly things out into a tiny paper bag, then passes it to him. 'I know you're not supposed to take sweeties from strangers, but trust me: they're good.'

He takes one and puts it in his mouth – all nippy and sour and sweet at the same time. 'Thank you.'

She holds his hand and walks him out of the shop. 'Now, let's see if we can't find your daddy.'

Of course they will. Otherwise the plan won't work.

The pretty lady has a nice voice, like the people on the radio, smiling and swinging his hand in hers as they walk down the narrow street. 'And all the tiny mouses sing, "What use have we of golden rings? / All we want is bits of cheese, and socks to warm our feet and knees, / And pies and biscuits by the tonne, and lemon drops for everyone."'

There aren't any shops down here, but she doesn't seem to mind the smell of the bins.

'But Santa frowned and asked again, "Mice, have you seen the silly hen?" / "Oh, no, Santa we have no want of shoes to fit an elephant, / Or zebra shorts, or lion hats, or spats to fit a pussy cat."'

She does a little skippy step every time something rhymes.

There's one parked car on the road, the boot standing open, a man pacing back and forth beside it, wringing his hands. He's the only other person here.

Justin points and breaks free of the nice lady. Runs across to him. 'Daddy!'

Father spins around, eyes wide, then beams and kneels on the cobblestones, sweeps him into a hug. 'Justin! Oh where have you been? I was worried sick!'

'The nice lady helped me, Daddy.'

He lets Justin go and stands. Holds his hand out to the lady. 'Bless you!'

She goes pink in the cheeks. 'Nah, it was nothing. He's a lovely wee lad.'

'Ever since his mother left us…' A sigh. '*Bless* you.'

She shakes his hand. 'My pleasure. It's not every day you—'

The fist is fast and only makes a noise when it slams into the side of her head. Then the nice lady's legs buckle and she slumps. But before she's even halfway down, Father sweeps her up in his arms and bundles her into the boot. Wraps her wrists and ankles in silvery sticky tape. Puts another strip of it over her mouth. Slams his fist into her face twice more. Then closes the boot.

Justin stands perfectly still, hands behind his back. No trembling. No crying. No anything.

Father grins at him. 'Who wants chips for tea?'

24

Brookmyre Crescent hissed in the rain. Drops bounced off the glistening tarmac, gathered in the gutters, spreading out in a tiny lake that lapped around the tyres of a new-ish Toyota. Their pool car sent a mini tidal wave sploshing against its hubcaps.

Callum unfastened his seatbelt as they drifted to a halt outside number 16, with its collection of naff garden ornaments. 'You still want to be the one that tells them their son's dead?'

'Why, you think I'm not up to it?' Franklin hauled on the handbrake. 'Think I'm going to—'

'Fine. Whatever.' He shook his head. Winced as a thousand tiny ants dug their pincers into what was left of his ear. 'You know, sometimes, just occasionally, *maybe* you could try not treating everything I say as some sort of insult to your gender, ethnicity, professionalism, or dress sense.'

She stared down at herself. 'What's wrong with my dress sense?'

'Try a mirror.' A cheap shot, but hey-ho. He grabbed a high-viz jacket from the back seat and clambered out into the rain, hauling it on as he hurried up the lock-block driveway to the door. Turned up his collar and rang the bell.

Rain drummed on his shoulders, hammered at the pampas grass growing around that hideous wishing well and even more hideous gnomes.

Franklin locked the car and jogged her way through the downpour. 'There's nothing wrong with my suit!'

'Keep telling yourself that.'

A light came on inside the hall, filtering out through the fanlight above the door.

'Why don't you stick your—'

The door swung open and Lurch from the Adams Family blinked down at them. He'd swapped the butler's outfit for a brown cardigan and mustard-coloured corduroys, but the huge hands and pale slab of a face were a dead giveaway. But his voice wasn't a deep ringing bass, it was a sharp-edged tenor, clipped and precise. 'Can I help you?'

Callum produced his warrant card. 'Mr Harrington? Can we come in please?'

The only sound was the sibilant hiss of the rain on the drowning world.

Franklin pulled her card out as well. 'It's about Ben.'

Lurch rolled his eyes, then turned and lumbered back down the hall. 'You'd better come in then. Make sure you wipe your feet.' He led the way into a living room lined with bookshelves. No TV, just a fancy stereo surrounded by stacks of vinyl. Leather armchairs that looked worn and soft.

He took up position in the middle of the room, straightened up to his full height, put his hands behind his back. 'If this is about drugs, I can promise you I don't want to know. I told him he was on his own if he *ever* did anything so stupid again.'

Franklin put a hand on the nearest armchair. 'Maybe you should sit down, Mr Harrington? I'm afraid we've got some bad news...'

'How's he holding up?' Callum fished the teabags out of the mugs and dumped them in the sink.

'Not well.' Franklin puffed out a breath and settled back against the worktop. Ran a hand across her face. 'Doesn't help they had a massive falling out last time they spoke. And now his son's dead and there's nothing he can do to fix it.'

The kitchen was nearly as big as Callum's whole flat, all marble and oak with a huge fridge freezer and a glass-fronted fridge just for white wine. A set of French doors led out onto a patio with wicker furniture dripping in the rain, and a set of steps leading down into a tidy garden with thick borders besmirched by more sodding gnomes. And beyond the fence: that view. Even in the pouring rain it was spectacular. Oldcastle, laid out beneath the heavy lid of grey, slivers of copper and gold caressing the Victorian cobbled streets of Castle Hill as the last gasp of daylight forced its way through the gloom. A slash of Kings River shining like a sharpened knife.

Much better than looking out on a railway line, a manky cluster of allotments, and some tenements.

How the other half lived.

Callum put the milk back in the oversized fridge. 'I called Mother, she's sorting out a Family Liaison Officer. And, according to McAdams, Brett Millar tried to bite off a nurse's fingers, so they've chucked him into a secure psychiatric ward. Straitjacket, padded walls, and twenty-four-hour surveillance.'

'That's the trouble with druggies, once they get the taste for human flesh...' The smile faded. 'Sorry.'

'Should think so too.' He put the mugs on a tray along with a packet of gingersnaps dug out of the cupboard above the kettle. Nodded at the door. 'Go on then.'

He followed her through into the book-lined lounge.

Mr Harrington was crumpled in one of the armchairs, his huge frame shrunken into itself, massive hands wrapped around his knees. Nose and cheeks red, as if he'd been standing out in the rain.

Callum put the tray on the floor and handed him a mug. 'Milk, two sugars.'

A sniff and a nod.

'Is it OK if we ask you a few questions about Ben?'

The lips curled on that slab of a face. 'My son's name is *Benjamin*.'

'OK. Yes, Benjamin.' He took his own tea and settled on the front edge of the other armchair. 'Benjamin bought a flat with his friends, Brett Millar and Glen Carmichael.'

'Gah.' Ben's dad stared down at the mug. 'The Millar boy was always trouble. I should've expelled him, but his parents were just as bad. It didn't matter that their horrible son was a bad influence on our boy, they made it very clear what would happen if I took the appropriate action. Drugs, on school premises!'

He made himself smaller in his chair, knees coming up against his chest. 'Of *course* they were the Millar boy's drugs. Benjamin didn't do drugs, we brought him up better than that, and now these jumped-up little *nobodies* are standing in my office telling me they'll go to the papers and say it was all Benjamin's fault.' Ben's dad grimaced into his tea. 'I should have expelled them: Bret *and* Benjamin. I should have expelled them *both*. A headmaster has to have principles. He has to be uncompromising. He has to be the rule of law.'

Callum nodded. 'But you didn't.'

'How could I? Christine would have died from the scandal. So I

174

made the whole thing go away, and the Millar boy continued to be a bad influence. It's amazing Benjamin got into university. A BA in aquaculture: it should've been law, or medicine. And does he *use* his degree? No, he buys a worthless flat in a horrible part of town with his two useless friends and thinks he's going to be the next big property magnate.'

'And did Benjamin mention anyone else? Maybe someone he'd met recently? Someone new to their circle?'

'What, a woman?' Ben's dad shook his head. 'We should be so lucky. Oh, don't get me wrong, he isn't *gay* or anything like that. He's just too busy being a conceited selfish little child to have a proper relationship.'

Franklin cleared her throat. 'Can we look at Benjamin's room, Mr Harrington?'

He wrapped his arms around his knees. 'It's upstairs, down the hall, at the end.' Then he laid his forehead on them and cried.

'Getting dark out there.' Franklin stood at the window, one hand on the *Star Wars* curtains, looking out at the rain.

The bedroom was immaculate: no oil slick of socks and pants on the floor; all the books in neat little rows on the bookshelf; a fancy workstation with a big monitor, printer, and ergonomic keyboard, all lined up perfectly square; bed made, with the Pokémon duvet cover tucked in tight like they did in hotels.

'You think he tidies up himself, or does his mum do it for him?' Callum snapped on a pair of blue nitriles and tried the bedside cabinet. Socks. Pants. Hankies. Mickey Mouse watch.

'His father's *lovely*.' Franklin put on a slightly deeper voice, mimicking the clipped accent. '"He's not *gay* or anything like that." Homophobic dick.'

'Check the wardrobe.'

She opened the doors and squatted down in front of it, rummaging through the neat rows of shoeboxes arranged in the bottom. 'Do you buy that whole "everything was Brett Millar's fault" act?'

'Yeah, well Brett Sodding Millar isn't exactly on my Christmas card list this year.' Callum pulled the drawers all the way out and checked the undersides. Nothing Sellotaped there. But there was a pair of socks in the gap beneath the bottom drawer. Probably fell out and popped down the back. 'Wasting our time here.'

'Probably.'

He pulled the socks out, frowned. There was something hard in the middle, something stuffed inside them. They got turned inside out on the bedspread, covering Pikachu's smiley face. 'Or maybe not.'

'You got something?'

'Flash drive shaped like a Lego man, and a wee ziplock baggie of pills.' He held the bag up. The contents looked like small green jelly beans. 'I'm guessing Benjamin was into Temazepam. Don't know about the flash drive, though.'

She pointed at the tower unit sitting under the workstation. 'Could find out easily enough.'

'And compromise the chain of evidence? No thanks. Whatever's on there, I want it admissible in court.' He pulled an evidence bag from his pocket and slipped the flash drive inside. Scribbled down the time, date, location, case number, and both of their names. Did the same with the pills. 'Probably won't go anywhere, but you never know.'

Callum stuck the bags in his pocket. Frowned at the room: the Pokémon duvet cover, the *Star Wars* curtains, the shelf covered with little SpongeBob SquarePants figurines mounted above a row of kids' books. The framed *Finding Nemo* print on the wall. 'It's all a bit … childish, isn't it? Like Ben's mum and dad are infantilising him. Keeping him young so they can control him.'

Franklin rolled her eyes, then stuffed the shoeboxes back in the wardrobe. 'You've never met a hipster before, have you? All this crap is "ironic". Watching *My Little Pony* and getting cartoon characters tattooed all over your body. Listening to bands no one's ever heard of and wearing glasses you don't need just because the frames are "retro". Beards. Haircuts. Tight trousers.'

Callum slid the drawers back again. 'When I was a kid, people dressed up as goths. Or grunge was still a thing. Just.' He stood. 'Not me, obviously.'

'Too cool, were you?' She rifled through a stack of vinyl records.

'The home wouldn't let us wear make-up, or grow our hair. Not even the girls.' His blue nitrile gloves snapped off, got bundled in with the evidence bags. 'Billy Jackson came home from school one day with a pierced ear. Someone did it for him at break-time with a needle and a strawberry Mivvi. Mr Crimon beat the living hell out of him and made him sleep in the bath for a week. Couldn't stand up straight for ages.'

'I mean, look at these bands: Sui-psychedel-icide, the Burning Yesterday Collective, Gerbils from Saturn, Stalin's Wardrobe... Who *listens* to stuff like this?'

'He runs a garage in Kingsmeath now. Still got a bit of a hunch on him.'

'Ooh, spoke too soon.' Franklin held up an album with a woodcut illustration of a rabbit and a cat dancing in a graveyard on it: *Open the Coffins*. 'Mind you, Harrington's probably only listening to it *ironically*.'

'Meh, the book was better. And speaking of which,' Callum pointed at the bookshelf, with its collection of textbooks and YA novels, 'how about we give this lot a quick rummage, then head?'

'Might as well.' She plucked a thick book from the middle shelf. 'Urgh. Listen to this: *Adaptive Governance*, colon, *The Dynamics of Atlantic Fisheries Management*, brackets, *Global Environmental Accord*, colon, *Strategies for Sustainability and Institutional Innovation*, close brackets. Sounds *fun*.' She turned it spine-side up and riffled through the pages. Nothing fell out. 'This home you grew up in: did *you* have to spend nights in the bath?'

'If you were really bad, they half-filled it with cold water first.' He flicked through something about a teenaged spy. 'I guess some people just love working with kids.'

She dumped the textbook and tried another one. 'You report them?'

'You think no one listens to women?' The next book was about the same teenaged spy. How was an eleven-year-old boy supposed to disarm a nuclear weapon? 'Try being the kind of kid that gets labelled "challenging".'

'Hmmm…' Another textbook.

'R.M. Travis came to our school once. Signed my copy of *Ichabod Smith and the Circus of Doom* and drew a little picture of a rabbit too… I was so nervous I nearly wet myself.' In the next one, Junior Superspy was foiling a global plot to wipe everyone out with Ebola. 'Course, I was too stupid to keep my mouth shut when I got back to the home. All puffed up and proud and showing the book off to all the other kids. So Mr Crimon confiscated it. Never saw it again.'

'Think we should seize the computer?'

'Can if you want, but the IT lab won't do a thing with it till someone bigger than you or me sets a flamethrower to their backsides.' He'd run out of boy-super-spy novels, so Callum moved onto a series about a boy vampire caught up in the Napoleonic wars. 'Maybe we should start with the flash drive and see how we get on?'

They flicked through every book on the shelf and only managed to turn up a voucher for guitar lessons that had expired three years ago. So much for that.

Franklin stuck the last YA novel back on its shelf. 'That's me.'

'Yeah.' Callum made for the door, then stopped as his mobile launched into song. When he pulled it out, the word 'HOME' sat in the middle of the screen. He gave Franklin a wee grimace and pointed towards the stairs. 'I'll catch you up.' Hit the button. 'Elaine?'

'Hi... Peanut was wondering what time you'd be getting home.'

'No idea. Late. Probably. You know what it's like with a murder investigation.'

'Well don't binge on kebabs and pizza, I made tuna casserole for tea. Just make sure you call me when you're heading home so I can pop it in the oven.'

'Yes, Boss.'

'And while you're obeying my every whim, can you pick up some pickles and Nutella on your way home? Doesn't have to be the fancy ones with the white-and-green label, any dill cucumbers will do.'

'Anything else, Your Imperial Majesty?'

'Love you.'

'Me too.' He hung up and headed downstairs.

Through in the living room, Ben's dad was still in his seat – all curled up with his forehead against his knees. A living mummy.

Callum cleared his throat. 'Mr Harrington? Is there someone who can stay with you? Maybe a neighbour, or a friend? It's probably—'

The front door rattled and a voice boomed out in the hall. 'Oh for God's sake, Anthony, what have I told you about leaving your muddy shoes on the carpet? Honestly, it's bad enough I have to clean up after idiots all day without coming home to it too.'

A small woman appeared in the doorway, peeling off a leather jacket. 'You can come help me with the shopping, it's...' She stopped. Stared at Franklin, then did the same to Callum. 'Anthony? Anthony, what's going on? Who are these people?'

Franklin held out her warrant card. 'I'm afraid we've got some bad news, Mrs Harrington.'

25

'No, Marline, I don't. And I'll tell you why I don't, because I never did nothing with him, OK?' Honestly, Marline was *such* a bitch. 'If he says I did, he's *completely* a liar.'

No noise from the other end of the phone – Stupid Central.

Ashlee slumped back on her bed and scowled up at the posters on the ceiling. All four members of Mister Bones, shirtless and smiling perfect smiles on some sunny beach somewhere *way* nicer than crappy old Oldcastle. The three guys from Four Mechanical Mice in a swimming pool, all glistening and muscles and that. $ick Dawg, posing on a motorbike in leather jacket and jeans, all those tattoos on his naked hairless chest. Sexy and mysterious with a superhero mask and utterly cool-shaped moustache/goatee thing. Even if he did have a load of completely thin bitches in the background, posing in their bikinis and showing off. Skanky cows.

'*He said you did.*'

'What did I tell you? *Completely* a liar.'

He was too. As *if* Ashlee would ever touch Marline's sloppy seconds. Wasn't even that good looking. And he was a crap kisser. All fat slimy tongue and weird little grunting noises. Freak.

'*He said you snogged him outside the chipper, Sunday.*'

'Ungh. Who you going to believe, Marline: Peter – who utterly dumped you on your birthday – or your best friend in the world, AKA: *me?*'

More silence.

Taylor from Mister Bones was *definitely* the hottest guy on her ceiling. He had these lovely teeth and a way of singing into the camera that made you know he was doing it just for you. Of course, she wouldn't say no to Zeb from Four Mechanical Mice either. Not with that lovely long hair.

It was nicer than hers.

Mind you, that wasn't difficult these days – hers was like straw. God she was *so* disgusting.

Why would Zeb or Taylor want to go out with a fat pig like her?

Didn't matter how little she ate, or how many times she did sit-ups and squats and went jogging and everything. Here she was, practically living on rice crackers, sneaking off to throw up after every one of Mum's disgusting fatty meals of slop, and she *still* wasn't thin. Not *properly* thin.

She risked a look down at the lines where her ribs poked out beneath the tank top, the hip bones making twin rails through the boxer shorts, the gap between her thighs. There was *completely* a roll of fat around her middle. Like a beer belly, or something. And she never even drank beer. How was that fair?

'I'm sorry, Ashlee. I know you'd never do that to me.'

A long low *'Brrrrrrrrrrrrrrrrrrrrrrrrrrrrrrrrrrrrrrrrring...'* rang out from downstairs.

'Ungh.' She sat up. Yup, that was massively a roll of fat. 'Someone's at the door.'

'He's such a liar, isn't he?'

'Always was. You were *utterly* too good for him, Marline.' Not true, but that was what you were supposed to say, wasn't it? Not, 'You were a matching pair of bookend freaks.'

She yanked open her door and stuck her head out into the dark hall. Put her phone against her fat-cow chest and shouted down the stairs. 'Door!'

'Brrrrrrrrrrrrrrrrrrrrrrrrrrrrrrrrrrrrrrring...'

For God's sake, did she completely have to do everything round here?

'DOOR!'

Her mum's voice came up from the kitchen. *'Well answer it then, I'm busy.'* Probably making more lardy yuck for tea.

'I'M ON THE PHONE!'

'So call them back!'

'Aaaargh!' God, it was like ... North Korea, or something. 'Fine. Whatever. Don't bother yourself. I'll just stop what *I'm* doing, shall I?' Back to the phone as she stomped down the stairs. 'Marline?'

'Everything OK?'

'Yeah, if you think my MOTHER BEING AN ENTIRE BITCH is OK.' Nice and loud to make sure she could hear it.

'*You want to get wasted for my birthday next week? I can utterly rob a bottle of voddy from my gran.*'

'Yeah, why not. You only turn fourteen once, right?'

The hall, of course, was *completely* Arctic Circle, because being an entire bitch means you're too tight-fisted to put a radiator in the hall. Not like it's chucking it down winter outside or anything, is it? Noooo.

Ashlee shuffled her feet into a pair of Mum's furry slippers, then grabbed a raincoat from the rack of hooks by the door and pulled it on. Hiding her disgusting fat body.

'*My step-dad wants to have a party down the bowling alley. Laser Quest, dodgems, and burgers, like I'm, I dunno, six years old or something. He's such a* complete *spazmoidal—*'

'Yeah, hang on, Marline.'

'*Brrrrrrrrrrrrrrrrrrrrrrrrrrrrrrrrrrrrring...*'

'OK, OK. Jesus.'

Mum appeared from the kitchen, wiping her hands on a tea towel. Typical: turns up when all the hard work's done to take the credit. The lazy cow flicked hair out of her eyes – maybe a decent haircut would help with that? And a proper dye-job too. Honestly: going out in public with an *inch* of brown roots showing. Never mind the chunky thighs and revolting saggy boobs, because *apparently* it's OK to massively turn into a slob when you hit thirty. She draped the tea towel over her shoulder, like she worked in Starbucks or something. 'Who is it, Ashlee?'

'Yeah, because I'm COMPLETELY PSYCHIC! Jesus.' Honestly, how thick could you get?

Ashlee twisted the snib on the Yale lock and pulled the door open till the chain jerked tight. Crammed as much scorn into her welcome as she could: '*What?*'

She's wonderfully thin. *Magnificently* thin. Glaring up at him, her whole skull visible through the pale thin skin.

He blinks at her, making his bottom lip tremble. His eyes are all red and puffy, like he's been crying – amazing what you can do with a dab of vinegar on a fingertip. He clears his throat. Puts on his best fake Dundee accent, because that makes it a bit more interesting, doesn't it? Being someone else. Someone who doesn't *burn* inside. 'I'm ... I'm sorry, but I'm trying to find my son.'

'And?'

181

He pulls a sheet of paper from his pocket, printed out at home. 'Missing! Have You Seen Samuel (4)?' Underneath the headline is a photo of a wee boy – dark hair and freckled cheeks, a dimple in his chin. 'Please: his name's Sam. He's only four.'

A chunky woman walks up the hallway behind the angry young girl, a tea towel draped over one shoulder. Blonde. Curvy. Maybe a bit curvier than Father would have liked, but still pretty with it. 'Ashlee, don't be rude to the nice man.' She reached past her and unclipped the chain. 'Is he missing?'

'Some woman picked him up from playschool. They said she had dark hair and glasses?'

'Oh, you poor man.'

The girl, Ashlee, folds her arms and rolls her eyes. 'Oh very classy, Mother, completely get your hormones on.'

'Don't listen to her; please, come in.'

'Honestly, ever since "Uncle Eddy" left you've been *completely* horny. Disgusting in a woman your age. Old people shouldn't be allowed to have sex, ever.'

The mother's cheeks darken, but she forces a big smile anyway. Brave little soul that she is. 'You said his name's Sam?'

'Sam. Yes.' Justin steps into the house.

Father never did get it. All that lying and play acting, dressing up like a priest to make people trust him, using Justin as bait. Silly, when you think about it. Unnecessary.

You don't need a little boy pretending to be lost if you wanted to meet women, you just need an *imaginary* boy and a photo printed off the internet.

Much easier.

Justin smiles.

Strange, it's been years since he's used that name, but all this thinking of Father has brought it back. Comfortable and warm as an old jumper, or a pair of cosy socks.

So Justin takes his smile and follows the girl and her mother into a kitchen warm with the vanilla smells of baking. Reaches into his pocket and pulls out the knife.

26

EMERGENCY CALL – 09 Sept at 19 hours 52 minutes and 13 seconds

OPERATOR: Police Scotland, what's your emergency?

CALLER: Oh God, oh God, oh God. [Sobbing]

OPERATOR: Hello, can you tell me what's happened?

CALLER: He's killing them, he's… They're screaming!

OPERATOR: OK. I need you to give me the address.

CALLER: Please come… He's killing them.

OPERATOR: Where are they? I need an address. Give me the address.

CALLER: [Screaming] HE'S KILLING THEM! YOU NEED TO COME NOW!

OPERATOR: I need you to calm down. Listen to me. Listen, we can't come if you don't tell me where you are.

CALLER: I'm at home. I was on the phone to Ashlee and she was answering the door and the man came in and he said he was looking for his missing kid—

OPERATOR: There's a child missing?

CALLER: No, you're not listening! He said he was looking for it, but he … he … [Sobbing] and they let him in and now they're screaming!

OPERATOR: OK. Where are they? I need an address. Where does Ashlee live?

CALLER: With her mum. Two Twenty-Three Johnson Crescent, in Shortstaine. Please, he's got a knife…

OPERATOR: Hold on. [Keyboard noises] Cars are on their way. When did it—

CALLER: Hurry! You've got to hurry, they're screaming!

OPERATOR: It'll be OK. There's police and an ambulance—

CALLER: No, listen. They're on my mobile…

[Crackling]

YOUNG WOMAN: [Sound is distorted] [Screaming] GET OFF HER! GET OFF HER! GET OFF HER!

WOMAN: [Sobbing] Don't hurt my baby! I'll do anything you [Screams]

YOUNG WOMAN: NO!

[Grunting] [Banging] [Sound of glass shattering]

CALLER: Please, you have to get there!

OPERATOR: They're on their way. Can you tell me your name?

CALLER: Marline. Marline McFadden. You have to hurry up!

WOMAN: I didn't… I didn't…

MAN: [Shushing noise] It's OK. It's OK.

YOUNG WOMAN: Mummy?

MAN: I'll take good care of you [Too quiet to make out] forever. Won't that be nice? Forever and ever.

YOUNG WOMAN: Oh God, she's dead. She's dead. She's dead.

OPERATOR: Marline, I want you to record the call for me, will your phone let you do that?

CALLER: I… Yeah, completely! I've got, like, this app that'll—

YOUNG WOMAN: Get away from me!

MAN: They'll worship you. You'll be a god and they'll worship you.

YOUNG WOMAN: [Screaming]

27

Mother stood with her back to the room, facing the murder board with its growing lines of actions and outcomes. 'You know what I think? I think they need to let us speak to Brett Millar.'

The blinds were open, letting in the darkness from outside. What little streetlight that managed to make its way around to the back of the billboard tainting the shadows with orange and brown.

Watt curled his lip, upsetting the bum-fluff line of ginger pretending to be a beard. 'I talked to a Professor Bartlett over there,' he said, and I quote, "Mr Millar is too volatile to remain un-sedated while in this establishment. I will not put my staff, or other patients, at risk."'

McAdams shook his head. 'A doped-up Millar? What use is that to us all? We seek a killer!'

'Then we'll just have to go round there tomorrow and give this professor the opportunity to change his mind, won't we?' Mother turned to face them. 'Right: home time. You can all go get yourselves a good night's sleep and come back bushy-tailed and bright tomorrow morning. Briefing will be seven o'clock sharp.'

Callum stuck his hand up. 'What about the flash drive?'

'The IT Lab have got it, so we should find out what's on the thing by …' she checked her watch, 'about the dawn of the next Millennium.' Then Mother stared at them all. 'Well, come on then: off you go. Home. Shoo.'

Dotty whizzed her wheelchair around in a tight circle. 'Pub?'

'No.' Watt marched out of the room, pulling his jacket on.

McAdams cupped his hands into a loudhailer: 'And remember to sign out this time!' Then a shake of the head and a sigh. Finally a smile pulled at his stubbly-grey Vandyke. 'Come, fair maiden Dot. Let us go from here to a bar. There to drink much beer.' He took hold of the handles on the back of her chair and steered her out into the corridor, throwing a parting shot over his shoulder, 'Dumbarton Arms. Last one there buys the crisps.'

'Boss?' Callum powered down his computer. 'If it's all the same, I'm going to stay and see what's on the drive.'

'Don't be daft, the IT Lab won't even *start* looking at it for weeks. Dorothy's right: pub o'clock. It's about time Rosalind here did some team bonding.' Mother stuck her hands in her pockets and sauntered out of the office. 'And it's karaoke night down the Bart, how more team bonding can you get?'

Franklin watched the door close behind her. Then groaned. 'I am *not* singing karaoke.'

Callum crept his way between the empty tables, balancing two pints of Stella, a half of Guinness, a pint of Old Jock, a gin-and-tonic, and a packet of dry-roasted on a wee tray.

The Dumbarton Arms wasn't exactly bustling at nine o'clock on a Wednesday night, which was probably why they'd turned the PA system up to a near-deafening roar. The only other patrons were an auld mannie and his Labrador, and a pair of students – young men that were more spots than skin. All of them blinking up at the little stage where a shiny-faced Franklin and Dotty were belting out an old Meatloaf standard about shagging in a car.

Doing a decent job of it too.

Callum lowered the tray onto the table and slipped back into the booth. Passed McAdams and Mother their drinks. Then gave Mother her change.

McAdams took a sip of Guinness. Raised his voice over the musical onslaught. 'I'd count that if I was you.'

'Oh, don't be such a misery guts, Andy. Callum has been in the wars and deserves a bit of sympathy.'

'Thank you.' Callum helped himself to one of the Stellas.

She nodded at the stage. 'Rosalind's settling in nicely, isn't she?'

Up there, Franklin was getting to the bit about sleeping on it.

Mother glanced at him. 'She says you probably saved her life, earlier. Could've died, running into traffic like that, but you stopped her.'

A shrug, then a gulp of cold lager. 'We need to find out what's on that flash drive.'

'*Really*, Constable MacGregor?' McAdams let his mouth hang open. 'I hadn't thought of that, you must be some sort of genius!'

'Andy, what did I tell you?'

McAdams chewed on his face for a moment. Then, 'Sorry, Mother.'

'Better. The problem, Callum, is that there's a backlog of stuff waiting to be processed by the Forensic IT people. A *huge* backlog. You can probably see it from space.'

A nod from McAdams. 'I took a laptop off a dealer six months ago and they haven't even powered it up yet.'

'Yes, but this is a serial killer investigation. Surely we can bump it up the priority list.'

Mother grimaced. 'Easier said than done. I've got no favours left in the IT Lab. How about you, Andy?'

'Do you think I'd wait six months for a laptop if I had?'

Callum scooted forward in his seat as Franklin and Dotty got to the finale. 'How about we call a press conference and tell the world we can't catch this guy, because Police Scotland won't give us the forensic resources?'

Mother and McAdams shared a look, then burst out laughing.

The last triumphant chord battered through the bar. Everyone clapped. Franklin and Dotty took a bow. Then the two spotty students scrambled for the stage as Oldcastle's finest made their way back to the table, grinning.

Dotty wheeled herself in next to McAdams. 'Phew, I'm roasted, is that mine?' She grabbed the pint of Old Jock and gulped at it.

Mother beamed at her and Franklin. 'That was *lovely.*'

Up on stage, the young men launched into ABBA's 'Dancing Queen'.

'You see, my dear Constable MacGregor, if it was that easy everyone would do it.' McAdams took a deep draught of Guinness, getting himself a little white moustache. 'Police Scotland do not give a toss about being showed up at press conferences. All that'll happen is they'll send some bigwigs up from Tulliallan to take over the case, kick us off it, then kick *us*. Hard. Probably in the genitals.'

Mother patted him on the shoulder. 'He's right.'

'I know it might feel like your career's halfway down the chunty right now, but they'll pelt it with used toilet paper and flush like madmen.'

Oh.

'Well...' Callum had a good long hard look at his pint. 'Can we put pressure on the Chief Superintendent instead? He's not going to want an unsolved serial...' Sodding hell. 'It'll be the same with him, won't it?'

'And the penny finally drops!' McAdams gave him a slow round of applause.

'Not telling you again.' Mother slapped the sarcastic git's hands. 'Callum, Andy and I had to fight like wounded badgers so they'd let us keep this case. *Any* excuse and it's gone.'

The whole team slumped a bit at that.

Up on the stage, the boys danced and warbled their way towards the end of 'Dancing Queen'.

Dotty gulped down the last of her beer. Stuck the empty back on the table with a diaphragm-rattler of a belch. 'So sod them. We find another way!'

Franklin, Mother, and McAdams just shrugged.

'Come on, are we the Misfit Mob, or aren't we?'

McAdams sniffed. 'Suppose.'

'I can't hear you, soldier!'

He rolled his eyes. 'Ma'am, yes ma'am.'

'Could you be more enthusiastic, Andy? I've done jobbies with more life in them than that.'

'Enthusiasm brings me out in a rash.' McAdams downed his Guinness. 'It probably doesn't matter, anyway. Unless Brett Millar is our killer, whatever's on the flash drive has nothing to do with Imhotep.' He stood. 'Same again?'

'But it *might*.' Franklin was barely halfway down her pint. 'Anything that helps has to be a good thing.'

'Ah, the naive enthusiasm of youth.' He grabbed the empties and lumbered off towards the bar.

'Dancing Queen' finished with a lot of fist bumping and whooping.

Franklin rubbed her hands together. 'Who's up for a bit of *Grease*? Callum? I'll even let you sing the man's part.'

'Yeah... *No*. Can't.' He threw his Stella down his throat. 'I've got a pregnant girlfriend to get back to, and Nutella and pickles to buy.' He pulled on his coat. 'You kids have fun, though.'

'Dotty?'

'Oh hell yes.' And the pair of them wheeched and wheeled themselves off to the stage.

Mother ripped her way into the peanuts. 'Andy's not a bad man, Callum.'

'Does a good impersonation of one.'

There he was, standing at the bar, knocking back a sneaky whisky while the barman pulled the pints.

'They've got him on another round of chemotherapy. Being ... colourful is how he copes.'

Great. Callum puffed out a breath. 'I'm sorry he's dying. But now and then, it *might* be nice if he was "colourful" at someone else for a while, because I'm tired of being everyone's kicking post.'

Callum squelched around the supermarket aisles, wheeling a trolley and dripping on the polished floor. Pickled dill cucumbers: check. Nutella: check. Tesco own-brand high-strength paracetamol – not on the official shopping list, but his ear ached like a visit from The Claw, so: check. Bottle of shiraz – *definitely* not on the official shopping list, but what the hell: check. Multipack of Wotsits: also check, because what was life if you couldn't push the boat out now and then?

One of the fluorescent lights flickered down the end of the cold-meats-and-ready-meals aisle, making the packaging glisten and buzz like something out of a horror film. Up above, the corrugated metal roof pinged and thrummed in the rain.

Be nice to pick up a curry meal-deal for two, but there was tuna casserole waiting at home. Maybe that could be a Friday treat, and sod the budget.

His phone blurted into life.

'Hello?'

Silence.

Checked the screen: 'Number Withheld'.

'Hello?'

Callum squelched on through the flickering light, towards the check-outs. 'Hello? Willow, is this you?' More silence. 'It's OK, Willow, you can talk to me. Is someone threatening your mum?'

And the line went dead.

Might be an idea to pop round there tomorrow and make sure her mum hadn't *accidentally* developed any more bruises.

But first: cycle home through the bucketing rain. Dry off. Painkillers. Wine. Tuna casserole. More wine. Bed.

A decent end to an incredibly crappy day.

And about sodding time…

The bike's lights flickered back from thick dark puddles. Their reflections swept across the dark canopy of leaves overhead, like tiny spotlights. Caught the drips of rain that worked their way through the canopy and made them shine, before disappearing again.

Camburn Woods lurked in the darkness either side of the path. A huge animal, breathing and rustling in the downpour. Waiting. The council still hadn't fixed the streetlights in here: most were topped with broken plastic globes and covered in spray-painted swearing. But the occasional one still glowed a pale gold, casting small pools of light to be swallowed by the forest.

A jogger puffed and plodded into view. A miserable-faced middle-aged man in lycra, lots of wobble as he exercised his way towards a heart-attack. Didn't even nod as Callum cycled past. Too busy sweating.

Probably wasn't the only one out there, sweating and panting in the woods.

Always a lovely thought.

Callum stood in the saddle, legs pumping as the path climbed up over a narrow railway bridge. Freewheeled down the other side. About fifty feet further on, the old familiar footpath led off to the left. Soon be home and...

He coasted to a stop.

Looked back over his shoulder.

The bike's back light cast a blood-red glow that barely touched the forest gloom.

Could've sworn he'd heard something.

A broken streetlight stood sentinel where the footpath snaked off into the undergrowth, leaving the whole area wrapped in darkness.

Callum pulled the bike around, twisting the handlebars, sending the front lights sweeping across the path, the trees, the bushes. 'Hello?'

Nothing. Just the staccato drip-drip-drip of rain on the canopy floor. The muffled grumble of traffic on the dual carriageway a quarter mile away. The dark-brown bitter-sweet tang of decaying leaves.

No one there.

So why were all the hairs standing up on his arms?

Yeah...

Maybe cutting through the woods wasn't the best of ideas at this time of night.

He turned the bike and *pedalled*. Onto the footpath, branches flashing past – caught for a moment in the front light before disappearing behind him. Heart thumping in his chest like a bear in a cage. On, through the gloom, and then BANG, he was out of Brothers Grimm territory and back in the real world.

Oh the glorious joys of tarmac and concrete.

Callum skidded to a halt on the pavement beneath a *working* street-light. Sat there in the rain. Panting. Staring back towards the maw of Camburn Woods.

No sign of anything following him.

And breathe.

Of course there wasn't anything following him.

Stupid.

He ran a hand through his wet hair.

Come on. Home.

The windows on Flanders Road glowed like welcoming beacons. Even if it was mostly rabbit-hutch houses and rabbit-hutch flats. Could see his and Elaine's one from here. Well, the side of it anyway. Top floor, third flat on the left, this side of the street. The light was on in the bathroom. Where he was going to take a long hot shower, thank you very much.

He cycled up the pavement and onto the road, lined with bottom-of-the-range hatchbacks and battered estate cars. Let himself into the communal lobby and chained his bike to the rack beneath the stairs. Picked up three small stacks of mail from the windowsill by the back door, and squelched his way up the concrete stairs.

Urgh.

Socks were like sponges, water oozing out of his lace holes with every step.

Callum took his jacket and rucksack off on the third-floor landing, gave them a shake to get rid of the water. Mrs Gillespie's cats had been at Toby's pot plants again – kicking soil in a fan-shape across the concrete in exchange for a little brown 'present'. No wonder his spider plants looked half dead as they sprawled their way up and around the far corner of the landing.

Well, if he didn't want them piddled and crapped in, he shouldn't leave them outside, should he?

Callum poked Toby's mail through the letterbox, then did the same for Mr and Mrs Robson. And, at long last, unlocked the door to his own sodding flat. Light caught the little brass plaque they'd screwed to the wood above the letterbox: 'CALLUM, ELAINE, AND PEANUT ~ THE MACGREGOR-PIRIE CLAN!' He slumped inside and thumped the door shut behind him. Sagged in place, and dripped on the laminate flooring for a moment.

Puffed out a breath. Worked his way out of his shoes and left soggy footprints all the way to the bathroom.

Raised his voice. 'Elaine?' Dumped his wet jacket in the corner and stripped off his shirt. 'We have *got* to get ourselves a car. It's like trying to cycle through a swimming pool out there.'

191

Trousers, socks, and pants in a damp little pile. Then he cranked on the shower and stepped inside as soon as steam curled up from behind the curtain. Ahhhhh… Blissful heat.

Should probably keep his bitten ear out of the water, but the taped-on wadding was already drenched from the rain. So too late now.

A clunk as the bathroom door opened. 'Callum?'

'I know it's not top of our priority list, but a car would make life a lot easier when Peanut comes. Nothing fancy. You remember Billy Jackson? Bet he could get us a wee second-hand hatchback on the cheap.'

The curtain clattered back a couple of inches on its metal hoops and Elaine peered in at him as he soaked up the warmth. 'Where have you…' Her eyes widened. 'What happened to your head?'

'Want to get in with me? Be like old times, all soapy and slippery?'

'Callum, your face is all scratched and you've got a *bandage* on your ear!'

'Come on, when was the last time we took a shower together?'

'Get out of there, now!' She jabbed a finger towards the bathroom door, mouth curled down at the edges. 'You've got a visitor.'

'Who?'

'DCI Powel.'

Callum screwed his face shut and thumped his forehead off the tiles.

Wonderful.

28

Poncy Powel sat on the sofa – in Callum's spot, thank you very much – in his fancypants suit, top two shirt buttons undone, no tie. A mug in one hand. Look at me. Look how at home I am, slumming it with the common man.

Callum loomed in the middle of the room, with a bathsheet wrapped around his middle. Dripping onto the rug. 'What do *you* want?'

A sigh, then Powel pinched the bridge of his nose. 'Constable MacGregor … Callum, I'm here to give you a bit of friendly advice.'

'Aye, right.'

'Suit yourself.' He put his mug on the coffee table. Stood. 'But don't say I didn't try.'

Callum didn't move.

Another sigh. 'I don't like you. I don't think you're a good police officer. I don't *trust* you.'

'If this is more crap about me taking a bribe to get Big Johnny Simpson off a murder charge, you can—'

'I understand you arrested Ainsley Dugdale yesterday.'

He bared his teeth. 'So?'

'I got a tip-off this afternoon from a nasty piece of work who breaks people's legs when they don't pay their loan shark. Dugdale's going round shooting his mouth off about how he's going to end you.'

'Ainsley Dugdale can pucker up and kiss my soapy backside.'

'Just … watch yourself, OK? Elaine here,' Powel pointed at her, 'swears blind that you're not as big a disaster as you look, so I'm doing you a favour. Dugdale is *dangerous*. It's not just the drugs and the protection rackets and the punishment beatings, he's implicated in at least two murders.'

'Fine. Consider me warned.' Callum tightened his grip on the towel. 'Now, feel free to sod off.'

'Callum...' Powel dropped his head back and stared at the ceiling. 'I couldn't give a toss if Dugdale kills you, hacks you to bits and chucks them in the Kings River, but you've got a *pregnant girlfriend* to look after. You're going to be a father in two weeks. Try to think of someone else for a change.'

Think of someone else?

It wouldn't take much. Just two steps and slam a fist right in the middle of the smug git's face. They weren't on duty: it *probably* wouldn't count as assaulting a superior officer.

Elaine put a warm hand on his arm. 'Callum, *please*. He's trying to help.'

But it would still count as assault.

Deep breath.

He relaxed his hand. Uncurled the fingers. 'Right.' Cleared his throat. 'Thank you.'

'I'm not your enemy, Callum. And you're not the only one he's threatened.' Powel buttoned his jacket shut. 'Well, I'd better get going.'

Damn right you'd better.

'Thanks for the tea, Elaine.'

She squeezed Callum's arm and he stepped back, let Powel past. Then she smiled at the smug-faced lump of yuck. 'Thank you, Reece. I appreciate you letting us know. Callum will be careful, won't you, Callum?'

What choice did he have? 'Of course I will.'

He stayed where he was as Elaine let Powel out of the flat. Sagged when he heard the front door lock thunk shut.

A home visit from DCI Powel and death threat from Ainsley Dugdale. Lovely.

She reappeared a minute later. 'Are you proud of yourself?'

'Since when were you and Poncy Powel on first-name terms?'

'Since we worked that murder/suicide last January. And he's trying to look out for us, OK? You didn't have to be so aggressive – beating your peely-wally chest like a wee shaved monkey. I'm amazed you didn't just drop your towel and measure dicks with him.'

'*He's* a dick.'

'You know what, Callum MacGregor? Right now, so are you.'

194

And the worst bit was, she was right.

'Yeah.'

She closed the blinds, shutting out the dark night. 'But you're *my* dick. Now go get dried and I'll heat up some tuna casserole.'

The flats on the other side of the railway line were mostly dark now. Lights off, time for bed. Wasn't much brighter in the lounge, where only the red glow of the answering machine fought against the night.

A faint rattling snore sounded in the bedroom, muffled by the wall. God knew how they were going to manage with a new baby in a one-bedroom flat. Wasn't as if they were rolling in cash here, even with Elaine's maternity pay.

But they'd make it work. Wouldn't they?

Course they would.

Callum toasted the faint reflection in the window and took another sip of wine. Dark in here, dark out there.

Powel was such a dick. *Dugdale's going to end you.* Yeah, right.

Unless it was Dugdale in the woods – the noises in the gloom – following him home...

Goose pimples rippled their way up his arms and across the back of his neck.

Yes, but it was cold in the living room with the heating turned off.

He'd beaten Dugdale once, he could do it again. In a fair fight, anyway. Which it wouldn't be. Dugdale wasn't a Queensberry rules kind of guy, he was a jump-out-of-the-bushes-with-a-baseball-bat/knife/illegal-firearm/attack-dog/three-friends-with-crowbars kind of guy. The kind you never heard coming until it was too late.

And what if he came after Elaine and Peanut?

What if all those silent phone calls *weren't* some firm of PPI-claim tossers? What if it was Dugdale?

Something hard and sharp rolled over in Callum's chest.

First chance he got, it was off to the B&Q in Cowskillin for some heavy-duty locks. Fit them to the flat's front door. Maybe rig up a panic button or something? They probably wouldn't let him put a grade-one flag on his *own* flat, but Poncy Powel could do it.

Worth a try anyway, seeing as he was suddenly all concerned for their wellbeing.

The Callum in the window shifted from foot to foot. Licked his lips. Blood fizzing at the base of his throat.

Dugdale wasn't taking his family away from him, and that was that. He couldn't.

Callum drained his glass, picked a book from the bookshelf, and went back to bed.

Nothing could.

— the four-minute warning —

"I'm not sure about this," said Russell. "My nose is twitching like it does when there are goblins around, and goblins are *never* a good thing."

"Don't be silly," giggled Martha, wriggling under the fence. "We're rabbits! No horrible old goblin could ever catch us!"

But little did they know that the Goblin Queen had sent her minions to the library for books about traps and snares and how to cook silly rabbits who stray into the deep dark woods...

R.M. Travis
Russell the Magic Rabbit (1992)

My mother didn't love me, so she gave me away.
*Man I hate that b*tch, every God-damned day.*
If she could see me now, she'd be proud as can be,
Standin' at the stage door, with her hand out for my money...

Donny '$ick Dawg' McRoberts
'Mothers' Day'
© Bob's Speed Trap Records (2014)

29

'…extensive roadworks for the next three weeks, so you're going to want to find an alternative route. Jane?'

'Thanks, Bob. It's competition time and we're giving away three pairs of tickets to Tartantula, this very weekend, folks. Stay tuned for how to win those. But first, how about some words from our sponsors?'

'Here.' Elaine held out the Sainted Tupperware Box of Lunch. Her pink furry dressing gown hung open, revealing the huge swell of her bulge. It poked out of the gap where her jammies didn't meet any more, outie bellybutton on full display. 'Tuna casserole buttie, with cheese and hot sauce.'

Callum tucked his shirt into his trousers. 'You *do* know I'm not the one who's pregnant, don't you?'

'Funny. You're a funny guy.'

'…that's right, this week only, you can get two ScotiaBrand tasty chickens for just eight pounds. They're fan-chicken-tastic!'

'How's the ear?'

A fresh wad of cotton covered the throbbing remains, glued to his head by half a dozen sticking plasters. Looked terrible, but at least it stayed on. 'Have you seen my red tie?'

'Cupboard.'

He had a rummage through the box. Frowned.

'…deal of the century at Mad Mark's Motors! You want a new car? You got it! Nought percent finance? You got it! Easy payment terms? I must be mad, cos you got that too!'

There was a yellow silk tie in there. A proper one, not a clip-on. He picked it up between two fingers, as if it was likely to hiss and bite him as it uncoiled. 'What's this?'

'*...confused about the new tax rates for business? Don't worry, Davis, Wellman, and Manson – chartered accountants – are here to help...*'

'It's a tie.'

'Yes, I can *see* it's a tie, what I want to know is: what's it doing in my box?'

'*...Oldcastle's premier pizza parlour just got even better!*'

'Isn't it yours?'

'I have clip-ons. Police officers don't wear real ties unless they want throttled by lunatic members of the public.'

'*...three toppings and get another two absolutely free! That's right: free!*'

'Hmm...' She took it from him, turning it over in her hands. 'I found it in the living room, beside the couch. Thought it was yours.'

Oh great. It really was a snake. 'It's Poncy Powel's, isn't it? He waltzes in here like he owns the place, takes his tie off and leaves it. What a *dick*.'

Elaine gave his arm a little punch. 'You should be nicer about Reece. He was only trying to help.'

'Bet he doesn't have to go to work with a tuna-casserole buttie.'

She rolled the tie into a neat little sausage and slipped it into Callum's jacket pocket. 'You can give it to him when you get there. And say thank you *properly* for coming round to warn us.'

'Gah...'

'And you mock the tuna-casserole buttie, but trust me: Heston Blumenthal wishes he thought of it first.'

Yeah, right.

Franklin beamed, showing off those perfect teeth of hers. 'You look like crap, by the way.'

'Thanks.' Callum settled into his seat and covered a yawn.

'*And* you missed a great night. We got everyone up for "We Are the Champions".'

He wrapped himself around his coffee. 'Thought you hated karaoke.'

'That was before I tried it.' She turned as Dotty wheeled herself into the room. 'Dot!'

'Am I late? Have we started yet?'

He checked his watch. 'Still got five minutes.'

'Oh, Callum, you missed *such* a—'

'"We Are the Champions". Franklin told me all about it.'

Dotty wheeled Keith across to the tea- and coffee-making facilities, pausing to share a fist bump with Franklin on the way. 'Rosalind, my man.'

'We have *got* to do that again.'

More grinning.

'Where's Whiney Watt the Wanky Waster?'

'Not in yet.'

'Good.' Dotty spooned coffee granules into a mug. 'I'm off to interview Brett Millar this morning. Assuming he's not still doped off his monkey. Anyone want to come? Rosalind?'

'Sounds good.'

Callum groaned. 'Noooo. Don't leave me with...'

The office door opened and in stormed everyone's favourite sour-faced git. Watt glowered out from beneath his greasy floppy fringe. 'What?'

'Speak of the devil.'

'Oh go bugger yourselves.' He hung his coat on the rack by the filing cabinets, straightened his nasty brown tie, then thumped himself down in his seat. Powered up his computer. Had a wee seethe on his own.

Ah, the joys of a happy team.

He was still sulking when Mother sailed in, towing McAdams in her wake. 'Gather round, my lovely ones. Time for assembly.' She perched on the edge of Dotty's desk. 'Andy, would you like to lead morning prayers?'

McAdams pulled some sheets of paper from a folder. 'Listen up, both young and old, / For a tale of woe you must behold, / Attention pay, so you may see, / The path of others' misery.' No applause. 'To wit, other stuff on the O Division books we don't actually care about, but have to pay lip-service to. One: they've still not got an ID for any of DCI Powel's severed feet. Two: someone set fire to an abandoned house, about halfway between Castleview and Auchterowan. Third house in a week, so there's an arsonist on the loose who isn't scared of a bit of graft. Three: someone ram-raided the Poundland in Logansferry, *again*. Guess some people just want to reach for the stars. Four: aggravated assault outside the Paris Casino on Holland Street. A group of young "ladies", he made the quote marks with his fingers, 'attacked a taxi driver and left him with serious internal injuries, a fractured skull, and no sight in his left eye.'

'Ooh.' Dotty bared her gritted teeth. 'Not good.'

'Also not good is number five: mother and teenaged daughter abducted from their home in Shortstaine. Best friend was on the phone at the time and recorded the whole thing. And last, but not least, they got a DNA match from one of the bodies found at the tip on Monday:

turns out Karen Turner *didn't* run off to Portugal with another man, like her husband claimed. She was too busy being battered to death with a golf club and stuffed into bin-bags.' McAdams put his papers down. 'Now, would anyone like to contribute anything to these ongoing cases? No? Didn't think so. Moving on.' He pointed. 'Detective Constable Watt.'

Watt's eyes narrowed, little gingery beard bristling. 'What?'

'When I say you're supposed to sign out at the end of a shift, what I mean is: you – have – to sign off – at the end – of a shift. Not: "Do whatever the monkey-spanking hell you like." Am I getting through to you? Knock once for yes, twice for no.'

'It wasn't—'

'Don't even bother – I checked. And I don't *care* how you did things in G Division, in O Division you clock off!' He pointed. 'Don't think I won't pull down your pants and spank you in front of the rest of the class.'

Watt's face went redder than his beard.

'Exactly.' McAdams rubbed his hands together. 'Now, children mine, police divine, / Tell me, what do you propose, / Our mystery to diagnose? DS Hodgkin?'

Dotty nodded. 'Rosalind and I are heading up the infirmary to see if we can get any sense out of Brett Millar.'

'Good: feel free to lean on the medical staff. I want a statement off Millar, A.S.A.F.P. Emphasis on the F. And that leaves naughty DCs Watt and MacGregor to canvas every smokehouse in the district. And not just phone calls: I want boots on the ground and signed statements.'

Callum sagged in his seat.

Why did God hate him? Wasn't sacrificing a quarter of his ear enough?

'After that, you can start on Dr McDonald's list: pubs and nightclubs where Ben Harrington, Glen Carmichael, and Brett Millar might have met Imhotep. Start from whatever's nearest the flat they were renovating and work your way out. Probably the Dockmaster's Yard? Let's see if we can't progress the plot a bit today.'

Watt folded his arms. 'I work better on my *own*. Why don't I take the smokehouses and leave the pubs to MacGregor?'

McAdams smiled and fluttered his eyelashes. 'Because I don't want you to be lonely, Detective Constable, that's why. Now off you trot like a good little boy and let's not have any nonsense about you two not playing nice. OK?' A nod. 'OK.'

Mother clapped her hands. 'And that's your lot. Keep me and Andy updated as you go. Class dismissed.'

As everyone else filed out Watt folded forward, elbows on his knees, head held in his hands.

Thanks for the vote of confidence.

'If it's any consolation, Watt, I'm not too thrilled being lumbered with *you* either.'

He stayed where he was.

Fine.

Callum reached into his jacket pocket and produced the lemon yellow tie, all soft and slippery. 'Right, I've got to go see DCI Powel. In the meantime, do you want to get a list of smokehouses together? Or are you just going to sit there wallowing in your sulk?'

Nothing.

Oh today was going to be lovely.

He wandered out into the corridor. Down the end to the stairs. Clumped his way up to the fourth floor.

The Major Investigation Team had the whole level to themselves, complete with multiple meeting rooms, a series of open-plan offices with swish computers and new furniture, their own mini canteen... All right for some.

Most of the rooms bustled with uniform and plainclothes officers, making phone calls and writing things on whiteboards, tapping away at keyboards that didn't look as if they'd fallen off the ark.

The second door from the end was ajar, its brass plaque polished to a high sheen: 'DETECTIVE CHIEF INSPECTOR REECE POWEL ~ MIT'.

Callum went to knock, then stopped – knuckles half an inch from the wood – as Powel's voice growled out from inside:

'*No, Anita, I don't. ... Because I don't, that's why. ... No, you listen to me for a change: marriage counselling didn't work, the second honeymoon didn't work, salsa classes didn't work. I've had enough. Enough of your sniping and your complaining and your nasty little comments. I've had enough of you poisoning my own children against me.*'

Yeah. Probably shouldn't be eavesdropping on this. Still.

'*You know what? Cry all you like. It's over, Anita. ... No: it's over, because I deserve better than this. I deserve better than you.*'

He had a quick check the corridor was still empty.

'*Of course I am, why do you think I packed a bag? I'll be round for the rest of my things in a couple of days, and if you even think of touching anything, I'll do you for destruction of private property. Are we clear? ...*'

203

You better believe I will – they'll march you out of there in handcuffs.
.... I don't care: my lawyer will be in touch. ... No, you know what, Anita?
You go screw yourself. Christ knows I never want to again.'

Then a clattering thump.

Presumably that would be Mr Telephone Handset being forcibly
reconciled with Mrs Base Unit.

OK.

Count to five, and knock.

Silence.

Callum pushed the door open. 'Guv?'

Powel was behind his desk, face a threatening cloud of red and
fury, glaring at the desk phone. Hands curled into fists either side of
it, as if weighing up the pros and cons of smashing it into tiny little
bits.

It was a pretty nice office, with a view out across the rooftops and
up the hill towards the castle. The spire of St Jasper's, in the middle
distance, jabbing at the low clouds. Big wooden desk, a pot plant fern
thing, filing cabinets bereft of dents and scratches, framed certificates
and news clippings on the walls, a whiteboard broken up into rows and
columns full of neat little letters. A small couch, two chairs, and a coffee
table. Very swanky.

'Guv?' Callum held up the tie. 'I think you left this at our house.'

He pulled his face up and round, clenched like his fists. His cheeks
darkened even more. 'Constable MacGregor.'

'Elaine thought it was mine.' Callum laid the tie on the desk.

'I see.' He uncoiled a hand and picked the thing up. Slipped it into
his pocket. Looked somewhere else. 'And how much of that did
you hear?'

Innocent face. 'How much of what, Guv? I just walked up and saw
your door was open. Took a chance on you being in.'

'Right. Yes.'

'Can I ask a favour? Not for me, for Elaine.'

Powel took a deep breath. Hissed it out. Then sat back in his seat.
'I'm listening.'

'We've been getting silent phone calls. And someone *might* have
followed me home last night. After what you said about Dugdale, I
thought, just in case, if we could put a grade one flag on the flat?' A
shrug. 'Probably nothing, but if Dugdale does try anything and I'm not
there...'

'Yes. Of course.' Still not making eye contact. 'How is—'

A knock on the door and one of Powel's minions stuck his head in. All short-back-and-sides, baggy eyes, and sunken cheeks. An Aberdonian accent you could stun a sheep with at fifty paces. 'Sorry, Boss, but we've got a nine-nine-niner. Some wee wifie's turned up a heid in a shoppin' baggie.'

Powel stared at him. 'A head, in a *carrier bag*?'

'Aye, hacked off at the neck and dumped in Holburn Forest aff nae far frae een o' the car parks. Div yis want ta gan oot and see it in situ?'

'God almighty...' He curled forward until his forehead rested on his desk organiser, talking into the interlocking biro doodles. 'Get a pool car, I'll be down in a minute. And get the pathologist as well. And the SEB. And a PolSA. And DS Blake. And about a dozen search-trained officers to do a fingertip.'

'Aye, Boss.' DC Teuchter pulled a face at Callum, then ducked back out into the corridor and shut the door behind him.

Powel didn't move. 'It never just rains, does it? No, it has to sodding *bucket* down.' He looked as if someone had driven over him, then reversed a couple of times to make sure he was never getting up again.

Maybe Elaine was right? Maybe Powel was doing his best?

Callum cleared his throat. 'Are you OK?'

'Never better.' A sigh. Then he sat up in his seat. Made a note on a Post-it and stuck it to his monitor. 'OK: grade one flag on your flat in case Dugdale goes after Elaine. Anything else?'

'Actually...' OK, so it wasn't very ethical to take advantage of the man when he'd just split up from his wife, but nothing ventured: 'Don't suppose you've got any pull with the IT Lab, do you?'

Mother blinked at him. 'You're kidding...'

'I'm not.' Callum grinned. 'Probably a once in a lifetime thing, but if we go right now we might get it done before he changes his mind.'

She stared at him, then the Lego man flash drive in its evidence bag, then back to him again. 'Quick as you like.' Her chair juddered back on squeaky wheels and she was off, out of her office and marching down the corridor, pulling out her phone and fiddling with the screen. 'Andy, it's Mother. Callum's got Powel to— ... No, of course I'm not checking up on you. But while I've got you, how's it going? ... Oh, OK. ... No, no we're fine. You stay where you are, that's much more impor-tant. Listen to the nice doctors. ... Yes. ... Yes I will. ... OK, bye.'

They pushed through the double doors to the stairwell. Waited for the lift to creak and grind its way down from the top floor. When the doors dinged open, they revealed a filing cabinet and a stack of file boxes abandoned in the middle of the lift. Like it was a cupboard.

Mother squeezed inside anyway. 'Room up top for a small one.'

Urgh... He forced his way in, pressed hard up against the filing cabinet.

She thumbed the button for the sub-basement. 'Does it hurt?' Pointing as the doors groaned shut and the lift juddered into life. 'The ear?'

'Yes.'

'Brett Millar *does* seem to like biting things, doesn't he?' She dug a little paper bag from her pocket. 'Have a jelly baby, it'll make you feel better.'

It probably wouldn't, but Callum took one anyway.

They stood and chewed in silence, squeezed in like beans in a tin.

Yeah, this was comfortable.

Now Mother's breath smelled of strawberries. 'I think it would be nice if we got a card for Andy. Wish him well with his chemotherapy. Maybe get him a cake or something?'

Because that would make *all* the difference.

Mother popped another jelly baby, humming a happy tune as she munched.

For God's sake, how long did it take a lift to get to the sub-basement?

Callum shuffled his feet.

Stared at the numbers changing on the display above the doors.

Ding.

He was first out, popping into the dull grey corridor like a cork from a bottle.

Mother marched out through the double doors and into the warren of corridors and rooms that lurked deep below O Division Headquarters.

He followed her through the maze to a black door with a plastic plaque with 'Forensic IT Lab' on it.

She wiggled her fingers, as if she was limbering up to play the piano. 'Remember: I do the talking.' Then pushed through the door.

Callum followed her into a room crammed floor-to-ceiling with metal shelving racks, each one packed with computers, laptops, and cardboard boxes with cables poking out of them. More boxes, hundreds and hundreds of them, each the size of a paperback book, were stuffed into the racks, six or seven deep. A workbench sat against the wall by the door, with a row of computer monitors mounted above it and more dangling cables.

A thin woman in a once-white lab coat was hunched over a netbook, tapping away at the keyboard with purple-nitrile fingers. Tongue poking out the side of her mouth. Glasses balanced on the end of a long straight nose.

Mother knocked on the wall and she flinched hard enough to make her wheelie office chair trundle back from the bench.

'Aaargh...' Mrs Thin turned and scowled. 'Don't *do* that!'

'Ruby, this is DC MacGregor. We need you to access whatever's on here.' She held up the evidence bag with the Lego man flash drive in it.

The woman in the lab coat raised both eyebrows, then burst out laughing. 'You're kidding, right? Of *course* you're kidding. Do you have any idea how many bits of electronica are in the queue ahead of you? Let me give you a clue, Flora, it's *hundreds*.' She spun her chair around and waved at the little paperback-sized boxes. 'I've got nearly a thousand mobile phones in here, not to mention everything else. And every time your lot arrest someone another lump gets added to the pile.'

Mother placed the evidence bag on the countertop. 'I know, but we've had the nod from DCI Powel: he wants this bumped to number one priority.'

Ruby's eyes narrowed. 'Oh yes?'

'Yes. It's all been cleared with Cecelia too, you can give her a call if you like. Check.'

She reached for the phone on the desk, then froze. 'This is on the up?'

'Cross my bypassed heart and hope to die.'

That thin pink tongue slithered out between her lips and Ruby picked up the evidence bag instead. 'OK. I guess I can spare five minutes.'

She scooted her chair down a couple of monitors and clicked an ancient black laptop into life. 'We'll run it on a virtual machine, just in case it's chocka with viruses.' She scribbled an entry into a form, copying down all the info from the bag, then pulled the Lego man's legs off and stuck his exposed connector into the side of the laptop. 'Any idea what we're looking for?'

'Not a sausage.'

The machine whirred and clicked.

Mother lowered her voice. 'I like your hair, by the way. Very nice. Frames your face.'

'I was thinking of going blonde.'

'Oh, no. Auburn suits you much better.'

A window appeared on the screen.

'Here we go.' Ruby fiddled with the mouse. 'Looks like it's password protected, so let's see what Aunty Ruby's box of magical tricks can do...' More fiddling. 'Edward Snowden didn't know the half of it.'

Numbers and dialogue boxes flashed in and out of existence.

Mother perched herself on the only other chair in the room. 'So, are you still seeing Charlie from the Finance Team?'

'Not for ages. He was a bit...' She pulled a face. 'I didn't mind the spanking so much, but the PVC all-in-one suit did terrible things for my dermatitis.'

'Spanking?'

'Well it seemed to make him happy, though God knows how he managed to sit down the next day for work. Men are funny creatures, aren't they?' A quick glance at Callum. 'Sorry, but it's true.'

The screen flickered with more boxes. Numbers. Lines. Boxes. Numbers. Lines.

Then the whole thing cleared, leaving a dialogue box.

Ruby hunched over the keyboard, tongue poking out again, and clattered her fingers across the keys. Sat back and smiled. 'Why people never use proper encryption is beyond me. Have you got a clean drive?' She held out her hand and Callum dropped a plain grey USB stick onto her palm. 'Thank you kindly.' It went into the slot next to Mr Lego.

Lights flickered on the stick.

'Just take a minute.'

Mother smiled. 'Next time I bake, you're getting brownies.'

'Brownies are good.' The machine pinged and she pulled out the USB stick. Handed it to Mother. 'You want a quick squint while you're here?'

'What's on it?'

The mouse clicked. 'Looks like we've got a bunch of video files and some word docs. Let's try ... this one.' She clicked on an icon in the shape of a piece of film and a new window filled the screen. Black as it loaded. Then...

Mother's eyes widened. 'Oh.'

Callum hissed out a breath. 'Bloody hell.'

But Ruby just nodded. 'Now *there's* something you don't see every day.'

30

Oh God, they were *completely* going to die here. Ashlee sniffed back a drip, mouth a trembly wobbling line, cheeks wet with tears. Eyes darting back and forth, pulling shapes from the darkness. How was this fair? How come it couldn't happen to Marline instead? How couldn't *she* be the one chained up in here? At least Marline would've deserved it!

Another wave of shivers rattled its way through Ashlee, making the water ripple.

Gah. If it *was* water. The stuff smelled like piss and vinegar and that manky potpourri Mum brought back from Barcelona on her last holiday with 'Uncle Eddy', before he realised how utterly a slob she was.

A metal tank full of cold piss and vinegar and manky potpourri. Like the world's crappiest hot tub.

Ashlee gulped in a big shuddery breath. 'Mum?' Her voice was tiny, high-pitched like a mouse or something. 'Mummy?'

She craned her neck to the side, pushing it as far as it would go, till the chains dug into her skin. 'Mummy, I don't feel so good...'

But Mum didn't move. She just sat there, with her back against the wooden slats, the chain around her neck tight from there to the wall, because she'd slumped a bit to one side. All naked and pale and bloaty.

The bruising was getting worse. It wrapped all the way over the left of her face, dark and purple in the gloom.

The bandages around her hands and wrists were spotted with red and yellow, arms dangling loose at her sides.

'Mummy?'

Ashlee's head fell back, making a dull ringing noise when it hit the metal tub.

They were completely going to die here. Alone and hungry and thirsty, in some crappy wooden room that *stank* like a chimney fire.

Quiet little sobs popped and crackled from her mouth.

Why couldn't it be Marline?

'Shhhh...' A voice in the dark.

Ashlee froze, eyes widening till it was like they'd pop free or something. 'Please. Please don't hurt me.'

'I'm not going to hurt anyone.' He stepped closer, settled his backside on the edge of the metal tub. Almost invisible in the gloom, like he was a ghost or something. Hands pale as a dead fish. But his voice was all, you know, warm and cheery – like he was a drama teacher or a kindly relative or something, instead of completely a psycho. 'I bet you're thirsty. And cold and tired and lonely. You *must* be hungry.'

She shrank back, but the chains wouldn't let her go any further. 'I'll scream.'

'That's OK: I've got a few minutes before I head back to work.' He put his fingers in his ears. 'You go ahead if it makes you happy.'

So she did. Long and loud and hard. Over and over till her throat was sandpaper raw and her head rang from the noise.

Ashlee slumped back in the filthy water, panting.

'There we go. Was that good?'

'Please don't...'

'Here, this'll make you feel better.' He pulled one of those plastic sports-bottle things from his jacket, the kind with a pop-up top so you can drink and cycle at the same time. He held it out. 'It's herbal water. It will cleanse away your sins. You'll be pure and free.' Gave the bottle a shoogle. 'You want to be cleansed, don't you?'

Ashlee stared past him, at Mum with her chains and her bruises. 'I want my mummy.'

'Come on, you need to keep your strength up. You're going to be a god.'

'If you let me go... If you let me go, I *promise* I won't tell anyone. I swear! Just let me go and—'

'Drink.'

'You can keep my mum! Let me go and she'll be *completely* grateful. Mum's like utterly dirty and—' The slap snapped Ashlee's head to one side. Leaving her face stinging.

'Shhh...' He stroked her hair with his free hand. 'New Mummy isn't dirty. New Mummy will keep us all safe and warm and loved, with her pretty yellow hair and soft cosy lap. New Mummy loves us.'

'You're off your mental nut. We… Just let us go, yeah? *Please.*'

'Don't you want to be a god?' He held the bottle to her lips.

'GET OFF ME!' She flinched back, till the chains yanked tight. 'You're completely a psycho! You're utterly and complete— Ulk.'

He grabbed her face with his other hand, fingers digging into her cheeks, forcing her jaws open. Jamming the sports bottle in and squeezing. Bitter cold water flooded her mouth, full of bits and yuck and no way in hell was she swallowing that crap.

The chains clanged and rattled as she grabbed at his wrists. Sobbing. The whole front of her face burst into flames, burning from the inside out, as that horrible water burst out of her nostrils.

He grabbed her nose and squeezed it shut. Forced more water into her mouth. 'I know it's nasty, but it *is* necessary. You *have* to drink it.' Held on tight. 'You want to be a god, don't you? You want people to worship you?'

Her fingertips scrabbled at his forearms. 'Ghhhhhhhaghhh!'

'Shhhh…' He dropped the bottle and forced her mouth shut again, keeping everything inside. 'It'll all be fine. You just drink up.'

Ashlee bucked and thrashed, sending water slopping over the edge of the tank.

Can't breathe.

Can't breathe.

CAN'T BREATHE.

So she did the only thing she could do: she swallowed the horrible bitter water.

He let go of her face. 'There's a good girl.' Smiled as she coughed and retched. Then scooped the plastic bottle out of the tub. 'One mouthful down, six more to go.'

Oh God…

The walls pulsed and groaned, twisting round through ninety degrees before snapping back into place and twisting again. And again. And again. Like hammering back a quarter bottle of Marline's gran's voddy in one go. No coke or nothing.

Ashlee blinked, screwing her face up tight. Bared her teeth.

Don't be sick, OK? Not again.

The bits were still floating all around her from last time. Because the manky bathtub water wasn't bad enough.

His voice came from a long way away, echoing and slow. 'How are you feeling?'

She could barely turn her head, it weighed *so* much. 'Gnffffmmmmmnt...'
Why wouldn't her mouth work?

'Good.' His face swam in and out of focus, pulsing in time with the
walls. 'I envy you so much. You're going to be a god. Isn't that great?'

'Plnnnnssss...' Her chest was full of rats. Rats and seagulls. And bees.
Scrabbling and flapping and buzzing deep inside her.

'They'll worship you and you'll save them, because you'll be a god.'

Rats, seagulls, and bees.

His voice faded away. 'I have to go to work, but I'll be back to check
on you. That'll be nice, won't it?' Faded away until there was nothing
left but the noises in her chest. Scrabbling, flapping, and buzzing.

'They'll worship you: you'll be a god.'

A hole opened up in the base of Ashlee's skull, and the whole world
fell through it...

It's her eighth birthday, and all she wants is a pretty princess cake and
the new Nerf Elite Hail-Fire blaster, cos you can shoot *a hundred and
forty-four* darts seventy-five feet. Which is as long as a swimming pool.
And it would be utterly cool, cos Marline's got an Alpha Trooper CS-18
and that only holds eighteen darts.

But what Ashlee's got is Mum and Dad screaming at each other
downstairs in the living room.

She sits on the edge of her bed, picking at the scabs on her left knee.
Peeling away the hard bits of skin, making the shiny pink under it bleed.

Then there's a thump and a crash and the sound of heavy feet on
the stairs.

Dad throws her door open. 'You. Downstairs. *Now.*'

'But—'

'NOW!' He's bigger than a bear, teeth all shiny, and eyes like burned
things. Hands like crushers as he grabs her arm and pulls her out onto
the landing. Drags her down the stairs. Shoves her through into the
living room.

A blue and red smear is all that's left of her Princess Merida cake,
sagging its way down the wallpaper by the window. The coffee table's
cracked and broken. Mum's on the carpet next to it, on her hands and
knees. Sobbing.

'Tell her!' Dad spits on the back of mum's head. 'TELL HER WHAT
YOU DID!'

'I'm sorry. I'm so sorry.' Her pretty yellow dress is all ripped up the
side, showing off blotchy purple-and-yellow skin.

Dad drops down to one knee and pulls Ashlee round, so she's got no choice but to look into those burned-thing eyes. 'Because of your slut mother, I'm going to have to go away. That's *her* fault. She's making me leave.'

Ashlee doesn't say anything, just stands very still.

'I wanted to take you with me, and you could be my little princess, and we'd have adventures all over the world, and we'd be together forever.' He smiles like broken glass. 'But your mother's spoiled it. And I'm going to have to leave you here. With *her*. And I want you to know, it's *all* her fault. You could be happy, but she won't let you.'

And then he stands and sweeps out of the house like a storm, crackling lightning and thunder, slamming the front door behind him.

Ashlee bites her bottom lip.

All she wanted was a princess cake and a Nerf Elite Hail-Fire blaster.

Mum cries and moans. 'I'm sorry...'

Then Ashlee blinks away tears, turns, and goes back upstairs to her bedroom.

Slams the door.

Just like her dad.

Marline swallows, shudders, and passes the bottle of voddy. Hisses out a breath. 'Gaghh...'

Ashlee takes a swig. God, it's *horrible*. The stuff makes her teeth itch and her mouth fizz, numbing her tongue before she forces it down. Hot and burning. 'Ghaaaa...' She shakes her head from side to side as her eyeballs pop and crackle.

Then it hits her stomach like burning petrol, spreading its fire through her whole body.

Marline pops one shoulder up till it's pressing against her ear. 'Smooth.'

The car park's empty, all the little people headed home for the night. Now there's nothing left but empty spaces and security lights. All the shutters are down on the shopping centre's windows.

Ashlee swings her feet back and forward, back and forward, holding onto the railing with her other hand. 'What you wanna do?'

'Dunno.' Marline takes another scoof of voddy. Shudders. 'Ghaaa...' Holds the bottle out. 'Ooh: you know Peter, right? Sits behind me in English?'

Oh yes. Peter with his squinty eye and his funny teeth. Peter with 'Assassin's Creed' printed across his school rucksack in flaky enamel paint.

Ashlee helps herself to another mouthful. 'Yurrrrgh...' The warm numbness is getting bigger. Stuff isn't *brilliantly* revolting when you get used to it.

'Well, Peter completely wants to go to Dougie's party with me.'

'Pfff...' She closes her eyes and listens to them crackle. 'Yeah, that's how it starts. "Oh, go to the party with me. I love you so much." Next thing you know he's trying to finger you in his dad's shed and if you say no he'll tell everyone you're a frigid bitch.'

'Peter?' Marline's voice wobbles, that one word catching and tearing like damp toilet paper.

Ashlee puts the bottle down and wraps her arm around Marline. Gives her a hug. 'No. I'm sure Peter's not like that.' Even though he probably is. They all are.

'Oh, yes, that's *very* pretty.' Uncle Eddie folds his arms and looks her up and down. Smiles like a crocodile. 'Very pretty indeed.' He licks his lips. 'Now, why don't you try on the red one again?'

The city's spread out before them like burning jewels in the darkness. It's not even that cold, perched up here on the edge of the old castle wall, legs dangling over the edge. Way below, the dual carriageway is a ribbon of streetlights, taxis, and the odd bus. Wouldn't think it was nearly Halloween.

Peter turns to her, with his wonky eye and his funny teeth. 'Are you sure it'll be OK?'

Ashlee swaps the half bottle of Smirnoff to her other hand, then reaches over and cups her hand around the crotch of his trousers. What's inside is hard like a spanner. 'You chicken?'

'But Marline—'

'Marline's an utter munter.' She parts her lips and leans in. 'And I'm *mint*.'

Off in the distance, an airplane roars into the October sky.

The ground rushes up, closer and faster and she's screaming a broken-bottle scream and—

Ashlee fights her way up through the duvet, till she's sitting up, dripping with sweat. Shivering and shaking. Mouth hanging open so she can haul in deep juddery breaths.

Gah...

Just a nightmare. Nothing to worry ... about.

There's someone in her room!

She grabs the bedclothes and pulls them up to her chin, scrambling backwards till she thumps into the headboard.

It's Uncle Eddie. Smiling. Her old manky teddy bear sitting in his lap. Covering things while he zips himself up. 'Sweetheart.' He leans forward. 'It's OK, you were having a bad dream. I wanted to make sure you were all right. You're all right, right?'

Ashlee nods.

'Good. Now, you lie down and go back to sleep and I'll stay here to make sure no monsters get you.'

Too late.

''Snot … 'snot fair…' Marline's back heaves as she spatters out this massive flood of Bacardi, all mushed up with a shared poke of chips. 'Hurrrrrgkkk…'

Ashlee rolls her eyes, both hands full of her best friend's hair. Keeping it out of the way as she chucks away perfectly good rum. 'You're too good for him, Marly. He's completely a wanker.'

'How could he … could he… With *her*! Hurrrrrrrgkkkk…'

Because he was a man and that's what men did.

And he wasn't even all that good at it.

'I'm not eating this *slop*!' Ashlee grabs the plate in front of her and flips it up and off the table, sending it spinning till it clatters against the kitchen floor and shatters into three jagged chunks, spraying disgusting spaghetti bolognese everywhere.

Like she's going to eat that?

Spaghetti bolognese? How much fat and carbs are in that? Millions, that's how much.

One hundred and ten percent revolting.

Mum just sits there, bottom lip trembling. Look at the lardy cow cry: big fat tears rolling down her big fat cheeks.

Ashlee stands. 'No wonder no one loves you.'

Little waves lapped the walls of the tub, sloshing the filthy water around as Ashlee sobbed.

The man with blue eyes lied: she wasn't going to be a god. She couldn't be. She was a *monster*. And no amount of bitter water was going to change that.

Why did she have to be so horrible to Marline?

Why did she have to be so horrible to Mum?

To Peter. To everyone…

Spoiled and vile and horrible.

And now she was alone. In a rusty metal tank, in a manky smoky room, with nothing but the darkness and the cold and the itchy feeling in the pit of her stomach for company.

The seagulls and bees were gone – no more buzzing, no more flapping, leaving her innards full of rats.

Any minute they'd wake up and gnaw their way out of her, turning the dirty water a nasty shade of scarlet.

When did she eat the rats?

Why did she eat them?

Ashlee craned her neck round again.

Mum hadn't moved: still slumped against her chains, arms hanging loose at her sides, bruises ripe and dark.

'Mummy?' Ashlee kept her voice down so the rats wouldn't wake up. 'Mummy? Don't let them kill me…'

But Mum didn't answer, because Mum was probably dead.

Selfish cow.

31

'So?' Watt stared at him from the passenger seat.

'So what?'

The pool car thrummed over the cobbles, lurched across a disused set of railway lines, windscreen wipers making a squealing harmony with the screeching gulls.

'You know very well what: what was on that flash drive?'

Callum shuddered. 'I'd rather not think about it.'

The Logansferry docks probably didn't feature in Oldcastle's tourist brochures. It wasn't quaint and old-fashioned like the Kettle Docks across the river – with its gaily coloured wee boats and fishermen's huts – instead it was a rigid grid of huge grey slab-fronted warehouses and chandlers' yards ringed with chain-link fences and barbed wire. Hordes of camera-toting tourists didn't come here, even if they'd managed to get past the security gates they'd end up squashed beneath a forklift truck, articulated lorry, or shipping container.

Watt folded his arms even tighter. 'Don't tell me then.'

'Imagine the most horrible porn you've ever heard of, double it, and add a collection of dogs and farmyard animals. Gah...' The shudder worked its way from the back of one hand, all the way across his shoulders and down the other side. 'I'm never singing "Old MacDonald Had a Farm" ever again.'

'So absolutely *no* help on the case.'

'Thanks for making it sound as if that's *my* fault.' Callum took the next turning, along a narrow strip of cobbles. On the left, a waist-high wall separated the road from the river, nothing on the other side of it until the grey lump of Kingsmeath reared up the hill. Ancient stone buildings lined the right-hand side of the road, squat and solid, with

217

rust-reddened corrugated iron roofs and heavy steel doors. He pulled up outside one, two thirds of the way down. 'This is us.'

It had the standard barn-style sliding door, painted a faded blue with 'MEARNS FINE FISH PRODUCTS LTD' in chipped white paint the width of the building.

Watt undid his seatbelt. 'I'm only going to say this once: you are not going to cock this up, do you understand? I will lead the questioning, you will keep your mouth shut and don't touch anything.'

Callum turned in his seat. 'Tell me, *Constable*, exactly who the hell do you think you are, ordering me about?'

'I'm the police officer who doesn't take bribes to let murderers go free.' He climbed out of the car and slammed the door shut.

Oh no you don't.

Callum clambered out and slammed his own door. The air was heavy with the oily reek of raw diesel and rotting fish. Rain bounced off the pool car's roof and bonnet. 'You know what, you gingery-pube-bearded sack of wank? I've never taken a bribe in my *life!*' He marched around the car, closing the distance. Balling his hands into fists. 'And I am sick and tired of snide sneery comments from arseholes like you.'

Watt looked him up and down. Then stepped back. 'Big Johnny Simpson walked, because of you.'

'IT WAS A SODDING MISTAKE, OK?' He thrust his arms out. 'Have you never cocked anything up in your life? Are you so *buggering* perfect?'

The bleep-bleep-bleep of a vehicle reversing cut through the gulls' lament.

Behind Watt, the Kings River was a twisted swathe of pewter, dull grey in the rain. Cars on the other side had their headlights on. And up above the sky was the colour of ash.

'Well?'

A shrug. 'You expect me to believe that you didn't take *any* money from Big Johnny Simpson?'

Callum turned his back. 'Go screw yourself.'

The cobbles were slippery, so he picked his way across them to the big steel door, grabbed the cold metal handle and hauled it back far enough to let out the deep smoky tang of burning wood. Stepped into the gloom.

'Hello?'

The room was easily big enough to park a couple of buses in. Racks along the walls, pallets of boxes in the middle, what looked like a large walk-in cold room on one side with another one beside it. Puddles dotted the damp concrete floor.

'ANYONE IN?'

He worked his way through the boxes to a small office with a grubby window overlooking the warehouse. A thickset woman was behind the desk, wearing a hairnet, heavy-duty white plastic apron, and a bright red fleece. She waved at him and pointed to the phone in her other hand.

Fair enough.

The door rumbled shut, then Watt appeared at his elbow. 'You're a bit touchy, aren't you?'

Callum kept his eyes on the woman. 'You can talk. All you've done since you got here is moan.'

No reply.

Then Watt puffed out a breath. 'I did the right thing, and I got shafted for it. Half my team were on the take and when I went to Professional Standards do you know what happened? Suddenly *I* was the bad guy.' He folded his arms, tight. 'How is that fair?'

'Yeah, that's pretty crappy.'

'Oh, crappy doesn't even *begin* to cover it.'

The woman in the office threw back her head and laughed, setting quite a lot of things wobbling.

Watt shifted his feet. 'And just in case you're thinking this is some sort of bonding moment, it isn't. I'm telling you what happened to make it perfectly clear: I don't like bent cops. I *hate* them.'

'How many times do I have to say this? Eh? How can I make it any clearer? I – didn't – take – any—'

'Aye?' The office door opened and she peered out at them through a pair of black-rimmed glasses. 'Can I help you?'

Watt pulled his warrant card and thrust it under her nose for a second. 'Detective Constable Watt. I'm here to examine your premises.'

She raised an eyebrow. 'Oh aye?'

'And I'll need a list of your employees.'

'Will you now?'

He checked his watch. 'Soon as you like. We've got seven other smokehouses to visit today, so…?'

She folded her arms, making the fleece bulge. There was a lot of muscle in there – probably all that humping heavy boxes of fish about. 'So what?'

Watt leaned in close. 'So: chop, chop.'

Great.

Because *that* was how you got the public on your side.

'Actually,' Callum produced his own warrant card, nice and gentle, 'what my colleague *meant* to say was, we really need your help. Any chance you can show us around and answer a few questions?'

Watt stiffened. 'Thank you, Constable, but *I'm* dealing with this.'

'Please forgive him. He's been in a bad mood ever since he got back from the doctor. They can't do anything about his frighteningly small penis, and it's upset him a bit.'

'What?' Watt wheeled around, mouth pinched, eyes bugged, face darkening.

The woman in the plastic pinny burst out laughing. Then slapped Callum on the back, hard enough to send him staggering. '"Frighteningly small penis." Aye, he looks the type.'

'Hey!'

'Come on, I'll show you around. You too, Wee Willy Winky.'

Watt hurled himself into the passenger seat and slammed the car door.

A bunch of seagulls had taken it upon themselves to respray the windscreen and bonnet with grey and white spatters. All streaked in the rain.

Callum got in behind the wheel. Started her up and set the wipers going, turning the glass opaque. 'Who's next on the list?'

And explosion in five, four, three, two—

Watt thumped his hand down on the dashboard. 'WHAT THE BLOODY HELL DO YOU THINK YOU'RE PLAYING AT?'

A pull of the squooshers sent two streams of blue foamy liquid into the smears, thinning them. 'Are we having a grump?'

'How *dare* you tell that woman I have a small penis!'

'Well, you were acting like a massive dick, so I thought I'd even things out a bit.' The windscreen was almost clear, so Callum pulled back onto the road. Going slow as the wipers made gaps in the seagulls' art.

'You can sodding well—'

'Know what? I don't think people won't work with you because you clyped on your old team – I think they won't work with you because you're crap at the job.'

'You completely undermined me back there—'

'She wasn't going to tell you anything, Watt. You spoke to her like she needed scraping off your shoe, how was that going to help? You're rubbish at talking to people.'

220

'I AM SODDING NOT!'

'Marching in there like the King of Dickland. Look at me, I'm so important!'

'I'm going to report you.' Watt thumped back in his seat. 'Soon as we get back to DHQ, I'm putting in a formal complaint.'

'You can't treat people like that and expect them to *help* you, you idiot.'

They'd barely gone a hundred yards before the next smokehouse appeared in the row of ancient buildings. 'OLDCASTLE SMOKED SEAFOOD SPECIALITIES ~ FABULOUS FISH AT ITS FINEST' boasted a slick plastic hoarding above a stainless-steel set of double doors.

'I'm a *police* officer.'

Callum parked outside the front. 'I'm sorry, OK? I'm sorry I told her about your minute genitalia, but if you keep on acting like that people are going to assume it's microscopic anyway. At least this way we got a list of every staff member and their rota for the last month.'

The smokehouse had a separate glazed door for enquiries and what looked like a wee factory shop inside.

He undid his seatbelt. 'Are you coming, or are you staying here to sulk?'

Watt scowled at him. 'God, I *hate* you.'

'Course you do. That's because you're jealous of my jumbo-sized penis.' Callum climbed out, grinned at the rain-dulled river, then turned and hurried in through the glazed door.

After a beat, Watt slammed his car door and thumped after him.

SCALLOWAY HADDIES
(OLD-FASHIONED, HONEST, & BEST)
Unit 4, Harbour Road, Logansferry

Thick greasy coils of smoke filled the room, curling behind them as they stepped inside.

'And this is where the magic happens.' Mr Smug swept a hand upwards. His white coat almost gleamed in the gloom and so did the white porkpie hat.

Callum stood in the middle of the room and stared straight up.

Rows and rows of fish hung, head-down, above – each one suspended by the tail from stainless-steel poles turned yellow by the smoke. Had to be about a thousand of them in here, vanishing up into the smoky heights.

Three smokehouses in and Watt was still grumping. As if it was Callum's fault he'd been born with the kind of genital appendage that could only be seen with an electron microscope. Wasn't his fault that Watt looked like a tit – one hairnet flattening his floppy fringe, another covering his wispy pube-like beard.

A little oily drip splashed on his shoulder.

Callum turned to Mr Smug. 'Is this area ever left unsupervised?'

'What, the smokehouse?' He curled his top lip. 'Oh no, no, no, no. This is a twenty-four-seven operation: we supply haddies to *Harrods*. The only time we shut down is for five days in January to do a thorough deep clean.'

'How about the nightshift?'

'Three staff on at all times. Like I said, it's a twenty-four—'

'Seven. Yes. Thanks.'

ABERCROMBIE FISHERIES
(TRADITIONAL SMOKED FISH SINCE 1826)
14 Ship Lane, Logansferry

'Oh aye. Aye, aye, aye...' Mrs Lumps hauled an empty plastic box on top of the full one and laid out a layer of split herrings in the bottom with quick fluid movements. Then topped them with a fistful of salt, flung with casual precision. 'We've been smokin' fish here, ooh, since the eighteen hundreds. No me personal like.' She gave Callum a wink that bordered on the obscene, layering up more herring as she went.

'And how many people have access to the smokehouse?'

'Och, just me, Jeemy, and the boy Rodger – that's him in the dungers on the forkie. Big lump that he is.' She waved a handful of salt at a bear of a man in dungarees, driving a forklift truck laden with boxes of ice. 'He's our Siobhan's eldest. Well, it's a family business, ken? Has been since the start.'

'OK, so does—'

'We do a lovely hot smoked salmon with Drambuie, chilli, and lemon zest. Our Hot Toddy Salmon was on the TV, you know. We were a "Food Hero"!'

'Yes, that's great. But could anyone else have access to the smokehouse?'

'Oh I doubt it.' Mrs Lumps gave him a big gap-toothed smile. 'We've got the biggest sodding dog you've ever seen. Take your arms off soon as look at you would our Winston.'

Lennox, Bremner, & Wallace
(Luxury Seafood Specialists)
Unit 2 – 4 Consort Lane, Queen's Quay, Castle Hill

Mr Baldy stuck his hands in his pockets and rocked on his heels. 'And that's it. The grand tour. "*Y daith fawreddog.*" As they say in Welsh.'

Rain hammered down on the large concrete yard, bouncing off the piles of empty fish boxes and refrigerated containers. Made rusty streaks down the ten-foot-high walls that blocked off the outside world. The warm rich smell of smoke wafted out around them, billowing from the open double doors through to the processing plant.

Callum turned. 'Didn't know you were Welsh.'

'I'm not, no. But I *do* like leeks. So...' Shrug.

'Right. Great.' Why was nobody normal any more? 'You got a big staff?'

'Sixty-two last count. Most are part time – we went into this job-share scheme thing, couple years ago, and you wouldn't believe how many single mothers we've got working here now. Had to open a crèche.'

Which explained the Portakabin in the far corner, behind the containers, all covered in characters from *Winnie the Pooh* and *SpongeBob SquarePants*.

Callum shifted back a bit, till he was underneath the roof of the loading bay again. 'How many men?'

'Ooh, now you're asking.' He chewed on the inside of his cheek for a bit. 'Fifteen? No: eighteen. I forgot about Mitch, Spanner, and Dingle.'

'Dingle?'

'Don't ask. And Spanner's not much better. What's the point of employing people if they never turn up? I told, Marge, I told her: we need to fire these idiots, but she's soft as Angel Delight, she is.'

'How many in their mid-twenties?'

Mr Baldy did the cheek-chewing thing again. 'Might help if you told me what this was all about.'

Watt pulled down his beard net. 'Sorry, it's an ongoing investigation so we've got to be a bit discreet.'

Dear Lord, was Wee Willie Wattie *actually* talking to someone like a human being?

'Ah, right. Got you.' Mr Baldy nodded, as if that explained everything. 'I'd have to check the staff records, but I think I can help.'

32

Callum stuck the keys in the ignition and pulled out his phone. 'Hello?'

McAdams' voice drawled into his ear: *'An update I seek, dear Constable Useless, / On Imhotep – killer both nasty and ruthless, / The smokehouses visited, all must be—'*

'Yeah, I get the point. We've done five of the seven smokehouses in Oldcastle: seen round the premises, spoke to the managers, got lists of staff members: when they've been working and where.'

'I had another three verses.'

'Thought you were meant to be busy this morning.'

'If there's one thing you can say about sitting in the Grim Reaper's Soulless Anteroom of Death, with a drip full of poison seeping into your veins, it's that any *distraction is a welcome one. Even talking to a lump of gristle like you. Now: An update I seek, dear Constable—'*

'We've done five, so we've got two more to visit in town, and the one over in Strummuir, but...' He tapped his fingers against the wheel as Watt sagged his way into the passenger side.

'But?'

'I don't know.' From the car park outside Lennox, Bremner, and Wallace, there was a rain-greyed view across the river to Castleview. Left a bit and there was McKinnon Quay with its background of grim council flats. Squint a bit and you could almost make out the one where Benjamin Harrington died, facedown in bathtub full of brine. 'All these places: they have to conform to EU directives and health-and-safety and food standards. They get inspected by Environmental Health Officers – and you know what the Cheese Police are like: they spot anything, they shut you down.' He frowned out at the rain. 'No. These are commercial enterprises working six days a week, minimum. Someone would notice if you stuck a body in their smoker for a fortnight. It'd get in the way of the kippers.'

Watt wiped the water from his face and flicked it into the footwell. 'Who is it?'

'McAdams.'

'*What?*'

'Not you: Watt. Thing is, I think our boy's built his own smoker. Or he's got access to one that doesn't operate any more. Somewhere you can smoke a body for weeks without any chance of it being found.'

'*And that's supposed to help, is it?*'

'Don't know. Even if he's built his own smoker, he'll have to get the wood he burns from somewhere. Lucy down the mortuary reckons it's a mix of beechwood and oak. Maybe we should get in touch with whoever it is sells sawdust and woodchips to smokehouses? See how many sales they make to hobby smokers?'

Watt shook his head. 'If he doesn't have to comply with food standards, he doesn't have to buy commercial-grade sawdust. He can just get a big bag of it from the local sawmill, or someone that does firewood.'

'You get that?'

McAdams made a hrumphing noise. '*Or he could just—*'

'*Andrew!*' A woman's voice in the background: '*What did we say about mobile phones?*'

A scrunching noise, and his voice went all muffled. '*Oh bounteous nymph, I hear thy pleas, / but it's police business, so sod off, please.*'

'*And the "please" on the end's meant to make that all better, is it?*'

'*Yes. Now be a good nurse and see if you can rustle up a cuppa and a biscuit. I'm wasting away here.*' Then McAdams was back at full volume: '*Where was I? Ah, yes: Imhotep doesn't have to buy sawdust at all. He could just get himself a bunch of logs from the forestry commission and make his own.*'

True.

'Worth a try though.' Callum turned the keys, setting the blowers roaring. 'How did Dotty and Franklin get on?'

'*What am I, your secretary? Finish up with the smokehouses, then the pair of you get back to the shop and start chasing up wood suppliers.*'

'But—'

'*That's what you get for interrupting my poem.*'

And he was gone.

BUCHAN'S CATCH
(THE TRUE TASTE OF SCOTLAND'S FINEST FISH)
Buchan House, Brunel Street,
Shortstaine Business Park

Mr Suit held out his hand for the printouts. 'Thank you, Janice. Tell Ted I'd like to see him in the boardroom in ten minutes please.'

'Yes, Mr Telford.' She pivoted on her heels and clacked out of the room, no-nonsense bob swinging in time with her footsteps.

He scanned the paperwork then slid it across the desk to Callum. 'We have a strict vetting policy and rigorous health-and-safety training for all our staff. All references are followed up. Random drug tests. Etcetera, etcetera.' He made circular motions with his hand – like the Queen waving out of a carriage window – showing off two signet rings and a gold bracelet with his name engraved on it: 'NORMAN'.

The view from his office window wasn't really grand enough to justify the floor-to-ceiling glass. It looked out on the factory complex, in all its stainless steel glory. A ballet of forklifts and containers, hoppers of salt and preservatives, a row of industrial units with their processions of raw and smoked fish. And beyond that, a set of grey warehouse buildings with the ScotiaBrand Tasty Chickens logo on them: a smiling rooster making a thumbs-up with his wing, a mini pastoral scene in the circle behind him. Steam coiled up from the slaughterhouse.

'If you turn to the back, Detective Constable, you'll find Appendix B lists everyone we've had to let go over the last six months.'

Callum scanned the names, then passed the list to Watt. 'Any absenteeism?'

'Oh no.' Mr Suit shook his head. 'We disapprove of that kind of thing. My workforce is highly motivated and dedicated to the task of delivering the most cost-efficient smoked fish and fish-derived products to market.'

Sounded lovely.

'Quick question for you: where do you get your wood from, for smoking?'

'For our luxury *undyed* range? I'll have to check with procurement.'

Callum forced a smile. 'Thank you, that'll be a great help.'

He pressed a button on the desk phone. 'Janice? Get me Charlie.'

Callum nodded. 'Take your time.'

Seagulls screamed on the roof opposite, fighting over something grey and slimy.

Mr Short-And-Limpy curled his top lip, staring down at the printout.

It wasn't a big yard, certainly not compared to Buchan's Catch. Barely room for a stack of empty fish boxes; a couple of Calor gas bottles; a big yellow plastic container heaped with reeking bones, heads, and guts; and a garden shed with a set of folding chairs, a wee card table and an overflowing ashtray. The door wide open to let the cigarette smoke out.

Rain danced on the shed roof, making it rattle like a drum.

Barely room for the four of them in here, but it was better than standing out there in the rain.

Mr Short-And-Limpy shrugged. 'No idea.' He passed the sheet of paper to Mr Ageing Hippy. 'What do you think, Chris? Recognise any of them?'

'Hmmm...' A frown. Mr Ageing Hippy took the fag out of his gob and shook his head, setting the dreadlocks swinging. 'Nope, sorry.'

'Well, thanks anyway.' Callum took the printout back. Folded it so the picture of Brett Millar, Benjamin Harrington, and Glen Carmichael didn't get creased. And slipped it into his pocket. 'It's OK, you finish your break: we'll see ourselves out.'

Watt followed him down a dank corridor, past a billowing cloud of bitter wood smoke, and out into the rain again. 'You know this is a five-minute walk from the flat they were doing up on Customs Street, don't you?'

'Yup.' He ducked his head and hurried across the road to the pool car. Plipped open the locks and scrambled inside.

Bleak granite buildings loomed on either side of Admiralty Place. Ancient warehouses with boarded-up windows, five-storey terraces with rust-streaked fronts, the slow whirl of evil seagulls.

A *thump* and Watt was in the passenger side. 'Don't you think it's a bit of a coincidence?'

'Could be. Maybe.' He pulled out his Tupperware box and popped the lid. Today's note was just a message, no picture, no puns: 'I KNOW THINGS HAVE BEEN DIFFICULT, BUT NO MATTER WHAT HAPPENS

I Love You <u>EVEN MORE</u> Than Nutella And Pickles.' He slipped it into his jacket before Watt saw it.

'Oh come off it – there's a smokehouse right here, and up there Ben Harrington's lying in a bath full of brine, waiting his turn to be kippered. And... Can you not do that please?'

'I'm starving, OK?' Callum stared down at the sandwich – cut on the diagonal as if he were royalty – a bag of Asda's own-brand salt and vinegar, and a 'fun-sized' Snickers bar. 'It's well after two, and we've not stopped for lunch yet.' He pulled out one triangular half of the dubious sandwich and sniffed it. There was a faint whiff of mushrooms and a sort of savoury cheesiness.

Watt humphed.

'What?'

He looked out of the window. 'Left mine back at DHQ.'

Ha, ha, ha. Tough.

Callum caught sight of himself in the rear-view mirror.

Don't be a dick.

Ah well...

He held the half-sandwich out. 'Here.'

An articulated lorry grumbled past, hauling a pair of shipping containers.

Watt didn't move.

'I'll take it back if you don't want it.'

'Thanks.' Watt accepted the triangle and took a bite. Chewed. Frowned. 'Erm, what *is* it?'

Callum popped open the crisps, poured them into the Tupperware and stuck it on the dashboard in easy reach of them both. 'The thing is, if they're the ones smoking the bodies, why did they leave him to rot in the bath?'

'I mean, I'm not saying there's anything wrong with it, it's just ... unusual.'

'Why wouldn't you just pop up there one night, after dark, and bring him back for smoking?'

'No, but really: what's *in* this?'

'Why just leave him there?' Callum had a bite of his own half. Wasn't too bad. Maybe Elaine had a point after all? 'Leftover tuna casserole, cheese, and hot sauce.'

'Oh.' More chewing. 'I quite like it. Spicy.' He helped himself to some crisps. Crunched. 'You heard Dr McDonald: Imhotep is a perfectionist. Ben Harrington wasn't properly prepared, so he swells up in the bath as the bacteria get to work. His stomach bursts and he's not good enough to preserve. So Imhotep leaves him where he is.'

'Maybe. Worth checking, anyway.'

Fog gathered on the car windows, turning them opaque.

Callum finished his half. Sooked his fingers clean. 'When I was wee, we used to go on caravan holidays. Mum and dad were mad on them – bundle the family into the car and go live in some field, sleeping in what was basically a large aluminium shed. Eight or nine times a year, every chance they got.'

That got a noncommittal grunt from Watt, as he polished off the last of the crisps.

'Nairn, Banff, Sandend, Findochty – that kind of thing. But the favourite was Lossiemouth. Every year, regular as the swallows, the MacGregors would pack up the Travel Scrabble and migrate to their spiritual home, hauling a caravan.'

'Are you going to eat that Snickers?'

'Yes.' Callum unwrapped it. Sighed. Then cracked it in two. 'Go on then.' Popped his own half in his mouth. 'Every time we went to Lossiemouth we'd charge up and down the beach, go rockpooling, collect seashells. And we always spent at least one day in Elgin. Dad would go see some friends – which was code for the pub – and Mum took Alastair and me to the museum. They've got a Peruvian mummy there.' He frowned. 'All naked and curled up with hands against its chest, and its knees against its hands, and its head bent forward... Used to think it was the most fascinating thing in the world. A real live dead body.'

Watt let out a long contented breath and settled back in his seat. 'I wonder if it's worth checking with the planning department to see if anyone's put in an application to build a new smokehouse?'

'Then one day they had a display all about the guy who donated it to the museum. Turned out that in the area where it came from, the mummies weren't just dead people: they were elevated to the position of gods. That freaked me out. Stood there staring at it for ages.'

'And we should crosscheck all the staff lists, see if anyone's been doing the rounds. I'll get them rattled into a spreadsheet and we can sort them by name, or company, or start and end date. Should be pretty straightforward.'

'It wasn't a dead body, it was a god. I was standing there looking at a genuine, one hundred percent, real live Peruvian *god*. And I couldn't help wondering: what would happen if it woke up?'

Strummuir Smokehouse And Visitor Centre
(From Glen To Sea, Preserving Scotland's Heritage)
19 Chapman Street, Strummuir

Watt coughed. Grimaced. Leaned towards Callum, keeping his voice low. 'Is it just me, or are you getting fed up breathing in smoke?'

'Yup.'

Their guide waved at them to join him in the smokeroom. 'This is the best bit.' Mr Trendy had to be in his forties, far too old to be dressing up in skin-tight jeans and Converse trainers. *Star Wars* characters posed on his right arm, various X-Men on his left, all of them tattooed in bright LOOK AT ME!!! colours. A tweed waistcoat and a T-shirt with a badger on it completed the ensemble. At least he'd hidden his stupid auld-mannie haircut under the obligatory food-hygiene white hat.

Callum stepped through the big wooden doors and onto the concrete floor. Heat radiated off the pile of wood in the middle of the room, sending up tiny orange sparks and a constant barrage of pungent wood smoke. 'Yes. Very good.'

Mr Trendy pointed upwards. 'We don't churn out "product" like the industrial big boys, but hey, who wants to eat chemically dyed fish, stuffed full of preservatives and additives? Not me!'

Racks of hanging fish reached up into the smoky gloom above them, then the sun must have come out, because that grey mass turned a brilliant white, silhouetting the herrings and haddocks and God knew what else.

'We don't even use stainless steel – all our poles are beech, *sustainably* harvested from The Swinney.' He held his arms out, as if he'd just won a marathon. 'Isn't it beautiful?'

'Yes. Very good.'

Mr Trendy led the way back onto the processing floor. 'We think natural materials are *very* important. And it's not just tradition for tradition's sake: the fish tastes better this way. That's why our smoke-house is built from local larch and granite.'

Two men in jeans and T-shirts were layering and salting fish – in wooden boxes, not plastic, of course – listening to some sort of terrible accordion-and-banjo music on a non-traditional and non-sustainable iPod docking station. A walkway ran around the room, about twelve foot up, and a group of cagouled tourists leaned on the handrail, taking selfies with the action in the background. Thrilling.

'And we do a roaring trade in preserving courses for gourmets, gourmands, and the epicurious. But it's not just smoking: it's cheese making, charcuterie, pickling. We're building some wood-fired ovens for a bakery course, if you're interested? Or I run a foraging class, that's always popular – we don't have many hedgerows, but there's mushrooms, nuts, berries, sorrel, wild garlic?'

Watt dug the printout of Glen Carmichael, Brett Millar, and Ben Harrington from his pocket and held it out. 'Do you recognise any of these men?'

'Hmm...' Some heavy duty frowning. 'I think, maybe this one? On the end with the ink? Sure I've seen him somewhere.'

'What about your staff?'

'I don't know if they'd recognise them, I can ask though?'

Watt gave him a smile. 'Please.'

Mr Trendy marched off with the printout.

As soon as he was out of earshot, Watt lowered his voice again. 'What do you reckon?'

'Definitely has that hipster thing going on. Dr McDonald said he'd be able to blend in with Glen, Ben, and Brett. He's definitely got access to a smokehouse. *And* he recognised Brett Millar.'

A nod. 'I think Darth Wolverine just became Suspect Number One.'

'Darth Wolverine?'

'You know, because of the tattoos? *Star Wars, X-Men*?'

'Oh.' Callum shrugged. 'I was calling him Mr Trendy.'

Someone else in jeans and T-shirt lumbered in, pushing a hand truck stacked up with more wooden boxes. Short and compact, with a close-cropped haircut and the kind of faded-blue tattoos on his upper arms and wrists that screamed 'I've been in prison!' Mr Trendy waved him over.

Watt shook his head. 'Darth Wolverine's got more of a ring to it.'

'So: we do some digging.' Callum got out his mobile and called Control. 'I need a PNC check on one Finn Noble, mid-forties, don't have an address.'

'*Give us a minute...*'

Mr Hand Truck took off his glasses and frowned at the photo. Then up at Mr Trendy. Who pointed over at Callum and Watt.

Then a frown. A nod. And Mr Hand Truck was off, tipping his boxes, sending ice and gutted fish splashing across the flagstone floor as he darted back out through the door he'd come in.

Watt thumped Callum on the arm. 'We've got a runner!' He sprinted across the room as the tourists swung their mobile phones round, grinning and filming.

'Sodding hell.' It was nearly impossible to get up any speed on the ice-slicked floor, but Callum did his best, hammering after Watt – past Mr Trendy and his staring minions, skidding around a slew of broken boxes, and thumping through the door.

Down a short corridor.

BANG – out through the door at the far end and into a rainy court-yard with a walk-in fridge off to one side and a stack of wooden pallets in the corner.

Mr Hand Truck made straight for them, arms and legs going, head down, with Watt in hot pursuit.

A leap, and the wee tattooed bloke scrambled up the pile of pallets like a monkey. He didn't pause at the top, just hurled himself over the top of the courtyard wall.

Watt clambered up after him.

Come on, up we go...

Callum leapt, grabbed a handhold of splintered wood and hauled himself up the wobbly pile. Sprawled over the lip and onto the top one. The whole stack rocked when he stood up. Yeah, no way this was safe. He lunged for the wall, feet scrabbling at the whitewashed stone as the whole mound of pallets clattered to the flagstones.

Aaaargh...

One leg up and over. Then the other one and he was lying on top of the wall. A short section of roof sloped down towards the swollen river, the slates slick with rain. No sign of Watt or Mr Hand Truck.

Deep breath.

He launched himself onto the roof, crouching low, arms spread out as his shoes slithered on the damp slates. A wooden deck wrapped around the side of the smokehouse about ten feet below, complete with tables, chairs, and patio umbrellas. A handful of people standing and staring, some with their mobile phones out, filming something just out of sight.

Callum dropped onto his backside and slid the last three feet. Popped over the guttering and dropped. Landed with a grunt in the shattered remains of a wooden table and broken patio umbrella.

Watt was on his back next to the wall, wrestling with Mr Hand Truck – trying to grab his hands and failing. A fist smacked into Watt's cheek with a dull slap, sending his head bouncing off the decking.

Then Mr Hand Truck grabbed the patio umbrella's base: a round lump of cast iron, big as a manhole cover but twice as thick, with a foot of splintered wooden pole sticking out of it. Raised the whole thing above his head like a makeshift hammer, muscles in his arms bunching with the strain.

Watt's eyes went wide. He snatched his arms in front of his face. 'NOOOOO!'

Callum dropped his shoulder and charged, hurling himself into the base as it swung down, knocking it sideways into the wall.

Clang.

His hip thumped into Mr Hand Truck, sending him bouncing off the wall too.

A knot of arms and legs.

Some swearing.

Thumps.

Then pain ripped its way up Callum's leg – bursting out from his inner thigh. 'Aaargh!'

He snapped around and there was Mr Hand Truck with his teeth buried in Callum's trousers, about eight inches from his groin. 'GET OFF ME!'

Callum smashed the heel of his hand into the biting scumbag's nose. It made a satisfying crunch, and he reared back, eyes closed, blood exploding from his nostrils.

'Aaargh, you dirty...' He grabbed his inner thigh. Dear *God*, that stung...

Mr Hand Truck pitched backwards onto the decking, making groaning foamy noises as little bubbles of blood popped from his broken nose.

Callum was shoved into the wall again as Watt wriggled out from underneath.

'You!' Watt hauled out his cuffs, floppy fringe all bent and twisted. 'STAY DOWN!'

But Mr Hand Truck wasn't having any of it. He rolled over and fought his way to his feet then lurched off across the decking, scattering tourists all around him.

There was a gap in the railing – stairs down to the grassy river bank.

He staggered down the steps, leaving a trail of red drops on the wooden boards, Watt limping after him.

Callum hauled himself upright. Struggling on his unbitten leg. Gritting his teeth. Making for the stairs in painful hops.

A jetty poked out into the dark-grey water – no more than a dozen feet long, with a couple of rowing boats tied up on both sides. A week of constant rain and the river was in full bore, breaking over the jetty's uprights, pinning one rowing boat against the wooden posts while the other was stretched downstream pulling its mooring line tight.

Mr Hand Truck stumbled his way onto the jetty, both hands clutched over his nose.

Watt closed the gap. 'GET BACK HERE!'

'Urgh.' Come on, move. Callum limp-hopped down the stairs.

Mr Hand Truck came to a halt at the end of the small jetty, looked back over his shoulder, then jumped into the rowing boat on the upstream side. Which promptly overturned and dumped him in the river. 'Aaaaaaaargh!'

He disappeared under the roiling gunmetal water. Thrashed to the surface, snatching handfuls of air as if he could pull himself up with them. Disappeared underwater again.

Didn't come up.

No, no, no, no...

Callum managed a wobbly run, every other step sending rusty shards of metal digging into his thigh.

Watt paced the width of the planks, staring down into the dark water. 'Sodding hell.'

A huge fountain of spray and Mr Hand Truck burst into view again on the opposite side of the jetty. Coughing, spluttering, and screaming. 'HELB! HELB!' Arms flailing.

'Oh God.' Watt froze, his voice just audible as Callum lumbered closer – talking to himself. 'Don't do anything stupid. Don't do anything stupid... Argh!' Then he whipped off his jacket and dived into the water.

'No!' Callum staggered to a halt on the jetty.

Mr Hand Truck thumped into the other rowing boat. 'I CAN'T SWIMB!' His face dipped beneath the water, then he struggled back into the air. 'HELB!'

And there was Watt – bursting out of the gunmetal water right next to him. He grabbed a handful of Mr Hand Truck's T-shirt, his other hand catching hold of the boat.

The river made bow waves against them both, rising up and curling away in breaking white spray. Shoving.

'HELB! HELB!'

Watt bared his teeth. 'Stop struggling!'

Tattooed arms flailed, whipping up spray, eyes wide, mouth open.

Then *CRACK*, his elbow landed right in the middle of Watt's face, snapping his head back and knocking him under the surface. When he burst into the air again, blood made a dark pink slick down his chin. 'Gagh...'

'HELB!' Mr Hand Truck snatched at him, clambering up Watt like a ladder, forcing him down beneath the surface again.

Oh no...

Callum teetered on the jetty's edge.

Oh God, he was going to have to jump in, wasn't he? Into the fast-flowing dark-grey water. And hope he came out again alive.

He whipped off his jacket, ripped off his clip-on tie.

'HELGGggggggglllllbb!' The river took a firm grip on Mr Hand Truck's head and torso, yanking him back and around, breaking Watt's hold on his T-shirt and sending him spinning away into the torrent.

Oh Christ.

Too late. Should have leapt in straight away. Shouldn't have stopped to think about it.

Watt spluttered his way back to the air, snatched at the boat with both hands as Mr Hand Truck was swallowed by the Kings River.

Should've just *done* it.

Someone swore.

He turned and faced a barrage of camera phones, all pointed at the swollen water. Half the people who'd been out on the decking were leaning on the rail. The other half had made their way down the stairs to the river bank. And they were all filming.

Oh that was just great – the whole fiasco, captured for all eternity and uploaded onto YouTube. So everyone could see him standing there, doing nothing.

Why the hell hadn't he jumped? He'd hesitated and now someone was probably dead.

Yes, but Watt wasn't. He *still* needed rescuing.

Do it.

Jump.

Get your cowardly backside into gear and—

Watt hauled himself up the side of the rowboat and tumbled inside. Lay in the bottom of it, on his back, heaving in great gulps of air. Coughing, both hands clutched over his chest. 'Arrgh...'

There was no sign of Mr Hand Truck. Nothing but that roiling expanse of hungry water, growling away around the curl of the bank. He was gone.

And this was officially a monumental cock-up.

33

Callum wrapped one arm around the ladder and reached out with his other. Beneath his feet, the river surged, rain making dimples in the steel-coloured surface that merged and disappeared. Only to be immediately replaced. The rowboat's mooring line was just out of reach, so he tried again, leaning further out over the rolling water... Got it.

Watt was still flat on his back, soaked through, panting, eyes closed. Blood made a dark smear through his beard – bright red at the corner of his mouth.

So Callum pulled. Hauled. Braced his legs against the ladder's steel rungs and dragged the boat closer to the jetty, fighting the river all the way. Until the boat bumped against the bottom of the ladder.

Watt still hadn't moved.

'Anytime you like!'

A groan, then he sat up. Puffed out a breath. Crawled to the prow. 'Did you get him?'

'Can we talk about this on dry land?'

'Oh no.' Watt's face crumpled.

'Just get out of the sodding boat. This thing's *heavy!*'

A sigh, then he reached for the ladder and worked his way up till he was kneeling in the boat. 'I couldn't hold him.'

'I know.'

'I *tried.*'

'I know.' Callum shifted himself to one side, leaving enough room on the rung for Watt to struggle his feet into place. 'Come on. Up you go.'

Watt climbed, dripping water and blood. 'He wouldn't stop struggling.'

Callum let go of the rope and followed Watt up onto the jetty. Stood with him in the rain as he folded forwards and stood with his hands on his knees, coughing. Patted his back.

Then flinched as, 'YOU BASTARDS!' rang out through the downpour. It was Mr Trendy, marching down the path in his health-and-hygiene white trilby, flanked by the T-shirted guys from the processing floor. He cut a path through the onlookers with their mobile phones. 'YOU *KILLED* HIM!'

'Just calm down, OK?'

'WHAT THE HELL WERE YOU PLAYING AT?' Face dark and trembling, hands balled into fists. 'WHY THE F—'

'All right, that's enough!' Callum held his hand up. 'Calm – down.'

'What did he do, eh? Answer me that! WHY DID YOU—'

'I'm not going to ask you again.' He hauled out his mobile phone and called Control. 'I need urgent assistance: we've got someone in the water, being swept downstream from Strummuir Smokehouse. Individual is an IC-one male with tattooed arms. Said he can't swim.'

'Putting you on hold.'

A tinny rendition of something vaguely classical burbled out of the earpiece, and Callum turned back to Mr Trendy. 'What's his name?'

The chest went out. 'I'm not telling you *anything*. Tod was just minding his own business and you hounded him to his death!' A finger poked Callum in the shoulder, hard enough to force him onto his back foot. 'You should be ashamed of yourself.'

Callum kept his voice level. 'I'm going to ask you to back away, *sir*.'

Another poke. 'We've got a very good team of lawyers and I'm going to make sure they hang you from the nearest tree by your balls.'

Watt straightened up, still breathing hard. Spat out a gobbet of foamy red spit. 'All right, that's enough. You have to step back onto the grass, Mr Noble.'

'Don't you tell me what to do! This is *my* smokehouse and you're a murdering pair of...' His eyes bugged, then he took a swing – fist whistling through the rainy air towards Watt's face.

Only it never got there, because Watt blocked it then rammed his open palm into the centre of Mr Trendy's chest, sending him sprawling onto his back.

Stood over him. 'And you *stay* down, or I'm arresting you.'

Callum limped up the stairs and through into the main office, carrying two waxed-paper cups of coffee that steamed and nipped at his fingers. Every step sent jagged teeth biting into his thigh. The chafing didn't help, but that's what happened when you wandered about in wet clothes.

One glass wall looked out over the smokehouse car park, then a small line of shortbread-box houses, and out towards a line of trees. All of it buckling under the weight of the rain.

A couple of patrol cars sat blocking off the car park entrance, blue lights flickering. Keeping all the tourists in.

Watt had perched himself on a big leather couch, shivering, a crinkly silver thermal blanket wrapped around his shoulders – giving him the look of a grumpy baked potato. He held a tea towel full of ice cubes against his cheek and jaw. The skin was already darkening there, the first hints of purple blooming around the edges. Working itself into a decent bruise.

Callum handed him one of the cups. 'Didn't know if you take sugar or not.'

'Thanks.' He took a sip and winced. Reapplied the tea towel. 'Any news?'

'They've got the Diving and Marine Unit coming down from Aberdeen. Should be here just in time for rush hour.'

'Urgh.' Watt sagged back on the couch. 'He's dead, isn't he? I couldn't hold onto him, and now he's dead.'

'Wasn't your fault.'

More blue flickering lights made their way along the road, past the line of houses. It pulled up in front of the car park and one of its siblings reversed to let it, and the car after it, to enter, then closed the gap again.

Callum groaned. The second car was a horribly familiar, brand-new, red Mitsubishi Shogun. McAdams. Lovely. No doubt here to dump an industrial-sized lump of doggerel and sarcasm on their heads.

Watt sniffed. 'How's the leg?'

'Why does every scumbag in Oldcastle try to bite a chunk out of me?'

'Yeah.' Another sip of coffee. Another wince. 'Ow… I called Mother – she's getting the review organised. Professional Standards and some Chief Inspector from divisional.'

'Drew blood and everything. Lucky he didn't sink his teeth in a quarter-inch higher, or I'd be circumcised by now.'

'Never been involved in a death before.' Watt shrugged. 'I've seen dead bodies – you know, at crime scenes – and I've delivered death messages, but it's not the same as being responsible.'

'Don't be daft: you're not responsible. *He* ran. *He* jumped in. You tried to save him.'

'Should've tried harder...'

There was a knock on the door and Mr Trendy, AKA: Darth Wolverine, AKA Finn Noble shuffled into his own office. 'Sorry.' He'd ditched the stupid white hat, revealing a stupid haircut – short at the sides, all quiffed up with hair gel on top. He closed the door. 'Erm ... about earlier, I just wanted to apologise. It was...' He stared at the toes of his Converse trainers. 'I got a bit caught up in the moment. I would *never* try to punch someone. And you're a police officer, how stupid would that be?'

Watt scowled at him. 'Very.'

'Yes. Yes.' He twisted his fingers into knots. 'Like I said: I'm very, *very* sorry.'

Callum took out his notebook. 'Let's start with the man we were chasing: name, address, age, shift patterns. Everything you've got.'

'Ah...' Pink flushed in his ears.

'And I'll need the same for everyone who's worked here over the last two years.'

'Erm, no. Not without a warrant. I can't.'

'What happened to "very, *very* sorry"?'

'We operate an outreach programme, OK? A lot of the people who work here have done time. We help them get back into work, teach them a skill, and it's all rehabilitation, isn't it? Someone's working here: they're making a decent living wage, doing something productive, developing a bit of self-esteem. Not off mugging OAPs and stealing cars.'

'And what was Tod in prison for, Mr Noble?'

'It's not like we employ sex offenders, or anything like that. It's people who've had difficult lives, who've made mistakes, who need a second chance.'

'What – did – he – do?'

Noble licked his lips, all attention focused on those shoes. 'The gang here *have* to be able to trust me. If they thought I'd just hand over their personal details, rat on them, without putting up a fight? Nah.' He shook his head. 'I couldn't.'

Watt shifted the tea towel full of ice. 'I can still change my mind about charging you.'

'Yes, I know, but I *can't*. It'd undo all the good we've worked for. *Six years*, ruined.'

'OK, if that's the way you want to play it.' He stood. 'Finn Noble, I'm detaining—'

The door thumped open and in marched McAdams, back straight, face like a clenched fist. 'Well?'

A uniformed PC followed him into the office and shut the door. Stood behind him with her mouth shut and her arms folded.

Callum pointed. 'At approximately fifteen fifty, Detective Constable Watt and I were being shown round the smokehouse by—'

'Thank you, Constable MacGregor, but I think DC Watt can handle it from here. You're going back to the ranch.' No haiku, no rhymes, no mocking asides.

That couldn't be good.

'DC Watt did everything he could. We've got it recorded on about twenty mobile phones: he risked his life to save—'

'I said *thank you*, Constable MacGregor. Leave the pool car, DC Watt might need it. You can get a lift back with PC Crawford.'

'He dived in the river and—'

'*Now*, Constable!'

'Right. OK.' He put his coffee down on the desk. 'Fine.' Then followed Crawford out of the office, down the stairs, through the doors, and into the rain.

She didn't say a single word all the way back through Castleview, across Dundas Bridge, and through the windy streets of Castle Hill. It was like crawling along through rush hour traffic, being driven by a shop mannequin. Only with less personality. Crawford just sat there, with her face set straight ahead, ignoring every attempt at conversation.

Ah well, can't say he hadn't tried.

Some officers were like that, though. Couldn't actually talk to people unless they were arresting them. Eventually, the job would weed them out and they'd go utilise their lack of interpersonal skills elsewhere. Like teaching or local politics.

No loss.

When she pulled up outside the back entrance to Division Headquarters he hopped out and gave her a cheery wave. 'Thanks for the lift, it's been fun!'

It wasn't far to the rear doors, barely six feet, but by the time he'd pushed through into the building his clothes had gone from damp to wet again.

They hadn't exactly tried very hard when they were decorating this part: breezeblock walls painted an institutional beige; scuffed concrete floor with suspicious brown stains that were either dried blood or something worse; signs with 'Custody Suite →', 'Processing →', '← Interview Rooms', and 'Custody Sergeant →' on them. The delightful scent sensation that was microwaved cabbage, fresh urine, and pine disinfectant. A slightly gritty taste of stale digestive biscuits, free with every breath.

'MacGregor.'

Callum stopped. Turned.

A big man with Seventies sideburns was leaning against the back wall, rolling a packet of Fruit Pastilles back and forth in his fingers. DS Jimmy Blake.

Callum nodded. 'Blakey.'

The skin around both eyes had darkened like aubergines and there was a thick T-shaped chunk of plastic covering his nose with the arms of the T taped to his forehead. Clearly, when Franklin punched you in the face, you stayed punched. 'You got a minute?' At least he didn't sound quite so bunged up.

'How's the nose?'

He narrowed his bruised eyes, the left one focusing somewhere over Callum's shoulder. 'You tell your friend, the darkie bitch, I'm not done with her.'

'Yeah...' Callum bared his teeth and hissed in a breath. 'Maybe not the *best* idea, Blakey. She could kick your arse from here to Kingsmeath and back again without breaking a sweat. Mine too. Let bygones be bygones, eh?'

Blake just scowled at him from behind his plastic nose guard.

'Oh, and Blakey, I know you're bigger than me, but if you ever call DC Franklin a "darkie bitch" again I'll straighten your wonky eye with my fist. OK?'

Outside a siren kicked off, followed by a roaring engine and the screech of tyres. It faded into the distance. A phone rang somewhere in the custody suite.

'OK.' Callum patted him on the arm. 'Good talk.' He turned and limped down the corridor, towards the stairs.

Blakey's voice echoed off the breezeblock walls. 'DCI Powel wants to see you in his office. Don't keep him waiting.'

Sod.

34

Callum stopped outside Powel's door. Straightened his clip-on tie. Brushed at a dirty patch on his suit trousers. Probably dried blood, from when that cannibalistic little sod tried to chew his leg off... Yeah. Maybe best not to dwell on that, given what happened next.

Besides, there'd be plenty opportunities for blame and recriminations coming right up.

The stain didn't come off, just smeared into the damp fabric.

And yes: given this afternoon's monumental fiasco, an internal review was inevitable. Member of the public dies while being pursued by the police? The newspapers would be stumbling over each other, drunk with righteous-indignation and delight, competing to see who could give Police Scotland the biggest kicking.

But did the review have to happen right away? They couldn't even give him half an hour to put on dry clothes?

Of course not.

Ah well, no point putting it off. Callum pulled his shoulders back and knocked.

A voice from inside: *'Come.'*

Deep breath.

He opened the door and stepped inside.

Powel was behind his desk, face poker still. Mother sat on the couch with her back straight, looking disappointed. A bloke in uniform was next to her, with three pips on his epaulettes – that would be the chief inspector Watt mentioned, here to run the review. And last, but not least, everyone's favourite avuncular, fake-bumbling, non-sequitur-spouting, inquisitor from Professional Standards: Chief Inspector 'Call me Alex' Gilmore.

And they were all staring at Callum. Like a firing squad.

Oh joy.

Powel pointed. 'Shut the door, Detective Constable MacGregor.'

He did. Nodded. 'Boss. Detective Chief Inspector. Chief Inspectors.'

Gilmore pulled on a smile. 'I understand you had a spot of bother out at Strummuir, Callum.'

Understatement of the year.

'It wasn't Watt's fault. It wasn't anyone's fault. The guy ran, we chased him, he jumped in the river. Watt went in after him, but he struggled and the river swept him away.'

'I see.'

'It was filmed on about two dozen mobile phones – we commandeered the lot. Soon as they're checked into evidence, watch the footage and you'll see.'

Gilmore nodded. 'I did. At least five of them uploaded the whole thing: Twitter, Facebook, YouTube... We'll have to call in the Police Investigations and Review Commissioner, but it's just a formality. Nothing to worry about. As far as I'm concerned you both did everything you could.'

'Oh.' A smile crept its way across Callum's face. Thank God for that. 'Great. Watt deserves some sort of commendation, though. He blames himself, but he—'

'Moving on.' Powel produced a blue folder from his in-tray and pulled out a sheet of paper. 'We got a call this morning from a little old lady walking her border terrier in Holburn Forest. They'd barely gone twenty feet when "Captain Muffin" hauled a carrier bag out from beneath a bush. And do you know what was *in* that carrier bag, Detective Constable?'

Callum kept his mouth shut.

'Human remains. A severed head to be precise: female, sawn off between the fourth and fifth cervical vertebrae. Sound familiar?'

What?

Of course it didn't. Why would...

Hold on: yes it did. 'When I was in your office this morning, someone came in and told you about it. You went off to the scene.'

'And that was the first you knew of it?'

'Yes. Why?'

'I see.' Powel held his hands out in a pantomime shrug: all just a silly misunderstanding. Nothing to worry about. 'Then would you like to explain how YOUR DNA GOT ON THE BLOODY REMAINS?'

'My *what*?'

'Your DNA. On a severed woman's head!'

Mother looked away. 'Did you kill her?'

Callum just stared.

'Did – you – kill – her?'

'No, of course I didn't! Why the hell would I kill—'

'Then did you dump the remains for someone else?'

'How... What...' He threw his arms out. '*No!* I had nothing to do with *any* of it.'

'You see, Callum,' Gilmore took off his evil scientist glasses and huffed a breath on them, drawing it out as he polished the lenses on a hanky, 'you have something of a reputation for compromising crime scenes, don't you?'

'I haven't been to Holburn Forest for years, how could I contaminate anything?' He jabbed a finger at Powel. 'This is the lab cocking things up again. They couldn't find an angry squirrel in a bean bag, never mind pick out DNA. Just because they buy a machine doesn't mean they know how to use it.'

Powel pulled out another sheet of paper. 'The DNA's degraded, but your name came straight back from the database. Why? Who was she? Why did you kill her?'

'I DIDN'T KILL ANYONE!' Though that might change in the next thirty seconds. The blood thrummed at the back of his skull, pins and needles filling his throat, hands clenched into tight fists.

Mother stood. 'All right, Callum, that's enough.' She pointed at the spare armchair. 'Sit down.'

He stood there, trembling.

'Sit – down. *Now*, Constable.'

Callum lowered himself into the seat. 'I didn't kill anyone. I didn't interfere with the crime scene. I didn't *do* anything. It's a mistake.' Or maybe it wasn't a mistake. Maybe it was deliberate? Of course it sodding was. 'Someone's trying to fit me up.'

Powel went back to his folder and pulled out a photograph. Held it out so everyone could see. 'Who was she?'

'I *told* you: this is nothing to do with me...'

The woman in the photo had to be mid-twenties, early thirties tops. Her long blonde hair, so pale it was almost white, lay plastered against her head – glistening as if it was wet; dark circles around her unfocused blue eyes; skin like the thinnest bone china, speckled with freckles; puffy blue lips; a heart-shaped face; and a neck that ended three or four inches below her chin in a jagged dark-red line.

But that wasn't what made Callum's breath thicken in his throat, made his chest contract. It was her ears.

'Oh God...'

A Long, Long Time Ago

'Last one there's a bumhead!' Alastair was off running before he'd even finished speaking. Cheating bumhead. Sprinting across the pebbly beach, flip-flops sticking out of his back pocket, bandy net slung over his shoulder.

Callum ran after him, lumbering a bit because of the fish-and-chips sloshing about in Fanta in his tummy. 'Cheater!'

Sunshine sparkled across the water, hissing in and out against the little round stones.

A big fat crab – easily the size of Callum's palm – scuttered across the bottom of the rock pool, between the raspberry-jelly anemones and the floaty bright-green seaweed. All legs and nippers.

Loads of sand and shells and stuff lined the bottom of the pool, along with dull pebbly things that Dad said were bits of glass the sea had ground and ground till it couldn't cut anyone any more.

Alastair dug his hand into the pool and scooped up a bunch of bits. Then Callum reached in and did the same. The pair of them squatted at the pool's edge with dripping handfuls of shells and sand and grit, grinning at each other.

Mum was going to love this.

The lady in the little hut smiled as they tipped their handfuls onto the table. 'Well, let's see what we've got, shall we?'

The wooden walls were clarted with picture frames and animals made of seashells and bits of driftwood. Lots and lots of shelves covered in things covered in more shells: lamps, lumps of rock, more driftwood. Which was kinda cool and kinda dumb, all at the same time.

A sort of ray-gun thing sat in a wee stand, dribbling clear plastic goo from the barrel, making the air smell like the inside of Dad's car on a hot day.

Alastair pointed at a crab claw, still crunchy with sand. 'That one. Use that one.' His hair was full of sand too, his legs sparkled with it.

It was *everywhere*: in Callum's flip-flops, gritty between his toes, itchy on the back of his knees where it'd started to dry.

The lady made a 'Hrmmmm'ing noise. 'It's a lovely crab claw, but it might be a *bit* big. How about...' She moved her fingers through the piles and pushed a shell from each – one with a blueish edge, the other pink, both all ruffled and ridged like crinkle-cut chips, both no bigger than Callum's thumbnail. 'I think they'll be very pretty, don't you?'

'Oh come on, David, stop sulking – they're beautiful!' Mum tucks her hair behind her ears and flashes the tiny shell earrings. 'Aren't they beautiful? I have the bestest little boys in the whole wide world.' She kneels and wraps Alastair and Callum up in a big hug. 'I'm never taking them off. Never ever.'

Dad scowls. 'All I'm saying is, I got you a gold bracelet *and* a bottle of that Priscilla Presley perfume.'

'Well, I love *all* my presents.' She stood and spanked Dad on his bottom. 'Now get that barbecue fired up, Chief Chef Caveman, the Mighty Empress Birthday Girl demands a sausage-and-steak sacrifice!'

'Callum?' Mother leaned forward and poked him.

He jerked back in his seat. Blinking at the photograph.

Powel nodded. 'You recognise her, don't you, Constable MacGregor? Who is she? Who did you kill?'

Wasn't easy keeping his voice level, but Callum did his best. 'Is this supposed to be some sort of joke?'

'Oh I can assure you, Constable MacGregor, nobody's laughing.'

'Is this supposed to be *funny*?' He lunged, grabbed the printout from Powel's fingers and thumped back down again. Fumbled his wallet out with thick slippery fingers. Opened it and stared.

There, in the photo – Mum, with her big smile and her freckled cheeks. Her cartoon cat T-shirt. Her pale blonde hair, bleached by a week in the sunshine at Lossiemouth. Her earrings, made by a woman in a shed on a caravan site and paid for by two little boys who'd saved up their pocket money.

And the head in the other photograph – Powel's photograph – its ears were two delicate curls of translucent skin and cartilage, with a seashell earring in each lobe. One blue, one pink, both ridged like crinkle-cut chips.

Powel stood. 'You know her, don't you? Who – did – you – kill?'

But it *couldn't* be.

The walls pulsed in and out in time with each breath.

It was twenty-six years ago. Mum would be in her fifties by now.

He grabbed the photo tighter, as if that would stop the thump-and-hiss of blood in his ears as the room got hotter and hotter.

Maybe... Maybe it was a cousin, or something? A relative he didn't know he'd had.

His mouth flooded with saliva, but he couldn't swallow – his throat was full of brambles.

Which meant there'd been someone who could've taken him in. He didn't *have* to grow up in a care home. But they hadn't bothered their backsides to help a wee five-year-old boy abandoned by his whole family...

The whole world shrank to the size of the photograph in his hand.

But she was wearing Mum's *earrings*.

How?

'Are you OK?' Mother held out a mug of tea, steam curling from the surface, rain thrumming on the black skin of her umbrella.

From up here, on the station roof, most of Oldcastle was laid out like a tortured Monopoly board. Do not pass go. Do not collect two hundred pounds. Do not hope or dream.

Low cloud hid the upper reaches of Blackwall Hill and Kingsmeath. Scratched at the crest of Castle Hill. Even the tops of the hospital's twin incinerator towers were gone, the red warning lights at their top reduced to a faint bloody Sauron glow in the gloom.

Callum shifted his bum on the metal support and huffed out a breath – opaque in the cold air as rain dripped off the communications array and onto his shoulders. 'Thanks.' He took the mug. Sipped at the scalding liquid. Glanced up at the big metal and plastic drums above his head. At the Airwave transmitters. At the civil defence warning systems. 'Four minutes' warning. If it was you, would you set the siren off, or let the end come as a surprise?'

'You'll catch your death of cold.'

'Four minutes to panic and scream, knowing you're about to die, or blissful ignorance followed by a flash of light and *poof*. You're nothing but a shadow, burned into a concrete wall.'

She sighed and settled onto the support next to him, sheltering them both with her brolly. 'Professor Twining's finished the post mortem. Do you want the details?'

He raised one shoulder in a half-arsed shrug. 'What can you do in four minutes anyway?'

'Twining says the histology proves the remains have been frozen, apparently he can tell from the way the cell walls are ruptured. But we won't know for how long until they've finished the isotope analysis.'

All these years...

A severed head in a plastic bag.

'Say you're at work, or you're in Asda, or you're arresting some scumbag, or maybe you're breaking up a fight when the sirens go off. How are you supposed to spend your final moments? Not as if you can teleport home and be with your loved ones, is it?'

'I had the head of the laboratory on the phone, desperate to apologise for getting it wrong the first time. Someone mixed up the internal and external samples, so it came back looking like a degraded match.' Mother blew out a long slow breath. 'Anyway, Cecelia says your mum's DNA isn't on file; it was the Nineteen Nineties, they had different rules back then. And everyone thought it was a case of child abandonment. If they'd treated it as a murder, or an abduction ... but they didn't.'

'So what do you do, phone them? "Sorry, love, it's the end of the world and we're all going to die." Only everyone's trying to call their husband or their wife or their kids or their parents at the same time, the network goes down and you spend your last four minutes on earth swearing at your phone.'

'We're reopening the investigation. Well, Powel is. He's putting an MIT together right now to look into it.'

'Not exactly how I'd want to go out: lonely, pissed off, and scared.'

'Callum.' Mother put a hand on his leg, warmth seeping through the wet fabric to the skin beneath. 'It's OK to be upset.'

He frowned down into the depths of his mug. 'I'd leave the sirens switched off: let people live their last four minutes in blissful ignorance. No one wants to know they're about to die.' Not going by the look of utter horror on Mr Hand Truck's face as the river dragged him away.

How could anyone sane cope with that?

Here comes Death, and he's shouting your name.

Callum ran a hand through his wet hair. 'What about the guy who went in the water?'

'You've had a horrible shock and I want you to take some time off.'

'Let me guess: they haven't found his body. He'll be trapped against the river bank somewhere, or wedged under something beneath the surface, or on his way out to sea.'

'Callum, I'm serious: go home.'

'Yeah...' A fat raindrop dripped from the umbrella's edge and made ripples in the tea's beige surface. 'You've wanted rid of me from the start. Might as well *carpe* the *diem*.'

'You're a silly sod, you know that, don't you?'

'So people keep telling me.'

'I'm not getting rid of you, Callum.' Mother let go of his leg and wrapped her arm around his shoulders. 'Not when I'm just starting to like you.'

Rain thumped on the brolly. Dripped from the communications array. Hammered down on the buildings and the people and the streets.

She gave him a little squeeze. 'And I'd leave the sirens off too.'

35

Callum wheeled his bike in through the door, locked it up in the rack beneath the stairs. Stood there for a bit with his eyes closed, dripping, blood hissing in his ears like waves on a pebble beach.

All those years...

Deep breath.

Come on.

He flicked through the pile of letters, fliers, and leaflets on the windowsill – took the ones for the top floor and squelched upstairs.

Didn't matter what the weather forecasters said, it was never going to stop raining. Not until they were all drowned and dead.

Mrs Gillespie's cats had been at Toby's pot plants again, black soil spread out in a fan around a wilting rubber plant. A Mylar balloon bobbed in the breeze, the string tied around Mr and Mrs Robson's door handle. 'HAPPY 20TH ANNIVERSARY!'

Glad *someone* had something to celebrate.

Callum posted their mail then let himself into the flat.

'Elaine?' He peeled off his wet jacket – sodding thing didn't deserve the term, 'Waterproof' it leaked like a teabag. 'Christ, you wouldn't *believe* the day I've had.'

He dumped his backpack next to the non-waterproof jacket. 'I need a drink.'

The TV was on in the lounge. Some sort of soap opera, probably. Lowered voices and ominous muttering coming through the closed door.

He unlaced his shoes and squelched through to the kitchen. Hauled open the fridge door and helped himself to a Tesco own-brand continental-style lager. Clicked the metal tag and had a good long swig.

Not much else in there. Some open jars of pickles and olives, bit of cheese going blue at the corners, some butter, a wilting lettuce... Leftover tuna casserole. He clunked the door shut. 'I'm ordering takeaway. I know we're meant to be saving money, but sod it.'

He peeled off his soggy socks and slapped them into the washing machine.

Took his beer through to the bedroom.

There were two bags, sitting on the bed. One was his battered old suitcase with its wonky wheel and the strip of green fabric tied around the handle so it'd be easy to find on an airport conveyor belt. The other was an aluminium hard-shelled job big enough to fit a small child. Not a scratch on it, so probably brand new.

Callum's shoulders dipped even further.

Great. There he was, worrying about ordering takeaway and Elaine's busy buying expensive luggage off the internet. As if they were going to let her take something that size into hospital. You could give birth *in* it, it was that—

'Callum?'

He turned, and there she was, wearing a baggy black T-shirt with some sort of communist-chicken design – stretched tight over the bump – and a pair of baggy grey joggy bottoms.

'New luggage? Seriously? I thought we were trying to save up for Peanut's—'

'I'm sorry.' She bit her top lip and stared down at her bulge. 'I'm really, *really* sorry.'

He ran a hand over his face. Sighed. 'OK. Look, it's only a suitcase, not the end of the world.'

Someone appeared in the doorway behind her. Someone with sticky-out ears and silvery hair. DCI Powel. Wonderful. Just what the doctor ordered – a pain-in-the-arse.

Callum crossed his arms. 'What's this, more "friendly" advice? Cos I'm not in the mood.'

Elaine cleared her throat. 'I was sorry to hear about your mother.'

'Callum, I know the timing's horrible, but it was going to be horrible whenever it happened.' Powel put a hand on Elaine's shoulder.

'Yeah, well, there's never a good time for your mother's head to be found in a carrier bag, is there?' He reached for a dry pair of jeans. 'Anything else?'

A sniff, and Elaine finally dragged her eyes up to look at him. 'Please don't make this any harder than it already is.'

252

'I just want to get dry and changed, OK?'

'Reece has left his wife.'

'Good for him. But he's not staying here. Barely enough room for the two of us as it—'

'I packed you a bag.'

Callum froze. 'You packed *me* a bag?'

'It...' She rubbed a hand across her pregnant belly. 'God, why do you have to be like this?'

'I'm not being like anything! What do you mean, you packed me a bag? Why the hell would I need a—'

'It's not your child, OK?' Her voice was loud and trembling. 'Peanut isn't yours, Callum. He's Reece's. Don't you get it?'

The world shrunk to a tiny silent pinprick.

Then blood crashed against the pebble beach. Nails dragged across the caravan's aluminium hull. Thunder *roared*.

Callum blinked. 'He's what?'

'Don't you get it? I was making do. Reece was never going to leave his wife and you were better than nothing. But that's all changed now.'

'Are you kidding? Are you—'

'I *love* him, Callum.'

Heat rushed through his body, pins and needles crackled between his shoulder blades, fists curled so tight his knuckles burned. 'This was all lies? Peanut isn't... I was better than *nothing*?'

'For God's sake, Callum, listen to yourself.'

'I was good enough to raise someone else's kid, though, wasn't I? Good enough to lie to!'

Powel squeezed past Elaine, putting himself between them. 'All right, that's enough. I need you to—'

'You manipulative, two-timing, backstabbing, lying—'

'I said that's enough, Constable!'

'I took the blame. For you!' He pointed at Powel's child, growing in her belly like a tumour. 'For *that*. And it wasn't even mine?'

Her voice trembled. 'What was I supposed to do?'

'I FLUSHED MY WHOLE CAREER – FOR YOU!'

Powel's open palm thumped into Callum's chest. 'I'm not telling you again.'

And the thunder roared.

Callum grabbed two handfuls of Powel's shirt, yanked him forwards and off balance, then slammed him into the bedroom wall, hard enough to knock framed photos off their hooks. Did it again, harder. Cracks

253

rippled out through the plasterboard where Powel's head crashed into it with a splintering thump.

Kill him.

Callum let go with one hand and smashed his fist into Powel's face. More cracks in the plasterboard as his head bounced.

Kill him.

Elaine screamed, the sound cutting through the thick air like a bone saw. 'GET OFF HIM!'

Powel's eyes rolled up, mouth drooping open.

Kill him.

Getting heavier in Callum's hands.

Kill him.

Callum let go and Powel slumped to the carpet.

KILL HIM!

He drew back a foot, to kick the bastard's head in and—

'STOP IT!' Elaine grabbed at his arm, tried to pull him away. 'LEAVE HIM ALONE!'

Callum stumbled, turned, fist curling up...

She glared at him, tears rolling down her cheeks, face flushed and distorted. 'GET OUT! YOU'RE NOT WANTED, UNDERSTAND? YOU WERE *NEVER* WANTED!'

He lowered his hand.

Blood crashed on the stony beach.

She covered her eyes. 'Please. Just ... go.'

Callum grabbed his battered old case and marched out, scooping up his wet shoes and soggy jacket on the way. Slammed the door behind him. Stood on the landing, jaw clenched so tight his teeth ached. Dragged in a deep, jagged breath.

'Callum?' The door at the far end of the landing was open, just a crack, still on the chain – Toby's jaundiced face barely visible in the gap. 'Is everything OK? I heard screaming.'

'No. Not it's not, "OK".'

He turned and marched down the stairs, suitcase clatter-thumping its way along behind him, past open doors on the second floor – everyone peering out to see what was going on from a safe distance.

Callum unlocked his bike and hurled it out of the front door into the rain. Did the same with the suitcase. Pulled on his wet shoes and jacket, then stormed out after them.

36

Thursday night in the Bart wasn't much busier than the Wednesday.

Three auld biddies in the corner booth were playing dominos. A couple having an argument over by the pool table. A fat beardy bloke, playing with his mobile phone and glancing at the door every two minutes. Probably wondering how long he should give it before admitting defeat and accepting that he'd been stood up.

Callum fed another four pound coins into the jukebox with his left hand, pressed a few buttons and lurched back to the bar as Radiohead's 'Exit Music from a Film' oozed out from the pub's speakers again. Ignoring the groans from everyone else. Feeling no pain.

He tipped back the whisky in his swollen right fist and clunked the empty glass back on the bar. Winced. OK, maybe some pain. But there was an easy way to fix that: 'Same again.'

Hedgehog Dundee sucked a breath in through his teeth then let it out in a long slow hiss. A round wee man with an oversized goatee, shiny face, and long straggly hair, he looked as if his blood was about sixty-four percent cheese. 'Not that I'm ungrateful for your patronage, Constable MacGregor, but you're rather undermining the happy-go-lucky atmosphere we strive for here at the Dumbarton Arms.'

'Double Grouse, no ice or … or water. Pint of Cham-pi-on.' Had to focus a bit to get the word 'Champion' out, because something had gone wrong with his tongue, but it was the thought that counted.

'And while "Exit Music from a Film" is a well-constructed song, and clearly reminiscent of Gustav Mahler's later work, the fact that you've played it fourteen times in a row is beginning to take its toll on the other patrons' *joie de vivre*.'

'An a … an a packet of piggled … onion.' He wobbled his way up onto a barstool.

'Especially as you preceded this tribute to a somewhat lesser known Radiohead song about suicide, with a dozen playings of REM's "Everybody Hurts".' Hedgehog reached beneath the bar and came out with a folded sheet of paper. Placed it in front of Callum. 'This might be more beneficial to your state of mind than the further consumption of alcohol and depressive songs.'

It was a leaflet for the Samaritans.

Callum drained his pint and thumped the empty glass down right on top of the thing. Squinted one eye shut to keep everything in focus. Put on his best police officer voice: 'Hedgehog, I'm going to give you … you a choice. You can either get me my drinks … drinks an crisps, or … or I can call a friend at Food Standards Scotland…' OK, that sounded a bit slurred, but they were difficult words after five or six pints. And double whiskies. 'I'll … I'll get them to come down here an … an give your kitchen the kind of … *examination* that'd make … make a proctologist's eyes water.'

A sigh. Then Hedgehog turned and pressed a tumbler up beneath the optic of Famous Grouse.

Damn straight.

No one wanted a visit from the Cheese Police.

The whisky went on a coaster in front of him, followed by a foamy pint of dark brown beer, and a silvery green packet.

He fumbled out a tenner and laid it on the bar with exaggerated care, just to prove he wasn't drunk.

Hedgehog took it, then stared over Callum's shoulder, smiling. 'Oh thank the heavens for that: you came.'

'Callum?' Dotty wheeled herself over to his barstool and looked up at him. 'Are you OK?'

'You want … want a drink? I'm buying.' He thumped his left hand down on the bar. 'Hedgehog – pint of … pint of Old Jock for Dotty. Put it … on my tab. No, no, I *insist*. You want crisps? Course you want crisps. Give her some crisps.'

'How much have you had to drink?'

'I'm celebrating.'

'Oh, Callum…'

He took a swig of beer. 'No, it's great. All of it.' A soft warm smile spread across his face. 'My mum didn't … didn't abandon me, she got murd—' The burp tasted of whisky and prawn cocktail. 'Sorry. She got *murdered*. An ... an I don't have to raise ... raise someone else's baby!' The Grouse set fire to his chest on the way down, making it swell. 'Cos it wasn't mine. You see?'

Hedgehog leaned on the bar. 'Dear, sweet, Detective Sergeant Hodgkin, I would consider it a personal favour – nay, a veritable *boon* – if you would escort DC MacGregor to another establishment. Perhaps somewhere he can drink copious amounts of coffee, consume some carbohydrates, and prepare for what is no doubt going to be a most terrible hangover? He can settle up and collect his bike when he's sober.'

The song on the jukebox mourned to an end. Then started right back up again.

'Wasn't my baby, Dotty. It never ... never was.'

'Have you got somewhere to stay?'

He spread his arms wide, slopping beer across the bar. 'World ... world is my oyster.'

She puffed out her cheeks. Grimaced. 'OK, OK. You can stay in the spare room, I'm sure Louise won't mind. Probably. As long as you're not going to be sick – she hates that. You're not going to be sick, are you?'

He lowered his glass. 'They kicked me out of ... of my flat. My flat! I paid ... paid for it an every ... everything.'

'You have to *promise* not to be sick everywhere.'

'It was my flat.'

'I'm serious about the not being sick, Callum. Don't do that.'

'Cross my heart.' He blinked at her for a bit. Then held out the packet of pickled onion. 'You want ... want some crisps?'

Callum wiped his mouth, sighed. Spat out a bitter thread of bile. Rested his forehead against the cool wooden seat.

The shower's hiss disappeared for a moment as he flushed the toilet for the fourth time.

Urgh...

Then he clambered back into the bath again, holding onto the rails built into the bathroom wall to keep him upright. Rinsed the shampoo out of his hair. Then stood there and steamed for a bit, till the water went tepid, then cold.

Finally, he clambered out and dried himself off on a dark-blue towel. Wrapped it around his middle and crept back along the hall and into

Dotty's spare room. Stood there with his back to the door, arms hanging by his sides.

Dotty and Louise had gone to town in here: pink chintz cushions; pink floral bedspread; pink floral pillows, curtains, and pelmet; dried flowers on the pine chest of drawers.

It was like standing inside Barbara Cartland.

He sank down the door, until his towelled bum came to rest on the fuchsia-coloured carpet. Cradled his swollen right hand against his chest. Every time he tried to move his fingers it was like rubbing barbed wire into the joints. That's what he got for punching Powel in the face.

Might hurt now, but it felt *great* at the time. Standing over him, watching the blood seeping out through his open mouth.

Deserved all he got. And more.

How long had it been going on: Powel and Elaine? She was due in two weeks, so that meant at *least* nine months. Probably longer. Probably ever since they worked that murder/suicide.

All that time, screwing around behind his back...

He groaned.

Yeah, that explained why Elaine had been off sex since April – she was saving herself for sodding DCI Powel.

And what would've happened if Powel hadn't found the balls to leave his wife?

No way Elaine would've come clean, not when she had Callum right there to pay for everything. To change dirty nappies and stay up half the night feeding Poncy Powel's bloody baby.

To take the blame for cocking up a crime scene, so she could keep her paid maternity leave for a baby that wasn't even his. Manipulating him with little love notes and sandwiches. How *stupid* could he be?

No wonder she treated him like an idiot – that's exactly what he was. A moron. A halfwit. A mug.

Whose mother's severed head was lying in a refrigerated drawer in the city mortuary.

Yeah ... this had been a *great* day.

37

Didn't really matter any more, did it? Who was going to hear? No one.

So Ashlee stopped screaming. Stopped rattling against her chains. Stopped fighting against the darkness.

Just slumped back and let the cold filthy water seep into her bones.

The surface rippled with every shiver that juddered through her, making her teeth clatter.

Maybe the Man with Blue Eyes would come back and let them go?

He said he'd come back...

Or maybe he'd forgotten about them?

How long had it been since he left? Hours. Hours and hours and hours. And no sign of him. Nothing but the cold and the wet and the sound of her own screams.

Mum still hadn't moved. She was just visible in the pale-orange light that seeped through between a couple of the wooden boards. Slumped over to one side with the chain tight around her neck.

Poor cow.

All those years living with Dad, who was *utterly* a dick. All the shouting and the manipulation and the checking up on her and not letting her have any friends... And then one day he just walks out and never comes back, because occasionally even utter dicks can do something nice for their families.

All those horrible years with Dad, then some more horrible ones with Uncle Eddy who always wanted to tickle Ashlee and take her shopping for pretty dresses and go with her to the swimming. Breathing heavily as she stripped off in the changing rooms. Sitting in her room watching her sleep. Oh, yeah, *completely* not a paedo. Then Uncle Eddy finds himself another single mother with a much younger daughter and off *he* goes too.

Good sodding riddance.

And *then*, when Mum was finally getting herself back together – going out of the house instead of staying at home watching soaps and eating ice-cream and oven chips – this happened.

Ashlee closed her eyes and sobbed in the dark.

Howling it out.

Because who was going to hear her?

She was going to die here. Alone. In the dark.

— protect and survive —

Fallout can kill. Since it can be carried for great distances by the winds it can eventually settle anywhere, so no place in the United Kingdom is safer than any other. The risk is as great in the countryside as in the towns.

Nobody can tell where the safest place will be.

Stay at home – Public Information Film
© Crown Copyright (1975)

"There's no point crying, little girl," said the Bonemonger with his scissor-sharp smile. "No one will hear you, and nobody cares."

R.M. Travis
Open the Coffins (and Let Them Go Free) (1976)

You better beware, cos yo parents is nowhere,
You hear me? I swear, man, you ain't got a prayer,
Ain't no love in the air, it's just pain and despair,
You grown up in care, and this place is a nightmare.

Donny '$ick Dawg' McRoberts
'The Arsonist's Diary'
© Bob's Speed Trap Records (2015)

38

'Urrrgh...' The kitchen throbbed like the heart of a monster. *Boom. Boom. Boom.*

Obviously, Dotty's fridge, freezer, and microwave were plotting Callum's death with their horrible reflective metallic surfaces. Sending burning daggers of sunlight stabbing through his eyeballs and into his brain. Making *everything* burn.

He held the empty pint glass under the tap and filled it up again. Glugged it down, water dripping onto his old grey T-shirt.

Finished and slumped there with his head drooped, panting.

Oh God.

Never, *ever* again.

He had to put the glass down to turn the tap off – his right hand had swollen up to the size of a space hopper. All purple and yellow and stiff and full of rusty metal. Fingers twisted and rigid.

Callum used his left to fumble a couple of painkillers from the packet by the kettle and dry swallowed them.

His stomach lurched and gurgled.

'Urgh...' He curled forward, resting his elbows on the work surface, head hanging like a sack of burning tatties.

Stay down. Stay down. Stay down.

Please...

The pills stayed where they were and he gulped down another pint of water.

Shuddered.

The sound of breakfast TV burbled through the house and he slouched through to the living room.

It was a lot less chintzy than the guest bedroom – more 'Scandinavian functionalism' than 'Barbara Cartland's innards'. Flatpack furniture with lots of straight edges, Scottish colourist impressions of wee seaside towns, hills, and but-and-bens in big wooden frames. A display cabinet full of random ornaments and wine glasses.

The only book on display was a celebrity biography of someone he'd never heard of, sitting on a big glass-topped coffee table.

'Well, well, well, look what the cat threw up.' The black-leather couch's only occupant took a sip from a huge mug. Greying hair cropped close to her long face. Sharp black suit, red shirt, a pair of no-nonsense schoolmarm glasses perched on the end of her nose. 'You look like a tramp had sex with a wheelie bin.'

'Louise.' Callum wiped a hand down the front of his wet T-shirt. 'Sorry.'

On the TV, a man in waders was chest-deep in a river somewhere. *'...and that's the only good thing about American signal crayfish: they're very, very tasty. Back to you in the studio.'*

'Still, at least you didn't vomit everywhere.'

The picture jumped to a pair of presenters sitting on a curved red sofa with big animated screens behind them. The woman smiled. *'Thanks, Colin. Now here's Valerie with the weather. Any good news for us, Valerie?'*

'Sorry. I'll get packed up and out of your hair.'

Valerie was a sporty-looking type in a stripy dress. *'I do indeed, Claire, as you can see from the satellite map it's going to be a lovely day for the southeast all the way up to Manchester and Newcastle...'*

'Pfff...' Louise waved at him. 'Just because I'm a solicitor, doesn't mean I'm heartless. Dorothy told me what happened with Elaine.'

'Oh.' He sank onto the end of the couch. 'Yeah.'

'...best of the sunshine in Wales and Northern Ireland...'

'She worries about you, Callum. Dorothy thinks you've got a self-destructive streak a mile wide.'

'I do genuinely appreciate the bed for a night. She didn't have to take me in.'

'Stray kittens, puppies, injured birds – you name it, she wants to give it a home.'

'...stubborn band of rain clinging onto the northeast of Scotland, but other than that we've got all the makings of an Indian Summer...'

He nodded. Stared down at his swollen knuckles.

'I think it's because she's in pain a lot of the time. She's hurting, so she hates to see others suffering. Well, except for that idiot Detective Constable Watt.'

'I'll get a B-and-B sorted out today. Give you your spare room back.'

'All the muscles and nerves are messed up in her right leg, from the crash, but they won't amputate it. Doesn't matter how much she begs.' A sigh. 'How is that fair?'

'*Thanks, Valerie. Now, how many of you remember this?*'

A music clip played from the TV – an orchestra swooping through a guitar-and-bassline.

'Life never is.'

'No.' A small, sour laugh. 'I don't suppose it is.' Louise stood, took a couple of steps closer and squeezed Callum's shoulder. 'You stay as long as you like.'

Then a man's voice, dark and warm belted out over the top. '*Run, little rabbit boy, you'd better run like hell, / Cos the Bonemonger is coming and he's after you as well...*'

Louise gave Callum's shoulder another squeeze. 'Well, let's call it a week. Don't want you cramping our style.'

'*Slick and sharp and sickle-like he smiles his scissor smile, / and he'll catch you and he'll eat you, though you run for miles and miles...*'

Louise let go. 'Sod it: look at the time.' She marched from the room, voice getting louder as she disappeared into the hall. 'There's a spare key hanging in the kitchen – if you're going out, pick up some milk!'

Clunk, the front door shut and he was alone.

Urgh...

He slumped back on the couch. Rubbed his good hand over his eyes.

Probably wouldn't hurt to go back to bed. Maybe a couple of hours' kip would dull the hangover howling its way through his skull.

'*...lovely to have you with us.*'

'*Lovely to be here, Siobhan. Though watching that, I have to wonder what on earth I was thinking. I know it was the Eighties, but oh dear...*' A familiar laugh, dark and treacly. '*Can't believe the* Miami Vice *look used to be trendy.*'

Callum peered out through his fingers and an old man had joined Mr Suit and Mrs Casual Dress on the breakfast sofa. He was wearing faded jeans, scuffed cowboy boots, and a dark-blue shirt that had silvery bits speckling the sleeves, leather buckles on his wrists. On the screen behind him was a *much* younger version of himself in a pastel-green linen suit with the sleeves rolled up, no T-shirt, showing off a lot of chest. The hair on his head swept up and back: coiffured into a big blonde mane.

The mane was still there, but it was thin and white now.

A caption appeared at the bottom of the picture: 'LEO MCVEY ~ SINGER SONGWRITER'.

'So Leo, of course Open the Coffins *was a massive hit in the eighties. But it almost didn't get made, did it?'*

'Oh yeah. Man that was a hard sell. You should've seen the record execs' faces when I told them I wanted to do a concept album based on this children's book about a wee boy who gets turned into a rabbit and has to fight the Lord of Bones for his sister's soul. "No way!" they said. "You can't make this, it'll be career suicide!"'

Callum pulled out his phone, winced one eye shut and brought up his call history.

Oh thank God – no drunk-dialling the flat or Elaine's mobile.

'And then it's like, sixteen weeks at the top of the album charts. Just goes to show you how much guys in suits know.' A wink. Then he leaned over and patted the male presenter's knee. 'No offence, Brian.'

Next check: text messages...

A big sigh let all the pressure hiss out of his lungs.

No angry texts, or weepy ones, not even a big chunk of solid swearing.

'And of course, Ray and I became really *good friends when I was recording the album; have been ever since. Man, we used to hang out all the time. He'd even come on tour with us. And loads of people would bring their books and he'd be sitting out in the auditorium signing them during the interval, you know? Great guy.'*

There were three *incoming* texts, though. All from Elaine.

Oh.

'And a great writer too. That's why the album was so successful – the source material was just so great.'

Callum's thumb hovered over the first one.

Might be a better idea to just delete them, rather than sit here reading all about how it wasn't her fault and he had no right to judge her...

'So you can imagine how awful it was when we started losing him, yeah? How painful it's been watching Alzheimer's eat Ray. How this horrible disease is consuming the guy we all loved.'

The male presenter sat forward and oiled out a sympathetic expression. 'But you decided to do something about it, didn't you?'

Callum selected the first message:

```
What the hell is wrong with you?
How could you DO that to Reece?
```

```
        I'm at the hospital because of
        YOU!!!!
```
'Yeah, so me and the lads got together and we said, "We can't just let this happen to Ray!" So I got onto the organisers of the Tartantula music festival, in Oldcastle, and told them, how about we do some sort of benefit...'

The second message wasn't much better:
```
        You broke three of his teeth!!!!
        I used to know you, Callum, but I
        don't now. You can't come back
        from this. Know what? NEVER come
        back again.
```
'...came up with the idea of getting all these modern bands to join in and help us raise money for Ray's care and, you know, to help research into Alzheimer's too. And these young guys have been great, it's going to be a terrific gig.'

Number three:
```
        I can't believe I ever loved you.
```
'The feeling's mutual.'

'And if you can't get up to Oldcastle on Sunday, don't worry: we're gonna record the whole thing and it's gonna be this great live collector's edition CD thing and on downloads or whatever it is you kids do these days.' Another laugh.

Callum deleted the lot, then added her mobile number to his phone's barred list.

'And every penny's going to—'

He killed the TV with the remote and slouched back to bed.

Dotty's voice cracked through the kitchen like a whip. 'You're up!'

Callum didn't look up, just stayed where he was: slumped at the small table, wrapped around a bitter mug of milky coffee while his stomach growled and gurgled. 'Why did you let me drink so much?'

'Don't look at me. According to Hedgehog you'd had about half a bottle of whisky by the time I got there. Not to mention all the beer. You owe him about seventy quid and an apology.'

Seventy quid?

Oh God...

A groan broke free and Callum sagged even further. 'What happened to my bike?'

'You left it at the Bart.' A warm hand rested on the small of his back.

'I know this sounds terrible, but you know what it's like with a murder enquiry, so…?'

He wouldn't be taking a couple of days off after all. 'Mother wants me back at work.'

'Ah. No.' Deep breath. 'They want you to come in and formally identify your mother's remains today. I know they've got the familial DNA match, but they still need someone to come down the mortuary and confirm that it's her. Sorry.'

Of course they did.

He straightened up. 'Yeah.'

Dotty wheeled Keith back towards the door. 'How's the hand?'

He held it out.

'Ooh. Right.' She made a hissing noise. 'We probably better get you to A-and-E first.'

'Are you *sure* you don't want to go to A-and-E?' Dotty manoeuvred her wheelchair in front of him, blocking the corridor.

'Let's just get this over with.'

Clearly, whoever built Castle Hill Infirmary hadn't given a toss about the bowels of the building looking like what bowels usually contained. Down here, in the sub-basement, they didn't bother with all that fancy terrazzo flooring, calming paintings, and institution-green walls. The floor was concrete with a scuffed line of black paint down the middle, the walls brick and breezeblock. And instead of a fancy-pants suspended ceiling with moon-surface tiles, bundles of cables and pipes snaked their way through the gloom. Because putting in enough lightbulbs to actually *see* by was just pandering to people. Much better to leave the corridor looking like something out of a horror movie.

It was warm down here too, the air heavy with the weight of the building above, thrumming and ticking and clicking with distant hospital sounds.

'Callum?'

He blinked. Puffed out a breath. 'I'll get the hand seen to when we've finished. Promise.'

A nod, then Dotty spun her wheelchair around and squeaked off down the corridor. 'We're thinking of getting a carryout tonight. I fancy a Thai, if you want to join us?'

Callum limped after her. 'Dotty?'

'What, you don't like Thai food?'

'Thank you.'

'Nah,' she let go of Keith's rim and waved a hand over her shoulder, 'it's only takeaway, no biggie.'

'And not just for taking me in last night, for *everything*. You were the only one who didn't treat me like a deep-fried jobbie when I joined the Mob.'

'Yeah, well, I need *someone* to raid the vending machines for chocolate, don't I? Not like Wanky Watt the Wrinkled Willy-Wart is going to do it.'

The corridor took a sharp right, only a single working lightbulb to deflect the darkness. A sign on the wall was barely visible, 'Mortuary →'.

'Maybe you should give him a chance?'

'What, Watt? I'd rather give him a boot up the backside.'

'He risked his life yesterday for a nasty wee scrote who'd tried to kill him. And it wasn't an automatic, gut-reaction, jump-straight-in thing, either: I could see him thinking about it. He knew it was stupid and dangerous, but he did it anyway.'

'Hmmm…' She followed the little black line. 'He's still a moaning dick, though.'

'Oh, *totally*. But wouldn't you be if you were him? If you had to wake up with that face every morning?'

A pair of double doors loomed up on the right, lit from above by a small fluorescent tube that buzzed and flickered. They'd mounted metal bumper plates on the dark-green wood – presumably to protect it – the surface covered with dents, gouges, and scrapes. Unlike living patients, the dead didn't mind if you used the trolley they lay on as a battering ram.

Dotty let Callum do the honours. He held one side open as she wheeled herself inside, then followed her into that familiar dark-brown reek of human waste and disinfectant. Each breath hung in the air, like a ghost, before dissipating away into the cold.

The mortuary looked about two hundred years overdue for a make-over. Its floor was covered in black tiles, cracked and uneven, the walls with filthy ivory-coloured ones, stained like a smoker's fingers. Three stainless-steel cutting tables sat in front of a wall of refrigerated drawers, the other walls lined with metal work surfaces. Glinting in the harsh overhead light.

A tall man in pale-blue scrubs and white wellies worked a mop along the floor tiles, pushing a mini tidal wave of grey-beige water around. Ponytail dangling behind him, high forehead almost as shiny as the cutting tables.

Only one of them was occupied.

The body was huge and tallow pale. Naked. On its back. Thick bloated arms and legs. Dark wiry pubic hair like a mini forest, nestling at the end of a gaping wound that stretched all the way down from his collar bone. Skin peeled back, front of the ribcage removed, torso hollow and glistening. Beard like a bear, but blotchy and yellowed around the mouth. Thick bands of bruises around his wrists and ankles.

The only other person in the room was leaning back against one of the work surfaces, poking away at his phone. Blakey looked up as the mortuary door clunked shut behind them, scowling around that big plastic guard thing taped over his ruined nose. A nod. 'MacGregor. Hodgkin.' Then back to his text, or game of Angry Birds, or whatever.

Dotty parked herself in the middle of the room. 'Come on then, DS Blake, where's your organ grinder?'

Blakey kept on poking. 'Conference call in the office.'

A half-glazed door sat off beside the sinks, the glass frosted like a public lavatory. The word 'PATHOLOGIST' graced a brass plaque with 'PROFESSOR MERVIN TWINING CBE' printed across a laminated sheet of A4 beneath it. The sound of muttered voices was just audible over the chilly drone of the fridges.

'Callum?' Blakey stopped poking, but kept his eyes on the screen. 'I was sorry to hear about your mother.'

'Thanks.'

Dotty wheeled herself over to the opened body. 'Who's your boyfriend?'

Silence.

'In your own time, Blakey, we've nothing better to do.'

He pressed a couple of buttons then put his phone away. 'Fat Archie Benton. Bunch of public-minded citizens decided they didn't fancy their children sharing a tower block with a convicted kiddy-fiddler, so they invited him round for drinks to talk it over.'

Dotty wheeled Keith on a slow lap of the remains. 'Very nice of them.'

'Don't think Fat Archie would agree. They pinned him down, jammed a funnel in his gob and treated him to all the bleach he could drink.'

A clunk and rattle from the office door and Teabag stepped out, flicking the dark floppy hair out of his eyes. 'Detective Sergeant Hodgkin!' He gave Dotty a smile, making the dimple in his square-jawed chin deeper, light glinting off his little round glasses. He smoothed down the top of his purple scrubs, then leaned down and kissed her on the cheek. 'To what do we owe the honour?'

'Professor Twining.' She reached up and put a hand on Callum's arm. 'We're here about the female remains that came in yesterday?'

'Ah yes, the severed head!' His smile grew. '*Completely* fascinating. Let me show you.' He strode across the cracked black tiles to the wall of refrigerated units. Opened a door and rattled out the stainless-steel drawer inside. A small body bag sat on the surface, the kind used for children. He scooped it out and placed it on one of the empty cutting tables. 'Here we go.'

The zip hissed open, then Teabag pulled the plastic sides down, exposing the contents.

The breath solidified in Callum's throat. Spread down into his chest like setting concrete.

After all this time.

They'd closed her eyes. Which somehow made it ... *better*. Better than the thought of her lying in that plastic bag, with her eyes open, staring into the darkness, in a mortuary drawer, buried deep beneath Castle Hill Infirmary. Her skin was impossibly pale, the freckles looking as if they were fading away. Someone had washed her hair, or at least cleaned the gunk out of it, leaving it like silk. The hideous stump of her neck: wide and purple and gaping.

Callum swallowed something bitter. Stared.

'Now, the truly interesting bit is this.' Teabag snapped on a pair of blue nitrile gloves and picked her head up, turning it over and brushing the hair away from her ear. 'The remains were covered in some sort of gelatinous residue. Took us ages to figure out what it was.'

Dotty looked away. 'Actually, Professor—'

'If you freeze any sort of meat for long enough, it'll end up with freezer burn. Doesn't matter if you put it in a bag or not, if there's *any* air in there the meat will eventually dehydrate and oxidise. I'm sure you've seen it yourself lots of times: sausages, joints of pork, steaks, they go all pale and gritty looking?'

Twenty-six years...

'That's why producers put an ice glaze on prawns. But ice *sublimates*, so over extended periods the water molecules will migrate to the coldest spot, leaving the remaining surface exposed, and you get freezer burn again.'

All that time, while he was being shuffled from care home to care home, there she was. Hidden away in someone's freezer.

271

'*However*, if you're smart about it, you can get round that by preserving your severed head in aspic before freezing. That's what the residue was: aspic. Isn't that fascinating?'

Dotty's hand tightened on his arm. 'Callum? Are you OK? You look pale.'

'We had to clean it out of the aural, nasal, and sinus cavities with a syringe. Every available orifice was full of it. That's why the remains are so well preserved.'

All those years...

The room went grey around the edges, all colour focused on the head in Teabag's hands.

'Callum?'

'Something like this takes practice. Skill too – you'd probably have to fill all the cavities one at a time and let them set before doing the next one, or the aspic would just ooze out.'

Locked away in the frozen darkness...

'I suppose if you had a big enough bucket you could do it all at once, but you'd have to make sure you didn't leave any air pockets. Not easy.'

All that time...

Behind him, someone coughed.

'Constable MacGregor?' That was Powel's voice. Wonderful. Because things weren't bad enough. 'Callum. I ... I can only imagine how difficult this is.'

The words wouldn't come out, blocked by the knot of barbed wire twisting itself at the base of his throat. Callum swallowed and tried again: 'What happened to her earrings?'

'I'm sorry, but we need you to formally identify the remains.'

'They were in the photograph. Tiny shell earrings. One blue, one pink.'

'Is this your mother?'

'WHAT HAPPENED TO HER BLOODY EARRINGS?'

Silence.

He looked up, and there was Powel, staring at him with a look of utter pity on his bruised face. Left cheek all puffy and purpled at the side of his mouth. A scab on his split lip.

Powel nodded. 'They're in evidence. Don't worry: they're safe, nobody's stolen them.'

At least that was something.

Callum closed his eyes and let out a shuddering breath. 'It's her. It's my mother.'

272

39

The curtain clattered on its rail and Powel stepped into the little treatment booth. 'We need to talk.'

Callum eased his right hand into his jacket sleeve, taking it slow. When he'd finished, a wodge of fibreglass cast poked out of the end. They'd left his thumb free, but all four of his fingers were imprisoned to the tips – partially curled as if he'd been caught in the act of cupping something. 'You're pressing charges.'

Of course he was.

'You chipped two of my teeth and knocked a crown off.'

'Good.' Callum stood. 'You deserved it.'

Powel stared at him. Then looked away. 'Possibly.'

'And this'll be the perfect opportunity to get rid of me, won't it? Polish off your little vendetta.'

A sigh. 'It's not a "vendetta", Constable MacGregor. I don't know how you managed to fool Professional Standards, but you took a bribe and—'

Callum barked out a laugh. 'No. No I didn't.' He fumbled with his jacket zip, not easy using just a thumb and a wodge of fibreglass. 'She didn't tell you, did she?'

'This has nothing to do with Elaine.'

'You've got *no* idea what she talked me into.'

That pulled a half-smile onto Powel's unbattered side. 'If this is about International Women's Day, it—'

'I didn't take a bribe to cock up that crime scene, and do you know why? Because *I* wasn't the one who cocked it up. But Elaine couldn't take the blame, could she? Noooo. Not when she was *pregnant*. With all that baby stuff to pay for? We couldn't afford it without her maternity pay.'

Powel's smile died. 'You're genuinely trying to pin this on her?'

'I threw my career in the septic tank to protect *your* child. It wasn't even mine!'

'Don't be ridiculous. This isn't—'

'Every bloody day! I turn up for work and get treated like filth, so your bloody baby can have a fancy stroller and a crib and everything else.'

'For God's sake, Callum, *listen* to yourself. You lost, OK? Lying to get revenge won't change anything.'

He paced to the end wall, then back again, barely three steps. 'And you want to know the *really* funny part? I can't even go to Professional Standards and tell them what actually happened, because that's how completely Elaine's screwed me. I took the blame for her, I *lied* to an internal enquiry. FOR HER!' Jabbing his broken hand out in the general direction of Flanders Road.

'Callum, don't—'

'Ask her. Ask Elaine.' Another laugh burst free, tasting of bile and betrayal. 'Mind you, she hasn't told the truth for at least nine months, why would she start now?'

A trolley squeaked past in the corridor outside.

The hospital PA system crackled into life: *'Please keep your personal belongings with you at all times.'*

Someone in the next cubicle wailed out in pain.

Powel pinched the bridge of his nose. 'Let's park this for now. OK?'

'And what about the flat? I suppose you expect me to just hand it over?'

'I didn't come here to fight with you, Callum.'

'Because that's *not* happening. I've paid the mortgage for three years on that place. *My* name's on the title deeds.'

'I came to ask about your mother.'

All the air went out of Callum's lungs. He settled on the edge of the treatment table, broken hand clutched against his chest. 'Oh.'

'I've been reviewing the original investigation. Not that there's much left in the files after the Great Clear-Out of Ninety-Five. Why they treated it as a case of child abandonment is beyond me. Who abandons a wee boy, *and* the family car and caravan?' He sniffed. 'Is there anything you remember from that day? Anything at all? Doesn't matter how trivial or insignificant.'

'I was five years old.' Callum fumbled his wallet out and opened it. Showed Powel the photo of the four of them, grinning for the camera, all T-shirts and sunburn. Took a deep breath. 'We'd just spent two weeks on a caravan site outside Lossiemouth and on the way home I needed a pee...'

Steam coated the café windows, turning them nearly opaque. Little rivulets of water trickled across the back of the words 'THE TARTAN BUNNET' – vinyl lettering stuck to the glass in an optimistic arc. The red-and-white checked plastic tablecloth was scarred with ancient cigarette burns, and sticky to the touch.

A TV, mounted high in the corner, was tuned to some auction/car boot sale competition rubbish, with the sound muted and subtitles on, while a radio by the counter burbled out some cheesy pop tune from the eighties.

An auld mannie sat on his own in the corner, buried in that morning's *Castle News and Post*: 'BEST FRIEND'S PLEA FOR MISSING ASHLEE' above the photo of a painfully thin teenage girl.

Other than that, they were alone.

Powel poured a third sachet of sugar into his mug and stirred it. 'We'll do everything we can, but I won't lie to you: it's a cold case from over twenty-five years ago and we're stretched thin as it is. They won't let me stick a huge team on this while we've got modern-day killers on the loose.'

Callum sat back with his arms folded. 'So that's that, is it? Nothing happens?'

'No. It's going to take *time*, that's all I'm saying. DS Blake will—'

'Oh well, that's OK then. If Blakey the Octopus is on the case we'll get an arrest by teatime!'

A sigh. 'Callum, you can't just—'

'This is because I punched you in the gob, isn't it?'

'Don't you *dare.*' Powel jabbed a finger at him. 'I don't do "half-arsed", understand? I'm putting Blake on it because he's worked abduction cases before. I do *not* cock-up investigations out of spite.'

A saggy woman in a checked apron appeared at their table, a plate in each hand. No smile. Mouth surrounded by the kind of wrinkles that suggested she never did. Shiny forehead daubed with thin grey hair. 'Who's gettin' the sausage?'

As if there was any question.

Powel took a breath, then pointed. 'Sausage for him, booby-trapped for me.'

She clattered the plates down in front of them, then shuffled off.

Powel opened the soft white bap on his plate, revealing a thick smear of melting butter and a fried egg – brown and crispy at the edges, bright-yellow wobbly yolk. 'I know you don't think much of DS Blake, but he's like a pit bull with a small child. Once he sinks his teeth in he won't let go.' Salt and pepper on the egg. 'He'll do a good job.'

Callum slathered the inside of his buttie with tomato sauce. 'He's an idiot.'

'For God's sake...' Powel burst the yolk with a fork, spreading it around. Closed his buttie and took a bite. 'Elaine and I didn't set out to hurt you, Callum. It just happened.'

'What, and you think buying me a cup of tea and a sausage buttie, and saying "sorry" makes it all right?'

'No. It... We'd been working that murder/suicide and it was tough, OK? They drowned the kids in the bath first: two beautiful little four-year-old girls. Then Mummy and Daddy took turns eating a shotgun. Blood and brains everywhere.'

The ketchup bottle was the old-fashioned kind: glass. Nearly full. Heavy in Callum's hand. Just the sort of thing for battering Poncy Powel's head in.

'Elaine was upset and we went out for a drink, and it just happened. We—'

'Don't.'

Powel frowned at him over the top of his buttie, voice soft and concerned: 'Callum, I'm only trying to—'

'Well don't.' Callum thumped the sauce bottle down on the sticky tabletop. Stood. 'You want me to what, forgive you? Say it's all fine. All's fair in love and war?' He grabbed his buttie and tossed it across the table, sending the sausages spilling out to roll off the edge of the table and onto the floor, leaving a smear of blood behind them. 'Lost my appetite.' He marched for the door, grabbed the handle.

Powel's voice cut across the room. 'Word of advice, *Constable.*' He reached out a foot and stood on one of the sausages, grinding it into the lino. 'DI Malcolmson's right: you should take a few days off. You don't look well.'

And whose fault as that?

'Callum?'

He looked up from the bench and there was Franklin, wearing yet another Blues-Brothers-tribute-act suit – complete with white shirt and black tie. She'd wangled herself an official Police Scotland golf umbrella with the Crimestoppers' 0800 number emblazoned all over it. It trembled in the downpour.

She had a quick glance around. 'What are you doing, sitting out here in the rain?'

St Jasper's Cathedral reached up into the stained clouds, austere granite walls topped with sandstone spikes and gargoyles. The sandstone wasn't the genteel, pale, creamy-coloured stuff they used in the Wynd, but a dark dirty red like old blood. And nearly five hundred years of sleet and rain had made it bleed into the grey beneath. A big brown scab of rusty scaffolding covered the circular stained-glass window, the sound of a workman's radio burbling out promos for the music festival in Montgomery Park.

Callum toasted her with his can of Fanta. 'Detective Constable.'

Headstones stretched out all around him, most crumbling, many illegible. All those lives: their owners rotted away and forgotten, feeding the massive oak tree that dominated this part of the graveyard.

'I'm … sorry about your mother.'

He nodded. Stared out across the rows of the dead. 'You want to guess what I've spent the last two and a half hours doing? Trying to disentangle myself from Police Constable Elaine Pirie. Bank accounts, council tax, mortgage, electricity bill, BT, hire purchase on the TV...' He rested his elbows on his knees, the cast on his right hand tucked into his sleeve. 'I'd go home and drink a bottle of Bell's in the bathtub, but I don't *have* a home.'

Franklin stared up at the ribs of her umbrella, voice a low mutter. 'Why do men always have to be such babies?'

'Great, thanks for the pep-talk.'

'Fine, you sit there wallowing in self-pity.'

'Self-pity? My girlfriend's pregnant with someone else's child, I've been thrown out of my own flat, my career's in the crapper, my mother's severed head is lying in the mortuary, and they've put DS Blake in charge of catching her killer. Blakey the Racist-Sexist-Scumbag-Octopus. The halfwit you punched in the face is now the *only* person looking into my mother's murder. I think I've got every right to complain!'

A seagull landed between two graves, paddling its big orange feet on the grass, trying to lure a worm to its doom.

Franklin shrugged. 'So just sit there, then. Catch pneumonia. Play the tragic jilted hero. See if anyone gives a single toss about it.'

Rain pattered on the shoulders of Callum's jacket. Soaked into his wet hair. 'Feel free to spread your special brand of sunshine and joy somewhere else.'

'Or you can get off your moaning backside and *do* something about it.'

40

The smell of boiled cabbage haunted Division Headquarters' stairwells. Callum squelched his way down to the locker room, where it was joined by the ghosts of cheesy feet, eggy farts, and cloying deodorant.

Full-length metal lockers lined the room, each one with a number, nametag, and assortment of dents. Some were plastered in headlines and photos culled from newspapers. Some with celebrity photos from the tabloid magazines. Others austere and bare. Nothing to see here: move along.

More lockers made an island in the middle of the room, surrounded by a knee-high wall of slatted benching. Heavy-duty clothes rails were hung with stabproof vests and high-viz waistcoats.

A young PC sat in the far corner, folded forward with his elbows on his knees, face buried in his hands. Shoulders quivering. Making little sniffing noises.

Callum took out his keys and unlocked locker 322. Opened it. Stared at the wall of photos Sellotaped to the inside of the door.

Most of them were selfies of Elaine: grinning for the camera, making pouty duck-lips, flashing the peace sign, pulling faces, going from flat-stomached to swollen pregnant bulge. All nice and normal. A happy little family in the making.

There was even a printout of the sonogram – looking like a radar image. A fan of streaked grey, surrounded by black, and just off the centre of the image, a small dark kidney-shaped blob. Elaine had drawn a circle around it in red crayon and an arrow labelled 'GOD, IT LOOKS LIKE A PEANUT!!!!' surrounded by hearts.

He reached out with his good hand and ran his fingertips along the sonogram's smooth surface. Then curled them into claws and tore it from the door. Raked the photos down after it, letting them flutter and spill across the tiled floor. Peeled off his sodden jacket and wrung it out.

It wasn't easy with one hand in a cast, but he struggled through.

Water spattered down on Elaine's selfies. Soaked into Peanut's first picture.

He did the same with his shirt, trousers, socks and pants. Stood there in the nip, staring down at the puddled photos. Then swept them all up and dumped them in the nearest bin.

Done. Over. Finished with.

A wooden rack sat outside the door through to the showers. He helped himself to a towel from the pile – greying and frayed around the edges, sandpaper-rough to the touch. Scrubbed himself dry on the way back to his locker. Dumped it on the floor to soak up the wrung-out water.

His spare fighting suit was a little crumpled, but at least it wasn't damp. No idea when he'd last had it on. Been a while since someone was sick all over him. They tended to gloss over that bit in the recruitment posters.

Callum bundled up his soggy suit and shoved it into a bin-bag. Tied a clumsy knot in the top.

Then marched out of the room, leaving the PC to cry in peace.

Callum stomped his way up the stairs. Through the double doors and into the MIT's palatial abode. Marching down the corridor, past the meeting rooms, past the open-plan offices, past the mini-canteen.

Poncy Powel's door was shut – probably off getting someone else's girlfriend pregnant.

Good. The chance of Powel getting another punch in the face was about ninety-nine point nine percent. And there were far too many of his team knocking about for that to happen – they weren't exactly going to stand about tutting while Callum battered their boss into a squishy mess.

Across the corridor from Powel's lair was another door with 'SERGEANTS' OFFICE' engraved into its brass plaque. Callum didn't bother knocking.

Inside, six desks were arranged around the walls, all with laptops and monitor stands, ergonomic keyboards and fancy mice. An electronic whiteboard above each desk, displaying photos and timelines.

A large woman with a pixie haircut had her feet up, swivelling back and forth, a mobile phone pinned between her shoulder and her ear as she picked at her fingernails. 'No. ... Because I *say* it isn't, Limpy. ... Well, guess what: I – don't – care.'

Two desks down, a tall thin bloke was hunched over his keyboard like a praying mantis, squinting at the media player on his screen.

And there, right in the far corner, was DS Jimmy Blake: elbows on his desk, hands propping up his face so he could do some industrial-strength frowning at the stack of paper in front of him.

Callum nicked the office chair from the next desk, wheeled it over, and sat. Dumped his bin-bag on the nice new carpet tiles. 'Blakey.'

He didn't look up. 'Go away.'

Mantis Boy must've set his player going, because a young girl's voice crackled out of his computer's speakers. '*You want to get wasted for my birthday next week? I can utterly rob a bottle of voddy from my gran.*'

A slightly muffled answer, dripping with teenaged indifference: '*Yeah, why not. You only turn fourteen once, right?*'

Callum poked Blakey in the shoulder. 'Have you made any progress yet?'

A long-suffering sigh. Finally he turned and looked up, showing off the big plastic guard covering what was left of his nose. Eyes like a panda that'd been on a three-day bender. 'Do you have *any* idea how many cases I'm working right now?'

'*My step-dad wants to have a party down the bowling alley. Laser Quest, dodgems, and burgers, like I'm, I dunno, six years old or something. He's such a* complete *spazmoidal—*'

'*Yeah, hang on, Marline.*'

'Have you at least *looked* at the file?'

'What am I, Dr Who? When am I supposed to have the time?'

The muted sound of a doorbell rang out from the speakers.

'*OK, OK. Jesus.*' Clunks and rattles. '*What?*'

Callum poked him in the shoulder again. '*Make* the time.'

A man's voice, barely audible: '*I'm sorry, but I'm trying to find my son.*'

Blakey stared at him. 'You want me to just drop everything and rake through the ashes of a cold case from twenty-six years ago? No chance.'

The praying mantis swivelled around in his seat. 'Can the pair of you belt up? I'm trying to listen to this.'

'*—his name's Sam. He's only four.*'

'It's my *mother*, Blakey. Understand? It was *her* head in that carrier bag.'

Blakey looked away. 'You sure you want to know what happened?'

Was he deaf or something? 'Of course I sodding do!'

'Oh, you poor man. Please, come in.' A woman's voice this time. *'You said his name's Sam?'*

'Sam. Yes.'

'Callum, you know well as me: nine times out of ten, when the wife gets murdered it's the husband that did it. That's how people work.'

'It's not—'

'Right now your dad's probably sodded off to the Costa del Sol, or Australia, or something like that. Living under an assumed name with your brother and his grandkids.'

Because Alastair would be able to get *his* girlfriend pregnant. Wouldn't need some greasy Detective Chief Inspector to come in and do it for him behind his back.

'What are you doing?' The woman's voice again. High and panicky this time. *'No! Leave her alone!'*

Screams ripped out of the speakers.

'LEAVE HER ALONE!'

Callum stood. 'You're an idiot, Blakey. And I'm glad Franklin battered your nose to a pulp. Hope it hurt.'

He marched out to a soundtrack of screaming.

How anyone was supposed to find *anything* down here was a mystery. Rows and rows and rows of shelving units stretched away into the gloom, each one crammed full of brown cardboard file boxes. The air slightly crunchy with the earthy taste of mildew and dust. They'd followed the same lighting design as Camburn Woods – less than one in three strip lights worked. Most were completely dark, the odd one pinging and buzzing, letting out an intermittent flicker before going out and starting all over again.

Callum hauled another box from the shelf and wiped a finger through the thick fur of dust covering the 'CONTENTS' sticker. Checked the crime number. Nope. Stuck it on the floor, and tried another one. And another. Put them all back where they'd come from and tried the shelf below.

Twenty minutes of raking through years' and years' worth of ruined lives and horror.

Still, at least this lot seemed to be in the right kind of era.

His mobile jangled into life and he pulled it out. Who would've thought you'd get a signal down here, in the basement of DHQ? Wonders never ceased.

He hit the button. 'Hello?'

Silence.

'NUMBER WITHHELD.' glowed in the middle of the screen.

Great.

This again.

'Willow, if someone's hurting your mum you need to—'

'*Callum.*' Not Willow Brown, DCI Reece Scumbag Powel.

He clenched his face. 'What do *you* want?'

'*I've just had Elaine on the phone.*'

He pinned the phone between his ear and his shoulder and pulled out the next box. 'Well, I'm sure that makes a difference from having her in the bed *I* bought.'

Nope.

The next box joined it on the concrete floor.

Nope.

'You still there?' Wouldn't be a loss if he wasn't.

Next box.

'*You cancelled the mortgage payments. You know fine well, her maternity pay—*'

'Get stuffed. The pair of you manoeuvred me out of my own sodding flat, do you *really* think I'm going to keep paying the mortgage so you can shag in it?'

The last one was tucked away at the back of the shelf. Ah. That looked a lot more promising – no crust of dust. Someone had checked it out recently.

'*You can't just—*'

'I've been paying *your* bills, Powel. Who do you think bought that crib, or the Winnie-the-Pooh mobile, or all those sodding baby clothes?' Getting louder and louder. 'Who bought the Nutella and pickled cucumbers for the last nine months? COS I DON'T REMEMBER IT BEING YOU!'

His words managed a brief echo, before being swallowed by the ranks of shelves and boxes.

'*Are you finished?*'

'Damn right I am: finished being your idiot. Pay your own bloody mortgage.' He thumped the clean box down on the pile and checked the crime number. Had to be at least a dozen of them printed on the sticker in careful blue biro. And third from bottom was an exact match for the reference he'd dug out of the computer.

'*This isn't productive, Callum. We are where we are and throwing tantrums isn't going to change that.*'

283

'OK, I'm hanging up on you now. Feel free to take your phone and ram it up—'

'You need to collect your things from the flat.'

Right.

His back stiffened. 'And will Elaine be there?'

'I ... don't think that would be wise, do you?'

Definitely not. 'I want my books back.'

'She's staying with her mother for a couple of days. Come over any time after eight.'

'I'll turn up when I feel like it. It's *my* flat.'

'We've changed the locks, Callum. After eight. I'll be there to make sure you don't do anything foolish.' Powel hung up.

Callum lowered his phone, knuckles white, the plastic creaking as he squeezed it. Then he snatched his arm back, ready to hurl the thing into the darkness... Hissed a breath out through his nose. Turned away.

Then back again, slamming his foot into the nearest file box – sending its contents spraying out across the dusty floor.

'Something foolish.' Yeah, like battering Powel's head in.

His shoulders dipped.

There were files and evidence bags everywhere.

He sighed, squatted down, and cleaned it all up.

Powel might have been an adulterous two-faced slimy scumbag, but he was right about one thing: the case file was virtually useless.

Callum flipped to the end of the file and back again. Which didn't take long as it was only two sheets. They had Mum, Dad and Alastair's names, the date they abandoned Callum, a brief note about social services taking him into care, and scribbled on the back in pencil: the name of both officers who worked the case.

No interview notes, no witness statements, no sightings. Nothing of any practical use whatsoever. Not even the name of the rest area they'd left him in.

Either the Great Clear-Out of Ninety-Five was incredibly efficient, or PC Gibbons and DS Shannon hadn't bothered their backsides doing any investigating at all.

Callum jotted their details into his notebook, stuck the file back in its box, and the box back on its shelf.

He signed himself out of the archives and collected his bin-bag full of wet suit. Draped it over his bad arm, freeing his good hand to pull out his phone. Dialled as he slogged up the cabbage-scented stairs.

'Brucie? It's Callum. Do us a favour and run a check on a couple of oldies for me: PC Gibbons, DS Shannon.'

'You got shoulder numbers?'

'Nope. But they worked here twenty-six years ago.'

'Give us a minute...'

Callum paused on the landing. Rain battered the window, rattling it in its frame. The flickering blue-and-white lights of a patrol car faded in the distance, siren wailing. A double-decker bus grumbled past, going the other way.

'Right, you got Police Constable Maggie Gibbons – transferred to Strathclyde in 1999. And Sergeant Robert Shannon. Retired twenty-two years ago.'

'You got an address on Shannon?'

'What did your last slave die of?'

'Come on, Brucie.'

'You're lucky I'm in a good mood. Won fifty quid on a scratchcard this morning.' The sound of a keyboard being tortured clattered through the phone. *'Here you go: Robert Michael Shannon, seventy-one, lives at Canaries Cottage, Leveller Road, Fiddersmuir.'*

'Thanks.' Now all he needed was a car.

Callum eased through the double doors into the corridor. Wandered down to the manky little offices of the Divisional Investigative Support Team, nice and casual. Mother's door was closed and so was McAdams'. No sound of voices coming from within.

The main office was quiet too.

Which was nice.

He eased open the door.

Empty. They'd all be out trying to track down Imhotep.

Good. That meant no awkward questions, forced sympathy, crappy haikus, or complaints about him nicking one of the pool cars.

There was a little whiteboard, over by the kettle and microwave, no bigger than a sheet of A4 – split up into three columns. A magnetic hook sat at the bottom of each one, a printed number plate at the top. And a bit in the middle to write your name and why you were taking the associated car.

Dotty's wheelchair-adapted Vauxhall was checked out, as was the battered Audi, leaving just one set of keys dangling on its magnetic hook: the ancient dirty-brown Ford Mondeo estate. And it was an automatic, not usually a plus point, but perfect if you only had one working hand to drive with.

Callum liberated the keys with a 'Yoink!' then scrawled something unintelligible in the details section. Probably wouldn't fool anyone for long, but it was worth a go.

He would've got away with it too, if it wasn't for that pesky DC Franklin.

She was marching down the corridor, clutching a sheet of paper when he slipped out of the office. Stopped and stared at him. 'Callum.'

He wheeched his hand behind his back, hiding the car keys. Pulled on a smile. 'Thought everyone was out.'

'Had to hang about, waiting for this.' Franklin held up the sheet of paper. 'Warrant forcing Strummuir Smokehouse to hand over all their employees' details. I'm off to serve it.'

'Right.' Sod. That meant she needed the last pool car. 'So they've not recovered the body yet? From the river...'

'Could you look more shifty than you do right now?'

'I don't—'

'*And* you're meant to be on compassionate leave.'

'What happened to "get off your moaning backside and *do* something about it"?'

Franklin narrowed her eyes. 'What are you up to?'

'Me? Nothing. Nothing at all. Just changed out of my damp suit.' Callum forced the smile a little wider. Jiggled his bad arm and its decorative bin-bag. 'Tell you what, as I'm not doing anything right now, how about I come with you? You know: keep myself occupied. I'll drive if you like? Not a problem.'

'Hrmmm...' Then a nod. 'OK, get the keys.'

'Way ahead of you.'

41

Rain. Rain. Rain. It pattered on the pool car's roof, rippled the wind-screen – shifting everything in and out of focus.

The Strummuir Smokehouse car park was nearly empty. Six o'clock on a Friday night. The staff and visitors would be long gone. All except for the owner of the white BMW, parked in a spot marked 'RESERVED FOR MANAGING DIRECTOR ~ MR FINN NOBLE'.

Callum had a scratch at his thumb, where the skin poked out of the cast.

Clicked on the radio.

A weird dirge-like groan filled the speakers, slow and dark. *'And I burn inside like the stars, / A million thoughts and pains and scars, / Running away from you, Angelica...'*

He turned it down a bit.

Should've brought a book.

How? How was he supposed to do that when they were all back at the flat?

Yeah, well, should have thought about that *before* he stormed out yesterday, shouldn't he?

Sodding hell...

Callum thumped his head back against the rest, then peered through the window.

What the hell was taking Franklin so... Ah, there she was.

Franklin pushed out through the smokehouse front door and into the rain.

'See me burn, / See me run and hide, / See me dying, / See me cyanide...'

She hunched her shoulders and ran for the car. Clattered into the passenger side. 'Gah... Does it *never* stop raining here?'

'You get the names?'

'I swear to God, it's like Oldcastle's cursed.'

In so many ways.

'But no, / You can't see me, / You can't breathe, / You can't hear me...'

She shook the rain from her hair. 'And what are you *listening* to? Sounds like a funeral for depressed monks.'

'No idea.' He cranked the blowers up full, drowning it out. Turned the car around and headed back along the road, through Strummuir. Driving with one hand in a cast wasn't so bad when you didn't have to bother changing gears. 'So: names?'

'Yup.' She dug out her phone and poked at the screen.

'Planning on telling me at any point?'

'Hold on.' Franklin put her mobile to her ear. 'Mother? Yes, it's Rosalind. I got the employee details from the smokehouse. ... No, rolled right over soon as I flashed the warrant. ... Uh-huh.'

A right at the roundabout took them out past the rows of little Scottish houses with their grey-harled walls and slate roofs. Fields of green and grey on either side of the road, streaking past as Callum put his foot down.

'According to Mr Noble, the man Watt tried to save from the river was one Tod Monaghan. ... Hold on, I'll put you on speaker.' She held it in the middle of the car and Mother's voice fought against the blowers' roar.

'Monaghan, Monaghan... Right, here we go, Andy's just bringing it up now. Tod Monaghan, thirty-five. AKA: Toby Hutchinson, AKA: Timothy Liddell, AKA: Todzilla. Did six years for attempted murder. Released on licence eleven months ago ... da, da, da... Oooooh: form for indecent assault. That's interesting, isn't it? And there was a rape case, but the gentleman he attacked didn't want to go to court.'

'Sounds lovely, doesn't he?'

'You know what I think, Rosalind? Violent sex offender, attacks men, works in a smokehouse, does a runner soon as John and Callum show up. I think we might have found our Imhotep. Isn't that...'

Silence from the phone.

A little graveyard slipped by on the left, its church a crumbling ruin. Woods on the right.

Some auld biddie, walking her dog in the downpour, clambered onto the grass verge as they approached. Stuck two fingers up as they passed.

And finally Mother was back: *'Rosalind? Why did you put me on speakerphone?'*

Franklin glanced across the car.

Callum put a finger to his lips and mouthed, 'I'm not here!'

'I'm … driving. Don't have a hands-free set. Safety first.'

'*Oh, yes. That's a good idea.*'

A right at the junction with the main road took them back towards town.

'*Just in case, I'm going to run everything past Dr McDonald. And we better get a warrant sorted for his home address too.*' Mother's voice faded, as if she'd turned away from the phone. '*Can you sort that for me, Andy? Top floor left, thirty-nine Bellfield Road, Cowskillin. Thanks.*' Then she was at full volume again. '*Good work, Rosalind.*'

'Thanks, Mother.' The line went dead and she slipped the phone back in her jacket pocket. Then frowned as Callum took the next left onto a country road. 'I thought Division Headquarters was that way?'

'Ah, yes. It is.' He gave her his best smile. 'Just got a *quick* stop-off to make on the way. Ten, twenty minutes tops.'

Franklin's head fell back against the rest, eyes screwed shut. 'Not again!'

'Knew I shouldn't let you drive.' Franklin scowled out of the passenger window.

'Hey, you told me to get off my backside and do something. Remember?'

The pool car crested the hill and there was Fiddersmuir, sulking at the bottom of a wide dip in the landscape, bordered on one side by a dense swathe of dark-green woods. An irregular grid of streets sat around an oversized town square with a dirty big monument in the middle. A church and town hall on opposite sides, facing each other down in a competition of who could look the most joyless.

The dour grey buildings got smaller the further away from the square they were, three-storey merchant houses giving way to austere Edwardian terraces, and finally miserable wee cottages. Someone had stuck a small housing estate on the far side, all pantiles and cream harling. Looking about as out of place as a vegan in a slaughterhouse.

Franklin kept her face to the glass. 'I meant on your *own* time.'

'This is my own time. I'm on compassionate leave, remember?' Callum checked the address and took them down a wide road lined with unhappy buildings, around the horrible monument to Prince Albert, and onto Leveller Road.

'You're impossible.'

Right at the end, just before the limits sign, was a large cottage set behind a long stretch of drystane dyke. A small conservatory sat out front, along with a collection of water butts. Tidy garden, thankfully devoid of gnomes. The words 'Canaries Cottage' sat in bright-yellow letters on a green sign.

'Ten, twenty minutes tops.' He pulled up onto the driveway.

'You said that twenty minutes ago!'

'Well, there you go then.' Callum grabbed a high-viz jacket from the back and climbed out into the rain, holding it over his head like a cape. Hurried up the path.

A little laminated notice hung in the glazed panel by the front door: 'If You're Delivering Parcels, I AM IN!!! ~ Try the Polytunnel Round The Back.'

Fair enough.

Franklin appeared with her Crimestoppers umbrella, following him around the side of the house. 'This is a *complete* waste of my time. I should be back at DHQ, working on—'

'Oh stop moaning. It'll take McAdams at least an hour to get a warrant sorted. Probably longer on a Friday night. All you'd be doing is twiddling your thumbs, listening to Dotty and Watt snipe at each other.'

The back garden was huge: a vast expanse of neatly mowed lawn, peppered with trees and bushes, meandering paths and flowerbeds. Off to one side, the grey arched shape of a polytunnel sat beside a row of beech trees, the plastic quivering in the downpour.

Callum jogged along the path, feet crunching on bark chips. 'Anyway, shouldn't you be more worried about missing your boyfriend's work's do?'

'Ten minutes, then we're heading back to headquarters if I have to drag you there by the balls. Understand?'

Music oozed out through the plastic, something old-fashioned and familiar, turned up loud.

He opened the door and bundled into the warm moist air, full of the toasted bready scent of soil and compost.

Dear God, this thing was bigger than his whole flat. It stretched on and on and on, full of green. Raised beds ran down both sides, packed with sprawling courgette plants, trailing cucumbers, dreels of tatties, rows of spinach, ranks of fancy lettuces…

Come the Zombie Apocalypse you could feed a family of four for a year in here.

Inside it was obvious why the radio was turned up so loud – the whole tunnel rang with every raindrop that thumped into its plastic skin. Thrumming and vibrating like an outboard motor. Fighting against a soft-edged bouncy song about some woman wanting to be with Callum everywhere. Which was a lovely offer, if a bit presumptuous.

Unless she was singing about the only other person in the polytunnel?

He was halfway down, on his knees, footering about with some sort of bean plant. Blue jeans, trainers, grey T-shirt with '1902' across the back in big letters, a swathe of pink skin showing through the top of his close-cropped grey hair.

Callum reached out and clicked the radio off.

The guy stopped footering and turned, frowning at them through a pair of gunmetal-framed glasses. A well-spoken English accent cut through the rain's drumming din, slightly higher-pitched than expected. 'I was listening to that.' His beard was every bit as grey and short as the hair on his head.

'Robert Shannon?' Callum dug out his warrant card. 'We need to talk to you about a child abandonment case you worked in CID.'

'CID?' He levered himself to his feet, brushed the dirt from his hands on a little paunch belly. 'I haven't worked CID for ... ooh, has to be twenty-five years now. And it's Bob, not Robert.'

'I was the child.'

'Ah.' Call Me Bob nodded. Turned. And pointed down to the far end of the polytunnel. 'You'd better take a seat.'

The cast-iron patio furniture was comfortable enough: a small round table and four chairs – each with a green-and-yellow cushion, bordered by some recycled chests of drawers on one side and a row of beetroot on the other. Above their heads, the plastic skin trembled.

Franklin checked her watch. 'Why didn't you say this was what we were here for?'

'Would you have come?'

'You should've told me.'

'Blakey hadn't even *looked* at the crime file. I checked the archive register. He's meant to be SIO and he can't be arsed to read the file?'

Not that it would have done him a lot of good, given how little was actually in there. But he could have put the effort in.

She puffed out a sigh. 'Don't suppose your ex-DS Shannon's done a runner, do you?'

Callum leaned forward in his seat, staring at the polytunnel door. 'Speak of the Devil...'

Shannon hobbled in from the rain, cardboard file box in one hand, brolly in the other. 'Here we go.' He limped his way down to the table and stuck the box in front of Callum. Shrugged his way out of his jacket. Eased himself down into his seat. 'Sorry it took so long; it was right at the back of the attic.'

Franklin raised an eyebrow. 'Sore leg?'

'Hip replacement. Doesn't usually bother me, but all this rain?' A shrug. He took the lid off the box and dumped it on the empty chair. Smiled at her. 'Have a look in the chest of drawers behind you, should be a bottle of red and some glasses.'

'I'm on duty.'

'I'm not.' Callum dipped into the file box, coming out with an over-stuffed Manilla folder held together with elastic bands. They crumbled beneath his fingers.

'Men.' She shook her head and went rummaging. Came back with two large wine glasses and a bottle of Malbec. Folded her arms and sat back.

Inside the folder were a bunch of statements from what looked like Dad's work colleagues and the neighbours. More from people who'd been at the caravan park that week.

Shannon opened the wine and poured out two hefty measures. Held one glass out. 'They were going to destroy everything, so I took it home.'

Callum accepted the glass and took a sip. Soft and jammy. 'The Great Clear-Out of Ninety-Five?'

'No.' He settled back in his seat, swirling the wine round and round the glass. 'We've met before, do you remember? Maggie and I inter-viewed you about a dozen times after it happened. She had a sort of giraffe glove-puppet for you to talk to?'

'I don't...' A frown. There was something there: a soft kindly face with a beauty spot on one cheek. A splotchy orange-and-white animal that talked with an Irish accent. 'Sort of.'

'We spoke to everyone we could think of, put adverts in the papers, posters everywhere, appeals on the radio. I'm sorry, Callum. If we'd had even *one* witness, maybe we could have done more. I suppose we'll never know what happened to them.'

Franklin scowled at him. 'We know what happened to Callum's mother.'

'Wow.' A chuckle rippled free, bringing a smile with it. 'That's great news. Where has she—'

'Her severed head turned up in Holburn Forest.'

'Oh.' The smile faded. 'I'm sorry.'

Franklin stood. 'Well, maybe if you hadn't treated it as a *child aban-donment* case, you'd have had better luck!'

'Whoa! I'm going to have to stop you there: Maggie and I ran it as an abduction. We'd been on it for months – fighting hard, but getting nowhere – before the top brass pulled the plug. Shifted us off to other cases. Downgraded this thing to "child abandonment" so it would look better for the crime statistics. Thank you and goodnight.' Shannon toasted them with his glass and drank. Sighed. 'So I kicked up a fuss. Wouldn't believe how much trouble *that* got me into.'

Franklin lowered herself back into her seat, cheeks flushed. 'I see.'

'That was it, far as my career was concerned. Because I wouldn't shut up, they gave me a "development opportunity", AKA: chucking me out of CID and back into uniform. I was supposed to make DI by the time I was fifty, instead of which I got to spend my last three years juggling staff rosters and patrolling Harvest Lane at chucking-out time.'

Callum put the statements back on the table. 'What about the Slug?'

'Hmm? Oh, we don't get a lot of them in here. I was listening to Radio Four the other day and they were banging on about setting a few chickens or ducks loose to eat the slimy little monsters, but they're even worse for guzzling lettuces than slugs are. So I just hand pick them and throw them in the burn.'

'Not slugs plural, *the* Slug. The man in the toilets?'

'What man?' Shannon leaned forwards, light glinting on his metal-framed glasses. 'Describe him.'

'Paedophile, about six feet tall, hunched, balding, think he had a limp? Breath stank of butter-mint.'

'And this was when you went missing?' Shannon's voice had gone up again. Excited. Eager. 'All those interviews with Constable Giraffe and you never mentioned him once.'

'He...' Callum's mouth clicked shut. 'I didn't?' He cleared his throat.

It was like tying an anvil to his stomach and throwing it overboard. Being dragged down through the water, breath burning in his throat, pressure squeezing him, sunlight fading as the lake swallowed him whole.

'If we'd even had one witness, maybe we could have done more.'

All this time.

'Maybe we could have done more.'

They'd *had* a witness: Callum. And he hadn't told them about the Slug.

'This is going to be our little secret. If you tell anyone, I'll know. And I know where you live and I'll come get you. Understand?'

He hadn't told them, because he was too scared. Too cowardly.

'Could have done more.'

DS Shannon and PC Gibbons could have caught the bastard. Could have saved his family.

It was all his fault.

'Are you OK?' Franklin was only visible from the knees down, standing in front of Callum's chair.

'No.' He kept his head between his knees. 'I didn't say anything. I should have *said* something.'

'Callum, you—'

'The Slug said he knew where I lived. He would come get me if I told anyone. I was terrified of him.'

'You were only five. A wee boy.'

Callum sat up, let his head fall back and covered his face with his fibreglass cast. 'Arrrrrrrrrrrrgh...'

The rain thrummed on the polytunnel walls.

Stupid, stupid, stupid, stupid—

A hand, warm on his shoulder. A squeeze. Franklin's voice, soft and kind: 'It wasn't your fault.'

Her hand was still there when ex-DS Shannon returned.

'Right, I've put in some calls, but it's going to take a while. Everyone I knew on Nonce Patrol is either retired or dead. But Franky Campbell's going to have a root about in his shed, see if he's still got any of the case files from back in the day.'

Franklin's hand slipped from Callum's shoulder. 'Does everyone steal files from the station?'

'Be glad we did.' Shannon pulled a face and sank back into his chair. 'The Great Clear-Out of Ninety-Five. The archives were packed, no one wanted to pay for a new storage facility, so they binned nearly everything not connected to a major case. A lot of people took stuff home rather than see it hurled in a big skip.' A shrug. 'I suppose, in a lot of ways, Oldcastle Police managed to outsource its storage problem to our attics and sheds.'

She checked her watch. 'And is this Franky Campbell going to be long?'

'Hours. And hours. And hours. He's on a Zimmer frame. Arthritis. *Very* bad.'

Callum nodded, then stood. 'Thanks, Mr Shannon. I appreciate...' A frown. 'Wait a minute: when I asked if they were chucking the files on my family's disappearance because of the Great Clear-Out of Ninety-Five, you said "no".'

'That's right.' He topped up his glass with the last of the Malbec. 'Happened right after they decided to write it off as child abandonment, even though any idiot could see it wasn't.'

'Why?'

'Officially? Not cluttering up the archive with redundant materials. Unofficially: because they were fiddling the crime figures and didn't want anything hanging around that proved it was an abduction. And super-unofficially?' He pursed his lips.

Callum stared.

Franklin cleared her throat. 'Any time you like.'

'Well, and this is just a rumour, and it didn't come out till years afterwards, but *super*-unofficially: they knew who did it and there was no way they were ever going to bring that person to trial, because that person was famous and that person was protected.'

'Hrmmm...' She flexed her hand. 'If the next words out of your mouth are "Jimmy Savile", I'm going to slap the face off you.'

'Jimmy...? *No.*' Shannon shook his head. 'And it's all just rumours anyway. Oldcastle's never been a mecca for the rich and famous, has it? Too sodding wet and miserable.'

'So who was it?'

'No idea. It was someone's leaving do, a DCI was drunk and mouthing off. Probably just a wine box of supermarket Cabernet Sauvignon talking.' A shrug. 'You know what some cops are like with a drink in them: the Castle Hill Ripper was actually on the city council, Sensational Steve from the radio has a basement full of dead children, Lord Lucan spent his last three years chained to the wall in a warehouse in Logansferry.'

Yeah. Still.

Callum stood. 'Do me a favour: see if you can track down your drunk DCI. Might be rubbish. Might be worth a go.'

Shannon levered himself upright and shook Callum's hand. 'I'm sorry about your mother. I wish we could've done more.'

'Me too.'

42

'...*spectonkular!*' Grating honking noises blared out of the car radio. '*You're listening to this super bumper edition of* Crrrrrrrrrazy Colin's Rush-Hour Drive-Time Club *on Castlewave FM, my friend, and we're here live at...*' pause for dramatic effect, '*the seventh annual Tartantula music festival! Yay!*' The sound of a crowd baying in the background – whoops, cheers, and whistles.

Franklin turned in the driver's seat. 'It wasn't your fault.'

'*Are we having a great time, or what?*'

More cheering.

Callum frowned down at the cast on his right hand, little pink fingertips poking out of the end. 'I know. But it doesn't help, does it?'

'*That's right-a-roonie, campers: we're not going to let a little rain spoil our fun. And now, are you ready for your next act?*'

Cheers.

The pool car wheeched down the dual carriageway, heading south, back into town.

'*I can't hear you!*'

Cheers.

On the right, the tight spirals and cul-de-sacs of Blackwall Hill. On the left, the necrotic miserable sprawl of Kingsmeath.

'*One more time!*'

Cheers, going on and on and on.

'Callum—'

'I know, OK? I was only five. But...' He rubbed his good hand over his face. 'Maybe Shannon will come up with something. I mean, the trail's only been cold for *twenty-six* years. What could possibly go wrong?'

'Darn tootin' you are. Let's give a great big Oldcastle welcome to Overture for a Riot!'

And the crowd go wild.

A slow, thumping drumbeat wove its way between the screams.

Franklin shook her head. 'You haven't twigged it yet, have you? Yes: the initial incident is twenty-six years cold, but someone dumped your mother's head in the woods Wednesday evening or Thursday morning. That's current. Something's happened to bring him out of retirement.'

She had a point.

The drums got louder. Faster.

She reached across the car and thumped him on the arm. 'So?'

'So we chase up the SEB. Fingerprints on the bag, any foreign DNA found on...' He cleared his throat. 'On the remains.'

Not his mother's head. *Remains.*

'Correct. Then you put out an appeal for witnesses: anyone in the vicinity of the woods. Dog walkers, courting couples, maybe it's a dogging hotspot? Get Traffic to stick up a couple of those "Were you here on the eighth or ninth?" sandwich board things they leave at the site of an accident.'

A single guitar chord sounded, long and trembling.

'Yeah... Only they won't do it for me: I haven't got a budget to give them. It's Blakey's case and he'll do sod-all for as long as he can get away with it.'

'So go *round* him. Talk to his boss. Get him slapped down.'

Another chord, building on the first.

Callum stared at her for a moment. Then burst out laughing. 'His boss is the one who got my girlfriend *pregnant*!' He held up his cast. 'Whose face do you think I broke this on? Powel's not going to help.'

'HELLO, OLDCASTLE!'

Nothing on the radio but cheering.

Franklin pursed her lips for a moment, then nodded. 'You're buggered, then.'

Might as well get *that* tattooed across his forehead. Save time.

The Blackburgh Roundabout loomed up ahead, the library in the middle dark and lifeless, while lights blazed in Montgomery Park – just past it, on the right. Marquees and anti-aircraft spotlights, a blimp shaped like a massive tartan spider. Its legs trembled in the rain. Yeah, because *that* wasn't going to give all the kids within a three-mile radius nightmares for months.

'*Wicker Man, Wicker Man, they're dancing while you burn inside, /
Run and hide, Wicker Man, your heart's pumping formaldehyde...*'

Franklin's phone rang and she dug it out, tossed it across the car to
Callum, then killed the radio. 'Put it on speaker.'

He did, holding the mobile out and keeping his mouth shut.

'*Rosalind? It's Mother. Where are you? We've been worried.*'

'Coming up to the Calderwell Bridge, just heading back to the shop
now. Did you get your warrant to search Tod Monaghan's home?'

'*Change of plan – I need you at Kings Park, east entrance.*' Pause. '*And
you can tell Callum he can come too.*'

Franklin raised an eyebrow. 'Callum? I don't—'

'*They didn't make me a detective inspector just because I'm pretty,
Rosalind. Now, bottoms in gear, children. We've got ourselves a body.*'

Franklin hunched her shoulders, rain drumming on her Crimestoppers
umbrella, picking her way down the gravel path from the car park.

Callum limped along beside her, bundled up in a high-viz jacket,
sticking close to stay dry.

Wet grass glistened in the fading light, big rhododendron bushes
lurking in the gloom, leaves just starting to turn on the trees. The fancy
sandstone bulk of Dundas House lorded it over the manicured grounds
– a massive Brideshead Revisited tribute act, covered with pillars and
twiddly carved bits – caught in the glare of a dozen spotlights, making
it glow beneath the dark sky.

But that was nothing compared to the light show on the opposite
side of the river.

Montgomery Park was lit up like a Ferris wheel. Marquees bright
as lightbulbs. That looming spider dirigible. Spotlights raking the low
grey cloud, the beams solid in the downpour. The pulsing thump and
rumble of drum and bass pulsing out across the water like a giant
heartbeat.

'Which way?'

Callum pointed.

A line of blue-and-white 'Police' tape turned and whirled in the rain,
blocking off the path a hundred yards further on, where the ground
fell away towards the river.

They ducked under it and picked their way down the damp stairs
to another gravel path, this one bordered by a knee-high stone wall.
Probably there to stop the dog walkers and joggers from tumbling down
the six feet of muddy bank and into the Kings River.

An aluminium ladder was tied to a couple of metal cleats sticking out the far side of the wall.

Callum peered over the edge.

Down at the bottom of the ladder, two SEB technicians in blue Tyvek Smurf suits squatted beside the broken-ragdoll figure of a man. He'd lost his T-shirt somewhere along the way and gained a deep gash across his back, but the faded prison tats on his arms and wrists were all the ID needed. It was 'Tod' from Strummuir Smokehouse, skin all pale and blotchy in the fading light, face buried in the mud of the river bank.

'Hrmmm...' Franklin's face puckered. 'That him?'

'Yup.' Callum stuck two fingers in his mouth and battered out a harsh whistle.

One of the techs turned and looked up, face completely hidden by the facemask and safety goggles. 'What?'

'Have you gone through his pockets yet?'

'One smartphone, deceased. One wallet full of papier-mâché receipts, two soggy fivers, a couple of sodden business cards, and an Irn-Bru-flavour condom. One handkerchief. A pound eighty-six in change. And a set of keys.'

Callum turned and grinned at Franklin. 'And you know what keys mean, don't you?'

He pulled out his phone and called Mother.

Bellfield Road stretched away into the distance, a long straight street of three-storey terraced granite. No front gardens, just a slab of pavement in front of the slab-faced buildings. A wee shop on the corner was boarded up, tentacles of black soot reaching out across the grey stone. The corner opposite was an aromatherapist's with bars on the windows.

And three doors down, in a block acned in satellite dishes, was number 39. It was one of the few buildings with an attic conversion – an ugly Dutch-barn-style lump of black slate stitched to the top floor. Dirty windows in dirt-streaked UPVC surrounds.

An intercom unit hung by a couple of brightly coloured wires, but the flat numbers on the panel still had names attached. 'Tod Monaghan' was printed in green ink next to 'Top Floor Left'.

Callum struggled his way into a blue nitrile glove, not easy with one hand in a cast, and slipped the keys out of their evidence bag. 'We ready?'

Mother and Franklin nodded from beneath the Crimestoppers brolly. Standing off to one side, McAdams grunted, rain thumping on the wide brim of his brown leather hat. His face was paler than usual, the lines deeper across his forehead and chin. As if yesterday's chemotherapy had been carved there with a Stanley knife.

'OK.' Keys one through three didn't work, but number four did.

Inside, the building didn't live up to its grim exterior. Instead it was painted a cheery shade of sandy yellow. Bright hall lights in fake-Tiffany lampshades. Pot plants curling out across the landing windowsills.

Callum led the way up the stairs.

By the time they reached the top floor, McAdams was puffing and wheezing, one hand pressed against his stomach. Face pale and shiny.

Top Floor Left had a green door with a welcome mat out front and a potted lily growing in a stand.

Callum knocked.

Mother rubbed McAdams' back as he hunched over. 'There, there. It's OK. You just catch your breath.'

Another knock.

Still nothing.

So Callum went through the keys again. Number Three unlocked the green door with a *click*.

He eased it open with his gloved hand.

Gloom.

'Boss?'

She shook her head. 'You and Rosalind can go first. Andy and me – we'll wait here for a minute. Rest our old bones.'

He stepped over the threshold.

A small irregular-shaped hallway with a coat rack by the door. Leather jacket. Parka with furry hood. Dog lead hanging like a noose.

'Hello?'

A door led off to the right: bedroom. Shrouded in shadow, but clean, tidy, bed made.

Franklin looked back, over her shoulder. 'He shouldn't be out here.'

'Who shouldn't?'

Next door: a galley kitchen, barely wide enough to turn around in. Mugs hanging from hooks beneath the wall units. Plates, bowls, and glasses lined up in the dishrack on the draining board. Spotless cooker.

'DS McAdams. Why haven't they *forced* him to go off on the sick? He's clearly not coping. Should be at home, or in hospital.'

'He doesn't *want* to go home; he wants to make a difference before he dies. What's wrong with that?'

Straight ahead: bathroom. Dancing penguins on the shower curtain. Wooden toilet seat. Splodge-free mirror on the medicine cabinet. The sweet lemony scent of bathroom cleaner.

'He needs help. Look at him. How is that healthy?'

Callum glanced down the hall towards the landing. McAdams was still bent double, Mother rubbing his back and talking in a voice too low to make out.

'What are they supposed to do, suspend him? Even if they say they're doing it for health reasons, it'd be a PR disaster: "Police Scotland sack brave cancer hero!"'

'He's going to *die* here.'

Probably.

One door left. It swung open on a living room.

Oh…

The rest of the flat might have been immaculate, but the living room? Not so much.

Franklin squeezed past him. 'Bloody hell.'

One window gave a view across the rain-slicked rooftops to the vast steel and concrete bird's nest of the City Stadium. The setting sun turned everything to fire and darkness as it burned its way through the gap between clouds and earth. Painting the living room in warm shades of bronze and amber.

The other window didn't give any view at all – it was completely covered in hardcore pornography. Sheets and sheets of it, Sellotaped to the glass. The couch was pushed back against one wall, clearing a space in the middle of the room for a wooden coffee table covered in plastic sheeting. And right in the middle of *that*, a mahogany-coloured body, curled up on its side, hands against its chest, knees against them, head bent forward at an impossible angle so the face was hidden.

The air was thick with the cosy enveloping smell of wood smoke.

Callum licked his lips. 'Yeah…'

Franklin puffed out a breath. 'Bloody hell. It *was* him. Tod Monaghan was Imhotep.'

And now he was dead, washed up on the river bank, facedown in the mud.

It was over.

No one else was going to die.

301

43

Ashlee's head made a dull ringing noise as it thumped back into the metal tank. She sniffed. Blinked. Stared up into the darkness. 'And I'm sorry, Billy. I'm sorry I made fun of your lisp in Mrs Roslin's class. I'm totally, *totally* sorry.'

The rats were asleep again, but they'd hollowed her out. Now the only things left were the jabbing pain in her stomach and the throbbing fire in her skull. It washed against the back of her eyes, like waves on a pebble beach. *Hissing.* In and out. And in. And out. And in. And out…

'And I'm sorry, Mr Khan. I'm sorry I used to steal Mars Bars from your shop. I'm sorry, I was stupid, and I'm sorry.'

There weren't many tears left, and the words were getting more and more difficult to make with her scorched-earth mouth and sandpaper throat. A tongue like a strip of cork matting, like they used to have in the kitchen before Dad ripped it out. Before he ripped *everything* out.

The words hurt, but what else could she do?

Dying.

All alone.

Here in this tub of manky water that she can't drink without being sick.

Dying.

In the dark.

There was nothing left, but to say sorry. Sorry for every horrible thing she'd done in her thirteen long horrible years on this cold horrible earth.

Saying it over and over. Grinding through her life: full of lies and petty hurts and jealousies and spite and spit and cruelty. Again and again. Remembering new horrors with every repetition.

Like binge-watching the worst box-set ever.

'And I'm sorry, Marline. I'm sorry for everything.' She scraped in a deep, gritty breath. 'I'm sorry for not being a better friend. I'm sorry for saying you looked like a fat minger all those times. I'm sorry for stealing your lunch money in primary seven. I'm sorry for breaking your hair-straighteners and blaming it on Sarah MacIver. I'm sorry I told everyone you had herpes in second year when it was just a cold sore. I'm sorry for snogging Peter and saying I didn't. I'm sorry for *shagging* Peter and saying I didn't.'

A little laugh turned into a sob. 'He was crap, by the way.'

The darkness blurred, and when she blinked, the shapes lurking out there refused to come back into focus. Her mother was little more than a fuzzy blob, slumped against the wall, chain tight around her neck.

'And ... and I'm sorry, Mummy. I'm completely utterly sorry. I was so horrible to you and you didn't deserve it and I'm a horrible bitch and I lied all those times and I stole and I cheated and...' Her breath rattled like a half-empty cereal box. 'And I let him *in!* Oh God...' The metal tub rang with the sound of her slamming her head back against it. Once. Twice. Three times. The chain around her neck rattling and clanking. Smashing her head back harder and harder till it drowned out the burning waves inside her brain. 'I let him in and now you're dead and I'm *sorry*. I'm sorry, Mummy. It's all my fault...'

But her mother couldn't forgive her, because her mother was dead.

So Ashlee waited till the sobbing stopped, and the stabbing pains in her stomach faded to a muffled scream, then went back to the start.

'I'm ... I'm sorry, Mrs Buchan, for ... for stealing money from your purse when you babysitted me...'

Because what else could she do?

44

Callum's phone *finally* went to voicemail. He gave the old man in Flat Six a pained smile. 'Sorry about that.'

Heat pervaded the living room, throbbing out of the fake coal fire beneath the fake mantelpiece. A single standard lamp glowed in the corner, fighting against the dark rainy night and losing. Not one picture or photo on the wall. No books on the shelves, just a collection of dusty porcelain cat ornaments.

The old man's shoulders rose beneath the threadbare cardigan. 'Don't matter.'

Curled up in his lap, an evil-looking ginger cat scowled out at Callum: *You're not welcome here, this is* mine.

'And you don't remember seeing any visitors, or anything like that?' He crossed to the window. Good view of the street from here, even at this time of night. Tod Monaghan's building was directly opposite, but this side didn't have an attic conversion, so Callum had to crane his neck up to see the flat. Even from this close, it was impossible to tell that one window was clarted in hardcore porn. Doubtful the old guy could have seen anything more than shadows on the ceiling from here. Like the ones playing across it now; hunched figures thrown into stark silhouettes by the occasional hard-white burst of a camera flash gun.

Two patrol cars blocked this bit of Bellfield Road, one at each junction, their blue-and-whites spinning solid bars through the rain. A dirty Transit van sat outside the building across the road, a slow progression of SOC techs in Smurf suits making their way in and out again. All caught in the streetlights' sickly yellow glow.

The old boy scrunched his face up and let out a huge sneeze. 'Urgh…'

He wiped his nose with his fingers, then rubbed them dry on his cardigan. 'No. No visitors. Keep ourselves to ourselves, don't we, Tannhäuser?'

The cat gave Callum another stare. *We hate you: go away.*

'Right, well, if you remember anything: give me a call, OK?' Callum left a Police Scotland business card on the mantelpiece and let himself out. Stood on the drab grey landing and pulled out his phone. Checked his call history. 'HOME ~ INCOMING, TODAY 21:05' was right there at the top of the list.

Lovely.

He pressed the button. Listened to it ring. Then Poncy Bloody Powel's voice sounded in his ear.

'Callum. We said eight o'clock. It's gone nine.'

'Oh I'm *sorry*, is our serial-killer investigation interfering with your evening? Because while you're sat on your backside, on *my* couch, I'm doing door-to-doors here.'

'Callum, we agreed.'

'No, *you* agreed. I'll get there when I get there.' He hung up on Powel and called Mother instead. 'Nothing doing. A whole building full of people and not one of them saw a single thing. Ever.'

'Ah well, it was worth a try. Thanks, Callum. Get yourself back to the Mobile Incident Centre and we'll call it a day.'

'Will do.' He thumped down the bare stone stairs and out through the front door. Into the rain.

The Mobile Incident Centre – AKA: DS McAdams' red Shogun – was parked not fifteen feet away, its paint turned the colour of dried blood by the streetlight, exhaust curling up into the cold damp air.

Callum hurried across the road and scooted into the back. 'Any luck?'

Franklin had the other half of the seat, Crimestoppers brolly wedged between her knees. 'Kingdom of the blind. Never seen so many people who never look out of their windows.'

'Welcome to Oldcastle.' Sitting in the passenger seat, Mother rummaged in a small paper bag, then passed it back, chewing around the words: 'Could be our Tod was just very good at not being noticed?'

Franklin helped herself, then tossed the bag to Callum. 'I know this might sound a little odd, but I was expecting a bit more ... I don't know, drama? It's never like this in the movies, is it? There's meant to be a big high-octane showdown when you catch a serial killer.'

McAdams turned in the driver's seat. 'Gwyneth Paltrow's head in a box.'

Mother's eyes bugged, then she hit him on the arm. 'Andy! Callum's mum...'

'Oh, yes. Indeed. Sorry, Constable MacGregor.' As if bringing up severed heads was nothing more than a minor faux pas right now.

Callum glared at him.

Mother hit him again. 'Andy, apologise *properly*.'

Sigh. Then a nod. 'Constable MacGregor: I'll admit that I enjoy winding you up, but I would never *ever* joke about someone's dead mother. It was thoughtless of me and I'm genuinely sorry if my comment upset you.' At least he sounded sincere.

Callum shrugged. 'Fine.'

'Good. Now, where were we? Ah yes, the story's emotional climax. Let's make it ... "Jodie Foster being hunted in a darkened basement" instead.'

Franklin glanced at Callum for a moment, then back to McAdams. 'Don't get me wrong, I'm glad we caught him, but it feels like a bit of an anti-climax.'

'I understand. You wanted more drama.' McAdams shook his head. 'My dearest Franklin. Real life is never so bold. Death is a dull thing.'

Callum plucked a green jelly baby from the bag and sent it to its doom. 'Don't knock "dull". When it comes to serial killers, "exciting" is to be avoided at all costs.' He liberated an orange one and passed the bag to McAdams. Peace offering. 'Do you remember Ian Zouroudi?'

'Gah...' McAdams' shudder must've been contagious, because Mother caught it too.

'Changing the subject,' she retrieved her jelly babies, 'we should go out tonight and celebrate.'

Franklin scooted forward in her seat. 'Karaoke?'

Mother smiled. 'There's none as fervent as the recent convert. But I don't see why not, if...' She pointed through the windscreen. 'Clap hands, here comes Cecelia.'

A figure in full Smurf had stepped out of number 39 and peeled back her hood. Now she stood in the rain with her face to the clouds, little tendrils of steam rising from her damp black hair.

Mother poked McAdams. 'Give her a toot.'

He did, leaning on the horn just long enough to make her start. Stare. Then disappear into the filthy Transit van for a moment. When she returned she was clutching a little red umbrella in one hand and an evidence bag in the other. She wandered over and knocked on McAdams' window.

He buzzed it down. 'Four bargain buckets, three with corn-on-the-cob, one with beans, and a Diet Coke, please.'

'Oh. Ha. Haha. Oh.' Her face barely moved. 'Is this you practising your kerb crawling, Andy, or could you just not live without me?'

Mother leaned across the handbrake, smiling up at her. 'Sorry. Just wanted to know if you'd found anything. You know, significant?'

'What, other than the mummified corpse on the coffee table?'

'Hopefully.'

'Well, we've got a number of small ziplock bags full of mushrooms from the fridge *and* freezer that look pretty damn magic to me. And when we took off the bath's U-bend the thing was full of dark liquid with herbs and wee bits of bark and stick floating in it. Sound familiar?'

'Very.'

'And we found *these*.' She produced the evidence bag from behind her back with two watches, and an assortment of piercings, plugs, and rings in it. 'They were in a shoebox under the bed.'

McAdams held his hand out, as if his drive-through order had actually arrived. Cecelia passed it over and he peered at the contents. 'Looks like serial-killer trophies to me. This big leathery monstrosity, unless I'm hallucinating again, was Ben Harrington's watch.' McAdams held the evidence bag out in the middle of the car, like Mother's sweeties. 'Anyone recognise anything else?'

Difficult to tell, but then one piercing looked very like another.

Franklin pointed. 'I think the red-and-white flesh tunnel might be Glen Carmichael's.'

Callum raised an eyebrow. 'Flesh tunnel?'

'Don't be filthy. It's what they call those hollow tubes they stretch their earlobes with. Glen Carmichael had a red-and-white one with a skull-and-crossbones in it.'

McAdams held the evidence bag up to the car's inner light. 'And there it is. Ladies and gentlemen, our case officially has an airtight lid. The novel is finished. It's time for the epilogue.'

'Cecelia?' Mother gave her a little wave. 'Tell your little friends that we'll be celebrating tonight at the Dumbarton Arms. There *will* be karaoke, but the first round's on me.'

She took the evidence bag back. 'Deal.'

The sound of fingers battering away at keyboards filled the little office, everyone hunched over their computer, the printer in the corner making whirring clunks every now and then to break the monotonous clicking.

Paperwork, that was another thing they never mentioned on the recruitment posters. Join Police Scotland: spend half your time filling in forms and the other half being covered in other people's sick.

It wasn't easy, typing one-handed, but Callum finished off his final door-to-door report and sent it to the printer.

He powered down his computer, stood, stretched. 'And with that, our handsome protagonist was first to finish.'

Dotty swore.

Franklin and Watt just kept on typing.

'Still all to play for, Dot: silver and bronze aren't as good as gold, but at least you'd be on the winner's podium. It's...' He cleared his throat and nodded. 'Detective Superintendent.'

The woman standing in the doorway had a full-on Kingsmeath facelift – blonde curly hair scraped back from her forehead and imprisoned in an unruly bun at the back of her head. Her grey eyes narrowed as she tilted her head to one side and stared at Callum. 'And the *reason* you came to an undignified halt just now, Detective Constable MacGregor?'

He forced a smile. 'Just finished my last door-to-door report, ma'am.'

'And we thought we'd rub that in our colleagues' faces, did we?'

The tips of his ears went very warm. 'Yes, ma'am. Sorry, ma'am.'

'Good. Serves them right for being slowcoaches.' Detective Superintendent Ness held up a hand. 'All right, everyone, hands off keyboards for a moment.'

A bit unnecessary, as the whole team had already stopped typing and turned to see how much of a bollocking Callum was going to get. But they all nodded anyway.

Ness stepped into the middle of the room and gifted them a smile. 'I've just been in with DI Malcolmson and DS McAdams, going over Operation Imhotep, and I wanted to stop by and tell you all what a great job you've done. Now I know the Divisional Investigative Support Team often gets the smelly end of the stick, but you've done yourselves, me, Police Scotland, and more importantly: the victims' families proud.'

Even Watt sat up straight at that one, looking like a cat that'd just been offered a spoonful of caviar.

'This was a swift and efficient investigation and you got the right result.' A little sideways nod. 'Yes, it's a shame Tod Monaghan managed to kill himself, cheating the families of a trial, but the important thing is that he's not going to be hurting anyone else. So well done, all of you.' She even gave them a solo round of applause.

Dotty grinned. 'We'll be happy to do it again, ma'am. You give us another killer to catch, we're there.'

'Yes. Quite. Well, the Chief Superintendent wants to add his congratulations to mine. He's putting on a big press conference tomorrow and he'll be making sure everyone knows about your invaluable contributions to solving this case.'

A pat on the back *and* credit? There would be pigs fluttering past the office window any minute now.

'In the meantime, DI Malcolmson tells me you're all off to the Dumbarton Arms for a well-deserved drink. First one's on me, OK? OK. Good.' Ness wheeched round on her heel and marched out of the office. 'Just make sure your paperwork's up to date before you go.'

'...and one orange juice and lemonade.' McAdams lowered the glass in front of Callum as if it was full of lukewarm urine. 'Takes all sorts.'

Word must've got out about Detective Superintendent Ness paying for the first round, because the Bart was hoaching with off-duty police officers, SEB technicians, and support staff. All clamouring for their free drink. Laughing, shouting, showing off, enjoying themselves.

Made a nice change.

And at least, with the Bart being packed to the walls, Hedgehog didn't have time to corner Callum and demand payment for last night's binge session. Small mercies.

Mother clinked her wedding ring against the double whisky in her other hand, setting the glass ringing. 'All right, people, as my dear old gran used to say: "HUD YER WHEESHT A MINTIE!"'

The hubbub died down to a muted roar.

'That's better.' She held out her hand and McAdams helped her up till she was standing on her chair, looming over the crowd. 'Now, I just want to say—'

A big voice boomed across the pub. 'Thank you, DI Malcolmson, for getting this lot to quiet down for a change.'

Everyone turned to face the door, where a massive lump of a man stood in the traditional black T-shirt and epaulettes, a peaked cap tucked under his arm and a moustache on his face. He held up a hand. 'Now, I know what you're thinking: the old man's just here to make sure no one's sloping off early, but that's not the case. Not this time, anyway.' A dark rumbling chuckle.

He got a couple of sycophantic laughs from the brown-nosed members of the congregation.

Mother forced a smile. 'Ladies and gentlemen: Chief Superintendent McEwan.'

The head of O Division gave a little bow, as if he was expecting a round of applause. He didn't get one. 'Today is a proud day for Police Scotland. Operation Imhotep's excellent result just goes to show what can be done with teamwork and the right management-support from senior officers. This is the essence of modern policing in these challenging times...'

Callum's phone launched into its bland anonymous ringtone. The two officers nearest him pulled pained faces and backed away a couple of paces as he yanked it out of his pocket and hit the button. Keeping his voice low. 'What?'

'Callum? Callum it's Bob. Bob Shannon? Hello?'

'...grasp the nettle and forge a new alliance with the public to ensure not just policing by consent, but by active enthusiasm...'

He turned his back on the Chief Superintendent. 'Bob, hi. Sorry, I can't talk, it's a bit—'

'I know it's late, but I think I've got an ID for your public-toilet paedophile.'

'...not just a success for DI Malcolmson's Divisional Investigative Support Team, but for all of O Division...'

'There are three or four possibles, but our most likely lad is one Gareth Pike. Mate of mine in the Sex Offender Management Unit did him at least a dozen times for trying to interfere with little boys in gents' loos. Montgomery Park, Dalrymple Park, Kings Park, Camburn Heritage Centre, all the classics.'

'...challenges when I took on the role of Chief Superintendent, but I knew that with the right people behind me, I could make a real difference to this division...'

'Point is, Pike got fed up getting his collar felt, so he started to play away from home. Rest stops on the A90, the services at Montrose, that kind of thing. So a lay-by on the Aberdeen road would have been right up his street.'

'...but it's important to remember that the transformation in Oldcastle isn't down to the hard work and inspirational leadership of just one man...'

Callum fumbled out his notebook. 'You got an address?'

'I can do better than that. Tell me where you are and I'll come get you.'

*   *   *

'Callum? Are you OK?' Mother stood in the Bart's doorway, hands deep in her pockets, breath curling out into the rainy night.

'Yeah. Fine.' Callum tried a smile. 'Just...' He picked at the lining of his fibreglass cast – hadn't even been on a day and already the thing was getting filthy, all greyed and blotchy. Getting it soaked at regular intervals throughout the day probably wasn't helping. 'Elaine and DCI Cock-Face want me to move all my stuff out. Today.'

'Ah.' She winced. 'I heard Reece had left his wife. Didn't know it was for your Elaine. Sorry.'

'She's not *my* anything.'

Mother nodded.

Water rushed in the gutters like filthy little rivers, washed across the paving slabs, hissed against the sign above the pub door, turned the streetlights into glowing spots – septic and angry.

A taxi grumbled past, a couple screaming at each other in the back seat.

'Callum, do you want a hand moving? It's not going to be easy with just a bicycle.'

He looked the other way. 'Actually, I thought I might borrow one of the pool cars. You know, without telling anyone.'

'Hmmm... Better take the Mondeo, then. You'll get more in the back of an estate.'

'Thanks, Boss.'

She made a tutting noise, then patted him on the back. 'Have you got anywhere to store your things?'

Ah.

There was that.

Because if Powel and Elaine thought they were keeping all the furniture and kitchen stuff he'd bought for the flat, they could carve that thought on a six-foot granite slab and shove it up their collective backsides. And there was no way it was all going to fit in Dotty's spare room. Never mind all the books.

Mother rolled her eyes. 'Men: you're sweetly pretty things, and we wouldn't be without you for the world, but your little heads just aren't suited to the practicalities of life.' She pulled a jailer's bundle of keys from her fleece pocket and worked a small Yale from one of the many rings. 'Here. My Jack has a lockup in Cowskillin: twenty-three Washington Lane, round the back of the processing plant. I'm sure it's all pornography and empty whisky bottles in there, but try not to make too much of a mess.'

Callum took the key. 'Thanks.'

A small green Toyota hatchback pulled onto the street, headlights shining back from the wet road. It parked four buildings up, outside 'Dougie's "Famous" Chipper! ~ Pizzas Kebabs & Baked Tatties Too'. The Toyota switched off its headlights and sat there with the engine running.

'And if you finish before midnight, come back and have a *proper* drink. No more of that orange-juice-and-lemonade nonsense. OK?'

'OK.'

'Good.' Another pat. 'Better get going: I'm doing "Somethin' Stupid" with Andy in a minute.' She headed back inside. And thirty seconds later, the car parked outside the chip shop flashed its lights and pulled away from the kerb.

Slid to a halt outside the Dumbarton Arms, right in front of Callum.

The driver's window buzzed down, filling the night with Lennon, McCartney, and Harrison imploring a postal worker not to sod off without checking their bag again.

Callum hunkered down with his hands on his knees and peered into the car. 'Can I help you?'

Ex-DS Bob Shannon smiled out at him, voice raised over the Beatles. 'Detective Constable MacGregor. You and I have an appointment with a child molester.'

45

Shannon paused for a moment at the top of the stairs, face flushed and shining. 'Urgh. The *smell*... Why does everyone have to pee in the stairwell? Do they not have toilets here?' He mopped his forehead with a green-and-yellow scarf.

Callum lurched to a halt next to him, breathing hard. Thirteen floors of climbing through the eye-watering reek of other people's urine and his throat burned. The air even tasted of it: sharp and bitter. 'He better be in after this.'

Faulkner Heights had to be the mankiest of the seven tower blocks that enclosed this side of the Blackburn Roundabout. Oh, it didn't *look* manky from the dual carriageway, or the library, because the council had painted the sides of the building that faced that way. But they'd left the other two sides as dirt-streaked concrete, with all the windows boarded up on the bottom three floors – about as high as a wee scroat could chuck a rock.

They hadn't bothered painting the inside either. Or dousing it with disinfectant. Though, to be honest, setting fire to the place was probably the only hygienic option.

A pile of bin-bags sat by the lift – beneath the 'OUT OF ORDER' sign – leaking rancid brown liquid across the floor. A dull yellow stain marked the wall in the corner, flowing down across pale crystalline growths to the ground – the burning stink of fossilised piddle mingling with the bin-bag's gritty stench.

Graffiti scrawled across the walls: generations of the abandoned, marking their territory in a slightly more permanent way than by peeing on it.

Shannon bared his teeth. 'About time they pulled this block down and stuck up something nicer. Like a crematorium. Or an abattoir.' He pointed at Callum. 'Before we do this, we need some ground rules.'

Callum wiped his good hand across his damp forehead. 'Go on then.'

'One: I know you want to kill this guy, but you don't. Agreed? No beating the living hell out of him, no breaking his fingers, not so much as a Chinese burn.'

'He—'

'No. That *can't* happen. We're police officers, or at least I used to be, and that means something. If he's the one who killed your mother, he goes to prison for a very, *very* long time. He doesn't walk free because you played "Batter the Suspect".'

Callum blew out his cheeks. 'Fine.'

'Two: we're going to Good Cop, Bad Cop it, and you're playing the good cop.'

Seriously? 'Come on, you can't—'

'No. Non-negotiable. If you're playing Good Cop you're less likely to twat him one.'

Callum stared at him. Then away down the dull grey corridor with its graffitied walls. 'Agreed.'

'OK, then.' Shannon leaned on the doorbell, but nothing happened: not so much as a *bing-bong* from inside. So he drew his fist back and gave the door three loud hard knocks. The kind that let everyone know the police were outside and they were *not* sodding happy.

Which was probably par for the course down here.

Or, strictly speaking, as they were on the thirteenth floor, *up* here.

Shannon gave the door another three bangs.

No one came out of the other flats for a gawp. The police hammering on someone's door had clearly lost its novelty a *long* time ago.

Callum checked his watch. 'Maybe he's out?'

'Doubt it. From what I've heard, Pike's pretty much a shut-in these days.' Shannon rolled his shoulders. 'Think we should kick it in? I've not done that in *donkeys*.' A grin tugged his grey beard out of shape. 'I was listening to Radio Four the other day and this guy from the Met said modern UPVC doors can stand up to a battering ram for over half an hour. This thing? One good boot and it's in.' He rapped his knuckles against the tatty wooden door. Someone had stolen the numbers off it, leaving just the dents in the paint to spell out '13-15'.

'We haven't got a warrant. Thought you wanted to do things by the book?'

'I used to love dunting someone's door in. It was like opening a present on Christmas Day, never knowing what you were going to get. Would it be a selection box, a pair of leather football boots, or a druggie with a shotgun?' A sigh. 'Strange, the things you miss when you retire from the force.'

Callum raised his left fist to the wood. 'One more go.'

But before he landed it, there was a *thunk* from inside. Followed by a light flickering on behind the spyhole.

Then a gravelly voice, dark as gravy, oozed through the wood. Unmistakable, even after all these years. *'Who is it?'*

Heat crawled up Callum's back, spreading pins-and-needles across his shoulders. He swallowed, then held his warrant card up to the spyhole. 'Mr Pike? We need a word.'

'Ah. I see. Well, I'm sorry, but it's not convenient right now. Not convenient at all. I'm ... indisposed.'

Shannon raised his voice a bit. 'Let's kick it in. Right now. Boot the door right off its hinges.'

'No! No, don't do that. I... I need my door. Yes. I need it. Please don't do that.'

'Then open up, *Gareth*.'

A rattling sigh. *'Today doesn't seem to be turning out as well as I'd hoped.'* The clattering sound of a chain drawing back was followed by several loud clicks. Then the door swung open.

The man standing in the doorway was stooped over, but his large bald head still came within an inch of the frame. Big. Wide. Just like he'd been in the car park, only a lot thicker around the middle. And instead of the black overcoat he was dressed in a stained silk robe, socks, Crocks, an 'I ♥ OLDCASTLE!' T-shirt spattered with what *looked* like brown sauce, and a pair of polka-dot boxer...

Gah!

Callum recoiled a step. So did Shannon.

Gareth Pike smiled, showing off perfect white teeth. Raised his bushy white eyebrows. 'I did mention I was indisposed.' The front of his underwear was tented out, pointing straight ahead at ninety degrees. 'Now do you gentlemen still wish to come in?'

Pike waved a hand at the couch. 'Sit. Sit.'

No chance.

Piles of newspaper and ready-meal containers teetered against the walls. The carpet, if there was one, lay buried beneath a thick layer of hair and filth. Water stains on the ceiling and walls. A drift of scrunched-up tissues spread out from the couch in a fan shape: all crunchy and flaky. Their faint bleachy smell mingled with the rancid odour of a man who'd clearly fallen out with soap and deodorant.

The only picture on the wall was Mary, cradling the baby Jesus.

An old-fashioned cathode-ray TV was hooked up to a video player, the screen flickering with a close-up of Simon Cowell's sneering face.

Pike lowered himself into a greasy armchair, legs spread wide, tent on full display. 'Oooh… My knees. Not what they once were.'

Hard to believe that this was the man who'd given him nightmares for years.

Callum crossed his arms, just in case his hands accidentally touched something. 'You don't remember me, do you?'

Pike's face creased for a moment. Then, 'No.'

Shannon went to sit, but obviously thought better of it. 'Twenty-six years ago, Gareth. You were interfering with little boys. Public lavatories, mostly. Parks. Service stations. Lay-bys. Winter, summer, autumn, spring: there you'd be, fiddling away. A nonce for all seasons.'

A big fat shrug sent his chins wobbling. 'A wise man once said, "To thine own self be true." So: yes. I admit it. But I've atoned for my sins. Repaid my debt to society with ten years attending to Her Majesty's pleasure at Peterhead Prison.' His hand reached over the brow of his belly and scratched at the boxer shorts, making the tent-pole wobble. 'Oh, this was back when it was a *specialised* institution, not the modern monstrosity they have now where they'll take just anyone. No, it was a lovely establishment. Loads of character. And *characters*, too. I remember one time, I was taking tea with a kindred spirit called Haroun and who should walk in but—'

'Twenty-six years ago.' Callum took a step closer. 'It was a lay-by on the Aberdeen road, not far outside Blackwall Hill. A family of four: mother, father, two wee boys.'

Pike raised his bushy eyebrows again. 'Sounds delicious. Were the boys blond and pretty? I *like* them blond and pretty.'

'I'll blond and—'

Shannon grabbed his arm. 'Good Cop, remember?'

Callum closed his eyes. Took a deep breath of stench. 'It was April. I was five and you tried to touch me in the toilets.'

'Ooh.' Pike squeezed himself through the polka dots. 'You were one of *mine*? You must have been *very* pretty when you were younger.'

'Two men came into the toilets and scared you off.'

'How rude of them.'

'My mother and father and my brother were waiting for me in the car outside. With a caravan on the back. Do you remember *them*?'

'Mmmm...'

'I swear to God, if you don't stop touching yourself I'm going to—'

'Come on, Callum.' Shannon shook his head. 'We agreed.'

'DO YOU REMEMBER?'

Pike didn't even flinch. 'I remember all my pretty little blond boys.' He squeezed. And squeezed. 'They're all I have left.'

Shannon pulled Callum back. 'All right. Let's just calm down a minute, OK?'

'Ask him. Ask him if he remembers hacking off my mother's head!'

Pike let go of himself and sank back in his seat. 'Oh, no. I would certainly remember something like that.' He raised his squeezing hand to his nose and sniffed the fingers. 'I don't do "mothers". Or fathers, come to that. Grown-ups in general repulse me.' A finger came round to point at Simon Cowell's face on the TV. 'I wasn't sitting here wasting a perfectly good Viagra on him. I mean, I'm not *gay* or anything. I just didn't think you'd like to see what I'd *really* been watching. Hmmm?' He licked his lips, dark and slimy like twin slugs circling his mouth. 'It's amazing what one can purchase over the interwebs if one is ... discreet.'

Callum pulled his arm free from Shannon's grip. 'Are you saying you didn't kill her?'

'Well of course not. Why on earth would I *do* something like that? Can you imagine how messy it would be? No: I'm a lover, not a fighter.' He gave a little shudder. 'But I do remember *you*. You ran off and hid in the caravan, didn't you? You wouldn't come out to play.'

'You said my parents didn't love me any more. That they'd given me to you.'

'Oh we could've had such fun, you and I. Before you got so *old* and *unappealing*.' Sigh. 'I waited so long in the rain for you. I hope you didn't mind my taking care of myself while I waited. But you wouldn't come out and help.'

Shannon curled his top lip. 'Did you see anything? Anyone else at the toilets?'

'Would you like to see the video I was watching? It's very good. I know everyone's obsessed with digital technology, but I'm not supposed to have a computer. I *do*, of course, but there's something so deliciously nostalgic about videotape.' His eyes widened. 'The way it flickers and buzzes. Oh, my...'

'Did you see anyone else, or didn't you?'

'Sometimes I like to twist the tracking all out of line, so it's like the old days when a tape's been copied and passed around and copied again and again and again. You don't get that sense of tradition with these modern digital films.'

Callum unfolded his arms and balled his left hand into a fist. 'Answer the sodding question, or I'll break the tracking in your *head*.'

'Oh yes. I saw someone. I saw things you wouldn't believe, right there in that car park, all those years ago.' Pike fluttered his eyelashes. 'But it'll cost you.'

Shannon grabbed Callum's arm again. 'He's just screwing with you. It's what people like him do.'

'Oh, no, no, no. All I'm asking is that you sit down and watch my video with me. Me and the Boy Who Got Away, *watching*.'

'OK, that's it, I'm going to kill him.'

Shannon tightened his grip. Leaned in close and whispered into Callum's ear. 'He puts on the video, you do him for possession of indecent images of children, or whatever they're calling it these days. It's not an illegal search, because he's shown you it voluntarily.'

'Well, my once-pretty-little-blond-haired-boy?'

Grab the greasy fat slug by the throat and squeeze. Dig both thumbs into his windpipe and squeeze till his eyes bulge and his face goes purple. Squeeze till he judders and gurgles and dies.

And never find out what happened.

Callum uncurled his fists. Forced it all back down again. 'Go on then.'

Pike clapped his hands. 'Oh how jolly!' He knelt in front of the video player and ejected Simon Cowell. Replaced him with a tape in a grey cassette. Collapsed back in his seat and grinned. 'You see, I was so angry when those ruffians burst into the toilets and spoiled everything I was going to slash their tyres. Serve them right.' He dug a remote control out from between his seat cushion and the arm of the chair. Pointed it at the TV and pressed play. 'But when I got out, another pretty little blond boy was right *there*. I thought it was you for a moment, but he was wearing a different T-shirt.'

A wall of flickering pink filled the screen.

'So I thought, well, today's going to end delightfully after all. Look what the baby Jesus has sent me.'

Callum turned his face away from the TV. Tried not to listen to the muffled sobs and pleas.

'"But," said I to myself, "where are this *delicious* little offering's parents?" Here's a lovely boy, on his own, in a car park. Surely Mummy and Daddy can't be far away.'

Shannon had his teeth bared, a look of utter disgust slithering its way across his face.

'And then I saw them. Mummy and Daddy. And... Have you ever seen a wildlife programme when a lion meets the hyenas? Here's this magnificent apex predator, with his beautiful blond mane, king of all he surveys, and there's the hyenas. Dirty, squat, and evil. They're not noble like he is, but there's more of them than there are of him so they can chase him off and steal his prey.'

The Slug pouted, eyes fixed on the screen. 'I always thought *I* was the lion. The noble apex predator. But standing in the car park – watching him beat that man and woman with an iron bar, bind them with duct tape, and bundle them into the boot of his beautiful white Range Rover – I realised I was never the lion. I was the hyena. And there was only one of me.'

Callum cleared his throat. 'Who was he?'

'So I hid in the shadows and watched him take his prey. I watched him scoop up the pretty little blond boy, lower him gently onto the back seat, ruffle his hair, and strap him in. Then I watched the Lion drive away.'

'Who – was – he?'

A dark, slithery smile. 'Oh, you'd know him if you saw him. He's *famous.*' Pike leaned forward, trembling, the images on screen reflected in his bloodshot eyes. 'Isn't it magnificent?'

'I want a sodding name!'

'Shut up. Don't spoil it. This is the best bit.'

Callum grabbed the TV, wrenched it off its stand, and hurled it to the filthy floor. The cathode ray tube popped and crackled, sparks flickered inside the casing, smoke curled up through the vents in the back.

Shannon just stared at him.

'Gareth Pike, I'm arresting you for violation of Section Fifty-Two-A of the Civic Government Scotland Act, as I believe you to be in possession of indecent images of children. You do not have to say anything, but it may harm your defence if you do not mention something that you later rely on in court.'

Pike grinned. '*Finally*. I thought you'd never ask.'

46

'Interview recommenced at twenty-three fifteen.' Callum held up the evidence bag. 'I am now showing Mr Pike "Exhibit A". Do you recognise this video cassette, Gareth?'

Sitting on the other side of the interview room table, Pike smiled his slug-like smile. 'Of course I do. It's the video I bought from a lovely man in Doncaster, who, I'm afraid, shall have to remain nameless.' Pike raised a hand. 'Oh, I know, I know, but honour among pederasts, Detective Constable. I'd hate to disappoint the brethren of my ... shall we say *distinctive* congregation.'

Interview Room Two stank of fresh paint, the walls, door, and skirting remarkably clean and blemish free. Even the carpet tiles looked new. Bright-white vertical blinds shut out the night, swaying above the pinging radiator. All very clean and hygienic. Which somehow made the stench rolling off Pike all the more cloying.

The uniformed PC sitting next to Callum had her chair pushed as far back as it would go, putting as much distance as possible between herself and the man opposite. She had the same look of revulsion on her face as Shannon had, back at the flat. As if she'd trodden on something she couldn't wipe off. She wouldn't even rest her notebook on the same table Pike leaned on, holding it in her lap instead as she wrote down everything he said.

Just the three of them, steeping in the smell of fresh paint and stale BO.

Callum stuck the evidence bag in front of him, the dirty cast on his right hand clunking against the clean Formica tabletop. 'And you are aware of the contents of this video cassette, Gareth?'

'Oh indeed I am. Very much so.' Pike leaned forward. 'I've watched it many, many times. My favourite bit has worn almost through, but that just adds to the mystique, don't you think? The mind's eye is *so* much more powerful than reality.' He looked up, stretching out his chins, staring straight into the camera mounted in the corner. 'It's a pornographic video involving two pretty young blond boys and one *very* lucky man.'

Callum stared at him. 'Why?'

'Oh, because who doesn't dream of having two—'

'No, Gareth: why did you show us the video? Why didn't you hide it? Why did you choose not to have a solicitor present? Why aren't you sitting there saying, "no comment" to everything?'

He curled his shoulders forward, hunching over the table. 'You've seen my home, Detective Constable, would *you* want to live there? I miss my lovely cell, with its regular meals and its working radiator. I miss my friends. Out here, if I talk to someone with … similar interests, I'm breaking the law, but inside? Ah, the joy of discussing my passions and past triumphs without being spat at!' He winked at the PC. 'How I long to never see another face contorted in ignorance like yours, young lady.'

She glared back, but kept her mouth shut. Wrote it all down instead.

'You *want* to go back to prison?'

'Who wouldn't? Out here I get excrement posted through my letterbox; in there I can spend time with kindred souls and live in peace. Unmolested.' He spread his chubby fingers wide. 'Perhaps I could finally work on my novel?'

'So you're confessing to the charges.'

'It's about a little boy whose wicked stepfather beats him every night and locks him in the attic. But the stepfather doesn't know that there's a portal to a magical world up there, hidden in an old wooden chest from the First World War. And the little boy goes on adventures with his best friends – a talking cat and a world-weary teddy bear – to save Wunderwelt from the Darkening armies of King Dunkelheit.'

'Are you confessing to the *charges*, Mr Pike?'

'Oh most certainly.' A frown. 'I can't decide if the teddy bear should harbour the soul of the boy's dear departed grandfather: killed in the trenches, I think. Maybe mustard gas. Or would that be too dark?'

Callum just stared at him.

'Of course, it's semi-autobiographical. I didn't have a talking cat or a haunted teddy bear, but I *definitely* had a stepfather. I'll leave out the bits where he shared me with his friends, though. No one likes a tattle-tale, do they?'

321

Was that supposed to make him sympathetic?

Tough.

Callum held out his good hand for the PC's notebook, then slid it across the table. Passed Pike a pen. 'Sign at the bottom there. And date it.'

'I'd like a south-facing cell, if at all possible?' He scrawled his name across the bottom of the page, followed by today's date. 'Would that be possible?'

'You said you recognised the man who abducted my parents and brother.'

'I suppose it all depends on what's available, but it'd be nice to feel the sun on my bars.'

'You said he was famous.'

'Oh I said many things, Detective Constable. And now,' he poked the notebook with its signed confession, 'I've got what *I* wanted, so why should I help *you* with anything? Supply and demand.'

'All I want is a name.'

'I know. And all *I* want is a south-facing cell. Something on an upper floor so there's a nice view. If you can't supply me with that, then our business here is concluded.' A wink. 'So why don't you scurry off and see what you can do about my cell? Off you go. Scurry, scurry.'

Callum snatched the notebook back and returned it to the PC. 'I can't believe I was afraid of you, all those years. You're pathetic.'

'Oh, indubitably. And now I've got power over you all over again.' The slug smile grew. 'Isn't that *delicious*?'

Shannon leaned back against the wall in the cupboard masquerading as the Downstream Monitoring Suite, mug of tea clutched to his chest. 'Told you: men like him, they like screwing with people.'

Callum closed the door behind himself and slumped into one of the three office chairs lined up in front of the monitors – the screen in the middle had a view of Interview Room Two on it, peering down from the corner at the empty chairs and table. He covered his face with his hands. 'Did you see?'

'Oh, "indubitably". Urgh... I mean, who uses words like "indubitably" these days? Dicks, *that's* who.' A sigh. 'I should've let you play bad cop.'

'He saw him. He saw this guy, this "Lion", attacking my parents and he didn't do a thing.'

'We had twenty-six flights of stairs for him to fall down.'

'He could've called the police. Taken the number plate down. He could've *done* something.'

'I know.' Shannon's hand landed on Callum's shoulder and squeezed. 'Look on the bright side: at least now we know the rumour was true. That drunken DI was right, it was someone famous. And they drove a white Range Rover.'

'I was terrified of that lardy sack of crap...'

'Callum, it's OK. I'll get my OAPs to go digging through their notebooks and attics and sheds. We'll find out who he is.' One last squeeze. 'But it'll take a day or two. Meantime, you sod off home and get some sleep. I'll give you a call soon as we know anything.'

Callum thumped the Mondeo's door shut and stood on the pavement, in the drizzle, staring up at the third floor. Twenty to twelve and the lights were still on in the flat.

Home.

Or what used to pass for it.

He pulled his shoulders back and let himself in through the communal front door. Ignored the pile of post on the windowsill at the back. Marched up the stairs.

The cats had been at Toby's pot plants again.

Tough.

Callum took out his key and slid it into the lock of 3F-A. It didn't turn. And the little brass plaque above the letterbox was gone too, replaced by a white plastic rectangle with 'R Powel & E Pirie' carved into the surface. They hadn't even waited till his grave was cold...

So he bunched his left hand into a fist and gave the door the same three hard knocks Shannon had given Gareth Bloody Pike. *The police are here, and they're not sodding happy.*

Took a while, but eventually the door swung open and there was Powel, in jeans and a Rolling Stones T-shirt. Big white trainers that looked as if they'd never seen the outside world. He didn't seem as intimidating out of a suit, more like someone's dad trying to be trendy and 'down with the kids'. And failing.

He scowled out at Callum. 'I've been *waiting.*'

'Where's my stuff?' Pitching it as a challenge, rather than a question.

Powel closed his eyes and shook his head, then turned and marched back into the flat on his ridiculous white trainers. 'Elaine packed everything into boxes.'

'I'll bet she did.' Callum followed him. 'And did she pack the TV and the couch and the bed and the microwave and—'

'Oh for God's sake, Callum, will you grow up?' Powel turned, arms out. 'Yes, OK, I get it: you've been betrayed. We hurt your feelings. Everything's terrible and it's all my fault.'

Callum's left hand curled into a fist. Chest out. Shoulders back.

'Does that make you feel better, Callum? I admit it: it's – all – *my* – fault.'

Grab him by the throat and squeeze the life out of him.

'But do you think you were so easy to live with? Do you think Elaine didn't struggle every day, with your moods and your obsessions and your *neediness*?'

Kill him.

'We fell in love, OK, Callum? We reached out for someone and we found each other.'

Kill him right *now*.

Powel's arms dropped to his sides. 'She didn't love you, Callum. She was just going through the motions because she didn't want to hurt you. It wasn't a conspiracy, it just happened.' He walked through to the living room. Pointed at the cardboard boxes stacked up by the window. 'I know it doesn't help, but I'm sorry.'

They'd obviously raided the nearest supermarket, because the pile was a mixture of small boxes that used to contain wine, big boxes that used to contain frozen chips, boxes for toilet cleaner, crisps, bin-bags, cauliflower florets, and Stork vegetable fat. Each one sealed with brown parcel tape and marked with black pen: 'CLOTHES', 'CDs & DVDs', 'LEGO', and 'MISC'.

But by far the largest number were marked 'BOOKS'.

'Elaine packed your favourite mugs and cookery things. There's some ornaments in there too, and photos of the two of you. She says, if you don't want them just let her know. Don't throw them away: she'd like to hold onto them for old time's sake.'

There it was, his whole life for the last five years, all neatly packed up in scrounged cardboard boxes.

Callum stared at the floor. 'What about the furniture, the TV, the *crib*? All the stuff I paid for?'

A sigh. 'If I write you a cheque, will that make you happy?'

'Happy?'

There was a lamp, sitting on the empty bookcase at the back of the room. They'd bought that on a weekend away in Anstruther. Back before she'd got pregnant.

He picked it up, turned it over in his good hand.

Powel folded his arms. 'And we'll need to sort something out about the flat. Putting it up for sale isn't going to do much good, not with the market like it is.'

Pale-brown pottery, the colour of a hen's egg. A little scene of boats and dinky wee houses wrapped around it. Heavier than it looked. Seagulls on the blue shade. They'd been happy then.

'As I see it, we've got two options: I refund your mortgage payments and we get the title deeds transferred into my and Elaine's names, or we buy you out at the *current* market value and you pay off half the mortgage.'

Or maybe they hadn't been happy at all. Maybe *he'd* been happy, but Elaine was miserable. Maybe she was already shagging Powel behind his back. The pair of them laughing at how stupid he was.

'Though, if I were you I'd go for the first one. The market being what it is, you'd probably end up losing out on the deal. At least if you take the cash you'll get something out of it.'

Poor stupid gullible little Callum. Buying twee lamps, when everything around him was *lies*.

'What do you say, have we got a deal? Like adults?' Powel stuck out his hand for shaking.

Callum stared at it, then at the lamp.

Bared his teeth.

Slammed the lamp back down, grabbed the nearest box, and marched out of the flat.

47

Callum loaded the last box of books into the back of the Mondeo. Looked up at flat 3F-1.

Standing out here, you'd never guess—

Sodding hell. Callum pulled out his phone. 'What?'

Nothing.

He checked the caller display: 'NUMBER WITHHELD'.

Not this again.

'Look, whoever you are, I'm not in the mood, OK? I've had a crappy day, so you can take your phone and jam it up—'

'Piggy?' A little girl's voice, broken and jagged. Her breathing jerky and trembling, punctuated by damp gurgling sniffs.

'Willow?'

'He's here! He's ... he's come ... he's come back.'

Callum closed the Mondeo's boot. 'Who's come back?'

'Dad. Dad's come back...'

The man who'd broken his four-year-old daughter's arm as a farewell present.

Right.

Callum marched around to the front of the car and climbed in behind the wheel. 'Where are you?'

'He's in there with Mum and Pinky and the baby!'

'OK. You stay away from him. I'll be there soon as I can.' Callum turned the key and put the Mondeo into drive. Stuck his foot down. The fingers of his good hand reached for the '999' button mounted on the dashboard, and the car's siren wailed into the rain, blue-and-white lights flickering behind the radiator grille – reflected back by the wet road.

Callum fumbled his Airwave handset out, the thing lumpy and awkward in his broken hand, working the buttons with his thumb. 'DC MacGregor to Control, I've got report of a domestic at forty-five B Manson Avenue, Kingsmeath.'

'Oh aye?'

'Yes, "Oh aye". There's a grade one flag on that property, I need backup—'

'I'm going to stop you there, Detective Constable. There's no flag on that house.'

'I asked for one days ago!'

'Aye, well I'm looking at the system now, and there isn't.'

'Oh for God's sake...'

Shops and cars and cones flashed past the Mondeo's windows. Then the industrial span of the Calderwell Bridge.

'Who have you got in the area?'

'Dawson and Cooper, but they're dealing with an assault.'

Right at the roundabout, the tyres screeching on the wet tarmac.

'Soon as they're done, get them over to Manson Avenue.'

'Aye, well, I'll do my best, but—'

'But you can't promise anything. Yeah, I know.' He let go of the button. 'Thanks for nothing.'

Callum swung the car hard left onto Munro Place, tearing up the hill, over the top and down the other side. Threw the Mondeo around onto Manson Avenue.

The depressing rows of flat-faced houses with their tiny weed-strewn gardens reared up on either side, the road lined with parked cars in various stages of decay.

Thirty-nine. Forty-one. Forty-three. There: forty-five.

He jammed on the brakes and slid the car to a halt, right outside. Clambered into the rain, just in time to see a big black Mercedes disappear into the distance.

'PIGGY?' That same little girl's voice, shouting over the wailing siren, sounding so much younger than the last time they'd met.

He turned and puffed out his cheeks. 'YOU OK?'

Willow peered out at him from behind a parked VW Beetle. 'YOU CAME.'

'SAID I WOULD, DIDN'T I?' Callum reached back into the Mondeo and killed the lights and siren.

A couple of curtains twitched on the other side of the road, but other than that Manson Avenue was silent.

Callum nodded at the house. 'He still in there?'

She shook her head. Bit her top lip. 'I wasn't scared or nothing.' A sniff and a shrug. 'Just called you, you know, for *Pinky's* sake, like. Cos Benny was worried bout her, yeah?'

'Course he was.' The small drift of plastic toys had disappeared from the front garden, leaving it to the weeds. Callum marched up the path.

The front door lay wide open.

He knocked anyway. 'Hello?'

No answer.

The hallway was cold, the wallpaper stained and peeling in the corner above the door. A selection of brightly coloured kids' coats rainbowed a rack on one side. A cracked mirror on the other, reflecting back a spider's-web kaleidoscope.

'Hello? Anyone in?' Callum turned back to Willow. 'What's your mum's name again?'

A shrug.

Yeah, because when you're that age, 'Mum' and 'Dad' was all the name they needed. Assuming you were lucky enough to still *have* parents.

A flight of stairs sat beyond the mirror. He rested a hand on the newel post, staring up at the landing. 'Hello? Miss Brown? Are you all right?'

No answer.

A little face appeared around the balustrade: sticky-out ears and flat monkey nose. That would be the brother, Benny. AKA: Baboon Boy. Only this time there was no hooting, just a damp-eyed stare.

'Is your mum up there?'

He wiped his face on his sleeve and shook his head.

OK, search downstairs first.

One door at the end of the hall, one on the right. He tried the handle and it opened on a living room just big enough for a saggy armchair covered in throws, a small TV sitting on a tatty sideboard, a stack of kids' toys, two threadbare beanbags, and a flimsy-looking playpen covered in cartoon characters.

Willow's mum was in the corner, sitting with her back to the wall, knees drawn up to her chest, arms wrapped around them, blonde hair hanging over her face as she rocked. The toddler – Pinky? – was holding on to her, face a big flushed tear-stained knot of gristle and snot.

Callum peered into the playpen.

The baby was lying on its back, sooking one of its feet, surrounded by yet more plastic tat.

OK, so at least everyone was still alive.

He squatted down in front of the woman in the corner. 'Miss Brown? It's PC MacGregor. I was the policeman who brought back Mr Lumpylump? You remember?'

She peered out at him from behind her curtain of hair. Looked away.

Callum tried a smile. 'I came because I was worried about you. Are you OK?'

She rested her forehead on her knees, voice soft and mushy – as if she'd been drinking. 'Go way.'

'Willow and Benny's dad's been here, hasn't he?'

No reply.

'Did he hurt you?'

No reply.

'If he hurt you we can *do* something about it.'

No reply.

Honestly, it was like interviewing a career criminal. Callum settled on the edge of the lone armchair. 'I know this is hard. It's not easy when someone you love hurts you. Trust me, I know what I'm talking about.' He stared down at the filthy fibreglass cast covering his right hand. 'But, you know what? If they hurt us this much, maybe they never really loved us at all? Maybe they don't *deserve* to be with us. Maybe they never did.'

Willow's mum raised her head, parting that curtain of blonde hair with one hand. A deep red bruise covered one side of her cheek. Her bottom lip was swollen, split, and raw, blood making a wide trail to her chin. No wonder her words sounded slurred.

Another fledgling bruise was spreading across her other cheek. A necklace of them wrapped tight around her throat. Her eyes sparkled with tears. 'He wouldn't hurt me if I didn't make him so angry...'

'What's his name?'

'I shouldn't have had another kid without him. I should have waited for him to come back and not run around with other men like a whore. I ruined everything.'

'You didn't do anything wrong ... it's Isobel, isn't it?'

'Irene.' She picked at the knee of her jeans. 'And I *did*. He told me I did.'

'Yeah, well, you didn't and he's a dick.' Callum pointed at the playpen and its foot-sucking inmate. 'You love your baby, don't you?'

A little nod.

'Well then, there you go.' Callum fumbled his notebook and pen out. 'Now, the charmer who beat you: what's his name?'

Irene Brown blinked at him, then looked away. 'I fell. I tripped and I fell. Because I'm a stupid clumsy bitch.'

'Come on, Irene, you're not—'

'Please, just … just leave me alone.'

Callum poured boiling water into the two mugs. The kitchen wasn't huge, and nothing in it looked as if it'd been bought from new, but it was clean and tidy enough.

Willow stood in the doorway, watching as he mashed the teabags against the mugs' inner walls with a teaspoon. Not saying anything as he fished them out and dumped them in the bin. Or when he got the milk out of the fridge. It wasn't till he took the lid off the semi-skimmed and had a sniff that she broke the silence: 'We're not scummers, OK, Piggy?'

'Never said you were.' Both mugs got a dollop of milk. 'Force of habit – you can't trust a pint of milk in a police station. Never know *who's* been at it.' He took a wee sip of tea. Hot, but bearable. 'Does your mum ever mention your dad's name? Maybe she's got photographs hidden away somewhere?'

Willow rolled her eyes and stomped into the room. Picked the semi-skimmed off the worktop and stuck it back in the fridge. 'What happened to your hand?'

Callum pulled down his jacket sleeve, till it hid the filthy cast. 'You didn't answer the question: your dad's name. Photos? Anything like that?'

'Nah. Not a snitch, yeah? Mum's not a snitch neither. Benny's not fussed, but she dropped him on his head when he was wee, so you can't believe a word he says. Lives in a fantasy world, don't he?'

'This guy comes in here and beats your mum up, and you think it's more important to not be a clype? Thought you wanted to "break his little bitch legs"? Now you want to let him get away with it?'

Willow stuck her head on one side and shrugged. 'Would've kicked the crap out of him, but you know...'

'Sure you would.'

'Yeah, would've killed him right there, but he had this huge shit-eating darkie with him.'

Callum stared at her. 'You can't say things like that.'

'But see if he was on his own?' She mimed punching someone.

'Willow, I'm serious. You want people to think you're some sort of stupid racist lowlife? Because that's what it makes you sound like. You *think* it makes you sound tough, but it doesn't.'

330

She clamped her mouth shut.

'Thought you were better than that.'

'You're not my dad!'

'Yeah. Because he's been *such* a role model, hasn't he?'

Pink swept up her neck and into her cheeks, setting the tips of her ears glowing. Then she glowered at the kitchen floor for a moment, muscles bunching along her jaw, like she was chewing something. Deep breath. 'He had a huge black guy with him. All gold chains and that. He took Mr Lumpylump, cos Dad told him to.'

'They stole your mother's *teddy bear*?'

'I was hiding in the cupboard under the stairs and I saw him take Mr Lumpylump. Should've broken both their legs. Should've killed them both.' Seven years old, going on Charles Manson.

'So tell me his name.'

'What happened to your hand?'

The filthy cast itched. 'I hit someone. *Hard.*'

A nod. 'And I'm not a snitch.'

Callum stepped into the thin drizzle, closed the front door behind him, and slouched down the front path to the Mondeo: still parked in the middle of the street where he'd abandoned it, still full of all his boxes. Which was something of an achievement for Kingsmeath, even at this time of night.

He plipped the locks and sank in behind the wheel.

'00:35', according to the dashboard clock, and he still had to drive all the way to Cowskillin, unload everything into Mother's husband's lockup *and* drive back to Dotty and Louise's house before he could call it a night.

'Pffff...' Come on. Keys in the ignition and—

A knock on the driver's window made him flinch hard enough to drop the keys.

Sodding hell.

He turned and there was Baboon Boy with his jug ears and pug nose, standing close enough for his breath to fog the glass.

Callum buzzed the window down. 'Benny?'

Benny did a big pantomime of looking up and down the street, then over his shoulder, before turning back and lowering his voice to a whisper. 'They beat on my mum.'

'I know, Benny. But your mum won't tell me who did it, so there's nothing I can do to help her.'

He wiped his nose on the sleeve of his tracksuit top. 'I saw them. Willow thinks I didn't, but I did. Both of them. Cos I see things.'

Callum slumped back in his seat. 'I'm sure you do, but I'm completely knackered, Benny, so...?'

'My Dad's a rock star.'

'Is he now?'

'He's got a helicopter and a plane and a tiger and loads of bitches.'

'Bitches?' Maybe Willow hadn't been lying about Benny being dropped on his head when he was wee.

'In bikinis and stuff, for the dancing.' He did a sort of Michael Jackson crotch-grab-and-twirl thing, finishing off with a finger pointed at the low clouds. 'Owwwww!'

'Right. That makes perfect sense now.'

Benny lowered his pointing hand and nodded, face serious as an aneurism. 'Yeah. I seen him on the telly. With his bitches.'

'OK, well, thanks for letting me know, Benny. I appreciate it. But don't call women "bitches", OK? That's not nice.'

Another serious nod.

Callum scooped up the keys from the footwell. Paused. Turned back to the strange little boy with his snot-silvered tracksuit. 'You don't know your dad's name, do you, Benny? Do you know what he's called?'

Another pantomime check that no one was listening. 'No one's supposed to know.'

'Yes, but do *you* know, Benny?'

'Mum used to call him Donald when he'd been naughty. But you're not allowed to tell anyone.'

'Donald. Right. It'll be our secret.' Callum stuck the retrieved keys in the ignition and started up the Mondeo. 'Do me a favour? Look after your mum and sisters. ... And whatever the baby is.'

'Cos I see things.'

'That's right. And if you see your dad round here again, you give me a call, OK?' Callum handed over a Police Scotland business card.

Benny frowned at it, then put it in his back pocket. 'OK.'

And with any luck, next time, they'd catch the cowardly little sod in the act.

Callum put the car in drive, gave Benny a wave, and pulled away into the night.

The lockup wasn't full of pornography, but it *was* full of booze. Half a dozen demijohns blooped and gurgled on a reclaimed section of kitchen units, complete with worktop. Crates and crates of wine bottles were stacked up in the corner, and a couple of black plastic bins had tea towels draped over their gaping mouths. Everything had the earthy undead smell of live yeast.

Callum piled his boxes against the wall opposite – clothes and things on the bottom, books on the top. Just in case anything happened and there was a homebrew flood. Sod the clothes: save the books.

He stood staring at the boxes, then opened the one marked 'KIDS' BOOKS'. Pulled out a handful of battered paperbacks, their spines cracked and flaking from years of rereading. The ones he was going to read to Peanut, when he was old enough.

The House at Pooh Corner, The Lion the Witch and the Wardrobe, Black Beauty, Open the Coffins, Biggles Flies Again... A lifetime of books – every single volume he'd *ever* owned since he was little – now just a pile of supermarket-scrounged wine boxes in someone else's lockup.

Callum put the books back in their box.

Stared at them.

Then carried the box back out to the car.

At least now he'd have something to read.

— these bones beneath the earth —

The little chimney boy blew life into a candle, melting back the darkness. "There we is, my dear," he said to Justin. "You just hops yourself up on the kitchen table and I'll warms you a nice bath." Then he pulled a big brass pot from a cupboard, filled it with water, and put it on to simmer.

Justin jumped onto the table and sat there, his brand-new rabbitty ears picking up all manner of scary noises lurking in the gloom. "Why... Why are you putting carrots and onions in my bath?" he asked, trying to sound brave.

"Because they's dirty, and I wants you to wash them for me."

"And are the potatoes, leeks, and salt-and-pepper dirty too?"

"Why, Justin, anyone would think you doesn't trust me..."

R.M. Travis
Open the Coffins (and Let Them Go Free) (1976)

Cos them bitches be wide with their legs in the air,
But he can't barely stand, he's wrapped up in his warfare,
His booze and his dreams, his tattoos and his schemes,
He's f*cked up inside, and it's time for some screams here.

Donny '$ick Dawg' McRoberts
'Diary of a Motherfunkin' Legend'
© Bob's Speed Trap Records (2016)

48

McAdams held up a hand, eyes clenched shut, wrinkles deep and thick across his forehead. 'If we could keep it down to a deafening scream, that'd be nice.'

He wasn't the only one who looked as if he'd rented his skull out to a Death Metal band. Dotty was slumped in her wheelchair, one hand massaging her temples while the other clutched a large wax-paper cup of coffee. Franklin was wrapped around a bottle of Lucozade, making little grunting noises every time she moved. And Watt sported a pair of dark glasses and a pained expression.

Mother, on the other hand, sat back in her office chair with her knees spread wide, tucking into a bacon buttie and a big mug of tea. She beamed at them, washed down her latest mouthful. 'I don't know what you're all complaining about: if you can't do the time, don't do the tequila shots.'

Callum had a sip of tea.

Dotty buried her face in her hands. 'Urgh… Whose bright idea was it to have flaming Drambuies?'

Watt raised a finger and pointed it at McAdams. Who just stood there, propped up against the wall. Groaning.

'Now, dear children, our masters will be holding their press conference at one, so we have until then to dot-and-cross. Who wants the "i"s and who wants the "t"s? Don't all rush at once.'

Callum raised his mug. 'I need to go see Blakey about the paedophile I arrested last night.'

'When you've done that, get your little friend, Dr McDonald, to look over Tod Monaghan's details. I want a ribbon wrapped around him with a bow on top. Rosalind, how did you get on with our friends at Strummuir Smokehouse?'

Franklin took a scoof of Lucozade, gave another grunt, then picked up a clump of paper. 'The only one *without* a criminal record is the woman who cooks chips in the canteen. Everyone else has done time: armed robbery, fraud, assault, murder, possession with intent...' She was slumping lower and lower with every word, her other hand digging into her hair, keeping her head from hitting the desk. 'Urgh...'

'Well, we need to add interviewing everyone and checking alibis to the list. Andy? Stick it on the board. Dorothy, you and—'

A knock on the office door, and a spotty young woman in an ill-fitting fighting suit stuck her head around the door. 'Sorry to interrupt, Guv, but you've not seen DCI Powel on your travels, have you? The Super's looking for him.'

Mother turned. 'How's the head today, Erika?'

She pulled a sheepish grin. 'Vodka Red Bull and crème de menthe do *not* mix.'

'Thought as much when I saw you doing the Lambada with Sergeant Crilley.'

The rest of Erika's face went as red as her spots. 'Oh...'

'And no: I haven't seen Reece this morning. Anyone else?'

There was a chorus of noncommittal grunts.

Callum had another sip of tea.

'Sorry, Erika, your prince is in another castle. Now,' back to the team, 'where was I?'

The DC slipped out of the room, taking her blush with her, leaving nothing but a vaguely minty smell behind.

Mother frowned for a moment. 'Ah yes: *Dorothy*. You and John set a rocket under the lab: they're supposed to be getting us fingerprints on the first two mummified victims. I want those bodies ID'd: we leave no one behind.'

That elicited groans from both of them.

'Don't whinge. A spot of fresh air will do you the power of good. And John?'

'Grnnnng?'

'You actually signed out at the end of your shift last night! A round of applause for DC John Watt, everyone.' What she got didn't even pass for lacklustre. 'Let's see if you can make it two in a row today.' She polished off the last of her buttie. 'Rosalind, seeing as how you won the "Guess How Many Pickled Eggs DI Morrow Can Fit In His Mouth At Once" competition, you can attend Monaghan's post mortem.'

'Oh God...' Franklin's face went a bit more grey.

'Andy and I will stay here and produce briefing notes for Chief Superintendent McEwan, so he doesn't make a fool of himself while claiming all the credit for catching Imhotep.' Mother sooked the last smear of tomato sauce from her fingers. 'Right: off you go. Play nice and no running in the corridors.'

'Well, you've got no one but yourself to blame.' Callum picked his jacket off the back of his chair and pulled it on – wriggling the filthy fibreglass cast on his broken hand down the right sleeve.

Franklin took another scoof of Lucozade. Shuddered. 'I'm never drinking anything ever, *ever* again...'

He crossed to the door and stepped out into the corridor, just as Watt and Dotty disappeared into the stairwell, making for the lifts – the pair of them groaning and shuffling like a cut-price episode of *The Walking Dead*. Or, in Dotty's case, *The Wheeling Dead*.

Franklin slumped out of the office and followed him down the corridor. 'It's all right for you: you don't have to sit through a bloody post mortem.'

'You're an ungrateful sod, you know that, don't you?'

'No one else has to watch them hack Tod Monaghan up into little squishy pieces.'

He paused with one hand on the double doors at the end of the corridor. 'Teabag never starts his PMs till ten, so Mother's basically given you a free ...' he checked his watch, 'two and three-quarter hours to enjoy your hangover in peace.'

'"Enjoy" isn't the word I'd use.'

'Diddums.' Callum pushed through into the cabbagey reek of the stairwell.

Someone on the floors below was whistling the theme tune to *Britain's Next Big Star*, only flat as an ironing board.

Franklin grimaced one side of her face shut and held the Lucozade bottle against it as they started upstairs. 'This paedophile you arrested last night. It was your Slug man, wasn't it? Bob Shannon found out who he was.'

'You should go back to the office and lie down. Curl up under one of the desks for a bit.'

'And you went round and ... did he admit to killing your mum and dad?'

'Or the disabled toilets on the second floor are a *great* place for a kip. Well, as long as you don't snore. You don't snore, do you?'

'Callum!'

'No. He didn't admit to killing anyone. Says he saw who did, though.'

Through the double doors and into the Major Investigation Team's domain. A lot of the officers milling about here looked every bit as zombied as Watt and Dotty.

Brainzzz…

'So who was it then?'

Callum headed down past the meeting rooms. 'He won't say.'

Blakey was in the Sergeants' Office, scowling away at his computer, elbows on his desk, fingers in his ears.

The only other occupant was DS Praying Mantis, still sodding about with his audio file – the volume turned up far too loud:

'I need you to calm down. Listen to me. Listen, we can't come if you don't tell me where you are.'

Callum grabbed one of the empty seats and wheeled it over to Blakey's desk. Thumped down into it. 'Have you interviewed him yet?'

'I'm at home. I was on the phone to Ashlee and she was answering the door…'

No response, so he gave Blakey's shoulder a poke. 'Have – you – interviewed – Gareth Pike – yet?'

'Oh Christ, not you *again.*'

'…a child missing?'

Franklin settled on the edge of the desk, on the other side, hemming Blakey in. Looming. 'How's the nose, DS Blake?'

'…said he was looking for it, but he … he …' Sobbing belted out of the speakers.

Blakey turned, glowering out from behind his plastic nose guard. 'WILL YOU TURN THAT BLOODY NOISE DOWN!'

DS Praying Mantis stuck out his bottom lip. 'I'm trying to catch a killer here, is that OK with you?'

Callum poked him again. 'Pike's in the cells right now. He's up before the Sheriff at eleven for having indecent images of kids. Get your finger out.'

'Leave me alone!'

'…mum. Two Twenty-Three Johnson Crescent, in Shortstaine. Please, he's got a knife…'

'Blakey, he was there when my parents were abducted. He saw who took them!'

'…on their way. When did it—'

He dug his fingers into his ridiculous sideburns. 'I don't have *time* for this, I've got—'

'I swear to God: if you screw this up, Blakey, I'm going to end you.'

'No, listen. They're on my mobile...'

The computer's speakers screamed.

'GET OFF HER! GET OFF HER! GET OFF HER!'

Blakey shoved his chair back, yanked a drawer open and grabbed a grey stapler from amongst the pencils, pens, and usual office detritus.

'Don't hurt my baby! I'll do anything you—' More screams.

He spun his chair around and hurled the stapler at DS Praying Mantis.

It clattered into the guy's monitor, bounced and went skittering across the desk, shattering a mug of tea and sending the contents exploding across keyboard, paperwork and the Mantis's shirt. 'WHAT THE HELL?' On his feet, staring down at the big beige stain.

'...on their way. Can you tell me your name?'

Blakey's face was the colour of an impending stroke. 'IF YOU CAN'T HEAR, GET SOME BLOODY HEADPHONES!'

'Have you lost your mind?'

'ALL DAY, EVERY DAY!' Blakey lurched to his feet, fists clenched. 'THE SAME *BLOODY* AUDIO CLIP BLARING LIKE A *BLOODY* AIR-RAID SIREN!' Tears sparked in his eyes.

'Well *excuse me* for trying to do my job!'

'I'll take good care of you...'

'HOW AM I SUPPOSED TO COPE?' Spittle glowed in the office's strip lights. 'TELL ME?' Bottom lip trembling. 'HOW?'

'...forever. Won't that be nice? Forever and ever.'

Blakey's shoulders slumped. 'How am I supposed to cope?'

'Oh God, she's dead. She's dead. She's dead.'

He bit his bottom lip, then turned and stormed out of the office, one hand rubbing at his eyes.

DS Mantis just stood there, mouth hanging open.

'Marline, I want you to record the call for me, will your phone let you do that?'

Through the office windows, most of the MIT zombies stood or peered over their partition walls. Watching Blakey go.

'I... Yeah, completely! I've got, like, this app that'll—'

Franklin blew out a low whistle. 'Wow.'

'Get away from me!'

Callum sagged in his seat. So much for getting Blakey to actually *do* something about Gareth Pike.

'They'll worship you.'

Shouldn't have pushed him so hard.

'You'll be a god and they'll worship you.'

DS Mantis pulled at his shirt, flapping the soggy fabric. 'Absolutely soaked through.'

Still…

More screaming from the speakers.

'You know what?' The Mantis grabbed a handful of tissues from a box of Kleenex and dabbed at himself. 'I'm getting *really* tired of Blakey's crap.'

Franklin took another swig of Lucozade. 'So what now?'

Good question.

Shame Callum didn't have an answer. 'We can't *force* Pike to give up the name.'

'Well … maybe we can trick him into it?'

'Oh, so it's *my* fault Blakey's wife is shagging around on him, is it?' More dabbing. 'Maybe if he wasn't such a dick the whole time, she wouldn't have to.'

Callum looked up. 'Blakey's wife's cheating on him?'

Odds on it was DCI Poncy Powel.

'I mean, I get it: all this macho posturing and sexist rubbish is his way of overcompensating. "Look at how manly I am; no way *my* wife's having an affair!" But enough's enough.'

Nothing but crashing and banging from the speakers. Muffled cries. A sob.

'Marline? Can you hear me, Marline? Have you recorded the call?'

'I pressed the button. Please, you have to help them!'

'Well screw him, I'm making a formal complaint soon as Powel gets in.' DS Mantis dumped his soggy tissues in the bin. 'Bloody shirt was clean on this morning.'

'It's OK, Marline. We're on our way. We'll be there soon.'

'You have to hurry!'

Callum stood. 'Yeah well, I suppose we'll just have to…' A frown. He wandered over to the tea-stained desk. 'Can you play that last bit again?'

'I've put up with his crap for six months now and I'm not doing it any more. I'm not.'

'The last bit of the audio file: play it again.'

Mantis grabbed another handful of tissues. 'I should've marched over there and knocked his ugly block off!'

OK, fine.

Callum scooted around the desk and wiggled the mouse in its little puddle of tea till the cursor on the screen hovered over the media player. A couple of clicks and the audio jumped back in time again.

The authoritarian voice of the Control Room, slightly muffled. Like the recording of a recording: '*Marline, I want you to record the call for me, will your phone let you do that?*'

A young woman, sniffly and frightened: '*I... Yeah, completely! I've got, like, this app that'll—*'

A different voice, another young woman, screeching it out: '*Get away from me!*'

And then a man, barely audible over the shouts and screams, as if he was standing far away from the phone. But there was no mistaking his calm and reasonable tone, the pride in his words: '*They'll worship you. You'll be a god and they'll worship you.*'

Callum turned the volume up and clicked the mouse again.

'*They'll worship you. You'll be a god and they'll worship you.*'

Franklin stared at him. 'Callum?'

'I think we've got more victims out there.'

49

'They'll worship you. You'll be a god and they'll worship you.'

Mother sat back in her seat and grimaced. 'Well… Maybe?'

Callum pointed at the media player sitting in the middle of her computer screen. 'Dr McDonald said Imhotep was venerating his victims. The Peruvians used to transform their dead into gods so they could look after the village. This is what he does: he abducts people and he turns them into gods.'

She looked over her shoulder to where McAdams was slouching against the filing cabinet, stirring something white and fizzy in a glass. 'Andy?'

A shrug. 'Play the recording from the start again. Let's hear our boy's voice.'

Callum did, setting the speakers crackling.

They sat and listened all the way through. Frowning at the screen.

'They'll worship you. You'll be a god and they'll worship you.'

'You'll be a god and they'll worship you. Hmm…' McAdams stared off into the distance.

Mother stared at him. 'In your own time, Andy.'

'Thinking.' He bared his teeth. 'I know it's all muffled, but does our boy sound local to you? I think there's a big lump of Dundee in there.' The filing cabinet squeaked as he leaned back against it. 'And how did this Marline manage to record the whole call?'

'She's got an app that runs in the background, buffering everything on a loop. Likes to record her boyfriend so she can listen to him over and over again. Find out if he's cheating on her.'

'Ah, the delights of modern technology.' A nod. 'The lad may be right. Imhotep doth make them gods. Now we must find out.'

Mother sniffed. 'I like it better when poems rhyme.'

'Don't blame me, blame the Japanese, / Their haikus flummox, tease, and please, / Though sometimes they may cause unease.' He downed his white-and-fizzy in a single gulp. 'It could be that our story has a third-act twist up its sleeve and our dead serial killer is reaching out from the mortuary slab. Can our brave team of misfits overcome their differences to save Ashlee and Abby Gossard in time?' McAdams put his glass down. 'Well, assuming they're not already dead, tra-la-la.'

'Fair enough.' She nodded. 'All righty. Callum: you and Rosalind go check out this Ashlee Gossard. But do it quickly – let's not get caught out on the "i"s and "t"s, because we got distracted dotting the "j"s as well.'

Johnson Crescent was a big horseshoe development of tiny two-storey houses, all squished together into long tenement blocks.

Callum parked a few doors down from number 223, beneath the yellowing leaves of a sycamore tree.

Franklin sniffed. 'Least it's stopped raining.'

The sun had even managed to poke its way through the city's blanket of dove-grey clouds.

Wonders would never cease.

This side was still wreathed in darkness, though.

The rattle and clank of construction stretching from the Camburn Roundabout cut through the damp air as they climbed out and locked the Mondeo.

Callum stuck his broken hand in his pocket and wandered down the pavement to number 223.

A line of police tape was tied around the door, but there was no sign of anyone guarding it.

He let himself in with the keys from the case file.

A small hallway with stairs up the right-hand side. A row of coats. Laminate flooring with a long smear of dark red curling away down the hall and disappearing through the door at the far end. More smears on both sides, below knee-height, as if someone being dragged had tried to get purchase on the magnolia walls. Smudged bloody handprints on the architrave of the open living room door.

Franklin peered over his shoulder. 'Should we not be in SOC suits, or something?'

'DS McCready says the SEB have been and gone.' Though it had taken a crowbar to get that information out of the Praying Mantis, never mind the keys, or the case file.

345

Just to be on the safe side, Callum fought his way into a blue nitrile glove and picked his way down the outside edge of the laminate flooring, keeping as far away from the blood smears as possible.

The room they disappeared into was a kitchen.

'Yeah... That's not good.' Franklin stood in the middle and did a slow three-sixty.

She wasn't wrong. There was blood up the walls, little red dots on the ceiling, shattered jars spilling teabags and coffee granules, sugar and cornflakes. A small table lay on its side against the fridge, one leg snapped clean off and sitting in a sticky-looking puddle of scarlet. Two chairs, twisted to splintered bones.

Franklin curled her top lip. 'Why all the blood? Tod Monaghan didn't do this when he attacked Ben Harrington, Brett Millar, and Glen Carmichael. *Three* of them, and not so much as a drop anywhere. Why the overkill?'

Good question.

'Maybe Ashlee and her mum wouldn't eat the magic mushrooms?'

'Nah, you heard the nine-nine-nine call, he didn't even try. Soon as he was in the house that was it: screaming.'

Callum eased the broken table out from in front of the fridge. The white plastic door was covered in blobs of black fingerprint powder.

'And he's never attacked women before, has he? All the other mummies are men.'

And *that* was a good point.

'Well, I don't know, do I? Maybe he thought Ashlee Gossard was a better bet: you've seen her photo, she's either bulimic or anorexic. Less body-fat means less water, means easier to preserve.'

'Assuming Ashlee was the target and not her mum.'

Another good point.

Callum sat back on his haunches. 'The only way we'll know for sure is if we find them.'

'If they're not already dead.'

'Will you stop it with the good points already?'

That got him a frown.

He waved a hand. 'Never mind. How did your boyfriend's work's do go?'

'I'm just saying this doesn't look like Imhotep's handiwork. This isn't his MO.'

'I know.'

She opened and closed a couple of the kitchen drawers. 'Apparently the partners kept asking where I was. And he had a miserable time. And it was all *my* fault, because *I* wouldn't drop everything and go simper at his side like a little woman *should.*'

Callum stood. 'Want to check upstairs?'

'He's always banging on about how he supports my career, but every time it clashes with *his* career suddenly I'm being "selfish".'

There was a pool of blood at the foot of the stairs. A couple of dark footprints on the bottom three steps, then a smear down the wall to the ground again. As if someone had made a run for it, but didn't get very far.

Callum tiptoed between them and up the stairs.

Franklin followed him. 'You know what I think? I think Mark doesn't want me to work at all. He wants a trophy wife who'll settle down and do some volunteer work between squeezing out three kids and baking sodding scones.'

The landing was clear – no blood spatters.

She curled her lip. 'I *hate* scones.'

'Uh-huh.' Callum pushed open one of the three doors – small bathroom with a built-in shower over the bath. Every porcelain surface was clarted with fingerprint powder.

'And why should *I* sacrifice everything to have kids?'

'I like cheese scones.' Door number two opened on a double bedroom. Nothing fancy. Blue-and-yellow duvet cover with matching pillows. An array of bottles, jars, make-up, brushes, and associated things on a little vanity unit. Scottie Dog cuddly toy thing. A few framed prints of famous Scottish landscapes.

'You can bet if it was *men* who had to squeeze three and a half kilos of human being out the end of their penis, they wouldn't be so damned keen on a big family.'

'They're nicer if you toast them. Oh, and lots of butter.'

She stared at him. '*Children?*'

'Cheese scones, you muppet.'

Door number three: a single bedroom that looked as if a drunken baboon had been locked in there and told to go wild with the clothes and underwear. It was everywhere. On the floor, on the bed, poking out from *under* the bed, on the chest of drawers, hanging from the top of the wardrobe. Shirts, T-shirts, jumpers, tops, jeans, leggings, jeggings, socks, stockings, tights, shoes, and flip-flops. Add about two dozen bras and pants and mix liberally.

Callum sniffed. The harsh chemical taint of deodorant and air freshener. 'Someone's trashed the place.'

Franklin rolled her eyes. 'You've never been in a teenage girl's bedroom before, have you?'

A collection of posters were stuck to the ceiling above the bed. Popstars and boy bands, a couple of rap artists. Lots of bare chests, tattoos, and flowing hair.

One particularly oily-looking git was posing on a motorbike, surrounded by unfeasibly breasty women in bikinis. They were all pouting at him, as if he were God's greatest creation, instead of a wee nyaff with a shaved chest, stupid facial hair, and a tattoo of a fox poking out from the waistband of his Calvin Kleins.

Franklin followed his gaze. 'Look at them. How are little girls supposed to develop a healthy body image when they're confronted with the Size-Zero Silicone-Mammary Brigade at every turn?'

Callum settled onto the edge of the bed, between a pink fluffy jumper and a pair of leather shorts. Frowned out at the devastation. 'Long as I live, I'll never understand you lot.'

'Try harder.'

He picked up a green sock with orange penguins on it. 'Monaghan raped a guy in Blackwall Hill, but the victim dropped the charges.'

'So?'

'Not sure.' The sock got tossed onto the floor so Callum could pull out his mobile phone and scroll through the contacts list till he got to 'McDonald, Dr A'.

She picked up on the first ring. *'Hello? Ash?'*

'Alice, it's DC MacGregor. From the Divisional Investigative Support Team?'

'Oh... I see.' Not doing a very good job of hiding her disappointment. *'Anyway, thanks for sending over the file on Tod Monaghan, I've been through it and compared it to the behavioural evidence analysis we did on the initial victim set, well, I say "initial victim set", but it isn't, is it? I mean we don't know who the first victims were, we just know about Glen, Brett, and Ben, but then we can't factor in the first two without an ID to do a victimology work-up from, does that make sense?'*

Sort of.

'Monaghan might have grabbed someone else. We've got a crime scene in Shortstaine, mother and daughter abducted, blood everywhere.'

Franklin leaned back against the chest of drawers, arms folded. Watching him.

'To be honest, that doesn't sound likely, I mean we've got all these other victims and they're all men and it's very *unusual* for a killer like this to cross a gender gap once established and—'

'The daughter's anorexic and she was on the phone to a friend when it happened. Her friend recorded the whole thing. And right at the end, he tells them, "They'll worship you. You'll be a god and they'll worship you." So I thought…?'

'Ooooh, now *that* is interesting. It's conceivable that there's someone else going around Oldcastle abducting people and turning them into gods, but it'd be a huge coincidence, wouldn't it, I mean absolutely massive, so if we work on the assumption that it *was* actually Tod Monaghan, then we'd need a compelling reason to justify his sudden change in victim-gender selection, because it tends to be pretty consistent with serial offenders, oh, it's different if they don't differentiate to start with, but when they make a definite choice they tend to stick with it.'

'But we're not likely to have two god-making nutbags on the go, are we?'

'There would have to be a reason for him to suddenly stop selecting male victims and you shouldn't call people "nutbags", these are human beings just like you and me only wired a bit differently due to their brain chemistry and upbringing. Dehumanising them by calling them "nutbags" doesn't help anyone; it doesn't matter how horrible the things they do are, they're still *human beings*. We should try to remember that.'

Which was pretty much the same speech he'd given Willow last night. 'Sorry.'

'According to the notes: eight years ago, Ted Monaghan goes to a picnic area in Moncuir Wood that's a well-known pickup spot for gay men, only there's an argument, the young man he wants rejects him and Monaghan becomes violent. Leaves. Comes back half an hour later with a hammer and tries to beat the young man to death. At the trial Monaghan insists he wasn't looking for sex, because he isn't gay, and that the young man attacked him. The jury doesn't agree and he serves six years for attempted murder.'

Franklin waved a hand at Callum. 'At least put it on speakerphone.'

'Sorry.'

He pressed the button and a tiny Dr McDonald voice sounded in the pigsty room. 'Five months after Monaghan gets out of prison he's back in Moncuir Wood, only this time he doesn't go looking for a willing partner, he attacks and rapes a different young man. When questioned, Monaghan claims he isn't gay and that he's the real victim. Again. The *young man later drops the charges when his car gets set on fire.'*

'So we know Monaghan's violent.'

'Well, yes, but when he starts turning people into gods, they're always young men, probably because it's young men that he likes, only he can't admit that, because it contradicts his self-image as a manly man, even though he's been having sexual fantasies about them for as long as he can remember, which is why he hangs out in this bit of the woods where it's easy to find someone to explore his sexuality with, only he can't reconcile his sexual needs with his strict upbringing and ends up venting this cognitive dissonance destructively, until one day he rationalises it into something more positive.'

How did she manage to keep talking for so long without taking a single breath? How was that physically possible?

'He decides to take the objects of his sexual confusion and turn them into gods, he's venerating what he can't allow himself to physically realise, so their gender is very important to him and the only way he'd change that pattern is if something serious happened, and I mean something revelatory, because he's been planning and fantasising about this for so long, but now it's all different, and it would send him right out of his comfort zone, so I'd expect to see a lot more violence when things don't go exactly as he's planned and he has to improvise his way out of trouble.'

Callum frowned. 'He didn't improvise anything. We heard him on the recording: he cons his way into their home – pretending he's looking for his missing son – and then attacks them. Blood all over the kitchen. Drag marks in the hall.'

'Ooh... Now that's interesting, I mean he's all softly-softly with the young men he attacks, but the women are there to be subdued quickly and violently. Maybe they don't deserve subtlety? Maybe women need to be put down hard and fast? What do we know about Monaghan's childhood?'

'Nothing that isn't in the file.'

'I think it's a safe bet he had a very difficult relationship with his parents. Probably an abusive father and a submissive mother. She's beneath contempt. She never loved him properly. Father had the right idea – women are dirty, subhuman things that have to be trained like dogs. Chained up and beaten...'

Silence.

Franklin checked her watch.

'Alice?'

'Sorry, thinking. Monaghan knew we were looking for him, it was

350

*in all the papers. He's feeling threatened and embattled and he needs
more gods to protect him. He's running out of time, so he has to cut
corners. You say the daughter's anorexic? Well, why starve a young man
when you can just abduct a young woman who's done all the hard work
for you?'*

Callum grinned at Franklin. 'That's what I said.'

She rolled her eyes.

*'That means the mother is surplus to requirements and if there's blood
everywhere, it's probably hers. It'll still take a few days to purify the
daughter to make sure she's worthy of godhood, but I'd be shocked if the
mother isn't already dead.'*

Sodding hell.

Callum stood. 'So there's still a chance we can save Ashlee?'

'Not much of one, but yes.'

'Thanks.' He hung up and turned to Franklin. 'Any ideas?'

'Monaghan had to transport them out of here somehow: car, or a
van.' She hauled out her phone. 'The initial investigation must've done
door-to-doors.' Her thumb poked at the screen for a moment, then she
held it to her ear and wandered out onto the landing. 'Yes. DC Franklin,
I need to speak to DS McCready...'

Two could play at that game.

Callum put a call in to the CCTV team. Listened to it ring. Crossed
to the window and pulled back the curtains.

The other side of the street still glowed like a packet of fluorescent
Fruit Pastilles. This part of Johnson Crescent formed the bottom curve
of a big U-shape, so anyone on the left or the right would have a clear
view of anything suspicious. Assuming they didn't come down with the
traditional Oldcastle amnesia and—

'Greetings!' A woman's voice, crackling with faux-American cheesy
cheer. *'You've reached the* magnificent *Closed-Circuit Television
Department, where dreams really* do *come true. How may I direct your
call?'*

'Voodoo? It's Callum.'

The accent disappeared. *'My God, there's a blast from the past! You've
not been on the scrounge for a favour since last Wednesday. I was beginning to worry.'*

'I'm looking for a car, or a van, involved in the abduction of a mother
and daughter.'

'What, straight into it? No foreplay?'

'Your husband says I'm not allowed to get you all fired up and horny.

Aggravates his lumbago. The vehicle would have been in the area this Wednesday evening, between seven and nine p.m.: Johnson Crescent. I need to know where they came from and where they went afterwards.'

'Got makes and models?'

'Depends if you believe the door-to-doors or not. Probably best to do it blind so we don't miss anything.'

'Hmmph, you're not asking much, are you? Let's see what we can see...' The sound of fingers dancing across a keyboard. 'There's no CCTV cameras on that street. Nearest I've got is Johnson Park, at the wee shopping centre.' More clicking. 'We're having a birthday party for Ian next week: sixtieth. You should come. Bring the lovely Elaine, we've not seen her for ages.'

'Yeah... Not so lovely. We've split up.'

'Callum MacGregor! You do not get a young lady pregnant and then—'

'I didn't. It wasn't mine.'

Clickity, clickity, clickity.

'Oh, Callum, I'm so sorry. I've got ANPR cameras on Camburn Roundabout, one at the traffic lights just before you hit the woods, and another outside ASDA on the Brechin road.'

'It's probably a van, but any car big enough to hide two bodies in the boot is worth a punt.'

'Are you sure the baby isn't yours?'

'She's been shagging DCI Reece Sodding Powel for about a year. Probably longer.'

'Then you should definitely come to the party. My daughter's just dumped her idiot husband and she could do with a shoulder to cry on.' Clickity click, click, click. 'This is probably going to take a while. I'll have to get back to you.'

'Thanks, Voodoo.'

'And I mean it about the party, Callum, you and Becky would be perfect together. She's smart; she's pretty; she's always got her head in a book; and she never, ever—'

'Bye, Voodoo.' He hung up. Stood there, staring out at the brightly coloured houses.

Maybe Oldcastle's answer to Yente was right?

Maybe her daughter was perfect?

And maybe he deserved to be happy for a sodding change?

It wasn't as if Elaine gave a—

'You OK?'

He turned, and there was Franklin, frowning at him. 'Hmmm?'

'Looked like you were miles away.'

'Any luck?'

'Couple of residents mentioned a small grey van parked up the road. One old lady saw a big blue Transit, but nobody else did. And there were three sightings of a big Red Land Rover driving erratically around the time of the nine-nine-nine call. McCready's got two DCs trying to chase them down.'

At least it was a start.

Callum went back to his phone and called Mother.

50

Franklin made a big show of looking at her watch. Again. 'We're going to be late.'

'No we're not.'

To be fair, the traffic was terrible. Whichever moron on the city council thought it was a good idea to dig up the main road through town on the same weekend as that stupid music festival in Montgomery Park needed a stiff kick in the backside. And then a punch in the balls.

The dual carriageway was down to one lane in each direction, crawling with eighteen wheelers; coaches; buses; cars; all blending in an exhaust-fume symphony of grey that stretched from the Camburn Roundabout as far as the eye could see. Didn't help that the rain was on again.

The line of cars ahead of them snaked through the slalom of orange traffic cones, crawling across the central reservation and onto the opposite lane. Then stopped.

Callum cleared his throat. 'OK: how do we trick Gareth Pike into giving up the name?'

'Lie to him.'

'I mean, it's not like I can threaten to put him in jail with a bunch of sex offenders, is it? That's his idea of a social club.'

'You could offer him something, then take it away? Pretend you've found another source and *they've* already given you the name, so the best Pike can do is corroborate it if he wants any concessions at all?'

'Might work...'

'He has to want something, everyone does. So what does Pike want?'

'South-facing cell with a nice view. Seriously: like he's reserving a room at the Ritz.'

'Good luck with that.' Franklin pulled a face. 'We're definitely going to be late.'

'Look, there's nothing we can do about the traffic, OK? Put the radio on or something.'

Franklin crossed her arms. 'Put on the blues-and-twos more like.'

He tried not to sigh, but it didn't work. 'We've been over this: you hit the nine-nine-nine button and the GPS starts recording, and the dashboard camera starts recording, and...' He tapped his fingers against the steering wheel.

She turned in her seat. 'What?'

Last night – outside Willow Brown's house. When he'd arrived, lights and sirens blaring, that big black Mercedes was just pulling away. Not exactly the kind of car you'd expect to see swanning about Kingsmeath. No: drive something like that down there and you'd be lucky to get home with all the wheels and doors still on it, never mind the hubcaps. So why was it there, on Manson Avenue? Why would—

'Callum!' Franklin poked him in the arm. 'We're moving.'

He blinked.

The cars up ahead had shuffled forward twenty yards.

A horn blared behind him, followed by a rising chorus of angry beeps.

He slid the Mondeo up to the car in front's rear bumper.

It couldn't have been Willow's *dad's* Mercedes, could it? He'd gone up in the world, if it was... Mind you, since when was being a wife-and-child-beating scumbag any barrier to success?

With any luck, the dashboard cam had got the Merc's number plate before it disappeared around the corner. Then it wouldn't matter how 'not a snitch' Willow and her mum wanted to be – a quick check on the Police National Computer would spit out the wee sod's name, address, and inside-leg measurement.

And speaking of PNC checks, what the hell had happened to the one he'd requested on all Irene Brown's old boyfriends? Have to chase that up. Honestly, you had to stand over people beating them with a stick to get anything done.

'...sometime today?'

'Hmm?' He looked up and the gap had opened in front of them again. 'Sorry, miles away.'

Franklin thumped back in her seat. 'Knew we should've gone the other way.'

'Everything round Montgomery Park is shut for the music festival, everything *near* the park is all tailbacks and diversions. Doesn't matter which way you go, you're just as stuck.'

'Gah...' She clicked the radio on and a throbbing bassline and kick-drum beat burst into the car.

A woman's voice, rich and dark, amplified over the top: '*Come on, let me see those hands in the air! Yeah!*'

More drum and bass.

Franklin stared out of the passenger window. 'What happened when you went to pick up your stuff, last night?'

'*Sing it with me: You are the fish in my sea.*'

A crowd roared it out, like a football chant. '*YOU ARE THE FISH IN MY SEA!*'

Callum's shoulders itched. 'You know: the usual. Powel banging on about how we're all adults and they didn't mean for it to happen.'

'*You are the birds in my tree.*'

'*YOU ARE THE BIRDS IN MY TREE!*'

His good hand tightened on the wheel. 'Said Elaine never loved me. She was just going through the motions.'

Franklin nodded. 'He is a bit of a dick, isn't he?'

'*You're the honey in my bee.*'

'*YOU'RE THE HONEY IN MY BEE!*'

She clicked the radio off again.

The traffic crawled forwards.

A cough. Then Franklin puffed out her cheeks and sighed. Picked at a stain on the dashboard. Sighed again. 'OK, so Pike wants to go to prison, yes? What if you threaten to take *that* away from him?'

'We caught him molesting himself to a video of two little boys being raped. He's going to prison and he knows it.'

'Hrmmm... What about telling him you'll put out a statement about how helpful he's been in exposing whatever ring he's part of? Soon as he gets inside they'll tear him apart.'

The traffic crawled forward another six foot.

'Or, how about— Sod.' She hauled out her phone. 'DC Franklin. ... Uh-huh. ... Hold on, I'll put you on speakerphone.' She pressed the button and held the phone up.

Dotty's voice thumped out into the car. '*...not telling you again!*'

Watt, in the background: '*You're not allowed to use a mobile phone while driving. It's illegal.*'

'*Oh, go bugger yourself with a loo brush.*' A pause. '*Rosalind, we've chased the labs up and guess what: fingerprints.*'

'You've already been in one horrible car crash, Hodgkin, let's not make it two.'

'Genuinely, it was the most disgusting thing I've ever seen. They soaked the hands in glucose, peeled them off the bones, and got one of the APTs to wear them like gloves. Urgh...'

'I'd like to go home tonight with both my legs, if that's OK with you?'

Callum raised his voice. 'Did they get an ID off the prints?'

'Oh, hello, Callum. Can you do me a favour and tell Watt he's being a big – girl's – blouse?'

'Do you two always have to do this?'

Watt: 'And you can tell her she's being petty, irresponsible, and childish! Traffic laws are there for a reason.'

He slid the car forward another length. 'Dotty, give Watt the phone.'

'I don't—'

'Just do it, OK? Please?'

Watt's voice came through loud and clear. 'Thank you. It's about time someone—'

'And you can stop being a dick. Stick us on speakerphone.'

'That's right, take her side. Everyone always—'

'Don't be such a Jessie! I'm the one—'

'OH FOR GOD'S SAKE, THE PAIR OF YOU! You're not six!'

Silence from the phone.

A gap opened up and Callum slid the car into it, crawling along as the line of traffic snaked back to its own side of the road. A massive road grader growled its way along the central reservation, flanked by soggy-looking men in dripping high-viz jackets and hard hats.

The Mondeo thumped over a hard line in the tarmac, marked 'RAMP'.

Still nothing from the phone.

'Fine: I'm sorry.'

Dotty sniffed. 'That's better.'

'You *are* six.'

'It's not my fault he always—'

'Did you get an ID off the fingerprints, or not?'

'Hmmph.'

Watt sounded a bit smug, as if he somehow thought he'd won something: 'I'll answer that one, shall I, Sergeant? Apparently they have to wear the hand in order to flesh out the fingers, so to speak. We got them to run the prints and they came back with two matches.'

A coach crawled past on the other side of the dual carriageway, full of pre-teen girls waving home-made placards with things like 'WE ♥ MR BONES!!!' and 'Marry Me Taylor!!!' on them.

Franklin scowled at the phone. 'This isn't *Who Wants to Be a Millionaire*, Watt. Stop milking it.'

'Sorry, had to check my notes. The body from the tip was one Roger Barrett. Did five years for armed robbery, got out last January. Hasn't been to see his probation officer in nine months.' That smug tone was back. *'And you'll never guess where he worked—'*

Dotty hammered in over the top: *'Strummuir Smokehouse!'*

'I was actually *telling them that!'*

'Rosalind's right: you were milking it.'

No wonder Mother went around with a pained expression on her face most of the time. 'So who's victim number two?'

'The mummy from the car boot was one Richard Duffy. No criminal record, but his prints are on file, cos someone broke into his house on Christmas Eve and stole a thousand quid's worth of electronics and jewellery from under the tree. So his wife got him a last-minute fill-in present: a charcuterie and artisanal curing-and-smoking course at Strummuir Smokehouse. He took it in January. His wife reported him missing in March.'

Which made sense.

Tod Monaghan was a creature of habit, picking his victims from the people he saw at the smokehouse. Too thick to realise that it left a trail leading straight back to Strummuir.

'We're on our way to break the news to Duffy's wife now.'

'OK, thanks.' Callum grinned across the car at Franklin. 'And Watt, Dotty? You did good. You make an excellent team.'

There was a small pause, then Watt's voice rang out loud and clear: *'Don't patronise me.'* He hung up.

Franklin shook her head. 'You did that on purpose, didn't you?'

'Oh hell yes.'

Franklin clambered out into the rain and hurried in through the overflow mortuary's front doors. Paused for a second to turn and wave at him, then disappeared inside.

Callum sat there with the windscreen wipers moaning. Pulled out his phone and called Control. 'What happened to the PNC checks I asked for *days* ago?'

Silence.

'Hello?'

A woman's voice stabbed out from the speaker. *'Do you want to try that again, DC MacGregor, using words like "please" and "thank you"?'*

Prima donnas. 'Please can you tell me what happened to the sodding PNC checks I asked for *days* ago? Thank you.'

'Good manners don't cost anything, you know. And I don't appreciate your sarcasm, by the way.'

'Fine. I'm sorry. *Please* can I have my PNC results.'

'That's better.' The sound of a keyboard being thumped into submission. *'I have eight names and details all emailed to you the day before yesterday.'*

Thursday. The day they accused him of murdering his own mother.

'Yes. Sorry I was... It wasn't a good day. I'll check when I get back to the office.'

'See: there was no reason to be all sarcastic and demanding, was there?'

'No. Sorry. Thank you.'

He hung up. Ran his good hand across his face.

Well done, Callum. Way to be a complete and utter dick.

'Urgh...'

Let's face it, with all this crap going on, he needed every friend he could get right now.

And speaking of which: he dialled Shannon.

'What?' The word barked down the line.

'Bob, it's Callum. This a bad time?'

'Oh, OK. Hold on.' It sounded like Marilyn Monroe was singing in the background, boop-boop-de-dooping her way into silence. Then Shannon was back. *'Sorry, it's been bloody government boiler schemes and green-energy review calls all sodding morning. Some people need stabbing in the ear with a trowel. Is it too much to expect to watch a film in peace?'* A grunt. *'Anyway, what can I do for you?'*

'Any news on that name?'

'The Old Age Police network needs time, Callum. I know it's important, but these guys are wading through nearly thirty years of junk to get at notebooks and case files. And even then, there's no guarantee.'

Of course there wasn't.

'Sorry.' He rubbed the fingertips of his broken hand across his brows. Trying to massage some life into them. 'Pike's up before the Sheriff at eleven and he's still not saying anything.'

'He likes screwing with people.'

'It's not like the name's any good to him.'

'He needs Viagra to have a wank, Callum, screwing with people is

probably the closest he gets to a natural hard-on. And even then, it's probably just a semi.'

Now there was an image.

'I don't know what to do, Bob.'

'We'll sort it out, don't worry. Now, if you'll excuse me, Tony Curtis is about to change out of his dress and into a blazer.'

Callum slipped the phone back into his pocket and sat staring out at the rain.

Checked his watch.

Half an hour and Pike would be making his guilty plea. Then a short car ride to HMP Oldcastle to wait for Social Work reports and sentencing. Taking his secrets with him.

And there was nothing Callum could do about it.

51

The old station house in Castleview had a weird sour coconutty smell, as if it'd got blootered on Malibu the night before and vomited all over itself. Maybe the Security Monitoring And Analysis Department liked to lube themselves up with suntan lotion of a Saturday morning?

Callum parked his backside on the windowsill and tucked his filthy fibreglass cast into his jacket pocket. Hiding it away. 'What do you think?'

The man in the blue hoodie was far too old to be wearing it, or the big fancy trainers, or the 'HALFHEAD ~ BONES & STONES WORLD TOUR!' T-shirt. He'd scraped what little hair remained on his head back into a sumo-wrestler's pigtail, glasses perched on top of his shiny scalp. 'Hmmm...' He picked at his soul patch – greying like the eyebrows. 'Why not: Winston Smith *likes* a challenge.'

The Mondeo's digital video drive sat in a little plastic cradle, connected to a silvery tower unit. A few clattering keystrokes and lights on the drive flashed green. A few more and the thing bleeped and whirred.

'Of course, I can't promise anything, yeah? Winston never knows what he's going to see till he sees it.'

The room was strangely empty. Just the desk and the computer, one very expensive-looking office chair, one filing cabinet, one window, and a radiator that pinged and gurgled like a fat man's stomach.

Callum checked his watch. Again. Ten past.

Pike would be on his way back to the cells by now.

'Right, here we go...' Smith's fingers flew across the keys and half a dozen little windows appeared on the computer monitor, each playing a view from the Mondeo's dashboard camera. Second-hand flickering lights and speeding streets. He fiddled with the mouse, closing all the windows but the one with yesterday's date – the dual carriageway roared past at triple speed, cars and traffic cones flashing by, over the bridge, round the roundabout, up into Kingsmeath.

Another click and the video slowed to normal speed.

The car swept around onto Manson Avenue.

Froze.

Wound back a bit.

'There we are, one black Mercedes.' Smith tapped the screen, where the back end of the Merc was just disappearing around the corner, partially obscured by an ancient Fiesta. 'Now, let's see what being a genius gets you these days...' He pecked at the keyboard and the window zoomed in on the car's number plate. The footage ran forwards and backwards a few times and the frown on his face deepened. 'Hmmm...'

'What?'

'Well, it's low light, which doesn't help, it's far away, which also doesn't help, and the camera lens isn't the cleanest either. This is as good as we can get.' A blurred and lumpy grey-and-yellow smear.

'Can't you do some sort of image enhancement thing on it?'

'This isn't science fiction, my friend. Winston is a genius, but he's not a miracle worker. These cameras record the image as a big block of pixels and write them to the hard drive. You can zoom in all you like, but there comes a point where all you're doing is making the pixels bigger. You can't magically wring more resolution out of the system, because it just doesn't exist.'

'Oh.'

Well *that* was a complete waste of time.

Callum stood. 'Well, thanks anyway.'

'Ah, ha, ha!' Smith held up a finger. 'Winston said he wasn't a miracle worker, but that doesn't mean he's incapable of the odd miraculous act. You see the pattern of blurring we've got here, the lights and the darks? That's been formed by the numbers on the number plate, and the way they combine in a given set of lighting conditions at a certain range. Winston can't make them any less blurry, but he can run a very clever bit of software to blur thousands of different number and letter combinations to see what produce the closest matches.' A wink. 'Told you: Winston Smith likes a challenge.'

He curled over his keyboard, face inches from the screen as he typed. Opening up programs, setting things running, clicking and clicking and clicking. 'You might want to grab a cup of tea, this is going to take a while.'

Callum took a sip of scalding hot tea, wandering the corridors. 'No, I just wanted to see if there was any news.'

Mother's voice crackled out of the earpiece as if she were on the other side of the planet, not the other side of the river. *'Well, Dorothy and John are off looking into Roger Barrett. Probably won't add anything to the stew, but it's better to err on the safe side, isn't it? I want us to have a good squint at Ashlee and Abby Gossard's movements in the run-up to the abduction. Monaghan must've bumped into them somewhere, and far as we know they've never been to Strummuir Smokehouse. Which reminds me: we've still not had anything back from the CCTV team, so if you wouldn't mind giving them a prod, that'd be nice.'*

'I'm there now.'

'Good. And tell Voodoo that Jack and I would love to come to Ian's party. I'll be bringing my famous spinach and artichoke dip. Jack will bring his infamous peapod burgundy.'

'Will do.'

The CCTV control room door was open, offering a view into a dim room lined with screens – each one displaying a different view of Oldcastle. Half a dozen support staff sat at the long central desk, working the joysticks that moved the cameras and eating cake.

'Callum?'

'Yes, Boss?'

'I hear someone broke Blakey this morning.'

That was one way to put it.

'Yes, Boss.'

'He's been signed off on the sick. Stress.'

'Oh for...' Callum closed his eyes and thunked his head off the corridor wall. 'So there's *no one* running the case?'

'I hear you think this paedophile, Gareth Pike, saw what happened to your parents?'

'How can there be no one running the case? Blakey was useless, but at least he was *there*!'

'When you get back to the station, we'll see what we can do, OK?'

His shoulders sagged. 'Yes, Boss.'

'Good. Now, in the meantime, go chase up Voodoo. And remember: spinach dip.'

Callum hung up, put his phone away. Thunked his head off the wall again.

Bloody Blakey. *Thunk*. Bloody useless half—

'I hope you're not putting dents in my lovely headquarters, Callum.'

He picked his head off the wall and turned, faked a smile. 'Voodoo.'

She was dressed in Police Scotland black, complete with shiny boots and epaulettes on the shoulders of her T-shirt. A small woman, with close-cropped grey hair and arms like a marathon runner. A big broad smile that made the wrinkles around her eyes deepen. 'I hope you're here to accept my party invitation?'

'Thought it would be wise to see a photo of your daughter first.'

'Cheeky sod.' Voodoo dug into her pocket and produced her phone, swiping away at the screen. 'I know you didn't come all the way over here for that, so what's the *real* reason?'

'Mother wants to know how you're getting on with the vehicle check for our Johnson Crescent abductions. Vans and big four-by-fours?'

'Ah yes. Walk this way, young man.' She turned and marched off, still fiddling with her phone. 'We've run through every ANPR camera in a half-mile radius, *and* the security footage from all public spaces in the area.' At the end of the corridor, Voodoo pushed through the double doors and hammered up the stairs, taking them two at a time. 'Keep up, Callum.'

It wasn't easy. 'Did you ... did you get ... anything?' Puffing and panting all the way. Tea slopping from side to side in his mug.

She stopped on the landing and held out her phone. 'There you go.'

A young woman smiled out of the screen: long brown hair, big brown eyes, long thin nose, suntan, huge smile, and a *tiny* blue bikini.

'That's our Becky. Still swithering about coming to the party?'

'Well, if I wasn't breathing heavy already...'

'Good boy. She likes sauvignon blanc.' And Voodoo was off again. 'I've got a long-list of about a hundred vehicles, but we've narrowed it down to three likely targets: a small grey Peugeot Bipper, a rust-brown Bedford Rascal, and a green Fiat Fiorino. There's a *lot* of four-by-fours, but these are the vans that get my juices flowing.'

A young man emerged into the corridor, did a double-take. 'Chief Inspector.' Then flattened himself against the wall as Voodoo strode past.

'Get the kettle on, Williams. I'm gasping.' She kept on going.

'Yes, Chief Inspector.'

She swung through a door near the end, and into a large office with one whole wall given over to at least two dozen TVs. A coffee table and a couch sat in front of them, along with a phone and a wireless keyboard. Voodoo perched herself on the edge of the couch and fiddled with the keyboard.

Pictures sprang into life across the screens: a curling cobbled street in Castle Hill, the bus station on Dalrymple Street, three views of Harvest Lane's rows of nightclubs, the car park just inside The Swinney, two views of Camburn Woods, then MacKinnon Quay, the school on Preston Row, Montgomery Park with its collection of marquees and big inflatable spider... On and on, peering into other people's lives – like being God, or GCHQ.

'Take a seat, Callum, you're making my office look untidy.'

'Sorry.' He sank into the couch next to her and stuck his mug on the coffee table as she did some more fiddling. 'Don't suppose any of these vehicles were registered to a Tod Monaghan, were they?'

'No.'

'Oh...' Well, it was never going to be *that* easy, was it? Monaghan would be driving someone else's van. Maybe without them even knowing.

The monitors divided up into three huge pictures, stretched across multiple screens. A green van in one, a manky orange-brown van in another, and a grey van in the third. All small vehicles, nowhere near as large as a Transit, and all waiting to go through a different set of traffic lights.

Their number plates sat in a caption box at the top of each image.

'We've got them going into the vicinity of Johnson Crescent between seven and eight, and coming out again between quarter past eight and twenty to nine. And by the way, you owe me six bags of doughnuts – getting my team to drop everything and slog through all that footage required bribery.' She poked at the keyboard again and the images on the screen pulsed like a slideshow as each of the vehicles were picked up on various CCTV and ANPR cameras across the city. 'We followed them as far through the system as we could, but ...' a shrug, 'sadly the powers that be won't let me put cameras on every street in the city. If they did, just imagine what we could achieve!'

'Constant and total surveillance, an Orwellian nightmare, only instead of "Big Brother" you'd be "Little Sister"?'

Voodoo smiled. Sighed. 'Ah well, a girl can dream, can't she?' Then jogged over to her desk and pulled a sheet of paper from a tray. Held it out. 'All three vehicles' registered owners and addresses, plus first and last confirmed locations on camera.'

Callum stood and took the sheet. 'Thanks, Voodoo, you're a star.'

'I am, aren't I?' She frowned at him. 'Callum, do you want a little friendly advice?'

No.

'You've had a bad run of late. Don't let it colour everything that happens to you.' She gave him a small hug. 'And come to my party: Becky's a yoga instructor. *Very* flexible.'

Winston Smith peered out over the top of his glasses. 'Well, yes, Winston did say you should go away and get a cup of tea, but the key part of that sentence is that you should *go away.*'

Callum leaned back against the windowsill again. 'You're all mouth and no trousers, aren't you?'

He narrowed his eyes. 'Winston is very much all trousers, thank you very much. He told you this was going to be a challenge, and he's not going to give up till it's done, but until then you should leave him alone and let him get on with his work.' He raised a hand from his keyboard and made shooing motions. 'Away with you. Winston will call when, ultimately, he is triumphant.'

Police Scotland *really* needed a moratorium on hiring freaks and weirdos.

'Fine.'

Callum headed back down to the car, phone clamped between his thumb and the fibreglass cast. 'Mother?'

McAdams' voice oiled its way into Callum's ear. *'She goes to stand firm. At the press conference. The top brass to save.'*

He clattered down the stairs. 'A simple, "she's not here" would've done.'

'Then: "she's not here," you artless spud. And she won't be back till two or three, so if you've got information: spill it.'

'Voodoo's done the CCTV analysis for us.' Callum pushed out through the old station doors and into the rear car park – surrounded by an eighteen-foot-high brick wall topped with barbed wire. 'They're nominating three small vans as possible abduction vehicles.'

'Good. Return your backside to DHQ; you and I are going visiting.'

Callum scuffed to a halt ten feet from the pool car. 'Erm... Maybe you'd be better off staying there and coordinating things? You know, if Mother's going to be tied up at the press conference? Somebody needs to be in charge?'

Fingers crossed...

'*Nice try, Constable.*'
Don't give up!
'And now I think about it, maybe Dotty or Watt would be better—'
'*Backside. Back here. Now.*'
Sod.

52

Division Headquarters was remarkably quiet for noon on a rainy Saturday. No clatter of boots on the stairs, no shouting in the corridors. No drunken singing echoing up from the cells.

A couple of PCs were having a heated argument by the coffee machine outside the Productions Office, but other than that: dead.

And there was still no sign of McAdams. *'I'll be down in five minutes.'* His arse.

Callum pushed through into the stairwell and froze, fingertips of his broken hand resting on the bannister.

That was Detective Superintendent Ness's voice, wafting up from the floor below. *'...problems. For God's sake, Reece, I know you're having a rough time at the moment, but that's no excuse for not turning up for work! This is* completely *unacceptable.'* The sound of feet pacing on the concrete landing. *'Look, call me when you get this, OK? If we have to rejig your workload till things calm down ... well, we'll sort something out. Bye.'*

A loud sigh. Then something muttered too low to hear.

Callum waited till the door below clunked shut before scurrying up the stairs like a rat. Along the corridor and into the Misfit Mob's office.

As if he was going to hang around, getting drawn into a conversation about DCI Bloody Powel. No thank you.

He scooted into his chair and logged back into his computer.

The email about Irene Brown's known associates was sitting in his inbox, between a memo about not leaving half-eaten takeaways in the pool cars and a lookout request for an OAP who used to specialise in jacking security vans.

Looked as if Irene Brown had lousy taste in men. Eight of them: all violent, all with criminal records.

What on earth was wrong with some women? How could they possibly find that attractive? Oh, you're an aggressive scumbag who steals things and deals drugs? That sounds *dreamy*!

Callum stuck the names into the Police National Computer and ran them again, just in case. Attempted murder. Drugs. Assaults. Housebreaking. Armed robbery. Stealing cars. Rape... Irene Brown certainly could pick them.

Going by the mugshots on file, she was into the sullen muscly type. Tattoos an added bonus. Like Bachelor Number Four.

Callum scooted forward in his seat.

Previous for shoplifting, theft, breaking into old ladies' houses and robbing them blind, nicking other people's cars, and that was it. Nothing on his docket for the last five years. Either he'd gone straight, he'd died, or he'd gone somewhere else. But the most interesting thing was his name: Donald Newman.

Benny, Willow's brother, said his dad was called Donald.

Mind you, he also said his dad owned a tiger, a helicopter, and "loads of bitches", so: pinch of salt.

But still. Bit of a coincidence if it wasn't.

And Newman was what, eight years older than Irene Brown? That was wholesome, wasn't it? A twenty-four-year-old wannabe gangster talking her into bed on her sixteenth birthday. Assuming he even waited *that* long.

Callum scowled at the screen.

It wasn't as if they could do anything about it, after all this time. If she was over sixteen it was legal. And if she wasn't, try proving Newman was in violation of sections 13, 14, or 15 of the Sexual Offences (Scotland) Act 2009, seven years after the fact. Assuming she even wanted to press charges after all this time.

Still might be able to do him for breaking his daughter's arm...

Mind you, even then, how would you *prove* it beyond reasonable doubt?

Might be worth getting in touch with Social Services, though.

Yeah, unless they took one look at Irene Brown and decided her kids would be better off growing up in care.

Sod that.

Callum slouched down the stairs, out the back door, and into the rain. Hurried across the rear car park and into the dysentery-brown Mondeo. Wiped the water from his face.

Checked his watch.

Detective sergeants were a pain in the backside at the best of times, but McAdams took the Jammie Dodger. Still no sign of him.

And you could bet your last fifty-three pounds and seventy-two pence that if anyone caught Callum hanging about in the office, doing nothing, they'd find him something unpleasant to do. Much better to hide out here, waiting for McAdams to turn up. And at least he could do something productive while he was waiting.

Callum took out his phone and made a call.

'Scenes Examination Branch.'

'Cecelia? It's Callum. I'm calling about the Gossard crime scene – two twenty-three Johnson Crescent. The abduction?'

'Oh I remember that one: blood everywhere.'

'Did you get any decent fingerprints or DNA?'

'Still working through the samples, but it's all the victims' so far.'

Sod.

A frown. What was it the posh-sounding bloke had said? The one on Dr McDonald's phone when they were going through Brett, Ben, and Glen's fixer-up flat... Right.

'Did you try under the taps and door handles? He would've been clarted in blood, he's not going to risk being spotted looking like an abattoir's floor. He'll have washed his hands.'

'Course we did. I got Brian to do it. Hold on...' There was a muffled conversation on the other end that escalated into a muffled argument. Then a sigh. And she was back again: *'I'll head round there soon as I've finished my tea.'*

'Thanks, Cecelia, you're a star.'

Callum hung up, stuck the seat back as far as it would go, pulled *Open the Coffins* from his jacket pocket and settled down to read.

A knock on the window made him flinch. He blinked at the dashboard clock – 12:15. A whole five minutes' peace and quiet.

McAdams slithered into the passenger seat and clunked the door shut. Sat there, staring across the car with one eyebrow raised. 'Any time you're ready.' He'd brought a slightly bitter aroma with him: like pear drops laced with marzipan and vinegar. An unwell smell.

Callum turned the page. 'Hold on, I'm nearly finished this chapter.'

'Oh for goodness' sake, not *more* kiddies' books. I'm beginning to think you've got an unnatural bent, Constable MacGregor.' He snatched the novel out of Callum's hands, shut it, and grimaced at the cover. '*Open the Coffins* is a ridiculous title for a kids' book.'

'It's a *classic.*'

'You know Travis stole that from William Blake, don't you? Or was it Milton? No, definitely Blake. "And by came an Angel who had a bright key. / And he open'd the coffins and set them all free…"'

Callum grabbed the book back and slipped it into his pocket. 'You said five minutes, *twenty* minutes ago.'

'And he's obsessed: rabbits as a symbol of male innocence and virility, cats as feminine cunning and treachery.'

He hauled his seat forwards, started up the Mondeo and stuck her into drive. 'The rust-brown Berlingo's closest: Milgarvie and Kirk, plumbing supplies and services, Cowskillin.'

'Justin Nevin gets transformed into a rabbit by the Wicked Witch of the Well as a punishment for his theft. And by the way, she's only stuck down the well because the villagers chucked her in there, but Justin thinks it's OK to steal the apples from the tree growing over the well even though they're her *only* source of food. Well, unless a child falls down there, I suppose.'

Callum slid them out of the car park, right, and onto Camburn Road. 'That's *why* she's got the apple tree there – so kids will try to steal the apples and fall in the well.'

'And that's something else he's obsessed with: witches eating children. Goblins eating rabbits. Monsters eating children. People eating rabbits that are actually children. It's a smorgasbord of transspecies consumption, posing as anthropomorphic cannibalism, but it's really about venal desire. Consume the flesh, violate the body, and absorb it into your own.'

They skirted the edge of Camburn Woods, steering clear of the main roads. 'They're kids' books. They're about magic and adventure, *not* sex.'

'Just because you read a lot, Constable, it doesn't mean you read deeply. Skimming across the surface like a water beetle, no idea of the pike swimming through the murky depths below.'

Past the cemetery on the left, where a yellow JCB was busy digging a six-foot hole.

McAdams turned to watch the graves go by. 'And what about Justin Nevin's sister, Arya? Nevin is Croatian for "innocent", Arya is Hausa for "false". So the main female character is *literally* called False Innocence.'

Callum took a right, up a street of Victorian houses with rail-ing-guarded front gardens, across the road at the end and into a narrow cobbled alley.

He pulled up outside a small shop with a dusty front window and an eight-foot-high gate wide enough to drive a bus through. 'MILGARVIE & KIRK ~ FAMILY PLUMBING SPECIALISTS' in big white letters across the blue-painted wood. 'You finished?'

'All I'm saying is that you've got a terrible taste in literature, and you should feel ashamed about it.'

'Screw you, Sarge.' Callum climbed out into the rain. Slammed the Mondeo's door. Then hurried into the shop.

'Nah...' The man in the overalls handed the photo of Ashlee and Abby Gossard back across a countertop littered with bits of copper pipe, valves, grommets, and washers. 'Sorry.'

Callum put the photo in his pocket and showed him one of Tod Monaghan instead. 'How about him?'

'Nah.'

'But you *were* on Johnson Crescent Wednesday night?'

'Fixing the most disgusting blocked U-bend you've ever seen in your life. Three women, sharing, and the amount of hair down the bathtub drain looked like they'd drowned a Womble. I can give you their number if you like? Manky cows...'

Dundas Bridge was jammed with cars and trucks trying to avoid the roadworks on the main route through Oldcastle.

McAdams grimaced out of the passenger window. 'Traffic's *terrible*.'

'And yet you made me drive all the way through it to pick you up, then all the way back again.' Callum tightened his grip on the steering wheel. 'Remember?'

'You know, moaning and whingeing isn't an attractive quality in a sidekick. You should watch that. I might have to trade you in for narra-tive purposes.' McAdams' face was the colour of damp newsprint, his breathing coming in little shallow pulses. The bags under his eyes had darkened since he'd climbed into the car, back at DHQ. He checked the dashboard clock, then reached out and clicked on the radio. 'Press conference should be starting soon.'

They were still doing their live coverage from the festival, only whoever was on stage right now couldn't sing in tune no matter how loud they tried. It wasn't even proper words they were bellowing, just noises.

Callum tightened his grip on the steering wheel. 'I'm *not* your sidekick.'

'Well you're obviously not the hero, are you? You're not even the comic relief – you have to actually be funny for that. All you do is moan and whinge. No wonder the readers don't like you.' McAdams held up a finger, the other hand pressing against his stomach. A grimace. Then: '*And* Arya gets transmogrified into a cat.'

That sickly pear-drop smell was getting stronger.

OK, so McAdams might be a pain in the backside, but still… Callum cleared his throat. 'Are you feeling all right, Sarge? Only you look terrible.'

'Remember the scene when she catches and eats that church mouse, even though it's got a family of six to care for? That's a metaphor for women being soft and fuzzy on the outside and all cruel violence on the inside. How they *consume* men for their own selfish ends.'

'Seriously, you look awful.'

A shrug. 'I'm dying.'

'You're not planning on doing it right now, though, are you? You can't believe how much extra paperwork that'd give me.'

McAdams smiled. 'I'll do my best to hang on till we get back to the shop.' He stretched in his seat, grimacing. 'Do you ever think about the end of your life, Callum? How it's all going to just … stop?'

'I'm not kidding: if you're going to drop dead do it to Dotty. Or Watt, he deserves all he gets.'

'The doctors say I won't see my forty-third birthday. Can you imagine what that feels like?'

Callum stared at him: the stubbly grey hair, the bags under the eyes, the wrinkles. 'You're only *forty-two*? God, that must have been one hell of a hard paper round.'

'The Reaper reaps all men, in time, / His hand has come to rest on mine…'

The song on the radio droned to a halt as they reached the other side of the bridge, replaced by cheering as Callum took them straight across the roundabout and into the posher part of Castleview. Where the streets were wide and lined with trees, and no one's corpse was floating in a bathtub full of brine and herbs.

'*Wooohooo! Wasn't that fan-chicken-tastic? That's Mr Bones there, sponsored by ScotiaBrand Tasty Chickens Limited, let's give them another big hand!*'

More cheering from a crowd that was either too polite to mention, or too drunk to care, that the band had been unable to carry a tune in a rucksack.

Callum navigated past a chunk of open ground, full of trees, and round onto a car park outside a small line of shops.

'And now here's Gorgeous Gabby with all your news and weather. Any chance of some sunshine, Gabby?'

'Sorry, Chris, but things might be looking up for Sunday. Here's the news. Police Scotland have announced they're not looking for any other suspects in the Imhotep Mummy Murder case, after a man's body was pulled from the Kings River outside Dundas House yesterday...'

He pointed through the window at a florist's, wedged between a domestic appliances shop and a Co-op funeral director's. A lumpy green van sat out front, the side door slid back so a young woman in trousers, shirt, and tie could load big floral arrangements inside. The number plate matched the one on Voodoo's printout.

'...over live to Oldcastle Division Headquarters.'

The sound of a general hubbub died down, punctuated by the occasional clack-whine of a camera going off. Then the Chief Superintendent's voice boomed out, amplified loud enough to cause a squeal of feedback. 'Ladies and gentlemen, I'm pleased to announce that O Division officers have successfully concluded the recent spate of mummification murders...'

Callum undid his seatbelt, but McAdams stayed where he was, clutching his stomach and grimacing. 'Do you want me to call an ambulance?'

A shake of the head. Teeth gritted. 'It'll be fine. I just ... need to sit here for a minute. Make sure ... the press conference goes OK.'

'...tireless work by the officers under my command, preventing further deaths at the hands of a deeply troubled individual...'

'Honk the horn if you change your mind. I can stick the flashers on and we'll be at CHI in ten, fifteen minutes tops.'

'I told you, I'm *fine*. Now ... sod off, you're talking ... all over the Chief Superintendent.'

He climbed out. Closed the door. Stood there for a moment, as McAdams grimaced and rubbed at his stomach.

Yeah, definitely *not* looking well.

Callum turned and marched over to the horrible green van. 'You Mrs Reid?'

The woman gave a little start and yelp. 'Argh, frightened the life out of me.'

'This your van?'

She stuck the last arrangement into the back and slid the side door shut. 'Course it's not my van. It's Mrs Reid's van. How could *I* afford a van?'

Up close she was a lot younger than she'd looked from the car.

'Are you the driver of this vehicle, then?'

Her mouth slammed shut, then she turned and hurried out of the rain, huddling under the overhang outside the funeral director's. 'You're the police, aren't you? Sodding hell.' She bit at her fingernails – already jagged and rough. 'If this is about that bitch's Porsche, I *swear* those dents were there before I parked next to her.'

He pulled out his notebook. 'Were you driving this van on Wednesday evening?'

'No.'

'You sure?'

Another fingernail disappeared. '*Please* don't tell Mrs Reid, OK? I'm not meant to take the van home, but I was out on a late delivery and my boyfriend had his parents' house to himself and we...' Colour rushed up her cheeks. 'Please don't tell Mrs Reid. I'm on my last warning as it is and I *need* this job.'

He clamped a pen between his thumb and the dirty fibreglass cast. 'I'm going to need his name, his address, and his number.'

A grey-haired woman emerged from the florist's next door, wiping her hands on a stripy apron. 'Is something wrong, Andrea?'

She slapped on a smile. 'No, Mrs Reid. This gentleman was just asking if we do funeral wreaths. I was giving him our number.'

'Well don't be long, that wedding's at three and I want those pedestals all set up by two at the latest.' She pursed her lips then nodded at Callum. 'I'm sorry for your loss.' Before disappearing back inside.

Callum produced his photographs again. No joy.

Two vans down, one to go...

53

'Are you sure this is it?'

Callum checked Voodoo's printout again. 'Postcode is right.'

The registered address for Van Number Three, the grey Peugeot Bipper, wasn't so much a house as a fire-blackened hulk slumped at the end of a track nearly halfway between Oldcastle and Auchterowan. Bordered on all sides by fields with a clump of woods in the middle distance. Its garden was a riot of weeds and grass, that looked as if it hadn't seen a lawnmower for at least a decade. No neighbours.

The damp undergrowth seeped cold moisture through Callum's trousers. 'Who's going to buy a second-hand van and register it here?'

McAdams howched, then spat a glob of yellowy-green into the rosebay willowherb. 'Oldest trick in the book: clone someone's number plates, or register your dodgy vehicle to someone else. Doesn't matter if you're speeding, or parking on double yellows, the police go after the registered keeper, not you.'

Callum called control on his Airwave, 'Brucie? Can I get a PNC check on a Paul Terence Jeffries, the Cloisters, by Auchterowan, OC25 8TX.'

'*Hud oan.*'

McAdams sniffed and leaned on the roof of the car. 'At least it's stopped raining.'

Overhead, the sky was a looming mass of grey, darkening from dove to charcoal at the horizon.

'*Right, Paul Terence Jeffries: did a six-stretch in the eighties for raping a mother of two, with three other offences taken into consideration. Couple of speeding tickets, then nothing since the early nineties. … Oh, and his house burned down.*'

Callum stood, looking at the soot-stained walls, blown-out windows, and partially collapsed roof. 'You don't say?'

'I do say. And there's no need to sound so sarcastic; it only happened Wednesday.'

The same day Ashlee and Abby Gossard were abducted. No way that was a coincidence.

'Thanks, Brucie.' He hung up and put his phone away as McAdams fought through the weeds to the front door.

Well, where the front door should have been – it was just a yawning black chasm now.

McAdams disappeared inside.

Silly sod.

Callum followed him as far as the threshold. Stuck his head in. 'Is that safe?'

A smile. 'I'm dying of bowel cancer. What's the worst that can happen: the walls fall in and spare me six more weeks of chemo and a slow lingering death? I'll take my chances.' He wandered down the hall, stepped into another room and was gone.

Just because *he* had nothing to lose, it didn't mean Callum had to join him.

It wasn't safe. Half the roof was still up there, sagging and fire-blackened, ready to come crashing down at any moment. Bang! Crash! Squish! No more police officers.

Callum groaned. Sighed. Then stepped over the threshold and into the burned-out house.

It reeked of smoke – the sweet scent of charred wood mingling with the acrid tang of fried plastics and fabric.

Every floorboard he stood on creaked...

Urgh.

McAdams reappeared at the end of the hallway, sauntering across and in through another door, hands in his pockets, whistling.

Three more doors led off the hall, one hanging open, revealing what looked like a corridor, one through into a grubby bathroom, and one leading down into the depths of the earth.

Callum peered into the partial gloom.

Stone steps, littered with bits of charcoal.

No chance.

What if the ground floor collapsed while he was down there?

McAdams appeared at his shoulder. 'What have you found here? A dark stairway to Heaven? Or one down to Hell?'

Deep breath.

He took the first step, then the second, then the third.

The floor above didn't fall on his head. 'You know, you can't just chop a sentence into chunks and call it a haiku.'

'Yes I can.'

'That's not poetry, it's bad punctuation.' Callum eased himself off the last stone step and onto a hard-packed dirt floor. 'There's a weird smell down here. Sort of sweet and tangy? Kind of herbal?'

McAdams limped his way down the stairs. Did a slow catwalk turn. 'Definitely what estate agents would call a "fixer-upper".'

The floor was littered with bits of wood from the floor above. Callum looked up, through the holes in the cellar ceiling and out to the heavy grey clouds. A faint wash of sunlight broke free, infiltrating the dark room, casting a warm golden glow onto the wall opposite.

'Ah.' McAdams sucked in a breath. 'Do you see what I see, Constable MacGregor?'

Three sets of chains were fixed to the stonework, each one with a rusty padlock making a noose on the free end. What looked like a melted plastic water bowl beside one of them. The burned frame of a metal bed, mattress gone, springs mottled by the heat, beneath another. An upended bucket by the third.

A fourth chain lay in the corner, still attached to the ring-and-plate that must have fixed it to the wall at one point.

McAdams pointed. 'Do you want to say it, or will I?'

Monaghan hadn't been keeping Rottweilers down here, these were for people. So Dr McDonald was right: *women are dirty, subhuman things that have to be trained like dogs. Chained up and beaten...*

The Peugeot Bipper was Monaghan's van and this was his lair.

Callum pulled out his phone and made the call.

'Rather them than me.' The Dog Officer sooked his teeth as a handful of Smurfs picked their way through The Cloisters' burned-out remains. He was a big man with a list to the left and hair poking out the neck of his black Police Scotland T-shirt. 'Had a friend got trapped beneath somewhere like this for two days till they could dig him out. Lost his arm in that one, retired to Portugal.'

McAdams sniffed. 'All right for some.'

'Nah: plagued with haemorrhoids. Big as a grapefruit.' He swept a hairy hand up and out, indicating another bit of the huge, overgrown expanse of back garden. 'Come on, Penguin, off you go, you lazy sod.'

A black lab in a wee high-viz waistcoat snuffled away into the damp undergrowth, nose down, tail wagging.

Callum turned, one hand held above his eyes like the bill of a baseball cap. A horrible little Fiat Panda was lurching its way down the track towards them, bringing a swirling cloud of grey-blue smoke with it. 'Mother's here.'

That got a grunt from McAdams. 'A pound will get you five, / That she'll skin us both alive, / For delving in the cellar, / Of this terrible Jeffries fellar, / And risking both our instant deaths, / "Reproach" shall be her shibboleth.'

The dog officer raised an eyebrow. 'Just make that up, did you? Cause rhyming "cellar" with "fellar" isn't exactly Wordsworth, is it?'

'Everyone's a critic.'

Mother's Panda came to a juddering halt behind the small collection of SEB Transit vans, gave one last *vrooooom*, then the gunshot retort of a backfire, and silence.

'I'm just saying: resorting to doggerel in the middle stanza undermines the poetic integrity of the piece. That's all.' Dog Man stuck a hand against his chest. 'For delving in the depths below, / Of this, our dark and deadly foe.' A nod. 'See? Much better.' Then he cupped his hands around his mouth. 'PENGUIN! WHERE THE SODDING HELL DO YOU THINK YOU'RE GOING?'

The black lab disappeared into a massive knot of brambles – five-foot high and covering at least a third of the garden.

'Sodding dog's a pain in my parliament, if you'll pardon the French.'

Mother climbed out, sleeves rolled up on her fleece, bare white arms semaphoring in the sunlight as she marched over to the nearest Smurf.

McAdams stuck his hands in his pockets. 'Save yourself, young Callum. Run away before she gets here. This will not be pretty.'

The Dog Officer nodded. 'A six-eight-six haiku. Very avant-garde. PENGUIN, I'M NOT TELLING YOU AGAIN! Stupid animal.'

Rustling and crackling came from deep within the brambles, but that was it – no Labrador to be seen.

The Smurf turned and pointed in their direction. And Mother was on her way.

'PENGUIN!' A shake of the head. 'Tell you, we get all the rubbish dogs in O Division. Anything that can't find its own tail: they send it here.' Deep breath. 'PENGUIN! OUT HERE NOW, YOU USELESS WEE SOD!'

379

Mother rounded the corner of the blackened house, shoulders forward, hands curled into fists.

McAdams stood up straight. 'We who are about to die, salute you.'

'PENGUIN!'

'Andrew Thomas McAdams, what in *God's* holy name do you think you were doing going down there? Are you *insane*?'

He just shrugged.

'PENGUIN, IF YOU'RE NOT OUT HERE BY THE TIME I COUNT TO FIVE, I'LL SKIN YOU AND WEAR YOU AS A POSING POUCH!'

Callum stepped in. 'If DS McAdams hadn't put his neck on the line, we wouldn't have found Monaghan and Jeffries' dungeon.'

'FOUR!'

She turned her scowl on Callum instead. 'And *you*! You should've kept him out of there, you know he's not well!'

'THREE!'

'At least now we know Monaghan wasn't working alone. There was no way he could prepare his victims at that tiny flat on Bellfield Road – he needed room to starve them before he gutted them and stuck them in the smoker. This is where he did it.'

'TWO!'

Mother thumped the Dog Officer on the arm. 'Would you *please* stop doing that while I'm giving these idiots a bollocking?'

'Cadaver dog, my fuzzy backside.' He zipped up his Police Scotland fleece, hauled on a pair of leather gloves, then stomped towards the brambles. 'PENGUIN!' He dropped to his hands and knees and crawled into the barbed-wire mass. 'AAARGH! SODDING SPIKY SONS-OF-A-BITCHING BRAMBLE ... GAAAAAARGH!'

Callum tried his best reasonable voice. 'Dr McDonald thinks there's still a chance to save Ashlee Gossard. Come on, it can't be a coincidence, can it? Someone spots the fire here and calls nine-nine-nine at six twenty – an hour and a half later, Ashlee and her mum are being attacked and abducted from their home. And a van registered to *this address* is right there in the vicinity.'

'I'M GOING TO KILL YOU, PENGUIN! YOU HEAR ME?'

Mother stared up at the heavy lid of looming clouds for a moment, then sighed. 'Andy, you *know* it was stupid going down there. What if the floor collapsed?'

McAdams smiled. 'There are worse things in life than death.'

'PENGUIN! WHERE ARE YOU, YOU STUPID...'

Callum pointed at the burned-out house. 'Look at the timing: Brett

Millar turns up at his parents' house in Blackwall Hill, this place is set on fire, Ashlee and Abby Gossard get abducted.' He held his hands out, like he was finishing a magic trick. 'Millar got free and escaped – that's why there's a loose chain in the basement, pulled from the wall. Monaghan and Jeffries can't risk him leading us back here, so they torch the house. Only *now* they don't have anyone to mummify, so they go out and abduct themselves a pre-starved teenaged girl instead. Jeffries is still out there, and he's going to kill her soon as he thinks she's ready to become a god.'

Mother shook her head. 'Yes, well done. All very logical and exact. Only your Paul Terence Jeffries isn't "out there" or anywhere else: he's dead.'

Oh...

'HELLO?'

'I got John and Dotty to go a-rummaging. The Cloisters belongs to an ecclesiastical trust. Jeffries was some sort of lay preacher, so not only did he live here rent-free – they paid him a wee stipend too. He stopped cashing the cheques, wouldn't answer any letters, they couldn't track him down anywhere, so they went to court and eventually had him declared dead. That was twenty years ago.'

McAdams sniffed. 'So who's been staying here?'

'That's the trouble – they didn't know they still owned it, till Dotty phoned and made them go through the files. Turns out they've been paying council tax on a derelict property for over two decades. Not the most efficient biscuits in the tin.'

'HELLO, CAN YOU HEAR ME?'

'Your hairy friend doesn't shut up, does he?' Mother shrugged her shoulders. 'Anyway: even if Jeffries *was* still alive, he'd be in his seventies by now. Doesn't sound very abducty, does it?'

'So Monaghan knew Jeffries was dead, knew his house was abandoned, and registered the van to this address, in a dead man's name, because he knew no one would ever check.'

'I'M NOT KIDDING ABOUT HERE!'

McAdams spat into the long grass. 'The Dog Man is stuck. Inside the brambles' clutches. Their thorns bind him tight.'

Mother nodded. 'Exactly. So we need to ask: *how* did Monaghan know? Does he have some connection with the ecclesiastical trust? How many other empty properties does he know about? Because one of *those* is where he left Ashlee and Abby Gossard before jumping in Kings River.'

'ARE YOU BUGGERS DEAF OR WHAT? SOMEONE NEEDS TO GET IN HERE, NOW!'

She scowled into the brambles. 'Callum, I hate to ask, but can you go see what he's yelling about?'

Oh, lovely.

Callum stayed where he was. 'Maybe we should get this ecclesiastical trust to go through their financial records and find out what other empty properties they've forgotten about?'

'SOON AS YOU LIKE!'

Callum growled out a breath. Buttoned up his suit jacket. 'ALL RIGHT, ALL RIGHT! God's sake...' The long grass was sodden with weeks of rain, making his trousers stick to his legs, soaking through his shoes and into his socks. Urgh...

Dog Man had flattened a path into the brambles and he followed it. Dropped to his hands and knees and picked his way into the spiky mass of horrible bloody stabby jabby— 'OW!'

This stuff was worse than barbed wire. At least a million times sharper. And the bloody thorns came off and stuck in his good hand and they grabbed at his suit jacket and— 'OW! AAAAARGH! I *HATE* BRAMBLES!'

He battered at them with his filthy fibreglass cast, but they just bounced right back at him. Only now they were angry. 'AAAAAARGH!'

Another ten feet of horrible jaggy stabbing needle-jabbing horror and he emerged into a little hollow, ringed with the old yellow-grey corpses of long-dead brambles. Officer Hairy the Dog Man was sitting off to one side, but Penguin the useless cadaver dog was right in the middle, surrounded by what looked like burrows. Not tiny ones like you'd get with rabbits, but bigger. Maybe a fox, or a badger?

Penguin was lying down, tail thumping against the earth – dry in here under the canopy of horrible spiky tendrils.

Callum sat back on his thighs, still hunched over to avoid their spiny crown. 'You better have a damn good reason for dragging me in here, ruining my suit, and look at my *bloody* hands!' Literally – covered with scratches and puncture marks seeping red, peppered with dozens of tiny brown thorns. Even the fingertips of his bad hand were lacerated where they protruded from the cast.

Dog Man pointed at a white rock poking out of the ground near one of Penguin's front paws.

Only it wasn't really white at all, it was a sort of off-ivory colour, the size of a half-deflated football. The rock had holes in it, exposed where it poked out of the dirt: one roundish, one an arrow shape. Wait a minute, were those *teeth*?

It was. It was a skull, lying on its side, one eye socket and half the nasal cavities exposed to the air, the rest buried beneath the ground. And it was definitely human.

Maybe there was a good reason no one had heard from Paul Jeffries for over twenty years.

— Father —

"If there's one thing I've noticed," purred the Goblin Queen, "it's that the people who pretend to be the bestest, and the nicest, are almost always the worstest and most horrible."

"I'm sorry we ate your cabbages," Russell said. "We were hungry and lost and we didn't know they belonged to anyone!"

"That's very honest of you. You're a good little rabbit." She patted him on the head. "But I'm going to have to eat you all the same."

R.M. Travis
Russell the Magic Rabbit (1992)

And ma dad beat the f*ck outta me as a kid,
Got his bones in a box with a button-down lid,
And I'll never forgive all them things that he did,
But he ain't doin' them no more, cos the b*stard is dead.

Donny '$ick Dawg' McRoberts
'F*ck U (Daddy Dearest)'
© Bob's Speed Trap Records (2014)

54

Paul smiles and nods. Wise and trustworthy as the fat bitch in the cardigan drones on about 'Jesus' and 'love' and 'forgiveness' and all the rest of the *crap* people like this always drone on about.

The vestry is hot and sticky, even with the windows open.

That's the problem with Catholics, though, isn't it? The lingering heat of Hell is never far from their guilty little consciences.

She's still talking – that glistening mouth with its red liver lips. All pious. Like she's never sucked a dick in her life.

Blah, blah, blah.

On and on and on.

A thick floral stench rolls off her, mingling with the sweaty taint of corpulence.

You know what would be nice?

No, what?

Strangle her. Right here, right now. Wrap your hands around that greasy throat and *squeeze* till her eyes bulge and all the blood vessels burst and flood with red and keep *squeezing* and *squeezing*…

'…don't you think, Father?'

Paul blinks. It's not the fat bitch, it's the priest in his long black robes. Dressed like a jackdaw. Desperate to be strung up on the back fence to act as a warning to others.

He clears his throat. 'I do indeed.' He gives them the smile and the nod he's practised so many times in front of the mirror. The one he uses to pretend he's human like the rest of them.

But the stench in here is getting too much to bear.

387

So he makes a big show of looking at his watch. Rolls his eyes and tuts. 'Sorry, I'm afraid I'm going to have to dash. But perhaps we could pick up where we left off next week?'

The man in the dress nods. 'Oh, we'd like that, wouldn't we, Margery?'

'Oh yes. Yes indeed.' She puts one of her flabby hands on his arm, warm and sticky even through his jacket and black shirt, globbing into his skin. 'Do come again. I'm so glad we could help.' Then she hands him the cheque with his name on it.

He slips it into his jacket. 'And please, pass on my thanks – and the thanks of all those poor neglected children – to your kind and generous congregation.'

The fat bitch stops at the threshold, but Father Crossdresser follows him out into the church.

There's a wee boy singing somewhere: '*Sanctus, Sanctus, Sanctus, Dominus Deus Sabaoth...*' the sound echoes off the walls like an air-raid siren for the damned.

'Well, Father Jeffries, I must say, I'm deeply impressed by the work you do with these poor deprived youngsters. It's an inspiration, it truly is.'

'*Pleni sunt caeli et terra gloria tua. Hosanna in excelsis...*'

Paul gives him a little modest shrug. 'We all must do what we can.'

'*Benedictus qui venit in nomine Domini. Hosanna in excelsis—*'

'NO! NO, DAMN IT, OLIVER!' The exasperated voice of some poor sod trying to make a kid do what it's told. '*How many times? It's pronounced, "ex-chel-cees". We're going to stay here and do it again and again until – you – get – it – right!*'

Paul turns, and there's his own little burden, sucking his thumb like a baby. Five years old and he's *still* sucking his thumb. How is he ever going to be a man, acting like that? So Paul raised his voice over the wailing chorister. 'Justin, thumb out of the mouth, eh, champ?' He forces a smile. 'You're a big boy now.'

Going to have to beat that out of him.

He'll never learn otherwise.

Beat it out of him till he learns his bloody lesson.

After all, it never did Paul any harm, did it?

The back garden sways and lurches as he ... he ... why is he out here again?

Oh, yeah, right.

A swig of beer from one hand, while the other fumbles ... fumbles his cock from his trousers.

Used beer splashes into the compost bin, adding its steam to the heap's.

Dark out here. Just the light of the moon filtering through clouds. Watching everything.

Never mind God an Jesus an … an all the rest of that *crap*. Moon. Moon was … what they should be worshipping. Like the old days with … you know … with virgins an sacrifices an … yeah.

Bitch in the basement … crying. Always crying. Specially afterwards.

Pff…

He's not a *bad* man. No, he's a *priest*!

A proper one.

Not a shep … shepherd.

No.

He keeps his flock … his flock in line the *old* way. Proper way. Unner the Moon's eternal … eternal eye.

A wolf.

Paul takes another hit of beer, an … an throws back his head an howls out his devotions.

'That's very generous. Thank you so much.' Paul takes the cheque and smiles, even though it's barely half what he got here a year ago. Doesn't do to burn the goose, even if it *is* only laying silver eggs right now. 'The Romanian orphanages will make good use of this.'

The skinny bitch in the twinset shows off her dentures – stained with dark red lipstick. 'I'm *so* glad we could help.' Protestants, just as bad as the Catholics, only without the sense of theatre. Holier-than-thou on the outside, deviant scumbags on the inside. 'Now, we *must* get a photograph for the church newsletter.'

He sighs and shakes his head. Puts a hand on her revolting shoulder, among those nasty little flakes of dandruff. 'I'm just His humble servant, I don't deserve all that limelight and praise.'

'Oh, but—'

'No. *You* should take the credit, Mrs Ingram. After all, *you're* the one who raised all this money. I'm just the one who's lucky enough to spend it on a very good cause.'

'Lies and *liars*. All of them.' Paul takes the last swig from his tin of Special, crumples it in his fist and hurls it into the corner. 'And *morons*!'

The living room sways slightly, the wallpaper twisting like the tattoos on a topless dancer.

'Boy! Justin, or whatever. Gimme another beer!'

After all, can't celebrate without beer, can you?

No.

And whisky.

He takes a swig of Glenmorangie, straight from the bottle. It tingles on the way down like a thousand little watch fires, flickering in the darkness.

'BOY!'

And there he is, the horrible little snivelling boy. Standing there in his stupid shorts and cartoon T-shirt. Eyes all big and shiny, like he's going to burst into tears any moment. Pathetic. He's six, for Christ's sake. Far too old to be acting like that.

He holds up a tin of Special, dew beading on the outside, and Paul snatches it off him. 'About time.'

'Sorry, Father.' That annoying, wobbly little voice.

'You should be happy.' Paul grabs him by the back of the neck and pulls him close. 'I saved you, boy. You know that don't you?'

'Thank you, Father.'

'Damn right.' He pushes the little shite away. 'I saved you from the grey. From the beige. From all the crap they shovel down kids' throats.' He rips the tab from the beer and swigs down a mouthful. 'Your mum didn't love you, Justin. She would've killed you and eaten you. I know. I've seen it before.'

'Thank you, Father.'

Better. Bit of respect for his elders and betters.

Paul swills beer between his teeth.

After all, he's a rich man. He *deserves* respect.

And soon as he's spent it all, there's always another congregation of pious pricks desperate to throw money at him for all his 'good works'.

He toasts the crucifix on the wall. His generous benefactor.

Oh yes, today is a day to celebrate.

'Boy?'

'Yes, Father?'

'Tell your new mummy to wash herself. She's going to be blessed tonight. And if you're a *very* good boy, I might even let you watch.'

55

Callum turned his back on the garden, the thumb of his broken hand poked into his right ear, phone clamped to the other. 'Sorry, Cecelia, can you say that again?'

The roar of small petrol motors battered back and forth, screaming, then falling, then screaming, then falling as three Smurfs with brush cutters fought against the thicket of brambles. Chopping it down to the ground. Making good progress too – half of it was already gone, the curled jagged stems carted away, leaving the ground grey and bare.

'*I said, we've finished our second sweep of the Gossard house.*'

'Cool.' He marched away from the noise, following a wheelbarrow-pushing Smurf around the side of the burned-out house. 'Anything?'

'*Won't know for sure till we analyse it, but there was a tiny smear of blood under the knobs on the kitchen taps. Nothing in the sink, or on the knobs – so he's tried to clean up after himself – but there's always traces.*'

Professor Whatshisface might have been a bit of a dick, but he obviously knew what he was doing.

'Let me know, OK?'

Wheelbarrow Smurf tipped his load of bramble clippings into a skip parked outside the house.

'*I heard about Elaine.*'

Great.

Callum ran his fingertips across his forehead. 'Can we not do this just now?'

'*I just think it's a good time to tell everyone the truth about who really cocked up that crime scene.*'

'Who's going to take me seriously? They'll all think I'm lying to get back at her for shagging Powel behind my back.'

391

'*Don't make me stage an intervention, Callum.*'

'Bye, Cecelia.'

Mother appeared from the house's blackened doorway, SOC suit rolled down and tied off around her waist. Talking into her phone as she wandered down the path. 'Is he? That's great, thanks, Duncan. ... No, we'll be there soon as we can. ... OK. ... I owe you one.' She hung up, turned and waved at him. 'Callum, how's it going?'

He pointed back towards the garden. 'Another couple of hours to finish clearing the scrub then they can get the Ground Penetrating Radar in. They'll find the rest of him.'

'Good. Now do me a favour and give Dotty a call: see if she can find us a connection between Jeffries and Monaghan. She's good at digging things up and I get the feeling our boys knew each other.' Mother held out an arm and he took it, helping her balance as she shimmied her way out of the Smurf costume. 'I miss the white Tyvek suits, don't you?'

'Nah.' He pulled a face. 'I always thought we looked like a bunch of sperm in those. Everything You Always Wanted to Know About Crime Scene Investigation But Were Afraid to Ask.' He pulled out his notebook. Flipped through to the details he'd copied down. 'Assuming the ecclesiastical trust people started proceedings on the day Jeffries died, that's twenty-seven years ago. Monaghan would have been eight.'

'Probably not *best* friends, then.' She puffed out her cheeks and turned to face back towards the house. 'What does your gut tell you, Callum: are these Paul Jeffries' bones?'

'Bit of a coincidence if they're not. Jeffries goes missing twenty-seven years ago, but he never even leaves the property, just turns to bone in a shallow grave.' Callum sniffed. 'Well, it's that or he killed someone, buried them in his back garden, and did a *very* thorough disappearing act.'

'True.' She stood there, frowning at the burned bones of a long-dead house. Then turned, 'Anyway, there's no point hanging around here, is there? They'll call us when they need us. In the meantime, I think you and I should go on a little field trip, don't you? Spend some quality time together.'

Why did that sound ominous...?

The Fiat Panda roared and spluttered, coughing like an old man on sixty-a-day as they lurched around the City Stadium Roundabout and into the long queue of traffic heading west on the dual carriageway.

Orange cones and brake lights stretched ahead of them, fading into the gloom as the first drops of rain splashed against the windscreen.

Fifteen minutes and they'd barely gone a mile and a half.

Callum sat in the passenger seat, with his hands in his lap. Because otherwise there was a risk of touching something in here. The dashboard had developed a new feature: someone had written 'Muck!' in the dust. With every lurching gear change, bottles clinked in the back.

Something sticky glistened in the passenger footwell and Callum shifted his leg away from it. 'I'm worried about DS McAdams.'

'Welcome to my world.' She cracked the window an inch, letting the drone of traffic *in* and a fat black fly *out*. 'Rosalind seems to be integrating well, doesn't she? Dotty speaks very highly of her. Very efficient.'

'I'm serious. He's holding his stomach and wheezing, sweating. I've seen bottles of milk with more colour in them.'

'He's dying, Callum. This round of chemo...' Mother sighed. 'I remember the good old days, before the old ticker started acting up.' She tapped herself on the chest. 'It was Andy and me that arrested Ian Zouroudi. We caught Dani McGiven. We nailed Joanne Frankland, even though everyone thought her brother Stephen did it.'

'Maybe ... I don't know. He shouldn't be at work, he should be home resting.'

'Then there was that counterfeiting syndicate, operating out of a charity shop on Dresden Street.'

'Tod Monaghan's dead: McAdams got his last serial killer. We'll find Ashlee Gossard and that'll be that. Everything else is just tidying up. Send him home.'

A smile tugged at Mother's cheeks. 'I remember one time, we'd spent all day chasing down an armed-robbery witness, and Andy—'

Callum's phone burst into song, buried deep in his pocket. 'Sorry.' He pulled it out. 'Hello?'

Elaine's 'angry schoolteacher' voice scratched in his ear: *'Did you pick up your stuff? Because I don't want you turning up at the flat pretending you forgot something.'*

'Oh for God's sake.'

'If I get home from Mum's and you've—'

'Bye, Elaine.' Callum hung up. Checked his call history and barred the number she'd dialled from.

The hairs prickled on the back of Callum's neck, and when he turned his head Mother was staring at him. 'What?'

'Do you want to talk about it?'

He folded his arms. 'No.'

'You're going to have to deal with this sooner or later, Callum. That's how relationships work.'

The industrial estate ground past on the right.

Callum kept his arms folded. Scowling out at the traffic in its depressing slow-motion waltz. Brake, two-three. Inch forward, two-three. Brake, two-three. And repeat. On and on till the end of the world...

Up ahead, a big metal sign announced that all this traffic chaos was going to continue for at least the next six weeks. Because everyone wasn't miserable enough already.

'I'm serious, Callum.' Mother indicated, then drifted right into a turning lane marked out with another stretch of orange cones. Sat there with her turn signal clicking. 'Are you going to spend the rest of your life avoiding her?'

He kept his scowl pointed out of the passenger window. At the cars full of miserable people, stuck in their miserable lives, stuck in miserable traffic, in the miserable rain.

A sigh. 'What's going to happen at work, then? When Elaine comes back after the baby?'

Someone coming the other way flashed their lights, leaving a gap in the traffic and Mother put her foot down, sending the car kangarooing across the opposite lane and down a road lined with dark-green gorse.

'And what about Reece? He's still going to be a Detective Chief Inspector, no matter how much you hate him. He'll *still* be able to give you orders. And if you're fighting with Elaine, he'll win that argument every time.'

'I get it, OK? I'm screwed. You happy? I – am – screwed.'

'That's not what I meant, Callum. You're going to have to make your peace sooner or later. And the longer it takes, the more it'll hurt.'

'Can you just leave it, please?'

A sigh. 'Well, no one can say I didn't try.'

She indicated and turned left, down another gorse-lined road, bordered by fields. A patch of woods. And just beyond them, the hulking grey lump of Her Majesty's Prison, Oldcastle. The kind of building not even an architect could love: brutally minimalist, with featureless walls and a three-storey glass block built out front that had a wide concrete portico like a Seventies hotel.

Mother pulled into the car park, and the Panda did its roar-and-backfire trick again, before dying into silence.

He unclipped his seatbelt. 'Going to tell me what we're doing here?'
She just grinned at him.

Oh joy...

They'd made a bit of effort with the interview room: framed prints
of landscapes screwed to the wall; a fake rubber plant in the corner;
flattering mood lighting; one of those automatic wall-mounted air-
freshener things they sometimes had in toilets, puffing out the occasional fruity whiff. But even that couldn't disguise the fact that this was
an eight-by-ten windowless box in the west wing of a prison.

It didn't do much to shift the underlying sour whiffs of grease and
BO either.

Mother sat at the interview table – chipped and scarred, with initials
and swearwords scratched into the Formica. She poked away at her
phone, playing Candy Crush by the look of things.

Callum stood by the radiator, drying off his damp, bramble-ruined
trousers. 'Still don't know what we're doing here.'

'Good things come to those who wait. You just have to have faith
and patience, and—'

The interview room door opened and a small balding man in thick-
rimmed glasses and an ugly jumper sidled into the room. 'Flora. It's
lovely to see you again. I was so shocked to hear about your ... *incident*.
I trust you're fully recovered now, yes? Good. Excellent. Yes.' A nod for
Callum. 'You must be the young man, Flora's told me so much about.
Nice to meet you.' He stuck out his hand – surprisingly warm, strong,
and dry when Callum shook it.

Mother put her phone away. 'Is he ready, Duncan?'

'Oh yes, yes. Yes indeed.' Duncan clasped his hands together. 'Now,
I know you've been here before, but there are a few formalities to
take care of. You're not to give the inmate anything, and you're not
to take anything *from* him. That includes messages to, and from, the
outside world. You're not to let him use your mobile phones. We
disapprove of physical contact. And a staff member will be present at
all times. OK?'

She spread her hands wide. 'How can I refuse?'

'Good. Yes. Well, let's get started, shall we?' Duncan stuck his wee
baldy head out into the corridor. 'You can bring him in now, Rachael,
thanks.'

Gareth Pike had to duck to get into the room, his rounded shoulders
brushing the door frame. His pale scalp gleamed like a freshly polished

395

cue ball. He paused and pulled on a slow sticky smile. 'Constable MacGregor, how delicious to see you again. Are you here about my south-facing cell?'

Pike.

A prison officer appeared behind him, closing the door and standing with her back to it, at parade rest, face blank and jaw set.

'Hello, Mr Pike.' Mother pointed at the chair on the other side of the table. 'Or can I call you, Gareth?'

'This one's new.' Pike slithered his way into the other seat, and sat hunched forward with his elbows on the table. Like a bear stuffed into a highchair. 'I'm not sure I like her yet.'

'I can quite understand that, Mr Pike. My name's DI Malcolmson and I'm here to formally apologise on behalf of Police Scotland for Detective Constable MacGregor's behaviour.'

What?

Pike's eyebrow climbed an inch. 'Are you now? Well that *is* interesting, isn't it?'

'I've reviewed the footage of your interview and I have to say that I'm more than a little disappointed. After all, you're not a well man, are you, Mr Pike?'

'No, I'm not. And please,' he reached across the table and took Mother's hand, 'Call me Gareth.'

'You've got type-two diabetes, angina, high blood pressure, gallstones, impotency...'

'These are my burdens to bear.'

Mother turned in her seat and stared at Callum. 'Officer MacGregor, is there something you'd like to say to Gareth?'

'What? No. I'm not—'

'Apologise, Constable.'

Was she insane? There was no way he was—

'*Now*, Constable.'

Silence.

The prison officer didn't move.

Duncan tugged at the hem of his ugly jumper.

And Pike smiled his big slug smile.

Mother sighed. 'Or perhaps you'd like another spell in front of Professional Standards?'

All that caring-sharing crap in the car had been just that: crap. She hated him as much as everyone else, and now she was rubbing his face in it.

That's what he got for trusting her. That's what he got for trusting anyone.

So what choice did he have? Apologise to this vast slimy sack of sick, or get a formal kicking by the rubber heelers for something he didn't even do. *Again.*

Callum cleared his throat. 'I'm sorry, Mr Pike, if I caused you any offence.' Every word burned like battery acid on his tongue.

Pike's smile got bigger. 'Oh, pish and tush, what's a little banter between friends?' He raised his other hand. 'You are forgiven, Constable.'

Mother nodded. 'You're very kind, Gareth. And to show that we in Police Scotland are big enough to admit our mistakes: I've had a word with the Sheriff.' She pulled a bit of paper from her pocket and held it up. 'Given your medical condition, he's agreed to give you a Community Service Order instead of a custodial sentence. You'll be able to stay in your own flat, and only have to spend a few hours a week helping out at the Kingsmeath Animal Shelter. Cleaning out the cages and things like that. Health permitting, of course.' She tucked her paperwork away again. 'Isn't that nice?'

Pike's smile slipped. Then his mouth hung open, eyes widening. 'Oh. Well … it's a very *generous* offer, but I sincerely fear that my chances of recidivism are—'

'No, let's not hear another word about it. It's the least we can do.' She prised her hand free and stood. 'I'm sure they'll make your stay here as pleasant as possible until the Sheriff makes it official on Monday.'

'But, no… You can't… I mean, I've *forgiven* Officer MacGregor. I don't expect any special treatment.'

'I wouldn't hear of it.' She turned and clicked her fingers at Callum. 'Come on, Constable, Gareth's had a long day, he'll be needing his rest.'

'But I'm a pederast! You saw the tape, it's got kids on it and—'

'As you say, Gareth, you're impotent. The Sheriff feels that puts you at a much smaller risk of causing actual harm.'

The prison officer put her hand on Pike's big round shoulder. 'Come on, time to go back to our cell.'

'But I'm dangerous! I…' He stared at Callum. 'Tell them. Tell them how dangerous I am! I tried to abduct you!'

And now it all made sense.

'You *were* dangerous, but like Mother says, you need a little blue pill to get it up these days. And with *your* blood pressure?' He sucked a breath in through his teeth. 'You're more of a risk to yourself than other people.'

Pike's mouth flapped up and down for a bit, but nothing came out.

Mother patted him on the arm. 'There, there. I know it's all a bit overwhelming, but the knowledge that you're on your way home is thanks enough.'

'I DON'T WANT TO GO HOME!'

The prison officer tightened her grip. 'Easy now.'

'You don't?' Mother frowned.

'I live in a shit hole: don't send me back there!'

'Oh dear and here's me already made that deal with the Sheriff. If only there was *something* I could do...' She tapped a finger against her forehead, frowning down at the tabletop. 'Come on, Flora: think.' A pained expression. 'I've no idea... Callum? Can you think of anything?'

And for the first time since arriving at the prison, Callum smiled. 'Oh, I'm sure I can come up with *something*. Won't that be fun, Gareth?'

There was a pause, then Pike bared his teeth. '*Never.*'

'Ah well. We tried, didn't we, DI Malcolmson?'

'We did indeed, DC MacGregor.'

'That's not fair: YOU SET ME UP!'

'Tell you what,' Mother nodded at Rachael the prison officer, 'this nice lady will take you back to your lovely clean comfy cell, with ... what was it: three meals a day and the convivial company of like-minded fellows? And you can have a nice *long* think about living in that manky little flat on the thirteenth floor, surrounded by people who hate you. Who knows, maybe you'll change your mind?'

They waved as he was pulled from the room.

'YOU SET ME UP!'

56

Watt folded over his desk, curling in around the phone in his hand. 'Yes, I *know* it's seven o'clock on a Saturday evening, but as I told your colleague, this is very, *very* important.'

The rest of Mother's Misfit Mob sagged in their chairs, McAdams perched on one of the spare desks, Mother leaning against the wall by the whiteboard – twiddling a marker pen.

Dotty sighed. 'Told you *I* should've phoned. He's useless.'

'No, I understand that. ... Yes. ... Yes. ... Here's the thing,' Watt thumped a hand down on the desk, 'there's a thirteen-year-old girl who's going to die if you don't get us that list. How does that sound? Does that get your ecclesiastical juices flowing?'

'See: he's blown it.'

He stuck the phone against his chest and birled around in his seat. 'Will you *please* shut your fat cakehole?' Back to the phone. 'Sorry, what was that? ... Yes. Right. OK, soon as you can. Here's my email address John— No, J for Jumper, O for Osprey, H for Hawk, N for November...'

Dotty dropped her voice to a barely audible growl: 'I'll give you a "fat cakehole", you gingery wee twat.'

Mother chucked the pen so it bounced off Dotty's desk partition. 'If you kids can't behave, there'll be no jelly and custard.'

Callum stretched in his seat and stifled a yawn. 'Pfff...'

'...dot *police* dot UK. ... Uniform Kilo. ... Yes, UK. Soon as you can, thank you.' Watt hung up and slumped back. 'God save us from religious bawbags.'

'Anytime you're ready, John.'

He grimaced at Mother. 'They thought it'd be OK to stop work at five, as it's a Saturday. Apparently, in their sparkly little world, you only have to comply with a warrant if you've got nothing better to do. They're going back to it now, but it's going to take hours – nothing's on computer, it's all filing cabinets. Be lucky if we hear back by Monday.'

McAdams buried his face in his hands. 'For God's sake.'

'Rosalind?' Mother wandered over and collected her hurled pen.

'Every traffic car, community warden, uniform, and special constable is keeping an eye out for Monaghan's grey Peugeot Bipper. He must've parked it somewhere, but so far no one's spotted it.'

'Dorothy?'

'He shouldn't have called me fat! It's not my fault I'm in a wheelchair, is it? You try exercising when you're stuck in one of these things.'

'Please, Dorothy, we're all tired. How did you get on?'

'The council's sent through a list of all properties currently registered as empty for council tax purposes. It doesn't include buildings considered uninhabitable.'

'What about some sort of Monaghan–Jeffries connection?'

'Still looking.'

'Callum?'

He pointed at his screen. 'I've been through the planning department's records and there's no sign of anyone applying to build a new smokehouse for over forty years. And the last one was converted into, and I quote, "a stylish four-bedroom family home, with off-road parking, outdoor hot tub, and a well-appointed garden" two years ago.' Callum frowned up at the map of Oldcastle pinned to the wall above the kettle. 'Look, according to Voodoo's CCTV search, Monaghan's grey Peugeot Bipper came from somewhere east of Caven Street, Logansferry, and disappeared somewhere north of the Royal Williams Hospital in the Wynd. We could try narrowing our search by getting rid of anything in between?'

Franklin pulled a face. 'Risky – he might've dropped them off en route.'

'True.'

Mother thumped down into the only vacant chair. 'Urgh... Ashlee's going to be dead by the time we get there, isn't she? Assuming we *ever* find her.'

The only sounds were the humming computers and someone squeaking past in the corridor outside.

In the end, it was McAdams that broke the silence. 'We'll find her. We just have to hope she can hold on till Watt's religious time-wasters get back to us.' He hopped down from the desk. 'In the meantime, we go home. Get some rest. There's sod-all we can do here till we get that list.'

57

'Mmsrrry...' Ashlee's head rolls back against the metal tank. The chains clank and click. The walls *thrummmmmmm* in the darkness.

Every muscle aches. Not just from being sick all the time, but from ... don't know. Just aches.

'Mmmy. Mmmmy mmsrrry...'

Her mouth barely moves now, all crusted and covered in scabs. She can taste them on the tip of her dry tongue. Split and bleeding, then scabbing over, then splitting again.

Probably all the salt in the water.

It's gritty between her fingers, makes a tidemark of pale-grey crystals around the tank, makes the water undrinkable, no matter how thirsty she is.

'Mmsrrry...'

And she is sorry. Totally, *totally* sorry.

Sorry she let him in. Sorry she was such a crappy friend. Sorry she was such a crappy daughter. Sorry she was ever born.

But it'll be over soon.

There was this TV show a couple months ago, all about how stupid people died in the woods and deserts and up mountains and at sea and crap like that. Places no one with even *one quarter* of a brain would go. The woman with the utterly ugly anorak and frizzy hair was banging on about being adrift in a lifeboat, or something. And how there was all this water, but you couldn't drink it, or you'd die.

Cos of the salt.

It does something to your insides and you die of thirst even though you're drinking water. Even if you throw it up again, it screws with your kidneys and you die.

But you're going to die anyway, aren't you?

Cos *not* drinking anything screws your kidneys and you die.

Her throat is like the road outside the house on a hot summer's day, all dark and sticky, and every horrible breath is like ripping off a sticking plaster.

Maybe dying's not so bad?

Got to be better than this.

Her head lolls to the side, and there's Mum. Still slumped with the chain around her neck. Still not moving. Cos zombies aren't real, are they.

It's better being dead, isn't it, Mum?

Yes it is. It's a relief, to be honest with you. After all the years of struggling and fighting, trying to make ends meet. Trying to make friends. It's nice just to have a bit of a rest.

That's good.

You should try it too, Ashlee. You'll like being dead. Nothing hurts any more.

I will, Mum.

No more lying in that dirty bathwater.

No more.

Maybe you should have a wee drink? That'll make you die of dehydration quicker, won't it? Like they said on the programme? After all, what's the point of hanging on? No one's going to come and save you.

I know, Mum.

It's just you and me, alone in this stinky room that reeks of smoke and puke. And I'm probably going to start smelling a bit soon too. Sorry about that.

It's OK, Mum, you're dead, you can't help it.

Thanks, Ashlee. You're a good girl. And I love you, I always have. Now, why not have a little drink.

So thirsty...

It's OK, no one's looking.

Ashlee lets her head fall further and further, until the salty water stings her broken lips. It's bitter and horrible and wet and sour and fiery and soothing and—

Her stomach clenches and the water sprays out again, frothing from her mouth, burning out of her nose. A hacking cough rattles her back and forth against the metal tub. The chains clink and jitter. The water slops around her in waves.

And finally the coughing fades and she sags, panting in those sticking-plaster breaths in her hot-tarmac throat.

Then, like someone turning on a kettle, whatever's in the water pops and fizzes through her. Getting louder as it boils. Pushing up into her skull and making the insides float. Up and up. Until all the colours sound the same.

He said she was going to be a god, but then he left and never came back.

She's not going to be a god, she's going to be trapped here for all eternity. In the dark. In this filthy metal tub. With this chain around her neck.

I'm sorry, Ashlee. I'm sorry, sweetheart.

Why can't she just die?

— open the coffins —

"Isn't my kingdom wonderful?" asked the Bonemonger. "All these graves and mausoleums and charnel pits, just waiting for someone to wake up their slumbering guests."

Justin backed away, until his furry shoulders pressed against the cage. "I won't do it!" he shouted, defiantly. "I won't and you can't make me!"

"But, my dear little Rabbit Boy, if you don't, your Sister Cat will sleep forever beneath my darkening ground."

R.M. Travis
Open the Coffins (and Let Them Go Free) (1976)

All them bones in the dark, and he's proud as can be,
Cos he'll open the coffins and let them go free,
And you better believe he's as sharp as a church key,
He'll cut you to shreds and swallow you whole, see?

Donny '$ick Dawg' McRoberts
'Little Rabbit Boy (The Bonemonger's Waltz)'
© Bob's Speed Trap Records (2015)

58

'OK, thanks, John.' Callum hung up and slipped his phone back in his pocket.

Thin morning light seeped through the battleship clouds, making the back garden mud glitter and shine. Would have thought, after all this rain, the smell of smoke would've dissipated, but if anything it was stronger than ever, oozing from the burned-out house like fog.

The brambles were gone, but a little village of blue SOC tents had taken their place, arranged almost at random across the garden, each one with 'PROPERTY OF SPSA SCENES EXAMINATION BRANCH – OLDCASTLE' stencilled in white on the side. The nearest had, 'TENT F' added to the end.

Callum pulled up the flap and ducked inside, his blue Tyvek suit rustling and crinkling.

Inside, a small diesel generator growled away in the corner, hooked up to a handful of high-powered work lights on stands. They glared down on a pit in the middle of the tent, five-foot deep and roughly rectangular. All the soil was piled up to one side, a couple of Smurfs on their knees in the hole, trowelling more into a black bucket.

McAdams stood at the head of it, staring into the depths, the hood of his SOC suit thrown back, arms folded. Face pale and shiny.

'That was Watt.' Callum stopped at the opposite end of the trench. 'The ecclesiastical trust must've pulled an all-nighter, because a list of every property they own just arrived in his inbox. All six-hundred-odd of them. They've got some marked as unoccupied, but given they were clueless about *here*...' A shrug.

McAdams didn't look up. 'Have you ever contemplated your own mortality, Callum?'

'He's doing some spreadsheet thing so he can combine their list with the data we got from the council tax people. At least then we'll know what's officially sitting empty. But again: the trust were paying full whack for an abandoned building, so who knows?'

'Ever stood at the edge of a grave and thought, "This will be mine soon. Maybe not this one, but one just like it"?'

'We're going to need a whole heap of bodies on it – visit every single property the trust owns and see what we can see.'

'"For what is man, but doomed to die? / And here within the earth to slumber, / Till naught but bone remains of him, / The merest breath of gods gone by."'

'That's cheery. Pam Ayres again?'

'Stephen P. Dundas, you ignorant spud.' He squatted down and tossed a little clump of dirt at one of the Smurfs. 'Well?'

'Ow!' The Smurf turned, clutching its head with a purple gloved hand. 'What the hell was that for?'

'Have – you – found – anything – yet?'

'Looks like female remains.' He pointed at twin lines of pale grey, just protruding above the black earth. 'That's a forearm, radius and ulna. Going by the scarring, she broke her wrist at *least* six times. See how it's a bit zig-zaggy? That's because it wasn't treated, just left to heal on its own.'

McAdams grunted. Nodded. 'Any buttons or zips? Bits of clothing?'

'No. If she was wearing anything when she went into the ground, must've been all natural fibres. It's long gone.'

'Same as all the others then.' McAdams stood. Dusted off his hands as he marched out of the tent. 'Seven female bodies, one male. All the women went in naked, but there are buttons and zips in with the man's remains. The women's bones are covered in scars, but not his. What does that tell you?'

Callum closed the tent flap. 'He was a rush job.'

'Show your working.'

'They're all in deep graves, five-foot down at least. Far as we can tell, he was about two, that's probably why the badgers got at him. The women were prepared for burial – stripped, probably washed. He was just tipped in, fully clothed.'

'I'll buy that.' McAdams unzipped his SOC suit and stood with his arms spread wide, steam rising from his chest. 'I want X-rays of all the skulls – see if we can get a match off dental records. And get them to run stable isotope analysis too. How long have they been buried here, how long were they kept here before that, where did they come from? Then we go through every missing persons' report till we find a match. I'd put money on the male remains being Jeffries, but let's widen the net a bit, just in case.'

'Sarge.'

'Urgh…' He let his arms drop and turned, staring out at the SOC tents. 'Seven women. Can you imagine what it must've been like for them?' McAdams shook his head. 'I don't think they were prepared for burial: those chains in the basement have been there a long, long time. They were shackled down there. Naked in the dark. Beaten, raped, and brutalised for months. Maybe even years.'

A depressing thought, but probably right.

'And then, when he was bored with them, he didn't bother stopping: he kept on going and beat them to death. Then buried them in his back garden, and went out to get a new one. Because that's what women are to him: disposable.'

'Sounds lovely, doesn't he?' Callum kicked at a little knot of brambles, still clinging on to the muddy ground. 'You think maybe Monaghan grew up here? That's why he turned out the way he did?'

'Who knows? Maybe it was always in him? Or maybe you just can't live through something like that and not come out broken.' A frown. 'Suppose it doesn't matter in the end.' McAdams pulled out his phone. 'I'll tell Mother, you go get the car warmed up.'

Major Incident Room Two buzzed with the low murmur of voices. A dozen officers sat at the desks, half in uniform, half plainclothes, all staring towards the front of the room as Watt pointed his wee remote at the projector on the ceiling. The screen behind him filled with a spreadsheet – all bars and colour-coded bits and numbers and addresses.

'This is every property N.E.T.H. own within a fifteen-mile radius of Oldcastle. I've ranked each by distance from where Ashlee and Abby Gossard were abducted, where the grey Peugeot Bipper appears on the CCTV system, and where it disappears off again.'

McAdams leaned over and whispered in Callum's ear – breath sticky and sour. 'Because colouring it up like a rainbow is going to sodding help.'

'As you can see here,' Watt poked a button on the remote and a little red dot shone onto the screen, 'I've cross-referenced the dataset with council tax records. Everything marked with a grey arrow is currently registered as vacant.'

'I bet he was touching himself when he put that together. Never seen anyone so turned on by spreadsheets before.'

Mother stood and held up two bits of paper, stapled together. 'Pair up. Each team of two takes one of these. You visit *every* property on your list and you look for anywhere that could be used as a smokehouse. That includes big sheds, by the way.' She stuck her list back on the pile and handed everything to the nearest uniform. 'Best estimates are that it takes *at least* a week to cold smoke a whole human being. The neighbours are going to notice something like that. *Ask* them.'

The uniform took one of the stapled lists and passed the rest on.

'If you see anything, and I don't care how tenuous or irrelevant it seems – if it makes your spidey-sense tingle, you call it in. Understood?'

Everyone nodded.

'Ashlee Gossard is thirteen years old. There's a chance she's still alive, but it's getting smaller every minute. *You* can save her.' Mother gave them all a big smile, then pointed at the door. 'Now get out there and make me proud.'

Callum, Dotty, Watt, and McAdams stayed where they were till everyone had filed out.

Soon as the door closed behind the last two-person team, Mother slumped back into her chair and rubbed at her face. 'Urgh… Someone tell me it's all going to be OK.'

McAdams picked up one of the remaining lists. 'How many properties are we looking at?'

'Tell me we're not just clutching at ghosts here.'

'Northeast Ecclesiastical Trust Holdings Limited own six hundred and twenty-four properties all over Scotland: from a block of flats in Kirkcaldy to a B-and-B in Cromarty, via a chip shop in Oban.' Watt wheeched his laser pointer across the screen again. 'I've marked commercial properties with a skull-and-crossbones. Fifty-two of them, in total.'

A grunt from McAdams. 'Assuming Monaghan had access to their list of properties at some point. Assuming he's been smoking them locally and not off up the coast in Buckie or Fraserburgh. Assuming he hasn't just built himself a DIY smoker somewhere deep inside Moncuir Wood, or the Swinney, or Holburn Forest. Assuming. Assuming. Assuming.'

Mother let her arms fall by her sides. 'Thanks for that, Andy. I feel *much* better now.'

'Glad I could help.'

'Does anyone have anything constructive to say? Any ideas at all? The floor's open.'

Franklin was sitting at the back, arms and legs crossed, face tight and angry. 'Public appeal. Any suspicious behaviour. Have you seen smoke coming from your neighbour's shed on a regular basis?' She bared her teeth. 'Heard any screaming lately?'

Mother frowned at her. 'OK... Well, I've got a media briefing at ten, and that's on the list. But you know what's going to happen: every well-meaning citizen, idiot, and attention-seeking special-little-snowflake will be ringing up within the hour. And they're only giving me ten support staff to man the phones. So that'll be fun.' Back to the rest of the room. 'Anyone else? I will literally consider *anything* at this point.'

Dotty held up her hand. 'I've been looking for any connection between Monaghan and Jeffries, and if there *is* one, I can't find it. So how did Monaghan get access to all these Northeast God-Bothering Trust properties? Even *they* didn't know what they owned till we made them look.'

Watt rolled his eyes. 'He doesn't have to have access to *all* of them, just a couple. Obviously.'

'Don't you "Obviously" me, you gingery wee—'

'Children! That's enough.' Mother stood. 'We stick with the plan, till someone comes up with something better. Rosalind: you and Callum take a list. Dorothy: you and John clearly need to spend some quality time together—'

'Aw, sodding hell...' Dotty folded her arm over her head.

Watt bared his teeth. 'I'd rather staple my scrotum to a leaky tumble dryer full of angry wasps.'

'—give you a chance to bond. And maybe act like grown-ups for a change. Wouldn't that be nice?' Mother clapped her hands together. 'Off you go.'

'Arrrgh. Fine.' Dotty wheeled herself from the room. 'But if I end up killing him, it's *your* fault.'

Mother waited until Watt snatched a stapled list from the pile and stomped out after her, before grimacing at the ceiling – both hands curled into claws. 'Arrrrgh...'

'Oh, you love it really. Our book is reinvigorated: we have *fresh leads* to follow. The readers know a big reveal is coming soon and are relishing every page.' McAdams picked up the last remaining list. 'Want to take your car or mine?'

She sagged. 'I can't. I've got a dozen of DCI Powel's cases to review,

411

teams to organise, updates to hear, rotas to organise, overtime to authorise, budgets to work up, etcetera, etcetera, etcetera...' Mother scrubbed a hand across her face. 'Could Reece have *picked* a worse time to go AWOL?'

Callum stared down at the tips of his shoes.

Don't get involved.

Don't say anything.

'Pff... Anyway. No point hanging about here feeling sorry for ourselves. We've got a missing teenager to find. If she's even still alive.'

Callum held the picture of Ashlee Gossard out again. 'And you're sure you've not seen her? Or her mother?'

The crooked lady in the twinset shook her head, setting free a little flurry of dandruff from her long grey hair. 'Sorry.'

'That's OK. Thanks anyway.' He waited till she'd gone back inside and shut her door before dragging a red pen through address number four on the list.

Franklin was already behind the wheel by the time he got back to the car. Still wearing her best Everyone-In-The-World-Needs-To-Die face.

Oh joy.

He slid into the passenger seat. 'Come on then: who climbed up the drainpipe and crapped down your chimney?'

'This is a waste of time.'

'Have I done something? Because I don't remember doing anything.'

She wrenched the steering wheel around, executing an angry three-point turn. 'We're just out here chasing our backsides.'

'Only you've been chewing a wasp all morning.'

She scowled across the car. 'You're all the same, aren't you?'

'Ah, here we go. Let me guess: Mark?'

'I don't want to talk about it.'

The terraced street gave way to another one, winding back towards the centre of town. 'Suits me.' He checked the list for address number five. 'Hang a right here, then left at the end of the road onto St John Crescent.'

More identical, depressing, featureless houses. Sulking beneath the rain.

Franklin banged her hand on the steering wheel. 'I mean, look at us. Going round and round, achieving nothing. How's that supposed to help Ashlee?'

'Well, if you've got a better idea, we're all ears.'

'The question we should be asking is: who killed all those women?'

'Fair point.' He nodded. 'My money's on Paul Jeffries. Those bodies have been buried at least twenty, thirty years, right? And Jeffries did time for rape. When he gets out of prison he pretends he's put all that behind him and found God, but it's all just a front. He's still a raping little wankmonger, he's just learned how to keep his victims from going to the police.'

'By keeping them chained up in the basement. Then burying them in the back garden when he's done with them.' Franklin took the turning onto St John. More horrible little houses. 'Which begs one *more* question.'

'Who killed Paul Jeffries and stuffed him into a shallow grave in his own private cemetery?'

She tapped her fingers against the steering wheel. 'Monaghan?'

'He'd only be a kid at the time. More likely Jeffries was part of some sort of ring and he had a falling out with one of his nasty friends.' Callum pursed his lips. 'Course, if this was a film, it'd be one of his victims' husbands. Jeffries gets careless and leaves a clue behind. Our man tracks him down, tortures and kills him, then buries him in his own back garden. And if it's a *good* film, he finds and saves his wife just in the nick of time.'

Franklin groaned. 'All hail the great male hero!' A snort. 'Sexist piggery. Why can't it be one of the victims' sisters doing the rescuing? Or maybe one of the women escapes and gets revenge on her abuser. Why does it *always* have to be a man saving the day?'

'True. We are horrible.' A smile. 'Just look at your Mark.'

And just like that, the muscles in Franklin's jaw were clenching again.

Yeah … probably shouldn't have done that. Seemed like fun at the time, but *he* was the one who'd have to suffer the ensuing foul mood.

Callum flicked through Watt's list of properties: four down, sixteen to go.

Six teams of two, plus them, plus Dotty and Watt. Eight teams. Twenty buildings each. Hundred and sixty houses and/or businesses. Plus whatever odds and sods McAdams was looking into. 'N.E.T.H. Limited have got a *lot* of interests in Oldcastle. And over six hundred properties Scotland-wide. Must be worth a fortune. Millions.'

Franklin just chewed on her sulk, glowering through the windscreen.

'Right, opposite the chip shop.'

She thumped the steering wheel again. 'I mean, where does he get off, dumping an ultimatum like that on me?'

'Didn't think there'd be so much money in Religion.' Callum stuck the list back in his pocket. 'Why don't they just liquidate the lot and give the proceeds to the poor?'

'What the hell happened to, "Your career is every bit as important as mine"?'

'Mind you, it's a *trust*, isn't it? Do you think it's all priests' pensions and bishops' investments?'

'Are you even listening to me?'

A shrug. 'Thought you didn't want to talk about it.'

'All the sodding same.' She took the turning at the chip shop.

'I get it: your boyfriend, Mark, is a dick who thinks whatever *he* wants is more important than what *you* want.' The houses were getting bigger with every street. 'And do you know *why* he thinks that?'

Franklin scowled straight ahead, mouth clamped shut.

'Because he's a dick.' Callum turned in his seat. 'And do you know what? He's a merchant banker – that was your clue, right there. Take a left at the roundabout and it should be about halfway down.'

'He wasn't a dick when I met him.'

'Yeah, well, you know the old saying: some men are born dicks, some have dickishness thrust upon them, and some achieve dickosity all on their own.' He gave her a smile. 'I'm paraphrasing a bit.'

'I am *not* giving everything up to be a bloody housewife with a bloody pinny, two-point-four bloody children, and a Cocker Bloody Spaniel!'

Callum knocked on the passenger window. 'That's us there on the left, number thirty-two.'

She pulled into the kerb. 'I'm not.'

Number 32 was one of Watt's grey-arrow properties, all the windows sealed with chipboard. The garden looked almost as bad as The Cloisters, only without the constant parade of Smurfs, brambles, and body bags.

Callum undid his seatbelt. 'So ditch him. Tell him you've had enough of his crap.'

She chewed and chewed and chewed.

'Someone I know gave me a very good piece of advice once. You want to hear it?'

'No.'

'You can just sit there, playing the tragic jilted hero.' He climbed out

414

of the car, turned, and stuck his head back in. 'Or you can get off your moaning backside and *do* something about it.'

'...absolutely sod-all. Well, except for the fact I haven't throttled Detective Sergeant I-Do-Nothing-But-Moan Hodgkin. That's an achievement all in itself.'

Callum winced as Dotty's voice scraiked out in the background: '*Oh, you think you're such a delight, do you? You sour-faced, pube-bearded—*'

'*Go roll yourself under a bus.*'

'*I'll roll my boot right up your—*'

'For God's sake! Do you two never stop?' He swapped the phone to his bad hand, freeing up his left to massage the ache growing between his eyebrows.

Mother deserved a knighthood, she genuinely did.

A manky old Renault parked itself next to the Mondeo, a chubby bearded bloke and a thin blonde rock-chick type getting out and having a stretch in the drizzle, before hurrying off across the lay-by. Making for the burger van that lurked along a bit from the public loos.

Dotty was the first to break the silence, obviously trying to sound light and cheerful. And failing. '*What about you and Rosalind?*'

'Naught for seven. Thought we were on to something with a derelict house in Cowskillin, but nothing doing.'

'*Well ... there's plenty of time, isn't there? Ashlee's still alive. We'll find her.*'

'*Don't be naive.*'

'*I'm not being sodding naive!*'

And they were off. Again.

'*Tod Monaghan's been dead for three days – unless he left her with plenty of food and water, she's already died of thirst.*'

'*She could still be alive.*'

'Can we not go two minutes without you pair—'

'*All the other victims got starved and dehydrated before he stuck them in his smoker, so he's not going to leave her a fourteen-inch ham-and-mushroom with extra cheese and a big bottle of Diet Coke in case she gets peckish, is he? Use your head.*'

'*I have had just about enough of your bloody lip, Constable.*'

'*Blow it, Sergeant. Genuinely. Out your arsehole, like a trumpet.*'

What was the point?

One last go. 'I'm asking you both nicely: can you try—'

'*That's it: get out of my car.*'

'*It's not "your" anything, so—*'

'GET OUT OF MY BLOODY CAR!'

Silence.

Franklin emerged from the ladies' side of the public loos, wiping her hands on her suit trousers. Face wrinkled and sour.

'GET OUT!'

'*Fine. Great. You know what, I will.*'

'*Go on then.*'

'*I am.*' Some clunking and rattling. '*Here!*'

'*Don't you throw stuff at me! You—*'

'*It's your half of the list, you moron.*' Then the coffin-lid *thunk* of the car door slamming.

'AND GOOD RIDDANCE!' The sound of an engine revving, then growling, getting louder as she worked through the gears. 'GAAAAAAARGH!'

Franklin turned her collar up and marched over, weaving her way between the pothole puddles.

'*That man drives me totally insane! He's impossible.*'

'Dotty—'

'*Everything's an excuse to moan and be sarcastic and nip, nip, nip.*'

Franklin hauled open the driver's door and threw herself in behind the wheel. Shuddered. 'God, that toilet is disgusting.'

'*You know what I should do? I should turn this sodding car around and drive right over the top of him!*'

She pointed at the phone in Callum's hand. 'Anything?'

He pulled on a grimace. 'Don't ask.'

'*You heard what he said to me, Callum, didn't you? You heard.*'

'Look, you can't just abandon him, you're police officers. You need to work—'

'*Should turn right round and squash him like the turdbeetle he is! Leave nothing but a skidmark behind. You see if I don't! He can...*'

Callum held the phone against his chest. 'Dotty's thrown Watt out of the car, and driven off without him.'

'Children.'

A big sigh, then he went back to the phone.

'*...never hated anyone so much in my whole sodding life. Not even the wee shite who cost me my leg. He's that bad!*'

'Yeah, well, maybe he only does it because he's secretly in love with you.'

'Urrrrrrgh... Think I just threw up in my mouth a bit.'

'You're welcome. Now turn round and go pick him up. We've got a little girl to find.'

– Detective Constable John Watt –

'I HOPE YOUR SODDING WHEELS FALL OFF!' John steps out into the middle of the road and slams the palm of his left hand into the crook of his right arm, punching his fist up as DS Moron drives off into the rain.

Woman's a bloody disgrace.

No way she made sergeant on her own merit. No: must've been a bribe to stop her suing the force after the crash. Which was probably her own fault anyway.

John hurries back onto the pavement, stands under the awning outside a tat shop and has a squint at his watch. Half eleven.

Could head back to Division Headquarters, put in a formal complaint about his useless DS... But what good will it do him? No way they'll fire her, no matter how crap she is. So the only option is to outshine her. Show them how a *real* police officer does things.

He pulls the other sheet of paper from his pocket – the other half of their list.

DS Hodgkin is such a moron.

Did she actually think he'd printed all those addresses out at random? That he hadn't done a Bayesian statistical analysis, based on the property's location and the location of the victims, and ranked them in order of likeliness? And, having gone to so much trouble, that he wouldn't keep the best ones for himself?

She could've just ridden his coattails to glory, but no. *Hodgkin* had to be the thorn in his toilet paper, the nettles in his underwear, the razor blade in his sock, the bleach in his eyedrops.

John scans the list. Definitely going to need a car to get round all these.

That's OK, though. Just grab a taxi back to Camburn Road where he parked this morning, collect the Clio, and head out to save the day.

Goodbye, DS Dorothy Pain-in-the-Arse Hodgkin, hello promotion.

And speak of the devil...

Her crappy Wheelchairmobile drifts down the road again, windscreen wipers going. Stupid fat face peering out through the rain-streaked glass.

John ducks down behind the little blue van parked outside the tat shop.

Off you go, Hodgkin. Keep on driving.

There, that's much better, isn't it?

Bye-bye.

Don't let tomorrow's headlines hit you in the arse on the way past: 'Police Hero John Watt Saves Missing Teen ~ First Minister Pays Tribute To Brave Detective Constable...'

No: 'Prime Minister Awards Knighthood To Newly Promoted Hero Cop!'

Yeah, that's better.

John sticks his list in his pocket and hurries off to the nearest taxi rank.

59

'Here.' Callum thumped back into the passenger seat and held out a warm newspaper parcel.

Franklin took it. 'Mayonnaise?'

'They stuck a couple of sachets in there.' He unwrapped his fish supper, filling the car with the loving scent of hot batter and brown vinegar. 'Only chip shop in Oldcastle where they still wrap everything in newsprint. Well, if they know you.'

Steam paled the car windows, hiding the grey street. Rain danced on the roof.

She crunched on a chunk of batter. 'McAdams was on while you were out. The SEB did another sweep of Paul Jeffries' back garden and guess what they found.'

He popped a chip in his mouth, crisp and brown and salty, sharp with malt vinegar. 'Go on then.'

'The male body, with the clothes – there was another set of female remains buried underneath it. And it definitely wasn't like the others: covered in kerf marks. Whoever she was, Jeffries had a serious go at her with a knife.'

'Urgh… He just gets nicer and nicer, doesn't he?'

'That's men for you.' She crunked the top off her tub of mushy peas. 'How many have we still to go?'

The list was on the dashboard. 'Six: four private houses, a block of flats, and a disused green grocer's. Should be done by about four, maybe five o'clock?'

'If we're lucky.' Franklin dug in a chip and scooped out a splodge of neon green. 'Odds on we're—'

Her phone sat on the dashboard, buzzing as it launched into 'Dancing

419

in the Moonlight'. Again. For the third time in twenty minutes. She just grimaced at it. Then ate another pea-smeared chip. Chewing as the ringtone came to a sudden halt.

Callum broke off a chunk of flaky white haddock and tipped it into his mouth. Almost too hot to eat. 'Can I ask you a personal question?'

'No.'

'You don't seem to like this Mark of yours very much.'

'Maybe Monaghan never had access to Northeast Ecclesiastical Trust Holdings Limited list? Maybe he just knew *that* property was vacant?'

'Maybe.'

'So maybe he knew Paul Jeffries? Just because Dotty can't find a connection doesn't mean one wasn't there. Jeffries was a lay preacher, right? Maybe that's how Monaghan knew him? He was in the congregation.'

'So, if you don't *like* Mark, why are you still with him?'

Franklin chewed, frowning straight ahead at the opaque windscreen. 'We should find out where Jeffries preached.'

'Life's too short: take it from me.'

'He must have neighbours of some kind, right? They might know a bit about him.'

Callum peeled the outer layer off a pickled onion with his teeth. 'Can't believe I wasted five years of my life with Elaine.'

'You're not helping.'

'Fine: he's a lay preacher. What do lay preachers do?'

'Depends what flavour he was. But there'll be sermons, raising money for charity, organising trips for wayward youths, rescuing fallen women, visiting members of the congregation if they end up in hospital or their partner dies. So officiating at funerals too, probably.' She shovelled in more chips. 'Don't know if they're allowed to give people the last rites or not.'

'Nah, that'll be a union job. Demarcation and all...' Callum put the pickled onion down. 'Dying and elderly members of the congregation: they think Jeffries is God's representative, right? They want to keep in with God on their deathbed, don't they?'

'Argh! Of *course* they do.' Franklin sooked her fingers clean then pulled out her phone. Poked at the screen. Held the thing to her ear. 'Hello? Yes, it's DC Franklin. I need someone to get onto the Land Registry Office— ... I don't care if it's Sunday. We need to know if a Paul Terence Jeffries owned any properties. Probably left to him by grateful OAPs right before they died. ... OK. ... Right. Tell them it's urgent and call me back soon as you hear. ... OK, thanks. Bye. ... Bye.' She thumbed the screen, then slipped the phone away. Grinned across the car. 'We're onto something, I can *feel* it.'

Callum popped a chip in his gob and grinned back. 'We're going to save Ashlee Gossard.'

John's stomach makes a sound like an angry badger trapped in a bath. Should've stopped to grab a sandwich or something on the way. Too late now. Just have to wait till he gets back to town.

His Clio lurches and bumps along the dirt track, little stones pinging in the wheel arches as he slaloms left and right between the potholes.

The outskirts of Holburn Forest run along one side of the road, beech and sycamore giving way to the dark regimented mass of pine trees, stretching away up the hill. The other side is all gorse and broom, spines and spears, reaching down across plowtered fields full of reeds.

And there we go: Thaw Cottages. Number two on the *good* list.

There's three of them – two semi, one detached, all grey. They look solid enough, but the semidetached cottages are missing glass in their windows, front gardens bounded by a sagging wall with most of the harling hanging off. Nothing but thistles, dock, and nettles growing within its boundaries.

The house next door isn't much better – both front windows boarded up with rain-darkened chipboard, one chimney pot missing, a row of jackdaws glaring down with beady eyes as he parks the Clio outside.

Another sagging wall, another garden full of weeds.

Must've been quite something, living here. Probably *monumentally* crap in winter: trapped halfway up a hill, at the end of a long winding track, wolves roaming the woods behind the house.

OK, so maybe not wolves, but no way anyone comes anywhere near the arse-end of nowhere like this with a snowplough.

The view, though. That's something.

The hill runs down, past a tumbled-down church and its crumbling graveyard, then out along the River Wynd, nestling in a valley that opens up as it hits the outskirts of Oldcastle. Can see most of the city from up here, lurking beneath a blue-grey lid of heavy cloud tinged with gold and purples.

John zips up his jacket and reaches back between the seats for the umbrella. Scrambles out and opens it with one fluid movement. Pop.

Those two years of contemporary dance were *not* wasted.

421

Rain drums on the umbrella skin.

Might as well check the conjoined cottages first.

No sign of a path beaten through the weeds to the front door, but the road hooked around the back of the buildings. Probably garages and things there.

He hops the broken gate and pushes his way through the soggy horrible nettles, holding his elbows up and out to keep both hands away from the stinging leaves. The front door isn't locked, just tied shut with orange string – the kind farmers wrap around bales of hay. He unties it, pushes on the wasp-stripped wood, and steps inside.

Callum drew a red line through property number fifteen: a two-up-two-down on a housing estate in Blackwall Hill. Checked his watch. 'Five to go.'

Franklin started the engine again, and pulled away from the kerb. 'I know there's no point just sitting about till we hear back, but this is *such* a waste of time.'

'We've been over this.'

'Where's next?'

'Gordon Crescent, Kingsmeath. Back down to the junction then right at the roundabout.'

The car's windscreen wipers grunted and moaned.

Callum's phone joined in the general noise. 'Hello?'

'Ah, yes, is Winston Smith addressing Detective Constable MacGregor?'

Because today hadn't contained enough weirdos. 'He is. And does Winston have something for DC MacGregor?'

'Indeed he does.'

Rows of squat little houses slid by the Mondeo's windows, all slumped beneath the rain.

'Would he care to tell DC MacGregor what it is?'

'Winston told you he would be triumphant, and triumphant he is. His software identified one thousand three hundred and fifteen possible three-character number-plate suffixes that would provide a reasonable match to the car on your footage. He then ran that through the DVLA's dataset via a method he'd rather not discuss right now, and narrowed it down to cars that conformed to the manufacturer and make shown on your footage.'

The Mondeo climbed the hill, over the railway bridge and down the other side. Slowing as Franklin took them left at the roundabout.

'And will Winston be getting to the point sometime soon?'

'This cut the number of hits to a mere two hundred and ninety across the UK. He then took those and hammered the ANPR system to see if any had been spotted in the vicinity, and lo his genius was rewarded.'

From here the entirety of Blackwall Hill stretched away down to the river, the garish goings on in Montgomery Park standing out like a grenade in a kid's sandpit. Especially that massive inflatable spider.

'Callum's dying of old age, here, Winston.'

'Those last three characters are the letters D.W.G. and form the climax of a personalised number plate, currently appearing on a black Mercedes registered to Bob's Speed Trap Records Limited and insured for the use of one Donald Newman.'

So Newman hadn't died or gone away, he'd gone legit. Or at least as close as passed for it in the music industry.

'OK. Thanks.'

'You don't seem to grasp the celebrity status of the gentleman in question, DC MacGregor. Donald Newman's stage name is Donny McRoberts, AKA: Sick Dawg. The rap sensation and creator of such modern top-ten classics as "Rock, Paper, Shotgun" and "I'm-a Spit on Yo Grave, Irene".'

'You're sure it's him?'

'Winston does not make mistakes. And he has that very vehicle on camera entering Kingsmeath via the Blackburgh Roundabout not thirty minutes earlier.' A sniff. 'Now, he takes it your business here is concluded, Detective Constable. And that you will be providing him with a cost centre to write his time against?'

'Thanks, Winston. I'll get back to you.' Callum hung up before there were any complaints. Then checked his watch again.

So Donald Newman was Donny 'Sick Dawg' McRoberts.

Maybe Willow's brother had been right about the helicopter, tiger, and 'loads of bitches'.

Well, Donald was in for a very nasty shock as soon as Callum caught up with him.

Which probably wouldn't be any time soon.

No way they could abandon the search for Ashlee Gossard to go rattle Newman's teeth for him. No matter how much he deserved it.

Franklin took a right at the traffic lights and onto the dual carriageway, heading for Kingsmeath.

But he *really* sodding deserved it.

The house is dry and dusty inside, littered with ancient manky furniture riddled with little holes. And the drifts of tiny black 'Tic Tacs' all over the floor explain why. There's mould on the walls by the empty windows, ancient flock wallpaper curled and stained dysentery-brown.

John picks his way through to a bedroom – complete with rusty bedstead and sagging mattress. A wardrobe full of old lady clothes and more mouse droppings.

The bathroom is clean, but dusty. The kitchen cupboards still have tins in them, but they're bloated and furry with dark brown flakes.

As if someone just walked out years ago and never returned.

The kitchen window is dirt-greyed, almost opaque. John huffs a breath on the glass and clears a patch with the side of his hand, revealing an overgrown garden and a collapsed shed. Looks as if next door's is much the same, only there's a greenhouse full of dead brown stalks in there too.

Past the garden is an old bothy – stone walls, corrugated iron roof – and an ancient wooden barn surrounded by chunks of farm machinery slowly disappearing under thistles and brambles.

OK, so finish up in here, check the other two cottages and then—

'What the *sodding* hell did you think you were doing?'

John freezes. Licks his lips. Forces a smile and turns. 'Sarge. What are you doing here?'

DS McAdams is standing in the kitchen doorway, arms folded, face creased into a pale glower. 'Oh don't look so surprised: I knew exactly what you were up to, soon as you ditched Dotty.'

Oh crap.

John's mouth clicks shut.

'Have you any idea how much trouble you're in right now?'

'I was just—'

'I know exactly what you were "just", Detective Constable Watt.' His head falls back and he stares at the ceiling. 'Why me?'

'It wasn't my fault, Sarge, DS Hodgkin threw me out of the car.'

'Why do I even bother?'

'You *know* what she's like: incompetent and chippy.'

'I'm dying of bloody cancer, here. I should be lying on a white sandy beach, drinking margaritas, not standing in a manky wrecked house in the middle of nowhere SHOUTING AT YOU!'

John retreats a couple of steps, pulling on his best righteous-indignation face. 'I was only trying to find Ashlee Gossard before something happened to her.'

McAdams' shoulders droop and he runs a hand across his wrinkled eyes. 'You want to know how I found you? You left the USB stick with your spreadsheet on it in the incident-room computer. I went digging.'

'Dotty threw me out the car! It's not my fault she's hormonal and mental.'

'I always knew you were a devious wee shite, Watt. And you're not the only one who understands Bayesian statistics: I saw what you did to the spreadsheet.' He pulls out a sheet of paper. 'Fiddling the ordering so all the highest-probability properties were last to be printed out. So you could take them for yourself.'

John sticks his chest out. 'I'm trying to save a little girl's *life* here.'

'YOU COULDN'T GIVE A TOSS ABOUT ASHLEE GOSSARD!' A deep breath and McAdams presses a hand against his stomach. 'God damn it, Watt. If you wanted to save her you would have prioritised those addresses and we'd have sent a team to each one *first*. You don't care if she lives or dies, you just care if you can grab all the credit and glory for yourself.'

The only sound is the rain pattering in the long grass, like a thousand little feet. Running away.

McAdams sighs. 'I'm not surprised. I wish I was, but I'm not. *Disappointed*, but not surprised.'

Heat rushes up John's face. He looks down at the faded lino at his feet. The worst thing isn't being caught, the worst thing is that McAdams is right. 'Sorry, Sarge.'

'Watt, this isn't Hollywood, or some cheesy detective novel, you can't just go running around on your own expecting to solve the case. You've got to be a team player. You've got to work *with* your team, not piss them off so much they ditch you and drive off on their own.'

'Yes, Sarge.'

'Dorothy's been worried sick about you.'

'Has she, Sarge?'

'Of course not.' Another huge sigh. 'John, do you actually want to be a police officer? I mean honestly, *genuinely* want to do the job? Cos, believe me, you get one lousy brief stint on this earth and if you're not totally committed to being a cop then you need to find something else. Something you're passionate about. Something you care enough about to do *well*. Understand?'

It's like someone's tied a great big heavy weight around his bowels, dragging him down on the inside. John nods. Can barely squeeze the words out: 'Sorry, Sarge.'

'So: do you want to be a cop?'

'Ever since I was a little boy.'

A tut and a groan. Then a long slow exhale. 'OK. I'm not going to tell Mother about this. Or anyone else. But you have to *promise* me you'll try harder.'

'Yes, Sarge.'

'We'll divvy up the most likely addresses and get them out to the other teams. Maybe we can find Ashlee before she... Well, we can only do our best.' He spreads his printout on the wobbly kitchen table. 'Which ones are most statistically significant?'

John points them out, ranking them in order – most to least – and McAdams nods, marking them up.

'Good. If anyone asks, *you* called *me* and told me these were our best chance. Everything else never happened.' He pulls his phone out and turns for the door. Then stops. 'Have you finished in here?'

'Only just started.'

'OK. Well give it a proper search before you leave. She's got to be out there somewhere.'

'Yes, Sarge.'

The smile looks pained, but at least it's there. 'Watt, you're a bright kid. You were honest enough to turn your old team in for being corrupt – that takes guts. You've got the makings of a good copper in you. Don't let the petty stuff get in the way.'

'Yes, Sarge.'

'Good boy.' McAdams sticks his hands in his pockets. 'And please, in the name of all that's holy, *sign out at the end of your shift.*' Then he limps away down the corridor and out the front door, disappearing into the rain.

John sinks back against the work surface and groans.

It's like every report card he's ever had: *Must try harder.*

Outside, the dark rumbling roar of a four-by-four sounds, then fades away.

Come on: search next door. Then the detached cottage on the end. Then the bothy and barn. Then onto the next address on the list.

After all, he can always claim credit for putting the list together in the first place.

That's got to be worth something. Right?

And with any luck, even if he isn't the one who actually finds her, someone will get to Ashlee Gossard before it's too late.

60

'Hold on a minute…' Callum nipped down the corridor and into the stairwell. The flats weren't bad, a clean six-storey block in a development of three. Landscaped gardens and a row of private garages. There was even a sculpture out front, though God knew what it was meant to be a sculpture of. Looked like a jellyfish having sex with an Oxo Cube. 'Hello?'

McAdams sounded even more tired than usual, the noise of an engine droning away in the background. *'Where are you?'*

'Thompson Court. It's all flats, so no chance anyone's smoking bodies in—'

'That's great. Listen, I've had a call from Watt. He's refined the spreadsheet and come up with eight high-probability targets for us to hit.'

Yeah, right. 'And he's just done this now, has he?'

Franklin appeared from the door of number 5, turned and said something to the householder.

'Don't be so cynical. The important thing is we've got a real chance of saving Ashlee Gossard.'

'Oh, no: I get it. He fiddled the list, didn't he? Kept all the likely properties to himself.'

Silence from the other end.

The flat door clunked shut and Franklin headed down the corridor towards him.

'I'm right, aren't I?'

'It's not as if you've never done anything wrong, is it, Constable?'

Franklin stopped in front of him, both eyebrows up.

Callum pointed at the phone. 'It's McAdams. I'll be down in a sec.' Then soon as she was out of sight he turned his back on the stairs.

427

'How many times? I – never – took – a – bribe! Is that clear enough for you?'

A sigh. *'I know.'*

'Do I have to tattoo it in six-inch letters on my forehead for you to… Wait, what?'

'Cecelia told me weeks ago. Your girlfriend messed up the crime scene, and you took the blame so she'd still get maternity pay.'

'You *knew*?'

'Can we get back to the topic at hand? I'm on my way to a disused warehouse in Cowskillin now, I need every team en route to the other seven properties A.S.A.B.F.P. Emphasis on the B.F.'

'Then why the hell have you been treating me like something you trod in?'

'Because I like screwing with you, Constable MacGregor. You're the gift that never quits.'

Down below, the flat's communal front door clunked shut and Franklin appeared through the window, hurrying along the path towards their cholera-coloured Mondeo.

'You're an arsehole, you know that, don't you?'

'I'm a dying man, Callum, I take my fun where I can find it. Now you and Rosalind get your pert little backsides over to number six Creel Lane. It's Kettle Docks, so you can't be more than two minutes away. And try to keep the sexual tension to a bare minimum for the next few pages, it distracts the readers.'

'Thanks a *lot.*' Callum thumped down the stairs, scowling out the stairwell window at the rain hammering down on the drab grey houses. 'Did you not *maybe* just think that things were hard enough with everyone else treating me like crap? Didn't need you piling in.'

'If it makes you feel any better: I'm sorry.' This time the sigh was long and rattling. *'I shall add that to my pile of regrets.'*

He pushed the door open and stood beneath the portico, just out of the rain's reach. Grudging every word: 'Are you OK?'

'There's so many things I'll never get to do, Callum. I'll never sing in a rock band. I'll never climb Mount Kilimanjaro. I'll never win the Booker Prize. Hell, I'll probably never even be published in my own lifetime…'

Franklin was staring out of the driver's window at him, pointing at her watch.

'I spent so much time in the procurement of material things, that I forgot to live. Grab every opportunity you get, Callum. You put them off,

thinking they'll always come round again, but they don't. One brief spin and we're gone.'

Now that was cheery.

'Is this us bonding now?'

'Maybe.' A small laugh. *'Yes, well, now that we're besties, you can tell me what the hell I'm going to do with Watt. He means well. Sometimes. When he's not being a gargantuan bell-end.'*

'You give him a good bollocking?'

'Thought he was going to cry at one point: "I'm not surprised, just disappointed."'

'Got to love the classics.'

Franklin leaned on the horn and a loud Breeeeeeeeeeep blared out through the rain.

'Do me a favour: keep an eye on him, Callum. He's his own worst enemy, but it's not for want of trying. There's a good cop in there some-where. Help him dig it out.'

Callum licked his lips. 'Are you sure you're OK?'

'Anyway, I've got the other teams to phone. You and Rosalind hightail it over to Creel Lane. Do me and Mother proud.' And he was gone.

Yeah ... no way that didn't sound like a last will and testament.

Collar up, Callum jogged for the car and slid into the passenger seat. Ran his good hand through his hair and flicked the water off into the footwell. 'That was McAdams. He says Watt has, and I quote, "refined the list".'

Franklin groaned and rolled her eyes. 'He rigged it, didn't he? So he'd be the one who found Ashlee.'

'Doesn't matter. He's done the right thing now.' Callum hauled on his seatbelt. 'And you and I have got a new address to search. Kettle Docks, and this time let's have a little mood music to help us on our way.' He reached out and poked the 999 button on the dashboard, setting the Mondeo's siren wailing and its lights flickering.

She grinned at him. 'About sodding time.'

Creel Lane: narrow and cobbled, lined on both sides with ancient, thick-walled buildings. Three and four storeys tall. The windows were small, the walls coated in harling and painted various shades of crum-bling beige. The road curled away to the right, following the line of the river. One set of buildings facing the water, the other crammed in between the road and a steep hillside, with another set of houses above that.

All very quaint and picturesque in the sunshine. But in the rain? Claustrophobic and grim.

A couple were cloaked in scaffolding, probably on their way to becoming extremely expensive flats.

Number 6 wasn't. It was on the inland side of the road, a flat-fronted building with an archway in the middle – big enough for a Transit van – sealed with a heavy wooden gate that went all the way up. All the windows boarded up. An official-looking notice scowled out from the wall, 'WARNING! PROPERTY IS UNSTABLE AND DANGEROUS!' in big unfriendly letters.

Franklin killed the siren and parked right outside. 'What do you think?'

'Maybe.' Callum hopped out and pulled on his high-viz jacket – the one with 'POLICE' on the back. Hurried around to the gate as Franklin joined him. He pointed at a big brass-coloured lump of metal securing both sides of the gate together. 'That looks like a brand-new padlock to me.'

She snapped on a pair of gloves and ran a finger along the hasp. 'Don't suppose you've got a crowbar?'

He snapped on his own gloves. 'Kick it in?'

'Kick it in.' She braced herself. 'In three, two, one, go!'

A booming thump rattled out into the rain. But the door didn't budge.

'Right, wait here.' Franklin turned and marched across the road to the nearest scaffolding-clad building. She was back a couple of minutes later clutching a claw hammer. 'Might want to stand back.'

BOOM, BOOM, BOOM. The metal head battered down on the padlock, achieving exactly sod-all. Then she flipped the hammer round and dug the claws in behind the hasp and yanked it down. Wood splintered. Metal groaned.

'Come on, you wee bugger!' Putting her weight into it.

And they were in.

The detached cottage is empty. Well, except for the dust. And the mouse droppings. And the *massive* wasp byke in the kitchen. Which only leaves the bothy and the barn.

John picks up the brolly and does his elbows-out march through the long grass and nettles in the back garden, clambers over the drystane dyke at the bottom, and brushes himself down on the track.

A bent piece of thin metal pipe is hooked through a hasp on the bothy door, keeping it shut. The wood's pale-blue paint is crackled and flaky. The guttering's missing. And this is a sodding waste of time.

He pulls out the pipe and pushes into the bothy.

Dark in here. And the floorboards look about as trustworthy as an angry toddler.

John creeps inside, testing the way before committing each foot.

It'll be just his luck if the floor completely—

'AAAAARGH!'

Sodding hell!

He drags his phone out and the music gets louder. Flips it open and presses the button. Takes a deep breath. 'Hello?'

'Watt? It's DS Hodgkin.'

Maybe it'd be better if the floor did collapse and swallow him. 'Sarge.'

'I got a call from DS McAdams. He says you came up with a new priority order for the houses.'

'Yeah, this isn't...' He rubs a hand across his forehead. McAdams was right: *Don't let the petty stuff get in the way.* 'Yes. I'm sorry about earlier.'

See, that didn't hurt, did it?

'Do you, you know, want to meet up and be a team again?'

John puffs out a breath. *You've got to work with your team, not piss them off so much they ditch you and drive off on their own.* No matter how much of a pain in the ring they are. 'You sure?'

'Course I am. Not as if I can do a lot of searching on my own, is it? Not in a wheelchair.'

'Cool. Where are you?'

'Shortstaine Business Park. The chandler's yard.'

'Give me...' Five minutes to finish searching, maybe ten minutes to get there if the traffic isn't too bad. 'Call it twenty minutes tops.'

'We'll find Ashlee. You and me: heroes.'

'I know. Be there soon as I can.' He hangs up. Lets his chin fall against his chest. 'Pfff...'

The first step is always the worst, though, isn't it? That horrible feeling the ground's not going to be there when your foot goes down and you're just going to fall and fall and fall...

'Here.' Callum handed Franklin a torch, and clicked on his own.

Daylight barely made it over the threshold, swallowed by gloom and shadows.

She swept the cold white beam of her torch across the floor. More cobbles, uneven and buckled, giving way to cracked paving slabs.

Callum did the same for the walls and roof: bare stones and crumbling mortar. A dangling wire with a broken lightbulb hanging from the end.

A single door off to one side.

She pointed at it, then clenched her fist – pumping it once, then flattening her hand out. Nodded at him for confirmation.

'You look like an idiot, you know that, don't you?' Callum marched over and tried the handle. The door was stiff, but a bit of shoulder made it groan open.

Her voice was a hissing whisper, 'We have no idea what's in there.'

'We know Tod Monaghan's dead. And we know the gate was padlocked from the outside, with no way to open it from in here.' Callum stepped through the door. 'So unless you're worried about ghosties and ghoulies, maybe we could get on with it?'

The torch beam picked out an empty room with decaying plaster walls, the lathe exposed like ribs on a carcass. Two doors and a staircase.

'There's nothing wrong with taking precautions.'

'Don't drag me into your SWAT team fantasies.' He put a foot on the stair. The wood creaked. 'What do you think, safe?'

'We should sweep the ground floor first. Work up level by level.'

'Fine.'

Door number one: a kitchen, complete with rusty range cooker and units buried beneath a duvet of grey dust. Door number two: another empty room with skeletal walls. Another door in the far corner.

Franklin held up a fist again. 'Padlock.'

It glinted in the torchlight.

She squared her shoulders, took a step back, then rammed her boot into the wood beneath the hasp. *BOOM* – but this time the door sprang open in a flurry of crackling splinters. Dust turned their torch beams into solid things.

A stairway led down into the darkness.

Franklin flattened herself against the wall. 'You ready?'

'Seriously, stop it.' Callum squeezed past and hurried down the stairs and onto a bare earth floor. A basement. Bare stone walls. Little archways set into them, lined with brick, the colour of blood in the torchlight.

Franklin crept down after him. 'Anything?'

'Nope. Just an empty...' Something glittered in one of the alcoves.

'What?'

'Shhh…' He edged across the dirt floor, playing the torch across the brick.

It was a chain, hanging from a metal ring screwed into the alcove wall at chest height. There was another one in the next alcove, and one in the alcove after that. Four in total, all hanging empty, all fixed to the wall.

Callum cleared his throat. 'Maybe we should check upstairs. *Now*.'

They scrambled back up to the ground floor, through the kitchen and up the creaking wooden steps.

Four doors leading off the landing.

He jammed his torch under his bad arm and dug out his phone. Scrolled through to McAdams' number. Waited for him to pick up. 'Hello?'

Franklin opened one of the doors and stepped inside.

'Callum, my new and bestest friend, / Tell me how to make amends, / For all the cruel things I've done, / Like kicking you right up the bum?'

'Shut up and listen. Six Creel Lane, it's got a basement kitted out like the one at The Cloisters. Chains fixed to the walls.'

'What about Ashlee, is she there? Have you found her?'

'Still checking.'

Franklin's torch beam cast long sweeping shadows out into the room.

'Well get off the bloody phone and check!'

'We *are*. And we need an SEB team over here – tell them to get a shift on.'

Franklin emerged from the other room, shaking her head. Marched over to one of the other doors and disappeared again.

'Got to go.' He hung up, got his torch and phone sorted. 'Franklin?'

No sign of her.

Callum tried door number three – a big empty room with fancy cornices and a big ceiling rose. Probably the kind of place you hung a chandelier if you were the kind of person who owned a chandelier.

Back out into the other room.

'Franklin?'

Nope.

He pushed through door number two. 'Where the hell are…'

This wasn't a room, it was a cavern, three storeys tall, dug into the hillside. Or maybe it was natural and they'd just built the house over the front, sealing it in? either way, it was massive.

He'd emerged onto a landing about six foot square, with no handrail. Stone steps descended to the floor twenty, maybe thirty feet below – dim and grey at the very edge of the torch's reach.

There was another torch down there, though, sweeping across a set of wooden structures – like self-contained rooms, or exhibition stalls. The smell of wood smoke, warm and sweet, mingling with the pungent taint of old fish.

Franklin's torch swung up towards him, voice echoing back off the stone walls. 'CALLUM!' Callum... Callum... Callum...

'ARE YOU OK?' OK... OK... OK...

'I'VE FOUND SOMETHING!' Something... Something... Something...

He picked his way down the stairs, hugging the wall, torch pointed at the steps beneath his feet.

'WILL YOU HURRY UP?' Up... Up... Up...

No.

He walked out onto hard-packed earth, stained almost black.

She was standing in front of a big wooden box, about the size of a large shed, made from rough planks of wood. It stood right next to a big drying rack thing, a good eighteen-foot tall, criss-crossed with notched poles, like the ones they used at Strummuir Smokehouse to be all olde worlde and sustainable.

'They've probably been smoking fish here for generations.' Callum shone his torch across the box, setting another padlock shining. Fish, and other things.

Franklin pulled the claw hammer from her jacket and wrenched the hasp from the door. The padlock clattered into the dirt.

He nudged the door and it swung inwards.

John wades through the grass to the barn door. Gah... Trousers are absolutely sodden now. But he had to take a short cut from the bothy, didn't he? Couldn't go the long way round, by the road, no, that would be too sensible.

Rain batters against his brolly, rolling in, up the valley, in thick grey curls.

Does it *never* stop raining here?'

The barn has one of those old-fashioned pin-and-bar catches. He clicks it up and pushes through into gloom and the cloyingly familiar scent of wood smoke and dead fish. Nasty and sticky, like every smoke-house he's visited with DC MacGregor.

A smile creeps across his face. Maybe?

The barn's walls are stone on the outside, but wood on the inside, the space divided up into three. An area at the front where old wooden fish boxes are piled. An area on the right set up so poles can be hung at various heights over an open fire – there's still a pile of ashes on the floor where the last burn died out. And last, but not least, an area on the left, sealed away behind a door. No lock, just a metal pin poked through a hasp to stop it opening.

'PRIME MINISTER AWARDS KNIGHTHOOD TO NEWLY PROMOTED HERO COP!'

John takes a deep breath, pulls out the pin, and steps inside.

61

Callum edged inside. The darkness was a solid thing, pushing against his chest and throat, thick and syrupy in his lungs. The torch's beam sliced through it, but the mass healed again soon as the blade was gone.

A metal tank sat off to one side, about the size of a big bathtub, its sides streaked with pale-brown rust.

He edged over, Franklin just behind him, and shone his torch into the tank.

The smell in here isn't just wood smoke and fish, it's tainted with a bitter-scented sourness and something that's half sweet, half horror film.

The gloom seeps out from the walls, leaving just a pale spot of light from the open door.

Should've brought a torch with him.

Too late for that now.

John steps forward. 'Hello?'

Another step.

Then another, scuffing his feet along the dirt floor.

His foot hits something soft and he freezes until his eyes adjust a bit.

'Oh crap...'

It's a woman, sitting on the floor slumped to one side, the chain around her throat stretched tight between there and the wall. No point feeling for a pulse, not with her eyes half-open like that, but he does it anyway. The skin's cold and clammy beneath his fingertips.

At least that explains where the other smell's coming from.

His stomach does a little lurch to one side and he huffs out a breath.

No being sick. This is a crime scene. They'd never let him live it down.

The rest of the room is finally seeping out of the gloom. Rough wooden walls. Another chain, dangling empty from a metal ring. And a metal tank.

He stands. Marches over, back straight.

'Pff...'

It's hard to tell if the body in the tank is male or female. A skeleton, coated in a thin layer of pale skin – crusted with salt just above the filthy waterline. The chain around its neck is looped around a metal pole at this end of the tank, with just enough slack to stop the head disappearing beneath the surface and drowning. Lank, greasy hair, long enough to sink under the surface.

'Ashlee?'

John drops to his knees and reaches for her neck, two fingers touching the point just beneath her jaw where—

Her eyes snap open.

'Aaaaaargh!' He flinches back and goes sprawling on his arse. Sits there, breathing hard. Then laughs. Scrambles forward again. 'Ashlee, my name's John, I'm a police officer. We're going to get you out of here, OK? You're safe now.' Another laugh. 'You scared the living crap out of me, by the way.'

She just stares at him, making little hissing noises from her cracked and bloody lips.

'It's OK. It's OK.' He pulls out his phone. 'I'm going to—'

There's a sound, like ripping fabric. White and cold as the ground rushes up and—

DS Hodgkin hurls a scrunched-up ball of paper at him. *You're such an arsehole, Watt!* She—

The sun's warm on the back of his neck, bees and wasps buzzing through the beer garden as Big Malky gets another round in, all grins and winks, no idea that he and his team are getting a visit from Professional Standards soon as—

Everyone files out of the grubby office. Mother sighs and pats him on the shoulder. 'Maybe you should try being a bit nicer to people, John? Might stop them—'

His father kneels on the sandy beach, holding out a curly shell as big as his fist. 'If you put it up to your ear, you can hear the sea.' He smiles—

Waves crash against the walls and floor.

Why is he lying down? Why isn't—

Mary kisses him, her body pressed hard against his as their song plays on the—

His phone's still in his hand, screen turned towards him, waiting for an input.

Mary. Skin like moonlight. Soft and warm beneath his fingers. That smell of strawberries and sandalwood. A smile like sunshine on a cold winter's—

The light on his phone's screen goes out.

Darkness.

'What do you think?'

Callum ran his torch around the room again. Then back to the tank. Dirty-grey crystals twinkled in the light, all the way down the sides. The bottom of the tank lumpy with them and what looked like bits of twig. 'Difficult to tell for sure, without the SEB, but that looks a hell of a lot like what was in the bathtub at Customs Street. Well, if you left it there for a couple of months till all the liquid evaporated.'

Franklin did a slow three-sixty. 'Chains on the walls, tank full of brine...' A sigh. 'How many more of these torture chambers do you think he has?'

'Can't be many. Too risky. What if Northeast Ecclesiastical decides to sell the property, or turn it into flats?'

Callum stared down into the tank. 'Maybe that's why he abandoned it? He saw all the building work across the road and cut his losses. Found somewhere safer.'

'Doesn't help Ashlee Gossard, though, does it?'

'No. But we've still got the rest of Watt's list to search.' Callum pulled out his phone. Frowned at the screen. 'No signal.'

Franklin turned and marched out of the makeshift wooden tomb. 'Then we'd better get our backsides in gear.'

62

Justin drops the spanner and it clatters off the floor, bounces, spins, then lies on its side like a wounded bird.

He hunkers down and stares at the fallen police officer. He's like a wounded bird too: blood trickling out of his nose and ear.

Hadn't meant to hit him that hard. But hey ho. Eggs and omelettes.

He's still got his mobile phone in his hand, so Justin picks it up. Presses the power button. The screen is a photo of a woman with pale skin, smiling like she's the happiest person that ever lived. Pretty enough.

Justin holds her over the tank of sacred water … and lets go. She splooshes into the liquid, the screen flickering and fizzing as it sinks. That's the trouble with modern electronics – nothing's built to last.

He grabs two handfuls of the poor lad's jacket and drags him over to the wall, where New Mummy is. Or at least, where she *was*. She's gone now, leaving nothing but a shell behind.

Poor New Mummy.

Justin wipes his hands, then kneels and brushes the hair out of her eyes. Blonde and pretty, just like Father wants. Wanted. Whatever.

He shuffles a foot or two to the side, then lies down with his head in her lap. Cold and soft. Just starting to smell. Shame. It would've been nice to just rest here. Sleep with her hand resting on his chest. The two of them joined together in fear, waiting for Father to wake up and the nightmare to start all over again.

He clears his throat. 'Can you hear me, Ashlee?'

A faint hiss sounds in the gloom.

'You're almost there, sweetheart. Soon you'll be a god.'

Silence.

Justin curls his knees up. Wraps his arm around New Mummy's legs. 'Once upon a time, there was a little boy and he had a happy life full of ice cream and adventures. And he had a brother and a mummy and daddy who loved him very, very much. Then one day everything changed...'

Once Upon A Time

'Here you go, Champ.' Father hands him a burger, all wrapped up in greaseproof paper, with 'WIMPY' written all over it.

Seagulls wheel and scream overhead as Justin takes a big bite.

The sun smiles down on them like a happy god.

Father sits on the bench next to him and wraps an arm around his shoulders. 'We're going to visit Mrs Mason after lunch, that'll be nice, won't it?'

She smells of wee and cats, and shouts cos she can't hear anything, and never gets out of bed, but Justin nods anyway.

'Soon as she signs the will, we're in the money. New car, maybe even a holiday somewhere nice?' He lets go of Justin's shoulders and ruffles his hair instead. 'And you're not going to do anything to cock it up for me, *are* you?'

The burger turns to gravel in his mouth.

New Mummy shudders and sniffs, holding in the sobs because she's a brave little soldier. Her naked back and shoulders quiver, one arm clutched to her front. Justin creeps down the stairs, pausing with every step to stare up at the cellar ceiling, ears stretched like a bat's for any noise from upstairs.

But the only sound is Father snoring.

Justin gets the blanket from the corner and carries it over to New Mummy.

She flinches as he wraps it around her shoulders, then she blinks up at him, biting her lip and nodding. Her eyes are red as a sunset, tears all over her cheeks and snot dripping from the end of her nose.

The bruises had almost healed from last time.

Justin takes the corner of the blanket and dabs at her face, drying it. 'Shhh...'

It's meant to be calming, but it's a warning too: don't wake him up.

She stares down at the twisted lumpy bits between her elbow and her hand, skin all purple and red and blue and yellow. Like a rainbow, only more horrible.

Justin climbs up onto the bed next to her, curls up on his side, with his head in her lap, and he cries too.

The pair of them sniffling away in the basement.

Because what else can they do?

'Ahhh...' Father licks his lips and smiles, rolling the whisky around in his glass, making it sparkle. Then he picks up a tin of beer and swigs it dry. Crushes the empty in his hand.

It's not the usual cheap beer from the bottom shelf of the supermarket, but stuff in a white tin with a red stripe. And the whisky's all fancy too: with a cork instead of a screwcap.

Father is happy.

He raises his glass. 'Here's to the highlife, Slugger. Think we deserve it, don't we?'

'Definitely. We deserve it.' A big grin and a nod. Because if Father's happy, Justin's happy. And nobody has to get hurt...

The only thing spoiling it is New Mummy. She's not even hiding it, just sobbing and crying and bawling. Like she doesn't care. Like she *wants* Father to go back down there.

His face turns into an angry-dog snarl and he stamps his foot on the floor. 'I'M NOT TELLING YOU AGAIN!'

The screaming doesn't stop, but it goes all muffled, like she's stuffed something in her mouth to kill the noises.

Father holds the crushed empty out to Justin. 'How about another beer, Kiddo?'

Justin takes it and runs into the kitchen. Yanks open the fridge. Grabs another fancy striped beer and runs back to the living room. 'It's nice and cold.'

Father cracks the ring-pull and drinks. 'Think it's about time you got a new mummy, don't you, Champ?' He takes a deep breath. 'ONE THAT KNOWS HOW GOOD SHE'S GOT IT!'

Another drink and he nods. 'A nice new mummy.' He smiles at Justin. 'There's this little blonde piece, works in a garage outside Ellon. Very sweet. You'd like that, wouldn't you?'

Justin tries not to move. Stares at his shoes. 'Father? Can't we keep this one? I ... I like her, she's nice to me. The others were all angry all the time.'

Father stares at him. Stares and stares and Justin's going to pee himself and then the shouting and hitting and kicking and—

'Why not.' Father reaches out and ruffles his hair. 'Just for you. We're celebrating, right?' He raises his tin. 'Here's to Mrs Mason, and the stroke that carried her off. Thanks for the house and all the savings. May you burn in hell, you stinking corpulent bitch.'

Father grunts. His trousers are all muddy and dirty, the ribby bits in his shoes clogged up with earth. He's taken off his shirt, showing off the faded blue tattoos and the little white curly hairs that grow through them. Black soil under his fingernails. Grey dust on his arms.

He's lined his empty tins up on the coffee table in front of him, like little soldiers waiting for orders.

Father throws back the last mouthful of beer and hurls the empty at them, sending his soldiers running for cover. Scowls as they clatter and click. 'Boy: beer!'

Justin grabs another tin from the fridge and holds it out.

He snatches it. Scowls at it. Scowls at everything.

Downstairs, New Mummy is screaming again.

Because she knows what's going to happen.

She knows why Father has been digging that big hole out in the garden.

So she screams and sobs and moans.

Father cracks into his new soldier and throws back a mouthful of beer. The words start out squeezed between his teeth and end up making the whole world tremble: 'Does that *bitch* never SHUT UP?'

Now the scowl comes round to rest on Justin.

Father's eyes are narrow and pink, one squinted up tighter than the other as he wobbles in his chair. '*You.*'

Justin backs up a step.

His voice goes all high and whiney: '"Oh, *please* can we keep her? I *promise* she'll be good. She's so *nice* to me..."' He attacks the soldier again. 'I kept her because of you, AND SHE NEVER SHUTS UP!' Father stamps on the floor. 'ALL THE BLOODY TIME! SHUT UP! STOP CRYING!'

But New Mummy keeps on sobbing.

Father bares his teeth. 'I should never have *indulged* you. I'm too kind, that's my problem. Too *soft.*'

This is how it starts. The first rumble of thunder that brings the storm.

'Well, I'm done being soft. YOU HEAR ME?' He swigs at his beer.

442

'I should never have rescued you. I should've left you with your stupid mother and your stupid father.' The smile is cold and cruel. 'That's right, you're not even my *real* son. Did you really think something as ugly and stupid as you could come from my cock? You're just some stupid kid I kept, because I thought it'd be a laugh. You're a joke, Justin.' Father sits forward and laughs in his face. 'That's not even your real name. You don't *deserve* a real name!'

Father drinks from his beer, then hurls the nearly full can at Justin. 'YOU'RE NOTHING BUT AN EMBARRASSMENT! A SNIVELLING, WORTHLESS, USELESS LITTLE BABY!'

Justin doesn't move as the beer soaks into his jumper.

'No wonder no one ever loved you.'

He does not move and he does not cry. Because crying only ever makes it worse. Doesn't matter how much the words hurt, the beating will hurt even more.

Father curls his lip, then spits on the carpet. 'Get out of my sight: you make me sick.'

Justin gets as far as the kitchen, before Father's voice bellows out from the living room again. 'AND GET ME ANOTHER BEER!'

Another beer.

He opens the fridge and does as he's told.

Father's spade leans against the wall, leaving little blobs of dirt on the floor.

It doesn't matter how much the words hurt. It *doesn't*.

It doesn't.

He's seven years old now, a big boy.

And Father's *wrong*. New Mummy loves him. She said so. She loves him, even if Father doesn't. Because he's a good boy.

'WHAT THE HELL IS TAKING YOU SO LONG?'

A good boy.

Justin goes to the kitchen drawer and pulls out the biggest sharpest knife that'll fit in his hand.

Then walks back into the living room.

The lightbulb flickers, making the basement shadows jump and dance as Justin creeps down the stairs.

He bites his bottom lip. Wipes his eyes on his sticky sleeve.

New Mummy is curled up on the floor by the bed, arms wrapped around her tummy, sobbing.

She's not the smiley pretty lady they picked up at the sweetie shop any more. The one who gave Justin sherbet lemons and sang a song about Santa and the Christmas Mice. The smiley pretty lady who laughed and skipped and smelled of sunshine.

Father's seen to that.

Her nose is twisted and bent, flakey with blood. Both eyes all swelled up and purple. Missing teeth like broken windows when she opens her mouth to wail out another scream. All those bruises. All that pain.

He stops in the middle of the basement. 'Mummy?'

Justin's hands are wet and sticky, his jumper hot where it clings to his arms.

She shrinks back against the wall. 'Please...' The word is all soft and mushy, because her lips are puffy and split.

'It's all right, Mummy. It's all right.' He spreads his sticky red hands so she won't be scared. 'Shh...'

Every finger on her left hand is pointing in a different direction, the joints all swollen and horrid. 'Please...'

He kneels in front of her, reaches out and strokes her hair.

She flinches back.

'It's all right. He can't hurt us now. He *can't.*' Justin's fingers leave dark smears on her yellow hair.

She squints at him with her puffy eyes. At his face, at his dirty hands, at all the blood on his jumper. 'What did ... you ... do?'

'He won't hurt anyone.'

Her battered eyes flick to the ceiling. Then widen. Then she stares at him. 'Let me go. Please. Please let me go unlock me let me go unlock me unlock me unlock me let me go!'

'I—'

'Let me go, let me go *now!*'

Justin nods. Then digs in his pocket and pulls out the little leather pouch he's not allowed to even look at, never mind touch. 'I've got Father's keys.'

'LET ME GO!'

'I'm doing it.' But his fingers are all red and slippy and the keys fall to the ground and he has to pick them up.

'Unlock me, unlock me, unlock me!'

He flicks through the keys, till he gets to a big brass Yale one. Slips it into the lock and twists. *Click.*

Justin grins at her. 'We can go away and we can be free and he'll never hit us again.'

New Mummy slumps forward, shrugging off the slithery chain.

Crawling away from the wall she's been fixed to for months and months. 'Oh God…'

'Come on, Mummy. You can do it.' He helps her to her knees, then up onto her feet. Only one of them doesn't work properly because there's a big lump on her right ankle and her foot's all dangly.

She hisses and groans every time she tries to stand on it.

So Justin takes as much of her weight as he can. A big brave boy as she hobbles and hops and cries and swears her way up the stairs. Slow and painful. Till they're standing in the hall.

Then New Mummy stops, her good hand against the wall, holding herself up, swollen eyes fixed on the open living-room door.

One of Father's legs pokes out from behind the door, trousers matted with dirt and blood. Not moving.

Justin reaches up to take her hand. 'I told you, he won't hurt us ever again.'

'Oh my God…'

'We can be *free*.'

'Where's the phone? There has to be a phone. *Where's the bloody phone?*'

He points at the living room and she hobbles forwards. Peers around the door.

'We can be free and we can live happily ever after, like in the stories!'

New Mummy limps inside.

The phone is on a little wooden table beside the television. All big and black and forbidden. She stumbles over and grabs the handset from its cradle. Works a shaky finger into the dial.

'We can get a nice house at the seaside and go for walks and eat ice-cream and get a dog! Can we get a dog, Mummy? Can we get a great big—'

The slap sends him crashing against the wallpaper. He leaves a dark red smear of Father's blood behind. Stands there, bottom lip trembling. 'Mummy?'

'I'M NOT YOUR MOTHER!' Little bits of spit land on Justin's cheeks.

'Mummy?'

'You helped him. YOU HELPED HIM KIDNAP ME!'

'But I was scared and—'

'You could've gone for help anytime, you could've called someone, YOU HELPED HIM!'

Justin shrinks back. 'But… But we're supposed to be *together*.'

'GET AWAY FROM ME!'

Justin bites his bottom lip. Blinks back the tears.

Doesn't matter how much the words hurt, the beating will hurt even more. Remember?

Only how could any beating hurt as much as this?

She goes back to the phone, sending the dial clicking around. Nine... Nine...

'Mummy?' He reaches for her. 'Mummy, I—'

'I SAID, GET AWAY FROM ME!' She shoves him away with her good hand, hard enough to send him tumbling across the bloodstained carpet.

The knife is right there. Right at his slippy-sticky red fingertips.

Justin picks it up.

The sun peeks over the hills, turning the sky to blood.

The birds are singing, making sure everyone knows they're awake and ready to do whatever it is birds do.

Sweat drips off the end of Justin's nose as he heaves another shovel of soil into the hole.

It took a long time, dragging New Mummy out to the garden and into the hole Father dug for her. Then shovelling in some earth. Then hauling Father out and dumping him in there too. Then more dirt, till the hole is full up to the top again.

Probably should've dug another hole for Father. New Mummy wouldn't like him sleeping on top of her for ever and ever. And maybe if she'd *loved* Justin, he'd have dug a new one for Father and she could've been all alone in the ground. But she didn't. So he hadn't.

If she'd loved him, they could've had a house by the seaside and a doggie and ice-cream and everything would be nice and happy and they'd sing songs and walk on the beach...

But she didn't.

He wipes his soggy face on his dirty jumper.

Father's lawn is all scuffed and flattened, with nasty red scrapes from here to the kitchen door. He'd have hated that.

And now Justin is all alone.

So in the end, nobody gets what they wanted.

He leaves the spade and trudges back into the house. Locks the kitchen door behind him. Tomorrow he'll have to decide what to do, but for now he's going to curl up in the Naughty Cupboard and sleep and sleep and sleep.

It's been a busy day.

63

Callum jumped back into the car. 'Nothing doing.'

Franklin scored address number seventeen off the list. 'Three more to go.'

'Two thirty-six Banks Road. Next right, then on to the roundabout and left.' It was the same in every direction: bland grey houses for bland grey people living bland grey lives. Callum let out a sigh. Checked the list again. 'Fancy some music, or something?'

'Yeah, OK.'

They both reached for the knob at the same time: their fingers touching. Then flinching back as if they'd been burned.

'Sorry.'

'No, it was me.' Franklin's cheeks darkened.

Callum cleared his throat. Buzzed his window down a crack. Definitely getting hot in here. 'Do you want me to...?'

'I don't mind.'

'Cos we don't have to, if you...?'

'Yes. It's OK.' She kept her eyes fixed on the road.

'Right.' He reached out and clicked the radio on, getting a raucous banjo-and-bagpipe rendition of Pink Floyd's 'Wish You Were Here' in return.

More grey houses went by.

The rain rained.

Franklin made a noise.

'Did you say something?'

'No. I was just ... humming along.'

'Right. Yes.'

And then Callum's phone went off.

447

Oh thank God.

He pulled it out. 'Hello?'

It was Mother: *'Please tell me you've got good news.'*

'Sorry. SEB are hammering six Creel Lane now, but going by the brining tank, Monaghan hadn't been there for months. Maybe years.'

'Damn it.' A clicking noise, like someone drumming their nails on a desk. *'Ashlee Gossard's going to be dead by the time we find her, isn't she?'*

Of course she was. She was probably dead already. 'There's still houses to search.'

'Gah...' A sigh.

'You OK?'

The street gave way to tiny detached houses with steep slate roofs, like a model village for gnomes. A miserable couple wheeled a pushchair through the rain. A bus sat at a bus stop: its driver had an OAP in a headlock, struggling with her in the gutter as the passengers looked on, cheering.

'Anyway, there's some good news: Gareth Pike has had a chance to think about the error of his ways, and he's decided to identify the man he saw abducting your family. Isn't that public spirited of him?'

A fire burst into life, right in the middle of Callum's chest. 'Who was it?'

'He won't say till I promise he's definitely going to prison.'

'So talk to the Sheriff again! Tell him Pike—'

'Callum, Callum, Callum... Pike's a paedophile, you caught him with a horrible video and got a confession. There's no way he was ever not going to prison. Do you really think we'd let him walk free?'

'But you had a thing from the Sheriff, at the prison, I saw—'

'No, that was just a parking ticket. Should probably get round to paying that...'

More Noddy Toy-Town houses, then a community centre.

'So...?'

'None of the other teams have found anything, by the way. Andy's running round like a mad thing – which is definitely *not good for him – Dotty's sulking, and God knows where John's got to. Honestly, some days it's like trying to get an angry ginger tom into a pair of Lycra cycling shorts.'*

'What about Gareth Pike?'

Franklin took a left at the roundabout, heading up towards the railway bridge. 'Where now?'

'Make a right, after the postbox.' Back to the phone. 'Boss?'

'I'm sorry, Callum, but Gareth Pike will have to wait till we've done all we can for Ashlee Gossard. And don't moan and whinge: you know as well as I do.'

He curled forward until the seatbelt cut across his chest. 'We need to get it out of him tonight. Soon as he finds out he's got what he wants – that he's going to prison anyway – he'll keep his mouth shut just to spite me. This is *fun* for him.'

'We'll get him, Callum. I promise. Now you get out there and you do your best. There's a scared little girl hidden away somewhere, dying. Find her.'

The little old lady frowned out the back door as Franklin disappeared into the shed at the bottom of the garden. 'Are you sure she's all right in there? Unsupervised?'

'It's just procedure, ma'am.' Callum stayed where he was, huddled inside the porch, out of the rain. 'And you're sure you haven't seen either of these women?' He held up the photos of Ashlee and her mum again.

'Only, you know what these *coloured* people are like. It's always them in those London riots, isn't it? And shooting people.'

It took a lot of effort, but Callum managed a smile. 'I can assure you, Detective Constable Franklin isn't like that. And the majority of rioters were white, by the way.'

'What if she steals my lawnmower?' A sniff. 'And they're so *touchy* these days, aren't they?'

'You can't say anything or it's a "hate crime".'

'She's *not* going to steal your lawnmower.'

'When I was a wee girl they were called "nig-nogs" and no one ever complained. If you ask me, that Enoch Powell had the right idea.'

He stared at her. 'Yes. Well. These are more civilised times, aren't they? We don't just *accept* casual racism. And we *don't* call people "nig-nogs"!'

Callum fingered the tin of pepper spray in his jacket pocket.

We do not live in a police state. We do not live in a police state…

'Should send them all back where they came from.'

He pointed. 'She's from *Glasgow*.'

A nod. 'There you are then.' As if that ended the argument.

Franklin emerged from the shed and it didn't look as if she'd stuck the old cow's lawnmower under her jacket to make a clean getaway. Instead, she shook her head, brushing cobwebs from her jacket as she marched up the path to the back door. 'Thank you for your cooperation.'

Mrs Enoch Powell smiled at her. 'Not a problem, dearie. I'm only too glad to help.' She followed them through the kitchen, down the hall, and out the front door. Keeping both eyes fixed on Franklin. 'Mind how you go now.'

Callum sank into the passenger seat and clicked on his seatbelt. 'And that's us.' He drew a red line through their final address.

'So what's next?' Franklin pulled away from the kerb, heading back towards the town centre.

The little old racist stood on her front step, watching as they drove away. Probably expecting Franklin to pull a handbrake turn and steal everyone's lawn ornaments.

'Chase up the Land Registry Office?'

'Worth a go.' He took out his phone and called control. 'Brucie? Callum. I need you to light a fire under the Land Registry Office. Tell them there's a little girl's life on the line here.'

'Your usual slave's got a day off, has he?'

'Don't be a dick, Brucie. You know it'll sound better coming from you. More official.'

'Aye, right.' A sigh. *'I'll give them a shoogle.'*

'Thanks, Brucie, you're a star.' He hung up. Tapped the phone against his chin. 'There's nothing else we can do for Ashlee right now, is there?'

Franklin shrugged. 'Not till the Registry gets back to us.'

'Exactly.' He called Mother as the housing estate gave way to a short line of shops. 'We're nought for twenty-one. Anyone else?'

'I should be so lucky.'

A voice in the background sounded like McAdams: *'Watt, I'm not kidding about here: call me back soon as you get this!'*

'Trouble in paradise?'

'None of the other teams found anything. Not so much as a smoked sausage.'

McAdams got louder: *'I trusted you, you wee shite. I thought we had an understanding!'*

The windscreen wipers squeaked and squonked their way back and forth. The gutters were overflowing at the bottom of the hill, making a loch that stretched all the way across the road and about twenty foot long.

'We're heading back to the shop now.'

Mother groaned. *'I think we've blown this one, Callum.'*

'Where the hell are you?'

'It was always going to be a long shot.'

'I know, I know. We—'

'When I get my hands on you, Watt, I swear on my oncologist's grave I'm going to—'

'Andy! For goodness' sake: enough.'

Franklin slowed for the water feature, sending arcs of dirty grey splashing up and out.

There was silence from the phone, then a sniff from McAdams. 'Fine. Call me back, Watt.'

'And don't look at me like that, you know it's not good for your blood pressure.'

Callum cleared his throat. 'Boss? You know you said we had to do everything we could for Ashlee Gossard…?'

Her voice was flat as an ironing board. 'You want to talk to Gareth Pike.'

'Only, we've been through our list, we've got a request in with the Land Registry Office, and there's nothing else we can actually do right now.'

'Callum, I've got half a dozen of DCI Powel's cases sitting here on my desk, just waiting for someone to—'

'Boss, please. I need to know.'

A sigh. 'All right. But if something comes up—'

'Not a problem. You shout and we'll come running.'

And with any luck, by then they'd be one step closer to catching his mother's killer.

The interview room was every bit as depressing as last time. Callum sat at the table, left leg twitching and jumping away to itself, waiting.

Franklin checked her watch. 'What's taking so long?'

'He'll be dragging it out as long as he can. He's lost, and he knows it. Keeping us waiting is the only way he can exert power.'

'Hrmmm…' She paced to the fake rubber plant and back again. 'Even if he gives you a name, there's no guarantees. A lot can happen in twenty-six years.'

'Will you sit down? You're making me itchy.'

'And what if he's just messing with your head, did you think of that? Maybe he didn't see anything at all, and this is just him playing games.'

'I'm not kidding, sit your backside down and…' Callum sat up straight as the door swung open and the little man in the ugly jumper came back in.

'Now, I know you were here yesterday, Detective Constable MacGregor, but this bit is like the safety announcement on aeroplanes: we have to do it.' Duncan took a deep breath. 'You're not to give the inmate anything, and you're not to take anything *from* him. That includes messages to, and from, the outside world. You're not to let him use your mobile phones. We disapprove of physical contact. And a staff member will be present at all times. OK?'

'OK.'

'OK.' A smile. 'Now, please make sure your seats and tray-tables are in the upright position.' He poked his head back out into the corridor. 'All right, Rachael, bring him in.'

And there was Gareth Pike again, ducking to get in through the door, lowering himself into the seat opposite like a shaved bear. Sitting with his shoulders forward and his back hunched. Lights reflected in his bald head. His mouth turned down at the edges, as if he'd just swallowed something nasty. 'Before we begin this exercise in completely unfair manipulation, I want it made clear that I am only providing this information under the most terrible duress.'

Callum reached into his pocket and produced a sheet of folded paper. Laid it on the table between them. 'You're looking well, Gareth. Have you been polishing your head?'

'Furthermore, I must protest in the strongest terms about being kept waiting for so long. I'm not a well man and the stress is harmful to my conditions.'

'You have a name for me.'

The mouth turned down even further. 'I want assurances that I will not be given a *community service order*.' A small shudder set his jowls wobbling. 'Like some sort of track-suited youth caught shoplifting from Lidl. I will be placed in a suitable residential facility designed to cater for people with my proclivities.'

Callum tapped the piece of paper. 'Things have changed a bit, Gareth. We've found another witness. You're nothing but corroboration now.'

'And I want a south-facing cell.'

'Nope.' He put the sheet back in his pocket and stood. 'Have fun cleaning out those cages. I bet the dogs and cats make one hell of a mess.'

Pike glared up at him.

'Last chance.'

He bared his teeth. 'You're enjoying this, aren't you? After all this time, being the one with the power. No more the scared little boy, cowering in his daddy's caravan, sobbing like a baby and wetting himself.'

'Bye, Gareth.' Callum turned to Franklin. 'Shall we?'

'All right! All right.' Pike balled his chubby hands into two enormous fists. 'I recognised the man who took your parents and brother. He was … I suppose in some circles he probably still is, famous. He's certainly in all the papers right now.'

Callum gave a big theatrical sigh. 'Come on then, Gareth: tell me who you saw and I guarantee you'll go to prison. No point kicking a man when he's down. Even a piss-poor excuse for one, like you.'

'I told you he was a lion, didn't I? That big blond mane of hair, the strut and swagger. A man used to being worshipped and adored.'

Franklin curled her lip. 'Stop milking it.'

Pink flooded Pike's cheeks. 'His name's Leo McVey.'

'No.' She stared. 'Wait, the rock star? *The* Leo McVey? Leo McVey abducted his parents?'

Pike's eyes widened. 'I know, isn't it delicious?'

64

'*Wow...*' Mother made a hissing noise. '*Leo McVey? The Leo McVey?*'

Callum tightened his grip on the phone. 'That's what Pike said. Said he attacked them with a length of metal pipe and forced them into the boot of his Range Rover.'

'*Wow...*'

'Can you stop saying that? It's not like this is a claim to fame, here.'

Franklin took them over the Dundas Bridge, windscreen wipers on full pelt. The cars coming the other way populated by hunched men and women, their faces soured by rain.

'*I'm sorry, it's just: Leo McVey. I had all his albums.*'

Right at the roundabout, following the river, picking up a bit of speed for a change.

'Of course, we've only got Pike's word for it.'

'*So what's your plan, Callum? The Sheriff won't give you a warrant on the word of one paedophile, and after twenty-six years...*'

'We're going to go see him.'

'*Leo McVey?*'

'One good thing about this music festival: we know where he'll be right now.' Getting ready to ponce about on stage with all his new showbiz mates. 'Franklin and me are on our way there now.'

'*I see...*' Her voice sagged a bit. '*Callum, this really isn't a good idea. You're too closely connected, you're upset, you're—*'

'Pike *saw* him.'

Silence.

A golf course drifted by on the right, trapped between the road and where the River Wynd emptied into Kings River. The fairway was more or less a lake now, punctuated with bunkers and the occasional flag.

'Boss?'

A sigh, then: *'Put me on speaker.'*

He did and her voice crackled out into the car.

'Rosalind? I'm relying on you to keep this under control. You don't leave Callum alone with Leo McVey. You don't let him say or do anything stupid. And most *importantly, you don't get me hauled up in front of the PIRC! Agreed?'*

Franklin nodded. 'We'll tread lightly.'

'Make sure you do. If there's one thing the seventies taught us, it's: celebrities sue. Even when they're guilty.'

'Yes, Boss.'

The man at the Portakabin door curled his top lip and stared down at Callum. 'You're kiddin', yeah?' He had to be at least six-five, with a crewcut, black bomber jacket, black jeans and Doc Martens. 'HATE' tattooed on one massive set of knuckles, and 'MUM' tattooed between the other.

A line of metal barriers sealed off this chunk of Montgomery Park from the rest of it, covered walkways keeping the important people's feet out of the shoe-sucking mud and their trendy haircuts out of the rain. Two lines of yurts and tepees were broken up by fancy-looking portable loos and outside-broadcast vans. A marquee with plastic windows was laid out as a fancypants dining room: tablecloths, waiters in black tie, and a real-life chandelier.

But *this* side of the barricade, the park was a litter-strewn swamp, full of muddy people in ponchos, bouncing up and down to whatever band was currently on stage and belting folk-rock out through the PA system.

And above them all, that *massive* inflatable tartan tarantula waved its legs in the rain.

None of which seemed to register on the big lump in the bomber jacket. 'You're not gettin' in. Now hop it.'

Callum checked his warrant card, then held it out to Franklin. 'Does this look like it came free in a box of Rice Krispies?'

She folded her arms, eyeing King Kong up and down. 'Are you interfering with a murder investigation, sir?'

He stuck out his chest. 'You're not on the list: you're *not* comin' in.'

'I'll tell you what's on the—'

'Hello, can I help you?' A trendy-looking specimen with sideburns and a quiff sidled up, clipboard under one arm, three or four lanyards

455

dangling around his neck. Call-centre headpiece cramping his haircut.

King Kong jerked a thumb at Callum. 'This one here thinks he can waltz in, just cos he's a cop.'

'I see. Right. Thanks, Charles, I'll take it from here.' Mr Clipboard clasped it to his chest. 'Now, how can I help?'

'We're here to see Leo McVey.'

'Ah... I'm afraid that's impossible. You see Mr McVey's on the main stage in just a little under thirty minutes. Twenty-seven minutes thirty-nine seconds, to be precise. And he's getting ready in the green room.'

'This won't take long.'

'Yes...' The plastic smile got a bit more stretched. 'Only he's the closing headline act of the whole festival, and we'd rather like him to be at his best when he walks out there to entertain twenty-six *thousand* people. Not to mention everyone listening at home, and anyone who buys the CD or DVD. So you see...?' A shrug.

'I didn't get your name, sir.'

Franklin reached out and took hold of one of the lanyards. 'Ryan Keen.'

'I see. Yes. Actually, it's *very much* not a good time and—'

'Have you ever seen the inside of a police cell, Mr Keen?'

He licked his lips. 'Ah...'

Mr Not So Keen stopped outside the door to an oversized yurt – like a cake made of brightly coloured canvas, topped with a big pointy hat. 'Now, *please* tell me you're A: not going to upset him and B: not going to make him late.'

Franklin put her hand on Keen's shoulder and eased him to one side. 'Thank you for your cooperation.' Then she opened the door and disappeared inside.

Keen fidgeted with his clipboard. 'I'm going to get fired...'

Callum followed her into the cake.

Inside, the sweet-sweaty scent of incense mingled with orange and apple. Oriental rugs overlapped across the floor, and a row of fairy lights twinkled their way around the outside of the large open space. Leather sofas were artfully arranged, with standard lamps casting little golden pools of illumination in the luxuriant gloom.

A woman in full-on French maid costume stood just inside, with a tray of bubbling champagne flutes.

Clearly, people took a lot better care of musicians than they did police officers.

Franklin flashed her warrant card. 'Where's Leo McVey?'

That got them a fixed death grin. 'Mr McVey's in the Absinthe zone.' She pointed at a small tunnel through the yurt wall. 'He's communing.'

'Good for him.' Callum marched over and through the tunnel, coming out in a separate domed expanse. Only this one was lined in pale green, with beanbags instead of leather sofas.

About two dozen people were gathered around a coffee table covered in mugs and glasses – some on the floor, some on the beanbags, others leaning back against the yurt walls. All of them beaming at an old man, as if he were the second coming.

Leo McVey looked just like he had on *Breakfast News*, Friday morning: tasselled jeans, cowboy boots, dark-blue shirt, leather buckles on his wrists. He leaned forwards. 'So there we are: Mick, David, Noddy, Lemmy, Ozzy, Alice, and me in the hot tub, and the only one with any clothes on is Mick.' He winked at them. 'That's Jagger, not Hucknall. And I have to admit I'd done *quite* a lot of acid at this point, so when Mick says—'

'Leo McVey, Police.' Callum held up his warrant card. 'We need to talk.'

McVey's smile grew. 'Not quite, but you're close, officer…?'

'MacGregor. Now, let's—'

'Hey, cop!' One of the acolytes stood, right shoulder forward, the other drooped, leather jacket hanging open to show off a shaved chest and a fox tattoo sticking out of the waistband of his underpants where *they* stuck out of the waistband of his baggy jeans. A golden dollar sign dangled around his neck on a shiny chain. Elaborate moustache and goatee decorating his chin. Both hands circled gangsta signs, pumping himself up with every word: 'You better stop, cos this man rocks, / And you pair of cocks better hit the bookshops, / And learn some respect, cos you incorrect, / I checked, and he ain't no goddamned suspect.'

A *very* large black man in a blue tracksuit nodded. An American accent so thick you'd need a chainsaw to cut it. 'Word.'

Franklin put one hand in her pocket – the one she usually produced her collapsible baton from, like a very violent magic trick. 'I'm going to need you to sit down, sir.'

Gangsta Boy gave her a good hard leer. 'Damn, bitch, you be *fine!*'

'Word.'

She narrowed her eyes. 'What did you just call me?'

He limp-swaggered closer. 'Bitch, you *know* I like my women like I like my coffee: strong, sweet, and black.'

457

'Heh, heh, heh. Word.'

'I'll give you strong, you pasty—'

'Ladies, gentlemen: chill, yeah?' McVey stood, both hands out as if he was about to bless them all. 'Donny, it's OK. I got nothing to hide from these nice police officers. I've not packed a stash since the noughties.'

But Donny just stood there, with his hairless chest puffed out. 'You sure, Leo, cos I can open up a can of righteous deliverance on these sons-a-bitches. Say the word and they *gone*.'

Another nod from the massive sidekick. 'Word.'

'You're very kind, but I'll be fine.' McVey smiled. 'Now, officers, any chance we can get this over with? I'm on in twenty minutes, and my bladder's not as young as it used to be.' He threw his apostles a peace sign. 'Chill here, guys. When I get back we're going to rock this city's socks off!'

They gave him a round of applause and some whoops.

Then Keen took McVey by the elbow and led him out into the main yurt, nearly bent double under the weight of his own obsequiousness. 'I'm sorry about this, Mr McVey. They assure me it won't take more than a couple of minutes. We'll get you out on that stage bang on time, don't you worry. You're going to be magnificent.'

'It's cool.' McVey wandered over to the hospitality table and helped himself to a bottle of beer from the fridge. Cracked it open. Then pointed at a door, hidden away in an alcove. 'Shall we?'

Callum followed him onto a section of decking set out with deckchairs and tables, beneath an awning covered in sponsors' logos.

McVey took a swig and settled his elbows on the railing. 'Amazing, isn't it?' Toasting the view with his bottle.

From here, the park sloped away towards the main stage – a big tessellated hemisphere surrounded by lights and speakers, flanked by a pair of screens three storeys high. Some sort of folk band were on the stage, leaping about and trying to get the crowd to join in.

There were thousands and thousands and *thousands* of them. All jammed together, waving flags, waving their mobile phones, waving their arms, apparently not minding the fact it'd been bucketing with rain for about a week and they were up to their welly-tops in sticky black mud.

Callum looked over his shoulder.

Franklin lurked nearby, her notebook out and pen at the ready. No sign of Mr Keen or his clipboard.

'So, who was Captain Bare Chest, back there?'

'Donny? He's great, isn't he?' McVey laughed and shook his head. 'Looks like he's barely into his twenties: turned thirty last year. Suppose healthy living and Botox will do that for a man. Well, that and a face-lift, a nose job, and three hours a day with a personal trainer.' Another swig of beer. 'But you didn't come here to talk about Donny Sick Dawg McRoberts.'

AKA: Donald Newman. Willow's dad. The man driving the black Mercedes. The 'man' who broke a little girl's arm. The *man* who beat his ex-girlfriend and stole her sodding teddy bear.

The man in serious need of a stiff bloody kicking.

But not quite yet.

Callum reached into his jacket and pulled out his father's wallet. Flipped it open. 'Twenty-six years ago, there was a family of four, just back from a fortnight in Lossiemouth.'

'And?'

'There's a lay-by on the Aberdeen road, just outside Blackwall hill.'

'Still listening, still not understanding.'

'They were attacked, Mr McVey. Mother, father, and a five-year-old boy were abducted. Never seen again.'

He shook his head. Took another swig of beer. 'Life can be pretty horrible, can't it?'

'Where were you on Wednesday evening, Thursday morning?'

'This week, or twenty-six years ago?' A shrug. 'Because if it was this week, I was in Brussels with the band. We've not toured in about fifteen years, got the feeling we'd be a bit rusty, so off we lurched to the conti-nent to get our swagger back.' He counted them off on his fingers: 'Hamburg, Friday. Berlin, Saturday. Dusseldorf, Sunday. Amsterdam, Monday. Rotterdam, Tuesday. Brussels, Wednesday. Cologne, Thursday. And back to Dear Old Blighty on Friday, cos I was on *Breakfast News*.'

'And you can prove this, can you?'

McVey laughed. Shook his head. 'Take a look online. There's got to be ten thousand photos of us all over the whatchamacallit: social media. Honestly, nobody actually watches a gig these days – they just stand there filming it on their mobile phones. In my day it was autographs, now everyone wants a selfie.'

'And what about the sixth of April, twenty-six years ago?'

This time he drained his beer. 'Spent most of that decade off my tits on various mind-expanding chemicals. How am I supposed to remember one day?'

459

'Because you were seen, Mr McVey. At the lay-by. You were seen assaulting the husband and wife with an iron bar. You were seen gagging them and tying them up with duct tape. You were seen loading them into the back of your Range Rover. You were seen abducting the young boy.'

'Doesn't sound like me.'

'You were *seen*.'

'Nah.' McVey pitched his empty bottle, overhand, into a recycling bin eight feet away. 'Ten points.' He stuck his hands in his pockets. 'Because I wasn't there. I didn't attack anyone. And this conversation is like Glam Rock: ridiculous and over.'

Callum stepped right in front of him. 'It's over when I say it is.'

'See, if you actually had anything on me, we'd be doing this down the station, wouldn't we? You're grasping handfuls of cloud and praying they're a parachute.' He raised his voice. 'Mr Keen, ready when you are!'

Shout and the creep will appear. Keen slithered onto the decking, holding his clipboard like a life vest. 'Mr McVey. That's great. I've got the car waiting; we're all set to wheech you over to the main stage.' He checked his watch. 'Don't want to keep your fans waiting...'

McVey turned and patted Callum on the shoulder. 'It's been fun. But if you want to do it again, better get a warrant.' He sauntered off, pausing only to wink at Franklin on the way past. 'Later, beautiful.'

'Mr McVey.' Was she blushing? She was. Unbelievable.

'Call me Leo.' He circled back, took her hand and kissed it. Then turned a wink on Callum too. 'And I never owned a Range Rover. A lot of my circle did, but I was always a Jag man. You got me confused with someone else.'

'Who?'

'Please, Mr McVey, we need to get you over to the main stage, so if we could just...?' Keen pointed at the door.

McVey put one hand against his chest, as if he was about to pledge allegiance to something, or stifling a burp. '"Isn't my kingdom wonderful?" asked the Bonemonger. "All these graves and mausoleums and charnel pits, just waiting for someone to wake up their slumbering guests."' He performed a little bow, then followed Keen out the door and away.

Franklin took a deep breath. Flexed her kissed hand like the fingers were brand new. 'I'm not sure how I feel about that.'

'Just because he's got an alibi for dumping my mother's head in Holburn Forest, doesn't mean he didn't abduct them twenty-six years ago.'

'I mean, eighteen-year-old me wants to never wash this hand again. Feminist grown-up police-officer me wants to rinse it in boiling bleach.'

'And what was that bit at the end supposed to mean?'

'Maybe Pike was lying all this time? He knew he was going to prison anyway, so he's just causing as much trouble as possible. Maybe he didn't see anything at all?'

'He said "the Bonemonger", so it's from *Open the Coffins*. But...' Callum chewed on the inside of his cheek. 'I don't know.'

'Still don't know what to do about my hand.'

'Wash it. *Definitely* wash it.' Callum pushed through the door and back into the yurt.

McVey was gone, but most of his acolytes were still there – probably waiting their turn in the car to the main stage.

And right there, in the middle, was Donald Newman, AKA: Donny McRoberts, holding court. 'Oh yeah, me and Leo: we go back years, innit? See when I was growing up in a home? He visited me, like *every* week.' Preening himself. 'That's how come I got him to duet on my very first album. Man's a star, right? Been like a dad to me.'

Leo McVey might have waltzed right out of here smiling, but this sack of vomit wouldn't.

Callum pulled out his warrant card again. 'Donald Newman.'

Newman's face pulled itself to one side, like he was about to spit bile. 'I don't know you, pig, but you better not call me that again. The name's Sick Dawg, yeah? Show some reeeeeee-spect.'

His sidekick folded his thick fat arms. 'Word.'

'You visited a Miss Irene Brown two nights ago, didn't you, Donald? In the black Mercedes your record company pays for.'

'Free country, innit?'

'You're a big man, surrounded by your mates. Think they'd still be your mates if they knew you beat up your ex on Friday night?'

Newman sneered. 'You can blow your lies out your arsehole, Piggy. Ain't nobody here buyin' what you sellin'.'

'You broke your daughter's arm three years ago, didn't you? She was four years old. What was that, a flying visit to abuse her between gigs?'

The sneer became a snarl and Newman lunged forwards, chest out, shoulders back. 'You wanna piece of this *action*? / Man I'm-a put you in *traction!* / Get my satisfaction from a violent reaction! / My fist and yo face gonna have *interaction*, / I'm-a beat you down *dead*, you don't swear a retraction!'

His sidekick stepped up beside him. 'Word.'

Franklin looked the guy up and down: the tracksuit, the heavy gold jewellery, the backwards baseball cap, the sunglasses. 'Nice. Play up to the thick black gang-banger stereotype, why don't you?'

That got her a laugh that set most of him wobbling. 'Hey, bitch, don't you be judging *me*, / Big Bobby B's got a master's degree, / I came top of ma class at M.I.T., / And they taught me for free, on a scholarship, see?'

Newman gave him a fist bump. 'Word.' He jerked his head towards the door. 'Better scram, pig, before I snap you in two.' Then pumped his chest at Franklin. 'Bitch, you can stay. I'm-a make an exception for your *fine* ass. Show you what a real man can do to it.' He took a handful of her backside, just to make sure she understood.

Ooh... Not a good idea.

Callum cleared his throat. 'Maybe you shouldn't—'

One second, Newman was standing there, posing, the next he was facedown on the Persian rugs, with his groping hand twisted up behind his back. 'AAAAAAARGH!'

Franklin leaned in and bared her teeth. 'Donald Newman, I'm detaining you under Section Fourteen of the Criminal Justice Scotland Act because I believe you've committed a crime punishable by imprisonment: namely making death threats to one police officer and the sexual assault of another officer.'

'GETOFFMEGETOFFMEGETOFFME!'

'You do not have to say anything, but if you do not mention something you later rely on in court it may harm your defence.'

His sidekick took a step forwards, but Callum got in the way. 'I don't think we got your full name, sir.'

Big Bobby B licked his lips. 'I'm cool.'

'BOBBY, HELP ME! GET THIS BITCH OFF ME!'

'You were there on Friday night, weren't you? When Mr Newman allegedly assaulted Miss Irene Brown. Witnesses saw you enter the premises.'

'Ah... Yeah. About that. I didn't have nothin' to do with beatin' on no woman.'

'BOBBY!'

'Are you *sure*?'

He nodded, setting off a Mexican wave of fat. 'Totally! That was all Donny. I was like—'

'YOU DIRTY TWO-FACED FAT BASTARD! YOU SUPPOSED TO BE MY NIGGA!'

'Hey, suck my balls, Holmes.' He turned and spread his hands. 'I was like, "Man you gotta *stop* hittin' that poor girl!" and he was like, "No way, this bitch gotta learn her some respect."'

The circle of acolytes backed off a couple of paces. Staring down at Newman as if he was a stain someone had trodden into the carpet.

'BOBBY!'

'Did he now? And what happened to the teddy bear he took from Miss Brown?'

'BOBBY, DON'T YOU DARE!'

'He got his stash hidden inside that poor girl's bear right now. Inna dressing room.'

'I'M-A KILL YOU, BOBBY! YOU HEAR ME? YOU DEAD, BITCH!'

Franklin twisted his arm a little further till the screaming faded to a tiny high-pitched whimper. She produced her handcuffs. 'Threats to kill, sexual assault, actual bodily harm, theft, and possession of a controlled substance. Not your day, is it, Donald?'

The yurt door swung open and Keen oiled his way in. 'Everyone, can I have act-one bands together, please? The car's...' His mouth fell open as he stared at Franklin and Newman. 'What... No... This...'

Callum patted him on the back. 'Looks like you'll have to get someone to fill in for Sick Dawg. He has to go take his medicine.'

65

Open the Coffins belted out of the festival's PA system – Leo McVey growling out the opening song about how boring life was in the village, and how sweet the apples growing over the well looked.

'I can't believe you said that.' Franklin thumped the car door closed and curled her lip across the roof at Callum. '"Sick Dawg has to go take his medicine." Genuinely?'

'Arya, it's just not fair; We're starving and nobody cares...'

'Oh come on, that was a classic action-film one-liner.'

'It was cheesy rubbish.'

'The bones protrude beneath our skin, / Oh, Arya, it's sickening...'

'Exactly.' He slipped into the passenger seat, turned and smiled. 'So, Donald. Any other offences you'd like us to take into consideration?' He held up the evidence bag with Mr Lumpylump in it. The threadbare bear looked a lot fatter than it had back at Irene Brown's house. Clearly the amphetamines-and-cocaine diet wasn't working. 'Or do you expect us to believe that this is it?'

'Above the well, so plump and sweet, the apples grow, / And it's not fair that we're both starving, here below...'

A scowl from the backseat. Newman was hunched forward against his seatbelt, both hands cuffed behind him.

'Nothing to say for yourself?'

'You recognise me, Piggy? You know who I am?'

'Ooh, and there it is: "Don't you know who I am."' Callum grinned. 'Trust me, Donald, if you have to ask that question, you're not going to like the answer.'

'Kiss my ass, Piggy.' He sat back. 'And I ain't sayin' another goddamn word till I get me my lawyer.'

'Probably just as well. You'd only say something stupid and make it worse for yourself.'

'The witch awakes inside the well, she's getting thinner, / She hears the children up above and dreams of dinner...'

Franklin started the car, easing them out of the 'FESTIVAL STAFF AND PERFORMERS ONLY!' car park.

'You don't know me, *Piggy*. You don't get to *judge* me.'

'No, but we *do* get to arrest you, and that's almost as much fun.' He tapped Franklin on the shoulder. 'Take a left here: cut through Blackwall Hill, miss out most of the roadworks.'

'Hey, you think it's easy? All them people worshippin' you, and kissin' yo ass, and you gotta get up there and, like, *perform*, man. Don't matter how crap you feel, you gotta make that goddamn stage come alive.'

'You broke a little girl's arm.'

'I grew up in a care home, Piggy. I got pain you ain't even heard of.'

The junction took them out on a road lined with shops.

'She was four years old.'

'I got beat every day I was growin' up, that leaves scars on yo *soul*, yeah? You wanna see some emotional scars?' He shoogled in his seat, struggling against the seatbelt. Then used his cuffed hands to raise the hem of his leather jacket. A patch of buckled skin, veined through with pale shiny bits, sat in the small of his back, about the size of a dinner plate. 'Bitch ran the place didn't like the way I washed the dishes, so she throws a pot of boiling tatties at me. I was seven.'

'Oh you grew up in care. Boo-hoo. We *all* grew up in care.'

Franklin shook her head. 'I didn't. My mum was a doctor and my dad worked for BBC Scotland.'

'All right for some.'

'Yo: bitch.' Newman was round the right way again. 'You dislocated my shoulder. Like it rough, do you? Like a bit of angry between your legs? That make you nice and moist?'

She glanced at him in the rear-view mirror, voice like a razorblade. 'Do you want me to stop the car? Because I will.'

Donald Newman licked his lips. Then shrank back in his seat. 'Nah, I'm good.'

'Yeah, I thought not.'

'Officer Franklin!' A grin spread across Callum's face. 'Stop flirting with the prisoner. You're—' His phone burst into song in his pocket and he pulled it out. 'Hello?'

'Callum.' Mother. Silence.

OK...

At the end of the street, Franklin took the main road West. Montgomery Park shrank and disappeared behind them, until only the huge inflatable spider crawled above the rooftops.

'Boss? Are you still there?'

'I need to ask where you were Friday night between nine p.m. and three a.m.'

'What? Why?'

'Callum, please. Just answer the question.'

'Hold on.' He dug out his notebook and flicked through it to the right day. 'Nine-ish we were doing door-to-doors on Bellfield Road – we'd just searched Tod Monaghan's flat and found the mummified body? Then we went back to the station and did paperwork. Then we went to the Bart for a celebratory drink. Then I got a call from an informant and arrested Gareth Pike in Kingsmeath.'

'What time?'

'Stopped interviewing him about half eleven? Then I went round to the flat and collected my stuff. Then quarter past midnight I got a call and went to a domestic on Manson Avenue. Franklin and I have just made an arrest on that one, it—'

'And was DCI Reece Powel at your flat when you collected your belongings?'

Callum frowned out of the window. Blackwall Hill sloped down towards the river in a patchwork of houses and small parks. All of it grey and miserable in the rain. 'What's all this about?'

'Was Reece there?'

'Well, yes, of course he was. Don't think they'd trust me there on my own, do you? I might have taken a crap on the carpet and spray-painted a few home truths on the walls. Now, what the hell is going on?'

'Callum, DCI Powel was found in Camburn Woods an hour ago. Someone tried to kill him; he's in surgery now.'

Oh.

The breath curdled in Callum's lungs. 'And you think, what, that *I* did it?'

'I need you to come back to headquarters, Constable MacGregor. I need you to come back right now.'

Chief Inspector Gilmore sat back in his seat and peered over the top of his evil-scientist glasses. 'I see. Yes.'

Sitting in the other chair, Mother just shook her head.

Some idiot had turned the interview room radiators up full, making sweat prickle between Callum's shoulder blades. He glanced up at the camera's dead black eye. Then down again. 'Of course it wasn't me! Why would I do something like …' he pointed at the photograph sitting on the scarred Formica tabletop, '*that*.'

DCI Powel lay sprawled on his back, in some undergrowth. Bushes behind him, the roots of a large tree to his left. His face was a mess of scarlet and purple: lumpen, swollen, and misshapen. More bruises on his arms, hands, and wrists where they poked out of his T-shirt. The same Rolling Stones one he'd been wearing that night in the flat, only now the graphic was smeared with blood. His never-been-worn-white trainers, filthy and scuffed.

Gilmore took off his glasses, huffed on them, then polished them with a hanky. 'Do you need me to list the reasons, Callum?'

Mother put another photo on the table, next to the first. A head-and-shoulders portrait of Powel, lying on a hospital trolley. Up close, the damage was even worse. It looked as if someone had driven over his head. Repeatedly.

'It wasn't me!'

'Your girlfriend was cheating on you with Reece Powel, he got her pregnant, you were paying for everything because you thought the child was yours. He told you about the affair the same day you learned that your mother had been murdered. You assaulted him that night and broke your hand…' Gilmore's eyes drifted down to the filthy fibreglass cast on Callum's right hand. 'Your DNA was found on his T-shirt.'

'Of course it was! He was staying in *my* flat. Sleeping in *my* bed. Sitting on *my* couch. Of course he's covered in my DNA!'

Gilmore popped his glasses back on again. 'Then there's the question of your … crime-scene indiscretion. I hear rumours that you now claim it wasn't you who messed up the evidence, it was Elaine. You took the blame so she wouldn't be blamed and fired. You destroyed your career to protect her maternity pay, so you could afford a baby that wasn't even yours.' He shrugged. 'Perhaps you can see why you come top of our list?'

Callum gritted his teeth. 'It *wasn't* me.'

'He was found an hour ago, by two young girls out playing in the woods. Can you imagine how horrible that must have been for them? And even worse for DCI Powel – the SEB think he'd been lying there for at least a day and a half. Outside. In the rain.'

'I didn't do it. Oh, don't get me wrong, I *wanted* to do it. I *fantasised* about doing it, but I – didn't – do – it.'

Mother folded her arms. 'I was just getting to like you as well.'

'How many times do I have to say this?'

Gilmore leaned forwards. 'You were there, at the flat, the night DCI Powel was attacked. You had *very* good reason to attack him. You'd already attacked him the night before.'

'IT WASN'T ME!' Callum wiped a hand across his sticky forehead. 'I'm not the only one who...' A frown. 'Dugdale! Ainsley Dugdale – it must've been him.'

'Ainsley Dugdale?'

Mother leaned in. 'Big, bald, bad-tempered. Runs loan-sharking and protection rackets for Big Johnny Simpson.'

'He'd threatened Powel. I know, because Powel came round to warn us about it on...' Warmth flushed Callum's face. 'Powel was already in the flat when I got home from work, Wednesday evening, wasn't he? He'd been with *her*. Pretended he'd only dropped by with a warning: Dugdale was shooting his mouth off about getting revenge on the pair of us.'

Gilmore made a note. 'On you and Elaine.'

'No. On me and *Powel*.' Idiot. 'Ask Elaine. Ask her, she'll tell you. Dugdale threatened Powel. That's who attacked him, not me.'

Mother stared at him. 'Elaine returned from Dundee at six o'clock today. She'd been staying with her parents for a couple of days, hadn't she? Keeping out of the way so you could collect your things. Wanting to avoid another fight.'

'I wasn't the one having an affair, OK?'

'She let herself into the flat and called nine-nine-nine to report that something horrible must have happened. Furniture overturned. Ornaments smashed. Blood on the floor. And DCI Powel was missing.'

'Then it must've been Dugdale!'

'She says you've been acting strange for weeks. You're prone to violent outbursts. She's frightened for her safety.'

'That's right: take her word for it. Elaine couldn't tell the truth if you paid her thirty pieces of silver.' He thumped back in his seat. Folded his arms. 'After I collected my stuff from *my* flat, I got a call to a domestic assault in Kingsmeath. I rushed straight over there. If I'd attacked Powel, I'd be covered in blood, wouldn't I? Ask the householder: Irene Brown. Ask her and her children if I looked like I'd just beaten someone half to death.'

'Callum, you have to see how bad this—'

'*Ask* them. And I'm not saying another word without a Federation rep and a lawyer.'

Wee Angie Northfield grimaced, then popped a roll-up in her mouth and set a lighter to the end. Sooked in a lungful, setting the tip glowing bright orange. Then let it out in a long hard sigh. 'You shouldn't have agreed to the first interview without representation, MacGregor. That was stupid.'

Rain played a staccato drum roll on the smoking shelter, running down the curved roof in rippled sheets. Splashing on the paving slabs.

Streetlights rocked in the wind, their thin yellow glow swallowed by the downpour, leaving Peel Place washed out and anaemic in the darkness. The war memorial on the other side of the street was a statue of three First World War soldiers, bayonets fixed, kilts billowing out as they charged. Someone had taken pity on them and provided each with a traffic cone hat to keep their heads dry.

Callum scowled out at the overflowing gutters. 'I didn't touch Powel, OK? Well, yes, I punched him *once* on Thursday night, but I didn't attack him on Friday. And I *didn't* dump him in the woods.'

'Worst-case scenario: the Procurator Fiscal thinks there's enough to charge you with attempted murder and you're off to the cells till it comes to court. Could be months.'

'It wasn't me!'

'Best case: they decide you *might* be telling the truth and go after Ainsley Dugdale for it. Either way you're looking at an immediate suspension pending investigation. Probably without pay.'

He let his head fall back till it boinged off the Perspex wall. 'Oh joy.' Then he dug a hand into a pocket and produced his wallet. Checked the contents: a fiver, two used bus tickets, and buy-one-get-one-free voucher for Big Bernie's Pizza Palace on Wallace Lane. 'So I've got to live on five quid and some pocket smush till they clear me?'

'Yeah well, that's how it's going to—'

'Constable MacGregor!' McAdams' voice boomed out from the main doors, cheery as a drunken accountant.

Even better. Now, on top of everything else, here came some sarcastic gloating wrapped up in half-arsed poetry.

Callum bounced his head into the Perspex again.

McAdams limped down the stairs, leaning heavily on the balustrade, and hobbled over to the smoking shelter. Grinned as he stepped inside.

He looked as if someone had taken a skeleton and dressed it in an inexpensive suit: cheekbones prominent and sharp, eyes sunken and dark. 'I just heard the news.' Heat radiated off him in sour waves.

'You look like crap.'

'Thank you. I'm dying, in case you didn't hear?' The smile got bigger and more cadaverous. 'Angie, my darling. Can you get our wee boy off, or is he now doooooomed?'

She shrugged, cigarette cupped in her hand. 'Fifty–fifty.'

'Then I have just the thing that may help.' He thumped Callum on the back. 'You, dear Constable Useless, can drive.'

'I can't go anywhere till they decide what's happening. Charge or release.'

'Oh, they've already *done* that. I've just come from Mother's office with the happy news: you're suspended without pay, pending an investigation.'

Wee Angie Northfield nodded. 'Told you.'

'Bloody hell.' Callum boinged his head off the smoking shelter's wall again.

'Ah yes, but I have a *plan*.' He flashed his death's head smile again. 'To the Misfit-Mob-Mobile!'

66

Rainswept buildings slid past the car windows, turned an unhealthy yellow-grey by the streetlights. Callum took a right, over Dundas Bridge. 'This would go a lot quicker if you told me where we were going.'

The Kings River stretched out on either side, swollen, dark, and angry.

Nothing from McAdams.

Off in the distance, Montgomery Park was lit up like a Wurlitzer. Spotlights raked the low clouds, making the huge inflatable spider glow every time they touched it. Colours flickered and burst out from the giant screens – too far away to make out any detail, just a changing smear of brightness that glittered back from the river.

'Sergeant McAdams!'

'Mmmph?' His head jerked up, eyes blinking. 'What?'

'I said, where – are – we – going?'

'Oh, right.' A long puffed-out breath and a little shake. His face gleamed in the dashboard light, greasy and unwell. 'We, my dear Callum, are going hunting for one Detective Constable John Pain-In-The-Backside Watt. Mother's worried.'

'You *do* remember I've been suspended?'

'Pff…' He waved a hand. 'Suspended is as suspended does. Besides, we're not undertaking an official investigation here, we're just out looking for a colleague, so I can kick his arse halfway up his back for him.' The sentence ended with a hacking cough that rocked McAdams back and forward in the passenger seat, leaving him panting and slumped.

'Are you sure you're OK to do this?'

'He's not answering his mobile or his landline, so we'll try his flat first. With any luck he's accidentally handcuffed himself to the bed in his favourite gimp suit.'

'Only you *seriously* look like you should be in hospital.'

'And if he's not there, we widen the search. I've been through his spreadsheet and we've got all properties accounted for. The only ones not searched by other teams are the two he did on his own: the old Patterson-Smith Warehouse in Wardmill, and Thaw Cottages out by Holburn Forest. We'll try those too.'

'I've seen post mortems on healthier looking people than you.'

'I've already checked with all the hospitals and both mortuaries.'

Well, no one could say Callum hadn't tried. 'Where's his flat, then?'

'Take a right at the roundabout.'

The old lady from number 5 lowered the keys into McAdams' palm. 'You sure I can't make you a nice hot cup of tea, dear? Only you look like you need one. It's no trouble.'

'I'd love to, but we're on duty.' He stood on the landing and waved at her until she went back into her flat and closed the door. Then McAdams slumped. Wiped the sweat from his forehead with a trembling hand. Sighed. And passed the keys to Callum. 'You can go first, I just need to catch my breath for a bit.'

OK.

Callum knocked on the door to number 6. Waited.

The only sound was McAdams wheezing.

So he took the spare keys and let himself into Watt's flat. Clicked on the lights. 'Hello? John?'

The hallway was small, but spotless: a wonky rhomboid with four doors leading off it. Kitchen, bedroom, bathroom, and living room. All neat, all clean, all tidy. Strange, would've put money on Watt being a Pot-Noodle bachelor, with posters of wrestlers on the walls and an impressive collection of used pizza boxes. Instead, it was like something out of a decorating magazine.

A row of sympathy cards were lined up on the mantelpiece in the living room, beneath a cheesy posed photo of Watt and a woman so pale she was almost see-through.

Callum picked up one of the cards: 'WE WERE SO SORRY TO HEAR ABOUT MARY. OUR THOUGHTS AND PRAYERS ARE WITH YOU ALWAYS, BILL AND AGGIE.'

He put it down again. As if holding it any longer would make it grubby.

The answering machine flashed a red light in the corner. Callum pressed the button.

'Have you had a bank loan or credit card in the last six years? Unsure if you're due PPI compensation? Well—'

He hit delete.

Marched back out to the landing. 'He's not here.'

Callum's torch beam wandered across the large breezeblock wall, catching the faded lettering: 'PATTERSON-SMITH ~ QUALITY FURNITURE YOU CAN DEPEND ON'. And now there was nothing left but dust and the dirty gritty scent of mildew and stagnant water.

McAdams limped out of a door through to the old office, brushing cobwebs from his suit jacket. 'There are spiders in there big as Yorkshire Terriers. I kid you not.'

'Sod-all out here either.' He did a slow turn on the spot. 'Have you tried getting Voodoo to put a lookout request on Watt's car? He jumped out of Dotty's – no way he slogged all the way out here on foot.'

'She's looking.'

'Oh. OK.' So much for that. 'Holburn Forest, then.'

'Holburn Forest.'

'Of course, what I don't get, is why he has to be such a dick the whole time.' McAdams held onto the grab handle above the passenger door as the Mondeo rocked and growled from pothole to pothole along the track, sending up arcs of water.

'Hello, Pot? I have Kettle on line one for you.'

The car's headlights caught the broom and whin crowding the road, sending jagged shadows racing ahead of them.

'That's different. I'm *dying*, I'm allowed to be a little—'

'Dicklike?'

'I was going to say, colourfully eccentric.' He shifted in his seat as a grating noise sounded somewhere under the car. 'You try being eaten alive by tumours, young Callum. See how altruistic you are then.'

'No thanks.'

The sky was a solid blob of orangey-grey, but a thick black stripe loomed on the horizon. That would be Holburn Forest, lurking in the darkness. Still no sign of any cottages.

'And don't get me started on the chemotherapy...' A thick, rattling sigh. 'You know, I wish I hadn't. Started on it, I mean. I could be dead by now, instead of lurching about like a broken clothes horse.' He nodded. 'But Beth won't let go, so I've got to hold on too.'

The headlights pulled tree trunks from the gloom as they reached the forest's edge. The track disappeared into it, but another track sat at right angles, skirting the boundary.

McAdams pointed. 'Left here, it's at the end of the road.'

Callum took the turning, thumping through another set of water-logged potholes. Off in the distance, the city lights glittered through the rain. A blanket of stars, draped across the landscape. 'Aaaargh!' The Mondeo lurched like a rollercoaster, setting free another grinding scrape from beneath their feet. 'Be lucky to have any bottom left on the car, after this.'

'You want a bit of advice, Callum?'

'Not you as well.' Why did everyone think he needed their sodding opinion?

There – up ahead – a line of three cottages, sitting between the track and the forest. Grass shone in the rowans, one of the chimneys looked on the verge of collapse. The gardens were full of weeds.

'Live your life like the future's never going to happen. Because before you know it: *plop*. It isn't.' He shook his head. 'Spent my whole life doing the right thing – being responsible, working hard – when I should've been out there *enjoying* life. Thought there would always be time for that later. Now look at me...' McAdams sighed. 'I'm down to my last few chapters, Callum. I don't think I'm going to make it to the end of the book...'

Three cottages: two semidetached, one standing on its own. Callum parked outside it. Killed the engine and sat there as the hot metal pinged and ticked. The rain got louder, battering off the car roof. 'We should probably check the graveyards.'

McAdams unclipped his seatbelt. 'You'd think, if someone buried him, they'd invite us to the funeral so we could dance on his grave.'

'There were sympathy cards in his flat. You ever hear him talk about someone called Mary?'

'To be honest, I don't know anything about his home life. He's always too ... blecccccch to spend that much time with.'

'If she's died recently, he could be visiting her grave. Or out getting hammered somewhere.'

A nod. 'Definitely worth a try.' Then McAdams levered himself out into the rain. 'Are you coming, then?'

Callum grabbed his high-viz from the back and hauled it on.

Hunched his shoulders as he followed McAdams up the path to the front door. 'He's definitely been here.' Pointing at a line of trampled grass and weeds leading around the side of the building.

'Of course he was. I *saw* him here, remember? Honestly, nobody pays any sodding attention.' McAdams pushed through into the house. 'He'd finished searching the cottages, I think. Or just about.'

The hallway smelled of long-dead mice, tainted with the sharp musky odour of fresh rodent urine, and the thick cloying tickle of dust. Other than them and Watt, it looked as if no one had been in here for years.

Callum slid his torch beam through the open door and into a living room. 'This is a complete waste of time. Why would he still be here?'

'Well, I don't know, do I?' McAdams limped past, playing his torch across the peeling wallpaper. 'It was all I could think of to do. He's not at home, he's not at the station, Dotty's not seen him since she turfed him out of her car. He's got to be *somewhere*.'

The bedroom floor sagged towards the corner, where a hole as big as an armchair was rotted through the floorboards. A pair of dark shiny eyes glittered in the torchlight, then disappeared.

'If you're that worried, send out a lookout request. Get the media department issuing statements and posters. Mobilise the nightshift.'

'It's probably nothing. You know what Watt's like – law unto himself, that one. Thinks he's too good to check in with anyone or clock off at the end of the day.' McAdams disappeared down the corridor. 'Nothing in the bathroom.'

The other bedroom was empty too. And the kitchen.

Callum's torch picked out manky worktops and kitchen units, little trails of footprints scrawled through the dust and mouse droppings. It sparkled back from the window above the sink. He opened the back door and ran it around the garden. 'There's outbuildings. A bothy and a big shed-barn thing.'

'I don't understand him, Callum, I honestly don't. You? You're a simple soul – a bran-flakes-and-marmalade kind of guy. But Watt?'

'Screw you. I'm plenty complicated.' He stepped back out into the rain.

'I thought I'd finally got through to him. "Don't be a dick," I said. "You need to work as a team," I said. "Oh yes," he says, "I promise I'll be a good boy from now on!"' McAdams spat into the wet grass. 'Dick.'

The bothy was a squat blocky thing with a rusty corrugated

roof. Something had been at the mortar, eating it away, exposing the rocks that made up the walls. It smelled even more of mouse than the house had.

McAdams followed him from room to room. 'See when I get my hands on Watt? I'm going to throttle the life out of him. You're going to have to alibi me. Kid-on he was already dead when we found him.'

An ancient kitchen with a lumpy range that was like a solid heap of decaying metal, floral wallpaper smeared with mildew. The ceiling had collapsed, exposing the roof beams, leaving chunks of plaster all over the floor.

'No, I won't throttle him. I'll tie him to the back of the car and make him run all the way back to Divisional Headquarters. Maybe drag him for a couple of miles too. That'll teach him to do what he's bloody well told.'

A line of swallow or house-martin nests lined the join between ceiling and wall in the next room. Stacks of old tiles and the rotting remains of kitchen units – probably dumped here when they did up one of the cottages decades ago.

McAdams wheezed. Leaned against the horrible wallpaper. Let his head hang.

Callum checked the last room – about the same size as the kitchen, only without the charm. Someone had drawn crude pornographic figures on the walls in crumbling chalk. And there was no way half of it was physically possible.

But no sign of Watt.

Back in the hall, McAdams hadn't moved.

'Right: soon as we've checked the barn, I'm dropping you off at the hospital.'

'I don't want to go to the hospital.'

'Tough. You think Mother's upset about Watt going AWOL? How do you think she'll feel if I let you snuff it out here?'

'I'm *not* going to the sodding hospital!'

'Keep telling yourself that.' Callum marched back out into the rain. Another trampled path led through the grass and weeds to the barn. So Watt had searched it too.

He took the path anyway, right up to the barn door. Flicked the catch open, pushed the door, and stepped inside.

Stopped.

Everything stank of wood smoke.

'McAdams?' Deep breath. 'MCADAMS! IN HERE!'

The room was split into two bits – one set out with a wooden frame above a pile of ash and burnt logs. The other was a little room, built of rough-hewn wood. Just like the smokehouse they'd found at Creel Lane.

A pile of old wooden fish boxes sat in front of it, still fresh enough to ooze the acidic tang of old seafood.

'MCADAMS!' Callum struggled his good hand into a blue nitrile glove and crept over to the sealed-off section. The door was slightly ajar. He eased it all the way with his foot. Then lurched back a couple of steps, covering his mouth and nose with his fibreglass cast.

The billowing, unmistakable, *greasy* stench of death collapsed out of the room.

Behind him the barn door thumped.

'Callum?'

'Over here.' He took a deep breath and stepped over the threshold.

A rusty metal tank gleamed in the torchlight. There must've been water in it, because it sent reflections sparkling across the wooden roof. He swung the beam right...

OK, that explained the smell.

A woman's body was slumped on the floor by the wall, held upright by the chain around her neck. Callum set the beam on her dark, swollen face. Abby Gossard. Definitely dead.

'Bastard...'

McAdams appeared in the doorway. 'I found Watt's car parked out back. What's... Oh Christ, is that smell what I think it is?'

'We've found Ashlee's mother.' He ran his torch across the floor around the tank, then back towards Abby Gossard... There was another body, lying against the wall, part hidden by a tarpaulin.

Please don't be Ashlee. Please don't be Ashlee.

Callum inched closer, picked up the edge of the tarp and folded it back.

It wasn't Ashlee.

If anything it was worse.

Detective Constable Watt lay on his side, one knee drawn up, head lying on his arm. Something black had dried in a thin line from his nose to his cheek. Another line down the side of his neck from his ear. His skin was so pale it fluoresced in the torch beam.

'Watt, you silly sod.'

McAdams cleared his throat. 'Is he...?'

Callum knelt beside Watt, laid the torch on the dirt floor, and pressed two fingers in under his jaw.

'Well?'

A tiny quiver pressed against Callum's fingertips. Then another. Faint, but definitely there.

'Call an ambulance! Call it *now*!'

67

Mother barged through the double doors, scattering a couple of paramedics in her wake. 'How is he?'

'Watt's in surgery.' Callum hitched a thumb over his shoulder at McAdams – slumped in a plastic waiting chair with his elbows on his knees and head in his hands. 'This one, on the other hand, probably should be.'

McAdams didn't even move at that.

She puffed out a huge breath. 'He's going to live, though, right? Watt's going to make it?'

'We don't know yet. Someone tried to cave his head in with an adjustable spanner. Nearly succeeded, too.'

'Gah...' She sank into the chair next to McAdams, put a hand between his shoulders and rubbed. 'Are you OK, Andy?'

'No.'

'Callum, get a doctor. Tell them—'

'Oh don't be so melodramatic.' McAdams creaked himself up till his back was straight again. His eyes were red and puffy, shiny in the overhead light. 'I was there, Mother.' He stared down at his hands. 'I was there at Thaw Cottages and I left him.'

'Andy, it's not your fault, it—'

'I gave him a bollocking, I gave him a pep talk, and then I got back in my car and I drove away.'

She cupped his neck with a hand. 'You couldn't have known.'

'If I'd stayed and searched the buildings with him, it might never have happened.'

'Shh...' Mother leaned in and kissed McAdams on the forehead.

Callum pulled up another plastic chair and sank into it. 'I've called

479

the SEB, the Procurator Fiscal, and Hairy Harry. SEB got there before the ambulance, everyone else is on their way.'

McAdams scrubbed a hand across his sunken eyes. 'Sorry.'

'Boss, we've got a problem: whoever tried to kill Watt, it definitely *wasn't* Tod Monaghan. Not unless he's stitched himself back together after the post mortem and broken out of the mortuary. He was working with someone.'

She stared at the ceiling tiles. 'That's all we need.'

'And whoever it is still has Ashlee Gossard.'

'Even better.'

'So, what if Paul Jeffries didn't die twenty odd years ago?' Callum scooted his chair closer. 'What if the male remains, in the shallow grave, were another victim? Not someone to sexually abuse, but someone to take the blame. What if Jeffries faked his own death and he's still out there?'

'Callum, Callum, Callum.' McAdams shook his head. 'Do you have any idea how many shades of stupid that is?' He held up a hand before Mother could do more than open her mouth. 'And I mean that with the greatest respect. One: if you're faking your own death like that, you need someone to actually *find* the body, otherwise what's the point? Two: Jeffries would be in his seventies by now, remember? And three: he was a sex offender with a thing for abducting and raping women. Why on Satan's shiny earth would he suddenly change to abducting young men to starve, brine, smoke, and turn into mummies? Think it through.'

Yeah. It was a bit of a stretch.

Callum shrugged as heat bloomed in his cheeks and ears. 'Just playing Devil's advocate.'

'Of course you were.' McAdams sighed, then stood. 'The brass aren't going to like this, not after the triumphant press conference and all the drinks. We're going to need a scapegoat, a statement, and another public appeal.'

'Urgh.' Now it was Mother's turn to curl up into a ball in her seat. 'They're going to blame me for this, aren't they?'

'Tell them it was my fault.' McAdams patted her on the shoulder. 'It *was*, after all. I should never have left Watt on his own.'

Callum checked his watch. 'If we hurry, we've still got time to get something on the Ten O'clock News. We can probably make the first editions too.'

She looked up at him. 'What are we going to appeal *for*? We have no idea who Monaghan's partner was. We have no idea what they look like. We have exactly sod-all clue what we're doing.'

McAdams pulled his bony shoulders back. 'We'll think of something. We always do.' A sniff. 'Well, usually, anyway.'

Mother rolled her eyes. 'It's official: we're doomed...'

Callum picked at the dirty lining of his cast. 'There's got to be *something* we can do. What about Brett Millar? He's still off his face on prescription meds right over there, isn't he?' He nodded at the windows lining one side of the corridor. Across a darkened courtyard, the merciless Victorian bulk of the secure psychiatric ward was just visible through the rain. 'We get a warrant and we force them to pump him full of something to bring him back down to earth. Then we sweat him till he tells us what the hell happened in that flat!'

'Andy?'

'They wouldn't give us a warrant yesterday, or the day before.'

Mother gave them a pained smile and a nod. 'Let's give it one more go, then.'

'Good.' Callum pulled out his phone. 'I'll call the—'

'Actually...' She looked away. 'Maybe you should leave it to us.'

'But—'

'Callum, you can't go ordering warrants if you're suspended from duty. I'm amazed you managed to get the SEB, pathologist, and PF to go visit Thaw Cottages. The Sheriff's not going to be that understanding.'

'Oh.' His shoulders slumped.

'I appreciate the thought, though.' She stood, rubbed at the small of her back. 'Right, Andy, let's get cracking. And see if you can drum up a uniform to stand guard at John's hospital bed. I don't want anything else happening to him.'

'Yes, Mother.'

She smiled at Callum. 'Go home. Read a book. We'll let you know if anything happens.'

He stood there, grinding his teeth as they walked away.

Mother and McAdams disappeared through the doors and that was it: abandoned again.

Lovely.

All because of DCI Reece Sodding Powel.

And Ainsley Dugdale, of course.

Callum ran his good hand across his face, straightened up and marched out. Through the double doors, down the corridor past waiting rooms and treatment cubicles and shuffling old people...

481

A large woman in a flowery blouse and pencil skirt emerged from a door up ahead. Stethoscope around her neck, sleeves rolled up to the elbows. She stepped into the middle of the corridor, hands on her hips, then marched away from him, shoving through the doors. 'Mr McAdams?'

Callum hurried after her, through into the reception area: lined with posters about healthy eating and venereal diseases; packed with miserable-looking people in various stages of despair, waiting their turn.

'Mr McAdams?' She was still going, stout little legs pumping, trainers squeaking on the pale grey floor.

Callum caught up to her as she pushed out of the main doors and into the night. She stopped there, under the hospital canopy, hands on her hips again. Staring out into the rain. 'MR MCADAMS!'

But there was no sign of him, or Mother.

'Oh, for God's sake. Some people just...' She clicked her mouth shut. Looked Callum up and down. 'Can I help you?'

'I work with DS McAdams.'

'Gah...' She rolled her eyes. 'Then can you do me a favour and ask him ... no: *tell* him, *force* him to call my office and set up an appointment. He's not impressing anyone with this he-man routine.'

'OK. And you are?'

She dug into the pocket on her blouse and produced an NHS Oldcastle card. 'Dr Fitzpatrick. And I'm not kidding about: he needs to call me and make a frigging appointment. Cancer isn't something that just goes away on its own.'

Callum frowned down at the card. 'Is this about his chemotherapy?'

'It would be, if he'd *actually* turn up to his clinical appointments.' She pinched the bridge of her nose. 'Please, just talk to him, OK? He won't answer any of my calls, or texts. We need to get him in and we need to get his treatment started. He's going to die otherwise. And I'm not talking in some obscure theoretical sense: he – will – literally – die.'

But...

'I mean it: he'll die.'

'Yes. Of course. I'll talk to him.'

'Thank you.' She spun around on a squeaky heel and pulled out her mobile phone, poking at the screen as she thumped back into the hospital. 'Angie: I need a CT scan for Mrs Stoltzman...'

Either she was helping herself to the contents of the medicine cupboard, or something very wrong was going on.

Callum hurried out into the car park, but the thing was huge, stretching all the way from here to the maternity hospital, broken into various chunks along the way. No way of telling where Mother would have parked her manky Fiat Panda.

So he ducked into a bus shelter and scrolled through the contacts on his phone. Clicked on the one marked 'DS CRAP POETRY'.

It rang for a bit, then McAdams was on the line, his voice muffled – almost drowned out by the grumbling engine. *'Are you missing me already? That's sweet.'*

'I just bumped into a friend of yours.'

'Did you now?'

'A Dr Fitzpatrick.'

The only noise from the other end was the engine.

'You still there?'

'No.'

'She says you've not been going to your chemotherapy sessions.'

'Well, that is interesting. Hold on, I'll have to text that information to you. … Yes.'

'What the hell are you going on about?'

'No, don't worry about it. Not a problem. … OK, bye.' He hung up.

Callum stared at his phone. Dr Fitzpatrick wasn't the only one raiding the medicine cupboard.

He dialled McAdams again, but it went straight through to voicemail: *'You've reached Detective Sergeant Andrew McAdams. I'm sorry I can't take your call at the moment, but—'*

Callum killed the call.

Five seconds later his phone buzzed and dinged an incoming text.

> What U playing at? Can't talk
> in front of Mother!!!
> Shes gt enough 2 worry abt
> already!

He leaned back against the bus shelter and poked out a reply:

> The doctor said you've not been
> going to chemo. You told us you
> were.

Ding, buzzzzz.

> I'll call U when we get bk to
> DHQ. Dnt B a dick about this!

Oh, so Callum was being a dick, was he?

> You're the dick! Why aren't you

taking your chemo treatment? Do
you WANT to die?
Ding, buzzzzz.
Yes.
Oh.

The Mondeo was where Callum had left it, double-parked across a pair
of matching four-by-fours. He unlocked the door and slid in behind
the wheel.

So McAdams was skipping his chemo and didn't want Mother to
know about it. Fair enough. It was his life. What was left of it.

Callum rested his forearms on top of the steering wheel. Rain
bounced off the car's bonnet, clattered on its roof, made a small river
in the gutter, overflowed into a spreading loch in the car park.

Suspended.

Of no use.

Abandoned.

Well, sod the lot of them. Ditch the car back at Divisional Headquarters
and hit the Bart instead. Pick up his bike from Hedgehog. Maybe have
a pint or three. Or four.

After all, it wasn't as if he had anything better to do.

Not now they'd chucked him off the case.

Something upbeat and poppy was playing as he walked into the room.
The Dumbarton Arms was virtually empty, just a pair of youngsters
trying to climb inside each other in one of the booths at the back. All
hands and tongues.

Callum shook the rain from his hair and stepped up to the bar.
'Hedgehog.'

The barman froze in the middle of loading a case of Bacardi Breezers
into the fridge. 'Oh dear.'

'Is that any way to greet a valued customer?'

He straightened up and turned. Tucked his hingin-mince hair behind
his ears and faked a smile. 'Detective Constable MacGregor, how
delightful of you to grace us with your patronage once more. I trust
things are on a more cheerful footing with your good self?'

'Pint of Trade Winds and a packet of pickled onion, thanks.'

'Only I don't think I could realistically survive another night of
suicidal music playing on an endless loop.' He pointed at the couple in
the corner. 'And it would ruin our young lovers' *esprit d'amour*. Please?'

Callum hauled himself up onto a barstool. 'Thanks for taking care of my bike.'

'Does this mean we'll be permitted to enjoy a Radiohead-slash-REM-free night?'

'Promise.'

All the breath flopped out of Hedgehog. Followed by a smile. 'In that case, dear Detective Constable, this first libation, and its accompanying comestibles, comes to you courtesy of the Dumbarton Arms in fulsome gratitude.' He pulled the pint and set the glass down in front of Callum. 'And while we're talking of fulsome gratitude, will we be settling our bar tab from Thursday at some point today?'

'Ah...' He dug out his fiver and his small handful of change. Set the lot down between them.

'Five pounds, eighty-three pence. And a button?'

'They suspended me without pay, Hedgehog. You're looking at all the cash I've got in the world right now.'

A long, gravelly sigh. Then Hedgehog pushed the small pile of cash back towards Callum. 'In that case, shall we come to an accord? I propose the Dumbarton Arms retain possession of your bicycle until sufficient funds are at your disposal to make the appropriate remuneration. How does that sound?'

Irene Brown pawned her teddy bear and kids' toys to pay for food and rent. And here *he* was pawning his bike to pay for an alcoholic bender.

Proud moment, Callum. *Really* proud.

'Thanks, Hedgehog.' He took a sip of his pint, then swore as his mobile dinged and buzzed.

Incoming text message.

No prizes for guessing who that would be from: bloody Haiku Boy.

Callum pulled the phone out and stuck it on the bar top, next to his crisps. But it wasn't McAdams, it was ex-sergeant Bob Shannon.

> Callum, I've got some good news:
> the OAPs finally came up with a
> name!
> Where are you? I'll come get you.

He popped open his bag of pickled onion and crunched through a couple. Then wiped his fingers clean on his trousers and replied:

> Too late. Gareth Pike gave me the
> ID this afternoon. I've already
> been round - denies everything.

There was barely time for another mouthful of beer before his mobile burst into life. Shannon again. 'Bob.'

'*Callum. You went round to see him? What happened? Did he cop to it?*'

'Did he hell.' Another couple of crisps vanished in a hail of crunching. 'Said he wasn't there, he didn't attack my parents, he didn't abduct my brother. And if I want to talk to him again I'd better have a warrant with me.'

'*Pfff… What about the night your mother's head was dumped in the woods?*'

'Oh he's got an alibi for that. Hundreds of them: all over Twitter and Facebook.'

'*What?*'

'He was on tour with his band. There's loads of pictures online of him up on stage in Brussels.'

One of the heavy petters surfaced for air, then shuffled his way to the bar, grinning. 'Yeah, can I get a Glenmorangie and a bottle of the strawberry-and-lime cider?' He turned and waved at the bearded friend he'd left behind at the table.

'Bob, you still there?'

'*Sorry. Did you say he was on stage in* Brussels? *Brussels, like the one in Belgium?*'

Callum took another scoof of beer. 'Have you been hitting the Malbec again, Bob?'

'*No. Just surprised, I suppose. Didn't think he'd be able to perform any more. Given his condition.*'

'You're kidding, right? He's been all over the radio, TV, and papers for about a week, banging on about his grand-finale career-comeback gig tonight. In Montgomery Park?'

'*Erm … Callum, who are you talking about?*'

'The man who abducted my family: Leo McVey.'

'*Yeah. No. That's not the name I've got.*'

486

68

Shannon pointed through the windshield. 'That's us there.'

The house sat on its own, on the outskirts of Auchterowan, just visible through the trees bordering the property. Not quite a Georgian mansion, more a bungalow with delusions of grandeur. All the lights were on, its windows glowing, casting a warm golden glow out into the front garden. A winding gravel drive, threading its way between rhododendron bushes to the front door and double garage.

At least it had stopped raining. Up above, a patch of stars glared down at them from a hole in the clouds. About as welcoming as a mortuary drawer.

Callum puffed out his cheeks. 'Are you *sure* about this?'

'It was just a rumour, remember? I'm making no promises.'

'OK. Right. Only ... you know.'

A small hatchback sat in front of the garage, its boot gaping open like a hungry mouth. And as they sat there, parked on the road with the engine idling, a woman in a flowery pinny and yellow rubber gloves lurched out of the garage with a big bag and fed the hatchback with it. Wiped her forehead on the back of her arm, then went back inside.

Shannon nodded. 'We don't have to do this if you don't want to.'

'No, I do. But...' He cleared his throat. Took a deep breath. 'But it's R.M. Travis. The man's a hero to millions of kids, he *can't* be a serial killer.'

'I was listening to Radio Four the other day: someone's started a petition to get him on the New Year's Honours list. Can you believe that?' The car's wheels crunched on the gravel driveway. 'They'll be a bit embarrassed if Pike's telling the truth. Arise, Sir Murdering Tosspot!'

Callum shifted in his seat. 'Maybe Pike's lying?'

A modern extension poked out from one side of the building – a low long box fronted with floor-to-ceiling glass. It was a private library, lined with bookshelves, crammed with books, lit by artfully placed downlighters and standard lamps.

God... To own that many *books.*

'I wouldn't be surprised if he was.' Shannon pulled up outside the front door. 'That's the thing about people like Gareth Pike: lying's like breathing to them. It's a way of life. I don't think Pike would know the truth if it clambered up his bumhole and took up clog dancing.'

Callum undid his seatbelt. Grimaced. 'OK. We can do this...'

'Of course, maybe Pike gave you Leo McVey's name because he was protecting Travis? Maybe they go *way* back?'

'You think R.M. Travis is a *paedophile*?'

'Wouldn't be the first kiddy fiddler in line for a knighthood.'

Something deep inside his stomach lurched and gurgled. 'Yeah, but...' He hissed out a breath. 'I loved his books, growing up. The home had a complete set. If it turns out he ... you know?'

Shannon patted him on the shoulder. 'Look at it this way, we—'

There was a knock on the driver's window.

The woman in the pinny stared in at them, face creased and worried. Brown hair, greying at the roots. Bags under her eyes, going slightly jowly around the chin. Pale. As if she hadn't seen the sun for years.

Shannon opened his door and she stepped back.

'Can I help you?' Voice brittle and sharp.

Callum climbed out. 'We're looking for R.M. Travis.'

She grunted. Then shook her head. 'I'm sorry, but it's late and my father's not up to visitors. Please, he appreciates you reading his books, but he's not well.' She pointed down the drive towards the road. 'Now, if you'll excuse me, I've got things to do.'

He produced his warrant card. 'DC MacGregor.'

If anything, she went even paler. 'What's this about?'

'Can I ask your name, Mrs...?'

'Travis-Wilkes.' She laughed, brittle and high-pitched. Wrung her rubber-gloved hands together. 'And it's *Ms.* Emma. Divorced, single, writer: seeks tall strong man for walks on the beach, cheese toasties, and vigorous lovemaking.' She licked her lips. Cleared her throat. 'Sorry.' Pulled on a smile. 'We get so many fans coming here. Well, not as many as we used to.' A shrug. 'It gets a bit much at times.'

'You live here?'

'As carer, nurse, archivist, biographer, and general dogsbody. You've *no idea* how much work's involved in looking after someone else's literary legacy. I haven't written a single word of my own for years.'

'We need to ask your father a few questions.'

The laugh sounded forced. 'Good luck. He's not having one of his better days.' She brushed her fringe aside with the bright yellow gloves. 'Half the time he thinks I'm my mother. The other half he hasn't got a clue *who* I am.' Emma pointed back towards the garage. 'He switched off all the freezers last week. No idea why. You wouldn't *believe* the smell.'

'We'll try not to take too much of his time.'

'Wouldn't be quite so bad if he didn't have enough rubbish in there to survive a nuclear winter.' Sounding more bitter with every word. 'I swear on the Bonemonger's grave, he hoards leftovers like some people hoard money. We've got pot roasts in there going back to Margaret Bloody Thatcher's...' Emma cleared her throat. Straightened her pinny. 'Sorry. I shouldn't be talking about him like that. It's been a long day.' She sighed. Pulled on another smile. 'Anyway, shall we?'

She snapped off her gloves, stuffed them in the pocket of her pinny, and unlocked the front door. Ushered them into a wide hallway covered in framed book covers – most of their titles barely recognisable in foreign languages: 'ÖFFNEN SIE DIE SÄRGE', 'ZACZAROWANY KRÓLIK RUSSELL', 'LES MONSTRES QUI SONT VENUS DINER', 'EL CUBO DE BASURA MILAGROSO DE IMELDA'...

'I need you to understand, his grip on the real world is ... tenuous.' Down to the end of the corridor and left. More book covers. 'He goes off on these rambling discussions where he's playing all the parts. Arguing with himself. I used to just let him get on with it, then I sat down and listened to what he was *actually* saying.' She looked over her shoulder as they passed a big kitchen with gleaming work surfaces. 'I was trying to get him to talk about his childhood, but he was going on about how the Goblin Queen was rebuilding her army in the depths of the forest.'

A door at the end of the corridor opened on the library. The comforting smell of books mingled with the chemical floral whiff of air freshener.

'It was like he was writing another Russell the Magic Rabbit book. Only instead of battering it out on his old Underwood, he was living it all in his head.'

The bookshelves weren't just around the outside of the room, they made islands in the middle of the space too, dividing it up into discrete areas. Some with armchairs, others with little tables.

How rich would you have to be to own something like that? It was like Heaven, Nirvana, and Jannat ul-Khuld all rolled into one. A Valhalla for bibliophiles.

'So I started recording him. Sometimes it's about Russell, sometimes it's Imelda, sometimes it's Justin and Arya. Sometimes new stuff, sometimes just retreads of the books already published. The only person he never talks about is Ichabod Smith, for some reason.'

Over in the far corner, at a desk piled high with books and papers, was the bent-over figure of a man. White hair circled a shiny bald patch speckled with liver spots. He was curled around a piece of paper, one arm shielding it – like a small child trying not to let the cheat at the next desk copy off him – scribbling away.

'Sometimes I wonder if it's because, writing the books, the characters and worlds he created are more real to him than what happens out here with the rest of us. They say people with dementia find it easier to remember stuff from fifty years ago than this morning. He remembers them instead.' She took a deep breath. 'Dad?'

The man at the desk kept on scribbling.

Emma lowered her voice. 'Just don't be surprised if it all goes a bit surreal. Sometimes he's him, sometimes he's one of his creations. He was the Bonemonger for nearly a week once. That was … *disturbing*.'

Callum took out his phone. 'Thanks.'

She walked over and patted her father on the shoulder. 'Dad?'

He flinched. Turned, blinking up at her. 'Sophie?'

'No, Dad, it's Emma. Remember? Emma?' She turned and held out a hand. 'These nice police officers want to have a chat with you. OK?'

'I'm busy. Tell them to come back tomorrow.' He went back to scribbling.

She pulled a face at Callum, mouthing, 'Told you.' Then back to her father. 'Come on, Dad, it'll only take a minute. Do you need anything? A cup of tea? Some juice?'

'Sophie, I can't find my hat.'

'OK, I'll leave you to it then.' She kissed him on top of the bald spot. 'I've got manky freezers to clean out.' A small shudder, then she was gone.

Callum pulled out the chair on the other side of the table and sank into it. 'Mr Travis.'

No response, just more scribbling.

He produced his wallet and opened it. Laid it on the table between them, turned so the MacGregor family photo was the right way up for Travis. 'Do you recognise these people?'

'There's no point wriggling, little rabbit boy. You're for the pot whether you like it or not.'

'Look at the photograph, Mr Travis.'

'Don't eat me. Please don't eat me.'

'A mother, a father, and two little boys.'

'Don't be silly, I'm *hungry*. And you're a tasty little morsel, all plump and delicious.'

'Mr Travis!'

'But you can't eat me. I'm… I'm full of venomous poison. If you eat me, you'll swell up like a massive balloon and pop!'

Shannon sighed. 'He's not even in the room.'

'You'll pop and there'll be bits of ogre all over the walls and ceiling. And … and your heart will turn *black* and the crows will take it away to the bonegarden.'

'TRAVIS!' Callum slammed his hand down on the tabletop.

The old man flinched, head snapping up like a trap. Eyes wide. 'I don't know you. Why are you here?'

'Do you recognise them? This family, right here. Twenty-six years ago.'

'Where's Sophie? Where's my wife?' He blinked. Frowned at Shannon. Then back to Callum. 'I don't want to die.'

For God's sake.

Now that he was sitting upright, the sheet of paper he'd been scribbling on was visible. He'd drawn a long-eared rabbit in the middle of it, then surrounded it with the same words over and over: 'KILL AND EAT. DESTROY AND CONSUME. SIN AND INNOCENCE.'

McAdams was right – Travis was obsessed.

One more go. 'Do you recognise this family?'

'They're happy little rabbits. Hopping in the sun. Look at their white tails flashing.'

'Yeah.' Shannon sucked air in through his clenched teeth. 'I'd suggest throwing him down the stairs a few times, but I don't think it'd help.'

'They run and they frolic beneath the happy summer skies. Mummy Rabbit, Daddy Rabbit, and little Justin.'

Callum closed his wallet again. Stuck it back in his pocket. 'You're getting your books mixed up. Justin was a little boy, before he got cursed by the witch. He never had a rabbit mum and dad – they were people.'

'Into the pot you go, little rabbits.'

'Sorry.' Shannon put his hand on Callum's shoulder. 'It was a longshot anyway.'

491

'So I can't touch Leo McVey, and R.M. Travis is...' A sigh. 'What's the point? Even if it *was* him we couldn't put him on trial. And no one's sending him to prison like this.'

'Please don't eat us, we promise we'll be good!'

Callum pulled himself to his feet. 'Thank you for your time, Mr Travis. I loved your books when I was growing up. But I don't think I'll be able to read one ever again.'

'What's the point of catching a rabbit if you don't eat it?'

'Come on.' Shannon steered him away from the table. 'We'll go crack open a nice bottle of wine and bitch about the good old days.'

Travis scowled at them. 'Who are you? What did you do with my hat?'

Never meet your heroes.

They made their way back through the house.

'It was just a rumour anyway.' Shannon gave Callum's shoulder a squeeze. 'Gareth Pike was actually there and he *saw* Leo McVey. So that's what we focus on now.'

'I can't go near McVey without a warrant. And he'll lawyer up, soon as I do.'

Past the fancy kitchen and all the framed foreign-edition covers.

'So we go digging. My OAP network isn't the spryest, but never underestimate the power of bloody-minded old codgers with a lot of free time on their hands. We'll dig into McVey's past till we find something. Then use it to squeeze him till he squeaks.'

They stepped out through the front door and into a thin drizzle.

'Thanks, Bob. I appreciate it.'

'We'll get him. I promise.' Shannon unlocked the car.

'Yeah.' Callum sagged. Then turned. 'Suppose I'd better tell the daughter we're away.'

The back of the hatchback was still gaping open, most of the boot packed with black plastic bags. Not the thin domestic ones – proper thick rubble sacks. Because who wanted their car full of manky rotting meltwater?

He stepped into the garage and the cloying smell of turned meat.

Pff... Place was bigger than his whole flat.

Well, what *used* to be his flat.

Shelves and storage on one wall, a dusty green Range Rover dominating half the space. White paint on the concrete floor. A rack full of golf bags and clubs near a door that had to lead back into the house. A large collection of tinned beans, hot dogs, peas, macaroni cheese, jars of pickled beetroot, onions, mustard... Callum picked a tin of peaches off the shelf and blew a blizzard of grey off the faded label. Best before June 2001. Yeah. Maybe not.

A row of chest freezers and a couple of uprights sat along the back wall. Some lying open, others still sealed shut.

Emma Travis-Wilkes was bent over one of them, delving into its stinky depths. Divorced – and available – bum wiggling as she reached. A pair of rubble sacks sat on the ground beside her, one full and tied, the other still waiting for more rancid gifts.

He held up the tin of peaches. 'I see what you mean about hoarding food.'

'Gah!' She straightened up with a start. A freezer bag splotched to the concrete at her feet, sending a spatter of brown liquid out as it split. She turned, stepped in front of it. 'You startled me.'

'Sorry. Just wanted to say we're going.'

'Right. OK. Well ... thanks for letting me know.' She eased the freezer lid shut behind her. 'Sorry about the smell. How was he?'

'Confused.' Callum took a couple of steps closer. 'Did he ever mention anything about a family of four? It would have been about twenty-six years ago. They were in a lay-by just outside the city.'

'No nothing like that.'

'What about Leo McVey. They used to be close, didn't they?'

'I ... yes. They hung out all the time. Got stoned and drunk, trashed hotel rooms on every continent. Cocaine, groupies, and rock-and-roll. No wonder Mum left him.'

Another couple of steps. 'Did he ever say something about McVey that made you suspicious, or worried about him? Something that didn't sound right?'

'No. Thick as thieves, that pair. Uncle Leo could've crapped in the fish tank and Dad would have sworn it was the cat. And you don't want to *hear* the stories of when they went to Las Vegas.' Emma snapped off her rubber gloves and closed the gap. Stuck her hand out. 'I'm sorry you had a wasted trip.'

'Me too.' He handed her the peaches. Pointed at the rubble sack. 'I can dump that in the car on my way past. I'm going that way anyway.'

'No, you don't have to—'

'You wouldn't believe how strange it was, questioning your father. I was such a huge fan when I was a kid.' Callum marched over and grabbed the sealed rubble sack. Heavier than it looked. And the underside was pale and gritty with frost.

Eh?

493

Why would *defrosted* leftovers be cold enough to—

Something solid slammed into the back of his head and the world erupted like a million fire alarms had just gone off at once. Yellow and black spheres popped and crackled across the garage. The freezers. The rubble sacks. He reached out to steady himself and the something solid slammed down again.

Then Callum's knees buckled and the concrete floor welcomed him with open arms.

69

The tin of peaches gave a dull *bang* as it hit the concrete and buckled. Bright red covered the sell-by date, leaching colour back into the ancient label. It rolled around a lopsided circle and came to rest against Callum's chest.

Garage floor should've been cold. All that concrete. But it wasn't.

Warm and cosy.

Soft and comforting.

Emma's boots appeared, right in front of his face. Then she squatted down. Stroked his forehead. 'I'm so very sorry.' Her bottom lip trembled, eyes sparkling as the tears welled up. 'But I can't.'

The boots faded into the distance.

He blinked.

She was unloading the golf bags from the rack by the door – dumping them on the ground. In the gap behind where they'd been was a tall thin metal locker, fixed to the garage wall.

Warm and comfy, lying sprawled on the cosy concrete floor.

She pulled a bundle of keys from her pocket, sorted through them and unlocked the door. Pulled out a shotgun. 'It wasn't meant to happen like this.'

A *clack* sounded as she broke the shotgun open. 'But that's life, isn't it? One minute everything's fine and the next you're standing in front of the freezer, looking down at a human head. And it's looking *back* at you. And everything you've ever known about everything is a lie.' Emma wiped her eyes on her sleeve, then rummaged in a large leather satchel. Slid two red shells into the shotgun's breech.

Flipped it closed again.

Clack.

A dull throb bloomed at the back of Callum's skull. Spreading out in jagged waves.

'But you just have to cope, don't you? What else *can* you do?' She nodded to herself. Then walked out through the open garage door.

Shannon's voice came from outside, ramping up from normal person to police officer in the space of six words: *'What the hell are you... No! Emma, don't do anything stupid. We can talk about this. Put the gun—'*

BOOOOOM...

The squeal of tearing metal, the patter of shattered glass hitting the gravel drive.

'CALLUM! CALLUM, I'M—'

BOOOOOM...

Silence.

She stepped back into the garage. Sobbed. Stood there bent almost double beneath the weight of it. 'I ... I didn't want this. I *didn't.*'

Clack.

Emma broke the shotgun open again and the two spent cartridges spun into the air, twirling as they fell, leaving thin trails of smoke behind. Pinging as they bounced off the concrete.

This was it.

He was going to die here.

She dipped into the cartridge bag for another couple of shells. Slid them home.

Clack.

She bit her bottom lip. Sniffed.

At least it would be quick.

But she didn't shoot him. She took a deep shuddering breath and marched through the door that led into the house instead.

Callum forced a hand under himself. Pushed...

Nope.

The throbbing in his head got louder, sharper.

Maybe it was all for the best?

What else did he have going for him?

Crappy childhood. Failed relationship. Ruined career.

The only mark he'd leave on life would be right here on the garage floor. Eight pints of blood. And twenty minutes with a mop and a bucket of bleach would soon get rid of that.

A muffled boom sounded from somewhere deep within the house. Followed by another one.

So get up. Get your useless, *lazy,* good-for-nothing backside off the ground and *do* something. What if Shannon was still alive? What if he was lying out there, bleeding to death, because Callum was too busy wallowing in self-pity to get off his arse and help him?

'Grrrrah...' He pushed himself over onto his front, then back and up till he was on his knees.

The garage whirled and roared all around him, like being drunk on the waltzers, making his stomach churn.

Be sick later, get up *now*.

Emma reappeared through the door, her face flushed and shiny, tears glistening on her cheeks. Arms wrapped around the shotgun, like a teddy bear. 'Why does nothing ever turn out the way *I* want? Tell me that. WHY HAS IT ALWAYS GOT TO BE EVERYONE ELSE?' She rubbed at her eyes again. Then curled her shoulders forward and sobbed.

Get up, get up, get up, get up.

Do it now, while she's distracted.

But his legs just didn't want to.

She's going to shoot you. She's going to stick that shotgun in your face and pull the trigger. They'll have to scrape your brains off the floor with a shovel.

ON YOUR FEET!

Emma shook her head as the sobbing subsided. She blew out a shuddering breath. Wiped her eyes. Sniffed. Turned back to the gun cupboard and dipped into the shell bag again. 'I'm sorry.'

Callum grabbed the chest freezer and pulled himself up to his feet. *Clack.*

He held a hand out as she turned back towards him. 'Emma, you don't have to do this.'

'Why?' She stepped closer, raised the gun. 'Why did you have to come tonight? Why couldn't you wait till tomorrow?'

'Emma, the man you shot: Bob. There might still be time to save him.'

'It would all have been *gone* by then.'

'Emma, please, this can still end up OK, I promise.'

Closer.

The twin barrels of the shotgun were huge and dark.

She wiped her eyes again. 'It would all have been gone.'

Goodbye cruel world.

Callum nodded. 'I understand. I'm sorry, Emma, it...' His eyes went wide, staring over her shoulder. 'Bob!' Smiling as he stumbled forwards a couple of inches.

She turned.

And Callum lunged.

Shoved the shotgun to one side and hammered his fibreglass cast into her face *hard*.

She went over backwards, left arm pinwheeling as she fell, gun still held in her other hand.

It went off as her head cracked into the floor, a deafening roar that ripped a huge hole in the Range Rover's driver's door, shattering the window, tearing out through the roof.

He half jumped, half fell on top of her, pinning her gun arm to the ground. Smashing his cast into her face again. And one more time for luck.

Reared back as the shotgun clattered free of her limp fingers.

Grabbed the dented tin of bloody peaches and raised it high above his head, ready to crash it down...

A little bubble of scarlet popped from her squint nose. She coughed and more spattered out of her mouth, leaving her teeth stained dark pink.

Callum let the peaches fall back to the garage floor.

She shook beneath him, eyes screwed shut, tears dribbling down the side of her face. 'I'm sorry. I'm sorry...'

Wiped a hand across his mouth. 'Emma Travis-Wilkes, you're under arrest.'

'I'm so sorry...'

He dragged out his handcuffs. '"There's no point crying, little girl," said the Bonemonger with his scissor-sharp smile. "No one will hear you, and nobody cares."'

Callum lurched out of the garage and onto the driveway. The drizzle was like a soft kiss, cooling and fresh against his face.

Shannon's car was lopsided – the wing peppered with holes, the tyre flat, door hanging open with more holes punched through it.

'Bob?'

Gravel crunched beneath his feet as he staggered over to the door.

Shannon lay on his back across the front seats, one leg in the passenger footwell, the other dangling out of the car.

'BOB!'

A large dark stain covered the front of his yellow T-shirt, spreading across the word 'Norwich'.

Sodding hell.

Callum clambered around to the driver's side, hauled open the door and felt for a pulse. Swore. Dragged out his phone and called 999. 'OFFICER DOWN, I REPEAT, OFFICER DOWN!'

70

'And we're all done.' The doctor dropped his needle into the kidney dish. 'Excellent stitches, even if I say so myself.' A small round Teletubby of a man with a comb-over and Stalin moustache.

Callum just grunted.

'Now I'm going to write you a prescription for painkillers, but keep off the booze with them, OK? And just in case: get someone to stay with you tonight. Don't want you dying in your sleep, right? Right.' He taped a patch of gauze to the back of Callum's head. 'While you're here, we might as well change the dressing on your ear. Nurse, let's have some disinfectant…'

There was more, but it was just noise.

The treatment cubicle curtains opened and there was Franklin. She'd ditched the black suit and tie for a red lumberjack shirt, blue jeans, and trainers. Flashed her warrant card. 'Will he live?'

Dr Teletubby stepped back to admire his handiwork. 'Well, he's damn lucky she didn't fracture his skull, but other than that? Probably.'

Callum slid down from the table and picked up his jacket. The sleeves and back were stained brown and black. Some of it his blood, some of it Shannon's. 'What about Bob?'

Franklin grimaced. Shook her head. 'They did everything they could.'

Great.

Dr Teletubby pointed through to the reception area. 'Go park yourself for ten minutes while I sort out your pills and get you discharged.'

Callum followed Franklin back to the rows of plastic seating and the buzzing vending machines.

She pointed. 'You want a cup of tea or something?'

'Any word on Watt?'

'I'll get you a tea.'

Soon as she was gone, Callum folded forward till his chest rested against his knees. Wrapped his arms around his head. Pressing them into the gauze taped to the back. Squeezing. Making the stitches scream a sharp bitter song.

Shannon was *his* fault.

He should never have accepted that lift out to R.M. Travis's house. Should have made his own way there. Should've insisted.

Bloody hell.

Why did everything have to turn to shite? Why did it *always* have to—

'Callum? Are you OK?' Franklin settled in the chair beside his, the warmth of her body seeping through his dirty shirt.

'No.'

'Do you want me to get the doctor back?'

He blew out a breath. 'No. Thanks. But no.' Another sigh and he sat back up. 'Sorry.'

'Here: drink your tea.'

The plastic cup was scalding hot. And the contents tasted every bit as bitter and foul as he was inside.

Franklin put her hand between his shoulder blades and gave them a little rub. 'You didn't shoot him, Emma Travis-Wilkes did. She killed her dad, she killed Shannon, and she would've killed you too. It wasn't your fault.'

A nod. More horrible tea.

She gave a little laugh. Shook her head. 'This has been a *great* first week at work.'

He turned in his seat and smiled. 'Welcome to the Misfit Mob.'

'Oh, Callum, you're a poor sod, aren't you?'

'I'm a bloody disaster area.'

'No you're not. You're a good man, and Elaine was an *idiot* for throwing that away. Didn't know a good thing when she had it.'

Franklin's hand was warm against his back. Her thigh warm against his. Her smile warm and soft. Her lips...

He leaned in, breathing in the scent of her: lemons and jasmine and rosemary. Closed his eyes.

'Argh! Jesus!' Franklin's chair scraped back and she was on her feet. Backing away, staring down at him with her face curdled, as if he'd just coughed up a hairball into her lap.

Heat flooded Callum's face, prickled across the back of his neck, set his ears on fire. 'I'm sorry, I—'

'What is *wrong* with you? This is—'

'I thought there was a thing and—'

'I've got a fiancé!'

'I'm sorry! I didn't... Arrgh.' He curled up in his seat again. 'God's sake.'

'Just because I'm a black woman, doesn't mean I'm going to jump into bed with every pasty-faced horny bastard who knocks! You're just like all the rest of them!'

Idiot. Bloody stupid halfwit *idiot*.

He gritted his teeth and clenched his eyes shut.

Everything. Every *single* thing he touched.

Franklin's phone burst into song. Then silenced. 'What?'

There'd been a thing, hadn't there? Between them?

Her voice was hard and brittle. 'Oh, he's here all right.'

Idiot Callum. Such a bloody idiot.

'Yes. ... OK. Right. ... No, I'll tell him. ... OK, bye.'

He took a deep breath. Stood. 'I'm sorry. I didn't mean to make you feel uncomfortable or preyed-on or anything like that. I thought...'

She just glared back at him, arms folded, knuckles pale where she was gripping her phone.

'I don't know what I thought. Maybe it was Emma Travis-Wilkes trying to cave my skull in? Maybe that rattled something loose? Whatever. I wasn't thinking right and I'm sorry. I'm one hundred percent genuinely sorry.'

'I thought you were different, Callum.'

'Yeah, well apparently I'm a moron like every other man on the planet.' He struggled into his filthy jacket. Couldn't look her in the eye. 'It's OK. I'll get a taxi. Thanks for coming. You don't have to stay.'

A nurse squeaked up, clipboard in one hand, small white paper bag in the other. 'Callum MacGregor? I've got some painkillers for you.' She held out the clipboard. 'Just sign there where the X is...' A frown. 'Is everything all right?'

'No. I just made a complete and utter dick of myself.' He scrawled his name in the appropriate box, accepted the paper bag. 'Thanks.' Then turned and limped out through the doors.

Franklin followed him.

He kept going, out from beneath the canopy and into the rain. Stopped. Turned, both arms held out. 'I'm sorry, OK? My life's turned to shit and I'm *sorry*. That wasn't about you, it was about me being *fucking* useless.' Cold and damp seeped through his filthy jacket. He dropped his arms. 'Just go. Please. I've embarrassed myself enough for one night. I don't need an audience.'

She held up her phone. 'That was DS McAdams. The Duty Doctor's given Emma Travis-Wilkes a clean bill of health. They're putting her in Interview Four now.'

He turned and walked out into the night. 'Good for them.'

'McAdams says you can watch from the viewing suite, if you like?'

Interview Room Four looked bigger on the screen. Not so cramped.

'Are you sure you want to do this, Emma? These are very serious charges.' Mother's mop of bright ginger hair sat in the bottom right-hand corner of the TV, next to McAdams' hunched back in the bottom left.

Emma Travis-Wilkes shifted in her SOC paper oversuit – sperm-white rather than Smurf-blue – and glanced at the man sitting beside her: dark-blue three-piece suit, grey hair pulled back in a ponytail, little round glasses, pointy sideburns. Mr Slick gave her a tiny nod.

Callum sniffed. 'Here come the lies.'

He shifted his cheap plastic chair closer to the monitor. A line of little microphones, perched on the end of bendy metal sticks, poked out at him, each one dark and dead. Waiting for someone to flip the switch.

Franklin stood with her arms folded, leaning back against the door. About as far away as she could possibly get.

Yeah, well, couldn't exactly blame her.

Emma Travis-Wilkes took a deep breath. The left side of her face had swollen and darkened. The bruises taking hold from where Callum introduced her to his fibreglass cast. A sticking plaster made a pale stripe across the bridge of her nose. *'Having discussed the situation with my solicitor, I would like to make the following confession.'*

Mr Slick patted her on the arm, voice almost too low to make out. *'It's OK: in your own time.'*

'I killed them.'

There was a pause, then Mother leaned forward. *'Who did you kill, Emma? For the tape.'*

She stared back. *'All of them.'*

Franklin gave a little whistle. 'I genuinely didn't think it'd be that easy. Expensive lawyer like that? Thought he'd make her "no comment" for at least an hour or so. It's a bit of a let-down, to be honest.'

Callum didn't move. 'She's lying.'

'All of who, Emma?'

'I killed the police officer in his car – I shot him once in the stomach and once in the chest. Then I went through into the library and shot my father. Once in the...' She cleared her throat. 'Once in the chest and once in the head.' Emma stared at the ceiling. Gave a sharp, shuddering breath. 'Then I went into the garage and tried to kill the other police officer, but he was too quick and overpowered me. I'm glad he did. I ... wasn't myself. I needed to be stopped.'

'Hmph.' Franklin didn't sound impressed. 'That's the most half-arsed attempt to plead insanity I've ever seen.'

'I see, I see...' Mother patted McAdams on the shoulder. 'Let's try the photos, Andy.'

He dipped into a folder and came out with a handful of A4 printouts. Laid them across the table. 'I am now showing Ms Travis-Wilkes exhibits nineteen to twenty-seven.'

Difficult to see what they were of, from up here – the interview room's CCTV system wasn't high-res enough to show more than a row of grey and pink blurs.

'Do you recognise any of these, Emma?'

She licked her lips, then looked away. 'I killed them too.'

'Who were they?'

'I don't remember.'

'How many are they?'

'I don't remember.'

'You don't remember how many people you killed, cut up, and kept bits of in your father's freezer?'

'No. I don't remember. It was a long time ago.'

Mother picked up one of the pics. 'That's a human hand, right there, Emma. A human hand, severed at the wrist and put into a freezer bag. There's even a date on the label: April fourth, 2015. That's not so long ago, is it?'

'I don't remember.'

'Here's a bottom jaw, complete with lip, tongue, teeth, and part of the throat. November 2006. Who was he?'

Travis-Wilkes swallowed. 'I don't... Please.'

'Here's a severed head. We found it last week, behind some bushes in Holburn Forest. Do you recognise her?'

Travis-Wilkes stared.

'Oh, for God's sake, Dad, it's everywhere!' Emma jabs a finger at the kitchen worktops.

Tomato sauce. *Everywhere.*

He's splattered it all over the toaster and the wall, making bloodstains down the units, scarlet puddles on the floor.

'I *told* you I'd make you something.'

Dad doesn't even answer, just sits there at the breakfast bar, eating his cheese and ketchup sandwich. Chewing as he squints at that morning's paper.

'Could you not have waited *five* minutes? Look at this mess.'

He picks a pen from his pocket and circles something on the front page.

'Are you even listening to me?'

He circles something else, head on one side as if he's a cat considering whether or not to pounce.

'I said, look at this mess!' She marches over and snatches the paper off him.

'BODY FOUND IN CASTLEVIEW FLAT' sits above a photo of an ugly, soulless block of flats. There's another picture set into it – three people standing outside the building. A pretty black woman, a grey skeleton in a grey suit, and a man with a bruised face. He's the one Dad's drawn a circle around. Another around the name 'DC CALLUM MACGREGOR (31)'.

Her father looks up at her. Then over at the blood-smeared kitchen units. Frowns. Stands. And stalks from the room.

Emma hurls the paper down. 'I'LL JUST STAY HERE AND CLEAR UP AFTER YOU, SHALL I?' God's sake, he just gets *worse.* 'DON'T YOU WALK AWAY FROM ME!'

She storms after him, through into the double garage with its fall-out-shelter's worth of antique tinned goods, jars, and all those sodding freezers.

Dad's got one of them open, leaning in to rummage through the contents. Picking things from the deep-frozen depths and dumping them on the concrete floor. Tupperware boxes, freezer bags, carrier bags, lumpy tinfoil parcels thick with frost. They clatter and skitter away.

'DAD!'

Nothing.

'I swear to God, one of these days I'm going to get the shotgun out and blow your *bloody* head off. And then I'll shoot myself. Who'll look after your literary legacy then?'

He digs and rummages.

'I'm not your skivvy, Dad, I'm your *daughter*.'

Then he straightens up. Closes the chest freezer. Places something on the lid.

'LISTEN TO ME!'

He blinks at her. 'Sophie?' Then frowns.

'No: Emma. EMMA! MY NAME IS EMMA!'

'She was never as beautiful as you, Sophie.' A grin. 'But oh, how she *screamed*.'

Emma takes a step back. 'OK...'

'I can't find my hat.' He turns and walks back into the house, leaving her to clean up after him. Yet again.

'God's sake.' She gathers up the nearest frozen chunks. Marches over to the freezer and stops. Stares at what he's dumped on top of it as her mouth goes dry as a library shelf. 'Dad?'

Oh Jesus... It isn't, is it? It *can't* be.

But it is.

The Range Rover growls into the forest car park, headlights raking the surrounding trees, turning their bark monochrome. Emma parks as far away from the entrance as possible. Sits there, trembling.

Her breath hammers in her lungs, sharp and shallow, blood thundering in her ears.

She licks her lips and glances into the footwell.

The carrier bag is rippled with a layer of white frost, just visible in the dashboard lights.

Get rid of it. Get rid of it. Get rid of it!

She stumbles out into the cold night air and scrambles around to the passenger side. Grabs the carrier bag like an unexploded grenade.

The plastic burns her skin, right the way down to the bone.

Get rid of it!

So she hurls it, as far and as hard as she can.

It disappears into the gloom ... then cracks and thumps mark its progress down through a tree or a bush, finishing with a rattle and a thud.

Oh God.

She shuffles backwards, till the car's warm bonnet stops her going any further.

A head. A human head.

There was a human head in the freezer, with the leftovers and never-weres.

Oh God.

Emma runs a hand over her face.

Calm down. Calm down and breathe.

It's gone now. That's the important thing.

She scrambles back into the car, turns around and drives the hell out of there.

The forest ripples past the Range Rover's windows, caught for a moment in the headlights before vanishing forever.

It's gone. And there's nothing more to...

Her eyes widen and she slams on the brakes. Swears. And swears. And swears.

What if it's not the only thing in the freezers? What if there's other bits? What if the rest of the woman is in there?

Oh God.

Don't panic. It'll be OK.

Oh dear God.

Just... Just go back to the house and look.

And if there's more bits?

Then they go in ... bin-bags! Take them to the tip. NOT ALL AT ONCE! Do it gradually. A couple of bags at a time. To different dumps.

No one ever has to know about this.

Emma stares at herself in the rear-view mirror.

Because if they find out...

'Emma? I asked if you recognised her.'

'I ... don't remember.'

Mr Slick reached out and turned the photograph face down, then pushed it back across the table. A public-school voice with a superior drawl. *'I believe my client has made her feelings quite clear on this, Detective Inspector Malcolmson. Let's move on, while we're all young, there's a good girl.'*

No one moved.

Franklin bared her teeth. 'Sexist tosser!'

'He did it on purpose to rattle her.'

It didn't seem to work, because Mother just let out a big long sigh. *'Emma, Emma, Emma. I don't believe you killed all those people. Oh, you killed Bob Shannon and your father, and you tried to kill DC MacGregor, but the rest of them? No.'*

'I killed them all.'

'You see, I think your father killed them. I think he's been killing people for a long, long time, and when you found out about it, you did everything you could to protect his legacy. You think, if you take the blame, no one has to find out he wasn't the man they idolised.'

'I'm not protecting anyone.'

'How many people did he kill, Emma?'

'He didn't kill anyone! Why won't you listen to me?'

'Was it three? Four? Seven? A dozen?'

'NO ONE EVER LISTENS!' She battered her fists down on the tabletop. *'I did it. Not him: me.'*

'Detective Inspector Malcolmson: my client has cooperated with your enquiry and given you a full confession. Now – move – on.'

Mother tilted her head to one side. *'You loved your father, didn't you, Emma?'*

'Of course I do. My father is... My father was a saint. He had nothing to do with any of those ... remains.' She sat up straight. *'I'm the only murderer in our family. Me. Myself. I. Singular and accountable. I did it, because I'm sick and I need help.'*

Silence.

Then Callum leaned forwards and clicked the button beneath the nearest microphone. 'Ask her about Leo McVey. Him and her dad used to get off their faces on drugs and wreck things: hotel rooms, marriages, anything they could get their hands on.'

Mother flinched a little, then put a finger to her ear. Maybe she'd forgotten she'd put the earpiece in? *'Tell me about Leo McVey.'*

Emma's mouth snapped shut.

'He and your father were very close, weren't they?'

'I don't...' She glanced at her solicitor. Then back at Mother. *'No comment.'*

'The drinks, the drugs, the bad behaviour?'

'No comment.'

Callum hit the button again. 'Gareth Pike saw him attacking my parents. He never said McVey was alone in the car. McVey's always had Jaguars, but I'll bet you a hundred quid, R.M. Travis is a Range Rover man.'

Mother spread her hands on the tabletop. *'Your father's got a green Range Rover in the garage, doesn't he? You shot a dirty big hole in it.'*

'So?'

'He always drove Range Rovers, didn't he?'

'He liked to buy British. What's wrong with that?'

'Oh nothing, nothing.' She leaned in, lowering her voice to a pantomime whisper, *'Only we've got a witness who saw Leo McVey attack and abduct a family, twenty-six years ago: mother, father, and little boy. He bundled them into a white Range Rover. Only he's never owned one in his life.'*

Emma fidgeted with the sleeve of her oversuit.

'Now, wouldn't it be funny if I got on to the DVLA and asked them to search for all the vehicles registered to your father, and up popped a white Range Rover from exactly *that time?'*

'I...'

'Remember the severed head in that photo? It belonged to the woman McVey abducted with your father's car. It's been frozen all this time. That's funny too, isn't it?'

'No comment.' But she didn't sound quite so sure this time.

'And, of course, our witness said Leo McVey wasn't the only one in the car. He had someone else with him. That would be your father, wouldn't it?'

Emma blinked. *'It was—'*

'Actually,' Mr Slick put up a hand, *'I think this is a perfect place for a pause. My client and I need to confer.'*

Mother shrugged. *'Call it, Andy.'*

'Interview suspended at twenty-one minutes past midnight.' He stood. *'We'll be outside when you're ready to talk.'*

And the screen went blank.

Franklin groaned. 'Just as they were getting somewhere.'

'I'm genuinely sorry, you know.' Callum swivelled his seat round to face her. 'If I could take it back, I would.'

'Whatever idiot thought it was a good idea to let slimebags have a lawyer present during questioning, needs a good hard kick in the balls.'

'I should never have tried to kiss you.'

'"No comment" this and "I don't remember" that.'

'I'm serious. Can we just go back to how it was before?'

Franklin rolled her eyes. Took a deep breath. 'All right, all right. Just ... stop apologising. It's like watching a puppy grovel for scraps.'

'You're probably a crap kisser anyway.'

She scowled. 'I happen to be a *great* kisser, thank you very much.'

'I promise I'll never try to find out if that's true.'

'Deal.'

'I don't know, maybe a pizza or something? There's a takeaway on Harvest Lane that's open till three. They'll deliver.'

Franklin dug back into her packet of Wotsits. 'Suppose it's better than nothing.'

'Or, if you like curry, there's...'

The screen flickered back into life. *'Interview resumed at six minutes to one. Present: Detective Inspector Flora Malcolmson, DS Andrew McAdams, Miss Emma Travis-Wilkes, and Mr Reginald Flynn.'* McAdams sat back in his chair.

Mother nodded. *'Well, Emma?'*

She licked her lips. Stared down at the tabletop. *'My father wasn't in the white Range Rover with Leo McVey, it was me. I borrowed the car to go get more vodka and Uncle Leo came with me. He was already pretty wasted – we'd been drinking and snorting cocaine all day – so when I saw the family in that lay-by and decided to abduct them, he had no idea what was going on. I drove them off to the middle of the countryside and I killed them. I don't remember where, so there's no point asking. I dismembered the bodies and kept some parts in the freezer.'*

'I see.' Mother tapped her fingers against the tabletop. *'And how old were you at this point?'*

'Twenty-one.'

'Twenty-one? My, my, my. And did you and Leo McVey kill anyone else?'

'Uncle Leo didn't kill anyone. He'd passed out from the drink. I did it. All on my own. When he woke up that evening, I told him I'd let the family go. He doesn't know what I did.'

'Right. You see, the trouble is: I don't believe you.'

'It's the truth. And I have nothing further to say.'

Mr Slick nodded. *'You've had a full confession from my client. She won't be answering any further questions.'*

The custody area was nearly deserted, but the sounds of singing and swearing echoed through from the cell blocks. An after-midnight serenade, fuelled by cheap lager and low IQ.

Callum shuffled in and up to the desk – an oversized pulpit decorated with computer monitors and public safety posters. A stick insect in an ill-fitting wig sat behind it, leaning over a copy of the *Castle News and Post*, propping up his long thin face on one fist.

He didn't look up.

So Callum banged a hand down on the countertop. 'Shop.'

A flinch. Then he raised his head and pulled on a pair of oversized glasses. 'Ah, Constable MacGregor. We've been expecting you.'

Silence.

'Can we make this quick, Sarge, only it's been a *really* long day.'

'Of course we can. It would be my most delightful pleasure.' He rescued a mouse from beneath a stack of paperwork and wriggled it. Clicking away. 'Ah, here we are. Two things. One: when you're processing suspects, try not to cock up the DNA portion of the proceedings. It makes the rest of our lives a lot easier. And Two: your custody from this afternoon wants a word and he wants it with you.'

'Tell him to go screw himself, because I'm going home.'

A jagged smile. 'That's hardly the caring and compassionate face of Police Scotland we're tasked with presenting, is it, Constable?'

'Someone tried to bash my brains in today. A friend was shot and killed. I've been battered and bruised and humiliated. And I don't give a *toss* what some spoiled rap-star wank-badger wants. I'm – going – home.'

'He's up before the Sheriff at ten tomorrow morning. Make sure you see him before then.'

'I'd *love* to! Only I've been suspended without pay, so Mr Newman can go crap in his hat.'

Sergeant Stick Insect's eyes widened, magnified out of all proportion by his big glasses. 'Constable MacGregor, language!'

'Bye, Sarge.' Then he turned and marched out into the corridor, through the double doors, and away into the rain.

— the Bonemonger's waltz —

The old lady puffed on her long willow pipe. "Once upon a time there was a little boy whose soul was dark as the blackest cat. Whose eyes were green as jealousy. And whose skin was pale as the dead."

"What was his name?" asked Justin, eagerly.

"Why child, he didn't have a name back then, just an unpronounceable howl of pain and hatred. And he'd come down from the hills at night and steal skeletons from the villagers' graves. Then he'd take them out to the deepest darkest depths of the woods and dance with their bones till dawn."

R.M. Travis
Open the Coffins (and Let Them Go Free) (1976)

Ain't nothing so sad as a man in his prime,
Got dirt on his knees cos it's grovellin' time,
Shoot that poor f*ck in the back of the head,
Cos trust me, that b*stard is better off dead.

Donny '$ick Dawg' McRoberts
'Walter Peck, the Bugf*cker'
© Bob's Speed Trap Records (2016)

71

Mother glanced up at the clock on the office wall. 'Well, we'll just have to start without him.'

Which meant it was just Callum, Dotty, Franklin, and Mother for Monday morning prayers. No McAdams.

She clapped her hands together. 'First order of business: the doctors say John's going to be in the high-dependency ward for at least a couple of days, but it looks like he'll be fine. Ish. There might be some brain damage, but they won't know till he wakes up.'

Dotty stuck up her hand. 'I've got a card for everyone to sign.' She held that up as well – something with a teddy bear on crutches surrounded by love hearts. 'GET WELL SOON!!!' in big letters. 'And I've started a whip-round too. Maybe get him something nice so he knows we're all thinking of him.'

'Second: Bob Shannon and Raymond Montgomery Travis are down for post mortem today, starting at ten, if anyone wants to volunteer? Anyone? No?' A shrug. 'Fine, Rosalind, you can do those.'

Franklin sagged. 'Not *again*.'

'Emma Travis-Wilkes has confessed to the murder of Robert Michael Shannon, the murder of her father, and the attempted murder of DC Callum MacGregor. She's *also* confessed to the abduction and murder of Callum's parents and brother, and an unspecified number of other victims. Which I'm a hundred percent sure is a lie, but can't get her to admit it. She's up before the Sheriff at twelve – expect "remanded without bail" and "sentencing to follow psychiatric reports". But I'll eat my own fleece if she gets less than thirty years.'

Callum folded his arms. 'What about the freezers?'

'SEB are calling in the forensic anthropologists from Dundee Uni.

Could take weeks to work out what's human and what's not. How long it takes to identify who the bits *came* from in the first place is anyone's guess. Maybe years.' Mother perched her backside on Watt's empty desk. 'Which brings us onto a sticky subject.' She pointed. 'Callum is officially suspended without pay, pending an investigation into the aggravated assault on Detective Chief Inspector Reece Powel. If anyone asks, and I mean *anyone* – don't care if it's your best mate, your mum, or the blessed Chief Superintendent himself – you tell them Callum's here as a witness on the Travis-Wilkes case, and that's all. He is *not* working on any other cases. Understood?'

Franklin and Dotty nodded.

Callum frowned out at them. 'Just so you know, I didn't touch Poncy Powel. If anyone battered him, it was Ainsley Dugdale. Not me.'

'Just here as a witness, remember?'

He stared up at the manky ceiling tiles. 'Yes, Boss.'

'We're going back to the beginning. Tod Monaghan worked at Strummuir Smokehouse, so did one of his victims, and another victim did a course there. I know we've already interviewed every employee, but we need to do it again. Who did Monaghan hang out with? Did he mention any friends from outside work? Who was he killing with? Ask, ask, and ask again.' She clapped her hands together. 'Right now, Ashlee Gossard has the tiniest, slimmest, most infinitesimal chance of still being alive. Get out there and *find* her.'

Cecelia was hunched over her desk, poking away at her computer. Most of her long brown hair was tucked back, out of the way, but a strand of it – about as thick as a finger – disappeared into the corner of her mouth. Making little sooking noises as she chewed.

Callum knocked on the doorframe. 'Did your mother never tell you about that?'

'Gah!' Bolt upright, soggy hair swinging loose again. 'Don't sneak up on people, it's rude.'

'I got hauled in by the rubber heelers yesterday. Chief Inspector Gilmore told me he'd heard rumours I was covering for Elaine at that crime scene. Care to explain why?'

She pulled a face. 'Ah. Yes. No. No idea.'

'You're a terrible person, you know that don't you?'

'Oh definitely.' She sat back, swivelling her chair from side to side. 'You here about the freezers, or the lab results from the Gossard house? Because if it's the lab results, that's very much *not* my fault. I took the samples, I labelled them *properly*, so whoever arsed it up did it at the laboratory.'

'Officially, I'm just here as a witness, but unofficially: freezers.'

She picked a sheet of paper from the top of her printer. 'We won't know for certain until the anatomy gurus get here from Dundee, but I'd say you're looking at between six and twelve individuals spread among the eight freezers. That's assuming everything *else* is what the labels say it is. And that's not...' She pointed at his jacket as singing erupted from somewhere deep in his pocket. 'Are you going to answer that?'

'Sorry.' He pulled out his phone. 'Hello?'

A woman's voice that sounded as if it could crush walnuts just by shouting at them. *'Constable MacGregor? Sergeant Price: custody suite. I have a note here that you're to see a Mr Donald Newman this morning before he goes before the Sheriff?'*

'I can't. I've been suspended. I'm not on active duty.' He glanced at Cecelia. 'I'm not even in the building.'

'Nice try. I'll expect you here before ten.'

Oh for God's sake. 'But—'

'Don't make me come looking for you.' Then she hung up.

Wonderful.

Cecelia passed over the sheet from her printer. 'Take a look: going by the freezer-bag labels our human remains date from thirty-one years ago through to about twenty ten. The handwriting gets a bit shaky at the end. A lot of the stuff's been frozen, thawed, and frozen again, going by the state of it. Do you know they had bolognese sauce in there going back to the seventies?' She shuddered. 'And I thought my mum was bad for hoarding leftovers. The *seventies!*'

'Lovely.' He scanned the list of items recovered. Maybe one of the hands belonged to his father, or his mother? Or maybe the eyes? Or one of the hearts? 'Any sign of ... children's remains. Like a five-year-old boy?'

Alastair.

The bumhead.

In his cartoon-fox T-shirt.

Cecelia shook her head. 'But then I'm only going by the bits that are instantly recognisable. Who knows with the other stuff?'

'Thanks.'

'Now go away, I'm working.'

He backed out of the room.

'And stop sneaking up on people!'

Callum wandered back along the corridor and through into the stairwell, frowning down at the list. A dozen victims over a space of thirty-one years. Not the most prolific killer Oldcastle had ever seen – not even in the same league as someone like Jeff Ashdale – but still...

And the experts from Dundee might ID even more. So—

He jerked to a halt.

Sod.

Detective Superintendent Ness was standing right in front of him, jaw set, shoulders back. 'DC MacGregor.'

'Super.'

Her face barely moved as she spoke. 'I thought I suspended you yesterday.'

'Yes, Super. It... I'm here as a witness? The Travis-Wilkes' case is—'

'Tell me, Constable, why is there a *very* expensive lawyer sitting in my custody suite threatening to sue Police Scotland if you don't speak to his client?'

Oh sodding hell. So Donny '$ick Dawg' Newman had called in reinforcements.

'I can't speak to him, Super: you suspended me. It's not my—'

'Hello?' Franklin's voice echoed through the stairwell. 'Callum?' She came thundering down the stairs, two at a time. Nodded at Ness. 'Super.' Then back to him. 'Sorry, thanks for waiting.'

'I...?'

She turned her perfect white smile on the superintendent. 'We've been going over his statement from last night. I had to nip off to the toilet. Emergency situation. Anyway,' she took hold of Callum's arm, 'let's get you that lift home.' Another nod. 'Super.'

'Oh no you don't.' Ness held up a hand. 'Constable MacGregor isn't going anywhere until he's seen this Mr Newman and his solicitor. And I want you there for corroboration.'

Franklin's smile slipped. 'Super?'

'You will make sure nothing happens, are we clear, Constable? If I've got to spend the next six months tied up in court, you're going to find yourself doing every crummy crappy horrible job I can find.' A big bright smile. 'Off you go then.'

'Yes, ma'am.' Franklin led him away downstairs. Out through the doors at the bottom. Slumped back against the bare breezeblock wall. 'Oh God... Why did you have to drag me into this?'

'How is this my fault?'

'I don't know, do I? Maybe you antagonised Newman with your "everyone grew up in care" speech? Or maybe you just rub *everyone* up the wrong way.' She straightened up and poked him in the chest. 'I stood up for you with Ness, and you better not mess this up for me, Callum. You go in there and you be nice to this dick and you say "three bags full" if you have to. Understand?'

Lovely.

'Thanks. Thanks a heap.' He pushed through the double doors and into the custody area.

Peace reigned inside, just the ping and click of the central heating to spoil the silence. Last night's stick insect had been replaced by someone who would've looked more at home on the rugby pitch, or a boxing ring. That would be Sergeant Price. She had her brown hair pulled back in a ponytail, a pair of half-moon glasses perched on the end of her nose as she passed a form across the custody desk to Mr Slick – Emma Travis-Wilkes' lawyer.

So Mr Slick had got himself *another* celebrity client. That was quite the portfolio he was building: a murdering liar, and a misogynist scumbag druggie. All he needed was a kiddy-fiddling TV presenter from the 1970s to complete the set.

Slick took a fountain pen from his inside pocket and signed. 'Thank you, Sergeant.'

She pointed off to a row of easy-to-hose-down plastic seats. 'Make yourself at home and I'll give you a shout, soon as Ms Travis-Wilkes is ready.'

The room's only other occupant was a chunky middle-aged man in a rumpled suit. Head a combination of Yorkshire Terrier meets pickled egg. Bags under his eyes, stubble on his chins, fingers stained turmeric-yellow from too many cigarettes. He was slouched across a couple of seats, as if he'd forgotten to bring his bones with him.

Mr Slick walked over to the plastic seating, pulled a handkerchief from his pocket, and dusted a chair as far away from Captain Scruffy as possible, before lowering his tailored backside into it. Sat there with his briefcase on his lap. Still as a garden gnome.

Callum slumped up to the counter. 'I came, OK?'

Sergeant Price flashed him a smile. 'Constable MacGregor, is it? Good. Right. Mr Newman's solicitor has laid out some ground rules for your meeting: no recording, no harassing his client, and everything said is to be considered off the record.'

'He can make all the rules he wants: I don't *want* to meet his client. His client can go—'

'Poop in his hat. Yes, I do read the night logs.' She pointed at a plain veneer door. 'You can use the solicitors' briefing room. Fifteen minutes.' Sergeant Price stared at him with all the warmth of an iceberg. 'Do we have a problem, Constable?' And there was that walnut-crushing tone again.

'No, Sarge.'

A deep breath. A sigh. Then Callum wandered over to the room and pulled open the door. Not even bothering to look at Mr Slick. 'Come on then, let's get this over with.'

The consultation room had three chairs, a frosted window high up by the ceiling, and a Formica table covered in other people's initials and swearwords. Callum collapsed into the chair beneath the window. Franklin was next, leaning back against the wall, arms folded.

And two minutes later, Donald '$ick Dawg' Newman swaggered in. They'd let him keep his own jeans and trainers, but confiscated his belt, shoelaces, and leather jacket. Someone had lent him a scruffy Oldcastle Police polo shirt to cover his naked chest. He slouched into the chair opposite Callum, one hand tucked into the waistband of his trousers, stubble blueing the gaps around his high-maintenance facial hair. 'Sup, Bruv?'

But it wasn't Mr Slick who shambled in after him and closed the door, it was Captain Scruffy. He grunted his way down into the last free chair. Rummaged through his pockets and came out with a packet of nicotine gum. Popped a couple. Chewing through a broad Glaswegian accent. 'Right, gentlemen, youse is all aware of the ground rules, and that? No sneaky recording the conversation. Everything said in here is, like, *mega* off the record, man.'

This was the *very* expensive lawyer Superintendent Ness was so worried about?

Took all sorts.

Callum stared across the table. Not saying anything.

Newman grinned at him. 'You look like crap, Bruv.'

He clenched his good hand into a fist. 'I'm not your "Bruv".'

'Chill, man, we just talkin', is all.' He spread his hands on the tabletop. 'You been to see Irene, yeah? And the kids?'

'You assaulted her. You broke Willow's arm. She was *four*.'

'Yeah, well, I been through some tough times in my life. Grew up in care. Got into trouble. And it was the drugs, yeah? They made me do things I'm not proud of, Bruv.' A wee shrug. 'And you caught me, like, bang to rights, innit? Gonna plead guilty and throw myself onna mercy of the courts. Do my time. Get my life in order.'

Captain Scruffy gave a little snort. 'Trust us, Donny, no way you're goin' down. When I get through with the Sheriff, they're gonnae give you a medal for being an upstanding citizen.'

'I'm gonna make amends, Bruv. Gonna make it up to Irene: give that bitch a huge cheque, like an apology for what I did and all that child support I never paid. Bitch can get herself a nice house in Blackwall Hill or something.'

Callum picked at a set of carved initials in the Formica. 'You actually think that'll make it all better?'

'Yeah, I was a dick. Like I said: drugs.'

'And don't call her a bitch.'

There was a pause and Newman tilted his head to the side, one eyebrow raised. 'You still ain't got it, has you, Bruv?'

Outside, in the custody suite, someone coughed like they were trying to expel a lung.

Franklin shifted against the wall.

Captain Scruffy chewed.

Newman sat forward. 'Got into a fight when I was twenty – bit of a barney over who owed who for a load of skunk went missing – sons of bitches broke my nose and cheek and jaw. Had to get plastic surgery to fix it, Bruv. And I thinks to myself, while I is here, might as well get me some more handsome, yeah?'

'There a point to this?'

'You really don't recognise me, do you? *Bruv.*'

'I told you to stop calling me that, I'm not your...'

Oh yeah, me and Leo: we go back years, innit? See when I was growing up in a home? He visited me, like every week. ... Man's a star, right? Been like a dad to me.

It couldn't be, could it?

No.

There would be a family resemblance, or something, wouldn't there?

Looks like he's barely into his twenties: turned thirty last year. Suppose healthy living and Botox will do that for a man. Well, that and a face-lift, a nose job, and three hours a day with a personal trainer.

Newman lifted the waistband of his borrowed polo shirt, showing off his shaved washboard stomach with its tattoo of a cartoon fox. Not identical to the one on his T-shirt all those years ago, but close enough.

Sodding hell...

Callum licked his lips. 'Alastair?'

'There we go.'

'I thought you were dead...'

'Nah, Bruv, I's a superstar and that. Right, Mr McQueen?'

'Oh aye. That you are indeed, Donny.'

Callum stared. 'But ... what happened?'

'Tried to get in touch a few years back. You know? Googled you, like, a million times. Thought maybe you were a midfielder for Celtic, but he looks nothing like us, yeah?' The fake London patois was slipping. 'So I hired myself a private detective. And now here we are.'

'No: what happened to *you*? After that day. When you all got abducted.'

Newman ... Alastair folded his arms. Looked away. 'Too soon, Bruv. Too soon.'

'Look, you were there. You're a witness. You saw what Leo McVey did – we can put the bastard behind bars!'

Alastair sucked a breath through his teeth. 'Man's been like a dad to me.'

'Only because he helped R.M. Bloody Travis murder our *real* dad. And our mum!'

'Nah, he's—'

'He *helped*, Alastair. They'd be alive today and I wouldn't have grown up in sodding care homes. Neither would you. We would've been a family!'

Alastair slumped back in the chair again. Frowned at him. 'You want to do Leo for killing Mum and Dad?'

'Of course I sodding do.'

The only sound in the small room was Captain Scruffy's wheezy breath.

And then Alastair shrugged. 'I'm-a think about it, yeah?' The patois was back. 'You asking me to snitch on the man brought me up. That's cold, Holmes. I'm-a speak to my legal representative now.'

Captain Scruffy took the nicotine gum from his mouth and stuck it to the underside of the table. 'And that concludes our business here this morning.' He nodded at Callum. 'We'll be in touch, pal.'

72

Callum marched past the custody desk and pushed through the door into the custody suite.

Franklin was right behind him. 'Your brother's alive; why have you got a face like a badger's backside? Isn't this a good thing?'

'I'll just be a minute.' Grinding it out between his teeth. 'Five tops.'

She groaned as he shoved through to the female cells: a twin line of blue-painted metal doors. 'Please tell me you're not doing what I think you're doing!'

'Of course I sodding am.' He pointed at the hatch mounted on the door of each cell. 'Help me look. She's in here somewhere.'

'Callum, you're a witness. Worse: you're a *victim*. She tried to kill you. You can't just rock up and have a cosy wee chat with Emma Travis-Wilkes, the Procurator Fiscal will do her nut. Wilkes's lawyer will have a field day!'

'Five minutes tops.'

'Oh for God's sake...'

He slid down the hatches and peered into each cell, working his way along one side until there she was. Emma Travis-Wilkes.

She was sitting on the blue plastic mattress with her back against the wall, legs folded into the lotus position, forearms resting on her knees. A calm smile on her face, even with all the bruises.

Nice to see someone was enjoying themselves.

Callum thumped on the door. 'Hello, Emma. Remember me?'

'How's your head?' She turned the smile up a bit. 'I'm sorry I had to hit you.'

'This lawyer of yours, Flynn. He's not from around here, is he? His suit's worth more than I make in a year.'

'My publishers organised everything. I phoned my publicist, said, "I've just killed my father," and the next thing you know: ta-daaaa.' She unhooked her legs and stood. 'I wanted to thank you for arresting me. For … stopping me.'

'Oh, don't worry, that was a *real* pleasure.'

Emma padded across the concrete floor on her bare feet. Placed a hand against the door. 'Do you know what it's like to live in the shadow of a famous parent? … No. Of course you don't. Sorry.' She shrugged. 'Believe me, you were lucky. Living with someone like my father, looking after him and his bloody legacy. Did you know, just last week they were talking about putting him on a stamp? On a *stamp*. How is anyone supposed to compete with that?'

She closed her eyes and took a big breath. 'God, I'm finally *free*. I can write again. My *own* words. Ooooooh… No more adult nappies, no more spoon-feeding him on bad days, no more watching him crumble like a sandcastle as the tides of time rush in.'

'But you didn't kill my mum and dad, did you? It was him.'

'What does it matter? He's dead, isn't he? He can't do…' A frown. 'His legacy is more important than a few dead bodies. Oh, not to *you* – I get that – but to the world. If he was some sort of monster, parents wouldn't buy his books, would they? Generations of children would miss out on *Russell the Magic Rabbit*. No one would ever read *Open the Coffins* again.'

'So you're taking the blame to protect his literary estate?'

'I'll be free.'

'How much did they offer you?'

'I can write again!'

'Because I'm going to burn your phoney confession to ash. Then I'm going to do the same with your dad's reputation. And then I'm going after Leo McVey.'

Her eyes narrowed. 'You can't do that.'

Callum inched closer to the hatch and dropped his voice to a harsh whisper. 'I've got an eyewitness. The boy your dad and Leo McVey abducted? My brother. He's still alive. And we're lighting the fires.'

'Hmm…' Emma blinked at him a couple of times, then smiled. 'My lawyer's very, very good. He says if I plead guilty they'll sentence me to treatment at a secure psychiatric facility, where I can get the help I so desperately need. And after two, maybe three years, when they finally declare me cured and fit to return to society, I'll find a *very* supportive friend in my publisher.' The smile was as sharp as it was cold. 'Because that's the kind of caring socially responsible international corporation they are.'

'Let me guess – it's the same company that publish your father's books.'

'They've been extremely kind to me.'

'Oh grow up. They didn't parachute a fancy-pants solicitor in to look after *your* best interests, they sent him here to look after *theirs*. How much is your dad's literary estate worth every year: a million? Two? Probably more, now he's dead.'

Franklin grabbed Callum's arm. 'Come on, that's enough.'

'And your publishers don't want anyone to find out he was a serial-killing tosspot because it'll spoil their sales figures.'

A sharp woman's voice boomed out behind them. 'Can I help you?'

Callum turned and there was Sergeant Price, all puffed up, shoulders back. Looking every inch the prop forward.

Franklin stepped in front of her. 'We're looking for Emma Travis-Wilkes.'

'In this station we check with the custody sergeant *before* we talk to suspects.'

'Right. OK. Thanks. Good pointer.' Franklin took hold of Callum's arm again. 'We'll just be on our way.'

'That's probably a good idea.'

She dragged Callum down the corridor and out into the custody suite. Then through the doors and into the bare-breezeblock corridor. Shoved him up against the wall. 'Are you *insane*?'

'Her solicitor's manipulating her to—'

'If Wilkes tells him about your visit, he – will – have – you – fired. Is that what you want?' Franklin let go. 'Because if it is, you're on your own.'

Callum stared at her. The flared nostrils. The wide eyes. The bared teeth.

'Fine.' He pushed past her, out through the double doors and into the rain. Turned. 'Emma Travis didn't kill my mum and dad, OK? She didn't abduct Alastair. It was her dad and Leo Bloody McVey.'

'For God's sake!' Franklin jabbed a hand back towards the cell block. 'Even if Donny "Sick Dawg" Newman is telling the truth, even if he *is* your brother, he was five when it happened. Five years old. Do you have any idea how easy it'll be to rip his testimony into tiny frilly little pieces?'

'That's not—'

'And Wilkes *admitted* it. She killed her own father! She killed Bob Shannon. She nearly killed you! Who's the jury going to believe?'

He closed the gap. 'You didn't see her. She shot Bob and she was in pieces. Sobbing. Horrified. Does that sound like someone who's murdered and dismembered a dozen people? Who's been killing since she was *sixteen* years old?' He marched away a couple of paces, then back again. 'Because that's when the first chunks of human being went into a freezer-bag at Casa Del Travis: thirty-one years ago. And *apparently* she's been getting away with it ever since. But shooting a retired copper in a Norwich City T-shirt makes her break down in tears? You believe that?'

Franklin stared up into the downpour for a moment. 'It doesn't matter, OK? It'll all come out at the trial. Newman can—'

'There won't even *be* a trial! She pleads guilty this morning, and that's it. No jury. No witnesses. No trial. Emma Travis-Wilkes goes off to a rubber room for two years while her father and Leo McVey GET AWAY WITH BUTCHERING MY PARENTS!'

The rain hissed against the bland featureless back of Division Headquarters. Bounced off the patchwork tarmac of the rear podium car park. Drummed on the roofs of the parked patrol cars, pool cars, and assorted private vehicles. Soaked through Callum's hair and trickled down the back of his neck. Leached into his jacket.

He screwed his eyes shut. Bit his lip. Took a deep breath. 'Sorry. I don't... This is all a bit... It's a shock, OK?'

Franklin's hand was warm on his arm. Her voice: soft. 'Maybe you should take a couple of days off?'

'Yeah. Maybe.' After all, it wasn't as if he was already suspended or anything. He turned. 'They killed my mum and dad, they took my brother, and they're going to get away with it.'

'Raymond Montgomery Travis is dead.'

'That's not the point. He shouldn't get to stay a "beloved children's author" – he's a serial-killing dick-monkey. People should be spitting on his grave.' Callum wiped his hands across his face and flicked the water out into the soggy morning. 'They're going to put the bastard on a *stamp*. How is that...' Wait a minute.

'Callum?'

Parked cars circled the gap behind the buildings, the space in between broken up into individual bays. A familiar red Mitsubishi Shogun sat in the far corner, and there was someone slumped in the driver's seat.

'Callum, are you all right?'

He jogged across the car park, splashing through the puddles.

McAdams was a crumpled heap, head thrown back, hands loose in his lap, mouth hanging open. Skin pale as mist. Not moving.

Oh Christ. He was dead, wasn't he.

Callum tried the door. It clunked open.

A sour smell oozed out of the car, layered with the scents of wood smoke and menthol.

'McAdams? Sarge?' He reached in and shook McAdams' shoulder. 'Hello?'

'Nnnghmppph...' McAdams blinked. Shuddered. Then let loose a deep rattling cough. 'Whrm I?'

'You're going to hospital.'

'No. No hospital.' Another cough and he sagged back in his seat. 'I'll be fine.'

Franklin clunked open the passenger door and slid into the seat. 'You look like you already died.'

That got her a smile. 'I love you too, Rosalind.'

'Callum's right, you need to go to hospital.'

He didn't move. 'It's very sweet of you both, but I'm not going to the sodding hospital. Are we clear on that? No – hospital. *Je ne vais pas aller à l'hôpital.*'

'But you're—'

'Dying. I know. And I'm *not* going to do it in a starchy bed surrounded by strangers and machines that go *ping*.'

Stubborn old git.

Callum sighed. 'Fine, no hospital.'

'Good. Now, where are we going? You're both obviously headed out somewhere. Have we got a lead on Ashlee Gossard?'

'I'm taking Callum home, before he gets himself properly fired.'

McAdams raised an eyebrow. 'You're taking him home? Are you two...?'

'No, we are not.'

'Well, that's probably just as well, you have about as much on-screen sexual chemistry as a loaf of wholemeal bread.' He clicked on his seat-belt. 'Well, climb in, Constable MacGregor. I'll give you a lift. No point getting a nice clean pool car all wet. You too, Rosalind: you can catch me up on the morning's shenanigans.'

She pointed over her shoulder, towards the Divisional Headquarters. 'Maybe I'd be better off—'

'In you get, Constable.'

'Yes, Sarge.' She got in the front.

Callum slid into the back. 'You sure you're OK to drive?'

McAdams grinned. 'Let's find out.' He cranked the engine, setting it roaring, then slid them down the ramp and onto Peel Place.

Some civic-minded soul had removed the traffic cone hats from the war memorial opposite, and given the three bronze figures Oldcastle Warriors scarves instead. The blue fabric hanging limp and dark in the rain.

'Come on then, Rosalind: shenanigans?'

'Callum's brother Alastair's alive, only now he's calling himself Donald Newman, AKA: Donny McRoberts, AKA: Sick Dawg.'

McAdams slammed on the brakes and the Shogun slithered to a halt on the damp tarmac. 'Really? Congratulations, Callum! That's...' He turned and raised an eyebrow. 'Didn't you pair arrest him yesterday for beating up his ex, sexually assaulting a police officer, making threats to kill, and possession of Class A drugs?'

Heat bloomed in Callum's cheeks.

'What a jolly family reunion that must have been. Still, at least you'll know where he is for the next six to eight years.' A wink, then McAdams faced forward again, driving them past the front of Division Headquarters.

A crowd of media people jostled by the main entrance, sheltering beneath umbrellas, doing pieces to camera and taking photos. Behind them were a group of protestors, waving placards with things like 'BRING BACK HANGING!', 'FATHER-KILLING BITCH!', and 'YOU MURDERED THE MAGIC!!!' More people drifted in off the street. By lunchtime there'd probably be a full-on lynch mob.

McAdams pointed. 'It's been on the radio all morning. Tributes to R.M. Travis, from all his celebrity chums. Someone's started fundraising for a statue.' A sniff. 'Morons.'

Callum poked McAdams in the shoulder – all bones. 'Your oncologist wants you to make an appointment.' After all, why *shouldn't* he share the misery?

'Not this again.'

'You need to start your chemotherapy!'

DHQ faded in the rear-view mirror, swallowed by the rain.

'Have you ever tried it? No, didn't think so.' McAdams took a left, past a squat grey church and its peeling 'THOU SHALT HAVE NO OTHER GODS BEFORE HIM!' posters. 'So don't tell me what I've got to do. I'm not having another round of bloody chemo, and that's final.'

'Your oncologist...' Callum sat back. Frowned. 'Your oncologist told me you've not even *started* this course of therapy.'

'It's my life, and it's my death too.'

'But you were on the phone – you called from the hospital, wanting an update on the smokehouse searches. I heard your nurse in the background.'

McAdams flashed a smile over his shoulder. 'Good, wasn't it? I recorded four or five of them last time round. Now all I have to do is hit play and people don't bang on about me not going to chemo. It stops Mother worrying.'

Not just a stubborn old git, he was devious too.

'But you're—'

'Do you want to know what I do instead? When everyone thinks I'm strapped into my deathchair in the hospital getting poison pumped into my veins? I go and park outside the castle, or across the water by the golf course, or just a lay-by somewhere up on Blackwall Hill. I sit in my car and look out at the city. And I wonder if anyone's going to remember me when I'm gone...'

A row of little shops went by, windows all dark, waiting for the morning to begin.

McAdams coughed again. Grimaced. Swallowed. 'No one ever remembers the police officers, do they? Oh, if we cock something up it's all over the papers: public enquiries, questions in parliament. Heads must roll!' Right at the roundabout then left, drifting by the closed nightclubs, bars, and takeaways on Harvest Lane. 'And if we actually *catch* the bad guy, do we get the credit? Do they bang on in the media about our thousands of man hours and dedication and genius? Do they hell. It's all about the killer, isn't it? How many people they murdered. What they did to the bodies afterwards. All the gory sensationalised details.' He shook his head. 'No one ever gives a toss about us.'

Franklin shifted in her seat. 'That's not true.'

'Name a serial killer.'

'Andrei Chikatilo.'

'I'll see Andrei Chikatilo and raise you Dennis Nilsen, Peter Manuel, John Wayne Gacy, Ted Bundy, and Harold Shipman. Name the police officer who caught any of them.'

McAdams pulled up at the traffic lights. Rain battered the Shogun's roof. Outside, an old lady lumbered through the downpour, dragging a tiny terrier along on the end of its leash. The lights turned green and he turned, past a strip joint with 'WE ARE HIRING!' in the window.

'No?' He sucked air through his teeth. 'How about this then: Jeffrey

Dahmer. He's *properly* famous. Never mind who caught him, name one of his victims. Just one.'

Right, onto the main road.

'See, you can't. All people care about is the killer. The rest of us don't matter at all.'

Kings River lay just beyond the docks, swollen and dark, breakwater curling against the supports of Dundas Bridge.

'Oh, one exception: if the victim's famous. People care about them then. JFK, John Lennon, *they* get remembered. The rest of us are just footnotes in a true-crime book.' He slowed for a small coughing fit. Then shuddered. 'So Emma Travis-Wilkes will probably be famous for generations. A serial killer who murdered her bestselling-children's-author father.'

Callum poked him again. 'She isn't a serial killer, it's all lies.'

'Do you *really* still believe the popular press and prurient public care about the truth, Constable? How sweet. And where do you stand on the topics of Santa Claus and the Easter Bunny?'

The Shogun growled its way over the bridge.

'You are such a dick.'

'Oh, no doubt.' McAdams gave a small, sour laugh. 'You know what I did this morning? I went up and I sat in the barn behind Thaw Cottages. I shouldn't have left Watt there...'

Franklin turned to him. 'Mother says he's out of surgery and they think he'll be OK.'

'Do they? Oh that's good.' He nodded. 'That's something.'

'Of course he might have brain damage, but— Sod.' She pulled out her ringing phone. 'DC Franklin. ... Right. ... No, no put them through. ... Yes. Thanks.' Franklin held the phone against her chest. 'It's the Land Registry Office.' Back to the call. 'Hello? ... Right. ... Yes, hang on a second.' She produced her notebook, pinning it against the dashboard. 'OK. ... 14 Lehman Road, Blackwall Hill. ... Yes.' Wrinkles appeared between her eyebrows. 'How many others? ... Can you text them to me? ... Yes. Thanks. ... No, that's great. Bye.'

She hung up. 'According to the Land Registry Office, Paul Terrance Jeffries only owns one property – in Blackwall Hill. He inherited it from a Mrs Georgina Mason. But *before* that he was left another four houses from various old biddies. And guess who he sold them all to?'

Callum had a stab at that one: 'Northeast Ecclesiastical Trust Holdings Limited.'

'Remember when you asked if N.E.T.H. was some sort of pensions and investment pot for the clergy?'

'But he kept Mrs Mason's house.'

Franklin reached across the car and patted McAdams on the shoulder. 'Change of plan, Sarge. We're off to Blackwall Hill.' Then she was poking at her phone, holding it to her ear as it rang. 'Mother? ... Rosalind. I think we know where Imhotep's keeping Ashlee Gossard...'

73

McAdams threw the Shogun around the roundabout, siren wailing over the squealing tyres. Lights flashing, reflecting back from the wet tarmac.

Callum braced his fibreglass cast against the door, leaning into it as the car fishtailed out the other side. Holding onto his phone as tight as possible. 'No, I don't know what the nature of the emergency is, I—'

'Well how can you possibly need an ambulance if you don't know what the emergency is?'

'All right, here: one young woman, suffering from extreme dehydration, shock, and starvation. How's that for starters?'

The tyres screeched again.

Franklin clutched the grab handle above her door, pretty much shouting into her mobile phone as the traffic parted before them and the streets raced past. 'NO, *LEHMAN* ROAD. LEMUR, ECHO, HOTEL, MIKE, ALPHA, NOVEMBER. ... YES. I NEED A FIREARMS TEAM THERE SOON AS YOU CAN...'

'An ambulance should be with you in about twenty minutes.'

'No. Not twenty minutes, *now!*'

'...WELL WHAT USE IS THAT? ... NO, THAT'S NOT GOOD ENOUGH. THERE'S A YOUNG GIRL'S LIFE AT STAKE – TELL THEM TO GET THEIR GUNS LOADED AND THEIR FINGERS OUT!'

'Tell you what, I'll get every available ambulance to open its doors and turf out whoever they've got in the back, shall I?'

'Just get one there soon as you can.'

Assuming Ashlee Gossard was still alive.

He hung up. 'Ambulance is on its way.'

'YES. ... THANKS. OK. ... BYE.' Franklin turned in her seat. 'We're not getting a firearms team for at least half an hour.'

McAdams stuck his foot down, nipping between a bus and a Transit van, coming within an inch of losing the paint off his left wing – earning himself a blare of horns from both vehicles and a lot of rude gestures too. 'Well that's no sodding use, is it?'

'That's what I told them. Apparently they've got to get all the way back to DHQ to get tooled-up before they head out again.'

The Shogun roared through a puddle that stretched all the way across the road, sending a wall of spray slamming into a bus shelter full of people. 'What's the point of having firearms teams if they don't carry firearms on them? Might as well deploy a crack team of Morris dancers.'

Callum's phone went off again. 'Dotty?'

'*We're about ten minutes away. Maybe less if this sodding school bus will get out of the bloody way!*' The sound of a blaring horn cut through the engine noise. '*MOVE IT, PRINCESS!*'

'You got Mother with you?'

Some hissing fumbling noises, and Mother was on the line. '*Callum? Tell Andy he's not to wait for us, understand? You kick that door in and you save Ashlee. If there's any flack, that's on me. Priority one is saving that little girl's life.*'

'Yes, Boss.'

'*For God's sake, Dorothy, look out for that lorry! Arrrrrrgh...*' More blaring horns. '*I'll have to call you back, Callum. If we survive. Oh God, I can't look...*'

And they were gone.

McAdams wrenched the wheel left and they drifted sideways around the corner, under the railway bridge, and out the other side. 'Hahahaha!'

'Mother says we don't wait, we go straight in.'

'Excellent!' McAdams grinned over his shoulder. 'Dig into the boot, young Callum. Should be a couple of stabproofs and a bit of MOE gear back there. I *might* have forgotten to sign them back in after we searched Tod Monaghan's *pied-à-terre* of mummified delights.'

Callum fiddled with the back of his seat until the other side folded down, letting him drag stuff out of the boot. 'Heads up.' He passed a stabproof vest through the gap between the front seats.

Franklin took it, pulling at the Velcro fasteners.

He did the same with his one: opening it up like a tabard before sticking it over his head and fighting the front part in under the seatbelt as McAdams slid them around another corner.

Callum tossed a pair of thick leather gloves and a couple of elbow protectors to Franklin, then reached back in for the Method Of Entry gear, AKA: one hooley bar. A cross between a crowbar, an ice axe, and a claw hammer. Long enough to be a pain in the backside to extract through the gap where the seat was folded down.

A *crack* went off like a gunshot and the Shogun's passenger-side wing mirror went flying off.

'Whoops!' A hard right.

Franklin reached out and killed the siren. 'Almost there.'

'Listen up, children. A rescue plan we must have. To save young Ashlee.' McAdams slowed to a more sedate fifty miles an hour, semi-detached houses streaking past the windows. 'Callum: you take the hooley bar and pop the front door. Rosalind: you're on pepper spray and truncheon. We don't have time to fanny about here, so we go in hard and fast. Anyone *not* Ashlee Gossard is to be considered dodgy as hell and completely arrestable. Any questions?'

Franklin pulled out her pepper spray. 'What if he's got a dog? Or a gun?'

'Then we probably get bitten and shot. Try not to, though.'

'And that's our plan, is it? Try not to get bitten or shot?'

He jerked the wheel left, taking them uphill onto Lehman Road. 'Do you have a better plan?'

'Just saying.' She put one hand over the clip of her seatbelt.

Lehman Road was a bit more exclusive than the previous streets, and a bit more rundown too. A cul-de-sac lined with big detached houses – large front gardens secured behind waist-high brick walls topped with six-foot iron railings. Weeds growing out of the cracks in the pavement. Old drooping trees, their leaves already yellowing. A couple of cars crusted with sap and dirt that looked as if they hadn't moved in decades.

Mrs Georgina Mason must've been worth a fair bit before she snuffed it.

McAdams pointed. 'Count it down.'

Franklin nodded. 'Number six … number eight … number ten … twelve… Go!'

The Shogun put on a burst of speed, the front end swinging to the right – up across the pavement and onto the weed-strewn blockwork driveway. Screeched to a halt right in front of the house.

Bang – Franklin was out.

Callum did the same, hooley bar clutched in his good hand, and sprinted up the stairs to number fourteen's front door. Only a few wisps of paint still clung to the wood. He swung the pointy end of the bar at the Yale lock, sank the tip in just in front of it and wrenched the whole bar forwards. A pop and crack, then the lock sprang free of the wood. He twisted the hooley bar round forty-five degrees and swung again, burying the wedge into the gap between the door and its frame. Shoved.

BOOOM...

The door flew open and Franklin rushed past, extendable baton clacking open in one hand, pepper spray in the other. Callum charged in after her.

She stuck her head in through an open door. 'Clear!'

He did the other side – an ancient music room, coated in a thick duvet of dust, the chairs sagging and mouse-eaten. 'Clear!'

By the time he'd got out again she was doing another room. 'Clear!'

A wide set of stairs snaked up towards a landing, chairlift rusting away on one side.

The kitchen cabinet doors hung squint in their frames. A collapsed chair lurked by the back door. But a clear line of tracks snaked through the dirt to the sink and back – the dust around the draining board almost non-existent. 'Clear!'

McAdams appeared in the hallway, shaking the rain from his shoulders. He took a quick look around.

'Clear!' Franklin stepped out of the bathroom and made for the stairs, taking them two at a time.

But McAdams marched right past her, to a small door part-hidden under the stairs. Wrenched it open...

A mop, a broom, and a collection of cleaning things collapsed out in a huge billow of grey dust. 'Gah...' He backed away, coughing, one hand waving at the impromptu smokescreen. 'It's an old house: there's got to be a basement somewhere. Find it!'

Callum went back to the kitchen. What looked like a utility room led off from one side, behind the rusted remains of a big round-cornered fridge. Twin-tub washing machine, more sagging cupboards, a collection of rotting wellington boots slumped by a Belfast sink. And a door.

He grabbed the handle and twisted.

Locked.

Well, the hooley bar would soon see to that.

Callum smashed the wedge into the doorjamb and shoved, setting the wood cracking and splintering. Then the door sprang open, bounced back off the wall as he took the first step into darkness.

Should've brought a torch...

Instead, he made do with his mobile phone, holding it out in his good hand, the hooley bar tucked under his other arm. 'Ashlee?'

The wooden steps creaked beneath him as he crept down into the depths.

His phone lit up the wall beside him – brickwork streaked with white where the salt had leached out of the mortar. The air tasted of raw mushrooms, smelled of vinegar and mouse droppings.

'Hello?'

His screen cast a pale-grey glow that barely reached a foot from his hand. Picking out strange rounded shapes all around him. He reached out and brushed a sheet, probably draped over a piece of furniture. His fingertips sent up a little cloud of dust that danced and twirled like midges in the thin light.

The basement was big, had to be about the same length and breadth as the house above. And it was full of unidentifiable *stuff*.

'Callum?' McAdams creaked his way down the stairs. 'Anything?'

'Too dark to tell.'

'Luckily...' A muffled *click* and a beam of light swept across the room. Shining through the sheets and pulling the shapes of dining chairs and bicycles from within. McAdams played his torch around the weeping brick walls, then down to the floor at their feet.

A clear path was scuffed through the dirt, heading around a stack of tea chests and disappearing behind a supporting wall.

Callum followed it. 'Ashlee? Can you hear me?' Around the edge of the wall. 'Ashlee, it's the police. We're going to get you out of here.'

Assuming the path through the dust wasn't just a well-trodden route for rats.

It took a right, behind another supporting wall...

He froze.

A wooden door. With a brand-new hasp and padlock. A perfectly clean quarter-circle on the floor where it'd been opened outward.

'Well?' McAdams shoved him forward. 'Don't just stand there!'

Callum jammed the hooley bar's claw in under the hasp and shoved his full weight against it.

A groan, a squeal, then a crack as the whole thing ripped free of the wood and clattered to the floor.

He pulled the door open. Wood smoke enveloped him, slipped down into his lungs. Warm and inviting.

Orange light flickered low to the ground inside. Pale and indistinct, but definitely there.

Callum's footsteps echoed up and away, reverberating back from the walls.

The screen on his phone cast just enough of a glow to pick out the brickwork. It was a room, about six foot by twelve. Flagstone floor. It wasn't that warm, even with the fire smouldering away in the middle. He swung his phone up, but all that did was make the smoke glow.

And then a harsh white beam burst into life beside him, turning the smoke into a solid thing as McAdams stepped inside. 'Can't see a bloody thing.'

Something patted against Callum's shoulders. Like tiny raindrops in the dark.

He looked up.

Another drop hit his cheek and he wiped it away. Oily. Greasy between his fingertips. He stuck his phone in his pocket. 'Give me the torch.'

'No chance. Get your own—'

'Give me the bloody torch!' He snatched it out of McAdams' hand and kicked at the fire, scattering the glowing embers. Stood in the middle of the room pointing the beam straight up.

Drips pattered against his face.

Whether it was the door being open, or him kicking the embers out of the way, didn't matter. But something changed and the smoke swirled around his torch, thinning enough for the beam to reach up into the heights.

Rows and rows of filleted fish – tied together at the tail and hooked over the wooden rods that ran from one side of the room to the other – stretched up above him. And above *them*, a shadow.

And then the smoke cleared.

It was a person, or what was left of them, their skeletal remains hanging head-down, arms dangling free.

'Jesus...'

They'd finally found Ashlee Gossard.

74

McAdams hacked and wheezed on the top step, face buried in an oxygen mask as Dotty's Vauxhall screeched up at the kerb. Mother clambered out into the rain and staggered over to Callum, breathing hard.

He shifted, making room beneath the twisted warty tree, just behind the ambulance. 'Boss.'

'Is Ashlee…?'

'She's so dehydrated they can barely find veins to get fluid into her.'

The ambulance's back doors hung open, both paramedics hunched over the emaciated figure on the trolley. Fighting to get wires and needles and drips fitted. 'Ashlee? Can you hear me, Ashlee?'

'Yes, but will she *live*?'

'Don't know. Maybe. It's possible…' He puffed out a breath.

Franklin marched out through the front door, paused to pat McAdams on the shoulder, then joined them under the tree. 'The only room not covered in eight foot of dust is the DIY smokehouse in the basement. No one's lived here for decades.'

Mother rubbed her hands across her face. Turned her back on the struggling paramedics. 'Good work, both of you.'

'No.' Callum shook his head. 'It was Franklin who got the Land Registry to search for properties belonging to Paul Jeffries, otherwise we wouldn't be standing here. I just went along for the ride.'

Franklin's cheeks went a shade darker. She shrugged. 'Team effort.'

There was a clunk and the Vauxhall's roofbox hinged open, the mechanics inside whirring and bleeping as a black metal arm brought Keith out from his storage bay and lowered him down beside Dotty's open door. Then the arm retracted back out of sight again. As if there was some vast metal spider lurking in the roofbox.

'Well: we've got Ashlee Gossard, that's the important thing. And she's alive.' Mother glanced back at the ambulance. 'Just.'

Dotty popped Keith open, then levered her legs out and swung herself into the seat. Wheeled her way over to them, squeezing under the shelter of the tree. 'Is she alive?'

Callum pointed at the ambulance. 'We've just done that bit.'

'Oh...'

'Excuse me.' Mother walked up the path and settled onto the top step beside McAdams. Put an arm around his shoulders. Talking in a voice too low to hear.

Franklin crossed her arms and leaned in close to Dotty. 'Did you know the silly sod's been ducking his chemo sessions?'

'Didn't you?' She shrugged. Then grinned and slapped Callum on the bum. 'I hear *you* found your twin brother, and he's alive!'

'He's also an egotistical narcissistic drug-taking misogynist dick who can't decide if he'll help me catch one of the guys who killed our parents. Needs to consult with his lawyer first.' A sigh tore its way free. 'I don't know, Dotty, I genuinely don't. All these years...'

Dotty gave his leg a wee squeeze. 'Give it time.' She rubbed her hands together. 'So: are we any closer to catching Imhotep? Well, I suppose it's more like Imhotep Part Two, "*Son* of Imhotep!", isn't it?'

'No.'

Dotty pulled a face. 'Didn't think so.'

One of the paramedics hopped down from the ambulance and closed the doors. 'Ashlee's *very* weak, and I'd be shocked if her internal organs haven't started shutting down, but we've managed to get a little fluid into her. Maybe...?'

Callum handed him a Police Scotland business card. 'If anything happens.'

'We'll do our best.' Then he climbed into the driver's seat, set the lights going and the siren wailing. Pulled away from the house. Getting faster towards the end of the street. Flooring it on the way out.

Rain pattered on the leaves above them. Gurgled in the guttering.

Dotty stared off into the distance.

Franklin fidgeted.

Callum cleared his throat. 'OK, the question we should be asking is: why didn't Paul Jeffries sell this house to Northeast Ecclesiastical Trust

Holdings? He turned the rest of them over, presumably for a tidy chunk of cash, why not this one?'

'Maybe he didn't need the money?' Dotty shrugged. 'Or maybe he was planning on living here?'

'He's got that place out in the middle of nowhere, no neighbours to see what he's up to. Why move into town and risk getting caught?'

Franklin pulled out her phone and poked at the screen. 'According to the Land Registry, Mrs Georgina Mason left the property to him thirty-five years ago. Maybe *that's* when he was killed? He couldn't sell it, because he was propping up a shallow grave. And eight years later, the trust *finally* notice he's not cashing the cheques any more, and another seven to have him declared dead.'

Dotty smiled. 'Ahoy, hoy – the Smurfs are here.'

A battered Transit van grumbled its way down the road, three faces peering out through the smeared windscreen. They parked in the spot vacated by the ambulance and Cecelia wound down the driver's window. 'This the right address?'

Callum hooked a thumb over his shoulder. 'Top to bottom, we need to know who else has been in there.'

She climbed out into the rain. 'We'll do what we can, but the labs...?' Her two colleagues went round the back and unlocked the rear doors. 'I swear on Jools Holland's grave, I have *never* had this many lab-result cock-ups in my life. We've got to send about half of them back for retesting.'

One of her minions reappeared, already kitted out in his blue oversuit, and handed another one to Cecelia. 'You want us to start with the basement and work our way up?'

'Sounds like a plan to me.' She pulled the fresh suit out of its plastic wrapper and grabbed Callum to help her stay upright as she wriggled into the thing. 'You think them mixing up the internal and external samples from your mother's head was bad? That isn't even the foothills of Cock-Up Mountain.'

Callum stayed where he was until she'd got herself sorted. 'Well don't let them cock *this* one up. Whoever Monaghan was working with, they're going to abduct someone else. Soon. We need an ID.'

The minion reappeared. Handed her a facemask and some safety goggles. 'Hi ho?'

'Hi ho.'

He turned and marched off, picking up his mate along the way, the pair of them whistling the tune from *Snow White* as they disappeared with their kit into the house.

Cecelia gave Callum a pained smile. 'We'll do everything we can.'

Why did everyone keep saying that?

'Here.' Callum put the mug of tea down in front of McAdams, then settled into the seat beside Franklin.

Condensation ran down the inside of the Tartan Bunnet's window, mirroring the rain outside, the steamy air redolent with the round brown scent of frying bacon as the owner worked her sinister magic on a half pack of smoked streaky. All the other tables lay empty, their tops wiped to a sticky gloss, waiting for the next unwary diner to wander in. Like red-and-white checked carnivorous plants.

Dotty hunched forward in her wheelchair, working her way through a huge pile of chips with grim determination and lots of tomato sauce.

A grunt, then McAdams wiped himself a drippy porthole in the steamed-up window and peered out at the street. 'She doesn't look happy.'

From here, Mother was just a dark blob with an orangey bit on the top. Pale arms jabbing and poking as she spoke on the phone.

Franklin added two sugars to her coffee. 'What about going back to the psychiatric ward and *forcing* them to give us Brett Millar?'

Dotty sighed. 'Here we go.'

'He's the only eyewitness we've got and we're not allowed to interview him?' She waved her spoon at them. 'Who does this Professor Bartlett think he is? We're trying to catch a serial killer and he's playing doctors and nurses! It's—'

'Impossible.' McAdams turned away from the window. 'We need a court order to get Millar's treatment suspended, and no sheriff worth his silly white wig will give us one. And *believe* me, we've tried.'

'They're keeping him doped up so he won't attack the staff or patients, right? Well, we lock him in a cell and he can shout and scream all he wants. Eventually the drugs will wear off and he'll tell us who Monaghan was working with. We need to—'

'Detective Constable Franklin,' McAdams reached across the table and took one of her hands, 'with the deepest and most sincere respect, in the words of Mother's dear old nan: hud yer wheesht. It's not happening. What we *need* is another plan.'

Dotty pushed her plate across the table. 'Have a chip, Rosalind. It helps with the feelings of frustration, helplessness, and existential doom.'

There was a pause, then Franklin helped herself to two.

'And Callum, sulking. Tell us pray, what news from court? Your brother, sent down?'

'Yeah, they say, "Bite me, Sergeant McAdams."' Callum took a sip of his own tea, hot and sweet. 'Pleaded guilty. They released him on bail, pending sentencing.'

'He'll be on the first private jet to the Bahamas, if he's got any sense. You'll not see him again.'

Franklin scowled around another stolen chip. 'Don't, OK?'

McAdams fluttered his eyelashes. '*Moi?*'

'Yes, you. Try a bit of compassion for once in your life. Can you even imagine how difficult this must be to deal with?'

Dear Lord, was Franklin actually sticking up for him?

'Ah, my dear Rosalind, you're probably right. It's force of habit. Winding up DC MacGregor is one of the few pleasures I have left, in these my twilight chapters.' He held out his hand. 'I'm sorry, Callum. To lose a brother to prison, having only just found him, must be—'

The café's front door banged open and Mother stomped in, shoulders down, fists clenched, cheeks and nose red, eyes narrowed, hair smeared flat by the rain. 'Useless, half-arsed, idiotic, pain-in-the-backside, moronic, *turdwardens!*' She threw herself into the last remaining seat at the table, setting the rubber feet squeaking. Sat there and glowered at her latte.

McAdams grinned. 'Good news?'

'AAAAAAAAAAAAAAAAAAAAAARRRRRRRRRRRRRRR-RRRRRGH!' The scream echoed back from the walls, setting the cutlery ringing, then faded away into nothing.

The proprietor didn't even look up from her frying pan.

Mother slumped. Grabbed a handful of napkins and dried her face. 'I'm sorry, children, but I am *more* than a little upset.'

Callum pushed her latte across the sticky tablecloth, till it was in front of her. 'Is it the Media, Detective Superintendent Ness, or the high heedjins from Tulliallan causing problems?'

'You remember the swabs Cecelia took from under the taps at Ashlee Gossard's house and the flat Ben, Brett, and Glen were doing up? Well our oh-so-wonderful labs came back with the results.' Mother ladled sugar into her latte, thumping each spoonful in, as if she was punishing it. 'Would you like to guess who our prime suspect now is?'

'Lord Lucan.' McAdams still had that grin plastered across his skeletal features. 'No, wait: Anne Widdecombe. Oh, I know: J.R. Hartley! It was, wasn't it?'

She thumped him on the shoulder. 'Don't be facetious.' More sugar was thrown to its death. 'According to the labs, Imhotep is sitting right here. At this very table.'

'It's Callum, isn't it? I always thought his shifty little eyes were hiding something. You can tell by the way they're all piggy and—'

She hit him again. 'It's *you*, you spanner.'

'Ooooooh.' Both of McAdams' eyebrows made a break for the top of his head. 'Now there's a twist we didn't see coming: the trusted old police officer is actually ... dan-dan-daaaaa! A psycho killer! OK, so it's a trope of genre, but who doesn't love the classics?'

Mother stared at him. 'You're just all-the-time hilarious, aren't you?'

'I like to think I have a certain homespun charm, yes.'

'Gah...' She lumped in more sugar. 'If I *ever* get my hands on the idiot who awarded our forensic-lab services to the lowest bidder, I'll throttle them with their own innards.' She took a sip of her latte and grimaced. Pushed it away and helped herself to a couple of Dotty's chips instead. 'They're rerunning the tests again.'

'I was definitely in the flat after we discovered Ben Harrington's body in the bath. But I don't think I've ever been to the Gossard house, have I?'

Callum joined the free-for-all on Dotty's chips. Stuffing one in his mouth and chewing through the words, 'I'll bet it was the same idiot who cocked up the samples on my mother's head.'

'Oh, I can top that.' McAdams licked a smear of tomato sauce from his fingertip. 'Did you know that they IDed a strangulation victim as Wee Davey Roberts, last week? Didn't seem to matter that Wee Davey is, last time I checked, a fifty-four-year-old man with an artificial leg, and the victim was a twenty-one-year-old woman with all her own limbs. They thought they'd got a DNA match and that was it.'

Mother snorted. 'I heard one of their lab techs has come up as a positive match in *eighteen* murder cases. Keeps picking his nose when he's running the samples and forgets to change his gloves.'

'Well I heard they had our very own Constable MacGregor down for trying to batter DCI Reece Powel to death. And— Ow!'

Callum kicked him under the table again, for luck. 'Serves you right.'

'It's a disaster.' Mother flopped in her seat, head back, arms dangling. 'All right, we go back to the plan: interview everyone at Strummuir Smokehouse till they squeak. Someone has to know *something*. Don't they?'

Everyone looked away.

Rain clattered against the window.

'Oh for goodness' sake.' McAdams thumped Mother on the back. 'Look at you all sitting there with your faces like fizz. We should be *celebrating!*'

Nobody set off a party popper.

He shrugged. 'All right, so whoever Monaghan was working with has slipped free to strike again. And yes: the labs couldn't identify a breezeblock in a box of cornflakes. But we just saved Ashlee Gossard's life! She's alive because of us, and that's worth celebrating.'

Still no party poppers.

'Isn't it?'

Dotty drained her tea and banged the mug down on the sticky checked tablecloth. Fixed them all with a hard gaze. 'I'll get some more chips.'

Callum looked down at the Mondeo keys nestling in his palm. 'Are you sure?'

The road outside the Tartan Bunnet was packed with cars, parked with a studied disregard for the double-yellow lines on both sides. That was the trouble with police officers – no respect for the law. If they couldn't get a parking spot at Division Headquarters, why not abandon their cars on the surrounding streets?

At the end of Doyle Lane, the ugly Victorian red-brick bulk of DHQ loomed over the surrounding sandstone buildings, like an angry drunk challenging them to start something.

Mother nodded. 'Just don't crash it. Or run anyone over. Nothing that's going to cause me a backside full of paperwork.'

'Thanks, Boss.'

'I'm serious – don't make me have to explain to Professional Standards why I let a suspended DC borrow a pool car.'

He pocketed the Mondeo's keys. 'If you need any help chasing anything down, unofficially, off the books, give me a call, OK?'

She inched back a little, staying in the shelter of the café doorway as the wind shifted, keeping out of the rain. 'How did Andy seem to you? When you were searching the house, was he OK?'

Ah...

Callum licked his lips. 'He gets out of breath all the time. He looks like death. And he's developed a kind of sour funky smell. A bit like a cat that needs a bath?'

'I'm worried about him.'

'He blames himself for what happened to Watt.'

'He's skipping his chemotherapy treatments. He thinks I don't know, but I didn't climb out of a packet of Wotsits yesterday.' Mother picked at the front of her fleece, pulling off little bobbly bits. 'He turns everything into a big joke, but he's dying, Callum. He's dying and he's scared and there's nothing I can do about it.'

The door behind her swung open and Franklin squeezed into the doorway. 'You ready?'

Callum nodded. 'If you are.'

Mother reached out and took hold of his arm for a moment. 'Don't tell him I know. Please.'

Her cheek was soft and warm against Callum's lips. 'Our little secret.'

The kiss left her blushing. She mumbled something, turned, and headed back inside.

Franklin watched the café door close, then raised an eyebrow at him. 'So now you're trying to snog Mother? Just can't keep it in your pants, can you?'

'I can wait if you like?' Granite houses slid past the Mondeo's windows, stonework darkened to charcoal by the rain. 'Not a problem. I'm not doing anything anyway.'

Franklin poked away at her mobile phone, not looking up. 'I'll get a lift back with Dotty. We'll be hours.'

'I've got a book to read, I'll be fine. Be glad of the peace, to be honest. You know, after everything.'

'Callum, we've got to interview everyone that works there all over again. Do you have any idea how long that'll take? And you'll be what, pining away in the car, waiting for me? Like a lovesick Labrador?'

Straight through at the roundabout. 'Did it maybe occur to you that you're not as irresistibly desirable as you think?'

'Says the man who thought we "had a thing".'

'I'm just trying to be nice, OK?' Up ahead, the traffic had slowed to a crawl, backed up behind a council lorry laying out yet more orange sodding cones for yet more sodding roadworks. He took a left at the next junction. Cutting through Castleview proper. 'OK, you want the truth? I don't want to go back to Dotty's and sit in the dark, brooding about Alastair, and Leo McVey, and Elaine-and-Powel...' The big granite houses gave way to brick tenements. 'I don't know what to do any more. I've not been on my own since I started seeing Elaine.' Her name was bitter on his tongue. 'I've not had a family since I was five years old.

Everything's changed. It's all... It's like someone's cut the anchor free and all these big chunks of me are drifting away.'

Franklin looked up from her phone. 'Oh, Callum...' She reached across the car and squeezed his leg. 'Man up and grow a pair.' Then went back to texting.

'That's the last time I open up to you.'

'Good. Do us both a favour.'

He took a right at the lights. A couple of small tower blocks poked up from the surrounding houses. Gathered in a square.

Franklin put her phone down. Frowned out at the scenery. 'I thought Strummuir was that way?'

'It is. We're just taking a tiny detour. Ten, fifteen minutes tops.'

'Oh God, not *this* again. Why did I let you drive?'

He headed straight for the tower blocks. 'I'm suspended, remember? I needed someone with me who can still arrest people.'

'You never change, do you?'

The rows of brick tenements gave way to a semidetached council estate, centred on the quartet of tower blocks. And right in the middle of the blocks: some yellowing grass, a little play park, and a shopping centre that looked as if the apocalypse had come early and stayed for tea.

'Ainsley Tyler Dugdale, forty-one, last known whereabouts: the Silver Lady strip club on Calder Road. Home address: fifteen B, Bowmore Avenue, Kingsmeath. Divisional have been looking for him since yesterday.'

'So what are we doing here?'

Callum pointed through the windscreen. 'That.'

A small, old-fashioned-looking pub sat at the corner of the shopping centre. Whitewashed walls and a neon 'T' in the window. Its name was painted in a wide strip of hoarding that ran the length of the building, 'The Pear Tree'.

'Dugdale's favourite boozer. And if we're lucky, the devious little sack of crap himself.'

'We're supposed to be finding Monaghan's partner!'

Callum parked outside. 'Dugdale battered a police officer and left him to die in the woods. Doesn't matter if Poncy Powel deserved a kicking or not, he's still one of our own.' And besides, if they did Dugdale for the assault, Professional Standards would sod off and bother someone else for a change.

She sat there, face clenched. 'Five minutes.'

'Fifteen, tops.' Callum climbed out into the rain, locked the car when Franklin joined him, then hurried across the car park and in through the Pear Tree's front door.

Warmth wrapped its arms around him. The smell of beer, peanuts, and Far Eastern spices. It was as old-fashioned on the inside as it was on the out: bare wooden floor; little round tables; chairs, benches, and stools upholstered in red vinyl; hunting prints and landscapes on the walls; and above a crackling fireplace, an oil painting of a tree with a single golden pear nestled within its dark leaves.

About a dozen customers, most of them in their sixties, were gathered around the fire, playing dominos, eating curry, and drinking half-pints.

Callum wandered over to the bar.

The large lady behind it gave him a dimple-cheeked smile. 'What can I get you, love?'

'Looking for a friend of mine: Ainsley Dugdale. He been in?'

Her eyes flicked left for a tiny beat, towards a wooden door with 'GENTS' on it. 'Dugdale?' A frown. 'Dugdale, Dugdale... No, doesn't ring a bell, sorry.'

'Big guy, bald, boxer's nose. This is his regular.'

'Can't say I've ever seen him in here. Maybe you're thinking of another pub? Try the Hare and Goblin on Wisdom Road.' The smile got a bit more strained.

'Right.' A nod. 'I'll just nip to the bogs before I go.'

And the smile disappeared altogether. 'Toilets are for customers only.'

'Fine. I'll take a can of coke. To go.'

'You're barred.'

'Nice try.' He turned and waved a hand at Franklin. 'Shall we?' He marched over and shoved the door to the gents open. Stepped inside.

Black and white tiles on the floor, the grout yellowed and greying. More white tiles on the wall, chipped and broken by the line of three sinks on the left. The sour sharp piddley smell reaching out from the urinals on the far wall. A pair of cubicles on the right.

Humming came from one of them: an old Donna Summer disco tune, from the sound of it.

Then some rattling and a grunt or two.

The sound of a zip being done up.

A toilet flushing.

And the door opened.

Dugdale had kitted himself out in jeans and a black hoodie – hood up, earbuds in, the white cables disappearing into the pocket at the front.

His nose, chin and cheeks were a mass of purple and blue bruises, fading away to green and yellow. Willow Brown had obviously given him a serious kicking while he was lying unconscious on the pavement with a face full of pepper spray. But he still hummed along as he swaggered across to the sinks, throwing in a little hop-skip in time to the music.

Franklin nudged Callum. 'Well?'

'Let him wash his hands first. Be more hygienic.'

Another skip-hop-skip and Dugdale turned on the taps, swaying his hips and nodding his head.

Callum let him get as far as lathering up, before stepping right behind him. Reached out and tapped him on the shoulder.

A tiny high-pitched squeal broke through the humming and Dugdale spun around, eyes wide, mouth open. Then he saw Callum. Swore. And lunged.

Both soapy hands smashed into Callum's chest, sending him careering back, crashing into a cubicle door. Arms flailing, feet skittering on the tiled floor, trying to stay upright.

Dugdale was off – barrelling into Franklin.

She bounced off the toilet wall and went sprawling while Dugdale disappeared back into the pub.

Callum hammered after him, jumping over her as she struggled to her hands and knees. Out.

The OAPs were on their feet. One of them grabbed a bottle of Beck's by the neck and smashed its bottom against the fireplace – turning it into a glass dagger.

Dugdale battered out through the front door and Callum followed. Ducking as knives, forks, and dominos were hurled in his direction. Into the rain.

'COME BACK HERE!'

But Dugdale was off, arms and legs pumping, head down.

Well, he was out of luck this time. Callum yanked out the car keys and plipped the Mondeo's locks. Jumped in behind the wheel. Cranked the engine and whacked her into reverse, setting the tyres screeching on the wet tarmac. 'Come on, come on, come on...'

Dugdale was fast, but not fast enough.

Any second now...

He jinked to the right, skidding onto a section of grass, leaping down the bank and onto a path.

Callum hauled the wheel hard over, hauled on the handbrake, and the car spun on its axis, facing the right way as it lurched over the edge and thumped down the grass and onto the path. Slithering and fish-tailing as the tyres fought for purchase.

Dugdale risked a glance over his shoulder and his eyes widened again. Head back down.

Closer.

Closer.

Callum tightened his grip on the steering wheel. 'You're *mine*, sunshine!'

There was no way Dugdale could have heard, but he wheeched to the left – leaping over the waist-high chain-link fence that bordered the playground. Dodging the empty swings. Making for the other side.

Callum slammed on the Mondeo's brakes and the back end slid, caught the chain-link and yanked the whole car to a sudden stop hard enough to set off the airbags. The white balloon punched into Callum's face, forcing his head back, filling the car with the eye-scratching reek of spent fireworks. Leaving the air tasting of rotten eggs.

He coughed and spluttered his way out of the car. Stood in the rain and watched the tiny figure of Dugdale disappear into the distance – vanishing between two houses. And gone.

'SODDING HELL!'

He limped around to the back of the car.

Most of the rear wing was gone, torn off and dangling on the end of a metal fencepost. What was left was gouged and tattered.

Yeah, Mother was going to kill him.

75

Franklin climbed out of the car, stared at the passenger-side wing then ducked her head back inside. 'You're right, Mother's going to kill you.'

Behind her, Strummuir Smokehouse slumped in the rain, a long curl of white snaking up towards the heavy grey clouds.

Scraps of white dangled from the middle of the steering wheel and the dashboard above the glove compartment. Callum gripped one and yanked it free. Dropped it into the footwell. 'Because *today* wasn't bad enough, was it? No. Course it *sodding* wasn't.'

'Maybe you could get a garage to fix her up before Mother finds out? Weld on a new panel. Fit replacement airbags…?'

He let his head fall back against the rest. 'If anything happens, if you find out who Monaghan's killing partner was, let me know, OK?'

'We'll do our best.' Then Franklin turned and headed in through the smokehouse doors, leaving Callum alone with the rain.

There was a figure in the office above the main entrance, partially silhouetted in the floor-to-ceiling windows, on the phone. Stupid 1930s haircut, both arms covered in tattoos – *Star Wars* down one side, *X-Men* down the other. Skinny jeans. Finn Noble, the smokehouse manager. What was it Watt had named him, Darth Wolverine? He raised his other hand and waved at Callum. Then turned and disappeared back into the room.

Idiot.

Oh, he looked all trendy now, but give it five years when the fashion had moved on to something less lumberjacky. What was he going to do with all those tattoos then?

Callum shook his head, turned the wheel, and steered the crippled Mondeo back towards town. A strange ticking clunk came from the back end now, the engine sounding a lot louder and more gravelly than it had.

He clicked on the radio to drown the noise out, getting a bland poppy number for his troubles.

'Ooh baby, you know I need you; And I want you; And I'll be true...'

Maybe Franklin was right – get the car to a mechanic and hope they could hide the damage before anyone else found out. Assuming no one had caught the accident on their mobile phone and uploaded it to YouTube already.

'Together, we can be free, / We can make love, / Have a baby...'

'Good luck with that.'

There was Billy Jackson's garage in Kingsmeath. He might do it for cheap with bits from the scrap yard. As long as he matched the colour, who'd know? And it wasn't as if Billy didn't owe him a shed-load of favours.

'Oh girl, you and me, / Living life, / Raising a family...'

Blah, blah, blah.

Sodding Dugdale.

The song chuntered on as the Mondeo clicked, rattled, and growled its way across town.

'Face it, Callum, it's not your day today.' A little laugh broke free. 'Day? It's not my week. Month. Year. Hell, it's not my sodding *life*.'

One final close-harmony dose of blandness and the song died.

'There we go, Mr Bones and "Babylove" from their most excellent live set at Tartantula last weekend. Stick with us, we've got loads more where that came from on the Lunchtime Sea of Sound *with me, Chris Pilot! But first it's quarter past one and here's Gabrielle with the news and weather.'*

'Thanks, Chris. Tributes continue to pour in for R.M. Travis as news of his death spreads around the world—'

'Dirty murdering bastard.' Callum stuck two fingers up at the radio.

'—lead singer of ninety's rock band Wolfrabbit.'

A man's voice: *'Yeah, it's a total nightmare. I mean, he meant everything to us when we were growing up. I know people chuck about the word "genius" like it means nothing nowadays, but he was a genuine hundred percent genius. There's no other word for him.'*

'How about "serial-killing dick-hat"?'

Technically four words, but it was the thought that counted.

A woman: *'It's completely devastating. How could anyone take R.M. Travis from the world? It's insane. I can't believe it.'*

Maybe the garage could fix the radio too, so it wouldn't pour crap out into the car?

Another man: '*R.M. Travis was a not inconsiderable landmark on the British literary landscape. They worship him all over the world, he's practically a religion.*'

And the newsreader was back. '*Staying close to home, Donny McRoberts, more commonly known as "Sick Dawg" appeared in court this morning on charges of possession of class A drugs, making death threats to police officers, and sexual assault. His lawyers issued a statement outside the Sheriff Court.*'

Callum turned it up.

Captain Scruffy's broad Glasgow burr filled the car: '*My client deeply regrets that the pressures of work have led him down the path of substance abuse and is* determined *to get clean.*' Though the accent was still there, he'd dropped all the Weegieisms. '*He wants to be a positive role model for his millions of fans, and understands he has a lot of work to do to regain their trust.*'

Not to mention all the violence against women and breaking his daughter's arm.

Callum slumped in the seat.

All these years wanting a family, wishing he still had a brother... Why did Alastair have to grow up such an arsehole?

'*We're asking the court to take into account Donald's very difficult childhood. And I'm afraid I can't say anything else about that at this time, but we will be making a further statement when we can.*'

'*McRoberts was released on bail to his record company who say he will be honouring all tour dates on his schedule. Local news now and police are appealing for witnesses—*'

Difficult childhood.

Suppose that was a bit of an understatement. Growing up in care was bad enough, but God knew what kind of horrors Alastair would have seen the day they were abducted. Did Leo McVey and R.M. Travis make him watch while they killed and dismembered Mum and Dad? Did they *do* things to him?

The plastic steering wheel creaked in Callum's good hand. Knuckles swollen and pale.

How long did they keep him for, before dumping him on social services as Donald Newman? Then McVey, visiting him in the care home, year after year...

Poor little sod.

Maybe it wasn't surprising Alastair had turned out the way he had?

'*—missing four-year-old was last seen outside the Templer's Vale Shopping Centre in Logansferry. If anyone has any information—*'

Callum's phone went off and he dragged it out. Pinned it between his shoulder and ear so he could turn the radio down. 'Hello?'

Mother, sounding as if she'd just been run over. '*The doctors have been on the phone.*'

That couldn't be good. 'Ashlee's dead, isn't she?'

'*It's John, Callum. A blood clot broke free and … he's had a stroke. They're trying to see how much of him they can save…*'

Oh no.

'Is there anything we can do?'

'*I'm just letting the team know.*'

'Right. Yes. Look, if there was ever a good place to have a stroke it's in the Intensive Care Unit of a big hospital, isn't it? He's going to be OK.'

There was a sniff and a shuddering breath. Then a cough. '*Of course he is. You take care of yourself, Callum. I'll give you a call if I hear anything else.*'

'Thanks.' He waited till she'd hung up to put his phone away.

'*—finally looks like we're going to see an end to this weather. There's high pressure moving in from the Atlantic and that means clear and dry conditions from Wednesday onwards. Best of the sunshine will be on Saturday and Sunday, so bail out your barbecues and get ready for a good weekend.*'

'*Thanks, Gabrielle. Now, who fancies a bit of the Bay City Rollers?*'

'No chance.' Callum switched the radio off again.

'Oooh.' The little man in the greasy grey overalls sucked a breath in through his teeth. Wiped his hands on a rag. 'You've totally buggered that one, haven't you?' He ducked down again and peered into the rear wheel arch, making the hunch between his shoulders stick out even further, showing off the bald patch at the back of his head. 'What did you hit, an elephant?'

'How much, Billy?'

Two cars sat on ramps over matching inspection pits. Shelves and drawers lined the walls, along with a couple of risqué calendars, a portrait of the Queen, a stack of alloy wheels, and a welding kit. A small office off in the corner. The garage's roll-up door was open, letting in the never-ending hiss of rain. It didn't dent the overwhelming smell of old motor oil and diesel though.

Billy stood and sucked his teeth again. 'Your rear wing needs replacing, and the suspension's wrecked, and you're gonna need a new tyre, and the airbags are gone, and the exhaust's loose, and—'

'Bare minimum, on the cheap: how much?'

'Then I've got to order the parts in from Ford, and you know what—'

'No.' Callum held up his hands. 'No dealership parts. We need to salvage everything from the nearest scrap yard. On the cheap, remember?'

'Pffff...' He puffed out his cheeks. 'Depends what I can get my hands on.'

Callum stared at him. 'How long have we known each other, Billy?'

'Oh come on, I'm trying to make a living here!'

'Did I, or did I not save your backside when you set fire to Mr Crimon's car?'

'I've got an ex-wife, two kids, and a cat to support!'

'He caught you, remember? With your jeans all clarted in petrol.'

'That was twenty-two years ago. Just because we grew up in a home, doesn't mean—'

'He was going to kill you, Billy. Literally. Crimon was going to hold you under the bathwater till you *drowned*.'

'It's not—'

'Who hit him with that crowbar? Because it wasn't the Tooth Fairy.'

'Gaaaaagh...' Billy stared at the roof. Slumped. Rubbed at his hunch. 'All right, all right. Much cheapness.'

'Thanks, and much quickness too, I need it back before anyone notices what's happened.'

'I'll make some phone calls.' He produced a battered mobile phone and wandered off, poking away at the screen.

And all Callum had to do now was figure out how to pay for it. Because, somehow, it was doubtful Billy would accept – quick check in the pockets – three pounds, twenty-one pence, and a button for fixing the battered Mondeo.

Couldn't even offer his bike in part exchange, not with the Dumbarton Arms still holding on to it as collateral. And the way his luck was running, buying three scratchcards and hoping for a windfall wasn't going to work either.

So Callum settled back against the workbench to wait. A couple of red-top tabloids sat next to a mug of coffee with 'WORLD'S WORST HUSBAND!' on the side. The front page of both was dominated by a photo of Emma Travis-Wilkes and her father at some sort of black-tie event. The pair of them smiling for the camera – him clutching a chunk of Perspex with a sponsor's logo on it and something trapped inside. 'BOOKED FOR HER FATHER'S MURDER' was one headline. 'THE MOST HATED WOMAN IN BRITAIN?' on the other.

Going by the crowds outside Division Headquarters that morning, she certainly had to be in the running.

There was a small story sharing the front page with Britain's most hated woman: a sidebar with a photo of Alastair with his shaved chest, baseball cap on backwards, and the tattooed cartoon fox poking out the waistband of his pants.

'MY LIVING HELL WITH RAP STAR DRUG FIEND'

Looked as if Irene Brown had sold her story to the papers.

Continued on page four.

Good for her. With any luck she'd got a whole heap of cash for it.

He flipped through to page four.

They'd given her a two-page spread with more photos of Alastair, AKA: Donald Newman (31), AKA: Donny '$ickDawg' McRoberts rapping away on stage. But right across the top was a big picture of Irene Brown (23), sitting in her living room, surrounded by her adoring children. Willow (7) and Benny (6) were striking rapper poses, arms crossed in ridiculous fashion with hands throwing gang signs out the ends. Pouting like ducks. Their little sister, Pinky (4), was dressed up in a long white dress with her hair done up in side buns like Princess Leia, sucking her thumb and clutching a lightsabre – not your standard Disney princess, but it still counted. The baby, Elsa (5 months) sprawled in Mum's lap, all pink arms and legs.

Irene hadn't put any make-up on for the photographer, letting the split lip and bruised cheeks shine through instead.

The article was in full-on tabloid sensationalist mode. The sex: rough. The drinking: constant. The drugs: hard. The violence: all the time. Living in grinding poverty while '$ick Dawg' was off drinking champagne, travelling first class, and not paying a penny in child support. And right at the end, they'd asked her why she'd finally found the courage to confront the aggressive drug addict who'd fathered three of her kids.

Callum raised an eyebrow.

Apparently it was all down to *him*. There it was, in print:

> "Detective Constable Callum MacGregor was the
> first person to be kind to me in years. I'd lost faith
> in the police, because no one ever cares about
> people like me," said Irene, holding back the tears.
> "But he did. And I owe it to him to stand up and
> tell the truth about what Donny did to us."

Dear Lord…

Something went pop deep inside his chest, spreading warmth across his lungs and down his spine.

Wow.

He closed the paper. Smiled. He'd *actually* made a difference.

Then frowned. Opened it back up and stared at the photo of the Family Brown again.

Donald Newman was really Alastair MacGregor, so that meant Pinky, Benny, and Willow were Callum's nephew and nieces. He had a family.

A grin spread across his face.

He actually had a family again.

OK, so Willow was a little monster, Benny was *different*, and Pinky was…

Pinky – dressed up as Princess Leia.

Darth Wolverine – standing there with all his tattoos.

The happy warm feeling seeped away.

Callum dug out his phone and called Franklin. 'Yeah, hi. Just wanted to know how you were getting on.'

'Believe it or not, we're coping without you. But only just.' It shouldn't have been possible, but the sound of Franklin rolling her eyes came down the line loud and clear.

'Sarcasm. Lovely.'

'Go watch a film, or read a book or something. Some of us have work to do.'

He wandered over to the roll-up door, standing on the threshold, just out of reach of the rain. Looking out on a manky grey alley in manky grey Kingsmeath. 'Listen, I was thinking about Darth Wolverine. Has anyone—'

'Darth what?'

'Watt came up with it: it's a tattoo thing. Finn Noble, runs Strummuir Smokehouse.'

'Is this going to take long? Only I've got eight more people to interview before the building shuts at five.'

'He's probably the trendiest hipster there, right?'

'Callum, can we not—'

'He's had access to the smokehouse all along. He's the one who decides which ex-cons get to work there. He runs the courses – smoking and charcuterie and all that – so he knows the names and addresses of everyone who attends. He's in charge. He can come and go as he pleases.'

'You think he's Imhotep?'

'You didn't see him when Monaghan went into the river: shouting the odds, swearing. He even took a swing at Watt. Bit extreme for someone who just employs the guy, isn't it?'

'Well...'

'And Noble said they never hire anyone who's a sex offender. Tod Monaghan had form for indecent assault, and he raped that bloke who wouldn't press charges. How is that not a sex offender?'

'If the victim wouldn't press charges, maybe Darth Windolene didn't know about it? They probably don't put soft intelligence on file when they send people for work placement.'

'But they'd put the indecent assault in, wouldn't they?'

'Hrmmm...'

Outside, a couple staggered past – the pair of them in ripped jeans and baggy T-shirts. Soaked to the bone, laughing, and sharing a half-bottle of vodka.

'Think about it. He teaches people how to smoke things. He's more hipstery than Ben Harrington, Brett Millar, and Glen Carmichael put together. He'd fit right in, just like Dr McDonald said Imhotep would.'

'Callum—'

'He teaches a foraging class too. That means mushrooms. How much do you want to bet he can get his hands on all the psilocybin he wants?'

The laughing couple dissolved into the distance, consumed by the downpour.

Callum turned his back on the rain. 'Come on, Finn Noble's *got* to be worth a closer look. You said the only person without a criminal record there was the woman who did the chips. What was Noble in for?'

Nothing from the other end.

'You still there?'

'I'm looking at my notes.'

557

'Just ask him where he was when Watt was attacked. See if he's—'

'Thank you, Constable. I might just be a lowly woman, but I do actually know how a police investigation works.'

Callum closed his eyes. 'OK, OK, I'm sorry.'

'Should think so too.' A sigh. *'He's gone out for lunch, but Dotty interviewed him this morning. I'll check with her, see what he said.'*

'Great. And call me back?'

'You're a pain in the backside, you know that, don't you?'

'Yup.'

'Right, you're in luck.' Billy stuck his head out of the little office. 'Frazer McFee and Son have a diarrhoea-brown Mondeo estate in stock – engine's completely seized, but everything else is salvageable. And they'll let you have the bits you need for three hundred.'

'Pounds?'

'No, Jelly Tots. Of course pounds. Cash, so no VAT, and… What?'

Callum fiddled with a spanner. 'I'm a bit, strapped.'

'Oh for God's sake.' He disappeared back into the office. 'They'll give us a ten percent discount if we dismantle the thing ourselves. And *you'll* owe *me*, understand!'

Callum followed him into a gloryhole of paperwork, files, and random bits of machinery. 'How long?'

Billy filled a little kettle from a little sink and stuck it on to boil. 'If I abandon everything else? Lunchtime tomorrow.'

That would be doable, wouldn't it? He'd just have to keep his head down till then and hope Mother didn't ask for her Mondeo back. 'Thanks, Billy, you're a star.'

'Just don't tell anyone.' Billy shook his head. Sighed. 'I'm a fool to myself.' Then delved into the filing cabinet. 'You want a Pot Noodle? Got chicken-and-mushroom, or Bombay Bad Boy.'

Easy. 'Chicken. Why would anyone—' His phone went off and Callum swore. Pulled it out and checked the screen: McAdams. 'Sorry, got to take this.' He walked back out into the workshop while Billy peeled the foil lids off the pots. 'Is Watt OK?'

A small pause. *'He had a stroke. How would he be OK?'*

'When Mother called she sounded … I don't know. Anyway, if it's not Watt, what do you want?'

'I'm dying.'

This again.

'I know.' Callum settled back against the workbench and flicked

558

through the other paper. Sex scandal. Sex scandal. 'MY DRUG BINGE HORROR' by some nonentity from a reality TV show.

'*We need to talk.*'

Murder. Sex scandal. '"I'M PROUD OF MY CELLULITE!" SAYS CURVY CORRIE BABE'.

'So talk.' Cellulite-Pride Week seemed to be nothing more than an excuse to print pictures of celebrities in their bikinis. Germaine Greer would be so proud.

A cough rattled down the phone, followed by another one. And another – hacking on and on.

The next page was an editorial about what a genius R.M. Bloody Travis was, and how everyone would miss his magical imagination.

McAdams' coughing gave way to wheezing gasps.

Callum scrunched the page up in his fist, spat on it, then lobbed it at the bin. Missed.

A wheezy voice sounded in his ear again. '*Callum? You still there?*'

'No.'

'*Where are you?*'

'Kingsmeath, visiting an old friend.'

Another cough rattled out of the earpiece. Followed by some panting. '*Urgh... My house. And bring some milk – full fat. No point wasting life on that semi-skimmed rubbish.*'

'McAdams, I'm not traipsing all the way across—'

'*We – need – to – talk. In person. Now.*'

Wonderful.

He didn't bother hiding the sigh. 'I'll see what I can do.'

Callum hung up and went back to the office, where the smell of rehydrating soya product filled the gaps between the oily diesel fug. 'Have you got a car I can borrow? Something's come up. Sorry.'

Billy pulled two forks from his desk drawer and stuck one in each pot. 'I need the truck to go get your Mondeo bits, but I've got something that might help. It's not fancy but it'll get you there.'

'Anything's good.'

That got him a very disturbing grin.

'What?'

'Nothing.' The grin got bigger.

Yeah ... why wasn't that reassuring?

76

BILLY JACKSON MOTOR SERVICES ~ MOTs WHILE YOU WAIT didn't stretch to a courtesy car. Instead, Callum wobbled along the side streets, both knees clamped together, buttocks clenched, holding on to the scooter's handlebars as if they were the only thing keeping him from a humiliating and messy death. The crash helmet rattled about on his head, about a size and a half too big, but it was the only one that would go over the gauze padding covering his ear and the back of his head.

This was clearly Billy's way of getting his own back on Callum for abandoning him to dismantle the scrapyard Mondeo on his own. Not to mention the matter of paying for the parts and repairs with an IOU. But still...

Spray made twin arcs either side of the front wheel, there was nothing to keep the rain off, it was freezing cold, and the engine sounded like an angry wasp attacking a PA system.

Sodding DS Sodding McAdams.

Why couldn't he just discuss whatever it was on the phone like a normal person?

Because that would be too easy, that's why. Because then Callum wouldn't have to drive a horrible little scooter through the pouring sodding rain.

A four-by-four passed by, going in the opposite direction, sending up a wall of water that crashed across Callum's arms and chest.

'Aaaaargh!'

That did it – cancer or not, McAdams had to die.

*   *   *

'What took you so long?'

Callum stood on the doorstep, arms outstretched, legs apart, dripping. Plastic bag dangling from his good hand. 'I'm going to kill you.'

'You look like you swam here.'

'I swear to God, if you don't get out of the way and let me into the dry, I'm *seriously* going to murder you right here.'

A slow smile spread across McAdams' skeletal features. Then he stepped back and gave Callum a low bow, sweeping one hand out to indicate the corridor.

'Gagh...' Callum stepped over the threshold and squelched his way along the parquet flooring and into the tiled dining-kitchen. All slate and black granite, beech units, a big fridge and another one right next to it just for wine.

Must be nice to marry someone with a trust fund.

'Perhaps, dear Constable MacSoggy, / You should change out of your clothes so damp? / You look just like a half-drowned moggy, / You sopping squishy squelchy scamp.' Then there was a wobble. A grimace. And McAdams lowered himself into one of the dining chairs. 'Help yourself to tea, coffee, or a nice glass of wine.' He waved a bony hand at the fridges. 'The Sancerre is particularly good. Far too expensive, but it's not like I can take it with me.'

Callum dumped the plastic bag on the draining board, wriggled out of his sodden jacket and wrung it out in the sink. Hung it over the back of a chair. Kicked off his shoes and poured their contents down the drain. 'This better be important.'

'I'll take a glass, if you don't mind? I'd get it, but my legs don't seem to be cooperating right now.'

His socks splatched and squished against the slate tiles all the way to the kettle. He clicked it on. 'Mother wants you to start your chemotherapy.'

'The glasses are in the cupboard on your right.'

'I'm serious. She's worried about you.' He pulled a white wine glass from the cupboard and stuck it on the countertop. Had a rummage till he found the mugs and stuck one next to it. Opened the tin marked 'Tea'.

Curled his lip.

The tin was full of bits. 'Gah... Don't you have any *proper* tea?'

McAdams smiled. 'That *is* proper tea. Beth gets it from a little shop in Aberdeen. One spoon for you, one for the pot.' He pointed at the wine fridge. 'Now: there should be an open bottle of Sancerre at the front.'

Callum pulled the bottle out. Unscrewed the cap. 'Stop being a dick and go to your bloody chemo.' He filled the glass and squelched over to the table. Stuck it in front of McAdams.

'Oh, Callum.' The smile softened at the edges. 'It's too late for that. All the coughing? My lovely cancer has metastasised. I'm riddled with it. Like an old building with rats. Eating the wiring, making holes in the skirting boards, and covering everything in crap.'

The kettle bubbled and growled.

'How long?'

'A week. A fortnight. A month. Does it matter?' McAdams took a sip of wine, eyes closed, then sighed. 'You sure you don't want a glass? It's lovely.'

'You should be in hospital.'

'I'm lucky. The drugs keep most of the pain at bay, for now. And I've still got all my marbles.' A wink. 'For now.'

'Matter of opinion.' A click and the bubbling subsided. Callum dumped two spoons of grey-black bits into the pot. Drowned them with boiling water. 'And for your information: proper tea comes in a teabag. It doesn't look like something you scraped out of the vacuum cleaner.'

'Philistine.' He produced a little notepad and flipped it open to a page covered in cramped handwriting. 'I'm making my bequests while I still can. Dotty's getting a case of Bowmore, because she loves her whisky. Mother's getting a cruise: the Norwegian fjords, because she likes pickled herring and deserves a decent holiday. Watt...' A frown. 'I wasn't sure what to get him. We don't even know if he's going to live now. Maybe his own electric wheelchair, if he pulls through? Or I could send him on holiday too, so he can recuperate?' McAdams took another sip of wine. 'Rosalind gets a diamond necklace. Nothing too flashy, but something dangly that will nestle between those magnificent breasts of hers. Because, let's face it, who wouldn't want to do that?'

Callum stirred the tea. 'What about your wife?'

'Oh, Beth's off to Edinburgh for the week. Apparently I've been a bit more *colourful* than usual and it's getting on her nerves. Or did you mean, "what does she inherit"?' He took another sip of Sancerre. 'She gets the house and the car and the bank account and the timeshare in Tenerife. Which is peanuts compared to what her dad left her, but there you go.' McAdams put his glass down. 'Which brings us to *you*, Callum.'

'I'd settle for a towel and a go in your tumble dryer.' He filled his mug from the pot, then pulled a four-pint carton of milk from the plastic bag on the draining board. Sploshed in enough to turn his tea beige.

'It was surprisingly difficult to find something appropriate to leave you. You're a simple soul, yes, but you've got dark depths, don't you? A compelling backstory for crime fiction: family abducted, growing up in care, unlucky in love, rumours of corruption. A mediocre officer in a troubling world, who spends his life trying to get justice for his mother, father, and brother.'

'Hmph.' The fridge was packed with jars and bottles and Tupperware containers. A whole shelf dedicated to kippers. He stuck the milk into the door pocket. Frowned at the shelves. 'You've got enough kippers here to feed an army.'

'And that's why you're so hard to buy for.'

'I didn't, by the way: spend my life trying to get justice.' He unclipped his tie and draped it over the taps. 'Everyone said my family abandoned me: dumped me in the lay-by and sodded off. All my life I thought I'd done something wrong.'

'But I think I finally got you the perfect gift.'

'I became a police officer, because I grew up in the care of people who shouldn't have been allowed within two hundred yards of children. I joined the job, because I wanted to put scumbags that prey on the weak behind bars.'

McAdams nodded. 'Indulge a dying old man and look in the drawer by the toaster.'

Callum did. It was a brown paper parcel, about the size of a ream of paper, only twice as thick. It flopped like a ream of paper when he picked it up too. He held it out. 'This?'

'That.'

Someone had printed the words 'A Dark So Deadly' across the front, in black Sharpie. 'I'm guessing it's not a holiday.'

'It's my book.'

Oh joy.

Dotty got a case of whisky, Franklin got a diamond necklace, Mother and Watt both got fancy trips, and what did *he* get?

'Oh, don't look like that. Everyone else got material stuff, but you: you're a reader. There's so few of you about these days, Callum. So I give you my book. My life's work, distilled into one hundred and ninety-four thousand, five hundred and twenty-eight words. Single-sided double-spaced on A-four.'

Callum put it down. 'You got me to drive all the way across town, on a scooter, in the pouring rain, because you wanted to give me a copy of your book? You said it was urgent!'

'I also needed milk. And how was I to know you'd be on a scooter? What happened to the car Mother lent you?'

Ah...

'Nothing. Thanks for the book.' He cleared his throat. 'Now, any chance of that towel?'

Rain.

It pounded the garden on the other side of the window, battering the bushes into submission, hurtling down from a charcoal sky, turning everything grey. The floral scent of fabric softener filled the utility room, mixing with the tickly smell of warm dust.

Callum tightened his borrowed towelling dressing gown and leaned back against the *whomp-whomp-whomp* of the tumble dryer. Warmth stroked the back of his legs. 'He what?'

Franklin sounded as if she was sucking on a wasp. *'You heard me: Finn Noble's dead.'*

'How the hell did that happen?' Callum pinned the phone between his ear and his shoulder, freeing up his good hand for a sip of tea. 'Was it an—'

'We sent a patrol car round his house: No answer. So the uniform peers in through the windows, and there's Finn Noble: hanging from a noose in the hall. He'd tied one end to the balustrade and jumped.'

'He *killed* himself?'

'There's more. He left a suicide note.'

The tumble dryer bleeped then fell silent.

Callum opened the door and hauled out his suit – all hot and crackling with static electricity. 'It's him, isn't it? Imhotep. He knew we were closing in and he chickened out before we could nab him.' The towelling robe went on the worktop and Callum pulled on his pants – all warm and clingy. Grabbed the edge of the washing machine as the world did a quick swirl when he stood up again. 'Whoa...' Blink. Sniff. 'You still there?'

'We've sent a copy of the note to Dr McDonald, but it's basically claiming credit for the killings, justifying his actions, and complaining that we

spoiled everything by capturing his gods before they could save the world.'

'AKA: nutjob.' Callum hauled on his trousers, fingers flinching at the hot zip and buttons. Struggled his fibreglass cast down the sleeve of his shirt. 'I can be there in…' Callum checked his watch. Then froze. How *exactly* was he going to turn up on a scooter and not have everyone asking questions about the missing Mondeo? Borrow McAdams' car? 'Maybe fifteen minutes?'

'*Don't be daft, you're suspended.*'

'Yes, but—'

'*No buts.*'

'Fronting up Finn Noble was my idea! How can you not… Hello?' Silence. 'Franklin? Hello?'

She'd hung up on him.

Perfect.

Thanks. Thanks very sodding much.

He buttoned his shirt. Pulled on hot socks. Checked his shoes – perched on top of the boiler. Twenty minutes up there, stuffed with crumpled-up bits of the *Daily Record*, and they were *still* sodden through. Callum changed the damp newsprint for dry bits. Grabbed his jacket then headed back through the door to the kitchen.

The contents of his pockets were where he'd left them, sitting on the kitchen table. He loaded up again. Paused. Sniffed the air. 'Why can I smell smoke?'

McAdams stood in front of the hob, stretching a sheet of clingfilm over a frying pan. 'That's the trouble with most people: no idea how to treat a kipper. It's already cooked, you don't need to grill or fry it – that just dries the flesh out – you stick it in a deep-sided frying pan, or roasting tin, and you pour hot water over it. Seal it for a couple of minutes and you're good to go. Jugged kippers.'

'Finn Noble's hung himself.'

'Has he?' McAdams clattered two plates onto the worktop. 'Let me guess—'

'Left a suicide note, admitting everything.'

'Thank God for that.' He sagged a little, one hand propping himself up. 'Get a couple knives and forks. You like kippers, don't you?'

'Franklin said everyone at Strummuir had a criminal record. What did Finn Noble do?'

'Of course you like kippers. Who *doesn't* like a proper kipper?' He tapped at the clingfilmed surface, making the condensation form into little round droplets. 'It's the drugs, they mess with your palate. Kippers are one of the few things that still taste right to me. That and the wine. And whisky, of course.'

'McAdams: what did Finn Noble do?'

'Hmmm? Oh, him. Yes. He was arrested for indecent exposure twice – decided it was a good idea to get his willy out on Stone Terrace, outside the youth hostel. Possession of a Class A drug on three occasions. And a handful of burglaries. Nothing major, except for the willy waving.'

'What was the Class A?'

'You know, I think these are just about done.' McAdams peeled back the clingfilm and used tongs and a spatula to manoeuvre one out of the water and onto a plate. Held it out to Callum. 'Why don't you guess what controlled substance Finn Noble was caught with.'

'Magic mushrooms.'

'Give that detective constable a kipper.' He went back to the pan for the other one. 'Try a knob of butter on it, melts right into the smoky flesh.'

'Woops.' Callum sat at the dining table a bit harder than he'd meant to, making the seat creak. 'Mother sent you home, didn't she?'

A shrug. McAdams lowered himself into a chair. Groaned. Then peeled the skin off the top of his kipper. 'She seems to think I'm taking too much on. Well, what am I supposed to do? Hang around here like Banquo's ghost? Eat your kipper.'

The skin was thin and papery, the flesh beneath it plump and moist. Smokey and full of horrible little bones. He worked them to the front of his mouth and picked them out. Wiped them off on the edge of his plate. Looked up to find McAdams smiling at him. 'What?'

'It's like a metaphor for life, isn't it? The flavour is magnificent, but every mouthful comes with a cost. And in the end, all you're left with is a pile of skin and bones.' McAdams reached for the butter dish, dug a chunk off with his knife and dolloped it onto his fish. 'You remember our discussion in the car? You me and Rosalind talking about how no one ever remembers the police officer or the victims, they only remember the serial killer?'

'People remember Gandhi, he wasn't a serial killer.' Callum picked out another mouthful of bones and laid them with their comrades. Like little pale thin soldiers. Took a swig of tea to wash down the saltiness.

'Gandhi doesn't count. He's remembered because he made a *difference*. What difference are you and I going to make?'

566

More little soldiers. All lined up on parade.

McAdams put his knife and fork down. Topped up Callum's mug from the teapot. 'Normal people don't change history. Normal people die and get forgotten.'

How many bones were there in a kipper. A thousand? Two? A million?

They caught the light and … sort of *glowed*. Little bone soldiers.

'Callum?' A sip of wine. 'Do you believe in God? Or gods? Or anything at all?'

Yeah, McAdams needed to cut back on the wine. His voice was getting a bit wobbly and boomy. Like the grown-ups in a Snoopy cartoon. Whah, whah, whah…

Somewhere, off in the distance, a phone rang. And rang. And rang.

'Don't worry, the answering machine will get it.'

All those glowing bone soldiers.

Bleeeeeeeeep.

'Andy? It's Cecelia. I'm sorry, I don't know what the hell they're playing at, but the labs have buggered it up again. I'm putting in a formal complaint.'

Callum blinked. The soldiers left bright orange streaks on the inside of his eyelids.

'Are you all right?'

He shook his head and the world lurched round by thirty degrees, then slowly drifted back again. Urgh… 'Think I'm coming down with something.' Not helped by driving a scooter all the way across town in the sodding rain.

Or had he said that already?

'The idiots have taken a liking to you: those samples from the Gossard house and the Carmichael flat have come back as a match again. And now they've got you driving the abandoned Kia Picanto. You know, the one we found Richard Duffy's body in the boot of?'

So thirsty.

Must be the kipper.

Have another gulp of tea.

'I've told them: I'm going to make you do these ruddy tests over and over till you get them right. Honestly, it's like trying to teach a lawnmower about particle physics.'

'Callum? You don't look too well.'

His hands made whooshing sounds when he moved them.

'Can't feel my tongue…'

567

'Anyway, just wanted to say sorry. I know it's not our *cock-up*, but still. Give me a call when you get this, OK? Bye.'

'That's a shame.' McAdams stood, wobbling like one of those inflatable men they stuck outside car dealerships.

'Oh, and speaking of Callum, if you see him, tell him the Dundee lot have done a preliminary sweep through the contents of Travis's freezers. They can't be a hundred percent, but they say it looks like it's all adults. No children's remains, if that helps? OK, that's definitely it this time. Bye.'

Bleeeeeeeeep.

Callum reached for his mug, but the thing wasn't where it was meant to be and his fingertips caught the handle, tipping it over. Pale brown and beige spread out across the tabletop. 'Sorry...'

'It's all right. It's only tea.' McAdams patted him on the shoulder. 'Well, not *only* tea, but mostly.' He wobbled over to the worktop and came back with a dishtowel. Laid it out on the beige puddle. The fabric darkened. 'You should've had the Sancerre instead.'

'Mmmph?'

'I only wanted to make a difference. Not a huge one, just a little one. Before I die.' McAdams mopped up the spilled tea. 'It would've worked too, but you...' A sigh. 'Well, I suppose you were only doing your job.'

'Nnnnmph.' The walls lurched in, then out again. Boom. Boom. In time with his pulse. Like waves. In. And out. In. And out.

'But couldn't you have left me with *one*?'

In. And out.

'Just one god for me. To fix all this? To make the world whole again?'

Callum grabbed hold of the tabletop. Dug his fingers into the slippery surface as the grain, buried deep in the wood, twisted and flowed.

'One by one I had to give them up. I didn't want to, but what choice did I have?' His hand was hot on the back of Callum's neck. 'I thought I'd have enough time with Ashlee, she was coming along so well. She'd purified. Made amends. She was ready to transcend.'

The tea. There was something in the tea.

'But now she's gone, back to the venal flesh and dust and darkness. You want to hear a secret? I think surrendering her was probably the hardest thing I've ever done.' A tiny laugh. 'Such a terrible waste. Don't get me wrong: in a weird way, I'm glad she's still alive, but I would have made her *immortal*.'

Callum scraped his chair back. 'Nnngh...'

'I know, I know. Come on.' He hooked his hands under Callum's armpits and pulled him to his feet. 'It's all right. In the end I couldn't help Ashlee, but I can still help you, if you like?'

'Nnnn.'

'Shhh… Here we go. It's going to be fine. Watch your feet on the steps, it's a long way down to the basement.'

77

'There we are, that's better, isn't it?'

The basement floor was warm and soft, like R.M. Travis's garage. Dusty soft warm concrete. The brick walls pulsed – in and out, in and out. Shifting in time with every single one of Callum's breaths. 'Gnnnmmph…'

'Shh… It's OK. You're going to be fine. Trust me. It's all going to be fine.'

Callum's arms were lead, dull and heavy, his fingers like wet balloons.

'You just sit up here. That's right.'

McAdams hauled him into a sitting position.

'Here we go.'

The chain was cool against Callum's neck. The padlock's click reverberated through his skull. Click. Click. Click. Click.

'All safe and secure.'

'Nnngh…'

A sigh. 'I feel bad about Finn, but look at it from my perspective: if I hadn't killed him and written that suicide note, we'd still be looking for Imhotep, wouldn't we? This way it's all finished nice and neat. We've come to the end of the book.' His hand was warm and dry, stroking Callum's cheek. 'You made an excellent antagonist and I *mean* that. Sincerely. And now you're going to be a god. They'll worship you and you'll be a god. How's that for an epilogue?'

In and out. In and out.

He gave Callum a sad little smile. 'It's all been a bit of a disaster, hasn't it? I didn't mean for the first body to end up in the tip, but Beth came home early and the body was ruined and I panicked, and, and, and…' He rolled his eyes and pulled a face. 'I know, I know: exposition.

570

Anyway, you wouldn't *believe* how much finessing it took to make sure we got the investigation when they found it. Couldn't have anyone else sniffing around my gods, could I? Of course not.' He leaned forward and kissed Callum on the forehead. 'Don't worry, though: no one will ever find you. You won't end up in Professor Twining's mortuary, like some sort of natural history exhibit. You're going to be a god. You're going to be immortal.'

'Gnnnnnnnnnnngh...'

'I'm going to get you some more tea. You wait here and—' He froze. Staring up at the ceiling as the doorbell gave out two death-knell rings. 'Tsk. Some people just have no sense of timing, do they? Never mind, they'll go away and we can—'

The bell tolled again.

'Oh for goodness' sake. Sorry about this. I'll be right back.' A smile. 'Promise.'

Callum closed his eyes and the walls stopped moving. The sound of McAdams' feet scuffed away then thumped up the stairs. Then the basement door clunked shut. Then silence.

'Urghnngh...'

Die.

Going to.

Going to die.

They'll worship you, you'll be a god.

Muffled voices came from up above. McAdams and someone else. Someone familiar.

Mother.

'Mmmmnnnfffrrr...!' He took a deep breath, but all that would come out was the same mushy grumble.

The tea. Should never have drunk the tea.

It took a lot, but he hauled his lead arm up and worked wet balloon fingers between his lips. Past his graveyard teeth. Across his slimy tongue. And into his throat. They felt big as—

'Hurrrrkkk...' Pale beige liquid splashed down his wrist, hot and sticky.

Barely a mouthful.

Again.

He dug his fingers in deeper.

'Hurrrrrrrrkkk...' This time his whole stomach heaved, curling his shoulders, hunching his back as tea and kippers splashed out onto the basement floor. 'Hurrrrkkk...' Chewed ribbony chunks of Pot Noodle.

'Hurrrrrrrrrrkkk…' More. Every heave like a kick in the stomach, leaving him hanging on the end of his chain. Spitting bile onto the concrete.

Callum slumped back against the wall.

Blinking.

The bricks started to pulse again.

In and out. In and out.

Mushrooms. It had to be mushrooms. And probably something else as well. Something to make him drowsy. Something to make him weak.

Probably still got enough of the crap in his system to keep a whole squat full of druggies tripping for a week. But at least he'd got rid of the rest.

His whole mouth tasted like an old wheelie bin smelled, though.

He spat again.

Ground his eyes closed.

Pulled his head forwards, then smacked it back into the wall.

A dull ringing flooded through his skull.

Again.

Harder this time.

The gauze padding softened the blow a bit.

Again.

Fire ripped across his scalp, followed by a thousand razorblades. Slicing through the stitches back there. Wrenching his eyes open.

Oh, dear *Jesus*, that hurt.

But it worked.

He shook his aching head and the walls stayed where they were.

Coughed.

Spat out another string of bitter yellow bile.

Basement. He was in the basement.

The concrete floor rippled beneath him. Hissing.

McAdams had made a wall out of dusty cardboard boxes, blocking this part off from the rest of the room, creating an alcove no more than twelve foot by eight. Three sets of chains were fixed to the brickwork, all of them shiny and new. One for Callum, one dangling above a bare mattress on the floor, and one going around the neck of the woman slumped opposite.

Brown hair with grey at the roots. Naked, except for a grey cardigan that was threadbare at the elbows and cuffs. Knees covered with scratches and bruises.

She didn't say anything. Didn't move. Just slumped there.

Callum cleared his throat. Fumbled his slippery sick-covered fingers to the chain around his neck. Then worked his way back along its length to where it fastened to a ring, bolted to the wall. Gave it a pull.

Nope.

Key.

Get the key.

And how the hell was he meant to do that, chained to the basement wall?

Upstairs, the muffled voices went quiet, as if someone had turned off the radio. Then a solid *thump* rattled the floor above.

Oh God.

He wiped his fingers on his once-clean, once-dry, shirt.

There was a creak, followed by the sound of something being dragged down the stairs. Thunk. Thunk. Thunk.

McAdams appeared around the boxes, shuffling backwards, bent double, pulling Mother by the armpits. She was limp, on her back, one shoe dangling off as he hauled her over to the mattress.

He struggled her into place, then sat back on his heels, wiping his forehead. 'I'm sorry, Mother, but you couldn't have picked a worse time.'

The chain clattered and rattled as he wrapped it around her neck, fastening it with another heavy padlock and slipping the keys into his pocket.

'But it's OK. It'll all be OK. You'll see.' He leaned forwards and kissed her on the forehead. 'It'll be better than OK.'

Callum slumped against the wall. Groaned.

McAdams turned. 'I know this isn't what we planned, Callum, but we'll make it work. And *now* we've got a New Mummy to look after us and love us and keep us safe. Isn't that great?' He nodded. 'But, you need more tea, don't you? Right.'

Another groan.

Wrinkles deepened between his eyebrows. 'Have you been sick?'

Callum's head lolled to the right, making the walls pulsate again.

'Oh dear. Never mind. It's OK. It's not your fault.' McAdams stood and walked over. Hunkered down right beside him. Took out a hand-kerchief and wiped Callum's mouth. 'It can be a bit harsh at first, but the tea's good for you. It purifies your body and your mind. It'll make you ready for divinity.' He brushed the damp hair from Callum's forehead. 'They'll worship you, you'll be a god. You'll be a— Gllllk!'

Callum's good hand slammed into McAdams' crotch. Took a firm grip and *squeezed*, twisting the contents of McAdams' pants like he was opening a jar of pickled onions.

There was a wet, strangled, scream, then McAdams collapsed to the floor and coiled into a little trembling ball, sobbing while Callum squeezed and twisted.

The words were lumpen and saggy, but Callum forced them out anyway. 'Say hello to … *The Claw!*'

78

Mother was breathing, but there was already a lump growing on the back of her head.

Callum unlocked the padlock from the chain around her neck. 'Boss? Can you hear me?'

He gave her a small slap on the cheek, but it didn't help.

She was still breathing though, that was the important thing.

The lady in the grey cardigan flinched when Callum touched her. So definitely still alive.

'It's all right, I'm a police officer. See?' He pulled out his warrant card. 'Can you tell me your name?'

Her eyes were wide as a rabbit's, waiting for the oncoming car.

'Hello?'

Nope.

Callum unlocked her too, but she scuttered away, squeezing herself into the corner of the room, arms wrapped around her knees. Staring out at him from beneath her greying fringe, with those glittering rabbit eyes. Probably off her face on McAdams' magic mushroom tea.

And that just left the man himself. Still curled up on the basement floor, wrapped around his tortured groin.

Good.

Callum hauled both of McAdams' wrists behind his back and slapped on the cuffs. 'Andrew McAdams, I'm detaining you under Section Fourteen of the—'

'Don't you want to be a god?' Face flushed and shiny. Tears and snot shining on his cheeks. 'Why? What's wrong with you?'

'You're going to prison, *Andy*. It's over.'

He stared. 'It's not too late, I can fix this. I'll get you some more tea.

You can be a god, Callum. You can watch over us all. You can fix *everything* that's wrong!'

'You're a psycho nutbag, and you're going to spend every last miserable day you've got left being someone's bitch in a six-by-six cell.'

And at that, McAdams threw his head back and laughed. Not a fake laugh either, a full-on belly laugh. 'I'm dying of cancer, you idiot. I've got weeks to live. You think they'll lock me up? I won't even stand trial and you know it.'

'I'm detaining you under Section Fourteen of the Criminal Justice, Scotland, Act—'

'You still don't get it, do you? All you've done is stopped me saving everybody's lives. We could have fixed everything. And you ruined it!'

'—because I believe you to have committed an offence punishable by imprisonment—'

'But you know what? It doesn't matter if I die, now. No one ever remembers the cops or the victims, they only remember the serial killer. I get to live *forever*.'

Callum licked his lips. 'You get to die in prison.'

'They'll write books about me – *Sunday Times* bestsellers. They'll make films about me. Maybe even a TV series. They'll talk about me in hushed whispers when they tuck their children into bed.' A grin. 'Andrew McAdams. Imhotep. Immortal.'

The walls throbbed in time with Callum's heartbeat.

Kill him.

It was the only way.

Arrest him and he'd barely see the inside of a courtroom.

Kill him.

Make it look like suicide – just like McAdams had done with Finn Noble – so everyone would think he just couldn't cope with the cancer. Then get rid of anything incriminating in the house, so no one would ever find out that he murdered all those people. Don't let him take *anything* from this.

Don't let him win.

McAdams grinned up at him, eyes like polished buttons. 'They'll worship me, I'll be a god!'

'No.' Callum tightened his good hand into a fist. 'No, you won't.'

79

'Ow! Get off me.' Mother slapped the paramedic's hands away. Tried to stand. Got pushed back onto the wheelie-stretcher thing that took up nearly one whole side of the ambulance.

'You've got concussion. Do you *want* to die? Doesn't bother me: I get paid either way.' The paramedic held out the disinfectant and the wad of gauze again. 'Now, are you going to sit still, or not?'

The ambulance's blue-and-whites spun in the downpour. Throw in the three patrol cars, all with their lights going, and the crime scene was transformed into a very damp, very miserable disco.

Callum climbed up into the back, joining them. 'That's Cecelia and her Smurfs of Doom just arrived.'

Mother nodded. 'Tell them I want— Ow!'

'Well sit still, then. And you're going to need stitches.'

'I don't *need* stitches.'

'God's sake.' The paramedic handed his gauze and disinfectant to Callum. 'Try to talk some sense into her.' Then he hopped down from the back and walked off under the eaves of the house. Took out a packet of cigarettes and lit up.

Callum peered at the back of Mother's head. 'Yeah ... you're going to need stitches.'

'I can't believe Andy hit me. He *hit* me!' She looked away. 'How's Beth?'

'They've taken her straight to A-and-E. No idea how long he's had her chained up in the basement, but she's gone full-blown psychotic episode.'

'His own *wife*. I was at their silver wedding anniversary.' Mother let her head fall back, then winced and straightened up again. 'Ow!'

'Look on the bright side: it could've been a lot worse. Remember what he did to John?'

'Urgh...' She wiped a hand across her face. 'Andy was my friend, Callum. I've known him for years. I don't even know who he is, now.'

'We're all still alive. He can't hurt anyone else. We've escaped our chains.'

She looked at him, then smiled. 'No more sodding haikus.'

'Deal.' He put a hand on her shoulder and she took it. Gave it a squeeze. Nodded.

'You did good, Callum. You did really, really good.'

'Thanks, Boss.'

'I think, in the circumstances, you can call me "Mother".'

The scent of deep-fried sausages filled the Downstream Monitoring Suite, underpinned by the sharp-sweet tang of cheap tomato sauce. Dr McDonald ripped another bite from her buttie and leaned closer to the screen, chewing as she stared.

Mother folded her arms and slumped back in her seat.

Callum licked tomato sauce and melted butter off the back of his hand. 'Sure you don't want one?'

'Surprisingly enough, I'm not hungry.'

On the screen, Interview Two was full – McAdams and his solicitor on one side of the table, facing the camera; Detective Superintendent Ness and a short fat DS on the other.

'No comment.'

Ness sighed. 'Andrew, you know how this works. You've been here often enough.'

'No comment.'

McAdams' solicitor looked as if she was auditioning for a Tim Burton movie. She tucked a strand of jet-black hair behind her ear. 'I believe my client has made himself very clear on this point, Detective Superintendent. He's quite happy to answer any questions, but only to DI Malcolmson.'

McAdams stared directly into the camera. Smiled. 'And Callum, of course. Only fair to include him. He deserves that much.'

Dr McDonald took another bite. 'He doesn't even look bothered, does he? It's like he's there to pick up a Chinese takeaway.'

'You know we can't do that, Andrew. You assaulted them both. It's a conflict of interest.'

'It's a shame he's dying of cancer, isn't it?' Dr McDonald got even

578

closer, till her nose was only inches from the screen. 'I mean it'd take years to unravel what's going on inside his head, and that would be *very* interesting wouldn't it and I'd love to have a go, but I don't think they'd let me, do you think they'd let me, or does that sound a bit creepy because of the serial killing and dying thing?'

Mother stared at her. 'Yes.'

'*My client is prepared to make a full confession, but only to DI Malcolmson.*'

'*And have the whole thing ruled inadmissible in court? We'll pass, thanks.*'

McAdams stuck a hand against his chest, as if he was about to pledge allegiance '*Then, "no comment" is the only thing, / That I will mumble, say, or sing, / "No comment" now, "no comment" then, / "No comment" time and time again.*' Then the smile slipped, as a coughing fit sent him rocking back and forward in his seat, bent over, head nearly touching the tabletop. Leaving him panting and wheezing.

The solicitor patted him on the back. '*I* insist *you get my client medical attention, right now!*'

Mother groaned. 'I know this is going to sound harsh, but I don't think I like him very much any more.'

— dearly departed, —
we are gathered here today

And when the Bonemonger raised his arms, the earth gave a great rumble as one by one the graves collapsed. Then, from the dark depths below, each and every coffin rose to the above, steaming in the cold morning air.

"Please, don't do it! I've changed my mind!" screamed Justin. "Stop!"

"It's too late," laughed the Bonemonger, "see what we have done!"

He clapped his bony hands and the lids flew off, revealing the dead in all their mouldy finery. They yawned and stretched and sat up in their satin-lined boxes. Then climbed out into the last morning there would ever be. For he'd opened the coffins and let them go free.

R.M. Travis
Open the Coffins (and Let Them Go Free) (1976)

You better believe I'm-a keepin' it real,
Cos there ain't no reprieve when The Man makes you kneel,
And I know you all grieve, but I'm gonna appeal,
Got some tricks up ma sleeve an' my will's made of steel.

Donny '$ick Dawg' McRoberts
'The Day Them F*ckers Done Fitted Me Up'
© Bob's Speed Trap Records (2017)

80

'I'm sorry for your loss.' Callum shook McAdams' wife's hand.

Beth had put on a little weight in the last week and a bit, but it'd probably be a long time until she lost that chained-up-in-the-basement hollow-eyed look. She stared back at him. 'He was a bastard, and I'm glad he's dead.'

'Yeah.' Callum nodded. 'Me too.' Then moved on to join what was left of the Misfit Mob. Everyone dressed in various shades of black.

Dotty looked up at the bright blue sky. 'Well, at least he got a nice day for it.'

Franklin shuddered. 'I hate crematoriums. Always give me the creeps.'

'Mother? You OK?'

'Hmmm?' She turned, blinking. 'Sorry, miles away. It was a lovely service wasn't it?'

'I thought your eulogy was very good.'

She patted Callum on the arm. 'I know it sounds odd, but I miss him.'

'He tried to kill me. He very nearly killed Watt. He murdered *at least* six people. And he was going to keep you chained up in his dungeon with his drugged wife. Probably thought he could take turns.'

'When you put it like that...' Mother puffed out her cheeks. Clapped her hands together. 'Right, we'd better get back to work, I suppose.'

Rain drummed against the office window, a counterpoint to the buzzing rattle coming from the radiator.

Callum sat back in his seat, both feet propped up on his desk. Finished the page he was reading and moved on to the next one.

McAdams' book was ... different. Not bad, exactly, but a bit long-winded and self-indulgent. Not to mention self-important.

Franklin backed into the room, laden down with box files. 'Working hard are we?'

'Yes.' He nodded towards the pile of paper, sitting on its opened-out brown paper wrapping. 'McAdams believed in the old adage: "write what you know". It's all about Imhotep's quest to save the world, told from the perspective of a little boy called "Justin". Abduction, physical abuse, trauma, desperate need for affection he tries to fulfil with the women his "Father" keeps chained up in the basement.'

She dumped the files on her desk. 'You coming tonight?'

'We don't need to worry about catching Paul Jeffries' killer – it was McAdams. Stabbed him for killing the last in a long line of New Mummies. Then Justin goes into care. More trauma and abuse. But he finally gets himself a nice foster family, changes his name, and everything starts to go right for him. Good exam results. University. Career in the police force. Sense of belonging and self-worth.'

'I mean, it was weird enough going to his funeral, but a wake too?'

'Then he's diagnosed with cancer and it all comes flooding back. That's when the killing starts.' A smile. 'And he would have hated that much summary narrative.'

'I've never been to a celebration wake before. Don't get me wrong, I'm all for celebrating someone's life when they've died, but actually celebrating the *fact* they've died?'

Callum pointed at the remaining stack of paper. 'Haven't got to the end yet, but five quid says there's nothing in there about getting his balls crushed by The Claw, then being arrested, charged, remanded without bail, or an epilogue where he gets stabbed twenty-three times in the throat by the very disturbed young man from the cell next door.'

'Thought it was nine times?'

'Artistic licence.' Callum marked his spot on the page. 'And, apparently, Tod Monaghan was nothing to do with it.'

Her eyes went wide. 'You're *kidding* me.'

'Nope. According to chapter forty-two, McAdams just took advantage of the fact Monaghan was dodgy, dead, and in no position to complain about mummified human remains being planted in his living room. Turns out "Justin" sacrificed a god to make it look like Imhotep had drowned himself in Kings River, so we'd stop looking.'

'What about Finn Noble?'

'Haven't got to that bit yet.'

'Wouldn't it be lovely if every murdering wee scumbag wrote their confession out as a novel?' She picked up a sheet of paper and read aloud: "'There's a jackdaw hanging on the fence behind the house. Like a little black kite, caught on its own strings.' That's cheery.' The page went back on its pile. 'So, are you coming tonight, or not?'

Callum shrugged. 'Don't see why not. I might even have a bash at karaoke.'

'Just seems … *weird*, doesn't it? Mind you, I suppose the signs were there – no sane person spouts haikus and bits of doggerel all the time.'

'Hmm.'

'And that thing he did, where he pretended he was doing a literary critique of his own life? Not right in the head.'

'Looks as if McAdams was right, though: he didn't make it to the end of the book after all.'

'Still, I suppose…' She frowned, then pointed at Callum's warbling phone. 'Are you going to get that?'

Might as well. He picked it up. 'Hello?'

A small pause. *'Piggy?'*

Not *again.* 'Willow, we've talked about this. It's "Uncle Callum", not "Piggy".'

Silence.

Franklin raised her eyebrows, then made a letter T out of her two index fingers and pointed at the kettle.

He gave her a thumbs up – not easy with his right hand still in the cast, but she seemed to get the idea. 'Willow, are you there?'

'Piggy, I need… Mum needs you to come over.'

'I could probably pop past later on, after work? We could maybe get a pizza or something?'

'No, Piggy: got to be now, yeah? It's urgent, like.'

He sat up. 'What happened: is it your dad? Is he hitting her? I can get a police car there in five minutes.'

'No! Nah, no. It's not Dad. That prick comes here, me and Benny gonna kick his little bitch arse for him. Gonna kick it good.' But the bravado didn't sound as brash as it usually did. It sounded brittle. Shaky.

'Are you OK?'

'Just do it, yeah?' A muffled voice in the background was too low to make out. *'Gotta go.'* And she hung up.

Callum tapped his pen against the desk.

Franklin waved at him. 'We're out of teabags. You want coffee instead?'

He stood. 'Thanks, but I've got to go out for a bit.' Then struggled into his jacket. 'Don't fancy a hurl, do you?'

'Can you see the pile of work I've got on my desk? Every single sodding case McAdams ever worked on, and I have to review the lot.'

'Come on, it'll only take twenty minutes. Thirty tops.'

'Another one of your "wee errands", is it?'

'The woman my brother beat up wants to see me. Apparently it's urgent.'

Franklin smiled. 'Maybe she wants her teddy bear back?'

That was a point. And it wasn't as if they needed it now.

'Why not?'

'So I was thinking, maybe curry?'

Callum shrugged, taking the Mondeo around the Calderwell Roundabout and into Kingsmeath. 'Bit unusual for a wake, but yeah. Sounds good. Get a bit of ballast in us before we hit the Bart.'

Sunlight glittered back from the satellite dishes and double glazing that graced the houses lining the road. Not a cloud in the sky. Even the river was settling back to its normal sedate sludgy grey.

Franklin nodded. 'I know Dotty's getting in some sausage rolls and wee scotch eggs, but I always end up feeling cheated if I don't get a proper dinner.'

'Can't go wrong with fish and chips.'

'True.'

And it'd be quicker than going out for a curry, so there'd be plenty of time to finish reading McAdams' book before heading out to celebrate his death. Would be good to get it finished. Move on to something else. Something a bit less ... deranged and *murdery*.

Wonder if anyone would publish it?

Might be an idea to see where they stood, legally, with that one. Suppose the rights would belong to McAdams' wife.

Left, up Munro Place. Over the top of the hill and down the other side.

Maybe they could publish it and all the proceeds could go to the victims' families? Or would that just be fulfilling McAdams' little fantasies of immortality and success?

Callum slowed for the turning onto Manson Avenue. What if they—

Franklin hit him on the arm.

'Ow! What was that for?'

'You haven't been listening to a word I've said, have you?'

'Curry then karaoke.'

She rolled her eyes. 'That was five minutes ago. I was talking about

Mark wanting to get back together again. Maybe take a trip to Thailand, or New Zealand.'

'Thought he was "an entitled dick who didn't respect you as a human being"? And I'm quoting there.'

'I don't know why I bother telling you anything.'

'You were the one who said it.' Callum pulled up outside number 45. The block looked pretty much as horrible as it had the last two times, only now the weeds crowding the front garden were bigger. About time Irene cashed her dirty big cheque from Alastair and traded up for somewhere better.

'I've always wanted to go to New Zealand.'

'Mark's a dick. You know it. I know it.' Callum climbed out of the car, then reached into the back for the teddy bear lying on the passenger shelf. *'Everyone* knows it.'

She caught up to him halfway along the path. 'The most exotic holiday we ever had was a three-day trip to Belgium. And that was only because he had to go to a conference.'

'So, what: you're going to take him back, shag him, laugh at his horrible jokes, all because he's going to take you to New Zealand? You do *know* what they call women who only sleep with men to get things, don't you?' Callum stuck his thumb on the doorbell, setting it ringing deep inside the house. 'Because it isn't nice.'

'Oh go bite your own backside.'

'At best, you'd be a gold digger, and at worst—'

The door opened, and there was Benny, in his blue tracksuit and backwards baseball cap. His eyes were small and pink, ringed with red. Cheeks shiny. A glittering trickle of snot on his top lip catching the sunlight. He held up his arm. 'Uncle Callum!'

'Benny, are you OK?'

He looked up at them, bottom lip wobbling, then turned and ran back inside.

Franklin raised an eyebrow.

'He's a bit … odd.' Callum stepped over the threshold. Raised his voice. 'Miss Brown? Irene? Hello?'

'All kids are odd. They don't stop being odd till they hit their twenties, and even then it's—' Franklin's phone launched into 'Dancing in the Moonlight'. She sighed. Dug it out. 'Mark? Is it important, because I'm in the middle of something. … I'm not being "like" anything. … No, I'm…' She rolled her eyes at Callum. 'Yes. But you remember what I do for a living, don't you?'

Callum pointed into the house and pulled a face.

She nodded and turned back to the path. 'There's no need to get all defensive about it, Mark. If we're going to give this another chance, you need to respect my boundaries. ... Yes. ... I didn't *say* that.'

He left her to it.

Down the hall. 'Irene? You there?' He held up the bear. 'I've got Mr Lumpylump.' Into the living room.

And there she was. Irene Brown. On her knees in front of the room's saggy armchair, one hand covering her mouth, blood dripping between her fingers. The other hand scrabbled at the carpet for what looked like teeth.

What the hell was—

The door battered into him, hard enough to send Callum thumping sideways against the wall, then tumbling to the floor. Sending a plastic tidal wave of kid's toys clattering across the carpet.

Then a boot connected with his ribs, hurling him into the wall again. Slamming all the air from his lungs and setting fire to his whole side. Another boot caught him on the forehead, snapping his head back. Drowning out all sound with a deafening booming ringing noise.

Then a hand grabbed the front of his shirt and hauled him up. 'Think you're clever, don't you? Think you got away.' Ainsley Dugdale grinned at him, the bruises on his butcher's-slab face fading away to a dirty smear. He folded his other hand into a fist. 'See when I take money for a job? I do the job. And you *don't* get away.'

The world snapped around ninety degrees and everything tasted of hot copper wire.

Callum raised an arm, but the fist battered his face again making something inside his cheek go *snap*. The carpet rushed up and crashed into his chest. 'Ungggghh...'

'Think you're the only one can do detecting?' The boot cracked into his ribs again. 'I open my newspaper and what do I see? This bitch whining on about how her man don't treat her right, even though she's a total whore.' Another kick flipped Callum over onto his back.

Every breath was like running a cheese grater over his lungs.

He coughed and warm red spattered back down onto his cheeks.

'So I thinks to myself, "Oho, this bitch is friends with Detective Constable Callum MacGregor, is she? Let's see if we can't arrange a wee surprise party for him.' This time the boot stamped down on his chest. Once. Twice. Then one cracked his head off the skirting board. 'You enjoying your party? Want to blow out your candles?'

The room lurched, then settled down into a slow, dark throb.

Strange, the carpet looked all cheap and threadbare from a distance, but lying here it was soft and warm and comfortable. Like the floor of R.M. Travis's garage. Or McAdams' basement.

Didn't even hurt all that much any more.

All his arms and legs. Like rubbery lead. Heavy and warm.

Could just go to sleep, right here on the floor.

Dugdale's face was all teeth, shiny and brown, shown off in a grin as he pulled out a lighter and scritched his thumb across the wheel. Sparks. More sparks. Then a big yellow flame. 'What do you think: start with your eyes or your ears? Yeah, let's burn a—'

'Get away from Uncle Callum!' Benny jumped on Dugdale. Eyes wide, tears on his cheeks, snot glistening from his nose. Teeth bared. 'GRRRRRRRRR!'

'What the… Get off me you little freak! You're in for—'

He sank his teeth into Dugdale's arm, shaking his head like a terrier. Blood trickling down his chin.

'AAAAAAAAAAAAAAAAAAAAAARGH!'

'Benny!' Willow ran for him, grabbed her brother's arm and pulled. But Benny just bit deeper. So she let go and ran away.

Not so big and tough after all.

'AAAAAAAAAARGH!' A chunk of flesh came free, big as a chicken nugget, the hole it left behind: red and purple, fringed with yellow. Dugdale stared at it for a moment, mouth hanging open. Then he backhanded Benny, sending the little boy flying into the back of the armchair. 'YOU LITTLE SHIT!'

Benny bounced, eyes wide, blood all over his mouth and chin. *Grinning*. Snapping his teeth together. Then lunging again. Sinking his teeth into Dugdale's leg, right at the bulge of his calf.

'AAAAAARGH! KILL YOU!' Dugdale grabbed him by the throat, ripped Benny off his leg and held him up, like a mascot. Then slammed him into the wall hard enough to crack the plasterboard. 'YOU'RE DEAD, YOU LITTLE FREAK!'

'LEAVE MY BROTHER ALONE!' Willow was back, clutching a dirty big kitchen knife, the blade gleaming as she swung it at him.

It never made contact. Dugdale punched her, hard in the face, sending her spinning away to smash into the playpen. Tiny drops of blood glittered in the air, marking her path. The knife thunked blade-down into the carpet.

Dugdale bared his teeth. 'The whole bloody lot of you are going to pay for this. Understand?' He buried another boot into Callum's stomach. 'You're all going to...' His eyes bulged and he looked over his shoulder.

Irene Brown stood right behind him, hunched forwards. She staggered back a couple of steps and raised her hands to cover her mouth. As if trying to hide the horrified expression on her face.

And Dugdale turned to face her. Unsteady on his legs. Shaking.

The handle of the kitchen knife stuck out of his back, just above his belt. Blood darkened his trousers. 'No...'

Callum blinked.

The world pulsed in and out. Warm and inviting as a length of basement chain.

Difficult to keep his eyes open.

When did his eyelids get so heavy?

Dugdale collapsed to his knees, both hands fluttering at the small of his back, fingertips brushing the knife's handle. 'Oh God, oh God, oh God...'

Then the living room door burst open and Franklin charged in, flicking her extendable baton out with a hard sharp *clack*. 'NOBODY MOVE!'

Better late than never.

Callum let the warmth and darkness fold over him like a duvet.

81

'You ready?'

'Yeah.' Callum winced and levered himself out of the big blue hospital armchair. The little private room was far too sodding hot, even with the window cracked as far open as it would go. A handful of get-well-soon cards were pinned up on the corkboard above the telly, the remains of a clichéd bag of grapes going raisiny on the bedside table.

He stood there for a moment. Straightened up. Wobbled.

Mother raised an eyebrow. 'Are you sure? Because I can call a doctor.'

'Four days stuck in here with daytime TV and lukewarm Lucozade is quite enough, thank you.'

'Callum—'

'I'm *fine*. What's a few cracked ribs, fractured cheekbone, and bruised spleen between friends?' He struggled his way into his jacket. 'And there wasn't any blood in my pee this morning. How cool is that?'

McAdams' book was back in its brown paper wrapper. Callum slipped it into his backpack and fastened the catches.

'Did you finish Andy's book?'

'Yup. Want to know what happens in the end?'

She shook her head. 'Certainly not, we don't approve of spoilers.'

'OK. Well, in that case—'

A knock at the door and Franklin stuck her head in. 'Is he still malingering?'

'I am *not* malingering.'

Mother crossed to the bed and picked up his backpack. Paused to peer out of the window. 'Have you seen the crowd down there? That's an awful lot of people for a Wednesday afternoon.'

Callum grinned. 'Maybe they're here to celebrate me getting out of hospital?'

'Dream on.' Franklin pointed at the door. 'Can we go now? Some of us have work to get back to.'

He limped out into the corridor, following her and Mother out of the ward and along to the lifts. Wheezing like a leaky balloon.

Mother pressed the button and the doors slid open. 'Dotty sends her love, by the way. She'd be here, but they're testing her for her disabled parking badge. You'd think missing half a leg would make her a shoo in, but who are we to question Oldcastle City Council's mysterious ways?'

They shuffled inside.

The doors clunked shut.

Down they went.

Franklin stared up at the numbers. 'Dugdale's regained consciousness, by the way. They've had to remove a big chunk of his bowel, liver, upper and lower intestines, but other than that he's dandy. He'll poop in a bag for the rest of his life, but swings and roundabouts.'

'They pressing charges?'

'What, against Irene Brown? No. She was saving the life of her children and a police officer. They've nominated her for a Queen's Commendation for Bravery. Dugdale, on the other hand, is facing two charges of aggravated assault, two of assaulting children, and the PF's doing him for the attempted murder of DCI Powel too. Turned out Dugdale was shooting his mouth off all over Oldcastle about it.'

Mother sighed. 'Poor wee soul never was the shiniest spoon in the drawer.'

'Hmph.' At least that meant Callum was off the hook. 'Do me a favour: when he attacked me, Dugdale was going on about how he'd been paid to do a job and I wasn't going to get away. Get someone to find out what the hell he was talking about.'

'I can try. But don't get your hopes up. He's not a shiny spoon, but he's sharp.'

The lift gave a shudder, a grinding noise, a ping. Then the door slid open on the hospital's reception area.

Franklin pointed. 'We're parked over in the red zone. Want me to drop you at Dotty's?'

'Any chance we can go via the library?'

'And how long's *that* going to take?'

'Fifteen minutes. Twenty tops.' Callum limped through the reception area towards the long line of glass doors, when someone stepped in from the overcast afternoon. Alastair.

The murmurs of that huge crowd outside buzzed through the open door, then clunked silent as it closed again.

Alastair / Donny / Donald / $ick Dawg swaggering over with a dirty big grin on his face and a hand out for shaking. 'Bruv!' He'd ditched the shaved-chest-and-leather-jacket look for a simple white shirt and blue jeans. A pair of expensive-looking sunglasses perched on the top of his head. Facial hair neatly trimmed.

'Erm...'

Alastair grabbed his hand. Shook it. Stepped back. Beamed. Then wrapped Callum up into a hug. Lifting him off the ground. Making broken nails burst across his ribs. 'Ha-ha!'

'Arrrgh!'

'Oh, right, yeah. Sorry, Bruv.' A squeeze on the shoulder instead. 'Callum, this is Courtney. Courtney, this is my bruv.'

A woman in a sharp suit appeared – thin, long hair swept back, young and perky looking as she looked Callum up and down, talking in a low Estuary accent. 'I don't like the bruises, makes him look like a boxer or something, but I suppose I can work with it.'

'Courtney's my publicist.'

'Right...'

'OK.' She clapped her hands. 'When we go out there, Sick Dawg's going to make a statement to the media. Then I need you to talk for no more than two minutes: we want to get this on the evening news, so keep it snappy but accessible. How great it is to finally meet your brother, how you're looking forward to getting to know each other again, you've always been a fan of his music, etcetera.'

'But—'

'Great. Don't forget: no more than two minutes. I'll give you a copy of the itinerary once we've done the broadsheet interviews.'

'Itinerary?'

'*The One Show*, *Breakfast News*, *Lorraine*. I'm waiting for a call back from *The Graham Norton Show*, but fingers crossed.'

Callum stared at her. Then at Alastair. Then at Mother. 'But—'

'Excellent.' Courtney checked her watch. 'I've got a table booked at La Poule Française for eight tonight. We can go over any questions you've got then.'

'But—'

'I know, right?' Alastair wrapped an arm around his shoulder. 'Bit of a shock, innit, first time in the bubble? But trust me, Bruv, you is gonna be a natural, right?' He turned a smile on Franklin and Mother. 'Can you give me and my bruv a couple of minutes, yeah? You know, to talk, like?'

Franklin bristled, but Mother put a hand on her arm. Nodded. 'Of course. We'll be over there, raiding the chocolate machine.'

'Cool.' Alastair snapped his fingers then pointed at it. 'Courtney, treat these fine ladies to whatever they like.'

Last of the big spenders.

And as soon as they were gone, Alastair thumped down into one of the waiting room seats, legs splayed out as if they were barely connected, and grinned at Callum. 'Man, we is gonna be on the *front pages* tomorrow. Can't buy this kinda publicity.'

Callum half sat, half collapsed into the seat opposite. Licked his lips. 'Umm...'

'You always this quiet, Bruv?'

'*Breakfast News?*'

'Yeah, better get used to it. My agent called: we got a bidding war going on for our autobiography, like *big time*. And don't worry: they gonna get some ghost writer guy to do the words for us, we just gotta cash the royalty cheques and sign some books. Already got offers coming in for the film rights.'

'How's that going to work if you're in prison?'

'Nah, Bruv. Got sentenced to two weeks at a five-star rehab retreat. Perks of being a celebrity with a very expensive lawyer.'

Typical.

Callum cleared his throat. 'I want to go after Leo McVey. For what he did to Mum and Dad. For what he did to you.'

Silence.

A nurse squeaked by with a clipboard and a frown.

Someone in the distance coughed.

The machine whirred and clunked as Mother, Franklin, and Courtney threw caution to the wind.

Alastair frowned. 'I remember.' The patois had disappeared, leaving the hard Kingsmeath burr behind. 'Not everything. But some bits. I remember the cage Travis kept me in. I remember the dinner parties, where he'd wheel me out.'

'Dinner parties?'

'Man, you think he kept all those bits of people in the freezer because he was *lonely*? You've read his books.'

And that's something else he's obsessed with: witches eating children. Goblins eating rabbits. Monsters eating children. People eating rabbits that are actually children. It's a smorgasbord of transspecies consumption, posing as anthropomorphic cannibalism, but it's really about venal desire. Consume the flesh, violate the body, and absorb it into your own.

'Oh Jesus...'

'In the end, it was Uncle Leo got me out of there. Yeah, there was stuff went on before that, but he's the one changed my name. Got me into a care home. Hid me away so Travis couldn't find me.'

'He abducted you in the first place! He helped Travis kill Mum and Dad.'

Alastair picked at the stitching on his jeans. 'Yeah.'

'If we're doing an autobiography, it'll all come out anyway.'

'Yeah.' A small smile. 'Not easy being a superstar. Wearing all these masks, so nobody sees the real you.'

Callum sat forward in his seat. 'Are you going to help me?'

Silence.

Alastair cleared his throat. Kept digging at the stitching. 'I need to tell you something. Ainsley Dugdale: I paid him.'

'You *paid* him?'

A shrug. 'Yeah, but it was just meant to be a thing, you know? I tell Dugdale to hang around Irene's gaff, I phone in an anonymous tip so you know where he is, then when you turn up and he batters you, I wade in and save the day. Willow and Benny see me, and they're all like, "Whoa, our dad's a hero!" You're like, "My bruv saved my life!"'

Callum stared at him. 'The big black Mercedes.'

'Only I got too stoned and then you got crushed in the balls and I was going to jump in, I really was, but you pepper sprayed him and he fell over and Willow kicked the crap out of him and I was laughing so hard I nearly peed myself.'

Lovely.

At least it explained the whole weird coincidence thing.

'And then, when I heard about that Powel guy, I thought, "No way this scumbag's getting away with shagging my brother's woman. No way." So I got Dugdale to pay *him* a visit too.'

Callum folded forward and covered his face with his hands. 'Do you have any idea how much trouble that caused me?'

'Yeah, sorry, Bruv. It's the thought that counts, though. Right?'

No, it wasn't.

The silence stretched.

Alastair sniffed. 'You need to know: if you go sniffing around Leo McVey with your warrant card and your police mates, he's going to lawyer up like *that*.' Alastair snapped his fingers. 'Might have to do it ... a bit dirty, yeah? You ready for that?'

'You're not talking about fitting him up, are you?'

'No, I'm talking about *justice* for all them people they killed. I'm talking about *revenge* for Mum and Dad. I'm talking about pliers and a blowtorch in an abandoned building. I'm talking a shallow grave out in Moncuir Wood where no one's ever going to find him.'

'You want to...' Callum snuck a quick glance around: the nearest person was the receptionist, on her phone. Lowered his voice to a hard whisper: 'You want to murder Leo McVey? No. Not happening. No chance.'

'Hmmm.' A nod. 'OK, so we can't kill him. Courtney said you probably wouldn't go for that.'

'You discussed murdering Leo McVey with your *publicist*? Are you insane?'

'Cos she came up with a better idea: Plan B. We get ourselves a film crew and we go after Leo McVey and that scumbag R.M. Travis on our very own reality TV show. Investigate the background, dig up other victims, all that stuff you cops do, yeah? Play our cards right, we get two seasons out of it.'

'You *are* insane.'

'Yeah, like a fox.' Alastair stood. 'Right, we got us a press conference to rock. You ready?' He held out his hand.

Callum swallowed. Levered himself out of his seat.

Followed his brother out into an overcast afternoon and a barrage of flash photography.

Oh God...

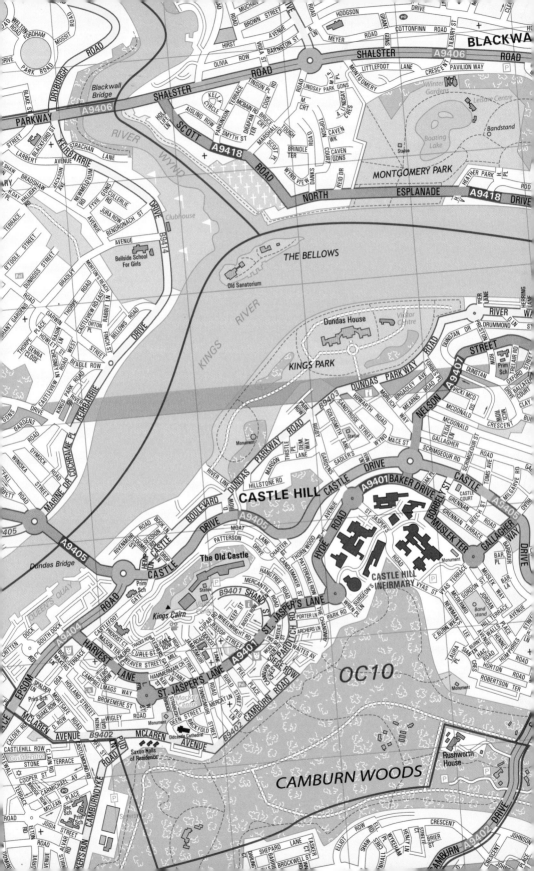